Whilst pursuing their studies in academic fields as diverse as astrobiology, rocket science and biochemistry on a distant, fragile, desolate and remote scientific world, three scientists, and the wider communities they belong to, experience a global catastrophe that sees the entire planetary population scrambling rapidly for safety elsewhere in the Nexus Cluster and beyond. Many of their number arrive safely on the nearest inhabited planet - the socialist world of Zeta Kotlin - with the ultimate goal of recreating the life they had enjoyed on their home planet. However, rival civilisations hear of the planetary exodus and seek to lure the scientists to their own worlds, with the aim of furthering fraught and ambitious agendas, and so the scientists find themselves drawn into the plans, rivalries and misfortunes of a set of very different neighbouring planets, and increasingly unable to recreate the home from home they had initially desired. Numerous journeys across the local quadrant of space, encounters with different peoples and a range of experiences on strange and bewildering planets sees the exodus ultimately give rise to a cascade of events that reconfigures the whole civilisational structure of the Nexus Cluster and its planets.

D1808557

Arrival in Utopia

Duncan Fraser

LULU Publications

Arrival in Utopia

First published in Great Britain by Lulu Publications 2021

ISBN 978-1-7947-9447-4

Lulu Publications
www.lulu.com

ACKNOWLEDGEMENTS

For all those seeking their own utopia

CONTENTS

The human race failed to look after its first home. Now it is trying again, but utopia is a contested concept.

PROLOGUE

The Message

Far out in the depths of space, in the distant realms of the near galaxy, a small, slowly rotating satellite traced out its lonely preprogrammed voyage around the outer circumference of a distant star system. So vast and so measured was its elliptical journey, that the curved nature of its trajectory could only have been discerned by an extremely distant observer. So far from its home star was the satellite, that its journey across the stellar depths went entirely unnoticed, shrouded in the permanent jet-black darkness that constituted the outer limits of the star system.

Viewed from such a great distance, the astral body at the centre of the satellite's orbit was little more than a slightly flickering pale yellow speck, located at the distant heart of the vast dark disc that marked out and signified the star's own unique stellar system. On occasions - as it journeyed through the freezing depths of space - the lonely sentinel would pass slowly through the icy debris fields of the local Oort cloud that surrounded the stellar body, but for the majority of its trajectory it simply journeyed through the vast array of cold dark nothingness. For decades the satellite had been barely noticed.

A small dish and antenna sat on the side of the shiny silver and green machine. Every sixty seconds, with metronomic regularity, its spinning body emitted - in perfect unison - a soft electronic sonic beep and a thin bright jade green beam of light that momentarily pierced the cold black icy depths through which it traversed. And, just as it broadcast its own regular emission, so the satellite waited for in-coming transmissions. For long months or years nothing would be received, until suddenly a short burst of incoming information was received, amplified by its processor, and beamed instantaneously towards the interior of the stellar system. And then, again, nothing but the empty silence of space, as it continued on its never-ending lonely trajectory around the outer limits of the star system. The satellite continued to spin, and its metronomic emission continued to be beamed out across space.

Long ago, a doomed civilisation had located the satellite there, a means of guiding its travellers through the immense depths of space - an astral lighthouse for all its starships to recognise, and for all its race to see. It provided a regular emission that the civilisation's voyagers could fix upon; a signal that helped them navigate their tortuous path across the deep, dark vastness of the inter-stellar spaces they had chosen to cross. It beamed out across the galaxy, navigating them towards the chosen stellar destinations of their unimaginably long journeys, embarked upon so many years before, as they sought to escape their dying planet.

For many decades, it had received few transmissions of any great importance, but now, after so many years of silence and solitude, an in-coming emission arrived for it to amplify and deliver to the planetary inhabitants, far away in the distant interior of its own star system. It told of a civilisation in crisis, a culture facing imminent collapse. The civilisation was abandoning its home planet and was seeking a new world on which to inhabit. The civilisation had discovered vast new swathes of advanced knowledge and learning. It had developed new understandings and new theories in cosmology, astrobiology, physics, astronomy, space travel and a whole host of other scientific fields. The civilisation came in peace and offered no threat, only a desire to continue with its academic endeavours.

The satellite duly performed the task of receiving, amplifying and delivering the plea for help to the distant inhabitants within its own local star system. The message passed through in mere seconds, but, far away, on the small insignificant planet that constituted the only habitable abode of the star system, the message arrived unheard and its impact barely even registered. The message, though, continued on its journey across the local star cluster and then out across the galaxy - to be received and amplified by identical satellites performing identical tasks as they circulated neighbouring star systems in exactly the same manner. And then, the satellite returned to its long, lonely, never-ending journey of following the circumference of the star system, the small green and silver lighthouse metronomically beaming out its position across the icy cold darkness. Its space once again fell eerily silent.

PART 1

The Diaspora

Arrival in Utopia

Ur-Tokar – the war begins

Topaz finally broached the top of the forested ridge, paused briefly to catch her breath, and then, with renewed vigour, made her way down to a small rock-strewn clearing overlooking the wider valley. Rogan had already set, but the pale orange light of the star continued to illuminate the twilight sky. Across the breadth of the sky, high above the dark mountains, a dazzling array of stars began to fill the crepuscular orange and yellow sky. To her left, and rising quickly into the night sky, was the large pale purple moon of Arioch commencing its transit across the chilly night sky. Far in the distance loomed the great curves and almost ghost-like peaks of the Zarozinian Mountains, their stark, bare, dark basalt rock glowing in the soft purple light reflecting down from Arioch. The central peak of Mount Zarozinia loomed large in the centre of the range, whilst beneath, its foothills dropped in descending curves towards both its northern and southern arms.

Immediately below her ran the Kauai River, flowing golden orange-yellow as it reflected the twilight sky, and snaking slowly into the diminishing distance. Thick forested ridges of both pine and gnarled bare oaks flanked its sides, shrouded in darkness as they sloped down gently to arrive at the wooded banks of the meandering river. Far in the distance against the river's distant shore, barely discernible in the fading light, glimmered the faint orange-yellow lights of Greenback, nestling secretively in the foothills of the towering mountain. This was to be Topaz's destination, but there was no question of her arrival there tonight. Even with her considerable navigation skills, the journey through the thick dark forest was fraught with difficulties. She would need to bed down for the night and make for her destination in the morning.

The following day, as Rogan broke the mountainous skyline and the first rays of sunlight spread across the forested slopes, Topaz woke and after a short period of staring at the soft pink, grey and blue clouds stretching across the morning sky, she wrestled her way out of her sleeping bag. After the basic breakfast that her diminishing supplies allowed, she set off through the forest, keeping the river ever closely to her right. To remain on the lower slopes of the ridges and to avoid losing her way, she would need to follow its long broad curves, adding considerable distance to her already lengthy journey. Greenback was not actually that distant as the crow flies, but on foot and crossing the thickly wooded slopes of the lower mountain ranges meant she was still several hours from her destination.

By late afternoon she was closing in on her destination. Standing on an exposed rocky outcrop, she could just discern the thin trails of smoke slowly curling skywards from the chimneys of the small village. But, as she made her way unevenly downwards towards the wooded slope that would permit her final descent to the small wood and stone bridge that stretched across the river that allowed her to reach the village destination, she heard the distinctive noise of thundering hooves arriving from somewhere to her distant left. Her relatively low elevation and the dense compacted forest of pines and firs meant she had no means of viewing the origin of the noise, but she knew this was unlikely to be good news. Her people, who populated the high mountain forests, did not keep horses in any significant numbers, but the monarchist lowlanders certainly did, and the relationship between their two peoples had been deteriorating badly for some time now. In previous times the monarchists had left them to their own devices, but these were no longer normal times and a number of violent encounters had seen casualties inflicted on both sides.

From the direction of travel, she was sure the horses were heading towards the village, and they would be there long before her own arrival. A few minutes later, as she hurried through the trees with added haste, she could hear the sound of raised voices and then the sound of frightened cries, shrieking and the clash of swords. She came to an abrupt halt, momentarily paralysed as fear coursed through her body. She considered turning and fleeing, but she knew she had to witness the events that were unfolding and continued down to the banks of the river, all the time making sure she was not visible to those on the far side. Through the trees she could just discern a small band of monarchists, mostly on horseback, but currently being joined by foot soldiers coming from the direction of the houses. They had occupied the grassy area between the wooden village houses and the river bank, and at various points she was sure she could see bodies lying prostrate and littered across the grassy river bank. More bodies were being brought out from the houses and deposited close to the river by the foot soldiers.

Arrival in Utopia

The enormity of what was happening took a few seconds to dawn on her, for this was no brief skirmish or ill-tempered confrontation. It was the systematic extermination of the entire village. One by one the inhabitants of each house were being slaughtered until not a single villager was left alive. More horsemen and horse-pulled carts laden with supplies arrived along the narrow track that constituted the southern route into the village. An aristocrat, who must have been the leader of the monarchist band – a dark-looking middle-aged knight on a black horse – was issuing orders to the assembled foot soldiers. As she continued to watch, the contents of the carts were fully unloaded and it slowly became apparent to her that this was not just a massacre either, for the band of soldiers was clearly occupying the village – this was an exercise in replacing the entirety of the village's population. Finally, the dead bodies lying on the ground were dragged over to the river and cast carelessly into its icy cold waters. They began to float downstream in the slowly moving current.

Topaz could not believe what she was seeing. Violent conflict was relatively rare in her society and she had experienced nothing even approaching this level of violence. The callous manner in which the bodies were unceremoniously dumped in the water left her crying for several minutes. Finally she calmed herself, collected her thoughts and tried to make sense of the unexpected situation she now found herself in. She had journeyed here to collect some final supplies before the worst of the winter weather set in. Her original plan had been to make the return trip upstream by boat. She wondered if she could wait for nightfall and then surreptitiously remove one of the boats and make her escape under the cloak of darkness, hoping she would not be discovered. The alternative was to forget all about the supplies and track back through the mountains empty-handed living off the land as she went. This was well within her means, but it meant several days of hard slog and winter was closing in. Neither option particularly appealed to her.

Margalla – ecosystem problems

Akiko strolled casually into one of the spacious learning suites at the education section of the Community Centre and greeted the youngsters there with a warm hello. The students returned the greeting and made various jokey comments about her late arrival. Laughing these aside, she made a hot drink and then gathered her resources together. The computers were already up and running, and after some small talk with her students enquiring about their recent adventures and educational projects, she launched into her talk for the day. Akiko, well tanned, black haired and in her mid-twenties, specialised in environmental studies, though, as with all the inhabitants of Margalla, she was reasonably well informed with regards to most aspects of her planet - partly because they were not particularly extensive, but partly thanks to the broad education that was the norm amongst her people.

Her talk concerned some fairly advanced knowledge of various aspects of the ecosystems that were known to have already evolved on Margalla – the students had covered the more basic tenets of ecosystem theory in previous study periods. Akiko worked her way slowly through the visual aids that accompanied her talk, taking comments and questions as they arose. There were only a dozen in the educational group and of various different ages, but she tried to make the talk as interesting as possible and accessible to all the different educational levels. The presentation was interspersed with various images and video clips to facilitate a full understanding of the subject in hand, but also partly to retain their attention, though as all the children had chosen to study this subject anyway, this might not actually have been necessary. After about forty minutes she concluded her talk and the group then engaged in a lengthy discussion of the subject.

For the rest of the morning, the youngsters worked on the various projects they had commenced some weeks beforehand. Akiko circulated amongst the group to gain a better understanding of the latest developments in their research, offering advice and possible lines of future examination. As she did so, she could not help but being impressed by the wide variety of subjects chosen, the imaginative approach taken in their studies and the impressive level of detail that some of the projects were already achieving.

14

Arrival in Utopia

Some had taken a highly local approach and were studying particular aspects of their island's evolving flora or fauna, whilst others had tapped into the planet's satellite system and were working on much wider areas of study. There was still much work to be done on understanding Margalla's evolving ecosystems – particularly on its vast oceans – but Akiko couldn't help feeling that this newly emerging generation would have no problem in significantly advancing their knowledge of this particular subject, thus firmly facilitating the future direction of their civilisation.

Towards the end of the morning, the children began to drift away as they completed whatever section of the project they happened to be working on. Education, as elsewhere on Margalla, tended to be a morning affair in the town of Ascaso; if the children wanted to continue with their studies throughout the day that was perfectly acceptable, but most headed for the beaches and playing fields to participate in social-based activities as a means of occupying their afternoons and evenings. Akiko gave a talk at the centre once every three days, so she too was also now free to either spend her time on her own research or engage in more sociable activities.

Education at the centre was largely implemented on a rota-basis – there were no full-time teachers as such – though there were some who particularly enjoyed the activity, and thus spent more time at the education centre than the others. Various members of the community simply attended on a regular basis and imparted their specialist knowledge of various subjects to the youngsters who had chosen to be present for that particular area of knowledge. The topics and subjects taught were thus ones directly relevant to the lives of the people on the island - or sometimes nearby islands – and were thus likely to be of interest to the newly emerging generation.

Project work was also the norm in their educational system, as it was widely believed the best way for anyone to fully understand a subject was to actively engage in acquiring relevant knowledge for themself. Emphasis on self-discovery, creativity and a generally iconoclastic approach to education were strongly encouraged. This, it was felt, would keep naturally curious children attached to the educational process. Since the community believed education was a vital developmental process, but had no effective means of making it compulsory – other than showing social disapproval towards those that avoided it – keeping education as interesting as possible was ultimately an essential dimension to the process.

Akiko watched the last of the children head towards the beach, and after making herself a light lunch headed to one of the study rooms. She was particularly keen to follow up on one particular area of her own research, as she had noticed some puzzling recent developments in the coastal waters off her island, and for which she had no plausible explanation. To investigate the matter further, she had recently flown a mapping drone over the relevant area and asked for a quantitative appraisal of the situation from the planet's computer system. She would spend the afternoon studying the data; she was hoping this would result in an improved understanding of the dynamics of the coastal ecosystem that was still, contrary to what they had previously thought, clearly evolving and in unexpected ways.

The major concern was that it was not evolving in the manner in which their theories maintained it should; in fact the latest development was particularly perplexing – the evolution of the ecosystem seemed to be going into reverse and so far she had been unable to formulate a plausible explanation. That was, unless she was willing to consider the ultimate worst case scenario – that Earth-originating life-forms in the long run were just not suited to this planet. This was something Akiko was not yet ready to believe in, and she was desperate for a more mundane explanation, that some other simpler, but unknown factor, was affecting the development of their major ecosystem.

She sat down at one of the desks and considered her options. Slightly petite with shoulder length shiny black hair and often with a look of concern on her face, Akiko was a relatively self-contained person, but nevertheless always friendly and always willing to help. In most respects, she had enjoyed a standard upbringing on Margalla with long hours spent playing with her friends, intermixed with their highly flexible schooling system. She was initially raised by her father predominantly - though her mother made occasional short visits to the various communes they resided in, and they had moved between several of these over the years – though this was not unusual by Margallan standards – until he finally moved on to one of the other islands, and she decided to stay in Ascaso with her close friends.

Arrival in Utopia

Initially, she had been the usual outgoing, self-confident and well-adjusted Margallan teenager, until she had experienced an incident involving her and one of her best friends, Chinara, whilst out exploring a long rocky promontory at the end of the bay. An abrupt and sudden change in the weather conditions had created a series of freak waves that swept both of them off the rocks – Chinara being knocked unconscious in the process and drowned. Akiko had struggled desperately in the choppy seas, but eventually managed to make it back to the rocks, where she was found several hours later – after friends had noticed she was missing – exhausted, bruised and badly injured, emotionally shaken but fortunately still alive.

The incident had severely knocked her self-confidence and it was several months before she was back to something close to her old self. Feelings of guilt about her deceased friend, and an unjustified belief that an attempt to help them should have been made sooner, had left her suffering from occasional bouts of anxiety. In the long-term the incident had made her a somewhat more cautious person and, untypically, a bit of a worrier in what was a largely care-free society. This, to some extent, explained her continuing worries concerning the subject area she was currently studying, and a tendency to even consider the worst case scenario as a possible explanation for the developments that had been puzzling her.

Unfortunately, after a couple of hours of poring over the data she was still at a loss as to what was actually occurring. She decided it was time to call it a day. She needed more time to think about the matter and maybe approach it from a different angle. Discussing the subject with other members of her community might give her some different insights; maybe she was missing something fairly obvious, she thought. Before she did that, though, she headed back to the communal dwelling where she lived with about two dozen other members of her community, chatted to some of her friends, made the necessary arrangements for the evening's entertainment and slept for a couple of hours in the late afternoon heat. Finally she showered, dried her shoulder-length shiny black hair, put on some shorts and a loose top and headed out into the warmth of the early evening sunshine.

Later that evening Kendra and Zuri were the first to arrive in the communal area of the residence, followed shortly by Keyden, then Jairo and finally

Arrival in Utopia

Amara and Mylah rolled up last, even though they lived in the same dwelling as Akiko. They rifled through the various fridges and cupboards in the communal kitchen – having been fully replenished by an AI unit during the afternoon – and found most of the foods they were looking for. Anything unavailable such as certain fruits, salads and other vegetables they harvested from what was locally known as the 'community garden', but which was, in reality, a patchwork of communal orchards and vegetable allotments, situated around the environs of the residential dwellings. They were eating quite late - compared with others in the community - so a brief diversion into the garden was needed for some of the more favoured foodstuffs.

Once fully provisioned, they headed towards a large wooden table close to the beach, laid out the food buffet-style, poured out the locally-brewed beers and made a start on the various foods spread across the table – a mixture of fresh fruits and salads from the gardens and various protein snacks, breads and pastas brought from their ferming unit. As was usually the case on these occasions, the group was in a light-hearted and positive mood. Sazhina was setting on the western horizon and its dying rays illuminated the small number of clouds hanging motionless in the sky with various hues of pink, blue and yellow.

'Beer tastes particularly good tonight' noted Amara approvingly.
'Yeh, we've been trying to perfect the fermentation process. The water's purer now and we've adopted a technique to reduce the sugar levels. It's much crisper and lighter, smoother, more refreshing,' explained Zuri, who had made it his latest goal in life to develop better quality beer for the community.
'I'll drink to that,' quipped Mylah, and they all laughed and their glasses soon needed replenishing.
'Doing anything exciting these days Kendra?' asked Akiko,
'I've volunteered to help with the tidal generator at the western end of the island tomorrow – as I'm considered to be something of an engineer,' Kendra laughed self-effacingly. 'One of the AI units reported that the control unit is in need of replacement; it's beyond routine maintenance apparently. We're going over there with a replacement unit which was constructed by the printers in the mini-fab today. All the diagnostic checks have come out positive, so it should be ready to install tomorrow.'

'Can't it just be left to the AI units?' asked Jairo. 'Surely anything routine like that shouldn't be a problem for them.'

'It probably could, but they've reported one or two technical issues, so a couple of us are going along, just in case they run into unchartered territory,' Kendra replied.

'There won't be a problem with energy supplies tomorrow though I hope,' enquired Keyden.

'No chance of that, one thing we're not short of here is energy. Tidal's only a small part of the mix – the majority comes from solar, wind and some wave power and we're rarely short on any of those. But it's good not to be too reliant on any one source. You won't notice anything tomorrow, whilst the unit's off-line,' answered Kendra, aware that most of those present probably knew much of this anyway.

'What about the fish-counting Akiko, how's that going?' smirked Mylah, aware that her co-dweller had developed some major concerns regarding her current research project.

'I do more than just count fish, thank you very much,' replied Akiko deliberately faking offence in her voice. 'I'm looking at the whole coastal ecosystem now and it's not working in the way it's meant to. We thought we now had enough top predators – the reef and bay sharks – to finally keep the system in balance, but in recent months their numbers have dwindled badly. We've never seen this before, and it's throwing everything out of kilter. The numbers of snapper and snook fish have exploded and they're busily chomping their way through half the ecosystem. We're losing a whole range of plants and bottom-dwelling species as a result, but even worse, when that's all been consumed I'm concerned that the predator fish will either depart or die off. The local seabirds had finally reached what looked like self-sustaining numbers, but that's not going to last long if all this continues for much longer, and if they decline, so will the seahawks that depend on them.'

'But once the fish numbers decline, then all the others should recover, shouldn't they?' asked Jairo.

'Possibly, but I think it's going to be at much reduced levels, a really impoverished seascape. That's my worst fear, and I really hope it's not actually going to come to that, but it has to be considered a possibility,' answered Akiko, expressing concerns she had been developing for some time now.

'So, the sharks are the keystone species, then', Zuri interrupted
'Ooh, we learnt something in Environmental Studies, then,' quipped Mylah.
'I was a model student, I will have you know. No. It's all really interesting this stuff; it's fascinating how everything knits together and the complexity that develops naturally within ecosystems. When I've finished with my AI maintenance project, I might join Akiko and help search for the sharks', added Zuri with a knowing look.
'Does it matter much to us; after all, we don't eat any of these things. Can it have an impact on the islands?' asked Keyden.
The others looked slightly concerned at such a question, so he clarified his position. 'I know it's important, but does it have wider implications?'
'Possibly, it's impossible to be certain. Once ecosystems change, the results can be highly unexpected and very unpredictable. We might get swarms of flies or beaches covered in toxic algae or something even worse. It's impossible to know what the end result will turn out to be. Impoverished ecosystems are usually highly unstable, there's lots of space for existing or newly introduced organisms to take over - at least temporarily – and with unpredictable results. We really need to evolve and then maintain a rich and complex system that is capable of providing the stability that is really needed, like the one that's been developing on land over the decades since we arrived here.'
'Maybe the sharks have just gone elsewhere, and eventually they'll come back and restore order', suggested Zuri.
'I've considered that, but where would they go. Most of the oceans around us are deep and of little use to them, as far as I'm aware. I don't know where they would go. The nearest shallow seas are thousands of kilometers away – why would they travel there? Though, now you mention it, I have been wondering whether I need to ask the satellites to check out those areas,' pondered Akiko.
'How long have the sharks been here; presumably since the very beginning - they're not an evolved species are they?' asked Amara.
'Mmm, they might have evolved to some extent - I'd be surprised if they haven't. After all, our gravity, solar radiation, day length and tidal behaviours are all different to those on Earth - they must have evolved to some degree, I would have thought. But, no, you're right; they came in the 'primordial soup'. Sharks lay eggs, so it was easy to include them in the species mix that was

poured into the ocean when the 'genesis pod' first arrived here. The mix of species seems to have been quite good actually; the technicians back on Earth seem to have done a pretty good job with that. Ironic, really, given they destroyed their own biosphere,' she added. 'Perhaps, the technicians of spaceship Earth were not as totally inept as we like to think,' added Akiko, referring to a commonly held belief amongst her people.

'Are you indicating there's a more fundamental problem here? Is there any truth in that old idea that Margalla is actually a dying planet?' asked Mylah. I heard that's why the first stasis ships to find this place chose not to stay here, and went elsewhere.'

'There's no good evidence anyone got here before us; that's just a rumour based on some vague circumstantial evidence,' chipped in Kendra, keen to emphasise a belief held by most Margallans, and strongly held for a number of reasons they considered to be of great significance.

'I'm not sure this is even a dying planet,' replied Akiko. 'The seismic studies indicate there is considerable low-level volcanic activity. It's all occurring deep in the oceans, so it's not very noticeable and it's too far down to create new continents at the present time. This probably is an old planet - there are three very large shallow seas, for instance – all very distant from here – that were presumably once continents and are now the end product of millions of years of erosion. It does seem odd that volcanic activity has never replaced them elsewhere, but the satellite scans indicate the inner core is still hot. It's not going to freeze up any time soon,' confirmed Akiko.

'Is there some other problem with the planet, something more basic? Some problem with the fact that there's so little land, or with the geo-dynamics of the planet? Whilst I believe no one has ever found good evidence of indigenous life on another planet, have we actually looked hard enough here? Could indigenous life-forms be harming the sharks - primitive bacteria or something?' asked Zuri.

'We've seen no sign whatsoever of non-Earth based life-forms. Anyway, if there were any primitive indigenous microbes here, they couldn't harm Earth-based life – they wouldn't have the evolved adaptations required to attack us. They'd need some massive genetic mutational leap to achieve that; it's highly unlikely that could be achieved. Everything else seems to be doing well here, even thriving. Look at us, and the lizards, butterflies, dragonflies and suchlike flourishing across the islands. Why would only the sharks be affected? I think there must be a more mundane reason, but I can't work out what it is. We'll have to hope it's an isolated phenomena and not a sign of worse things to come – that our ecosystem is actually as robust as we've been assuming it is until now.'

Finally, Akiko ended with some surprise news, 'I've contacted the biological institutes on Zeta Kotlin and sent them the relevant data. They have whole university departments there devoted to the science of Environmental Studies. They won't know as much about the astrobiology of Margalla as we do, but they might have some theories or similar experiences on their planet that could help us understand this development. If the Opa-Loka should visit us sometime soon, I might even get the chance to go and study there myself. They might even have useful substitute predators we could bring back – though that would be a last resort; it's not a route I'd be happy going down.'

'There's also that nice pilot they have as well, what was her name – oh, yes, Jiaying – I seem to remember you spent some time with her,' smirked Mylah, looking at Akiko.

'And she wasn't the only one either, was she Jairo?' added Amara quickly.

'Yes, I wonder why they like coming here, given we have so little in the way of resources to offer them. I think I might know why,' laughed Kendra.

'Yeh, but the crew is never the same from one visit to the next, so it's actually nothing to do with that. I have no problems finding someone here anyway,' retorted Akiko, faking mock offence once again.

'Speaking of which, it's getting cold now, let's head back to the building,' suggested Amara. They paired up and headed back to their dwelling, all except for Akiko who decided to stay a little longer and wandered down to the shoreline.

She was now the only person on the beach, one that spanned the length of the pocket-sized bay. She walked slowly and thoughtfully as she made her way along the small waves that lapped gently and quietly onto the sandy beach. Was there something fundamentally wrong with Margalla, she wondered. Had she underestimated the enormity of the problem on their planet? She didn't think so, but sometimes small clues could be indicators of much larger problems. They had few actually functioning ecosystems on the planet and they knew they lived in a potentially fragile scenario. Until now, though, the few ecosystems that did exist all seemed to have been developing towards a greater level of stability. Was she witnessing the first signs of that development coming to a halt, or even beginning to reverse, she wondered.

She looked out across the dark ocean and could just make out the dim outline of the horizon across the calm waters. The night air was warm and still, with just the very lightest of breezes. After a while, she raised her eyes towards the starry sky and noted the small red and green moons of Rosa and Jade amongst the myriad stars, already well into their nightly trajectory across the starlit sky. In some way, she had always thought of them as good luck charms, but was their luck about to run out on Margalla. Surely not, she hoped.

Zeleyan – political unrest

The region of Outer Padnia stretched from the high northern hills - that long ago had marked the boundary with the vast grassy plains of the Northern Alliance lands further to the north - to the indented sea coves, bays and jagged headlands that constituted the coastline of New Europe in the far south-eastern reaches of the region.   Much of its extensive lands were constituted by verdant rolling hills - interspersed with drier, slightly-raised plateaus - that these days were largely turned over to arable farming; extensive crop fields and fruit orchards, that, in places, were highly productive. Between these hills ran long, narrow and fertile river valleys, all of which headed eastwards to the relatively flat and increasingly urbanised coastal plains, characterised by pockets of intense industrial activity, but also dependent upon the service sector activities of the major cities that dominated the coastal region.

For several decades now - ever since its incorporation into the pan-continental super-nation of Zeleyan – the region had mostly enjoyed political stability and a steadily developing economy, although periodically interspersed with the occasional recession and slower levels of economic growth. Politically, as with the rest of the supercontinent, it had experienced long years of repression, highly authoritarian rule, occasional political crackdowns, and lacked even the most basic of freedoms and civil rights. Its social and cultural life was strictly regulated, with an emphasis on maintaining and celebrating only traditions, practices and customs approved by the regime. Nothing was permitted without the express permission of the ruling party.

In the city of Jons, it was the height of summer and the region was basking in the typically high temperatures of the southern summer sun. White-washed houses, interspersed with the occasional pink or yellow interloper, packed tightly along the broad clean streets that constituted the entirety of the well ordered city centre. High-branching carob trees lined the streets at regular intervals, their long dark pods ripening in the heat of the late afternoon sun. Underneath them, individuals and small groups sought shelter in the shade they offered from the intense glare of Hedilla, the planet's large bright yellow sun, a picture that had altered little over recent decades. The city centre had hardly changed since the construction of its original carefully laid out design, nearly a century beforehand.

In other respects, though, events in Jons were far from typical, for political unrest had broken out across the region and rebellion was in the air. In normal times, all political activity, other than that conducted through the United National Patriotic Party (UNPP), was strictly proscribed. Unlawful gatherings, membership of outlawed organisations and unapproved media communications would all result in immediate arrest and summary imprisonment. Known troublemakers, simply disappeared. Such repression had mostly been borne stoically, particularly as living standards had been steadily and measurably improving. But, in the last few weeks, all of this had changed. A recent lowering of the approved and strictly tiered wage rates accompanied by a compulsory extension in working hours had come as a huge shock to a workforce, more used to seeing gradual improvements in their material circumstances. Such a development had been greeted with incredulity. The 'unofficial deal' was that they suffered the lack of freedoms without protest, but enjoyed an improved standard of living in compensation.

The result of the shock had been a spontaneous outbreak of illegal political gatherings and a series of strikes, particularly amongst the more skilled workers who knew they were more difficult to replace. It was for this reason that Colonel Davila had swept into the city early that morning at the head of a large military convoy of armoured vehicles that was normally stationed - for outbreaks of unrest such as these - in barracks further to the north of the city. Once in the city centre, he had positioned troops at strategic points across Jons, ordered the arrest of known subversives, and publically threatened workers with severe punishment if they failed to arrive at work on time. There had been some sporadic pockets of attempted resistance, but after a few hours the city streets were once again back to their perceived normality. Davila would maintain his military presence until it was believed the situation had been fully normalised.

The colonel, a stocky man with sandy hair, a short moustache and a pale complexion, was now with his senior officers and other high-ranking party officials at the party's headquarters in the centre of the city. Given that control of the city appeared to have been fully reestablished, he felt he could begin to relax a little and consider the wider situation. He was pleased that he had not needed to resort to the AI units that he had at his disposal, and that human soldiers alone had succeeded in restoring order. He regarded the AI units as inferior to his human troops – they did not understand the myriad complexities of conflict and the nuance of battle. In previous conflicts they had inflicted unnecessary massacres, shot innocent bystanders and even, on occasions, shot their own troops when the chaos of the battlefield had become too complex for their simplistic programming. On occasion, they could even be worse than conscript armies, he thought to himself.

His mind wandered elsewhere, as he observed the various elite figures circulating around the room, congratulating themselves on the restoration of order and a return to normality. Davila couldn't help finding it somewhat perplexing that the centres of political unrest in the uprising had been amongst the most prosperous areas of the region – it seemed a real paradox. Surely these people had the most to be grateful for - they should be the most ardent supporters of the regime, not out on the streets causing trouble. Some people didn't know how fortunate they were, he thought, whilst others – usually troublemakers - mistakenly, always thought they knew best. He continued to peruse the elegantly furnished room and observe, somewhat enviously, the ease with which certain 'establishment figures' struck up conversation and mingled amongst the different social groups.

His mind drifted back to his own awkward childhood and the long and difficult years spent both at home and in school. He had struggled with the subjects he was taught and had received no help with them from his own parents, who were usually more concerned with keeping their dysfunctional relationship alive than addressing his developmental needs. Neither had he excelled on the sports field. The other children had either ignored him or treated him as an inferior, and the teachers clearly thought he would amount to little or nothing. The other children in the school and neighbourhood always thought they knew better than him, had always belittled his efforts and opinions.

As he got older, little had improved for him – in some respects matters even worsened. Long years of ridicule had made him socially unconfident, and whilst his peers were experiencing early romantic encounters he remained depressingly single. As he approached the end of his schooling, his job prospects had looked dismal. The saving of him had been his patriotism and his love for his country. He might not have been able to be proud of himself, but he could at least be proud of his country. He had joined the youth cadet wing of the UNPP, and they had eventually encouraged him to join the military. Gradually he had gained in confidence and moved up slowly through the ranks, until now he had achieved the rank of Commander of the Eastern Forces.

History had vindicated him, he believed. It had been he who had been right all along, and the others – the mocking children – who had all been wrong. And it was now those kinds of people who were causing unrest in the region – leftist agitators who always thought they knew better than the regime leaders. They must be the explanation for the unrest, otherwise it made no sense. Elitist leftist elements convincing the ignorant masses that life could be made better by creating greater freedoms. In his experience, people who had too much freedom simply indulged themselves to excess, and it all invariably ended in tears. What people really needed was order, discipline and boundaries, otherwise they had no moral compass and no means of telling right from wrong. This was why he was more than happy to crackdown swiftly and brutally on the political unrest – it was what the people actually needed. For this reason, Davila had earned the reputation of being a particularly repressive military commander - 'the Sword of the East' - and it was a reputation he was keen not to dispel.

But why had Supreme Commander Vartin issued a decree changing working conditions in the first place, he wondered. There appeared to be no particular problems with the economy, quite the opposite in fact. Maybe there was something to these rumours that there were wider problems on the planet. He had heard accounts of increased activity at the spaceport of Gombos, accounts he considered to be from reliable sources. The site had experienced long years of neglect, but was now apparently a hive of activity. Others had mentioned a sudden increase in the number of satellites being placed in orbit, and that Space Fleet Commander Vice-Admiral Rosson was at this very moment visiting Rorque 4. How had Rosson – an incompetent bungler – managed to suddenly raise the profile of the space fleet - traditionally seen almost as an afterthought - he wondered.

Arrival in Utopia

Davila looked searchingly around the room but wasn't sure who he could trust; false rumours, he knew, were often bandied about to catch the unwary off guard. He needed to be in Vartin's inner circle, he decided – a promotion that had, so far, eluded him, and that was now beginning to rankle. How else could he know what was really occurring on Zeleyan? He needed to find a way of getting closer to Supreme Commander Vartin, he now confidently decided. He left the room quietly and unnoticed, whilst the great and the good of Jons continued to discuss their recent good fortunes.

Alpha Fraczan – stability issues

A single solitary silver autocar made its way rapidly across the dusty red plateau in a long straight unwavering line. As it did so it kicked up a trail of carmine-coloured dust behind the moving vehicle, that only slowly dispersed in the crisp cold air of the early morning. Interspersed amongst the carmine-coloured dirt, and the jumbled assortment of angular and jagged rocks of varying sizes that so characterised the rock-strewn plateau, occasional stunted scrubby yellow-green goat willow bushes struggled to grow in an otherwise dry and inhospitable landscape. The dark red plateau stretched out before the vehicle, until it suddenly and dramatically ended at the precipitously deep ravine that separated the plateau from the vast mountain range further to its south.

The thin jagged peaks and steep-sided valleys of the Kristos Mountains were already displaying the pale reds and deep ochres so characteristic of the planet, in the early morning rays of the sun. Where the sun's rays hit the mountain's vast array of quartz crystals the slopes sparkled softly in the distance, lending a certain shimmering quality to the mountains in the crisp early morning air. The self-driving vehicle followed the long straight dirt track cleared between the jagged rocks and bushes, until it reached the clearing on the edge of the precipitous ravine.

Once the autocar had come to a gradual halt at the end of the road, the engine cut automatically. A woman of average height and in her early thirties with a short black bob, pale skin and wearing sunglasses climbed out of the vehicle. Mila Lustrom straightened out her jacket and trousers and took in the expansive view before her. The mountains with their subtle but majestic beauty never ceased to impress her, but this was not the reason for visiting the ravine this particular morning. Lifting her gaze higher in the sky, she spotted the object of her intended attention and it really did seem to loom larger than usual in the sky; the bright yellow star that was now clearly visible above the lower peaks situated to her right across the broadest part of the ravine.

Lustrom gazed at the star for some time, finding it difficult to believe that the luminous object in the sky could prove the undoing of everything they had achieved on Alpha Fraczan. Was their civilisation really doomed? Was the

29

planet really in as much difficulty as her colleagues were maintaining? What could be salvaged from their work here if they were forced to abandon their home planet? Lustrom pondered several possibilities, unsure of what the solutions were, or even if any were actually needed. She was hoping against hope that the calculations would be proven to be wrong.

It had long been known amongst the university communities which constituted the entirety of Alpha Fraczan's inhabitants, that the orbit of Celestrina represented a possible major problem for the planet upon which they had chosen to build their establishments. Alpha Fraczan was the fourth planet of an average-sized red dwarf star known as Gannexon. The planet was actually considerably closer to Gannexon than Earth was to the Sun, but the relatively weak solar radiation given out by Gannexon meant that Alpha Fraczan was a somewhat colder, and thus drier, planet than that of Earth. To compensate for this cooler climate, the communities were largely based around the more equatorial zones of the largely dry rocky planet. Extensive ice caps dominated both the northern and southern regions of the planet, but did mean that a constant source of fresh water was available in the equatorial zone, since many of the glaciers that spread outwards from the ice caps melted to become rivers, some of which made their way through the enormous ravines that crisscrossed the planet's largely mountainous terrain.

It was one of these great ravines that Lustrom was now stood in front of, and as Gannexon continued its ascent in the morning sky she caught its gleaming orange-red reflection on the broad river meandering its way slowly across the floor of the ravine far below. Whilst standing at the edge, a sharp gust of cold northerly air suddenly blew from behind her and she pulled her jacket closer around her body for extra warmth. It looked as though it was set to be yet another wind-blasted day, as per usual. She was about to leave when she noticed the flight of a small dark brown warbler, its wings fluttering amongst the goat willow bushes that grew on the edge of the ravine, and stopped to admire its tenacity and ability to survive in such a harsh terrain. From the edge of the ravine precipice Lustrom returned to the autocar, and the silver machine made its way directly back to Sienna Pools University.

As she approached, the university buildings towered isolated but compactly above the flatness of the dark red plain, a mixture of sandstone and glass constructions that appeared curiously both modern and ancient at the same time. The need to keep out the frequent strong northerly winds – an almost constant feature of the climate in this region - meant that the complex possessed an almost fortified character, and as she neared the university she was reminded of heavily-fortified desert castles she had seen in old Earth movies. Her first meeting of the day was on the top floor of the central building and upon her arrival she was greeted by a number of colleagues who had clearly followed her return from the recent visit to the ravine, thanks to their lofty vantage point on one of the upper floors of the central building.

Mila Lustrom came from a family of struggling academics, who had suffered intermittent periods of unemployment as they had chosen somewhat unfashionable and esoteric subjects to study at university level. At lower school, she frequently struggled with both the academic and social aspects of life, had needed to move schools on more than one occasion, and was occasionally the subject of bullying and social ridicule. As a result of these early experiences, she was now somewhat more socially insecure than her present day peers and often struggled to make and retain friendships.

These formative experiences in life had also left her with a fairly pessimistic view of human nature; a belief that society was not particularly friendly, and neither was it likely to improve anytime soon. A number of problematic relationships in her teenage years had only added to her negative view of human behaviour. She often found herself feeling cynical about the motivation of others, seeing self-interest and deceit at the root of many of their decisions, rather than genuine attempts to engage with her or the issues at hand.

Nevertheless, her parents had eventually settled into their careers, and her life ultimately came to enjoy a suitable level of stability. She eventually progressed in the field of biology – a developing interest in plants had allowed her to reduce her level of contact with humans - though she had tended to focus on some of the more fringe areas of the science. Eventually, her focus gravitated towards the study of astrobiology and the manner by which life was evolving on the various different planets that had been colonised by humans. She had initiated contacts with several other newly-formed civilisations, though the receipt of information from other star systems was always very slow-going, and its arrival typically occurred in occasional intense and massive batches of data. As such, she was now fully engaged in comparative studies of life on different planets, and how it developed within the context of local planetary conditions such as gravity, length of year and day, strength of magnetic field, distance from star and the class of star involved.

With her shoulder length black hair, dark eyes and a slightly enigmatic smile, and a penchant for wearing dark sunglasses though they were rarely needed on Alpha Fraczan, she had gained a reputation within the University for being slightly quirky and occasionally withdrawn. As Mila entered the room, she could see her colleagues looking out through the huge windows that ran the length of the upper floor, and after the brief greetings she stated, 'it really does appear to be getting visibly larger, though I guess it could just be my imagination – or maybe it's just confirmation bias, not sure either way really.'

Itzel Anderson, tall and slim, with short blonde hair and in her early thirties, and another leading member on the university committee turned away from the huge window and looked across the wide stone table that stood between Mila and the others, and stated very precisely, 'we know for certain its trajectory is bringing it closer to Gannexon, but it's no longer looking like fine margins to me. What's worrying me more than anything is that the satellites are already picking up a discernible increase in the rate of tilt. Our obliquity was very gradually changing even before Celestrina's recent approach, but now it seems to be significantly amplified by its increasing proximity. It's looking like our worst fears could easily be confirmed.'

'I assume the whole planet is aware of this development, after all we always knew it was a possibility, though personally I thought it would probably be many centuries before this was actually likely to happen. The geological studies indicated the planet has been largely stable for probably several millennia, perhaps even many more; there was no reason to believe we would get unlucky quite this quickly. Celestrina makes a near approach our star system every 37.5 years; this happens on a regular basis, it clearly makes no significant difference normally,' Mila responded, still unwilling to believe the worst.

Arrival in Utopia

'We're in constant communication with all the other universities on Alpha,' Itzel informed Mila. 'There's a general consensus that we need to continue to run and refine the data, and extrapolate from the readings on a continuous basis. The models so far are not fully clear whether a major tilt is on the cards but they're certainly not ruling it out . . . but in my opinion it's looking more and more likely. We need to start considering our options with regards to a worst case scenario actually occurring, I'm afraid to say.'

Mila could still hardly believe what she was hearing and was about to say as such again, but thought better of it. Her other colleagues looked equally concerned but said little. Mila assumed that they had already discussed the situation and that Itzel's pronouncements were pretty much the consensus of the whole group. She started to think about the implications for her own work on the planet. She was an astrobiologist and figured she could probably pursue the main body of her research pretty much anywhere, but following a particular new theory she had developed, she had recently taken a much keener interest in the plant life on her own planet, and was concerned this would now come to a premature halt. This was definitely not what she needed at this particular point in her career.

She looked around the room, but the silence following Itzel's pronouncement continued and many of the assembled group returned their gaze out across the plateau towards the shimmering red mountains, the early morning wind now howling around the university towers. The large windows of the upper floor of the university building had been constructed for the very purpose of providing far-reaching views across the dramatic landscape – indeed the university's location had been chosen as much for this as for the suitably flat terrain that facilitated easy construction. That, and its proximity to the fresh water lagoons which were situated slightly towards its eastern side, and which could be found nowhere else on the vast plateau landscape.

As she had anticipated, the wind's strength was now increasing and carmine-coloured dust clouds were beginning to lift from across the flatness of the plateau, spreading their dimming gloom, as the cold winds from the north once more blasted the bare surfaces of the flattened landscape. Today was proving to be yet another ordinary wind-blasted day on Alpha Fraczan, Mila considered. Indeed, in most respects it appeared a totally ordinary day, little different from any other in the more than a century that the world had been inhabited by the academic communities. Yet, in one major respect, this seemed to be a day with implications unlike any other in the planet's short history.

Arrival in Utopia

Rorque 4, Cosmic Solutions – plans for the future

Christine Sanchez leaned back in her executive chair and gazed once again at the latest quarterly figures on the screen in front of her. No matter how she viewed them they made for depressing reading. Lower than the previous quarter, even lower than the equivalent quarter in the year before, and still on a general downward trend. Even worse, this was the quarter when the recovery in the corporation's fortunes was meant to have kicked in. Their big new project – the one that would see them emerge from what seemed like endless years of economic malaise – had made no discernible difference to their latest profit margins. It wasn't even slowing the downward trend. She could almost feel the vultures circling. It had taken grit and determination to hold things together even this long; but she was beginning to run out of scapegoats and excuses for failure. Whether she could manage to hold things together much longer was anyone's guess.

She gazed out the window from the thirty-fifth floor of the headquarters of Cosmic Solutions, one of the oldest and most prestigious companies on Rorque 4, out across the city of New Galtville. It was another swelteringly hot day and she could see the shimmering heat haze rising rapidly from the city streets and buildings far below, distorting the shapes of the figures and vehicles that moved distantly through the heat of the afternoon sun. In places, the buildings appeared as if they were almost melting, so intense was the movement of the rising air.

Eleutheria, the star round which Rorque 4 orbited, burned brightly in the cloudless azure-blue sky and she further dimmed the windows to reduce the increasing glare. Her gaze returned to the screen and she flicked through various images. She stopped at one of the planet Morpheus, at the heart of her corporation's supposedly life-saving project. Discernible progress was clearly being made. The shallow oceans that had been established were clearly visible from space now, and the areas of green on the landmasses surely signified that the atmosphere was now approaching habitation levels. But, all of this, she could not help feeling, was occurring far too slowly.

Cosmic Solutions had set its sights on terra-forming one of the neighbouring planets of their star system. The hopes of the corporation were that this newly habitable planet could attract an ever increasing population, thus launching a concerted and prolonged economic recovery and expanding markets, and thus formulating a return to lucratively high levels of profitability. The corporation's directors had identified the root cause of its current profitability problems as resulting from a lack of new markets into which it could successfully venture. For a whole host of reasons, none of its previous efforts had seemed to work on Rorque 4, and so they had now finally turned to an extra-planetary solution. Here too though, the company had encountered a whole range of major difficulties in its new and highly ambitious endeavour.

Firstly, space travel was still a relatively slow process and operations between the two planets seemed to be interminably drawn out, with one costly delay after another slowing their progress. Secondly, they were still struggling with formulating a viable plan for reigniting the inner core of Morpheus. The sister planet was thought to be considerably older than Rorque 4 and had therefore cooled earlier and effectively died – a development marked by the end of any meaningful volcanic activity deriving from the planet's core. However, their surveys indicated that the planet clearly had possessed oceans and volcanoes until relatively recently – at least in geological terms - and so the core probably did not need too great an energy infusion to make it sufficiently molten to once again power the volcanic activities needed to effectively keep the planet alive.

Sanchez had, not surprisingly, recruited the brightest and the best of the scientific and engineering community for such a huge endeavour. In the early days of the project they had met her expectations and delivered for the corporation, but recently she had increasingly felt that they were running out of solutions to the mounting difficulties they faced, and seemed to be just playing for time now – probably just trying to retain their contracts for as long as they possibly could, she thought. The corporation needed some major engineering breakthroughs, but she could not see from where they might be forthcoming. As such, her position was becoming untenable; she had tried everything she could possibly conceive of, but now she was running out of options, though she was not about to openly admit this to anyone.

She had been schooled at great expense by her wealthy family, who had expected her to follow a career in law – like most of her family – and eventually reach the upper echelons of the judicial hierarchy. She, however, had found the legal profession far too dry and its rules-based culture far too stifling. She had rebelled against her upbringing - and fallen out badly with her family – and opted for a career in business instead, which had taken her surprisingly quickly into the upper echelons of Cosmic Solutions. School connections, wealth, ambition and being an astute judge of character - but above all a pathological desire to prove to her family that she was right and they were wrong - had all helped her rise rapidly up the corporate ladder and eventually to the position of Chief Executive. Despite, or perhaps because of, her success, she had persisted with her innate sense of self-righteousness and rarely, if ever, admitted to her mistakes

So, in many respects this was an unusual predicament for Sanchez, for she had built her career on a reputation for blue sky thinking, unorthodox ventures and a knack for spotting popular trends. In the popular media her persona was one of being slightly oddball, a bit wacky and anti-establishment, but with a hint of genius. Although her long wavy ginger hair and penchant for wearing brightly multi-coloured dresses gave some credence to this portrait of her, it was effectively at odds with reality, for the image had been carefully crafted by media figures within her own company. In reality, as with all the leading figures of corporate life on Rorque 4, she had been educated at the one of the most expensive Liberty Schools and derived from a thoroughly establishment background. The unorthodox image had simply served to cloak her underlying drive and ambition, and had fooled many of her erstwhile rivals, allowing her to eventually arrive at the highest echelons of one of the planet's leading corporations.

As she idly perused the streets far below, she could not but notice the general paucity of people out and about on the streets below. Given it was the middle of a working day this was quite puzzling. She had occupied this office for the best part of a decade now, and she was sure the streets had traditionally been busier than was currently the case. Intrigued, she looked more carefully at the few figures that were moving around below and soon discerned that most of them were actually AI units – their gait was discernibly different from that of humans, since attempts to perfectly mimic human motion had never been perfected. She wondered whether the lack of actual people on the streets below might be linked to the increased heat of recent weeks; it was far more pleasant to remain in an air conditioned office, retail centre or eatery than to be out in the baking heat of the city centre streets. But there were not even that many AI units out on the streets and the heat issue was irrelevant to them.

She was suddenly reminded of a missive sent to her some months ago by the Head of Marketing. During the course of exploring the recent sales for a newly developed product placed on the market and aimed at the younger generation, the department had discovered that the number of units shifted was significantly lower than initial projections had indicated. On exploring why this was the case, the department had concluded that the product was actually selling quite well, it was just that the size of the population cohort it was aimed at was significantly smaller than they had originally believed to be the case; thus sales fell far short of what had been originally projected.

At the time she had wondered if the department had simply been making excuses for poor performance, but her latest observation and a number of other recent experiences made her wonder if they had in fact been correct – the planet's population might actually be declining, and possibly quite rapidly. The corporation would need to look into this more thoroughly. Maybe this phenomenon was linked to the persistent economic problems the planet had recently been experiencing. If it was true, it also had worrying implications for their plans to terra-form and colonise Morpheus. Sanchez was suddenly even more concerned than she had been a few minutes earlier.

Earth - Climate Catastrophe

Across the many peoples and planets of the inhabited galaxy the exact details of the exodus from Earth were still the subject of continuing argument and debate, and far from clear now that several generations had been born, grown old and died in the intervening passage of time. Increasingly lost in the mists of time, shrouded in argument and counter-argument, the various different inhabited planets tended to emphasise the particular developments that fitted with their own special narrative of how and why they had departed from the mother planet. In reality, each narrative held at least some grain of truth, but where exactly each put their emphasis was largely borne of the particular dreams and desires of that specific planetary people.

For the inhabitants of Earth, though, the writing had clearly been on the wall once the East Antarctic ice sheet began a series of concerted and prolonged melt sequences; huge ice-floes and bergs slipping dramatically into the Antarctic Ocean every southern summer. At this point it became obvious to the entire world that it was only a matter of time before Earth would inevitably experience a seventy metre sea level rise of devastating consequences. Nearly a billion people, and most of the world's great cities, were faced with the imminent or eventual problem of severe flooding, if not outright and total submergence. The coastal plains and fertile agricultural deltas of the planet would no longer be there to feed huge swathes of the world's population. Before long, the many inhabitants residing around the Bay of Bengal proved to be the first to experience such permanent inundation and the subsequent forced migration that would later become familiar across much of the planet.

Whilst the wealthier sections of these populations might be able to head for higher ground or the, relatively empty, interior of the various continents at higher latitudes, for the vast majority of the affected peoples no such option realistically existed. Planet Earth faced the ever increasing prospect of experiencing possibly several billion climate refugees on the move, desperate for new homes and livelihoods. To all intents and purposes there was no serious possibility of this number being accommodated anywhere anytime soon. Humans needed somewhere to emigrate to, but the rapidly heating interiors of the major continents offered little in the way of promise for the desperate soon-to-be-starving masses.

The first collapses of the ice sheet came a short time before the Earth's human inhabitants reached a peak population of slightly more than ten billion individuals in the early 2080s. Global resources had just about coped up until this landmark, but there had long been signs of stresses and strains within an international economy faced with the twin dilemmas of a rapidly changing climate and a human population approaching peak numbers and seeking ever more affluent lifestyles. Across the entirety of the global economy a profound malaise set in as agricultural areas were swallowed up by the oceans, and the world's leaders could only look on in alarm as the greatest calamity in human history loomed alarmingly across the decades before them.

A minority had hoped that the melting of the ice sheets, permafrost and glaciers – particularly at the higher latitudes of the formerly frozen Northern Hemisphere – might offer promising new possibilities for large-scale farming and urbanisation, but the speed of change, the geophysical instability and the nutrient-poor soils of the newly-unfrozen lands, together with a whole host of legal, political and economic barriers meant these hopes were never to be fulfilled. At best they would have only housed a fraction of the coastal refugees anyway.

The prospects of runaway climate change had been on the cards for several decades beforehand and there had been plenty of warning signs posted along the way. The much vaunted early attempt to limit global warming to two degrees Centigrade had signally failed by the early 2030s. This marked a crucial turning point in the catastrophe that was soon to envelop the entirety of the planet. Previous to this point the host of climatic changes had, to some degree, been manageable – persistent droughts in India, central Africa and the southern states of the USA, intense summer fires in the Australian outback and the Mediterranean oak forests, ever strengthening hurricanes and cyclones in the western Pacific and Atlantic seaboards and heatwaves and flash flooding almost everywhere else. All could be accommodated in some way within the existing structures.

Arrival in Utopia

But from the 2030s onwards, accelerating warming had breached various tipping points and unleashed one positive climatic feedback system after another, warming the planet in a vicious circle by which one warming event inevitably gave rise to a further episode of heating. First to go was the rainforest of the Amazon basin, quickly followed by the other rainforests of the world. As their soils and peatlands heated and dried, so they released further massive deposits of carbon, which in turn caused the eventual melting of the Siberian permafrost and even greater release of the potent greenhouse gas methane into the atmosphere in what became, as the century progressed, an unstoppable spiral of one climatic disaster after another.

Elsewhere, the increasingly rapid melting of the ice-sheets was accelerated by an albedo affect caused by ever-darkening seas, and so the polar regions melted at a far faster rate than anyone had ever predicted. This too led to the release of vast amounts of methane gas from the methane hydrate pockets historically trapped for millions of years under the frozen seas. The rapidly warming atmosphere that ensued soon produced equatorial regions that experienced semi-permanent flooding from increasingly intense and prolonged downpours, frequent monsoon episodes and ferocious storms. Straddled around this region like two great belts around the planet, the sub-tropical areas rapidly baked in the ever increasing heat, with worsening droughts, dramatic sandstorms, expanding desertification and frequently intense fires and heatwaves. Crop yields plummeted and people starved. Even the temperate latitudes faced acidic oceans, desiccated soils, frequent droughts, sinking islands, wildfires, heatwaves and flash flooding as they experienced the traumas of runaway climate change.

For those inhabitants of distant planets looking back on this period of Earth's history it was one of eternal puzzlement as to why and how its human inhabitants could have allowed such a self-induced catastrophe to develop in the first place, never mind to be allowed to continue to the point of near-total global destruction. It was not as though they were unaware of their impending doom – the problem had become widely known and discussed in the closing decades of the twentieth century. But if they had been able to travel back through time, their puzzlement might have been at least partially answered. Earth's human inhabitants had spent the previous two centuries

41

on a rapid, prolonged and almost totally uninterrupted drive for material comfort, luxury and prosperity. This may well have been understandable, but it was done with almost no thought for the planet upon which they actually inhabited.

Ultimately, almost all of Earth's human inhabitants had acquired a vested interest in pursuing a course of action launched centuries earlier by their forebearers. Several generations had spent their entire lifetimes acquiring heightened levels of comfort, and were not about to abandon their hard fought gains overnight. Lifestyles based on unlimited construction, throwaway fashion, over-consumption of meat, mass transit systems, flights to foreign holidays, air-conditioned buildings and all the other trappings of modern living had by that point in history acquired an air of complete normality. Those parts of the world's population not actually enjoying such benefits were determined on joining the wealthy regions as fast as was humanely possible. Everyone wanted to join the party. By contrast, alternative less-damaging lifestyles seemed, for most, to be either undesirable, or entirely unnecessary.

Those time travellers would have also noted an almost universal inability to take personal responsibility for the impending catastrophe. Private corporations seeking ever-larger profit margins had few incentives to alter what had always been a highly profitable economic process. Consumers waited for the corporate leaders to take a decisive lead in halting the climate catastrophe, whilst continuing to consume the very products they knew were exacerbating the problem. Corporations waited for politicians to implement the necessary legislation, afraid to be the company that took an isolated and expensive lead that led only to their premature collapse and bankruptcy. Politicians, wary of losing their supporters, waited for voters to show a decisive support for greener alternatives over ever increasing materialism.

Developing countries – those suffering most from the climate catastrophe - implored the wealthy nations to switch to sustainable practices, whilst the wealthy countries demanded an end to the damaging practices pursued by the impoverished economies. Nations dependent upon the extraction of fossil fuels changed absolutely nothing as the rest of the world continued to consume the products they produced, but knew were leading to impending catastrophe. Trust seemed in very short supply, competition precluded cooperation, and for many it was simply someone else's responsibility to take decisive action.

Ultimately, despite the warnings and despite the ever worsening forecasts of doom and disaster, there were far too few humans who were willing to break decisively with their newly acquired lifestyles and opt for a distinctly different way of running their lives. Numerous excuses could be made – the enormity of the task that lay ahead, the lingering doubts as to whether catastrophe really was about to happen, the powerlessness of the majority to effect control over their own lives, the prevalent atomised individualism that prevented collective action in the face of impending doom, or the fact that some even welcomed such an apocalypse as an opportunity to start out all over again.

Whatever the excuse, nothing could detract from the fact that the human race seemed to have wholeheartedly engaged in a gigantic act of self-imposed destruction. It really did seem to be the fable of a failed race. Whether future generations would condemn or understand such a development, there was no escaping the fact that the changes occurring were now irreversible, not just for the planet that they lived on, but for the destiny of the human race forever more.

Alpha Fraczan - history

The official history of the planet of Alpha Fraczan had, not unsurprisingly, initially been written by the respective History departments of each of its universities, shortly after their esteemed organisations had been officially established. The first full and official planetary convention of the Society of Historians of Alpha Fraczan a few years later had, however, noticed discrepancies in the different accounts – mainly over the relative contributions of various individuals, departments and subjects in the initial creation of the planetary civilisation - and had, after prolonged argument and debate, agreed to formulate a committee that would oversee a collective revision of the different historical accounts with the aim of producing a unified planetary version they could largely agree upon.

Given the short history of the planet and the relatively minor areas of disagreement this was duly completed within a few short years. Whilst the finished document did not fully satisfy all interested parties, it was passed by a healthy majority of those present and became the first official history of the planet. The committee had thereafter convened on a regular basis, collating and unifying the latest appraisals of Alpha Fraczan's history as it unfolded over the decades, updating the original document on a five yearly basis. The following account is a summary and adaptation of this official version.

Alpha Fraczan, as with several of the inhabited planets in the Nexus Cluster, had originally been targeted by a multiplicity of stasis ships. Data streamed back across space from the 'genesis pod' that initially terra-formed the planet had given the world a fairly high habitability rating, and so it had duly attracted the attention of a number of interested starships. Many of these starship communities had programmed their AI pilot crews to seek out particular planetary features and environments, largely based on the ideological, religious, political or scientific motives that had driven them out into space in the first place. Alpha Fraczan, for reasons that are still not entirely certain, ended up attracting several starships transporting largely scientific and academic communities, possibly because they sought out planetary locations that might help facilitate their uncovering of the remaining mysteries that outer space still retained. Whatever the exact reason, of the spacecraft that investigated the planet's potential, it was only 'scientific' stasis ships arriving at the small reddish world that decided to remain and make the planet their new home.

The initial information they received from the 'genesis pod' had proven to be largely accurate. Most importantly, a standard nitrogen-oxygen atmosphere had been created that closely replicated that of Earth. There was also fresh water on the planet and the multiplicity of microorganisms, phytoplankton, invertebrates, bacteria and other assorted organisms considered necessary for the basis of a planetary ecosystem – colloquially known as the 'primordial soup' – had been released onto the land and into the lakes and seas and had clearly flourished in suitable locations. A restricted range of plants had become established and a reasonable number of life forms such as fish, other marine creatures, insects and other invertebrates had multiplied from the billions of eggs released into appropriately selected marine and land locations.

The ecosystems that had developed were still fairly basic when the first ships arrived, but it had always been known that this would be the case on the newly inhabited worlds. Given the prevalence of non-Earthlike conditions on all the planets located by the 'genesis pods', and the short span of time in which life forms were given to colonise their new homes before the first settlers arrived, it was always assumed that there might be initial ecosystem difficulties. Such a scenario had been appropriately factored into the early difficulties the arriving space colonists would be facing.

Alpha Fraczan orbited a standard-sized red dwarf star known as Gannexon, and as a result of this was a relatively cool and dry planet. It was the fourth of the inner rocky planets in the planetary system, all of which were somewhat diminutive in size. This meant that as well as being cooler and dimmer than Earth, its gravity was also slightly lower. In addition, its diurnal rotation was slightly quicker than that of Earth, leading to both shorter days and nights. The long-term impact of these conditions on both humans and the rest of the planet's slowly developing biodiversity was considered uncertain, but it was felt by the initial settlers that it was likely to be on the negative side.

Given it was orbiting a diminutive red dwarf star, it was entirely unsurprising that Alpha Fraczan was covered by two extensive and extremely thick ice sheets at both its northern and southern poles, their vast icy coldness only occasionally broached by the highest and toughest of the planet's mountain peaks. These frozen wastelands extended for thousands of kilometers towards the centre of the sphere though eventually melted as they encountered the warmer heat of the sub-tropical and equatorial zones. In these central regions of the planet, mighty glaciers descended from the ice sheets, their meltwater forming twisting rivers and eventually pooling in wide but shallow basins, giving rise to what passed for the small, only slightly saline, seas that could be found interspersed amongst the numerous ancient high-standing red mountain ranges and dusty high plateaus of the central zone.

Further out into Gannexon's planetary system were what might be called two ice giants, though they were comparatively small compared with those found in some of the galaxy's other myriad star systems. The first of these was the larger of the two and named Amaranthus after the deep rich amethyst purple that constituted almost the entirety of its pristine-looking sphere. From Alpha Fraczan it could be seen easily in the night sky and seemed to sit spectacularly in the jet black starscape - only the occasional thin white wispy cloud-like formation drifting at a glacial pace across its shining purple surface interrupting its near perfect uniformity. Further out into the depths of the darkness orbited the smaller paler Cerula, an eggshell-white, slightly bluish and highly fragile-looking sphere that was circled by an almost imperceptibly thin ring of ice debris along its vertical axis.

Alpha Fraczan, itself, suffered a number of potential difficulties for those seeking a new life on its surface, and the travellers on the arriving stasis ships that entered into orbit around the planet in those early days had engaged in prolonged debates as to whether to actually colonise the planet or seek out somewhere more promising. Potentially most problematic was the fact that it was located within a loose binary star system, and it was therefore assumed that the danger of the planet experiencing occasional but significant gravitationally-induced periods of instability was very much a real one. This was thought to be particularly worrying as Alpha Fraczan possessed only two very tiny satellite moons. It thus lacked tides of any significance, experienced darker nights but, most worryingly, lacked the stability-inducing impact that large moons were considered to impart on their celestial host. However, careful modeling of the gravitational forces and a study of the planet's geology by the first potential colonisers seemed to indicate that the star system was perhaps more stable than they had initially feared.

Ultimately, it was probably the thought of going back into stasis for countless years - and the search for another uncertain destination - that had swung the argument in favour of commencing colonisation of the not entirely suitable planet. It was also widely known that only a small percentage of habitable planets actually possessed a large moon, and the opportunity to study a partial binary star system at first hand was not one that some of the scientists were willing to pass up. As such, the first arriving stasis ships soon commenced the disembarcation process that marked the beginning of Alpha Fraczan's history. The AI units on the original genesis pod had already constructed rudimentary habitation zones in preparation for human arrival and so disembarcation was a relatively straightforward affair. Over the space of the following decade, a total of ten stasis ships – all constituted predominantly by scientific and academic communities – chose to make Alpha Fraczan their home.

Each of the communities they created on the planet designated itself as a university establishment. This was not at all surprising, since the vast majority of the starship passengers were scientists and a range of other academics, and so the planet eventually become known colloquially within the local star cluster as the 'science planet'. In the intervening period of just over a century, a scattering of self-governing university communities thus emerged, all situated in, what for Earth humans would be considered, a cool temperate climate zone, even if it was actually located within the equatorial latitudes of the planet. The communities were organised and developed in such a way that scientific research and endeavour were by far and away the predominant economic activity on the planet.

Unlike some of the planets colonised elsewhere in the galaxy, the presence of suitable building materials on Alpha Fraczan was never a significant issue. Even at the beginning of the process there were plentiful quantities of easily mined sandstone and the much harder granite that seemed to be almost ubiquitous across the planet. Combined with the mini-fabs and advanced materials brought onboard the stasis ships, the AI units were readily able to fashion some impressive and grandiose looking centres of learning at suitably designated locations. Given the nature of the communities that constituted the planet's population, there was never a shortage of engineering ideas and expertise, and the novel problems thrown up by such a pioneering project were invariably solved by the combined brain power of the scattered communities and the hard work of the AI units. What all the university constructions shared in common though, was a compact almost fortress-like nature designed to protect them from what seemed like the almost constant blast of polar-originating winds - winds that whipped up the loose glacially deposited moraine that lay across much of the planet's surface and swept it in icy blasts across the plateaus and bare mountains of the central region.

Over time, as more sophisticated manufacturing units were constructed and a wider variety of quarried stones became increasingly available from the huge mountain ranges that dominated the planetary landscape, the governing bodies of the universities became increasingly ambitious in the sophisticated and impressive towering structures they constructed. Whether consciously or subconsciously, or perhaps as a result of working largely in sandstone and granite, all the universities came to eventually resemble the precipitous and jagged red-stone mountains that predominated across the central zones of the planet.

Typically, at the centre of each construction emerged an eclectic collection of towering sandstone and granite structures where the actual university research and teaching was carried out. As all the universities tended to be semi-collectivist affairs – meeting almost all of the needs of the communities – eating, entertainment and retail sectors grouped close together and spread out from around this central zone, whilst beyond these stretched small townships constituted by habitation pods, fruit and vegetable plots and the ferming units that were used to form food from the now plentiful supply of bacteria in the atmosphere. Around these invariably existed some form of walling or other structure to keep out the near-constant winds and their damaging dust-blasting.

In many respects, university life for the developing communities did not dramatically alter from the way it had been organised back on Earth. The one major change that proved crucial, though, was that the academic communities were no longer beholden to the dictats of states or private companies. This newly acquired level of autonomy offered significant advantages, and only a smaller number of drawbacks. The original generation of arriving vice-chancellors had sought to retain control of their establishments and to a large degree proved successful in this endeavour, though some significant compromises in terms of academic freedom needed to be granted to achieve this. All, though, felt this was an acceptable price to pay for retaining administrative control, since many academics could be highly individualistic, or at best somewhat partisan towards their own particular discipline. Material resources were initially limited and there was a need to organise some form of rationing and prioritisation. A free for all, it was believed, could easily degenerate into chaos and would invariably damage the level of excellence they would be able to achieve.

Not surprisingly, research and teaching were valued above all other activities, so tasks considered of a menial nature such as food production, construction, sanitation, transportation etc. were left to be performed by the AI units that were owned and largely controlled by the university establishments. Although owned by the university authorities, occasional consultations were held with representatives of the wider academic community to determine how exactly the AI units should be put to use, which activities should be prioritised and the degree to which they could be reassigned for new tasks and functions. The arrangement did not suit everyone, but it gave some degree of collective control to many in the community, and helped to preempt possible areas of conflict. Regular meetings between representatives and the administrative elite also served the purpose of allowing the different parties to understand each other's priorities.

The use of AI units for almost all non-teaching and research purposes left the community of academics with ample amounts of time and energy to further their chosen academic discipline, and an increasingly wide range of academic fields were soon pursued across both the physical and social sciences, though it was the physical sciences that continued to be valued above all else within the universities. A new planet with new challenges, new perspectives and a new spatial position in space ensured a continuous stream of ground-breaking ideas, research and theories. For many of the scientists and other academics these proved to be almost perfect circumstances. Freed from the political imperatives of states, and the commercial preoccupations of private companies, pure research could be pursued and ambitious theoretical agendas constructed, with only the existing level of technology and the material limitations of the planet holding back their progress.

Highly original, ground-breaking and ambitious theories were expounded across the fields of mathematics, physics, astronomy, cosmology and many others. Observations made from their newfound position in space, together with data collected by the 'genesis pods' and the stasis ships en route to their respective destinations, all combined to form a much greater understanding of the galaxy and the wider universe. The chemical sciences had a whole new planet and its different substances and compounds to investigate, whilst the biological sciences closely monitored how the living organisms brought from Earth adapted and evolved on a planet with a shorter day, lower gravity and lower levels of sunlight than the one they had evolved to exist upon. Additionally, information and data were being constantly relayed back and forth between the various planets opened up by the 'genesis pods' across the near-galaxy. This generated a whole new realm of research areas within the fields of astrobiology, terra-forming, planetary geology and the numerous other fields that were developing within the all encompassing one of cosmology.

The universities, under their newly refined social structures, were able to generate a fertile mixture of cooperation and competition which acted in significantly pushing back the boundaries of knowledge in their chosen disciplines. Each of the universities sought to outdo the others, and a range of prestigious awards and ceremonies were established for those recognised by their communities as making the greatest advances in their chosen academic field. Unsurprisingly, major theoretical advances and breakthroughs were claimed in fields associated with their now much improved understanding of the galaxy – the processes associated with star and planet formation, the realms of dark matter and dark energy, theories of exogenesis, developments in space travel and rocket science and a whole range of other disciplines.

As time passed, the years rolled by, the seasons slowly changed and the communities gradually expanded. The original social structures were occasionally tweaked and refined as the decades passed, but – successfully achieving their original purpose - remained largely the same throughout. Slightly more than three generations later and the communities had achieved a level of advanced knowledge they considered to be unparalleled in the known galaxy. Hunkered down in their wind-blasted, lofty red sandstone towers and compounds, high above the ravines and valleys that cut deeply into the planet's surface, they had devoted their whole existence to research, the pursuit of knowledge and higher levels of theoretical understanding. They had uncovered secrets not even dreamed of by previous generations, unlocked the mysteries of stars and galaxies, and fashioned intricate and highly elegant theories of both the known and unknown universes.

But now, these communities and their impressive achievements were all in severe danger of disappearing, of dying out like so many countless civilisations across the millennia had done before them. In the lofty granite towers, committees were hurriedly being organised, calculations pored over, proposals for the future formulated and heated debates conducted amongst their members. A sense of panic was sweeping through the seats of learning but none of their number possessed any definitive answers to their imminent destruction. Outside their esteemed walls, the icy blasts descending from the glaciers continued to howl around the towers, still sweeping down from the north, still blasting across the mountains and plateaus and still shrouding the plateau in a foreboding gloom of carmine-red.

Ur-Tokar – the awakening

Once darkness had fallen, Topaz slipped out from beneath the dense mass of fir trees and quietly made her way down towards the cold, dark and slowly-flowing river. The moon of Arioch had risen a quarter of the way through its ascent into the night sky, and its pale purple reflection on the river gave her just enough light to make out the fact that only a small number of guards were on duty in the village on the far bank. The nearby bridge across had been left unguarded – presumably they were not expecting any visitors – and so she made her way quietly across the old stone structure keeping as low as possible, headed towards the village and slipped over the wall onto the narrow sandy poorly vegetated shore that ran between the river and the raised grassy bank. A few moments later and she was in amongst the boats moored on the water's edge. Her original plan had been to take any boat that proved to be available, but once amongst the boats she spotted what she was certain was the boat laden with supplies intended for her settlement, and naturally opted for that particular boat. It would be heavier than the others, but she was sure she could still push it away from the shore.

Suddenly, noises came from the riverbank above. She crouched low by the boat, froze and tightly held her breath. Her heart beat so loudly she was sure the guards would be able to hear it. Whatever the noises were, though, nothing further occurred and after what seemed like an eternity, but was probably only a couple of minutes, she decided to make her move. She untied the boat, waded into the freezing cold water, took a long intake of breath and pushed the boat out as firmly and forcefully as she possibly could, out further into the dark river's depths and clambered quietly aboard. The boat wobbled back and forth a couple of times and then finally settled. She held her breath and lay as still as possible, face down on the boat. Slowly and silently it drifted outwards and slightly downstream. She continued to hold her breath. A quick glance back at the village indicated that she had not been spotted and the alarm she had half-expected to hear being called, never materialised. Finally, she stopped holding her breath, and breathed out a long sigh of relief.

She let the boat drift for a while, and when she thought it was safe to do so, took the oars and began very quietly to row the boat upstream in order to gain momentum and put some distance between her and the soldiers in the village. Once this was successfully achieved, she was able to start to relax a little, she seemed to be safe now, she thought, and was now moving comfortably upstream against the glacially slow flow of the wide river. Before long she was round the first bend and the village was no longer in sight. She wrapped herself more tightly against the cold in her thick woollen cloak and made the occasional pull on the oars to maintain speed and direction. After a while, and now fully convinced she was safe, she gazed into the star-studded sky above and her attention wandered over to Arioch, now somewhat higher on its journey across the heavens.

Leaning back in the boat, she surveyed the night sky in wonderment – one of her favourite occupations. Close to Arioch twinkled Luxotica, the sentinel star that so often seemed to accompany the moon on the journey it traced across the heavens each and every night. She marveled as a single descending moonbeam briefly illuminated a long high bank of altocumulus clouds in an otherwise cloudless sky. Further to her south, high above the river, amongst the stars of the Kadu Flyer constellation the luminous points that constituted the Southern Cross seemed to shine even more brilliantly than usual in the late autumn sky, she thought to herself. She knew most of the constellations and the brighter more prominent denizens of the night sky, and as she admired the myriad star formations, she wondered what lives might be playing out at this instant around those far flung points of light, far out in the deep dark infinity of space.

She continued for a while down through the night, until finally she was too tired to continue rowing. She found a suitably quiet side channel next to a low sandbank on a wide bend in the river and spent the rest of the night moored closely to the river bank. Next morning, shortly after dawn, refreshed and having eaten from the supplies on the boat, she continued her long slow and gradual ascent towards the darkland that constituted her home territory and its heavily forested mountains. As she did, the morning remained eerily quiet. Occasionally, a thin wisp of mist rose ghostly like a wraith from the river's mirror-smooth surface as the cool waters slowly warmed in the early morning sun. Out of the shadows of the forest emerged occasional deer and wild boar for an early morning drink on the banks of the river before, once again, disappearing silently back into the woods.

Arrival in Utopia

The day passed slowly, but she never tired of the subtly changing, ever spectacular but calm and peaceful landscape. At one point she spotted an eagle gliding majestically on broad outstretched wings as it hunted across an adjacent mountain ridge. On occasions, the speed of the river quickened and she needed to row with more determination, but for the most part she made good progress along the wide slowly meandering watercourse. Once in a blue moon she passed a remote cottage in the woods nestled by the banks of the river, but for the entirety of the journey she never saw a single other soul. As midday turned to afternoon, the mountains began to rise higher and higher, scree slopes stretching above the tree-line, snow capping their highest reaches. She knew now that she was approaching her intended destination.

Finally, towards the end of the day the contours of the land began to look increasingly familiar, until eventually she spotted the three towering peaks that rose dramatically behind the settlement of Lato where she resided. As she rounded the final bend in the river and approached the village she could see a sprinkling of small cabins dotted across the hillside stretching up from the river's banks, many with a candle burning softly in the open windows, illuminating the rectangular wooden shapes that were now only just apparent in the gathering darkness. She guided the boat across to the river bank that lay in front of the settlement and steered the boat as far as she possibly could up to the bank and then secured it to one of the moorings on the riverside. The settlement looked eerily quiet in the murky gloom; its houses either completely dark or only dimly lit as the night closed in.

She knew where many of the inhabitants would be at this time of night though and headed briskly along the main street and up the slope on her left towards the rear of the settlement. A few minutes later and she could hear the noise and see the lights of the best tavern in the whole settlement. Nestled in the shelter of the mountainside, flanked by pine forest and almost glowing in the darkness of the night sat the Hall of the Mountain Grill. Smoke billowed from its chimney stretching high above the sharply pitching grey-tiled roofs. The half-timbered upper level looked dark and almost foreboding, but through the arched lattice windows of the ground floor she could see the warm yellow glow of the tavern and the movement of its patrons.

Arrival in Utopia

She pushed her way through the large arched oak door and was met with a scene of warmth and light – all the more welcoming after the cold days and dark nights she had recently experienced in the forest and along the river. The tavern was just as it always was in the evenings; a bright fire burnt fiercely in the large stone hearth that dominated the end-wall nearest the door, but still gave off sufficient warmth to heat the whole of the long stone room. Tapestries depicting scenes from the forests and the mountains hung the length of the longer stone walls, whilst lights shone from the wooden circles slung across the low beams that crisscrossed the length and breadth of the roofing space. Groups of men and women sat noisily around the wooden tables eating the hearty meals the tavern was famed for, drinking beer and exchanging the latest developments in their lives with each other. At the far end, from behind the long wooden bar, staff attended to the needs and desires of the latest arrivals.

Several of the locals quickly spotted her and she was soon enjoying a series of firm hugs and warm welcomes. Her friends, Amethyst, Rowan, Autumn and Raven were amongst the first to greet her and she was ushered across to their table where she was soon consuming a large bowl of thick vegetable and lentil soup, warm crusty brown bread and a large flagon of beer. She ate ravenously after the exertions of the day and - between slurps of the soup - related the events of her tale to an increasingly attentive crowd of taverners. There were shocked gasps of alarm as she recounted the massacre of the villagers at Greenback – many had friends and relatives in the village – and much swearing and cursing as she described the aristocrat who had overseen the whole episode. Finally she finished with an account of her escape down the river, but the gathered crowd still looked shocked by the unexpected news. Her successful delivery of the winter supplies hardly received a mention.

'I always said this would happen sooner or later. Those bastards were never going to leave us in peace for ever. They've never liked our way of life, and the fact that we won't worship their idiot kings. Sooner or later they were going to try and impose their rule on us; I always figured this was likely to happen,' stated Hagan, a sturdy middle-aged man, who Topaz knew lived someway further up the river in an isolated homestead. He was known to her because her friends had noted his tendency to disappear for several days at a time without any clear explanation. He was considered as something of a jack of shadows – here today, gone the next – and she suspected he was involved with the groups that occasionally came into conflict with the lowlanders every now and again.

'But they massacred the whole village – that's not imposing their rule, that's wiping us out,' exclaimed Raven, named for his shiny dark hair, and a close friend of Topaz. They had shared many adventures together as they were growing up in the forests, and she had been particularly pleased to see his smiling face when she first entered the tavern after her long journey. 'That's worse than anything we had ever imagined they might do to us.'

'But why have they decided to do this now?' asked Autumn. 'We've not provoked them in anyway, we've done nothing to deserve this - well not as far as I know,' she added, suddenly wondering if the conflict between the two peoples had plumbed new depths she was unaware of.

'It's just their arrogant ways, the fact that they think they should be able to lord it over us, the same way they do with their stupid peasants. It's the only world they understand and our continued existence is a threat to their rule,' Hagan continued, feeling this was just the opportunity he needed to drum up support for his longstanding conflict with the lowlanders.

'Indigo told me she'd seen a party of them in the hills down that way a couple of months ago; she thought they were prospecting for ores higher in the hills to the north of Moonglum Heights. If that's right, this looks more like a land grab to me. It looks like they're trying to take control of that whole area away from us,' explained Raven, looking for a more reasoned explanation for the monarchist's behaviour.

'But even if that is the case, the Greenback massacre was entirely unprovoked. They have to pay for this. We can't let them get away with something as appalling as this. We've been far too forgiving in the past with those pompous bastards. This time we have to strike back', declared Hagan, hoping to finally convince everyone present that the campaign against the monarchists needed to be fought with far greater urgency.

Most of the tavern indicated they were in agreement, but only because they had run out of any other options. For long years they had been a peace-loving people keeping to their own ways, working closely with nature and protecting the pristine environment they populated. In recent years though, intermittent but increasingly violent monarchist provocations had gradually led to a changing of opinions. They had tried negotiating with the lowlanders but the promises they made had never been kept. The incursions, provocations and attacks had simply continued. Slowly but surely, a wind of change had passed through the varied communities of the Mountain People, and now they were decided on adopting an increasingly hostile outlook toward the monarchists.

They had never experienced a full-scale massacre like the one at Greenback and this seemed to indicate a whole new level of hostility between the two different populations.

'We all knew this was coming someday. This is the awakening. We once thought we could just keep quiet, stay out of their way and they would leave us alone. Then when the problems started we thought we could just resist them and push them back through a sort of low-level attritional warfare. This is the final proof that will never happen,' declared Hagan.

'So we're officially at war with the monarchists?' asked Rowan, a tall thin red-haired youth and one of Topaz's oldest friends. 'I can't believe it's come to this - and so dramatically.'

'You'd better believe it,' grimaced Hagan, 'we need to mobilise as many people as possible. If we don't, it's only a matter of time before we're the next community to be massacred.'

He put on his hat and jacket and headed out of the tavern. He had been expecting an event like this for some time, and had already formulated ideas about how they should retaliate. Soon he was on his way through the chill night air to meet up with some fellow travellers and plan their next move.

Arrival in Utopia

Alpha Fraczan – preparations

When it came to the science of space travel and rocket engineering, Alex Kim was probably second to none on Alpha Fraczan, clearly one of the planets leading experts in this particular academic discipline. His chosen field of expertise had, however, both a series of advantages and disadvantages. The traversal of space by thousands of stasis ships across many light years and for so many decades ago had produced a wealth of data and improved knowledge with respect to the subject of space flight, and had revealed a whole host of areas in which refinements and improvements could theoretically be made. As was standard practice with all the colonised planets, the original stasis ships arriving at his planet had been left in orbit and maintained and managed by their designated AI units. They were designed to make use of a range of potential energy sources – most notably solar - thus ensuring a constant and sufficient supply of power. This meant Alex could make frequent visits into near space to test and refine certain of his new theories and his perceived advances in rocket engineering.

However, flight on the planet itself was relatively infrequent. This was generally the case on most of the colonised planets; since none had possessed indigenous life in any significant sense, there were no fossil fuels available as an energy source. Those planets that did practice air travel tended to use small electric planes and little else. Additionally, on Alpha Fraczan, the various universities – sparsely distributed across the equatorial zone - felt little need to actually visit each other physically, since communication was easily achieved through the sophisticated array of orbiting satellites originally placed in orbit by the arriving 'genesis pod', once it had considered the planet to be potentially habitable. The few journeys that were undertaken between the universities simply used the original transportation ships that had been employed in the disembarcation process.

For Alex, this meant there was little scope for large-scale engineering or the creation of operational prototypes. In addition, Alpha Fraczan was effectively isolated as a planet – on the far edge of the Nexus Cluster and conducting no transactional relationships with its neighbours, or indeed with other worlds further across the galaxy. The universities – somewhat suspicious of the intentions of the other planets - had unanimously agreed to maintain this position and banned the removal of their stasis ships from the planet's orbit. The scientific communities were now well ensconced in their new home – despite its several drawbacks - and had little appetite for further space travel and exploration. The resulting lack of any meaningful space flight – other than continuously orbiting the planet – meant that most of Alex's work never went beyond the theoretical or laboratory stage. His university - Sienna Pools – had, perhaps for the above reasons, rated his department a low priority for material resources, a source of considerable frustration for Alex and his work colleagues.

Alex – impatient for success - had investigated the possibility of transferring to one of the other universities, possibly those of Rouge Mountain or Pine Ridge, but his enquiries there had uncovered the fact that his discipline was equally undervalued elsewhere – something he could not help but consider a supreme irony, given it was only thanks to his academic discipline that they were present on their new world in the first place. As such, he had remained in situ, continuing to pursue his research and teaching at the theoretical level, but nevertheless believing he had made some significant engineering breakthroughs, particularly in the field of rocket propulsion - small-scale engineering tests in the laboratory tentatively confirming even some of his most ambitious designs and theories. Recent tests had indicated strongly to Alex that he was actually now on the verge of a major breakthrough in his field, but a frustrating inability to engineer at a larger scale meant he was unable to definitively confirm this.

Alex, as with all the planet's inhabitants, was well aware of the problem that Celestrina was now thought to pose to both his very existence and his life's work. If the worst case scenario of Celestrina's celestial approach proved to be correct, this was occurring at exactly the wrong time for his career. However, as a leading rocket scientist, he and his team had been tasked by the university authorities with preparing the technical side of a possible evacuation from the planet. In this respect, he already knew that all the stasis ships in orbit and the transportation craft at Sienna Pools University were in good working order, since he occasionally used them for research purposes. Enquiries to the other universities indicated their embarcation craft were also still functioning and in good order.

As such, it had been relatively straightforward to establish a workable evacuation strategy and all the necessary procedures had now been put in place. The population of Alpha Fraczan was still relatively small, only slightly larger than when the stasis ships had first arrived more than a century ago. The highly educated individuals that constituted the vast proportion of the population were never likely to have chosen to parent many children, and even the establishment of communal nurseries and the availability of AI units as suitable child-carers for those that did, had done little to raise the birth rate. The latter barely breached the replacement rate, since two children per woman was considered more than adequate amongst a community that was far more interested in devoting their considerable talents and efforts to the pursuit of knowledge and scientific endeavour, rather than the raising of small children.

As such, Alex had established with considerable certainty that his plan could remove everyone from the planet's surface and safely into orbit within the matter of a few short hours. His connections at the other universities indicated that they too believed this was eminently achievable. What they would actually do once they were on the stasis ships he had no idea. Rumours were flying around as to the various possibilities, but he assumed the university authorities would be taking any final decision. As a young and healthy man in his mid-twenties, he was sure he would survive stasis without any major side-effects, but how long it would be before he could relaunch his research agenda was anyone's guess - the dislocation was bound set him back several years, exactly what he didn't need at this time in life, he had gloomily decided.

Whilst the technical side of the evacuation plan had been organised without any notable difficulties, this was far from the case with regards to choosing an ultimate destination. A heated debate on the subject had broken out amongst leading figures of the university in the vice-chancellors meeting room at Sienna Pools University. The fact that all those involved were able to view the grand sweeping vistas of the plateau, mountains and ravines from the upper floor windows – and ostensibly the planet looked the same as it ever had done - somehow gave the argument an even more surreal edge to what already seemed like a bizarre discussion. It had slowly dawned on the committee members during the course of the argument that they were actively organising departure from the only world any of them had ever known – including the sweeping vista that lay passively in front of them, and that in all likelihood would never be seen again – at least not in its current form.

Nevertheless, in the event of an evacuation – and as the hours slowly passed the data was indicating that this was looking more and more likely – they needed an agreed plan of action, but were struggling to find common ground, particularly on the question of where their intended destination should be. After a consideration of the relevant data and a summary of potential destinations, three options had gained a significant amount of support and were being actively supported by different members of the room's participants.

Itzel Anderson was proving to be the most outspoken partisan of the first option. Tall and thin, pale-skinned with very short blonde hair and a slightly aloof demeanour, she was a member of one of the more esteemed families on Alpha Fraczan, a pure physicist, but also a keen and dedicated historian of science. Intensely serious and highly studious, her readings of Earth's history had led her to believe that the academic disciplines had never been allowed to correctly flourish on the mother planet, since they had always been subjected to the diktats of the lesser educated and malignly motivated. In her learned opinion, academia had been the greatest invention of civilisation, but had never been allowed to fully flower and achieve its true potential. In fact, even worse, the perversions of other interested parties had meant its incorrect implementation had inadvertently led to the demise of civilisation on Earth.

Accordingly, she was a very strong believer in maintaining the absolute pureness of academia and was determined to keep it away from the clutches of business, political ideologues or any other distorting influences, seeing it as either corrupted, watered down or diminished in importance by those not fully understanding its aims, needs and desires. Partly due to this belief, but perhaps also due to her family background, she had achieved an elevated degree of status amongst a dedicated section of her fellow academics, who greatly appreciated her devotion to the profession. However, this grouping had historically been a smallish minority, since on Alpha Fraczan there was no immediate danger of other sections of society harming their academic efforts, since the universities effectively ran all the communities on the planet. As such, she had previously been regarded as effectively an idealist and a keeper of the purist torch, rather than as someone with any immediate relevance to their everyday needs and ambitions. Nevertheless, the present worrying situation had suddenly and significantly changed her status, making her ideas appear far more relevant, and she now found herself as one of the figureheads in the present, increasingly heated, debate.

'Our best option is to go back into interstellar space,' Itzel stated once again. 'Thousands of 'genesis pods' were sent out from Earth, and we know with complete certainty from the transponders, that new worlds have been established across whole sections of the near galaxy. I've already established a team which is working on which of these worlds appears to be the most promising. I agree we will need to be in stasis for years, more likely decades, but we will have the significant advantage of effectively completely recreating Alpha Fraczan for a second time. We will maintain the major benefit of retaining our autonomy and absolute control over our working lives. We've done it once before and we've learnt the necessary lessons. The next time we can do it even quicker and even more efficiently. I admit it's a major inconvenience - there's no escaping from that - but then all the potential solutions we have at our disposal have their own particular problems. We have plenty of time to prepare whilst we're in orbit if that proves to be necessary; we can run a skeleton crew whilst we establish our destination and then implement the desired protocols to the AI units and ships. If we find a suitable planet, we will have the additional benefit of several more decades, possibly a whole century, of planetary terra-forming development, both in terms of increased biodiversity and constructed habitation – it could actually be significantly better than what we found here on Alpha Fraczan when we first arrived.'

Mila Lustrom could see the benefits and attractions of such an approach but was still somewhat sceptical. 'I'm still not so sure of such an idea. Do we really want to stay in stasis for such a long period of time? What if we do reach this new planet and we find that it too contains another range of significant problems? Let's face it, we know that there aren't that many great planets out there anyway – they all come with their weird and wonderful problems. The space web has been telling us this for decades. I'm strongly inclined to stay in the Nexus Cluster. There are at least four well established and viable planets within a few short light years of us. I know they all have their particular issues and problems, but Zeta Kotlin and Rorque 4, at least, offer distinct possibilities for us. I think we'll give Zeleyan and Ur-Tokar a wide berth though – if recent reports are still correct, they are probably completely unsuitable for people like us.'

Itzel grimaced, 'but we'll lose control, we'll be subject to the dictats of people who basically misunderstand science, our ambitions, our lives and everything we're trying to achieve here. We lose our freedom and autonomy - we will serve the needs of . . .' Itzel struggled for an acceptable term, '. . . of idiots and the lesser educated, the kind of people who have always been our nemesis.'

Mila looked at the vista outside the long floor-to-ceiling window for a few seconds and then replied, 'but there are also many advantages for us. Their worlds have proven to be stable and highly suitable for human habitation. They possess significantly larger economies than we have managed to develop, a much greater range of resources and manufactured machinery and other products. They can supply us with scientific equipment and engineered products in quantities that are still way beyond are means. In turn, we have made huge advances in our fields of research and have much to offer these societies. They should welcome us with open arms. We should be able to negotiate special considerations that will preserve our freedom and autonomy.'

Itzel shook her head in frustration, 'but that just won't happen. They will seek to subordinate us and use us for their own ends. It's very naïve to believe otherwise.'

'I'm also aware that my proposal is the favoured option of the majority of the committees at the other universities,' said Mila. 'Personally, I would say it is best if we stay together united - if we can agree on a single plan of operation it will benefit us all in the long run and maintain our long-term aims.'

The third option always looked the least likely and was proving to be the least popular but was still being argued for by Zaid Collinson, a tall, elderly and slightly balding figure and a leading light in the Chemistry faculty. 'We still have the option of simply staying in orbit around Alpha Fraczan - in stasis if necessary - and waiting for the disruption to arrive at a natural end and for the planet to settle down again. Some of the calculations we have made indicate a number of the universities will not end up in the polar regions. It's also possible they might survive the ensuing earthquakes and floods. Once the tilt is over and Celestrina has moved further away from us, we can ascertain the level of damage and assess the possibility of returning to the surface. It's possible we might be able to remake our world.'

'I have major doubts about those calculations and no one knows for sure of the obliquity we are about to experience. I would be extremely surprised if any buildings were to be left standing after such a significant tilt event. There will be massive floods, the melting of glaciers, violent earthquakes and who knows what else. And, perhaps more pertinently, this tilt might happen again at some point in the future, even in the near future,' argued Itzel, now pacing the room and increasingly impatient with opposition to her preferred plan.

'But more likely, probably not for hundreds, or even thousands, of years though', retorted Zaid defensively, though he had realised all along his preferred option was the least popular of the three, and he was still clearly losing the argument.

'But it's always going to be a problem. It will never go away. The lack of a large-sized moon means there is always going to be an ever present danger of this occurring a second time', said Mila. 'And the planet has a number of other problems, as we are all aware of. Our founders knew this and we've never fully overcome them – the cold, the limited sunlight, the high winds, the paucity of land vegetation – we've always been living on a knife edge here. There already exist more suitable planets with better climates in this cluster alone; we need to seriously explore the possibility of joining the people who live on them. I'm sure we can continue to enjoy our high-level status – we're highly intelligent people, surely we can work something out to our benefit. It's almost certainly the least problematic solution,' argued Mila. 'Anyway, we can monitor Alpha Fraczan from the other planets in the cluster, and if a return looks possible, we are within easy travelling distance for a return colonisation,' concluded Mila, hoping this might lead Zaid and his supporters into backing her proposal, against that of Itzel's.

Despite Mila's attempts at some form of compromise, the arguments continued for some time further. As time passed it became obvious to everyone present that no form of consensus was going to be arrived at any time soon. Itzel and Mila's suggestions were clearly the most popular and eventually the committee reluctantly decided that they would need to move to a vote on the matter, as this would be the only means by which they could make their all important decision. In the event, Mila's proposal achieved a narrow victory, but she could see from Itzel's expression that this was probably not going to be the final word on the subject. The meeting subsequently dispersed and Mila was tasked with establishing a sub-committee to organise the finer details of the evacuation from the planet – if it ultimately proved necessary - and the exact destination of their dispersal within the Nexus Cluster.

Earth – early space travel

Towards the final years of the twenty-first century, it had become increasingly obvious to almost all of Earth's inhabitants that the world really was burning up, that the planet was in a particularly bad way and that its problems were not superficial ones, rather they reached down to its very core. Whilst they might question the sanity of what they had previously done, with runaway climate change, humans were no longer in control anymore, and desperately needed new solutions to their self-inflicted predicament. Not surprisingly, once the prospect of inter-stellar space flight was raised as a serious possibility, humans quickly took this offer of a helping hand. Initially, it was seen as simply a solution, as a means of solving a problem, but it soon became apparent that its organisers were also offering an added bonus. Inter-stellar flight offered humans a means to learn, to make their dreams their own, and not simply a way of leading them far away from a world they no longer recognised - a world that many were now keen to leave so far behind.

However, there were huge uncertainties as to how this endeavour might actually be organised. The prolonged economic expansion of the mid-twenty first century had generated a renewed interest in space travel after a significant hiatus during the damaging economic slumps and recessions that had characterised the depressed downswing decades of the thirties and forties. For the most part, this renewed interest had been driven largely by space entrepreneurs and private companies in their quest to deliver space tourism experiences to the super-rich. Inter-planetary excursions and short-stay vacations on the planets and moons within the solar system that had proven suitable for such jaunts, became the must-do experience of the seriously wealthy in the booming fifties and sixties.

Alongside this, there had additionally been several attempts at establishing scientific colonies and bases across both the inner and outer reaches of the solar system. Various proposals for establishing scientific research bases on an assortment of moons circulating Jupiter and Saturn had in turn been postulated, explored and ultimately abandoned as too costly and impractical. With Mercury and Venus offering no viable options, Mars had not surprisingly seen the greatest number of endeavours, with huge sums of money, enormous resources and vast amounts of scientific expertise thrown at the multiple problems facing any would-be colonists. Long vaunted as a possible target for human colonisation, a small scattering of settlements had finally been established on the red planet in the year 2065 through an ingenious mixture of public and private funding and scientific endeavour, most notably emanating from the USA, still just about the preeminent state power, though facing stiff competition from both China and India for this title.

With the stars and stripes flying above the red planet, the western media outlets were finally able to declare that 'Uncle Sam's on Mars', but their dreams of looking for life on the dead planet, and building settlements in the red sand all eventually came to nothing. The efforts in keeping the colonists on a hostile and alien planet proved beyond the abilities of the finest minds in space exploration. A host of problems persisted over the months and years and a number of significant mistakes were made, despite the best efforts of the scientists and entrepreneurs involved. These included the supply of necessary resources to the colony, the outbreak of major psychological issues amongst the settlers, the failure to establish sustainable local food sources and, of course, existing in the inhospitable climate and landscape of a dead planet. The dreams of extending the colony faced one serious setback after another and envisioned further settlements and interlinking freeways and intersections were eventually put on hold.

The colonisation effectively came to an end when in 2068 a serious viral epidemic swept through the small scientific colony, and finally ended what limited efforts had been achieved against all the odds. The small number of survivors was eventually evacuated back to Earth, though not before considerable delays had occurred, and the project was quietly, though effectively, abandoned by the authorities. Uncle Sam never got to extend his reach across the solar system, his imperial outreach ending with his dreams of digging in the red sand. The colony's supporters did manage, however, to snatch some small victories from the jaws of the defeat - improved knowledge of space flight and the details of how to go about the actual physical colonisation of a planet – but for the wider public, this particular avenue of exploration now appeared to have arrived at a premature conclusion.

Not that this had not been foreseen. Critics had always disparaged the idea of establishing any viable and sustainable society on Mars. Mars was a dead planet. Its small size – substantially smaller than Earth – had meant that its inner core had cooled long before life had even become established on Earth. With a cooling inner core there was no planetary volcanic activity, no atmosphere and no protective magnetic field surrounding the red planet. Humans had arrived at no plausible way of reigniting and maintaining the essential warmth of the core, so any artificial atmosphere and warmth that might be artificially created would eventually be blown away into the vastness of space, in the same manner that the original atmosphere had been destined to experience. Equally, the absence of a magnetic field meant no protection for the planetary inhabitants from the deadly cosmic rays arriving in the solar wind constantly emanating from the Sun. Effectively, no one had devised a viable means of turning Mars into a self-sustaining living planet, and so it was abandoned.

Yet, Mars had been the most optimistically touted of the new space homes within the solar system. With all the other various moons, satellites and planets of the solar system offering even less promising prospects, those considering an emigration into space faced a serious problem. The interplanetary solution was effectively a non-starter. However, some of those disparaging the inter-planetary option had long advocated a more ambitious, yet more realistic option – they claimed – the daunting task of establishing an interstellar colonisation, one where humans could and would spread out amongst the stars, rather than remain confined to a limited number of localised and inhospitable planets.

Finding backing for such an endeavour had always been an uphill task - to put it mildly - but the scientists promoting such a venture loved to repeat the mantra, 'just as humans came from the stars, so we would return to them.' Although, not precisely, as attention was actually turned towards the myriad exo-planets discovered by cosmologists and astronomers over the previous seventy years, not just to the stars themselves. Through a series of ingenious techniques and much laborious effort, it had been known for several decades that the galaxy was littered with literally billions of planets, as had originally been postulated by those who saw little reason to believe that the Solar system was in any way unique within the cosmos. Through a continuous refinement of techniques used for studying these exoplanets, a number of potentially Earth-like candidates had been tentatively identified.

They offered at least an outside chance of being habitable by humans and the other life-forms that had evolved on Earth. A short check-list of the criteria needed for such a colonisation included a similarity in size to Earth, possessing a rocky nature, and exhibiting a strong indication that the planet possessed water and continuing volcanic activity. Invariably they were to be found in the 'Goldilocks zone' of the star systems that had been studied. The most promising area of the night sky - at least in terms of an achievable distance – was thought to be in the nearer sections of the Orion-Cygnus arm of the galaxy. Several clusters of stars here looked initially promising and it was to this galactic area that exploratory efforts were eventually concentrated upon.

Though long advocated and speculated upon, there were, unsurprisingly, vast technological difficulties facing any such human exodus. It was believed that the rocket engines of the spaceships developed for the space tourism industry and inter-planetary settlements, even after appropriate readjustments could, at best, reach only approximately a third of the speed of light, even over the vast and considerable interstellar distances that would be covered by the space colonisation effort. This was even the case for the latest series of plasma-fueled engines, recently developed, and lauded as a major breakthrough in space travel. The dreams of faster-than-light speed, or even simply travelling at the speed of light - so beloved of science fiction movies - were still just that - science fiction. Exploration by sail-powered sunship, hyper-fast nuclear drive or anti-matter propulsion engines simply remained as pipe dreams. Real space travel would prove to be considerably slower than in the movies and on television.

During the course of the booming fifties and sixties, a small number of exploratory spacecraft missions were launched with the task of exploring promising star systems, though given the vast distances inter-stellar being covered and the time needed for returning information to then be conveyed back to Earth after their arrival, it was many years before any significant amounts of useful data and knowledge could be returned and analysed.

Nevertheless, these first tentative steps beyond our own solar system would ultimately prove to be the prelude to much greater endeavours.

As the inter-planetary project ground to halt, the climate catastrophe intensified and humans sought a means of escaping the subsequent chaos, serious economic and intellectual investment in the inter-stellar project suddenly and dramatically multiplied. Though welcomed by those who had long promoted such a venture, this meant that the decision by those who desired to travel into inter-stellar space and launch a potential human exodus across the near galaxy were, to a large extent, travelling blind. Their decision to do so was based on limited scientific observation and information, and to all intents and purposes would require considerable quantities of luck, as well as endeavour, if it was to achieve any long-lasting and sustainable success.

Arrival in Utopia

Alpha Fraczan - evacuation

Mila was milling about on the upper floors of the glass and sandstone tower that constituted the central building of the university, one which comfortably overlooked all that lay around it. She was once again staring out the huge windows that looked out in all directions across the windswept plateau. To the south the sky was already a pinkish-yellow colour as Gannexon descended towards the southern mountains in the hours of the late afternoon. To the north, across a clean blue sky, pink clouds of all varieties and at all levels of the atmosphere stretched broken and torn along a north-south axis, strong northerlies driving them down towards the equator, the lowest of which scudded quickly over the outstretched plateau, casting small quickly moving shadows.

Like most other members of the university she was finding it difficult to concentrate on her work amidst so much uncertainty. She looked over to her right, beyond the sand-blasted walls that marked the outer perimeter of the campus, and noted small groups and individuals moving about the large brownish-red lagoons that pockmarked this particular region of the plateau - presumably the product of a bygone glacial age - and after which the university had been named. They appeared to be placing small stones and pebbles into their bags, presumably to act as momentos and keepsakes in the event of their likely departure from the planet and the only home they had ever known. Mila was reminded of her days spent wandering amongst the lagoons as a growing teenager, days spent developing her interest in the stubby grasses and sedges that grew around their shallow margins, and which ultimately led to the work she was now undertaking, memories that now filled her with a growing sense of loss and nostalgia. Eventually she wandered back to her workstation to continue her research, found she could achieve very little.

The evacuation order to depart from the planet finally came later that day in the late evening hours. Early the following morning, all inhabitants were to proceed towards their designated landing ship at the time notified to them by the university authorities. The worst fears of the population had ultimately been realised, and the latest planetary wobble had gone unnoticed by no one who was awake at the time. Computer modelling had shown that the planetary wobbles were now forming a regular pattern and each one was a proportionate amplification of the previous one. It was now possible to calculate the eventual angle of tilt and a 22.5° shift towards the orbit of Celestrina was being predicted as the most likely outcome; this prediction was considered to hold an 87.6% degree of likelihood.

These were odds that no one was willing to gamble with, and though some projections showed slightly lesser tilts, these had a lower probability of actually occurring, and even these lesser tilts were likely to result in widespread chaos across the entirety of the frosty red planet. Whole sections of the extensive ice caps would melt, whilst newer ones would begin to form at the regions moving into the polar zones. All the climatic regions would dramatically alter with catastrophic impacts on the still slowly evolving vegetation belts. Increased seismic activity had been detected in the planet's interior, and so the prospect of prolonged volcanic activity and severe earthquakes were considered an odds on certainty. In short, the planet would be temporarily uninhabitable, unless you really wanted to take your chances with the floods, tsunamis and other natural disasters that were soon to manifest themselves erratically across the unfortunate world.

In the event, the evacuation went almost perfectly to plan. The transportation craft at the various universities departed as timetabled, and the thousands of scientists, researchers, engineers, and other assorted academics and their families were transported safely and without major incident to the stasis ships still orbiting around the planet. However, the question of their final destination, as Mila had anticipated, had still not been fully resolved. As the evacuation process was being implemented, it became increasingly apparent that arguments similar to that occurring previously at Sienna Pools University had been replicated across many of the other university campuses. There was still considerable dissent with regards to the plan Mila had advocated and instituted, which came as no surprise to her at all. She knew the narrow victory margin of the vote and Itzel's determined advocacy of the alternative, meant that this had remained a distinct possibility. She had also heard rumours that Itzel's team had now identified a specific destination planet that was considered eminently habitable, had contacted all the other universities with the information and was still actively seeking support for her alternative solution.

Arrival in Utopia

As the evacuation progressed, it became increasingly obvious that to avoid outright mutiny and even a possible outbreak of physical violence – almost unheard of on Alpha Fraczan – all departing inhabitants of the planet would need to be given a vote on the matter. Mila and many of her supporters were still hoping the whole academic community could be held together as a priority, but it was equally the case that others were clearly more concerned by the issue of the working and living conditions they would experience at their recently chosen destination. Electronic voting meant the process could be implemented rapidly – thus causing no unwanted delays - and it was considered that the planetary tilt was unlikely to damage the spaceships and satellites in orbit, though they were moved to a higher orbit just to be absolutely certain. The need to leave the planet was pressing, but a delay in departing orbit was thought to be less of a concern.

The vote occurred without mishap, and initially seemed to have settled the matter, with slightly over seventy percent favouring the plan supported by Mila, and only thirty percent opting for that proposed by Itzel. However, it quickly became apparent that the dissidents were still extremely unhappy and after a considerable amount of bad-tempered negotiation, it was ultimately decided that three of the stasis ships would head off deep into interstellar space. Itzel's team had identified a planet named Alchemy as their potential new home, further out in the Orion-Cygnus Arm towards the Pleiades Cluster. It would probably take three decades to reach their destination, but as the entirety of the journey was spent in stasis those advocating this were not too concerned by the length of the journey. The transportation craft were used to hurriedly shuttle around those voting for this option to the three ships designated for the much longer journey and the rest - those supporting Mila's favoured option – were retained on the remaining seven stasis ships.

The majority seven ships had already decided to plot an initial course for Zeta Kotlin, which with its present orbit was calculated to be a travelling distance of slightly less than two years. This was somewhat ironic for two reasons. Firstly, the initial founders of Alpha Fraczan had rejected a similar move over a century ago. On discovering the geophysical difficulties facing them on their newly found planet, some of their number had suggested joining the established and already developing colonies on Zeta Kotlin. However, a wide range of objections had been raised against such an idea. Zeta Kotlin's society was deemed to be far too egalitarian for the academic project they were planning to pursue. Many thought that their scientific research would not be given sufficient respect; it might even be derided as elitist. They were concerned that their work would be subject to populist control, severely limiting their freedoms.

In addition, recent communications received by their satellites were indicating that considerable political unrest had broken out on Zeta Kotlin. Many within the science communities were highly doubtful as to whether an egalitarian society could ever prosper, and these reports seemed to confirm that the emerging society was already in difficulty. They had no desire to reside within a troubled, unstable and potentially doomed society. As a result, the scientists ultimately decided to remain and settle on Alpha Fraczan, despite its known planetary difficulties. Eventually, it became known through satellite communications that the political unrest on Zeta Kotlin had not been what it initially seemed, but by then the full-scale colonisation of Alpha Fraczan had already commenced and there was effectively no turning back at that point.

Secondly, Mila herself had wanted to plot a course for Rorque 4, largely for personal reasons as she considered its ideological outlook came closer to that of her own. The sub-committee tasked with deciding which planet within the Nexus Cluster they would actually make their new home upon had, however, opted for Zeta Kotlin for the reasons that it had a relatively large population, a significant amount of unpopulated land and was believed to possess a well developed and diverse economy. It appeared that it contained enough space for the construction of new universities, and that the political regime there was now sufficiently benign as to present few problems for their community. It was also by far the closest known habitable planet, so represented the least amount of time spent in stasis. Given that groups within their community were already at odds with one another, Mila had decided not to raise objections to this decision - she figured she could address the issue at a later date – but it was far from being her preferred destination.

Both sets of starships followed the standard protocols that had long ago been established for journeying safely through the myriad dangers that existed within inter-stellar space. The vast majority of the stasis ship's travellers were placed immediately in the immense banks of stasis pods that constituted the bulk of the spacecraft, whilst skeleton crews were established to oversee the initial and final stages of their respective journeys into space. All the universities on the planet had, as standard, kept the entirety of their research journals, papers and other publications on the space web, so both sets of ships were able to depart with the complete suite of knowledge acquired during their, ultimately short, period of residence on Alpha Fraczan.

Before the final departure, Mila looked down upon the planet, the only home she had ever known. She hoped that one day she might return – even if only to discover what had eventually become of her native planet. Would it be a scene of utter devastation and destruction or would life cling on precariously to her semi-frozen, wind-blasted, diminutive world. From the viewing deck, she could easily see the extensive ice-cap stretching across the frozen northern regions, and the small dark fragmented oceans dotted across the central zone, isolated amongst the vast stretches of land – great stretches of carmine red plateau and dramatic orange-red mountain ranges. She wondered where exactly her own home was amongst the mass of multi-coloured reds – the city of lagoons as she had affectionately known it - and for a brief moment she thought she might discern the extensive pools that surrounded her former university. She looked nostalgically at the planet one final time and turned away.

Once the various spacecraft had safely cleared the outer edges of Gannexon's planetary system – though in diametrically opposite directions - the skeleton crews were able to pass control over to the AI units and the ship's computers, locked down using the security protocols, and joined their co-travellers in the stasis pods as the spaceships accelerated rapidly out into the vast interstellar darkness. The two sets of ships rapidly gathered pace as they departed into the endless silent icy-cold depths of deepest space, the darkness closing in around them as they carried their precious cargoes to their very different destinations. For one set of travellers it would be many decades before they were to once again recommence the normality of everyday lives, though under very different circumstances. For the other set of travellers it was only the beginning of an entirely different conjunction of circumstances that would see their lives and their small corner of space transformed in ways they could not even have begun to imagine whilst still ensconced on their small isolated home, a home that was now itself the scene of increasingly dramatic transformations.

Margalla – history and society

The civilisation that had developed on the relatively unknown planet of Margalla possessed no such concept as an official history, as this was simply not the manner in which matters were practiced on the anarchist planet. Most of what had been recorded or remarked upon over the decades was still present for all to see – either in a physical form or in the memory banks of their computer systems – but no particular individual or grouping had ever felt the need or desire to actually collate the stored knowledge into one coherent and collective narrative.

For those who might wish to undertake such a task, there was the additional problem that, in reality, not a great deal of historical note had ever actually occurred on the planet since its initial inception. The settlement and development of the various islands of the lonely isolated archipelago had proved to be a straightforward, peaceful and largely uneventful process. With no class system – and thus no significant economic disparities - or political or other groupings in dispute with one another, wars and violent conflicts were effectively unknown. In addition, having successfully implemented a post-scarcity economy neither were there famines, epidemics or other similar disasters to create frictions between the different settlements and islands, or indeed for anyone to analyse, evaluate or remark upon at any great length.

Effectively, Margalla was a civilisation in a state of highly stable socio-economic equilibrium, and thus with no realistic prospect of any significant systemic change likely to occur within the foreseeable future. Viewed within the much longer context of the history of the human race – from its first origins on planet Earth onwards - the people of Margalla could be seen to have reached the end of the human race's long journey, the much vaunted end of History, their own fortunate and final arrival in utopia. In short, little in the way of history had ever actually occurred in their own small corner of paradise, and neither was it likely to. Only the usual difficulties that all Earth-originating life-forms faced as they developed viable ecosystems on an alien planet had the potential to offer any significant instability to the utopian society, and so far this had yet to materialise.

There were, nevertheless, locally recorded mini-histories on each of the islands of the archipelago, usually compiled and collated by young scholars engaged on the various learning projects they devised at their respective education centres. Occasionally these were further developed by those showing a particular interest in the subject involved, but this was far from guaranteed and no comprehensive account was yet to appear. Given the small size of the Margallan civilisation and its short duration, however, the following account could easily have been formulated from these existing works and resources by anyone who was so inclined to do so.

Margalla was the fifth planet of what, for humans, was a fairly ordinary G class main-sequence yellow-white star known as Sazhina, though it was appreciably larger and hotter than that of the Sun. The four inner planets of Sazhina's system were all smaller than Margalla, and, unusually in the near galaxy, were all surrounded by thick, dense oppressive atmosphere's which were considered far too hot or toxic to support any form of Earth-originating life form. Beyond Margalla orbited the gas giant Zecrone, its giant mass dwarfing all the other planets of the system whilst its huge gravitational pull was assumed to protect Margalla from celestial bombardments of all kinds and natures. Its vast gaseous surface was divided into a central circling zone of white encompassed by numerous bands of blue of all varying shades and tones. In the white zone, moved mysterious darker cloud formations, their oscillations appearing to mirror the movements of the gas giant's darker blue rings.

Further out still in the planetary system lay the lonely ice giant Hiemal - circling like a massive, perfectly-formed frosty-white snowball, its lonely beauty enhanced by a deceptive electric-green shimmer that engulfed the entire planet, and was assumed to result from copper impurities in its thin icy atmosphere. Even further out, on the far fringes of the system, towards the heliopause, almost lost in the vast depths of space, orbited a collection of small rocky dwarf planets, thought to have originated from the disintegration of a once much larger planet, and forever in danger of colliding with one another as they followed their slightly elliptical chaotic orbits around the outer circumference of the stellar system.

Margalla, itself, was blessed with two medium-sized moons – Rosa which always emanated a coppery-red sheen thanks to the presence of ferrous minerals in its dominant surface rock, and Jade which glowed bright green thanks to the presence of high levels of the mineral olivine in its surface layers. The two had significantly different orbits in terms of both trajectory and duration, and their position with respect to each other could give rise to a complex set of phenomena both within the atmosphere and across the planet's surface. Their differing orbits gave rise to bizarrely different types of lunar and solar eclipse and occasionally complicated tidal systems across the planet's oceans, though, for a variety of reasons, this was mostly of little actual significance to its inhabitants.

Margalla itself was about nine-tenths the size of Earth, but the denser rocky material that made up the bulk of its core and mantle meant that the planet's gravity was of a similarity to that of Earth. The planet was, in many respects, highly suitable for human habitation except for one major drawback - its surface was almost entirely covered by deep blue ocean. There was a single large mountainous and completely frozen land mass traversing the higher latitudes of the northern hemisphere – known simply as 'the frozen north' – and which was considered, with good reason, to be entirely uninhabitable. The only other land on this wide watery world was an extensive archipelago of between sixty and seventy islands that stretched along a broadly south-west to north-east trajectory over the course of several hundred kilometers in the sub-tropical zone of the southern hemisphere.

The 'genesis pod' that had first arrived at Sazhina's planetary system all those many decades ago had, nevertheless, identified the planet as potentially inhabitable for humans, largely on the basis of the vast quantities of water present in its one enormous ocean. It had thus implemented the standard terra-forming process, developing a nitrogen-oxygen atmosphere, introducing the usual organic life-forms into the oceans, and transforming the archipelago from a barren collection of rocky islets into a verdant sub-tropical ecosystem fit for human habitation. Unsurprisingly, the process had been achieved relatively quickly compared with many of the other terra-formed planets, and a reasonably complex ecosystem had been established on the archipelago by the time the first stasis ships arrived in the Nexus Cluster.

The natives of Margalla still argued about the matter, but some were still convinced that their starship had not been the first to arrive at Sazhina's planetary system. There was a belief that at least one stasis ship, and possibly others, had previously checked out the planet, making brief landfall, but deciding not to remain. The paucity of land on the planet was cited as the deciding factor – there was, in effect, no real scope for population expansion or significant economic development. When asked to cite any evidence for this persistent - but undocumented - belief, mentions of additional satellites, ancient messages on the space web and the finding of pre-used habitation pods would all be raised, but to date there was actually no hard evidence to support any of these assertions, and they simply remained unfounded rumours. For the Margallans this was not just a matter of paranoia or a purely academic debate though, for as far as they were concerned, they had found paradise, and to this day continued to worry that these first-arriving stasis ships might return and lay claim to their idyllic utopia.

The original founders of Margalla's island towns and villages had arrived on one of the so-called 'utopia ships' - as the mainstream media on Earth had mockingly labeled them. Like so many of their ilk, it was a fairly small and underfunded affair, optimistically named The Spirit of The Age, and had transported a fairly eclectic and idealistic array of anarchists, radical feminists and social ecologists - originally hailing from all six of Earth's inhabited continents, but only numbering in their low thousands. Their fairly budget affair had only permitted the transportation of limited numbers of people, other life forms and necessary resources, and so the restricted nature of the planet's habitable land surface actually suited their diminutive but diverse and cosmopolitan population.

What they lacked in resources though, they made up for in the ambition of their vision. The utopian travellers aboard the stasis ship had always dreamed of a golden future and a never-ending peaceful existence. Their world would be one where freedom finally reigned, and where wisdom would last until the very end. Their vision was of a new home, a world of wonder and a life of unnamed joys and endless thrilling hours - one where the chaos and confusion of Earth was left long and far behind. So when they came upon Margalla they instantly identified the world as one where their dreams would come true, that this was their arrival in utopia – from where they would never need to look back, ever again. Their future here would be one of lazy days, of flowing wine, wondrous fields and nights around the fire - there would no longer be anything to fear, they would be forever contented in their newfound utopia.

And so they quickly settled. Firstly the larger islands were inhabited and clusters of small towns and villages developed rapidly on each of those, predominantly along their extensive coastlines. Over time, as the population underwent a slow but gradual expansion, habitations spread to the smaller islands, until almost all the islands of the archipelago were eventually populated. The climate of the archipelago was a relatively benign one – a semi-permanent sub-tropical high pressure system ensured that the islands remained warm, dry and relatively storm-free. Fortunately for the islanders, though, the seasonal shifting of the high pressure zone facilitated a rainy season which allowed the collection and storage of fresh water to last through the much longer dry season. Desalination units were available to the settlers, but the water, they believed, never tasted quite right, and so freshwater pools were to be frequently found across the islands to ensure a continuous supply of fresh water throughout the year.

Given the ideological beliefs and often high level of education enjoyed by the arriving settlers, overpopulation on Margalla was never likely to have surfaced as a problem, and the number of islanders did indeed stabilise after two or three generations – freely available contraception and natural abortifacients ensuring there were no difficulties in controlling fertility levels. Determined to put their negative experiences on Earth behind them, the first settlers had opted for an entirely egalitarian and communal lifestyle in keeping with their perception that they had truly arrived in utopia.

In fact, following a belief that anarchism was probably only possible in small and decentralised communities, the extensive archipelago seemed to be exactly what they were looking for. No unified system of government had ever arisen across the varied islands of the archipelago, each one remaining essentially self-governing. A rudimentary constitution had been established by the initial colonists, but other than establishing the absolute equality of all islanders, effecting a ban on the employment or any other form of subordination of one human by another, ensuring high levels of protection for the environment, and a few other standard rights and freedoms, it had remained a fairly limited affair.

With employment outlawed, no social class system had been able to develop. The land, manufacturing units, and most importantly - it was believed - the AI units all remained under strict communal control. Unlike living on Earth, the AIs had been programmed to accept orders from any individual, though protocols had been developed to prevent misuse, and a variety of restrictions concerning the youngest children had been established until they were considered mature enough to enjoy full access. Occasionally, usage problems arose, demonstrating that the system was not actually completely perfect, and that they might not be used in exactly the way that most people would have approved, but on the whole the system worked adequately well. There were occasional minor arguments and disputes when demand for them was high, but these were quite rare.

Effectively, the AI units carried out any tasks that the islanders themselves felt disinclined to engage in. These tended to involve the more menial activities associated with areas such as construction, sewerage, cleaning, repair work or anything else that was considered too difficult, tedious or unpleasant. The actual consideration varied from person to person and from time to time - on any given day an individual might, for instance, be keen to collect fruits and vegetables from the garden plots, but on another simply instructed an available AI unit to perform exactly the same task. Effectively, it was left to individuals as to how and when they would actually organise this matter, but since most activities were carried out for the benefit of the community, there were often few other demands being made of the AI unit at the same time anyway.

The islanders were, however, acutely aware that a finite number of AI units had arrived with the stasis ship and – with limited natural resources on the planet - the ones they possessed needed to be treated and maintained with considerable care. Power was never an issue – plentiful renewable energy supplies made certain of that – and the units were to some degree self-repairing whilst they were recharging anyway. However, if certain parts failed completely there was limited scope for manufacturing replacement ones. The island archipelago had limited natural building materials, being constituted largely of a limited range of different types of volcanic rock almost across their entirety, and thus very little in the way of metal ores or useful minerals. As time passed, and the occasional AI unit became unviable, its parts could be cannibalised, but this, they were aware, was not something that could be sustained indefinitely.

The planet did of course possess their one and only stasis ship - the one they had arrived in, The Spirit of The Age. It was maintained in orbit around Margalla – an arrangement that most, if not all, colonised planets had opted for – in the case that there arose the need to travel elsewhere in the local area of space, or in the worst case scenario that they found it necessary to actually evacuate their world and go in search of another planet to inhabit. The AI units, as per usual, dealt with all the routine maintenance issues on board the ship. There were occasional discussions as to how much of the starship they could use to help repair ageing AI units, but they were always mindful to maintain the stasis ship in good working order, so here too there was a finite limit to the resources available to them in terms of scarce materials they might need elsewhere.

It was for this latter reason that Margalla had somewhat reluctantly entered into a very loose trading arrangement with one of their nearest neighbours in space, the planet Zeta Kotlin, though the somewhat erratic and only very occasional visits of the latter's trading ship actually suited them down to the ground. The far more diverse and developed economy of Zeta Kotlin was able to supply them with valuable parts for the AI units, scarce minerals and metals, certain manufactured goods and occasionally even complete AI units. The major problem for Margalla was that it possessed a limited number of products it could exchange for this advanced technology. Fortunately, the ship's crew – typically about five or six individuals - never seemed overly-concerned by this, and was happy to take any surplus resources that happened to be around at the time. The crew would often stay for extended periods, well beyond the time taken to exchange resources, and then later return to Zeta Kotlin or whichever planet they were planning on trading with next.

Despite this, the Margallans were still not fully enamoured of this relationship. The persistent belief by some of their number that the planet had originally been discovered by other stasis ships, combined with the fact that they could not believe that other peoples would not want to inhabit such a fantastic location – and possibly even seize it by force - meant that they had taken certain measures to hide themselves from the rest of humanity across the star cluster and near galaxy. The location transponder that orbited the star system – a standard feature left orbiting around all the stars visited by the original 'genesis pods' - had been reprogrammed to emit a message stating that none of the planets in the system had been deemed suitable for habitation. Use of the space web was kept to an absolute minimum, and few emissions originating from the planet ever emanated across space. They hoped that this silence would continue to convince other civilisations that the star system was of no use and of no interest to anyone else.

To date, the Zetan trading ship was the only exception to this strategy, but so far its crews had proved trustworthy and they hoped matters would continue to remain as they had been now for several decades. They were acutely aware of potentially hostile regimes on a number of relatively close star systems, and possessing no means with which to defend themselves from external attack, a perceived non-existence appeared to remain their best form of defence. But all of this, suddenly, was about to be thrown into doubt and potential disarray, for the civilisation of their closest neighbour in space, Alpha Fraczan, was in the process of collapsing in spectacular fashion, resulting in a chain of events that would have profound implications across their entire quarter of space.

Arrival in Utopia

Interstellar Space - the diaspora

Given the rancorous disputes that had broken out during the actual process of departure, the eventual evacuation process from Alpha Fraczan had ultimately proven to be a fairly smooth affair. Looking back in hindsight, the scientists considered that the endeavour might have actually encountered far more difficulties than it ultimately experienced. It had, from the very earliest days, become standard practice for all planets to keep and maintain their stasis ships in orbit and in good working order. The original colonisation of space so many years before had invariably started with uncertainty, and no one could be sure that a premature departure from a newly colonised planet would not be needed. Alpha Fraczan was no exception in this respect and so rocket engines, energy supplies, life-support and all other essential systems had been carefully maintained, so that should interstellar travel be needed at any point in time, they could all be reactivated with relative ease. But no one could be one hundred percent certain all would go smoothly to plan.

Nevertheless, within a short period of time, the entirety of the planet's inhabitants had been safely ensconced in stasis, and given that nearly four generations had passed since the planet was first colonised, this was a novel and unexpected experience for all of them. On each ship the skeleton crew - kept out of stasis for a short period of time – found they needed to do little in terms of necessary alterations. Routine checks over the decades had been regularly implemented to ensure all engineering systems were functioning correctly, particularly the stasis pods and life-support systems. AI units had continuously monitored the structural integrity of the starships over the years and carried out running repairs, so there were few worries with regards to the physical condition of the ships. Shortly before leaving, a recorded message was beamed out across space to alert the rest of the Nexus Cluster to the disaster that had befallen the inhabitants of Alpha Fraczan. As the need for this had only been realised late in the evacuation process, it had proven to be a hurried affair.

Respective courses were plotted for Alchemy and Zeta Kotlin with the intention that the spacecraft would arrive at their destinations in the shortest time-span possible. Once all the passengers, including the skeleton crews, were safely in stasis, the ship's systems carefully monitored the thousands of sleeping passengers as they zoomed silently through the vast darkness of space towards their intended destinations. The ships were programmed to keep in regular contact with each other and autocorrect any deviations from their trajectory. A near continuous relay of inter-ship messages was established, whilst the AI units were deployed to effect any necessary and ongoing repairs or adjustments on board the ships as they hurtled through interstellar space.

To an observer scanning across the star-studded skies and locating the seven departing ships speeding through deep space towards Zeta Kotlin, nothing would have appeared out of the ordinary for the first nine months of their journey. The flotilla of ships followed their pre-programmed stellar trajectory always remaining within a short distance of each other and in a regular alignment. After nine months, though, one of the ships clearly slowed, dropping back behind the other six continuing ships, and then deviated dramatically away from its original course as it peeled away from the route followed by the rest of the cohort. It then continued on a rapidly slowing trajectory towards an entirely different destination. Six months later, a second ship also deviated away from the remaining group. The extremely gradual curvature of its trajectory would have left the observer initially unsure as to whether any deviation was actually occurring at all, but as time passed it could clearly be perceived to be heading in a significantly different direction. Whether the two incidents were connected in any way would have been left to the imagination of the observer. The other five ships continued unfalteringly on their initial trajectory and at their original speed.

Arrival in Utopia

Zeta Kotlin – the message arrives

Zeta Kotlin was a planet constituted by nine large continents and a vast array of islands of all shapes and sizes set in a series of largely shallow oceans. It possessed little in the way of significant mountain ranges, being dominated by vast plains interspersed by concentrations of undulating hilly areas and occasional deep ravines. It basked permanently in a relatively warm climate – the result of it orbiting a large G class star known as Aequitas. Even the continents closest to the poles remained ice-free all year round. As such, it had been relatively straightforward for the original settlers to commence the construction of what was now a well developed and largely decentralised economy. Its system of government was correspondingly decentralised, so the message from the dying civilisation of Alpha Fraczan - arriving at the planet a little short of seven months after being first emitted by the departing starships – was made freely available and widely disseminated across its numerous communities.

Once transmitted across the planet, the message quickly became the centre of much discussion and debate. Federal and community council meetings were held on a regular basis even in normal times, and the message was soon placed high on their agenda of items to be discussed. The attitude held by the Zetans – as they liked to call themselves – towards the scientists of Alpha Fraczan had historically been a fairly mixed one, but until now had been of little import or relevance. A reasonably widespread view was one of mild disapproval. It was known that the scientists once, many years ago, had passed up the opportunity to live on Zeta Kotlin, and some surmised that this was because the academics had considered themselves to be too important for a world that prided itself on its egalitarianism. Some of those belonging to this persuasion harboured suspicions that the scientists might be developing technologies and ideas that offered some form of potential threat or danger to Zetan society. Various ideas had been postulated as to what this threat might prove to actually be in practice, but in the absence of any hard evidence they remained little more than idle speculation.

Probably the more commonplace viewpoint, though, was that the academic communities that constituted Alpha Fraczan were largely harmless. In over a century, there had been very little engagement between the two planets and this was evidence that the Alphans offered no substantial threat to Zeta Kotlin. If the Alphans wanted to devote their entire civilisation and existence to the pursuit of science and theoretical knowledge, then that was their affair and they should be allowed to continue to be left in peace as they so desired. After all, Zeta Kotlin had pursued its own particular unorthodox socioeconomic approach, so it should respect others who chose to do likewise. Nevertheless, they also believed that if the Alphans were to create new and useful technologies, it would only be sensible and appropriate to share these with their neighbours – a development that had yet to actually arise in practice, though. Like all planets, Zeta Kotlin had its own fair share of problems and difficulties and some extra technology would not go amiss in helping to ameliorate or eradicate some of them.

Until this point in time, the differences in opinion had all been largely academic, but the Zetans quickly calculated that their planet would most likely be the chosen destination of the Alphan diaspora, though it was not a complete certainty. With the somewhat cryptic exception of the Sazhina star system, they represented the nearest inhabited planet. Knowledge of the existence of Margalla – the fifth planet of Sazhina - was generally hazy even for most Zetans; some were unaware it was even inhabited, although those with a better knowledge of planetary affairs were aware it possessed only tiny amounts of habitable land, and had actually been colonised by a like-minded people with which their own planet had established a highly intermittent trading relationship.

Zeta Kotlin, by contrast, contained several large open land masses, all of which still possessed plentiful amounts of space for new colonists. It was thus a far more suitable destination than the tiny archipelago existing on Margalla. It was also thought that there might be an outside chance that the starships would head for the more distant planet of Rorque 4. By contrast, it was commonly agreed, that given the nature of the types of society existing on Zeleyan and Ur-Tokar - and the additional time involved in reaching those two planets - these were highly unlikely destinations for several starships full of well-educated scientists and academics.

Of course, there was the consideration that they might simply exit the Nexus Cluster entirely in a quest to seek out and colonise an entirely new planet for themselves; but it was not too long before Zetan satellite systems dispelled this possibility – several ships were definitely following a trajectory that would see them arrive in Zeta Kotlin's stellar system in a little over a year's time. This at least gave the Zetans plenty of time to deliberate on the matter and decide what their approach to the forthcoming dilemma should be. Given the typically slow-moving nature of the highly decentralised governmental system on Zeta Kotlin this was a definite benefit for their society.

The economy on Zeta Kotlin was characterised by collective community control over all its main features, and, in particular, community control of the AI units was considered to be of paramount importance. This meant that the pattern of habitation across the varied continents and islands largely resulted from a combination of geography and the direct wishes of the people, rather than the requirements of big business or an over-powerful government. With plentiful building materials, almost limitless amounts of renewable energy, and AI units providing most of the labour, the towns and cities constructed by the inhabitants of Zeta Kotlin had, as the decades passed, increasingly been an exercise in indulgence. Many had been constructed in quite spectacular locations such as those clinging to the sheer cliffs of notable ravines, precipices or offshore islands. Others topped plugs of volcanic rock that rose high above the surrounding plains. Many hillsides had seen a spate of semi-cavernous glass-fronted constructions built into them – their inhabitants enjoying spectacular views across the valley before them and the passing of the sun throughout the day.

One such exotic location was Kapal, built on a high and ancient linear ridge of hard igneous rock that ran longitudinally across the Plain of Xestron. It had initially started as a small and compact settlement but had gradually lengthened along the length of the ridge as its attraction and fame grew. Accessed by a single road running along the western side of the ridge, the habitations along its entire length enjoyed unrivalled views across the extensive plains in both directions – their distant horizons framed by the low dark hills and cordillera only just perceptible in the far distance. Such an arrangement allowed the viewing of both sunrise and sunset throughout the entire year, the deep orange-red ones of the slightly cooler winter months being particularly dramatic.

In political respects, though, Kapal was like any other settlement on Zeta Kotlin, holding regular community meetings, the votes of which fed into the wider planetary decision-making processes. The community council meeting of Kapal called to discuss the eventual arrival of the Alpha Fraczan scientists had been typical of conversations held across the entirety of the planet. As per usual, advanced notice of the agenda had been posted on the local web and no one was surprised that contributions to the discussion were more numerous than in usual gatherings. The latest events, thoughts and information on the subject had already been widely disseminated across the various communities of the planet. Attendance at their fortnightly meetings could often be patchy - it depended on the particular issues that were being discussed and voted on – but this meeting was much better attended than many others.

As with all the other communities on Zeta Kotlin, Kapal also possessed an administrative committee chosen at random and by means of computer through the process of sortition. Being only a small settlement, it had decided that only four members would be needed on the committee and each would perform the task for a duration of three years only. This calculation meant that each member of the community would probably be chosen for membership of the committee at least once during their lifetime. More populated communities tended to select larger committees with members serving shorter periods of office for the same reason. Zetans invariably took membership of an administrative committee seriously – knowing their community depended upon their good governance for its continuing high quality of life.

Such a political arrangement had both advantages and disadvantages. First and foremost, with administrators being chosen at random and for short periods of office (and probably only once in their lifetime) there was little danger of an oppressive and powerful political elite class developing to destroy the planet's egalitarian society. Secondly, it also meant that most citizens had direct experience of community administration at some point in their lives, and appreciated many of the difficulties entailed in the process. This meant committee members often received helpful advice from the rest of the community, especially over awkward matters and issues.

Arrival in Utopia

On the other hand, new members had little experience of administration and there was always the danger they might initially engage in poor decision-making. However, the fact that they invariably attended an initiation session held by the outgoing committee offering much needed advice, that the role largely consisted of implementing decisions previously made at community-wide meetings, and that the planetary web – where all community administrations logged their decisions and actions - was available to help out with tricky situations, meant that this disadvantage could be significantly ameliorated.

Membership of the committee was not particularly time-consuming – especially in a small community like Kapal – and largely entailed following the decisions made in the monthly community meetings. Mostly this entailed allocating sufficient AI units for routine maintenance and repair of community buildings, services and the general local environment. Occasionally they might be requested to hold tribunals regarding behaviour by certain individuals considered unacceptable by other community members, though these often turned out to be the result of a breakdown in communication, and could usually be resolved amicably. Other than these, there was often little of great importance to be involved with.

Zeta Kotlin had very little in the way of official legislation. Private ownership of land and AI units was strictly forbidden, as was the employment or subordination of others. With all property being owned by the community there was little need for property legislation and theft was effectively next to non-existent. In a post-scarcity society, communities enjoyed material security, and property items could usually be replaced with relative ease. In addition, as children were made aware that their peaceful and prosperous existence resulted from their membership of an egalitarian and communitarian society, from an early age they were encouraged to respect themselves, their fellows and their wider community. In such a climate, there was little in the way of violent behaviour towards others, or any other forms of anti-social behaviour.

As such, committees were only infrequently called on to make judicial-type decisions and, on those occasions, they typically reverted to community-based tribunals, with relevant members of the community in attendance and contributing significantly to any decisions that might be arrived at. Mostly communities tried to ensure differences were resolved in a way that suited all parties. Often this simply involved long discussions where all could equally voice their opinions and interests, and collective solutions then arrived at. Only on rare occasions did this prove insufficient; and in the event of prolonged personality clashes, usually one or the other, or even both parties, would usually move to a different commune long before the situation became disturbingly out of hand.

All in all, the administrative committee of Kapal usually had little of major import to discuss or implement at its regular meetings, so it came as a major surprise that so early in its tenure it found itself needing to engage in a discussion with planetary-wide implications. Given the importance of the matter, it decided to hold an extraordinary community meeting that turned out to be particularly well attended. The committee's four members – Zhang Li, Pedro, Rishaan and Catriona - as would be expected, initially took the lead in the important matter to be discussed.

Zhang Li commenced the meeting. She was one of the more elderly residents of Kapal and had joined the community more than two decades previously, initially attracted by the tranquility and solitude offered by Kapal's unique location. Even after this length of time she still remained enraptured by the spectacular vistas across the plains, and had indeed spent much of the day doing exactly that as she socialised earlier in the day with other members of the community. 'I think it's safe to assume that the scientists of Alpha Fraczan will all want to settle on Zeta Kotlin – there's little reason in arriving here other than for that purpose. Assuming all the passengers are in stasis, there's no advantage in simply using Zeta Kotlin as a staging post for a more distant destination. That would make no sense at all. I think our priority should be determining exactly how we incorporate them into our society. Clearly we will need to consider their needs and desires, but we also need to establish our own position,' she stated confidently.

Entering old age and with whitening hair, calm, serene and collected, she possessed a highly philosophical approach to life, was well versed in forms of contemplative thought, and extremely good at seeing all sides of an argument. Empathic, caring and considerate, her priority in all situations was the common good, maintaining peaceful relationships and ensuring everyone could make the most of their lives without harming or inconveniencing others. Though no one on Zeta Kotlin followed a profession as such - simply engaging in activities they found personally interesting and which were of use in some way to the wider community - Zhang Li had spent much of her life helping others through psychologically difficult periods, though she readily admitted that compared with some other planets she could mention, the problems she dealt with were relatively mild ones.

The health status of the wider population on Zeta Kotlin was generally a good one. Unlike on Rorque 4, say, citizens were not subject to long, strenuous and often unsociable working hours with all their attendant physical and mental health issues and problems. All sections of the Zetan population had access to good quality and sufficiently nutritious food, high standards of sanitation and readily available healthcare, whereas on Rorque 4 this was always done on a strict ability to pay. In addition, on Rorque 4, it was common practice for corporations to encourage their customers to consume products – food, medicines, beauty products, clothing and the like - that were of dubious or questionable safety as they pursued their drive for higher profit margins. On Zeta Kotlin no such pressures existed.

Additionally, on Zeta Kotlin communities were not crammed into densely-packed and unhealthy living conditions, whilst, by contrast, they did enjoy full control over local affairs and were never subjected to powerful corporations or governments imposing unwanted or undesirable developments upon them with all the stress, anxiety and depression this might entail. All in all, health standards were generally high on Zeta Kotlin, so the expertise of people like Zhang Li was not in particularly high demand, and her life as a mental health practitioner was not a particularly demanding one. Thus, despite occasional difficult scenarios, she had always gained great satisfaction from helping those who sought her advice.

'Can we safely assume that the passengers are all in stasis?' asked Rishaan, a tall elegant middle-aged man and intermittently also a longstanding member of Kapal's community. 'They are, as we know, all highly educated scientists and engineers – along with their children, of course. What if they've invented more advanced forms of space flight and improved forms of technology. They might have dispensed with stasis. It's possible they might have intentions other than simply settling here. We'll need to discover what they might be, but I'm not sure we can take that completely for granted.'

He paused for a moment. Middle-aged and in good physical shape, Rishaan was outgoing and active, full of life and keen on physical activities. He liked to get involved with life as much as he possibly could, but also had an impetuous streak running through him. He had spent significant sections of his life travelling and exploring the different continents of the planet, but had also travelled around the islands and, unusually for Zetans, spent some time at sea. For Zetans travel was a relatively easy pastime to enjoy, since they were unencumbered by employment, material scarcities and the necessity of bringing up children. All transport was public, fully automated, maintained by AI units and flexible enough to meet the needs of all its users. Despite all of these advantages though, few had travelled to the extent done so by Rishaan.

As he had explored the planet, he had enthusiastically helped with the various projects being pursued by the communes he stayed in. These often involved helping to improve the biodiversity of their ecosystems – a persistent concern on various parts of the continents - and occasional alterations to the system of food production, though he frequently found himself helping with educational and child-care matters. Zetans had very rounded educations as they were growing up, and once the basics had been covered, learnt about any and every subject that might interest them. Only as they grew older did they tend to focus more on specialised areas. With the planetary web containing huge amounts of knowledge and data – freely and easily available to all – it was not too difficult to quickly become well versed in any subject of choice, and so be capable of helping with the children's education.

After a few moments of thought, Rishaan continued, 'they might simply be headed here to acquire supplies or other resources we possess and they are in need of, and then simply depart for some as yet unknown further destination. The message indicates they've made significant advances in spaceflight technology – maybe that's what's being alluded to. After all, they've been there over a century now and never shown any interest whatsoever in our planet before.'

'But that's simply because they've not needed us before. The message clearly indicates they're looking for a new home; I personally believe it's highly likely that they're heading for Zeta Kotlin for habitation purposes, and they probably know that we have sufficient space to accommodate them here - we're still a generally sparsely populated planet, especially on some of the remoter continents. That's why they're heading here. We are their obvious first choice. Margalla is far too small for their purposes, and the other inhabited planets in the Cluster possess far less appealing civilisations than our own. We have everything they could possibly need – geographical space, an advanced economy and a stable civilisation,' surmised Catriona, one of the youngest and more optimistic members of the community. One of her oldest friends, and a former member of the Kapal community, Jiaying, had been heavily involved in Zeta Kotlin's space trading mission for several years now, and through frequent contact with her friend she possessed a good working knowledge of the planets in the Nexus Cluster, and clearly believed Zeta Kotlin was their obvious choice of destination.

Young, dark-haired, caring and sympathetic, Catriona often felt the pain others experienced and was thus highly empathic. She was also a keen ecologist and determined to ensure that the seventy per cent of Zeta Kotlin's land surface set aside from human development processes was maintained to the greatest extent possible, despite occasional pressures, especially from a desire to pursue leisure interests in some of the more attractive locations. This, she believed, would ensure that the planet's climate would not be adversely damaged in any significant manner. She and her fellow ecologists were also hoping that abundant biodiversity would eventually evolve, despite some initial imbalances and a lack of complexity within the early ecosystems. As such, she was actively involved in various biodiversity projects whilst also studying the evolution of the plants and animals brought to the planet in earlier times. In this respect she was quite fortunate, as most communities were keen to see their environment enhanced and improved for the better, with very few pressures to act otherwise.

Pedro was the fourth member of the present committee and easily the most sceptical of the four. 'Are we definitely certain we can take their message fully at face value? Are we absolutely certain they are coming in peace? Maybe it's a ploy and they're actually planning some form of invasion or takeover of our society. Maybe - over all those years - they've been developing advanced weaponry and some form of invasion force. Our planet is so much more benign than theirs; it wouldn't surprise me if they had a hidden agenda of some sort. Remember we have no military forces of our own. We have no effective means of defending ourselves from a military invasion. This could be potentially highly problematic for us, even devastating,' he interjected.

Pedro was a dark middle-aged man, quite thick-set, with dark hair and bushy eyebrows, down to earth and pretty matter of fact about most things. Invariably he would be most concerned with the practical details of any issue that was raised in their meetings. He was also not the most sociable of people, and thus never seemed completely at ease at them either. As one of the more sceptically-minded members of the community, he typically took little at face value and was concerned that there might be far too much complacency on this particular matter, both at this meeting and across the planet in general. He was part of the minority tendency on the planet that was somewhat suspicious of the intentions of the Alpha Fraczan diaspora.

As an individual he was also highly innovative and creative, and as a maker of jewelry and other decorative artefacts, he was considered something of a skilled craftsman. His work was well-known for its intricate patterns and use of unusual materials and was popular throughout the region. He had lately developed an interest in sporting activities, though had mainly become more physically active to address a health condition that had developed during his late twenties. Sport on Zeta Kotlin was mainly engaged in for a combination of pursuing good health, to develop team-building qualities and as a form of social and leisure pastime, and rarely for competitive reasons. In this respect, Pedro was typical of his fellow inhabitants. Few were prepared to devote the huge amounts of time and effort – and loss of social life - needed to acquire the levels of expertise achieved back on Earth, and there was thus little in the way of competition - leagues and tournaments, for instance - other than local friendly rivalries.

Arrival in Utopia

Catriona shook her head vigorously at Pedro's suggestion of possible invasion. 'The astronomers on Mount Xestron don't think this is the case. They've confirmed that Celestrina is currently making its nearest approach to Gannexon for many centuries, and they've detected orbital anomalies in the whole of its planetary system. Alpha Fraczan has very likely experienced a major catastrophic event and they've had to evacuate their planet as quickly as possible. It's far more likely to be a genuine emergency, than any form of planetary takeover,' responded Catriona confidently.

'The message has the air of a real last minute affair – in fact, it looks to be a pretty amateurish effort, in my opinion. I very much doubt this is some form of covert military operation, I think we should take it at face value; these are people facing the destruction of their civilisation and we should do everything possible to help them,' added Zhang Li, smoothing back her short white hair, and then pouring herself another glass of water.

'I agree, and I think we need to look at this in a positive way and consider the possible advantages, both for the Alphans and for our own civilisation. We're actually well placed on the Xestronian continent to take a large number of settlers – there's plenty of space on the eastern side of our continent, for instance. A whole new community of academics and scientists could make life here significantly more interesting,' stated Catriona, warming to the idea of accepting an exodus of people who were in dire need of help. 'Despite all the successes we've enjoyed here, we still face a number of problems, ones that their expertise might be able to help us with.'

'My main concern is that they must accept the basic features of our society. There's no question of them retaining private ownership of AI units or any other resources within our economy,' stated Pedro, still not fully willing to let go of his suspicions. 'I understand that's how they've been operating on Alpha Fraczan until now. We need to make sure they accept our political and economic structures. We can't have them pursuing the old oppressive and exploitative ways we left behind on Earth.'

'I agree with you there, there's no question of them retaining the bad old ways – and they definitely need to accept our egalitarian decision-making system of government. I've also heard that they still make use of the old ancient hierarchies and systems of private property we left behind on Earth,' added Catriona, trying to strike a conciliatory note that she was sure all present could agree with. 'We cannot allow those old unfair and damaging systems to be reintroduced here, especially if they have developed advanced technologies superior to our own. I admit that there, they could pose some real problems for us. We might as well have stayed back on Earth if we allow all that to occur again.'

'I also agree, as long as they follow our society's basic requirements, I don't see any reason for them not to settle here successfully. Hopefully they have developed useful ideas and technology we can use for our own betterment, but equally we can help them integrate into what, I am sure all here agree, are a better set of social arrangements than the ones they knew on Alpha Fraczan. It's certainly preferable that any advanced knowledge and technology is shared with us, rather than the dubious elements that control Rorque 4, or the fascists on Zeleyan,' added Zhang Li, making, for her, a rare critical comment, for even she could find little positive to say about the two planets.

'Yes, especially those fascist idiots on Zeleyan,' interjected Pedro – a comment that brought agreeing laughs from those assembled at the meeting.

After this, the meeting was opened up for comments from the wider community, though most contributions covered the ground already discussed. As the afternoon progressed, it became clear that the more optimistic position of Catriona and Zhang Li was the predominant one within their community, and they seemed to successfully assuage the doubts of those holding concerns about a more negative impact on their planet. When the discussion was finally concluded and all present had contributed to their satisfaction, they eventually went to a vote supporting a motion allowing the Alphans to remain on the planet, with the specific proviso that certain preconditions identified in the meeting were closely adhered to.

At around the same time, similar discussions and votes were occurring across the many continents and islands of Zeta Kotlin and the one at Kapal proved to be highly typical. Once the federal and community councils across the various continents had discussed the matter and submitted their opinions and decisions, the General Committee of the Federal Councils was fully convened. Like all such cross-planetary meetings it was conducted virtually - since it's various members were elected from all the regions of the planet - and televised live so any interested observers could follow the proceedings. Its discussion and decisions were informed closely by the soundings deriving from each region, and ultimately – very much in accordance with the wider wishes of the population - it was decided that due to the unusual circumstances and significant importance of this particular matter, the way forward should be to implement a cross-planetary vote of the entire population.

Given that the matter had already been widely discussed, it was decided that the vote could take place within the next fourteen days. The inhabitants were given a choice between offering the Alphans settlement on the planet - assuming that was what they wanted - but only on the condition they adhered to the basic Zetan political and economic structures - or alternatively to be told they could not stay and must find another planet to reside on. For two weeks the Zetans continued to debate and discuss the matter, but in the absence of any further significant information arriving from the ships or elsewhere, opinions did not significantly alter. A system of electronic voting ensured the decision made was a rapid one. Turnout for the vote was high - unsurprisingly given the nature of the issue - and a clear majority opted to allow the Alphans to stay, assuming they adopted the proviso that they must adapt to the established structures of Zetan society.

Once the decision had been made, they could then do little but wait for the starships to actually arrive. Messages were sent to the incoming starships informing them of the planetary decision, but also requesting further information of their intentions. All they received in return, though, were repeated standard emissions of the original message – presumably the AI units piloting the ships were following preprogrammed orders in respect to this matter. Discussions across the planet therefore turned to where any new settlements could be established, and how the Alphans might be integrated into Zetan society. Provisional plans were drawn up for the creation of new settlements and the necessary infrastructure and transport networks to effect this.

Interstellar Space, Web Weaver – change of destination

The first of the two ships that had departed from Alpha Fraczan and later deviated, nine months into their journey, from their preprogrammed destination of Zeta Kotlin, was the Web Weaver - so-called because its original occupants had desired to spread an intricate network of knowledge across the known galaxy. It had done so because the maintenance systems monitoring the life support systems aboard the stasis ship had moved to a critical level report. Initially, the problem had been investigated by the AI units running the ship but discovered it was not one they were able to immediately fix. The systems maintaining the artificial atmosphere required within the ship, and in particular for the stasis pods, were starting to severely malfunction, and the required oxygen levels were very gradually but clearly falling.

The passengers were not in immediate danger – temporary back-up systems had been activated - but there was no prospect of them reaching their designated destination; the required levels would drop well below a life-sustaining status several months before arrival at Zeta Kotlin. The situation would eventually endanger all passengers on board, unless the pods were switched off one by one, in an unedifying process of sacrificing the few to save the many. Given that their destination was still eleven months away though, even this would still result in an unacceptably high death toll. As such, the AI units did not possess the necessary protocols to commence such a procedure. The designated skeleton crew would need to be woken from stasis to make any appropriate decisions.

A standard skeleton crew in a stasis ship typically consisted of six members, and in the case of the Web Weaver they were all previously leading members of the academic institutions on Alpha Fraczan. Those awakened were Anna Dubois, the acting commander of the ship, and her associates Quiang Maduro, Masego Carlson, Agnetha Bertillon, Ning Frenzzy and Alvilda Schmidt. As was always the case after time spent in stasis, they all experienced an initial period of grogginess and nausea as they wakened fully to their senses. The AI units were programmed to deal with this process, and after several hours and it was registered that the six had been aided and deemed sufficiently recovered, they were fully informed of the current situation on the starship.

Once informed, Anna Dubois designated specific tasks to each member of the crew. Masego and Quiang were tasked with checking the maintenance systems to ensure that the initial AI unit analysis was completely correct. After a long series of detailed diagnostic checks they ultimately arrived at the same result as the AI units, which none of them were particularly surprised by. Whilst they were performing this process, Agnetha and Alvilda were tasked with calculating and exploring possible alternative engineering solutions to the emergency, but after several hours of investigation concluded that their options were highly limited.

Anna, working with Ning, checked the immediate vicinity of space for any possible sources of the gases and other resources they needed and also for emergency landing sites. This was not a particularly difficult task as one option clearly presented itself above all the others - the nearby star system of Sazhina. It was well known to the scientists of Alpha Fraczan, for no other reason than the fact that it was easily their nearest stellar neighbour in the Nexus Cluster. The system, for many years, had also been something of a puzzle. It was known that five rocky planets orbited within the inner section of the system, with a single ice and gas giant circling in its outer regions.

The four planets nearest the star, it was widely agreed, appeared to be enveloped by thick gaseous atmospheres, but various analyses of the fifth planet appeared to show the presence of large amounts of water and a benign atmosphere. Yet the message emitting from the stellar system's transponder clearly stated that none of the star's planets were habitable or realistically capable of being terra-formed. Various exploratory attempts had been made by the scientists to discern whether this was actually the case, but their attempts to make contact with the planet were met with complete silence, and the two probes sent to explore the system had both malfunctioned, though it was unsure why.

Much debate ensued as to what the answer to this enigma might be, and a variety of theories had been postulated. The exo-biologists on Alpha Fraczan had been particularly keen to mount an expedition to the stellar system to resolve the debate once and for all, but for reasons that were never made entirely clear, though seemed to be based on largely political and security issues, the university authorities had refused to give permission for such an expedition to go ahead. The exo-biologists continued to monitor the planet from afar, and various tell-tale signs convinced them that there did indeed seem to be life on the planet, though possibly only in very small quantities. Unable to investigate beyond this though, the planet thus remained something of a mystery to them.

All this information and data was readily available to Anna and Ning in the ship's data banks, and once the other two pairs had fully informed Anna of their findings, a relatively short discussion was held by the skeleton crew with regards to their possible options. It soon became apparent to them during the course of this discussion that the ultimate problem was that none of them were actually experts in space flight or rocket engineering, thus they were not in a position to make a fully informed appraisal of their predicament. Whilst the stasis ships did possess solutions to this particular eventuality, the options being offered by the ship's computer to them were well beyond their expertise and they were extremely uncertain as to how to actually proceed.

As far as they were concerned, there were only two options they fully understood – the gradual one-by-one sacrifice of passengers, or a deviation to the fifth planet of Sazhina. Given that the ship's computers strongly suggested that the fifth planet had exactly the resources they needed, it was not a difficult decision for the crew to ultimately make, and so the Web Weaver slowed, plotted an alternative course of direction and then departed on this trajectory. As it did so, it messaged the other ships of the diaspora, informing them of its dilemma and its chosen solution. The message was received and stored by the other six stasis ships.

Arrival in Utopia

Rorque 4 – the message arrives

A month later, the arrival of the message from the fleeing diaspora ships of Alpha Fraczan at Rorque 4 late one mid-week afternoon had taken the news agencies completely by surprise, but it was soon breaking news across the entire planet. The information bulletins quickly relayed the details of the message to their paying customers situated across the various cities and other habitations of the planet. By mid-evening, each news channel had managed to locate and gather a number of talking heads who were considered to have at least some degree of expertise in some vaguely relevant area, or who were known for their outspoken views on a variety of controversial subjects. They were duly invited onto the various talk shows to speculate on what disaster might have happened at Alpha Fraczan, the likely destination of the departing spaceships, and what might be the likely implications of this unforeseen and unexpected event.

And it was, indeed, largely speculation they expounded, for the message had been brief, lacked any significant detail and seemed distinctly ambiguous in places. Despite much argument and debate on the various infotainment shows, their guests were still able to arrive at something of a broad agreement that there had been a catastrophic disaster on Alpha Fraczan, that the starships were most likely to head for Rorque 4, and that this could offer some major investment opportunities for the hi-tech and science corporations, at a time when they really did need some new ideas, new products and an injection of optimism.

Whilst they generally acknowledged that Zeta Kotlin was logistically the nearest inhabited planet for the Alphans to head for in an emergency, there was also a general agreement that the backward nature of the Zetan economy and the lack of freedoms that existed there, would hold few attractions for scientists who were leading lights in their field of expertise, particularly ones looking to advance their research, careers and reputations. The journey to Rorque 4 might be considerably longer - not that the scientists would notice this anyway as they would all be asleep in stasis - but it would certainly be worth going the extra distance in the long run. The talking heads were confident that the scientists would make the obvious decision, choose

Rorque 4 as their destination, and everyone would eventually benefit from the arrangement.

It was not just the talking heads on the media who were confident that the spacecraft would head in their direction; some of the largest corporations on the planet had also arrived at a similar conclusion. Or, at the very least, they could not afford to allow their competitors first access to the arriving scientists, in the event that they did choose Rorque 4 as their preferred destination. In the event that the stasis ships did choose their world to reside on, they could not allow themselves to be in a position where they might lose out in the recruitment race that would invariably follow when they made landfall on the planet. And so, each of the large corporations quickly created a slick and highly attractive recruitment package and then used their own private satellite systems to beam their corporate message out towards the presumed-to-be-approaching starships. Given the vast distance that the messages needed to travel, the corporations could then do little but sit back and wait for a response.

Arrival in Utopia

Zeleyan – the message arrives

A couple of months after the Web Weaver changed trajectory towards the planet of Margalla, at the far end of the Nexus Cluster, Supreme Commander Vartin sat at his enormous desk in his equally large bureau on the highest floor of the party headquarters building situated in the centre of Zeleyan City. As was always the case, he started work late in the morning after a long leisurely breakfast with his political subordinates, allowing him the opportunity to take in the recent news, or other significant developments from the day before, and disseminate appropriate instructions. The national media outlets were checked to make sure the stories and information they had disseminated were in accordance with party orders, and plans for the day formulated.

Once in his office, his work routine followed a predictable order of business, which largely involved the further issuing of security orders to senior military personnel. But shortly before midday, unexpectedly, a knock came from the door at the far end of his extensive room. The guards in the corners of the room stiffened slightly and readied for any possible problem that might unfold. A slightly nervous looking junior army officer entered through the door, made the long walk across the room to Vartin's desk and delivered a large glossy white envelope to the small group seated around his desk. One of the senior officers present complained at the unscheduled interruption.

'High Command sent this as designated top secret and of the utmost urgency. It was considered to be too confidential to be sent electronically,' the junior officer explained apologetically.
Vartin looked at the junior officer briefly, 'very good lieutenant, dismissed,' and the young officer promptly made the long walk back to the door he had only recently entered by.

Vartin picked up an ornate letter-opener from his desk and expertly slit open the end of the envelope and read carefully through the single sheet of paper that had been delivered within the glossy package. He read it a second time to make sure he had not missed anything on the first reading. The other senior officers across from him began to look concerned as Vartin looked as though he might be about to lose his temper.

Arrival in Utopia

The message sent by the starships leaving Alpha Fraczan had finally arrived at Zeleyan, the last of the inhabited planets of the Nexus Cluster, taking a further four months than had been the case for it to reach Zeta Kotlin. For those living on Zeleyan, Alpha Fraczan was located at the extreme far end of the Nexus Cluster and was largely an enigma. They knew it was mostly or entirely populated by scientists and was believed to be singly devoted to the pursuit of knowledge. Other than this, little else was known of its affairs. However, for Vartin, with his highly suspicious and paranoid mind, Alpha Fraczan's claim to be simply engaged in pursuing knowledge and an advanced understanding of the universe could not seriously be taken at face value. He had always believed that there must be some form of covert agenda, possibly some attempt to undermine the existing order, or a hidden relationship with one of the other planets in the Nexus Cluster. The arrival of the message triggered a stream of paranoid thoughts within his mind, but whatever the actual truth of the situation, the dangers this development posed were clear enough, as far as Vartin was concerned.

Vartin managed to contain his temper and informed the senior officers of the contents of the message.
'If it's purely an evacuation procedure, will they head to Zeta Kotlin – that's the nearest inhabited planet, is it not?' asked Colonel Musson.
'That's a possible destination. And if they share their knowledge with that bunch of Zetan renegades, that must surely impact on the position of Zeleyan,' stated his immediate senior General Neumann.
'How will this affect our plans for Ur-Tokar?' asked Musson, but his question was left unanswered.

All of this and more had already occurred to Vartin. He paused and thought for a while; his senior officers had not been chosen for their expert knowledge or, indeed, for any tactical military brilliance or other form of expertise. As all despots had traditionally done, he had surrounded himself with yes-men, sycophants, loyalists and toadies. They could all be relied on to obediently follow orders - though unfortunately not always competently - but then they could always be replaced, he reminded himself as he looked across the table at the two officers.

Arrival in Utopia

General Neumann with his large grey moustache, reddish complexion and seriously deep voice was a tall and forbidding figure and very much a product of the Zeleyanian Military Academy. Orthodox in almost all respects of Zeleyanian society, his comfortable and privileged background meant he was a straight down the line orthodox fascist and obediently followed the every wish of his supreme leader. He was, additionally, a man who brooked no nonsense and was capable of meting out harsh punishments for anyone he considered as a transgressor. Not for no reason was he known by most Zeleyanians as 'the widow maker'.

With no existing system of human rights, civil liberties or rule of law, there were no effective restrictions as to what these punishments might entail, as long as he maintained the support of Supreme Commander Vartin, which was invariably the case – both realising that loyalty worked very much to their mutual benefit. As such, Neumann had been a natural candidate for inclusion in Vartin's High Command and his unfaltering loyalty ensured he maintained Vartin's support and approval. Vartin was well aware that Neumann would offer little in the way of innovative problem-solving or creative military strategies but his loyalty more than made up for this lacuna.

The colonel, by contrast, was a somewhat different kettle of fish. Even by the standards of Zeleyanian fascism, Musson was a quite sadistic and brutal character and particularly ruthless when dealing with opponents of the regime. From an early age he had been encouraged by an elitist family to regard himself as superior to those around him, and a series of achievements in his teenage years had only enhanced this behavioural trait. Effectively, he looked down on others with disdain, and tended to see only failure, weakness, cowardice and ignorance in so much of the society he happened to be a member of. Additionally, violence had also been a common feature within his family and frequent, often unjustified, beatings from his father had created a sadistic streak in him; he had resented the beatings and soon learnt to take his frustrations out on others, particularly those he believed to be of little worth and value – which happened to be most people.

These two combined features had created an arrogant and brutal elitist, and Zeleyan was just the kind of society in which such an individual could flourish. The Zeleyanian media was always full of divisive stories blaming other towns, regions or subversive groups for any failings occurring within the regime. There existed an endless number of potential groups and minorities that could be picked on and demonized when necessity called, and Musson – who was only too willing to believe the negative propaganda – was also only too willing to treat such groups with the disdain and brutality he felt they deserved.

Musson's contempt for the perceived failings of these scapegoated groups was, by contrast, matched only by his admiration and devotion to those who he believed lived up to the standards that could be achieved, if only more effort was put into doing so. Amongst those he perceived as living up to these high standards was the Supreme Commander and he was highly dedicated – in his own simplistic and straightforward way – to keeping him in power, the place he believed he should rightly be. Musson was thus exactly the type of commander Vartin placed within his High Command, and he was more than ready to overlook the Colonel's occasional bouts of brutality towards unfortunate others, knowing his loyalty could be entirely guaranteed.

Neither of his senior officers would, thus, ever challenge his ideas or thoughts, and he had to admit to himself at this moment, he really did need some extra input on the subject he now needed to turn his attention to. Vartin's knowledge of cosmology, space travel and everything associated with it was somewhat limited. He would need to consult his so-called Science Officer, Jonas Varela, to make a more thorough evaluation of this unwanted development. He eventually gave some cursory but non-committed answers to his officer's questions, and then suspended the meeting, dismissing his senior officers, and went for an early lunch, though not before issuing orders that his Science Officer should be summoned for a top secret meeting that same afternoon. The meeting was to be strictly private, even his personal security guards would not be present.

Jonas Varela was in his early forties, tall and thin, bespectacled, slightly balding and of a generally disheveled appearance. He was a quite gangly looking figure with a sardonic smile and often bemused look on his face, usually hiding the disdain he held for others. Varela would readily admit he was not the most likeable or sociable of people, but he invariably considered this to be a major benefit for his self-allotted task in life, that of preserving the true fascist nature of Zeleyan. If he needed to rub people up the wrong way, well that was what he needed to do, and he never held any regrets – no matter how much he displeased or annoyed those around him.

He was the product of an upper middle-ranking family and its associated school background and enjoyed all the benefits and privileges that went with the status of this particular grouping. From an early age he had always been a fervent supporter of the regime and its ideology – he knew which side his bread was buttered on – but at the top university he had attended to complete his studies, where he had rubbed shoulders with those from the highest and most important echelons, he had been alarmed to discover what he regarded as a worrying lack of ideological vigour amongst this elite group.

Rather than a fervent commitment to fascism and the official ideology of the planet, they appeared to show greater loyalty and devotion to maintaining the esteemed position of their own highly privileged class, and any commitments they did demonstrate towards the ideology seemed to rest solely on the fact that it furthered their own narrow class interests. Varela had become concerned that with power resting so heavily with such a pampered and self-interested group of, not particularly talented, individuals, there was a severe danger that the regime might collapse as a result of their short-sightedness or loyalty to their own selfish priorities. He was convinced that their preoccupation with their own class interests meant they had lost sight of the wider importance of maintaining a fascist regime, one which he firmly believed was ultimately of benefit to the entire population, though admittedly in different ways and as long as its members obediently adhered to certain basic requirements.

As such, Varela had made it his own personal mission to preserve the ideological purity of the political elite, and he had quickly recognised that in order to purse this particular pursuit it was imperative he should enjoy the close confidence of Supreme Commander Vartin. His subsequent involvement and success in a number of important political campaigns had brought him to the attention of Vartin, and once he gained a toehold amongst the senior elite, it was only a matter of time before he eventually came to be seen as an indispensable aide to the head of the government and the military. Fortunately, from his own particular point of view, Vartin appeared more politically aware than many of his fellow officer class, and more ruthless in his desire to preserve the existing power structure, even if this might mainly be out of pure self-interest.

Varela had, for some time now, found himself in exactly the position he wanted to be. He had been appointed as Science Officer by Supreme Commander Vartin several years beforehand, though some years after Vartin's attainment of the top job. Varela actually had no particular expertise in science, despite being highly educated and from a semi-privileged background. His highly motivated ideological disposition meant he showed utter contempt for anything other than his own fascist views - a quality Vartin had, over the years, found extremely useful, since his own perceived strengths lay largely elsewhere. Varela, motivated purely by ideology, offered no personal threat to Vartin, and over time had proven to be a very able advisor. On occasions, Vartin worried that his dependence on Varela might, in fact, have become too great, and he always remained on the look-out for additional 'political advisers', though there seemed to be something of a dearth in talent in this particular area at this moment in time, he had noted.

By the time Vartin arrived at the meeting after lunch, Varela had already read the message and given it some considerable thought before the two were due to meet. Vartin quizzed his Science Officer for his thoughts on this latest unwanted development.
'It simply means we need to move faster with our plans for Ur-Tokar. If the Alphans do actually possess advanced knowledge of space flight and improved weapons technology, it makes it all the more urgent that we advance our plans to an earlier date. We need to close the deal with Rorque 4 and ensure delivery as soon as possible,' he paused for a moment and scratched his head. 'I would say our plans need to be advanced by several months. If we hesitate and wait to see how this development plays out, there is a severe danger that we will suffer unnecessary delays and ultimately fail to complete the mission. If Zeta Kotlin obtains advanced space flight technology and military engineering from the Alphans that could scupper our plans entirely. It's imperative that we pre-empt this possibility and move as fast as possible', concluded Varela, who also liked to think of himself as a man of action and purpose, and not simply a hired political advisor.

Vartin smiled, acknowledging this appraisal of the situation; these had been his thoughts almost exactly. He was pleased he had not over-looked anything of major importance; indeed his appraisal of the situation had gone beyond the thoughts of Varela. This unwanted development might actually prove to be all the information he needed to advance his plans for his next, and so far greatest, moment of glory. Indeed, he now believed he could actually turn the unwanted development to his advantage, and that his plans for everlasting greatness should now be launched at the earliest opportunity available, a thought that was actually very out of character for the normally highly cautious Vartin.

The meeting with Varela concluded much sooner than Vartin had expected. He returned to his desk, and issued a series of orders to a range of functionaries and senior-ranking officers instructing the relevant organisations and agencies to bring forward his original plans by exactly six months. This would no doubt cause problems for various individuals lower down the ranks, but this was an opportunity, he considered, for them to show their value to the party, the nation and the Supreme Commander himself - by demonstrating their ability to meet the needs of the hour as and when necessary. Rewards and punishments were always available for those impacted by the decision, depending on how competently they responded to their new orders.

Finally, Vartin gave orders to message his Space Fleet Commander Vice-Admiral Rosson with a brief summary of the day's events and news. Rosson was at this very moment headed towards the Necron star system to conclude a business deal with one of the business corporations from Rorque 4. Rosson was to be informed that the matter was now one of even greater urgency than had previously been the case. The future of Zeleyan was now in the hands of the Vice-Admiral, and he was expected to perform his duties to his utmost abilities. Rosson was informed of the now more generous terms that Zeleyan was willing to offer to conclude the deal, but was left under no illusions as to the consequences of failure. Vartin's opinion of his Vice-Admiral was not an especially high one, but he did have to admit that Rosson's ability to get things done was occasionally capable of surprising him. His complete obedience to Vartin, by contrast, he believed, could be fully guaranteed.

Arrival in Utopia

Margalla – arrival of the Web Weaver

Kiyona had woken at what, for her, was an unusually early hour and was discovered she was entirely unable to fall back asleep. She shifted her gaze from the drawings on the bedroom wall to the sleeping Jairo lying next to her. She briefly contemplated waking him so she had something to do but quickly decided otherwise. She had been sleeping with him for several weeks now, but had recently realised she was now losing interest in him. Their conversations were no longer particularly interesting and she felt the relationship was not delivering what she wanted, though exactly what that was, she was even less sure of than had been the case even a short while ago.

She rolled out of bed as quietly as she possibly could, so as to not to wake the sleeping Jairo, gathered up her clothes and padded silently out of the room. She washed and dressed in the en-suite bathroom, carefully arranged her hair and then made her way through to the communal living space. As she had always assumed, no one was there at such an unsociably early hour – she was rarely one of the early risers – and a quick rifle through the communal kitchen cupboards highlighted the need to visit the fruit and vegetable gardens that surrounded the commune. She left the water on to boil and the pancakes to warm in the oven, and was soon back inside after a quick sortie to gather the fruit and salad vegetables she desired for breakfast. She left any surplus she had gathered in the very large communal fridge and headed to the veranda to eat breakfast.

Outside, the air was yet to warm in the stillness of the morning – Sazhina not having commenced its slow ascent over the distant ocean horizon. A few small cumulus clouds appeared to distantly hover low over the sea's glistening tranquil surface whilst the wide dark blackish-blue sky stretched infinitely above her in all directions. High above her she spotted the two moons, Jade and Rosa, still casting their pale green and red light further to the south-east. She spotted a small loose-knit flock of pale white seabirds headed northwards along the beach, no doubt heading towards deeper waters for a day spent fishing further along the coast. As she ate, a slight onshore breeze picked up – the rustling of the fruit trees being the only movement in the calmness of the morning.

She had no particular plans for the day, but the sea looked inviting, and after several days of lazing around she decided she needed some exercise, so after finishing her breakfast she headed down to the beach. The water was nice and warm, as it always was at this time of the year, and she spent the next thirty minutes swimming casually around the bay. The sea was crystal clear and she could easily make out various species of fish below her, crabs scuttling across the sand and even the occasional octopus making its way furtively through the marine plants and rocky formations that made up patches of the seafloor in the bay. A few months previously she would probably not even have noticed the sea creatures, but her close friend Nova had recently developed an interest in the local sea-life, and was keen to extend her new found knowledge to her closest friends.

After her swim, she made her way back to her commune, one of many dotted fairly randomly amongst the various orchards and thinly wooded groves that spread across the wide expanse of the broad shallow bay that constituted the greater part of the coastline on this part of the island. On her return, she showered once more, rearranged her hair again and chose a different set of clothes for the day. None her fellow communards had emerged from their bedrooms for breakfast as yet – even now the hour was still early - and so she made herself another cup of mint tea and sipped it slowly whilst she decided what she could do for the rest of the morning. Finally, after much indecision, she decided to head to the Community Centre, located further inland on the higher slopes of the bay. Nova's recent interest in the local fauna and flora had left her feeling that she too needed to do something more constructive with her time, and she resolved to make a start on devising her own personal project.

She made her way breezily up the gentle slope of the bay towards the centre of the loose-knit settlement. Towards the top of the slope she stopped and turned to take in the view. There was still no one else around. Sazhina was now only just breaching the horizon, and the sea was taking on a deeper aquamarine blue in the early sunlight. From her vantage point she could take in the majority of what might be called the township in which she lived. In reality, her settlement of Librado was just a loose scattering of low-rise communal buildings set within a hillside constituted largely of thinly wooded fruit tree orchards, occasional palms and small more open areas devoted predominantly to the cultivation of fruits and vegetables. Pathways criss-crossed the whole hillside, but only the occasional road snaked its way through the trees and between the communal buildings.

She turned and looked across the top of the hillside towards the still somewhat darker western sky and was slightly surprised to see the unmistakable sight of a space ship moving steadily across the upper reaches of the atmosphere. She assumed it was The Spirit of The Age, the one and only stasis ship that the planet's inhabitants possessed and which she had seen on numerous occasions late at night. A few seconds later though, she spotted a second ship following in its wake, moving along a very similar trajectory - that was odd, she thought, there really only should be one space ship up there! Momentarily she thought she must be imagining it, but the second ship continued its steady transit across the sky – it really was there and not a figment of her imagination. She thought hard, but could not recollect any talk of the Zeta Kotlin trading ship being expected at Margalla anytime soon – and anyway that was a dark-coloured ship that was particularly difficult to see against the backdrop of space. In fact, it had made one of its rare and irregular visits only a few months ago, so was not expected to return for a considerable period of time. A growing sense of worry and alarm rose within her.

With still no one else around to discuss the matter with, she hastened quickly to the Community Centre where she would be able to monitor recent satellite communications and check for any incoming messages that might have been logged. Kiyona wasn't entirely sure whether to be scared or to be excited. This was the most unexpected event she could recall for a long time. In many respects, she tended to be typical of her fellow planetary inhabitants in that she was an inherent optimist, and she was hoping there might be some form of benefit to this sudden and unexpected visitation. On the other hand, their community had an underlying concern regarding invasion from one of the more hostile civilisations that they knew existed out in the local neighbourhood of space, and with no means with which to defend themselves, this appearance could potentially spell doom and disaster for their small island paradise.

Margalla – Web Weaver in orbit

The Community Centre in Librado was pretty standard by Margallan standards, only its use of a variety of local building materials would have marked it out as distinct in any particular way from the other centres across the islands. Its many buildings, parks and gardens sprawled across the centre of the hillside ensuring that it was the social centre of much that occurred in the settlement. As with all the other centres across the islands, it served as an all-purpose utility space for the whole community. Almost any event of any significance was held here – town meetings, entertainment events, social ceremonies, healthcare, education and any other matter that the local community considered to be of importance.

When Kiyona reached it, there were only a tiny number of people in the Community Centre at this early hour and all were clearly busily involved with their various activities. She made some brief comments to one or two of them and hurried into the computer room. Kiyona possessed a generally average level of knowledge when it came to the use of the now somewhat archaic communications devices that were in standard usage across the planet, but after logging into the relevant data system, even she could very quickly see that no one had actually bothered to check the external communications systems for some months, though the images on the screen quickly demonstrated to her that there was actually very little to be concerned with.

To all intents and purposes, this was not actually surprising. Margalla had, long ago, effectively chosen to establish a form of communications silence with the rest of the cosmos, so there was little actual reason to carry out any regular checks. After first arrival on the planet, for a short while, the planetary community had collectively decided to monitor inter-planetary communications – a decision largely driven by their fear of a possible invasion - but the messaging they logged proved to be almost entirely constituted by routine communications sent between the various other planets and any passing spaceships, and little of any interest was ever really noted.

It quickly became clear to them that there was very little actual space traffic or intercommunication between the planets. Such a boring task had soon been passed over to the AI units, but even this had proven problematic as the

AI units, in practice, were unable to distinguish between what was actually important, what was possibly threatening, and what was of routine irrelevance. In addition, at most times, they were usually needed for far more important and practical tasks across the various islands of the archipelago. Ultimately, the community had largely lost interest in the procedure and decided that an alarm system would be activated for any communications deriving from the Zetan trading ship - the Opa-Loka - that occasionally visited them, and for anything that sounded distinctly suspicious, but everything else could be safely ignored.

The scan Kiyona initiated trawled through recent communications stored in the data banks, ignored the routine emissions, and quickly retrieved the message stored - for thirteen months now - from the dying civilisation of Alpha Fraczan. She listened to the message and quickly assumed the event was probably connected to the ship she had seen in orbit around the planet. She was not exactly sure how far Alpha Fraczan was in terms of space flight from Margalla but she knew they were in the same sector of the Nexus Cluster, and so figured that the ship was probably one of those that had departed in the disapora. But why was there only one? She checked for communications between vessels in near space and discovered the message sent by the Web Weaver to the other ships informing them of its difficulties. The presence of the starship now made complete sense. Feeling she had fully understood the situation, she locked on to the orbiting stasis ship's communications channel and sent a message asking the crew what exactly they needed from their planet. For a while there was no reply.

Shortly before, aboard the Web Weaver and high above Margalla's watery surface, Anna Dubois and the other five members of her skeleton crew had successfully placed the ship in orbit around Margalla, but after several rotations of the planet were somewhat puzzled. Apart from a large frozen polar continent in the northern hemisphere, there appeared to be no actual land, just one vast blue ocean. Margalla appeared to be simply one vast waterworld with little else of any note. The members of the crew situated on the viewing deck and were trying to make sense of the strange planetary situation.

116

Arrival in Utopia

'This must explain why the star's transponder unit is emitting a non-habitable message to the rest of the cosmos; yet our scans clearly show the atmosphere to be a breathable one. Something's not quite right here,' stated Anna Dubois carefully, possibly talking more to herself than the rest of the crew.

'Surely only a 'genesis pod' could have created this atmosphere, the chances of it occurring naturally must be thousands to one,' agreed Ning, who had happened to overhear Anna's remark.

'Did the genesis pods ever try to terra-form planets and then give it up as a bad job? Or did they just automatically terra-form planets with water, irrespective of the actual planetary conditions? Surely, they had better programming than that,' Anna pontificated, again more to herself, than the other crew members. Her field of expertise was pharmaceuticals, so she was a long way from being certain of what she was now dealing with.

'Maybe the atmosphere only became breathable long after the terra-forming process had been ended and the negative transmission established,' mused Agnetha, though as a geologist, she too was also unsure as to how the 'genesis pods' had actually operated more than a century ago.

'In addition, there's only the frozen landmass at the northern polar region that's potentially habitable, and I can't imagine many people actually wanting to live there, other than for research purposes. Maybe that's why they gave up on the planet. Perhaps they were hoping the ice would melt in the terra-forming process, but it never actually happened, so they then sent out an 'uninhabitable warning message' from the transponder,' added Masego, equally confused by the whole situation.

'Wow, we're receiving a message from down below,' interrupted Alvilda suddenly, 'where's that coming from – surely not from the ice sheet,' she added, shaking her head, not quite believing what she was seeing.

The ship's computers quickly calculated the precise origin of the planetary message. It seemed to be coming from somewhere in the sub-tropics, but initially they could only see yet more ocean there, until the computer magnified the area on the screen and suddenly a small archipelago of islands appeared across the viewer. The crew glanced quizzically at each other, almost not believing what they were seeing.

'That's the only habitable land on the planet! No wonder no one came to live here,' gasped Agnetha, at the same time suddenly wondering how such a geological scenario was even possible.

'Well, not exactly no one. Clearly there is some intelligent life here,' replied Anna, pleased to have resolved one conundrum, but now unsure as to whether this would prove a benefit to their predicament or a hindrance.

'Not much though, surely. Presumably, those islands can only hold a tiny population. I doubt there's any room for us, even if we were planning to stay,' added Ning, also still not quite believing the strange configuration of the planet. 'At least we don't need to use the ice sheet for landing anymore. Even the AI units might have experienced difficulties operating there, I suspect.'

Anna requested that Alvilda should reply to Kiyona's message explaining the exact nature of their predicament. They needed to fix their life support systems and then replenish them with various gases from Margalla's atmosphere so that they could recommence their journey to their original destination of Zeta Kotlin. However, they needed to move much faster than originally thought as their problem seemed to have recently accelerated in severity, and they now believed the stasis life support systems would soon be moving towards dangerously low levels. Oxygen levels, in particular, would reach critical within the next day or two according to the latest diagnostics.

In desperation, they had even identified engineering experts amongst their passengers, and recently brought them out of stasis, but their prognosis, so far, had also been a highly negative one, confirming that a visit to the planet of Margalla was by far and away their best hope of rectifying their predicament. As such, they needed to descend to the planet as soon as possible to commence the repair process. They had, in addition, informed their fellow starships of their newfound situation, and the fact that they believed they could now resolve their technical difficulties and soon rejoin them on their journey to Zeta Kotlin. Frustratingly, though, there was no immediate response to Alvida's communication and the crew waited impatiently, repeating the message on two more occasions.

Back on Margalla, the reason no return message had been received by the stasis ship was because a major dispute had broken out amongst the inhabitants of Librado. Excited, Kiyona had relayed her fantastic news to the others in the Community Centre, but they had taken an entirely different view of the situation. For them, it came as a great shock that an unknown and unexpected stasis ship had suddenly descended out of space and slowed into orbit around their planet, and Kiyona had been admonished by a number of her fellow townspeople. Concerned to keep their existence in the universe a secret – or at least a near-secret – they had been alarmed by her decision to send a return message to the orbiting stasis ship.

Almost immediately, Kiyona realised her mistake – she was well aware of her tendency to act on impulse without thinking through the consequences of her actions, and almost immediately began to regret her action. Why had she done such a stupid thing, she thought, once again frustrated with herself. She had just assumed the ship would have already seen the archipelago and registered their existence. Yet, she had once visited their own planet's stasis ship as part of a trip organised by the local community and now remembered just how tiny and almost invisible their archipelago actually was, and how surprisingly difficult it was to find from the edge of space, even when you knew roughly where to look.

Although she made immediate apologies to those present, she could not shake off the fact that she had received the disapproval of her community, and so she tried to make excuses and argue that perhaps her mistake would not prove to be the calamitous one some were predicting.
'They're on their way to Zeta Kotlin, and our existence is already known there - possibly not by all of their inhabitants - but our existence won't be a totally new revelation. Probably, nothing negative will actually come from this.'
'Well, we'll need to hope that remains the case, but there's no way of guaranteeing that. The Zetans have promised to keep our existence a secret, but how do we know these Alphan ships won't go elsewhere and spread knowledge of our existence across the whole cluster? What happens if we become known of on Rorque 4, or even worse, Zeleyan? They're ruthless cultures that won't give our needs and desires a second thought,' remarked Rajita, a middle-aged woman who had just arrived at the centre in order to meet up with a group who were arriving from one of the other settlements that morning, and who seemed particularly alarmed by what she was being told.

'We're a small and remote planet with very little that anyone could actually want. Why would they bother coming here anyway?' asked Kiyona, recognising the weakness of her argument, and still recognising the enormity of her mistake.

'Who knows, but if these Alphans really have developed improved spaceflight technology, that places us in an even more vulnerable position. In part, we've survived because of our remoteness, but if it's now quicker and easier for spaceships to arrive here, then we could be facing major problems. There might be any one of a number of reasons for them wanting to occupy our planet – military, commercial, political – who knows? If it's in their own selfish interests, they'll do it and they won't care how much damage they do to us in the process,' replied Rajita, expressing a viewpoint of the other civilisations they shared this corner of space with, that was highly typical across Margallan society.

As the morning progressed, it also became obvious that the townspeople of Librado were not the only Margallans who had noticed the arrival of the stasis ship. Several other communities across the chain of islands had also registered its appearance, and word had soon spread of this unexpected development. For most, this was disturbing news; especially once they were informed it was not one of the Opa-Loka's irregular trading visits. The message sent to Kiyona by the Web Weaver was relayed to all the community centres across the archipelago which helped to dispel some of the more outlandish and paranoid conspiracy theories that were being proffered to explain the ship's arrival. However, to all the communities of the archipelago it had become obvious that meetings needed to be quickly held to address this unexpected and unwanted development.

The spontaneous meeting that had already developed in Librado - as more and more people arrived at the centre - explored various possibilities with regards to what should be their course of action. Some highlighted the fact that the starship was in trouble and that people's lives were at risk. The community had a duty to help those in difficulty. Others were more cautious, concerned more with the security issues that were apparent to all present. Ultimately, it was realised that without further information from the Web Weaver they were unable to arrive at any definitive course of action. This was pretty much the position that most of the communities eventually came to, and though there was some opposition to the idea, it was felt that they needed to open up a continuous channel of communication with the crew of the Web Weaver in order to progress the situation.

Kiyona wanted to volunteer to be part of the process to make amends for her earlier error, but the event had also knocked her confidence, and a general lack of expertise with regards to spaceships and communications meant she held back from offering. A thin young man, with curly brown hair and the tanned skin so typical of Margallans, named Zhavia, was chosen to organise the negotiations with the starship, as others looked on. He was something of a communications and computer expert, and the community felt his expertise might increase the likelihood of a positive outcome for them all. Kiyona decided to remain on site, hoping that developments would pan out in such a way that her error would not prove to be a serious one.

As such, after a silence of several hours, the crew of the Web Weaver suddenly found themselves back in communication with the inhabitants of Margalla. Zhavia acknowledged that they had received the previous communication, and indicated they would offer any help they could to fix their technical problems, so that they could safely depart and quickly be on their way. Unfortunately, in the few hours that had passed since the previous dialogue, the engineers aboard the starship had decided that the life support problem was degrading even faster than had previously been predicted. They were increasingly of the opinion that it might take several days to actually repair the life support systems and several more to replenish them with the necessary planetary gases and associated materials. This was time they no longer possessed. They would need to wake the thousands of scientists and their children on board the ship and transport them down to the surface temporarily until the situation had been resolved.

Given the already existing concerns of most Margallan inhabitants, they most definitely did not like the sound of this idea. Some, particularly those of a more sceptical persuasion, even believed it might be a covert excuse for an invasion of their world. Those of a less suspicious inclination – probably the majority – were fairly sure that they lacked the space or resources to deal with such a huge and sudden influx of visitors anyway. They were also unsure as to whether there were sufficient shuttle craft to relay such large numbers of passengers to the islands in such a short space of time. It was overwhelmingly agreed that they were probably incapable of achieving such a massive logistical task. On the other hand, they did not want to be responsible for the deaths of the thousands of stasis passengers on the ship. As a result, further arguments, debates and discussions broke out for a considerable length of time.

It was during these discussions that Zhavia decided to point out that the scientists could possibly use Margalla's own stasis ship, the Spirit of the Age to solve their problems. Admittedly, it was a far from perfect solution – waking thousands of passengers from stasis, transporting them to another ship and then putting them immediately back into stasis was not going to be popular with those undergoing such a tedious exercise – but it was probably their best, and possibly only, option. The islanders, after extensive discussions between the various communities, felt inclined to go with this idea – it offered few inconveniences to them whilst at the same time it would save the lives of the scientists.

The Web Weaver's skeleton crew was somewhat more sceptical of this idea. They were already growing alarmed at the length of time it was taking the Margallans to organise a viable plan – time the crew simply did not possess. They could also anticipate the prolonged complaints and grumblings that would accompany such a transfer process. They might even face open mutiny. What would they do if one actually occurred? Was it even logistically possible to move so many people in such a short space of time? They were far from sure as to what the answers were. However, they desperately needed a quick decision now as the clock was very much against them, and they had come up distinctly short on any better alternatives. They made some quick calculations which indicated the transfer was just about possible, but they would need to start immediately and would need all available Margallan shuttle craft, as well as their own. As such, unable to offer a better plan, they messaged the Margallans and informed them that they were going with Zhavia's idea.

Margalla still had a small number of transport craft left from their first landing on the planet, and a small number of humans and AI units who still knew how to fly them. Relieved that the scientists had gone with their new plan, they were only too pleased to make them available for the transfer, space pilots included if necessary. The Margallan education system ensured that all members of the communities were brought up with sufficient knowledge and abilities to operate the various AI units, computing and communication systems that were used on a regular basis to ensure the functioning of their society. However, only a few used these to a technically high level, and an even smaller number had ever used the transporter craft that flew them to the orbiting stasis ship, since there were few reasons for anyone to ever visit the ship anyway. Most visits were for maintenance purposes, though occasionally visits were made for tourism, project research or scientific reasons, but these were not common. Amongst the few that had done so, were Akiko, living in the settlement of Ascaso, and Zhavia, and both volunteered to be involved with the transfer of the scientists from the one stasis ship to the other.

The transfer began almost immediately, and in the event, the evacuation of the Web Weaver's passengers to the Margallan ship went without any major mishaps, and only a few minor ones. Anna Dubois, as acting crew commander, had elected to operate a low level repeated alarm signal during the entire process. The passengers were woken in batches large enough to be transferred on each transporter craft and briefly informed of the nature of their emergency. With the alarm message broadcast by the tannoy system repeating regularly in the background, they were left in no doubt as to the urgency of the situation, and were then quickly placed back into stasis upon arrival on the Spirit of The Age. Though they cut the process fairly fine, the evacuation was only just completed within the time they had left. As they had anticipated, many of the scientists were displeased with this turn of events – a few needed lengthy explanations to convince them this was a genuine emergency - but disoriented and suffering from post-stasis torpor, there had been no major outbreaks of dissent, and fortunately no form of mutiny.

A very small number, did however, request to stay on Margalla. For the most part these were scientists who were interested in subjects such as oceanography, astro-biology or certain of the social sciences. There were also a small number who were struggling with the effects of post-stasis and could not face the thought of re-entering the stasis pods. This was not what the organisers of the evacuation had wanted or needed given the time constraints, but despite appeals to just go with the plan, a few could not be dissuaded otherwise. Some fraught discussions with the Margallans followed, but once they knew that only a tiny numbers of individuals were involved, and the reasons they had made this request, then permission for the small numbers involved to settle was granted.

Whilst the evacuation procedure was being hurriedly carried out, the details of the ship exchange was finalised by the two sides. The Margallans insisted that they wanted their spaceship to be returned immediately, once it had deposited the passengers on Zeta Kotlin, and that they would provide a skeleton crew capable of doing this. The crew would accompany the Alphans to their new home and then fly The Spirit of The Age back to Margalla. Once this had occurred, the Alphan AI units could then fly the Web Weaver to Zeta Kotlin – as it was assumed that the ship would have been fully repaired after this length of time. The Margallans would help with the latter process, particularly once life support had become possible on the ship.

This was not what Anna Dubois had wanted and neither had she expected this. The Web Weaver was actually a better class of ship than the Margallan one and she had assumed the Margallans would want to keep the better ship. Despite several attempts to persuade them otherwise, they seemed particularly stubborn about keeping to their chosen arrangement, and even more reluctant to offer a plausible reason for doing so. In fact, the more she tried to dissuade them from this idea, the more they seemed to want to keep with it. She suggested their AI units could accompany the Alphans instead of a human crew, but this idea was also rejected. She suspected their chosen arrangement was because they did not fully trust her, and since she was exchanging a severely malfunctioning ship – with who knows what other problems – she was also in a weak negotiating position.

Ultimately, she conceded to their demands, particularly once the Margallans insisted on retaining all the research and scientific equipment aboard the Web Weaver as some form of collateral. This was not actually a particularly major problem, she considered, though it might be useful to eventually reclaim it in the fullness of time. She had, though, made sure all the scientific data in the ship's memory banks had been transferred safely to the new ship

– she had initiated the download of data at the beginning of the evacuation and it had not taken too long to complete. Once the evacuation was completed, AI units were left on the Web Weaver to continue with its repairs, eventually with help from the Margallans and their own AI units.

Back on the planet's surface, the Margallan crew had been rapidly assembled – which greatly surprised Anna - and had arrived on various transporter craft, and now that the transfer was complete was waiting for her on the observation deck. She joined them as they looked together over their ocean world. Even after several hours of orbiting the planet, Anna could still not quite fully believe that a world constituted almost entirely by water was actually possible. With the exception of the shining white ice-cap, and the myriad white and grey cloud formations circulating in their different ways around the globe, it was a world of unrelenting aquamarine blue wherever you looked, without break and without interruption. There was almost nowhere for the eye to linger on, just unremitting blueness.

They all then transferred to the flight deck and initiated a final systems check of the entire ship. The Margallan AI units had always kept the stasis ship in perfectly good working order, and there was little reason to believe it was not capable of making the twelve month journey to Zeta Kotlin. The trajectory for the journey had already been logged into the computer system, and once the systems check was finalised and completed, the ship's computer slowly began to accelerate the massive starship out of orbit; the great silver space machine gradually pulling away from the planet's gravitational field, and soon entered into the cold, dark blackness of inter-planetary space.

The Margallan crew consisted of Akiko, Kiyona, Zhavia and three others named Zek, Arlo and Xander who had all, for an eclectic range of reasons – mainly involving a desire to experience space travel - volunteered to accompany the ship to Zeta Kotlin. Akiko had jumped at the opportunity to visit Zeta Kotlin, where she was keen to meet up with those studying the environment and discuss their latest theories and ideas. Kiyona was keen to make amends for her earlier error, and - if she was entirely truthful with herself - because she had decided this was could be her big opportunity to do something more useful with her life. Zhavia was interested in almost anything to do with the cosmos, rockets and space travel.

Very few Margallans had been interested in undertaking the venture – most had little reason or inclination to leave their utopia - and generally regarded space travel to other planets with some disdain. Journeys were considered long and potentially hazardous, with few compensations, and so the six actually wanting to make the journey found they faced no competition for places. They all now sat strapped into their chairs together, and as the ship accelerated through their star system they viewed the epic spacescape from the flight deck with avid interest.

They had all seen images of Sazhina's star system transmitted back to their planet by the various satellites that had explored their star system, but experiencing the depths of space at first hand was completely new to all of them. The crew had decided on a trajectory out of the system that would fly past both the gas giant Zecrone and the lonely ice giant of Hiemal and they were not disappointed by the impressive spectacle that passed before them. They all marveled at the sheer massiveness of Zecrone with its huge circling zones of synchronized blue and white, and the mysterious oscillations of the dark clouds that characterised the slowly rotating whites of the central zone. After Zecrone, they thought they had seen it all, until they stared in awe whilst witnessing the massive frosty-white snowball of Hiemal, mysteriously resplendent in its remote setting, separated from the all engulfing blackness of space by only the thinnest band of electric-green atmosphere, shimmering narrowly above the entirety of the sphere.

Beyond Hiemal they looked out into the cold dark infinity of inter-stellar space, its sheer overwhelming vastness. Only the numerous scintillating points of starlight punctuated the silent blackness.

'Wow, space is deep,' exclaimed Zhavia, who had seen plenty of footage relayed back from space satellites, but only now fully realised just how immense it actually was.
'And we're the only ones who have seen this,' added Kiyona, thinking of the tales should could tell her friends once they had returned to Margalla.
The others looked at her, but said nothing. Margallan society tended to disapprove of such egoising. They all continued to regard the vast star-

studded darkness before them for a while longer, and the immensity of the undertaking they had just embarked on slowly began to dawn on them. After a while, as they realised the scene before them would remain essentially unchanging, they eventually decided to leave the flight deck.

Once the starship was fully clear of Sazhina's planetary system, and after further flight checks, the ship's computer indicated that all systems were still functioning correctly and that the ship was on the correct course for Zeta Kotlin. Finally, a message was transmitted to the six ships currently heading towards Zeta Kotlin informing them of recent developments. With only the long black corridor of space now between them and Zeta Kotlin, both the Alphan and Margallan crews decided it was time to enter into stasis. Anna Dubois, as acting commander, made sure she was the last to do so, but before she entered her allotted stasis pod for the long space voyage, she reprogrammed a new journey destination into the spaceship's computer. Once this had occurred, all systems were finally locked down and the running of the ship was passed full over to the automated systems and AI units. For the rest of the voyage, the AI units then went quietly about their preprogrammed business, to the continuous background hum of the life support systems in the dimly-lit darkness of the vast hangars that dominated so much of the vast stasis ship.

Earth – interstellar space travel

When a whole host of political and commercial leaders on Earth finally made the decision to venture out and across inter-stellar space in significant numbers, the previous experiences of inter-planetary space travel and near-Earth colonisation bore heavily on the exact manner in which they decided to carry out this civilisation-changing endeavour. For the undertaking to prove even partially successful, it was decided - at a very early date in the process - that a number of essential features were key for interstellar space flight, and by and large these features continued to be adhered to throughout the entire period of exodus into space. The experiences of the interplanetary travel that had previously been undertaken by the space tourists and failed colonisers on Mars, though admittedly limited, had led to some distinct conclusions being drawn about the nature of space flight. Humans, it was concluded, were not particularly good space travellers, and the difficulties involved in transporting them across vast distances were highly problematic. Space travel – basically - was far from easy, and they needed to find a whole range of systems to address this problem.

A myriad of obstacles faced any would-be starfarers. Even putting a small number of travelers into space entailed the use of an enormously expensive amount of resources and energy. The additional paraphernalia needed to keep them fit and healthy during such long and distant journeys was considered to be a burden that was simply impossible to achieve and also to afford. Specially adapted plant life, food, water, medicine, furniture, entertainment, washing facilities and a whole host of other daily necessities would be needed on board the starships and in large quantities. They would need to be paid for, in some manner launched into space and then be maintained in working order on board the craft for the duration of exceedingly long journeys. This presented the starship designers with a range of challenges that were essentially insurmountable and unaffordable, except perhaps to only the very wealthiest of space travelers.

Equally, whether humans had a temperament suitable for covering such vast distances in the cramped and confined space of a starship over years and possibly decades, was widely doubted. The little empirical evidence already existing, strongly showed that a range of problematic physiological and psychological difficulties were unlikely to be overcome. In such an unnatural environment as a prolonged voyage in a confined spacecraft where there was no effective means of leaving the ship, it was thought that disputes, arguments – some leading even to fatalities - were highly likely to occur. This had been already been the experience of a small number of inter-planetary missions.

The worst incident had occurred when four passengers and crew had been killed on the Beagle 7 as it returned from a failed mission to Titan in 2067. Space travel before this had been largely unregulated, but following this particular incident, a whole host of rules and regulations had been deemed necessary in order to protect the lives of crew and fee-paying passengers. An investigation had identified the fatalities as resulting from the stressful conditions on board the spaceship – and this was considered to likely be a commonplace problem on any prolonged space mission into interstellar space involving thousands or even tens of thousands of voyagers.

This was even before the issues of protecting passengers from cosmic radiation, keeping them in good physical condition in near-zero gravity, and dealing with seriously contagious diseases were looked at in any significant detail. There were a number of star systems within a few years travelling distance of Earth, such as those of Alpha Centauri, Sirius and Epsilon Eridani, but the information being returned on the suitability of the planets found in these systems was not particularly promising. It was far more likely that settlements would need to be found much further and deeper into the galaxy. Even the shortest of colonisation journeys was now expected to be in the region of three or four decades, and many might last longer - considerably longer - than this. The logistics of keeping thousands of passengers alive, in good mental health and comfortable for this duration on a single craft was mind-bogglingly complex.

It was thus not difficult to arrive at the decision that all the space colonists would be placed into stasis for the entire duration of their voyage to the stars. Contemporary studies of hibernating animals were thought to have achieved an all-encompassing understanding of how the process occurred, and to have discovered all the necessary knowledge for this to process to be replicated in a modified form for humans. A number of test studies had proven promising with no significant health side-effects noted, and the minor ones identified had led to refinements and improvements of the processes implemented. It was considered that a standard and safe technique had been developed to counter muscle wastage, and a number of other potentially problematic conditions that had been observed in test subjects. It was expected that in stasis complications would arise in a small number of cases – even possibly leading to death – but if the percentage of cases could be kept to a minimum, then this was simply a price that was worth paying.

In addition, Artificial Intelligence systems were by then considered sufficiently advanced to pilot starships to any desired destination, and were also deemed capable of making suitable corrections in the face of any difficulties encountered en route. In a genuine emergency, crew members could be woken if it proved necessary to deal with complex or life-threatening decisions, but it was deemed desirable to keep these to an absolute minimum. All routine procedures and maintenance during the long space flights could be carried out by the AI units, which were largely self-repairing and easily replenished from the ship's energy systems.

Almost all the starship manufacturers opted for massive economies of scale. Whilst a large ship carrying several thousand stasis-bound passengers might initially prove more difficult and costly to launch, it was ultimately cheaper than launching several smaller and ostensibly more affordable craft. Large spaceships also had the additional benefit of delivering very large numbers of colonists to the same planet at the same point in time, offering the wide range of skills and talents needed in any incipient colony seeking to rapidly and successfully establish itself halfway across space.

Plasma-fuelled starships filled with row after row of stasis pods, and crewed by a small number of AI units, became the standard starship model, and eventually rolled off the production lines - across the six inhabited continents of the planet - in their thousands. By the mid-2080s large numbers of humans – facing the worst existential crisis in their history – had opted for the decision to leave for space in ever increasing numbers. Slowly, at first almost hesitantly, but with gathering pace, starships were launched from Earth, sometimes in groups, sometimes individually, towards their pre-programmed destinations amongst the stars.

Arrival in Utopia

For the passengers on board these thousands of spacecraft, their hope and desire was for a new life at a promising new planetary destination with all the opportunities that a clean slate appeared to offer. It was an opportunity to put the impending disaster on Earth behind them and to create a civilisation that might avoid the costly mistakes made on planet Earth. In reality, if they had seriously considered the harsh realities of cosmology, of star and planet formation, planetary geology, astrophysics and the processes of biology they would have realised that this was very much a huge gamble. Finding suitable new planets for humans to successfully inhabit was to prove a particularly tricky problem.

Interstellar Space, The Spirit of the Age – a new destination

For several days after leaving the planetary system of Sazhina, The Spirit of The Age followed a flight path that would have seen it eventually join the six starships that were still on course for their intended destination of Zeta Kotlin. But on the eighth day, the stasis ship began to slowly deviate from this original trajectory. Almost imperceptibly at first, it arced away from the originally chosen path, eventually effecting a deviation of approximately 80° and headed out across interstellar space in a completely new direction. No messages of explanation were sent to the starships advancing towards Zeta Kotlin, though its new trajectory was soon registered by the AI units crewing those ships. Messages of enquiry were duly sent by the six ships, but the AI units on The Spirit of the Age had been instructed not to respond, and so the enquiries went unanswered.

During the short time spent in orbit around Margalla, Anna Dubois had still managed to find time for a considerable rethink with regards to the destination of the starship she had recently found herself commanding, for the planned destination of Zeta Kotlin was really not to her liking. On Alpha Fraczan, she had been one of the senior principals of Seven Mountains University, a position which meant that she enjoyed a considerable range of privileges and was held in high esteem by many of her colleagues. Slim and elegant, with long blonde hair usually tied back in a ponytail, and with a reputation for being fairly straight-laced, Anna had enjoyed the typical childhood of a child born on Alpha Fraczan. Born to parents who were both scientists, she had excelled in school and could not understand why others performed at a lower level than herself, and had thus developed something of an elitist approach to life, believing others to be either less able or too lazy to put in the effort necessary for success. The ease with which she attracted boyfriends only added to her beliefs.

As she progressed successfully through school, she – unsurprisingly - gravitated towards the sciences, particularly chemistry and biology. As was widely expected of her, she had eventually graduated in the biochemical sciences and progressed fairly rapidly through the various administrative levels to eventually become a senior figure at Seven Mountains University. Her first priority in life was always her academic work, but she also sought to be widely recognised for her academic successes and endeavours, and she regarded career advancement as a natural part of this process.

Now in her mid-thirties, having already worked at three different universities and enjoyed a series of rapid promotions, she had still gained a reputation amongst her fellow academics as a strong believer in behaving in an appropriately correct manner, an appreciation that she always treated others with respect and that she could always be relied upon to aid her colleagues with advancing their careers. She possessed a strong sense of responsibility, but also a belief that she was capable of making decisions suitable for those around her. As such, she had been a natural choice to command one of the stasis ship skeleton crews when the diaspora was launched, and had found herself appointed as the Commanding Officer of the Web Weaver.

She had initially followed the general consensus that the flotilla of ships should head into the Nexus Cluster, but, like Mila Lustrom, had assumed the chosen planet would most likely be Rorque 4. She had raised significant doubts concerning the choice of Zeta Kotlin when it had been chosen as the favoured destination, but, despite these reservations, had nevertheless continued to support the majority opinion to preserve a sense of unity within the diaspora. As with Mila, she was hoping that if Zeta Kotlin proved to be an unsuitable destination upon arrival, the scientists would then duly proceed to Rorque 4 after a major rethink. She harboured major misgivings about the idea of settling on Zeta Kotlin, for a range of reasons.

If she was completely honest with herself this was largely because she feared she would lose her privileged position on a planet devoted to egalitarianism, though she also felt that scientific research subjected to democratic decision-making and the popular will of the masses was very likely to pursue the wrong objectives and concentrate on areas of research that would probably be mundane, unappealing and uninteresting. In all likelihood, she believed, life on Zeta Kotlin would prove to be highly damaging to her own personal research and career ambitions.

Her time spent in orbit around Margalla had only reinforced many of these misgivings. Her dealings with the semi-chaotic – and like Zeta Kotlin, egalitarian – Margallan society had increased her doubts about the wisdom of doing science in such a society. Her university on Alpha Fraczan had enjoyed clearly defined levels of authority, stated goals and purposes, lines of communication and responsibility which were clearly understood, and a generally well-ordered structure. For Anna Dubois, this was the society she had grown up in, flourished in, and in which she had achieved her ambitions and high status. It was what she had grown to expect and Zeta Kotlin, she believed, had little prospect of delivering such a good life for herself, in particular, and for the scientists aboard her starship, in general.

The more she thought about the situation, the more she believed it made increasing sense to simply cut Zeta Kotlin out of the equation and head straight for Rorque 4, a manouevre that should be straightforward, at least in technical terms. She wasn't sure how she would explain this to the rest of the crew and the scientists on board the ship on arrival at Rorque 4 – though she did manage to devise a few not entirely convincing explanations – but by then it would be too late anyway. They would be faced with a fait accompli.

Her position as Commanding Officer of the ship and former high status on Alpha Fraczan should hold her in good stead at their new destination, and secure her a suitably senior position at one of their universities. Surely, she thought, the authorities on Rorque 4 would only be too pleased with this new infusion of talent and expert knowledge she had brought with her. Ultimately, the scientists on board the starship might even come to thank her once they achieved positions of distinction and improved research budgets, benefits that would surely convince them to appreciate their new planetary home, and the decision she had made for them. As events unfolded whilst in orbit around Margalla, she toyed with the idea of relating her decision to the rest of the skeleton crew, but, fearing opposition to her plan, she decided to keep quiet and act alone and in secret.

The insistence of the Margallans on leaving their own skeleton crew on the ship to ensure its eventual return had thrown a potentially major spanner into the workings of her plan, and she had searched for reasons and ways to prevent this from happening, but had ultimately been unable to prevent them pursuing such a course of action. She guessed they would just have to spend longer in space than they had initially bargained for. Eventually they would be able to return to Margalla, just several years later than they had originally believed. This would only be a small price to pay – and after all, she thought, they would be in stasis most of the journey anyway.

So having arrived at her decision, she had waited until the two respective crews had entered stasis before she then pre-programmed the ship's computers to alter course to Rorque 4 a few days later - a manouevre that would take place once they had all been safely ensconced in stasis. She had worried that the Margallans might in some way attempt to disrupt her plans, but they had proven to be a very trusting group, and had shown little interest in any of the security procedures or protocols on board the ship. Before entering stasis herself, she also programmed the ship's computer to send out a communication informing the authorities on Rorque 4 of her intentions, and to alert her to any important messages that might be received in reply.

The AI units were also informed of the intended change of destination before she went into stasis – again there were no security issues here – and she made certain she was definitely the last person on the ship to actually enter stasis, ensuring that all systems were safely and fully locked down after she did so. The distance from Margalla to Rorque 4 was approaching two-thirds of a light year, so the ship would still need slightly more than twenty-two months to reach her chosen destination, but barring any further technical difficulties they should all be safely approaching Rorque 4 when she next awakened.

Before long, all returned to normal on The Spirit of The Age; the human passengers slept and the AI units went about their routine business. As they did so, the silver spacecraft continued with its long solitary journey across the vast darkness of inter-stellar space, all within it safely ensconced in stasis, but unknowing of their new destination.

Arrival in Utopia

Interstellar Space, the Avante – destination Rorque 4

A little more than two months later, a solitary man made his way somewhat unsteadily through the long corridors of the vast stasis chamber that constituted the enormous central section of the starship, the Avante. It was so vast that it possessed the air of some ancient gigantic aircraft hangar. The chamber was shrouded in darkness save for low levels of thin strip lighting flickering high above the corridors between the stasis pods. An endless array of grey metallic piping spread confusingly across the walls and ceilings – the ship, like all others, had been mass produced and costs kept to the minimum possible. The air was cool and slightly dry and all was quiet except for the constant low level hum of the ventilation systems in the background.

To both sides of Alex Kim, almost as far as the eye could see, were stretched bank after bank, column after column and row after row of stasis pods. Packed into sections of seven by seven, there were quite literally thousands and thousands of pods organised regularly as high as the ceiling, each line of pods stretching from one end of the vast chamber to the other. Inside almost all of them lay the sleeping scientists; only a small number of the pods on the highest levels remained empty. Long straight parallel corridors passed between the banks of the shiny grey and metallic pods, each one flanked by an array of electronic and hydraulic devices keeping the occupant alive whilst monitoring their vital signs. Fronted with transparent coverings, he was able to peer into the ones on the lowest levels as he made his way slowly along the corridor towards the front of the ship, but he couldn't say he particularly recognised any of the faces he saw inside.

His quiet and cautious progress along the corridor was almost certainly unwarranted, for there was highly unlikely to be any other human awake on the spaceship; the AI units would be performing their usual allotted tasks, but there should be no other wakened humans on board, other than himself. He was, however, fairly sure as to why he might have been brought out of stasis and he floated his way, somewhat clumsily, to the control centre at the front of the ship. The single AI unit on duty there registered his presence and informed him that a priority emission had indeed been received by the ship, as Alex had been hoping and expecting.

Arrival in Utopia

Before he read the message, though, he glanced casually out through the large viewing screen that dominated the wall in front of him. He was slightly confused and surprised to see the thousands of stars and galaxies of all sizes and colours that littered the cosmos the ship was passing through, as it hurtled towards its destination. The points of light twinkled and shimmered as their rays travelled across the light years of space dust that littered so much of the darkness. He had expected space to be darker and blacker, but slowly realised this was an assumption he had made based on terrestrial viewings of the night sky. After a short while he strapped himself into one of the chairs and turned his attention back to the received message, and listened with a growing sense of jubilation and justification running through his mind. A smile spread across his face. It was exactly what he had been hoping to hear.

Slightly on the stocky side, and with a shock of thick black hair, dark brown eyes and a friendly face and smile, Alex Kim had enjoyed the typical childhood of almost all those born on Alpha Fraczan. The son of scientist parents, his mother an engineer and his father a physicist, he had, from a very early age, been fascinated by the internal workings of all things mechanical. He had spent his childhood dismantling and reassembling all manner of machines and devices, eventually working his way up to computer systems and complex vehicles whilst developing a particular fascination for aircraft, of which - unfortunately from his point of view - there were not that many on his home planet.

Somewhat socially naïve and cosseted, he had shown little or no interest in any of the social sciences or wider society, and throughout much of his earlier years was part of a small and fairly tight-knit group of friends who also shared his passionate interest in machinery and engineering. Enjoying the typically comfortable and easy lifestyle of an inhabitant of Alpha Fraczan - as was equally the case for those immediately around him - he was given no reason to question or enquire into the wider society in which he lived. He had, however, been frustrated by the lack of attention shown to his chosen subject and also the lack of funding it attracted, though he had seen this purely as short-sightedness on the part of the university authorities.

Alex had used his position as one of the leading experts in rocket science, space flight and communications engineering to ensure he was selected for one of the skeleton crews appointed as the Alphan diaspora launched into space. Alex had also been the eventual author of the message beamed across the galaxy by the departing inhabitants of Alpha Fraczan as disaster hit their planet. The initial draft had been drawn up hastily at a late hour by a small group of senior committee members, but Alex had been tasked with actually emitting the final draft of the message. He had, at the very last minute, made some slight alterations to the original text message. The changes he included were, perhaps, not completely accurate, but equally, nothing that he added was factually incorrect, so he felt he could justify his somewhat dubious action, if he was ever to be found out.

In all the chaos of the dispersal, he had also managed to ensure he was on a starship with no particularly senior university officials – many of them had chosen to fly on the same ships, though he was not exactly sure why this decision had been made. Somewhat exaggerating his expertise and knowledge of space flight, he had also manoeuvered himself into the position of the ship's Commanding Officer. Following the sending of the original open official message, he had then devised an additional semi-encrypted and more personal secondary message that he had instructed the AI units to transmit towards Rorque 4. Shortly after all the passengers and crew had been safely put in stasis and lockdown – by himself – this instruction had been duly implemented and according to the schedule he had devised.

This was the reason that Alex had been brought out of stasis. Someone on Rorque 4 had replied to his transmission and the response was exactly what he was hoping for. Indeed, the offer being made by this particular corporation on Rorque 4 looked extremely attractive, way beyond anything Alex had actually been expecting. Still somewhat groggy from emerging out of stasis, he double-checked the incoming transmission to see if he had missed anything, but could find nothing of note. As such, he returned an encrypted message back to the sender on Rorque 4 accepting their offer and authorised the ship's computer to plot a new course, this time heading for the capitalist planet. Enquiries from the other six ships were to be answered with a standard and repeated message that this was simply a routine change of course. They would soon calculate where the Avante was headed for anyway, but he was fairly certain they would and could do nothing to interrupt his new laid plans.

He then scanned through the routine incoming communications to see if there was anything else of particular interest. It was at this point that he noticed there were only five other ships still accompanying the Avante. 'Where was the seventh ship?' he wondered. He checked the older communications logs and located the messages that had been received from the Web Weaver several months beforehand. He scrolled through the messages and discovered it had previously been in orbit around Margalla, and had been receiving help from the planet's small population of inhabitants. 'Interesting . . . so the planet is inhabited after all,' he thought, 'just as some of his colleagues had always suspected.'

Scrolling through further communications from the other five ships left in the fleet he then discovered that the new stasis ship now being used by the former passengers of the Web Weaver - The Spirit of The Age - had also parted company with their pre-designated flight path and was following a completely new trajectory, one he quickly calculated was taking it straight towards Rorque 4. He also discovered the fact that the ship was in communication with its new planetary destination, though semi-encryption made it difficult for him to know what exactly was in the messages being sent onwards to the planet's inhabitants. However, it wasn't hard to guess; it was highly likely it would be very similar to the message he himself had sent out fifteen months earlier – the ship's captain offering their expertise, skills and technical know-how to academic institutions and potential employers on Rorque 4. He checked the logs and discovered the Commanding Officer was Anna Dubois. She had spent a short time at his university, but he had only met her briefly on two or three occasions. He knew her more by reputation than by name, a reputation for seeking quick promotional advancement that had seen her soon move on elsewhere.

In some ways, this was something of a relief for Alex, since he now knew another Commanding Officer had clearly arrived at the same conclusion as himself – that Rorque 4 was a better choice of destination than Zeta Kotlin. Earlier, he had weighed the responsibility of redirecting a whole ship of passengers - without any form of consultation with them - against his own personal ambitions, and had harboured some doubts about the decision he had decided to make. He had wondered whether he had actually just abducted a whole ship load of passengers, and whether this might even be illegal, never mind somewhat morally dubious.

In other ways, though, he felt himself to be justified. He believed he had been overlooked far too often, forced to endure missed opportunities and lost chances, and generally seen his work neglected by the authorities on Alpha Fraczan – work that was potentially a major game-changer. In his opinion, the decision to head for Zeta Kotlin was only the latest in a long line of poor decisions overseen by the higher university authorities, who he assumed were mainly concerned with looking after their own privileged positions. He felt justified to be rebelling against yet another incorrect decision and, who knows, his fellow scientists might actually thank him for making this decision when they eventually settled into their new lives and careers on Rorque 4, since these would probably prove to be better than anything that could have been offered by Zeta Kotlin.

On the other hand, though, he also realised he now had some competition. Calculations made by the ship's computer indicated that The Spirit of the Age was likely to reach Rorque 4 approximately three weeks before The Avante, which itself was still nearly two years away from its new planetary destination. Alex thus issued a further set of instructions to the ship's computer and the AI units. These entailed ensuring that the ship pursued the fastest trajectory possible to Rorque 4, that the journey should remain completely uninterrupted and should not be altered or affected in any way by the five stasis ships still heading towards Zeta Kotlin. He also ensured that he should again be consulted if any new major developments came to light during the course of the rest of the journey. Approximately twelve hours after emerging from stasis, finally certain that he had made the right decision, implemented his instructions in the correct way and effected all the necessary security protocols, Alex eventually returned to his stasis pod for the duration of the voyage.

For those twenty plus months, his stasis ship blazed a lonely trail across the cold dark depths of interstellar space, on a trajectory that witnessed it gradually converging on the same destination as The Spirit of The Age, slowly closing the distance between itself and the less powerful starship, as though engaged in an overly long space chase through the long dark corridor of space, one that would eventually see the two ships arrive at their chosen destination within a few short days of each other. At this point they were not to know that events would follow a distinctly different course from those expected by their Commanding Officers. However, the increasing flurry of incoming messages from Rorque 4, offering the ship's passengers a whole range of unbelievably lucrative career opportunities and personal lifestyle benefits, might have given them some inkling of the very different civilisation they were soon to be immersed within.

Interstellar Space – the Alphan diaspora arrives at Zeta Kotlin

After passing through the long black corridor of interstellar space, the five remaining stasis ships of the diaspora began their slowing descent into the Aequitas star system. Their destination was the second planet of the system, Zeta Kotlin, but their plan was to use the gravitational forces of the two outer gas giants to sufficiently slow their trajectory, before coming slowly into orbit around the only inhabited planet of the stellar system. Skeleton crews had been brought out of stasis shortly before entry into the planetary system, messages transmitted ahead for the waiting Zetans, and final diagnostic checks run within the ships to make sure they were in sufficiently good shape to survive the gravitational forces they were now expecting to experience.

Aequitas was a somewhat brighter than average G class star but with an unusually sparse planetary system. The five slowing ships initially passed through the extensive debris field that constituted the star's own distinct Kuiper belt on the far-flung reaches of the stellar system, a zone comprising an indeterminate number of rocky dwarf planets that circulated the star at an immense distance and in a set of highly complex elliptical orbits. Once through the chaotic debris field, it was then only a short period of time before the stasis ships were looping around the first of the gas giants, Ampilion. The vast behemoth of a planet was a mass of white, bright neon green and subtle aquamarine blue, the colours swirling slowly and almost sedately across the planets enormous surface, and all of which became increasingly visible as the ships neared the colossus.

As they finally closed in on their approach, the gas giant loomed larger and larger until it soon became effectively impossible for the now transfixed crew members to comprehend the sheer enormity of the leviathan that lay before them. None of those present had ever travelled in space before, let alone viewed such a magnificent sight as the one that overshadowed all before them, and a hushed silence fell across the viewers, transfixed by its enormous majestic beauty. As the ships made their closest approach, the incredibly thin concentric green, white and translucent rings that circled the planet slowly emerged into view, and many of the crew members could only stare in wonderment at the sheer symmetrical elegance of the cosmic phenomenon before them. Tilted at a slight angle, the fragile-looking rings barely seemed to move, only the occasional glint of reflected ice-cold light hinting at their more dynamic nature.

If Ampilion had been a case of wondrous allure then the second of the gas giants, Ochron, was more an exercise in baffling bewilderment, for its gigantic mustard and cobalt coloured surface could - even from a considerable distance - be seen to be positively buzzing with electrical energy. Across its entire surface thousands upon thousands of lightning bolts were constantly being discharged into the cold darkness of the surrounding atmosphere, giving the enormous planet the impression of fizzing with a dull orange-yellow electrical glow. The Zetans had nicknamed it 'the fizzball' but were still at a loss as to explain its unique planetary nature. Ampilion had produced a hushed silence amongst the crews, but Ochron proved to be mind-blowing and left them mystified and puzzled. The phenomenon of luminosity could sometimes be a puzzling one, and extensive discussions broke out amongst the crews as to what might actually be causing this particularly intriguing one.

In fact, so fantastic and spectacular were the views of the two gas giants, that the crews were almost ashamed by the fact that they had not woken the entirety of the passengers on the ships to view such breathtaking spectacles. It was difficult to believe they would ever be able to experience anything quite so fantastic ever again. Those still firmly immersed in stasis would unfortunately have to be satisfied with the visual recordings being made by the ship's computer system, but those present felt this could never quite capture the sheer grandeur and enormity of the spectacle they had been so privileged to experience at first hand.

Having once swung past the two gas giants, the five stasis ships then traversed a series of smallish asteroid belts and soon found themselves approaching the inner sections of the star system. In what seemed like only a brief passage of time, the initially small indigo blue disc that represented Zeta Kotlin gradually grew larger and larger as they slowed further and finally approached their destination planet. Approaching their new home, little by little, the greens and sandy browns of the numerous continents, the indigo blue of the oceans and the white and grey of the clouds swirling high above them could be slowly but increasingly discerned by the watching crew members assembled on their respective flight decks.

Before long, mountains, plateaus, islands, lakes, forests and even the areas of inhabitation could be distinguished as their rendez-vous with the planet became ever closer. Eventually the ships fully slowed and descended safely into orbit around the planet. During their final approach, they had been messaged by the Zetan General Committee of the Federal Councils with a request that the Zetans should be allowed to use their transporter craft to send a welcoming delegation to the stasis ships in order to open discussions with the Alphans. The scientists had duly agreed to this, and soon they were awaiting their first contact with the planet's inhabitants.

Zeta Kotlin – the arrival of the scientists from Alpha Fraczan

The arrival of the five starships from Alpha Fraczan had, of course, been widely anticipated on Zeta Kotlin, and the General Committee of the Federal Councils, having received their mandate from the planet's population, was fully prepared for the talks that would ensue between the two peoples. Zeta Kotlin was one of the few local planets that had actively maintained a presence in space - albeit a very limited one - so they had no problem in launching one of their shuttle craft to transport members of the Committee to one of the starships, the Silver Shokeen – named after one of the great astrophysicists of the mid twenty-first century - designated by the Alphans as their preferred rendez-vous location. The Alphan skeleton crews had also come to a broad agreement as to what their negotiating positions would be – based on discussions conducted before their departure from Alpha Fraczan - and so the two sides quickly went into discussions once quarantine protocols had been observed and some brief introductions and associated pleasantries concluded.

As with all important meetings on Zeta Kotlin, the negotiations were live-streamed to the entire planet, to ensure the committee's mandate was adhered to, and so that there was no possibility of its members receiving or accepting special favours from their counter-parts. For the Alphans, on the assumption that suitable habitation could be found or built for them, their main demand was one of being allowed to continue with their various scientific endeavours, research projects and teaching practice. For the Zetans, their main concern was successfully incorporating the academics and their children within their existing socialist structures. There was clearly sufficient geographical space and material resources for a number of new settlements on the planet, and both the Zetans and the Alphans possessed a sufficient number of AI units to construct any new settlements that proved necessary, and to then serve their basic needs in both the near future and in the longer term. There was, in effect, little in the way of material practicalities preventing their successful settlement.

Nevertheless, some of the Alphan delegation had assumed they could use their specialised knowledge and advanced technology as bargaining chips in return for certain special considerations and possible exemptions from being incorporated into the Zetan social structure. It quickly became clear that this position was an entirely untenable one. Zetan society was one inherently based on publically shared resources and absolute equality, and shared knowledge was a key feature of this structural arrangement. There was simply no question of the Alphans using their ground-breaking knowledge and technology as a means of buying any particular desired end goal that involved special privileges, the continuation of their own hierarchal structures or engaging in research widely considered to be unethical by Zetan society.

It became apparent, very early in the negotiations, that Zeta Kotlin was considerably more affluent, better resourced and far more politically stable than the Alphans had previously believed. The Alphan delegation soon realised their negotiating position was actually a fairly weak one, whilst at the same time quickly discerning that there existed a wide range of benefits in being allowed to remain on the planet. This new world was far more amenable in climatic terms, better resourced than that of Alpha Fraczan, and with a well-developed economy that could provide them with much of the manufacturing and raw materials they had lacked on their now-devastated home world. It also possessed a well-ordered and peaceful society into which they could probably easily integrate. Their academic freedom would be largely guaranteed - as long as they adhered to the ethical standards of the existing polity - since the political structures were far more decentralised and democratic than their forebearers had led them to believe was the case. Zeta Kotlin also possessed its own universities and centres of learning and research, of course, so many of the Alphans could probably be integrated into these existing establishments, as well as founding their own new ones where necessary.

As much as the benefits of staying on Zeta Kotlin were plentiful, the alternatives for the Alphans were similarly limited. There was no question of them being allowed to settle on Ur-Tokar, whilst news reports over the years concerning Zeleyan had indicated this was not a desirable location – academic freedoms would be close to zero on a fascist planet! Within the Nexus Cluster, this only left Rorque 4, which was a distinct possibility for some of the Alphans. It was widely believed there existed a well-resourced economy there, with already existing universities, though they had also received reports in recent years of protracted economic difficulties. Rorque 4 possessed a highly competitive and individualised society that would presumably value high quality scientific research, although there would be the major problem that it would forever be subject to the vicissitudes of high finance, private corporations, shareholder dividends and the drive for ever increasing profits. And then there was the final option of swallowing humble pie and following Itzel back out into deep space for several decades to join her in establishing a new colony on Alchemy.

Finding themselves in a distinctly weaker negotiating position than originally anticipated and aware of divisions breaking out within their negotiating team, the Alphans requested to take a break from the negotiations to consider their position. They were divided roughly four to one in favour of staying at Zeta Kotlin, with the dissenting minority favouring a further journey and opting for residence on Rorque 4. Given that the skeleton crews were dominated by the upper echelons of the various university establishments, this was perhaps a somewhat surprising result. Accepting the political structures of Zeta Kotlin would mean relinquishing much of their power, privilege and status.

On the other hand, at heart they were scientists and academics, not administrators, and a return to their original educational passions and the intrigues of conducting pioneering research and the dissemination of knowledge was not an entirely unattractive proposition. Life on Zeta Kotlin appeared to be considerably better and more comfortable than they had previously assumed, and they had quickly become aware that their assumptions about the socialist planet had largely been handed down to them by their forbearers – the original settlers from Earth - and thus might be considered unreliable and outdated.

It was ultimately put to a vote, which split four to one as the direction of argument had indicated. The dissenting minority, led by Mila Lustrom, insisted on the right to take one of the stasis ships onwards to Rorque 4, and the majority somewhat reluctantly agreed, provided that this proposition should also be put to a vote of the entire scientific and academic community. This would entail waking the entire passenger fleet, explaining the situation to them and then implementing a further vote. It would possibly take a couple of days – given the mental and physical state of those emerging from stasis – and then involve transporting those choosing Rorque 4 to a specified ship ready for departure. There were just about sufficient supplies on the ships to provision such a process, but if the process proceeded much longer they would be needing extra help from the Zetans.

For many, this was an extremely disappointing outcome, and not really the bright new promising start they had desired at their chosen destination; five of their ships had already departed for other destinations – half their community - and this would fracture their people even further. Nevertheless, they were unable to convince the dissenters to follow the majority. The vote amongst the entire remaining Alphan community went approximately the same way as that amongst the skeleton crews, though split closer to five to one for staying at Zeta Kotlin, and for roughly the same reasons as those of the negotiating delegation. In addition, most did not fancy another extended period in stasis, and simply wanted to commence their new lives, and continue to make progress with their research and teaching as soon as was humanly possible.

As a result, the stasis ship, The Star Chaser, with a much depleted complement of passengers, was readied for the nearly two year journey to Rorque 4. Mila Lustrom, still keen on her original plan of settling on the capitalist planet, was appointed as Commanding Officer and set about ensuring the rocket systems were reenergised and that sufficient resources stocked on the ship for the voyage. Unfortunately for her and the rest of the passengers, though, a whole series of technical, fueling and resource problems led to a series of quite lengthy delays. It was nearly a full four months before the ship was eventually considered to be fully safe and prepared for departure – during which time the crew found themselves needing to be constantly provisioned by their Zetan hosts, a somewhat embarrassing scenario given they had just chosen to reject their civilisation.

During the process, Mila was frequently impressed by how often the Zetans proved friendly and helpful towards them, attempting to solve their frequent technical difficulties, and provisioning them with any additional resources they might need. It was true that their AI units were doing most of the hard work and heavy lifting, so it was probably not too difficult for them to do this, but she frequently contrasted their magnanimity with her own selfish behaviour and low expectations of human nature, and found her own approach very much wanting. Perversely, in some ways, it only encouraged her desire to depart from the planet even more quickly, for then she would no longer need to analyse her own shortcomings in this area, with all the implications such a process held. Eventually her desire to depart was finally met, and much later than anticipated, the Star Chaser finally lifted out of orbit and commenced its long voyage to Rorque 4.

Although there had been a small number of difficulties throughout the integration process, the Zetan population had generally been pleasantly surprised by the favourable outcome. The discussion sometime later at the local administrative committee meeting at Kapal was, as usual, fairly typical of those occurring around the planet.

'I was expecting greater resistance to our demands than was ultimately the case,' remarked Rishaan, opening the discussions. 'I also thought there would be more dissenters wanting to head to other planets. It seems to have proceeded much more smoothly than we had initially expected, which can only be seen as a good result for all involved.'

'Well, the fewer that go to Rorque 4 the better as far as I'm concerned. We really don't want large numbers of highly educated scientists helping those capitalist money-grubbers,' responded Pedro, who now seemed to have adopted a distinctly different approach to the scientists from that at their first meeting. 'I still think Rorque 4 will try to destroy us one day – we stand for everything they hate and despise, and they cannot let that last forever, as far as I'm concerned. We must be a constant reminder to workers on their planet that a much better alternative is available, and their leaders must hate that,' he added acerbically, and more in keeping with his usual brusque character.

'I suspect the Alphans expected far more difficulties than actually occurred; after all, the logistics of settling several thousand new inhabitants on a completely different world must have appeared highly problematic. It's lucky for them that we're such an optimistic people – starting construction so early on the new university settlements must have helped allow the process to run much more smoothly than would otherwise have been the case,' offered Catriona, with her usual positive approach to any such matters. 'I'm sure we could have provisioned the scientists for a certain length of time on the stasis ships, but essentially the quicker they settled on the planet the better for all involved.'

'I suspect we can all agree with that thought. Apparently, many of the Alphans have already settled into existing communities, and the new ones have largely been established as well. I've not heard of many major difficulties, so it sounds as though the whole process has been a remarkably smooth one,' agreed Rishaan. 'A few months ago, I would have thought that quite unlikely. Let's hope they are able to adapt to our way of doing things – there are still a few concerns there, though, I believe. How easy do you think it is to shift from hierarchal to egalitarian ways of thinking and behaving?'

After a few moments reflection, Catriona responded, 'well, their society already possessed some egalitarian elements, so it's not a completely new approach for them. In addition, human nature is fairly adaptable. They're now fully immersed in an egalitarian society and social structures, so their behaviours and thinking are bound to slowly change and conform to their newfound environment. I suspect some will find it more difficult than others, but if you want to thrive here – and I'm sure they all do – it's simply easiest to fit in and go with the flow.'

'And it's not as though we are expecting them to do anything unpleasant, harmful or against their will. They have the freedom to explore their new ideas and thinking and carry on with their experiments. If any of this proves beneficial it can be used for the good of the whole people . . . and if not, then we have the procedures and structures to prevent its implementation,' agreed Rishaan. 'As you say, I'm sure they'll adapt to our ideas and ways sooner or later.'

'And it could indeed be very beneficial if the scientists produce some productive ideas and technological breakthroughs that will prove useful for the whole of our society – how could they not be pleased with an outcome of that nature?' asked Zhang Li. 'Better that than simply remaining in some ivory tower on a remote planet, aiding a privileged elite or just pursuing some form of self-aggrandisement. Ultimately, all science and all knowledge should be for the benefit of the whole of humanity, not just to benefit the few, and if it is put to good use, then that is how it should be,' she added, with her usual desire to adopt a wider philosophical viewpoint on any subject they discussed.

Ultimately, as the administrative committee at Kapal had surmised, there were few significant problems with the resettlement process. The new universities were constructed, the scientists were homed, and the Alphans slowly integrated into their new egalitarian society. Life as usual returned to the inhabitants of Zeta Kotlin. The collapse of the civilisation on Alpha Fraczan had posed a number of potential difficulties and dangers to the people of Zeta Kotlin, but these seemed to have all been safely dealt with. As far as they were concerned, to all intents and purposes this appeared to be the end of the affair. This, though, turned out to be an entirely premature evaluation, for the cascade of events that was to result from the fall of the civilisation on Alpha Fraczan was, in reality, only just beginning.

Rorque 4 – messages returned

A few weeks later, largely unaware of recent developments on Zeta Kotlin, at the other end of the Nexus Cluster, seated in his small office in what was his favourite comfy chair, what really puzzled Ralph Parker was that the message he had just received seemed to indicate that only one of the starships from Alpha Fraczan was actually heading in the direction of Rorque 4. This meant the others really did look like they were headed towards Zeta Kotlin, as their corporate satellite system had earlier indicated, unless for some reason they were leaving the Nexus system completely, on a trajectory that just happened to take them in the general direction of the socialist planet. This was a development that both perplexed and worried him.

Rorque 4, had for a great many years now, held something of a contradictory position towards the scientific community on Alpha Fraczan. In the earlier years of planetary development, the corporations had reached out to the scientists, hoping that their knowledge could help resolve some of the technical problems they were experiencing on their new home planet. These, however, had been rebuffed by the scientists. Alpha Fraczan was at the far end of the Nexus Cluster in respect to Rorque 4, a distant planet in a somewhat unattractive looking star system. Interstellar communications between the two planets were slow and space travel even slower. The sheer scale of the distances involved meant that the logistics of working with the scientists were highly problematic, and some accepted this as the explanation for the scientist's lack of interest in their affairs. Others, though, took a much more cynical line, believing the Alphans to be far too high-minded; a group of overly-educated boffins who believed themselves to be above getting their hands dirty in what they regarded as the dubious world of business – a world they mistakenly believed to be murky, grubby and based on nothing more than filthy lucre.

For Parker, and his own particularly cynical mindset, the fact that the majority of the Alphan starship diaspora had either headed further into deep space to star systems unknown, or were travelling towards Zeta Kotlin seemed to indicate the latter as the correct analysis. This was also of considerable concern to the authorities on Rorque 4 for two significant reasons. Firstly, they believed it would be the Zetans who would be acquiring any advanced technological developments brought by the scientists, particularly that of improved space flight technology, and it was already known that Zeta Kotlin operated a limited space-trading operation. Better or faster spacecraft would surely give them considerable comparative advantages across the Nexus Cluster.

Rorque 4 itself had developed almost no space presence for almost all of its existence, though this was now changing; the Rorque Corporation had recently commenced mining operations in the adjacent Necron star system, whilst Cosmic Solutions was engaged in terra-forming Morpheus, one of their sister planets. They had, though, made no significant technological progress with regards to space flight since the original settlement of the planet, and, as with all the other planets they knew of, were still using starships that were constructed back on Earth nearly two centuries previously.

Initially, their major concern, as with all newly established civilisations across the galaxy, had simply been the actual process of creating new settlements and infrastructure on their recently colonised planet, and for many decades this had proven to be their all-encompassing endeavour whilst also a profitable exercise. As their economy and society matured, though, they did eventually start looking outwards into space for possible solutions to solving several material and technological issues that the corporations found themselves facing on an increasing basis. However, these efforts had ultimately been short-lived ones, and this was for one very straightforward reason - they could not find a way of making space travel suitably profitable.

The long interstellar distances involved meant large upfront costs, and long and uncertain waits for returns on investment. They had reluctantly accepted that the expertise of a human crew was needed on the spaceships for various particular purposes – AI units were highly suitable for mundane, manual and predictable tasks, but only humans were able to deal with some of the more complex elements of interstellar commerce – and the human crews demanded to be paid extravagantly high salaries. Using human crews also involved a number of risks; one starship, for instance, simply never returned - no emergency calls had ever been received, no word was ever heard from it, and it was suspected that the crew had simply chosen to settle elsewhere in the Cluster. This, and the general dangers of travelling in space, had resulted in astronomical insurance premiums. This multiplicity of difficulties had thus seen the quiet abandonment of interstellar commerce by the early corporations. That was until recently, now that the prolonged economic slowdown had forced the corporations, once again, to look skywards for an answer to their long-term economic malaise.

The second concern for the authorities on Rorque 4, was that the arrival of the scientific diaspora on Zeta Kotlin could represent a significant propaganda coup for the socialist planet. The long years of economic stagnation experienced on Rorque 4 during the last two or three decades had led to a great deal of public disaffection and disillusion, particularly amongst the planet's growing underclass. Whilst much of this had been safely diverted into non-threatening manifestations such as petty crime, gambling, drug and alcohol addiction, there had still been an increase in radical and extreme political movements, predominantly on the far right, but far left movements and parties had also continued to attract support from disparate sections of the population.

So far, they had achieved little in the way of effecting significant policy changes, but a comparison between the relative fortunes of the two planets, it was feared, might suddenly boost the political fortunes of the left. The corporations would make sure that their media outlets played down the whole Zetan situation and put a negative spin on this unforeseen development, but it was still possible that the far left groupings might see a significant boost in their popularity - and the corporations were already facing significant and intractable-looking difficulties as it was. Additional problems were definitely not needed at this point in time and so the Alphan diaspora event was proving to be a headache they really didn't need.

Parker had been tasked by his superiors at the Rorque Corporation with establishing and maintaining communications with the Alphan starships. Normally, recruitment was carried out by AI units, but in this particular case it had been decided that a more human element was needed. Initially, his role had simply involved creating and then sending repeated emissions of what amounted to attractive glossy recruitment packages to the scientists on the ships in the hope of attracting them to his own company, rather than their competitors. For the following months it had involved nothing but a waiting game, until today, when he had finally received a reply from one of the starships and one that expressed an acceptance of their offer.

However, this was not exactly what he had been expecting. Initially, it had not really crossed Parker's mind that the Alphan starships would head for anywhere other than Rorque 4. As far as he could see it was the obvious choice of destination. In his opinion - which was a common one across the upper echelons of the planet's population - the other planets were all dead-end backwaters, not worthy of any serious consideration. Unfortunately, for him, the corporation had not developed any truly modern long-range scanning devices and he and his AI units were having to work with fairly old technology. His ability to track the starships had been somewhat limited, but what little information he could glean from them seemed to indicate that most were, in fact, heading for Zeta Kotlin, whilst others had left the Nexus Cluster entirely and in a completely different direction.

Parker despised socialism – indeed any form of left-wing ideology – and could only assume that the Alphans had been the subject of some underhand duplicity or were entirely ignorant of what they were heading for. He found the latter difficult to believe, as they were supposedly intelligent people. Maybe, he thought, they might be academically intelligent but just lacked any real common sense - this was why they had made such a poor decision. Whatever the reason, though, Parker needed to demonstrate to his superiors some form of achievement for his efforts. Many in the corporation had been surprised by his sudden promotion to his current role, believing him to be wholly unsuitable for what was effectively a public relations exercise. Parker, by contrast, believed he had been overlooked for far too long now, losing out to fellow managers who appeared competent, but who in reality just knew all the correct buzzwords and latest fashionable jargon, but were actually fairly useless.

Parker relayed the good news of the starship response to his immediate superior, the managing director of the corporation, Colin Jamieson, who was currently away checking their new mining operations in the Necron system, and who was not expected to arrive back at Rorque 4 for several weeks yet. However, he did not specify exactly how many ships his good news involved – he was hoping more might ultimately respond to his transmissions – or exactly how many scientists were likely to be involved. The fact that Jamieson was absent visiting the Necron system, Parker realised, gave him the opportunity to play fast and loose with some of the finer details. It would also give him enough time to lord it over the other managers, and make sure all the other departments in the company knew of his success. He could start to initiate preliminary preparations for the arrival of the scientists, though his role in this task had been left somewhat vague by Jamieson. He would start by tasking the different departments with organising which of their corporation's universities would be taking the scientists and where they would be housing them. The enlargement of existing departments, or the creation of new ones, could be finalised later when they knew the specialisms of the arriving scientists, but Parker was sure that he was more than capable of commencing all these tasks whilst Jamieson was away on business.

A week later, in the sprawling city of New Galtsville, hundreds of kilometers away on the adjacent continent of Eastern Shala, Thomas Patel, Head of Communications at Cosmic Solutions, received a transmission from The Avante stasis ship informing the corporation of their keen interest in the employment packages that had been offered to the scientists on board the ship by the company. From the nature of the transmission, it appeared that on board The Avante was Alpha Fraczan's leading rocket scientist and authority on space travel, with all the beneficial implications that might entail for Cosmic Solutions recent business projects. Patel looked delighted and very quickly relayed the good news to his superior Christine Sanchez.

For Sanchez, seated in her office on the highest floor of the corporate headquarters, this was the best news she had received in a long long time. The project of terra-forming Morpheus was still progressing far too slowly, and largely, in her opinion, because of the slow nature of space travel. Faster space craft would be a major bonus for the corporation, and might finally deliver the project on time and with significantly higher profit margins. Additionally, she was certain this would also provide them with a major advantage over their main competitor, the Rorque Corporation, and whatever secret projects they had been devising recently. There were rumours swirling around that they too were looking to space-based solutions to reinvigorate their various companies. For the first time in many months she suddenly felt that matters might finally be moving in the right direction. Maybe this was the stroke of good luck her corporation had needed all along.

She poured herself a congratulatory drink, swiveled round on her chair and gazed out through the floor-to-ceiling window that ran the length of the room, out across the streets of the city centre. It was yet another sweltering day with record-breaking temperatures, and once again the volume of traffic seemed less than she would have expected. She really needed to employ someone to check the population statistics, she thought to herself.

Interstellar Space - the rendez-vous at Necron

The wide array of sensors on the viewing screen of the spaceship's flight deck finally indicated an approaching spacecraft was heading towards their immediate vicinity. It had taken a while to be sure it was an actual starship that was showing on their screens, but its purposeful trajectory, energy emissions and slowing approach had strongly indicated that this was a controlled craft rather than some random piece of space debris headed in their general direction. For the small crew aboard the ship monitoring the immediate vicinity of space, they were once again reminded that human progress with regards to space travel was still somewhat in its infancy. Their detectors only operated reliably over relatively short distances - at least by the standards of space travel - and all forms of communication and message transmission remained frustratingly slow. Matters were not helped by the fact that they had also agreed to keep inter-ship communications to an absolute minimum.

The estimated time of arrival of the approaching craft was still another two hours, and not before time, as far as the ship's chief passenger was concerned. Colin Jamieson sat impatiently in his chair on the viewing deck trying very hard to keep his temper. Agreed rendez-vous was supposed to have been nearly four hours ago, and by no stretch of the imagination was Jamieson a particularly patient man. The two members of the crew who were actually human could sense his growing unease and tried to keep out of his way as much as they were possibly able. Only the AI units continued to attend regularly and calmly to his various demands.

The ship they were waiting on, The Sunray, had been converted from one of the smallest class of stasis ships to have chosen Rorque 4 as its destination over a century ago. It had been refitted mainly as a cargo transporter and was now capable of carrying only a small number of stasis passengers relatively short distances across space, but little more than that. For the engineers who had converted the ship, the main problem they faced – and one they shared with many of the other inhabited planets - was that Rorque 4s economy had never grown to the size, nor developed the level of technical complexity, to sufficiently advance space flight technology beyond that developed on Earth so many years before.

Arrival in Utopia

Space flight was still no faster, nor more comfortable or advanced than it had been almost two centuries beforehand. As such, a limited suite of stasis pods had needed to be retained on board for longer voyages involving humans, and in case the ship ran into any serious difficulties. With their planet operating no form of rescue space service, it might be as many as several months before their corporation could be contacted and a rescue craft organised to retrieve them from whatever dilemma they happened to have experienced. The ship was able to hold around half a dozen people in relative comfort for perhaps a maximum of three months before its energy systems, life support and food supplies would effectively cease to keep its complement of passengers alive and healthy. Stasis pods were therefore still essential.

The ship was currently orbiting the only rocky planet of this particular star system, a satellite of a small red dwarf star that had been given the name of Necron, in the light of it possessing no habitable planets. Colloquially it was often known as the 'forgotten star', or occasionally as the seventh star, in light of the fact that many in the Nexus Cluster regularly overlooked its existence. In total, it's planetary system only contained a couple of ice giants, a small number of icy dwarf planets, numerous asteroid belts and this one smallish dry rocky planet. The planet had, nevertheless, been found to contain a wide range of useful minerals and ores, some in particularly rich concentrations, and so the Rorque Corporation had recently commenced mining operations here.

Space mining was a slow process, though, as only a single converted stasis ship and a couple of landing craft were available to the AI units being used for mining the ores and minerals. It was, however, reasonably lucrative; for the moment they faced no commercial competition since many of the minerals were not to be found on Rorque 4, so were effectively operating as a monopoly. The profits raised by the mining enterprise were proving to be increasingly important, as its operations in other sectors were facing significant difficulties during the prolonged economic recession that had blighted the planet. Whilst out here, Jamieson had taken the opportunity to look for means to speed up operations, but this was not the main purpose for his secretive visit to the Necron system.

Two hours later, the second ship finally dropped into orbit around the small rocky planet and a transporter craft shuttled quickly between the two ships, so that the passengers from the second ship could embark for their prearranged talks. Jamieson welcomed the boarding party - a small group of military officers led by a figure he assumed was Vice-Admiral Rosson, vice-commander of Zeleyan's space fleet. Jamieson had no direct experience of dealing with military figures – law and order on Rorque 4 was maintained entirely by private security forces - but immediately felt uncomfortable with their stiff, ultra-formal and quite abrupt manner. He was far more accustomed to the dealings of the corporate world, with the cut and thrust of the business deal, interacting with like-minded entrepreneurs who made you feel welcome and appreciated, but who equally knew you were determined to maximize your side of the deal. The stiff formality of the military officers gave him little to work with, and he immediately felt the need to find some weakness that could help swing the terms of the meeting in his own favour.

Vice-Admiral Rosson and his officers clearly did not seem to do pleasantries, and once strapped into their seats, and after some very brief introductions and the provision of drinks, the meeting moved to the matter of business in an almost unseemly and abrupt manner. This made Jamieson wonder about the late arrival of the military deputation. Had they deliberately kept him waiting as a means of demonstrating some form of perceived superiority – was this part of a suite of tactics designed to put him at a psychological disadvantage? What other tactics might the Vice-Admiral employ he wondered to himself, as he looked across the table at the military officers. An alternative explanation also occurred to him, though. Were the space capabilities of the Zeleyanian fleet actually more limited than he had been led to believe? This might, he thought, give him some purchase in the negotiations.

Almost immediately, though, any illusions that Jamieson had harboured about this being a typical business deal were brought to an abrupt halt; in fact, Rosson seemed like a man who had no expectation of entering into any negotiations whatsoever. With an almost alarming swiftness Rosson outlined the requirements of the Zeleyan delegation. They required a specific number of stasis ships, fully laden with fuel and delivered to Zeleyan with only AI units aboard in exactly eleven months time. He also requested that a significant amount of engineering hardware should be included on each ship – given with very specific details of their exact requirements. He then offered what seemed to Jamieson very good terms with regards to the resources Zeleyan was offering in return. Finally, he concluded the offer with some cryptic remark about them needing to deal with a common enemy, and that he was sure that his corporation would find the terms more than agreeable. He then waited for Jamieson's response, though it was obvious he was expecting compliance.

For a second time in the space of only a few minutes, Jamieson felt at a significant disadvantage, a feeling he was not used to experiencing. He wanted to give the military commander the sense that he was dealing with a man that would drive a hard deal, a business partner that was at the top of his game but with whom he could nevertheless still strike an extremely good deal. The already unexpectedly generous terms offered by the Zeleyanians meant there was little scope for such an approach, in fact it could prove distinctly embarrassing to do so, and who knew how the military men might react. He toyed briefly with the idea of holding out for more; the fact that he possessed something the Zeleyanians clearly wanted put him at a distinct advantage. But somehow Rosson looked like the kind of man who would not countenance any such nonsense.

Jamieson also knew Rosson had the option of going to the other corporations on Rorque 4 for the stasis ships they desired, and it was entirely possible they had already done so for all he knew. The precarious state of his company's financial position at the present moment meant that Jamieson really had no desire whatsoever to see this deal being concluded by the competition. But Rosson also appeared like a man in a hurry he had quickly concluded. This could be an advantage to him, but equally Jamieson probably didn't have the option of playing for extra time, of considering all the various implications, devising is own best position and then returning with an improved deal at some later date. The limitations of space flight completely knocked that idea on the head.

Still slightly flummoxed, he decided to play for time and asked for a short recess. Rosson looked distinctly annoyed. Jamieson retired to an adjacent room with his small team and they poured over the details of the deal at a slightly more leisurely pace. It really was as generous as he had first thought. He thus mentally decided to accept the deal, but went through the pretence of asking for the thoughts of his subordinates to see if he had missed anything. Whilst they did so, he also made some quick calculations and figured they could meet the terms of the deal with time to spare. His subordinates identified no particular problems with the deal and so his decision was confirmed. They returned to the main negotiating table and informed Rosson that the terms of the deal were indeed agreeable and that his company would give the contract their highest priority. Rosson could expect delivery of the ships with all the specified requirements on the exact date of delivery he had requested. Documents were signed to conclude the deal and Rosson and his team departed with as little fanfare as when they had arrived.

Jamieson watched the Zeleyan starship lift out of orbit away from the rocky planet and depart into the star-studded darkness of space. It traced a slowly arcing line across the night sky and eventually disappeared into the darkness of inter-stellar space as it commenced its journey back to Zeleyan. Presumably, they would soon be in stasis for the two month journey – a long journey, for such a short meeting, he thought, but given the secretive nature of the deal, also entirely necessary. Despite the strange and slightly unsettling nature of the meeting, Jamieson felt extremely pleased with the deal he had just concluded. This, together with the proceeds from the mining operation, might effectively help them see out the economic crisis.

However, he also felt a nagging sense of unease. A number of issues irked him, and not just the fact that he had not been given an opportunity to impress Rosson with his business acumen and leadership skills. The Zeleyanians also seemed to have an exceptionally good idea of what Jamieson's company was capable of delivering, in fact, far too good for it to be a coincidence. Contact between the two planets was sparse at the best of times - did this mean they had spies on his planet, even within his corporation? He would need to investigate the matter further. He would put security on the issue to see what could be discovered.

In addition, there was the slightly unsettling fact that he had just sold a large portion of his fleet of stasis ships to a militaristic fascist regime. He had thought this feature of the deal through several times, but ultimately decided that a business deal was a business deal. He would be able to defend it back on Rorque 4. The cryptic remark about a common enemy he assumed referred to Zeta Kotlin. What exactly were the Zeleyanians planning to do with their new spaceships? Surely Zeta Kotlin was too distant for an all out military invasion – the Zetans would see them coming from miles away! The Zeleyan authorities had previously talked about defensive capabilities – so were the Zetans more aggressive than was popularly thought? He was under the impression they had little in the way of military forces. They were an ideological nuisance, that was for sure, but he had no reason to believe they were a military one as well.

Jamieson had plenty of time to consider these issues at length on the long journey back to Rorque 4. He also faced the small matter of ensuring that the shareholders and board of directors approved his recently concluded negotiation – if you could call it that. His seniority in the company would normally make this a foregone conclusion, but given the enormity of the deal, he felt he would need some cast-iron and totally convincing arguments, just to be certain. As long as he had the backing of the shareholders, though, he should be home and dry. The quarterly dividend payment was due soon, his mining operations and the new deal with Zeleyan could deliver a remarkably good one, in fact a surprisingly generous one given the present economic circumstances. That should seal it for him. He ordered the AI units to transmit a series of emissions back to company headquarters on Rorque 4 to set his plans in motion, and swigged back a celebratory drink from one of the containers.

Arrival in Utopia

Zeleyan - return of Vice-Admiral Rosson

The return journey back from the Necron system to Zeleyan lasted for the duration of a little over two months. Vice-Admiral Rosson – ironically for a space fleet commander – had never been a particularly good traveller in ground-based vehicles, and space-bound ones had proven to be little different. Keen to avoid the debilitating effects of space sickness, he saw little reason to remain awake for the duration of the voyage. After ordering all the members of his crew to enter stasis, he had then joined them himself after initiating lockdown. The AI units duly piloted the stasis ship successfully through interstellar space, and after approximately two months of travelling awakened the Vice-Admiral and a small number of his senior officers as they approached the outskirts of the Hedillan star system.

Rosson had never flown in space before his journey to the Necron star system, but had, despite his other difficulties, unexpectedly developed a taste for planet tourism. As they had passed out of the Hedillan star system on the outbound journey to Necron, their trajectory out of the star system had taken them past the large outer planets of Keitzel and Muisson. Previously, Rosson had, like all Zeleyanians, known of the system's planets through science lessons and popular culture, but had never given them a great deal of thought. Witnessing them first hand, though, had been an astounding, even transformatory, event for the military commander. Never in his life had he experienced such astounding and breathtaking visions as those that loomed before him - the sheer enormity of their size and the majesty of their presence, dwarfing their little ship, made him feel as if he was in the presence of a god or some other form of mystical metaphysical cosmic power.

Once clear of Hedilla's system, and before entering stasis, with a whole gamut of ideas racing through his brain and still unsure of exactly what his recent experience actually signified, he had ordered the ship's computer to provide him with a visualization of the Necron star system. Upon noting the presence of two ice giants orbiting the outer reaches of the system he had ordered the ship to plot a course to his arranged meeting that would entail the ship passing both planets. This was why he had eventually been late for the meeting with Jamieson, the ship entering the system from a direction that the Rorquians would not have anticipated and slightly delaying Rosson's journey.

And Rosson's deviation to view the two ice giants had not left him disappointed. The first of the two ice giants was that of Sapphos. Initially it had appeared as a small blue marble lost in a vast sea of unaltering darkness, but as the ship approached the ever largening globe, Rosson marvelled at the deep cerulean blue sphere that loomed larger and larger before him. Eventually, they approached so close to the planet that nothing but the sheer size and intense blueness of the planet was visible from the viewing deck. As they did so, the finer visual details of the sphere became evident - long thin wisps of white occasionally disrupted the blueness of the planet, whilst towards the poles, thin bands of a deeper and darker prussian blue encircled the globe, almost imperceptible against the vast blueness of the giant sphere. Once more, Rosson felt himself to be in the presence of an almost unworldly and magical spiritual presence.

Whilst Sapphos was quietly and almost mystically awe-inspiring, the second of the two ice giants, that of Kristilla, was more of a breathtaking visual spectacle. The weak sunlight of Necron falling on the deeply uneven icy surface of the vast frozen world, was reflected in an intricate and almost mesmerically repeating pattern of coruscating soft diamond white light. The planet seemed to sparkle like a vast cold white planetary glitterball, its scintillating brightness in stark contrast to the pitch dark of its spatial surroundings. As the ship approached ever closer, the unevenness and imperfections of the pattern became more apparent, but, for Rosson, this was still a magnificent sight to behold. The ice giant proved to be a vast sphere of deep valleys, unimaginably high crystal peaks, deeply embedded canyons and impressively immense mountain ranges that apparently explained the glittering chiaroscuro effect of the planet.

For Rosson, all too quickly, the ship had hurtled away from the shimmering and scintillating sphere as the gravity sling shot took the small consignment of military officers to their prearranged rendez-vous with the businessmen from Rorque 4. After such mind-blowing spectacles, the meeting could only ever be regarded as an exercise in mundanity, a return to the preprogrammed order of military life. Nevertheless, he knew his career, possibly his life, and maybe even his civilisation depended upon it proceeding successfully. As he approached The Sunray he was still not entirely sure, though, as to how exactly he would conduct the meeting.

Following the successful completion of the meeting - one that had passed far more smoothly than he had been expecting - Rosson had ordered the ship, under the pretext of using their gravity as a slowing mechanism, to once again fly past the giant planets of Keitzel and Muisson on the return journey to Zeleyan. This would entail an extra few hours of flying time, but for Rosson this was now nothing of any great concern, in fact, he was seriously beginning to wonder whether this was the real reason he had been sent into space.

The first planet they encountered was the more distant of the two; that of Keitzel, and its enormous blue mass became increasingly apparent as the ship approached its first fly-by. As they neared, Rosson once again felt an almost mystical aura wash over him. Floating transfixed and silent on the observation deck he gazed intently, absorbing the repeating wave-like patterns of indigo blue and deep violet that seemed to sweep ever onwards against the pale cerulean blue background of the giant sphere. In the southern hemisphere, the patterns took on the appearance of crashing waves, swirling inexorably and unendingly across its vast pale blue circumference. A more nuanced, layered and almost dreamlike blue shift effect characterised the waving bands that spanned the northern half of the sphere.

As he gazed transfixed at the planet, Rosson began to believe he could discern subtle patterns of graduated change in the layers and degrees of altered shading that he was sure contained some form of hidden meaning. He wasn't quite sure why he believed this, but the feeling was so distinct he was entirely unable to get the idea out of his mind. Then, as the starship arced slowly away and across the curved edge of the gas giant, three of the vast sphere's small satellites emerged from out of its shadow, shining weakly in the dim starshine, appearing precariously close to the vast behemoth as they continued their slow but never-ending trajectory around the vast planet. He wondered whether this too had some form of metaphorical significance.

Arrival in Utopia

A short time later, and it was the equally gigantic gas giant of Muisson that stretched endlessly before them, its vast size absolutely dwarfing the small speck of a spaceship that travelled before its vast majestic beauty. Muisson, in contrast to Keitzel, emitted an aura of calm serenity and measured subtlety. Gently-waving whorls of pale mustard, cyan blue and cream formed intricately laced wave-like bands and rings across the entirety of its huge curved surface. The layers seemed to be somehow intangibly interlinked and tangled, forming an infinite number of complex interweaving patterns, that made Rosson again wonder whether they too were the timeless endeavour of some great cosmic force weaving its way across space, rather than the rational product of the physical and chemical forces of nature. Once again, Rosson searched for some hidden mystical meaning in their appearance, and once again was struggling to understand what this all actually meant.

As the ship travelled away from the gas giant, Rosson returned to his chair, strapped himself in and surveyed the viewing deck and his officers around him, and could not help but reflect on how suddenly different his life had become in recent months. He had been born into one of the more privileged families on Zeleyan and so an illustrious career had always been expected him. However, in his early years he had shown little sign of promise. His favoured activities had always been of an outdoor nature and he had engaged enthusiastically in a range of montane and riparian sporting and adventure activities, so much so, that his studies and social life had been severely neglected. Rosson often disappeared for days or even weeks at a time with whichever member of his small circle of fellow enthusiasts might be up for such similar adventures.

Eventually, though, his family had insisted on a career in the military and a marriage into an equally wealthy family. Neither had progressed particularly well. Although the marriage had produced two daughters, he struggled to feel any great attachment to his family. In a similar manner, his career in the military had progressed far more slowly than those around him would have liked. He struggled with the discipline of the profession, the stiff formality, the issuing of orders and it was only the occasional field exercises and war gaming activities that allowed him to endure such an existence, one which was largely consisted of long periods of tedium punctuated only very occasionally by much shorter bursts of excitement. His slow progress up through the officer ranks was presumably more down to family connections than any actual outstanding military brilliance.

It had therefore come as a great surprise to both Rosson and his contemporaries that he was suddenly promoted to Vice-Admiral of the space fleet. Admittedly, at this point in time, the space fleet was extremely small – in fact, only one solitary stasis ship – but he had been informed that all this was soon about to change. Rosson had absolutely no experience of space flight and had not even served in the maritime navy. His family, by contrast, was delighted and he was sure they had probably pulled the relevant strings. Initially, he had not known what to make of the promotion. He was unsure whether he would spend much time in space or how important his position really was. At first, there were far more questions than answers.

Within a short space of time though, he was soon made aware that his new position was, surprisingly, actually a highly important one. His first assignment had been that of meeting with Jamieson in the Necron system. He had been instructed in no uncertain terms, by Supreme Commander Vartin himself, that the meeting was, at all costs, expected to be a successful one. Failure was not an option. Rosson had only very limited experience of dealing with business leaders, and a life in the military had produced very little in the way of negotiating acumen. He had explored possible ways of conducting himself in the negotiations but had ultimately arrived at the conclusion that he could probably not outsmart an experienced captain of industry, and had simply opted for the stiff formality of a military approach. It was completely out of character, but he was simply clueless as to how else he could proceed.

Rosson had been equally unsure as to how he would cope with spending long periods of time in space, if indeed that was even to prove the case, since he figured there was a strong possibility of the position being a largely desk-bound one. In the event, his recent almost quasi-spiritual experiences in space, in addition to his recent rapid promotion, had left him profoundly puzzled and confounded. There was little in the way of organised religion on Zeleyan – other than the official religion somewhat half-heartedly promoted by the party - but Zeleyan society was rife with superstition, quasi-mysticism and nationalistic folklore. Rosson – no different in this respect - was now seriously wondering whether fate had finally smiled on him - after what seemed like a long period of penance in the military – and that he might now be entering some form of higher phase of his life in which he was gaining access to the mysteries of life and the wider universe. It was still something of a vague feeling and was not sure of the exact details, but was beginning to assume that as time unfolded he would eventually achieve greater clarity.

With the two gas giants left far behind, it was only a short matter of time before the stasis ship finally approached their home world of Zeleyan. Much of the sphere was constituted by blue ocean, but the huge supercontinent that almost stretched from pole to pole down one side of the planet soon hoved into view. Rosson noted how distinctly the vast flat green plains of the northern area were delineated from the rest of the huge landmass, the topography of which was distinctly more varied. Then, as they passed over the huge oceans, he occasionally thought he caught sight of one of the small island chains that looked so lost and isolated in the vastness of the cerulean blue ocean. As the ship finally descended to a lower latitude, he was able to discern the small southern polar ice-cap that lay almost half-hidden at the bottom of their world.

When the shuttle craft that transported them back to the spaceport of Gombos finally touched down, Rosson, now beginning to feel the effects of travel sickness, did so with mixed feelings. He felt disappointed to have left the ethereal charms of space tourism behind him and to be back on the day-to-day treadmill, returning to the humdrum and tedium of his desk job. However, he had successfully completed his first important mission, returned with extremely good news and would surely be congratulated on his success. Maybe, he thought to himself, his success would allow him a greater degree of freedom and latitude, and the possibility of shaping his new position to his own designs, rather than the expectations of High Command.

Shortly after touchdown, he was soon being whisked along a major highway back to the capital of Zeleyan City in the heavily-protected motorcade that had been waiting for him at the spaceport. It was now almost midnight in the capital and so this allowed Rosson some time to head home, get some proper rest and recuperate from the tiring journey he had just completed and recover from the travel sickness. Tomorrow he would be expected to duly report back to Supreme Commander Vartin and the rest of High Command. Vartin would be expecting a full and detailed account of the meeting at party headquarters the next day, but Rosson could not see how this would be anything other than a formality now.

Arrival in Utopia

Earth – how to colonise space

By the year 2070, the study of exoplanets was a well-established, even ageing, field of astronomy. An array of space-mounted telescopes orbiting close to Earth and the more distant tracts of the solar system had added enormously to the bank of knowledge gleaned as they peered out across the vast stretches of open space that existed between the stars. The existence of literally hundreds of thousands of planets spread across the galaxy was a well established fact by this date, and they had formed in all manner of planetary configurations. The solar system, as had been long suspected, was – if the near galaxy was anything to go by - a fairly standard planetary system. The vast majority of stars that had been studied intensively had been found to have at least a few, and sometimes many, planets orbiting around them. These ranged from huge gas giants, even larger than Jupiter, through to rocky Earth and Mars-type intermediates, down to tiny ice planets, frequently found on the outer limits of the huge number of systems studied.

Additionally, these studies demonstrated that a number of the planets that had been discovered showed promising signs that water might be present or even abundant on their surface, and not surprisingly it was to these planets that scientific and exploratory attention typically gravitated. Many planets also gave tell-tale signs as to the type of atmosphere that might be surrounding them, but few, if indeed any, appeared to possess oxygen-rich atmospheres. This was not particularly surprising to the observing scientists, since it was well-known that living organisms had created the vast majority of Earth's oxygen, and that there were few non-organic processes that might actually be capable of creating an atmosphere and ozone layer that was suitable for Earth-evolved organisms. Additionally, despite intense efforts, there was still little to no good evidence that life might exist on the exoplanets so far discovered and studied. Very few of the planets observed showed suggestive signs of life - such as, for instance, the presence of methane in their atmosphere. To all intents and purposes, Earth still remained the only known repository of life in the near galaxy.

For those wishing to colonise space, therefore, the standard thinking was that any planet space-colonists arrived at in the future, was highly unlikely to be immediately suitable for human habitation. Instead, some form of terra-forming process would be needed for a successful colonisation to be undertaken. It would also be clearly beneficial if this was commenced well in advance of any settlers arriving. The length of time needed to complete a terra-forming approach was completely unknown and a matter of considerable debate – though presumed to be heavily dependent upon the exact conditions on any individual planet. But, the idea that humans could orbit a planet for any significant length of time, confined to a spacecraft for the several years or decades before it became habitable, whilst at the same time remaining in good mental and physical health, was considered to be a complete non-starter.

The universally accepted solution to this problem was effected through an agreement to launch a huge fleet of Planet Transforming Advance Ships – quickly dubbed 'genesis pods' on social media – well in advance of the departing stasis ships. These were smaller, easier to build and launch, and free of the difficulties of moving large numbers of humans across space, and could travel considerably faster across space. Compact and relatively easy to manufacture, they were eventually sent out in their thousands to all star systems that had been shown to possess at least one planet that showed even the slightest signs of being suitable for habitation. The pods were piloted and controlled by preprogrammed AI units - their source of energy deriving from either self-perpetuating solar or dynamo-type processes - and were stocked with a very wide range of organic materials thought necessary to make the basics of life possible for humans on any planet deemed potentially suitable.

The bulk of the material on the 'genesis pods' was constituted by tanks full of an extremely dense but super-rich microorganism mixture cooled to a level where it was effectively in stasis. Chief amongst these were genetically-engineered phytoplanktons and other oxygen-producing organisms selectively developed to disperse and multiply at the fastest conceivable rate, whilst delivering a rapid and constant stream of oxygen into the atmosphere. Next were bacteria capable of breaking down rock to help form the basis of soil - a process that could also be aided by a mechanical action performed by specially-designed AI units - together with a whole range of seeds, fungi, mosses and other organisms considered necessary for developing the first soils. Finally, a whole range of eggs and larvae from thousands of different species of fish, insects and other invertebrates were kept in a variety of different tanks to be placed in aquatic, coastal, montane and plateau-like environments to be introduced as and where deemed appropriate.

It was thus hoped that by the time the first stasis ships arrived several years or decades behind the 'genesis pods', the rudiments of planetary life would have already been pre-established. There would be a nitrogen-oxygen based atmosphere, marine life established in the oceans, and plants growing in soils artificially manufactured on the land. The AI units were also capable of building suitable shelters for the first settlers, partly using advanced materials taken on the 'genesis pods' but also from locally sourced inorganic materials. Significant supplies of corbalite – the latest all-purpose advanced material to be invented – were taken to provide a flexible, dependent and relatively light building material for the buildings that would be erected before the arrival of the first settlers. If time allowed, there was even scope for growing the first trees, establishing agrarian areas and creating transport routes, in readiness for the arrival of the original colonists.

The commencement of the settlement process - once a 'genesis pod' had arrived and established that a particular planet was suitable for habitation – was to launch an array of satellite and other communications devices to orbit the planet continuously. These contained a host of scientific monitoring and measuring devices that could continuously collect and analyse vast quantities of data on all relevant aspects of the planet – its geology and geography, seismic activity, the salinity of the oceans, the nature of the atmosphere and the progress that life was making on the planet once it became established. Selected summaries of this data could be beamed back towards Earth for any approaching stasis ships, thus giving a comprehensive guide to approaching colonists as to what they could expect to find on the planets ahead of them. If a stasis ship were to eventually arrive, the entirety of this data was available to its crew upon arrival, and a rapid evaluation of the state of the planet could be made by the arriving settlers, thus helping significantly to shape the mode and manner of their initial colonisation.

In the event that none of the planets of a particular star system were considered habitable, the 'genesis pod' would leave a single transponder in orbit around the star system beaming out a message that stated why it had arrived at such a conclusion. It would then redirect itself to the nearest star system deemed as potentially habitable and which had not already been assigned to another pod. The designers of this process were also aware, however, that leaving the evaluation as to whether a planet could be made habitable or not to a machine might lead to a number of erroneous decisions, with a human analysis potentially arriving at a different conclusion. With this in mind, it was decided that in cases of uncertainty, a series of algorithms would rate the percentage likelihood of how habitable a planet might be, and if this fell into the outer limits of the range then a different message would be beamed out from the transponder, indicating that no planets appeared habitable but that this evaluation might need revisiting.

Once the logistics of how the Planet Transforming Advance Ships would operate were established, the commencement of their manufacture was an extremely rapid one. The need for them to arrive in sufficient numbers and years ahead of the stasis ships was considered of paramount importance, and so the various nations, regions and corporations of the world devoted great efforts to ensuring this would be the case. All across the globe, production lines churned out 'genesis pods', firstly in their hundreds, and then in their thousands, quickly followed by their launch from the proliferation of space stations spreading across the globe. The human race was thus set to embark on the greatest exercise in migration it had ever undertaken.

Rorque 4 – Rorque Corporation board meeting

Three days before The Sunray was due to enter orbit around Rorque 4 in the star system of Eleutheria, Colin Jamieson and his small team of managers were brought out of stasis by the AI units as previously instructed. Once they had recovered sufficiently from the awakening process, they then set about making preparations for their imminent arrival on the planet. In-coming transmissions over the preceding four months were checked and dealt with, whilst preparations were also made for the upcoming shareholders meeting. Notable amongst the transmissions was Parker's communication informing Jamieson of their contact with the starships of the Alphan diaspora, and it was to this that Jamieson paid the greatest attention.

As with so many of the messages he received from subordinates, Parker's had the usual ingratiating tone, but somehow, Jamieson thought, there always seemed to be a slightly mocking quality to those he received from Parker, a feature that he was finding increasingly irritating. He was never entirely certain that this was actually the case - rather than perhaps the product of his imagination – but the more messages he received from Parker, the more he was becoming convinced that he was not imagining any this. Parker had made the usual song and dance about the importance of his own role in the achievement – this was to be expected – but looking beyond the attention-seeking, he was quietly pleased with the outcome that the unexpected opportunity of the Alphan diaspora appeared to be delivering.

Despite the pompous and self-congratulatory tone of the missive, he could not suppress a brief smile. He was more than aware that Parker was not the most capable of his small team of managers, but he had been chosen for the role because he possessed qualities that Jamieson believed would be suited to what would probably prove to be a difficult set of procedures. Parker had a reputation for possessing a brusque manner and often rubbed up colleagues the wrong way with a range of insensitive insults. He seemed not to care when he offended his colleagues, indeed he often seemed proud of his dubious achievements. In other circumstances this would be a distinct problem, but Jamieson believed he could turn this personality defect to his own advantage if developments panned out in the way he was expecting.

Looking at the wider picture though, that the Rorque Corporation would soon be employing some of Alpha Fraczan's finest scientists, was great news for the company, and if there were any doubts about getting his recent deal with Zeleyan approved by the board of directors, this development should firmly scotch them. Nevertheless, it did mean he had some extra thinking and planning to consider. Parker's missive indicated that on board the Spirit of The Age were some of Alpha Fraczan's leading experts in aerospace technology. If this was correct – you could never be sure with Parker - this would be a major bonus for the corporation, and might deliver a number of positive repercussions in his dealings with Zeleyan. Jamieson subsequently spent much of the ship's arrival time with his team dealing with these implications and finalising his plans and preparations for the crucial meeting that lay ahead of his arrival back on Rorque 4.

A few days later, Jamieson and his team were seated on the highest floor of the impressive Rorque Building set in the heart of the business district of Rorque City. The towering headquarters of the Rorque Corporation had been quite deliberately built to transmit a message to all who saw it, that this was the most important and most powerful corporation on the continent, and quite probably across the entire planet. Taller by far than the host of other skyscrapers that nestled beneath its widely-spreading shadow, its long elegantly fluted metallic column projected high above its diminutive-appearing contemporaries to be capped by a huge circular, almost space-ship looking, gently-domed glass and metal disc structure that rotated slowly above the city streets far below it. Those gazing upwards at the high rise construction would see only the oblique underside of the disc, so could only guess at what was actually occurring within its all important walls. This was how Jamieson liked to keep such matters.

Seated at the central position of the grand old dark wooden table that dominated the centre of the conference room, Jamieson could not help but wonder if the meeting he was soon to commence was quite probably the most important in the entire history of the corporation. Seated comfortably around the long rectangular table was the complete entirety of the corporate heads, leading managers and large shareholders of the corporation, without a single exception. Before them, neatly arranged in a regularly repeating pattern lay the paraphernalia that typically attended such important meetings – pens, pads of paper, bottles of differently coloured waters, small bowls of sweets and a computer portal incorporated into the structure of the table at each plushly designed seat.

Like all those sat around him, and again without a single exception, Jamieson had been schooled at one of the top Liberty Schools and hailed from one of the planet's wealthier families. He had always been expected to do well in life, but had not been particularly academic or even good at sports at school. Nevertheless, he had all the right contacts, had enjoyed the best education money could buy, and had developed the high level of personal entitlement that typically went with such a privileged background. Family connections had quickly ensured a middle-ranking position in the Rorque Corporation, but he had, from a young age, acquired a desire to go all the way to the top, an ambition that he had eventually achieved some years ago.

The ride to the top had not been a completely smooth one, but what he lacked in intellectual ability he made up for in drive, ambition and an ability to read human nature. The singular nature of his character and his obsession with acquiring power and wealth might have delivered his present status, but it had also made him a difficult person to live with - he had been married three times and twice divorced, for instance. And there had been many other casualties along the way as he manouevred his way to the top of the corporate ladder. Competition for the top positions was intense and friendships had been broken, colleagues betrayed and lovers neglected as he used those around him for his own ambitious ends and then abandoned them once they had served their useful purpose.

Once at the pinnacle of the corporate ladder, a further desire to become the richest person on the planet – to climb above the other billionaires of his world - had maintained his competitive drive and his continuing ambition. He was long past actually needing the wealth he was acquiring – he possessed enough for his family to live on comfortably for several generations – but simply wanted to be ahead of the competition and those around him. All the acquisitions and mergers, lay-offs, redundancies, product development, promotions and demotions, legal actions, union-busting, pay cuts, worsening of employee working conditions and evasion of regulations were devoted to this one obsessive goal of his.

The meeting commenced promptly at ten in the morning. Jamieson, flanked by his immediate team of fellow senior managers, opened with a series of remarks that he felt befitted the potential importance of the meeting. Introductions were dealt with as quickly as possible and he moved to the first and only important item on the agenda – namely his recently concluded deal with the authorities on Zeleyan. Jamieson explained the terms of the agreement he had concluded with Vice-Admiral Rosson four months previously, and dwelt for some considerable time on emphasising exactly how impressive the terms he had negotiated actually were.

He outlined the difficulties with which he had needed to grapple with to achieve such an impressive payment from the Zeleyanians, the hard fought nature of the bargain, and the fact that this was exactly what the corporation now needed to put an end to the difficult economic times it had experienced, for what was now an unacceptably long period of time. Such was the impressive nature of the deal, he claimed, that it could quite probably provide the corporation with a large percentage of the investment it needed over many coming years, deliver a return to a suitable levels of profitability, and deliver impressive dividends to the shareholders. Failure to accept the deal, by contrast, could see the corporation go into free fall, and the demise of all they had previously strived for.

Effectively, he stated, they had tried everything else they could possibly think of in terms of opening up new and lucrative markets, but this looked far more promising than any of their previous unsuccessful attempts. Most of those around the table looked sufficiently impressed by Jamieson's speech and various nods and murmurs of approval came each time Jamieson mentioned the various positive aspects of the deal. Jamieson paused for a few moments, and a bespectacled elderly man in tweeds, Ethan Samuel Forster, who Jamieson knew to be a major shareholder of the corporation, unexpectedly took the break in his speech as an opportunity to launch into an old hobby horse of his.

'But is it actually true that we've tried everything available to us? What about the Medusa option? There are potentially huge amounts of easy money to be made from that market, but we always run scared from them. It's a highly lucrative market, far better than all this nonsense concerning Zeleyan. That's what the corporation should be concentrating on.'

Forster clearly achieved the reaction he had been expecting, for he smirked as various mutterings, snorts of derision and cries of disapproval emanated from those present around the table, though also a couple of knowing bursts of laughter. He was a fogeyish, very old fashioned, cantankerous figure and apparently descended from some ancient line of aristocrats back on Earth, and clearly delighted in the reaction he had provoked.

'We've been through that issue several times before. The lawyers are quite clear; it might initially prove lucrative, but once we've been dragged endlessly through the courts we'll end up being closer to bankruptcy, rather than earning a fortune. We're not raking over that old ground, yet again,' stated the corporation's vice-president, clearly irked by the intervention.

Unfazed by the interruption but also slightly annoyed, Jamieson promptly returned to his previously prepared speech. A few minutes later he came to a final conclusion and the assembled group was asked if they had any questions or comments with regards to the nature of the deal. Several of the shareholders voiced enthusiastic support for the deal, but, as Jamieson had expected, there was not complete agreement and it became necessary to field a number of questions and criticisms.

The first to do so was an elderly female member of the highly wealthy Minoche family. 'Whilst I support the stated ambitions of our Chief Executive Officer and appreciate the hard work he and his team have undertaken to achieve this significant and possibly historic agreement with the planet of Zeleyan, I also have some major concerns. For instance, can we fully trust the Zeleyanian government to keep their side of the agreement? We know little of them, and if they were to refuse to deliver on their side of the bargain what redress do we have. They are a military regime, I believe, and, of course, based on a planet on which we have no political or legal jurisdiction. Can we be completely sure of their trustworthiness? If not, we have little in the way of effecting rectification, if they fail to uphold their side of the bargain.'

'I would also like to express similar sentiments,' stated a representative of one of the leading corporate shareholders, now emboldened by the preceding remarks from a member of one of the leading dynasties on the planet. 'We are effectively selling to the Zeleyanian authorities almost one half of our entire corporate space travel capacity. I'm very much aware that we have found little use for these stasis ships ever since our original arrival on this world, but is this truly a wise decision? It could severely limit our future trading abilities in space if we chose to carry out such undertakings. We also know that Cosmic Solutions are seeking to expand their space travel capacity – should we really be doing the opposite to our competitors at this point in time?'

A third objection was raised by Ebony Whitlow, a recent heiress to a significant family fortune acquired over many decades. 'I am also concerned about a perhaps more political element to this somewhat risky deal. The planet of Zeleyan is run by a militaristic fascist regime. It is a regime that clearly rules by force and uses its military to pursue its ends. How can we be sure that their acquisition of our stasis ships is not part of some grandiose military conquest of space? What is there to safeguard us from the fact that they may turn their weapons upon us, and invade Rorque 4 using the stasis ships we sold them? I can also envisage our corporate competitors using this deal to scheme against us politically. We will shortly be involved in planetary-wide elections and this could well be used to turn the voters against us. Even if they fail to defeat us politically, I would not be surprised to see them mount legal attempts to halt this deal.'

Jamieson had expected a certain amount of opposition to his deal, but he had calculated that it would be less than he was currently experiencing. Nevertheless, he and the members of his team had prepared for such objections and they were able to offer convincing ripostes to each of the challenges, and as time passed he appeared to be gaining the upper hand within the room. The meeting increasingly seemed to be in the process of swinging his way, when Jamieson received what was clearly an important message from one of the AI units present, and after a brief discussion with his close associates, he asked the permission of the meeting to display an incoming news communication from the media section of their corporation. Curious to know what might be so pressing as to interrupt such an important meeting, there were no objections to his request.

Arrival in Utopia

The large bluescreen that dominated the inner wall of the room was illuminated and a news bulletin relayed the fact that five of the starships carrying the scientists from Alpha Fraczan had definitely arrived at Zeta Kotlin and this could now be confirmed beyond doubt – though the ships had actually arrived there a little over seven months earlier, the time it took communications to travel between the two planets. Satellites belonging to the Rorque Corporation had also picked up communications sent between the various settlements on Zeta Kotlin, and these emissions were currently being analysed by the corporation's executive and media department in preparation for broadcast later that day in an attempt to assess the implications of this development for Zeta Kotlin, but also the wider Nexus Cluster.

Discussions immediately broke out amongst the various participants seated around the table, with most clearly disliking the news they had just received. Jamieson had already calculated that news of this event should give him the final advantage he needed in the meeting. If Zeta Kotlin was to be a major beneficiary of the Alpha Fraczan diaspora then it was essential that their corporation should also be developing its own presence in space and across the Nexus Cluster. If Zeleyan had hostile intentions towards the socialist planet – which they considered to be highly likely - then the corporation might be wise to take advantage of this in any way that proved profitable.

After this event, the discussion tipped distinctly in favour of the deal with Zeleyan, and as Jamieson had anticipated, the vote eventually went his way - ultimately it was not even a close run thing. As the CEO of the corporation he could typically expect his decisions to be backed by the shareholders, who, at the end of the day, were only really interested in one single consideration – adding to their already considerable fortunes – and the deal looked very likely to facilitate this. For these highly wealthy and privileged people, the acid test was simply, 'would it increase the dividend payouts?' Jamieson closed the meeting assuring all present that the contract with Zeleyan would be implemented with considerable speed and would deliver exactly what they wanted.

Over the following weeks and months, the stasis ships owned by the corporation were, after some decades of relatively benign neglect, subjected to a process of intense maintenance and a degree of upgrading - measures that the corporation was sure would soon pay dividends. Their readiness for the journey to Zeleyan would only be a few short months; the task was predominantly one of ensuring they were fully spaceworthy and supplied with sufficient fuel to complete the six month voyage to Zeleyan. It would only be a short amount of time before the stasis ships were on their way to the fascist planet.

Despite his success at the meeting, though, Jamieson now had a more immediate and pressing problem on his hands. The news of the arrival of the Alphan starships at Zeta Kotlin had been anticipated for some time, but now that they had actually landed and this had been fully confirmed, the implications of this development were beginning to slowly sink in and Jamieson was becoming increasingly concerned about the matter. He would need to meet with the head of their Media department to decide on the exact means in which the spinning the Zeta Kotlin story could paint the socialist planet in an increasingly negative light. He had already developed some ideas on how this should be achieved. Additionally, he was now wondering how accurate the information Parker had relayed to him a few days earlier actually was.

Zeleyan – The Crusader leaves for Ur-Tokar

Knowledge that five of the starships containing the scientists fleeing from the disaster on Alpha Fraczan had definitely reached their chosen destination of Zeta Kotlin had arrived with the authorities on Zeleyan some six weeks previous to similar transmissions being received on Rorque 4. Supreme Commander Vartin had been visiting a garrison of troops in the eastern sector of Outer Padnia at the request of Colonel Davila when the unwanted, but expected, news arrived. Despite earlier successes by Davila, he had become concerned with new outbreaks of political unrest in the region, and he had decided his own personal input was needed in order to make an accurate appraisal of the situation, boost the morale of the troops, and advise Davila on how best to thoroughly crush the subversive agitation in the area before it developed into a full-blown insurrection.

Vartin had, of course, been expecting the news of the starships arrival at Zeta Kotlin; all the communications data and extra-planetary media transmissions the authorities were receiving were indicating such an outcome should be expected. Nevertheless, when the occurrence was actually fully confirmed he still felt a sense of unease and concern, one that now prompted him to press ahead earlier than he had intended with his plans for Ur-Tokar. To some extent, he now believed, he had been prevaricating for far too long with the momentous decision. This unwanted development gave him exactly the excuse he needed – not that he actually needed permission from anyone – but he could certainly now justify the decision to himself, and anyone else who might be foolish enough to question it. He would now take swift and decisive action immediately.

Firstly, though, he completed his designated series of meetings and inspections with Davila, and left the colonel in no uncertain doubt that he expected that the complete pacification of the eastern sector of Outer Padnia to be achieved within a matter of days. After dismissing Davila, he was put through to High Command and issued orders that all troops designated for the Ur-Tokar mission should be transported immediately to the spaceport at Gombos. This was followed by a series of instructions relayed to a small number of high-ranking officers and other designated personnel to immediately prepare and ready for their role in the extremely important undertaking. He then made arrangements for his own personal role in the mission.

The journey to Gombos the following day was an extremely straightforward one. He and previous Supreme Commanders had ensured that, largely for military purposes, all sectors of the continent were linked by rapid transit autoroutes. It would thus take only a few hours despite the lengthy distance. He was accompanied by two senior officers, but Vartin was not much in the mood for talking and spent much of the journey flicking through various transmissions, information files and simulated projections, or simply passed the time viewing the ever changing landscape from the heavily armoured and protected autocar. The southern region of Outer Padnia was a complex mixture of high and largely dry longitudinally-running mountain chains interspersed with deep green river valleys and thus provided ever-changing scenery. The autocar travelled at considerable speed through long tunnels, across high valley-spanning bridges and along the shores of the long shallow lakes that formed in the higher reaches of the valleys. Eventually, several hours later, it climbed consistently for the best part of an hour and finally emerged onto the high and largely barren plateau wastelands of the central interior.

The spaceport of Gombos was located on the extreme eastern edge of the region of Novo Salzar towards the centre of the supercontinent. Situated on an extremely wide, elevated and largely savannah-like part of the plateau close to the equator, it was effectively only visible from the air. The town itself was a relatively small and indistinct affair possessing little of significant note, since historically Zeleyan had made little use of the spaceport, as they had previously possessed no real space program to speak of. Vartin had anticipated this would no longer be the case in the future, and had recently undertaken a concerted modernisation and expansion of the spaceport facilities – an undertaking that had been particularly easy given the wide and flat nature of the plateau. When Vartin and his officers arrived later that day, Gombos was already a hive of busy activity, with a steady flow of fleets of autobuses packed with soldiers arriving from the north, and landing craft arriving and departing from the spaceport at regular intervals. A senior officer approached Vartin, saluted and then informed the Supreme

Commander that the whole operation was running extremely smoothly and to plan, and would be duly completed at the designated time.

Vartin and his senior officers and advisors in High Command had been planning the operation for several years now. The orbiting stasis ship, The Crusader - the only one to have survived the nationalist wars in the earliest years of the planet's occupation, and the one used by Rosson for his rendez-vous in the Necron star system - had been fully overhauled two years previously, and the AI units now had the starship functioning at maximum performance. The craft had already been thoroughly prepared for the eight month voyage that lay ahead of it, fully fuelled and fully provisioned for its mission on Ur-Tokar. All that was needed now was for the last complement of soldiers to be transported skywards to the ship and placed into stasis, so that the final details before the flight actually commenced could be concluded. As the embarcation process moved into its final stage, so Vartin and his senior officers were informed of the readiness of their shuttle craft, and a short while later they were boarding the orbiting stasis ship.

Waiting for them in the control room of the starship was Space Fleet Commander Vice-Admiral Rosson. The officers saluted each other, and, once strapped into their chairs, Rosson gave what sounded like a well rehearsed run down of how efficiently the whole operation was proceeding. With no visible evidence to indicate otherwise, Vartin made positive comments of approval and declared that the whole exercise would soon be deemed as a magnificent success. The party then moved through to the observation deck. The ship was currently passing high above the supercontinent, and Vartin looked out through the observation window and took the opportunity to gaze imperiously over the vast landmass that lay below him as though he was the designated king of the world.

The supercontinent of Zeleyan constituted over one-third of the planet's total surface. Far to the north, he noted the vast verdant plains of the Northern Alliance, the prairie stretching long, green and unbroken until it finally reached the shallow shores of the huge Bay of Vega. The bay always looked as though it was opening like a gigantic mouth as if to swallow the chaotic mass of the Identimate Islands that lay further to the north, the islands seeming to litter the colder climes of the northern polar region. Further to the south rose the precipitously high and jagged brownish-yellow peaks of the long sinuous Central Mountain Belt, sharply delineating the lands of the Northern Alliance from the two southern regions of Novo Salzar and Outer Padnia. Vartin continued his gaze and looked southwards.

On the northern coast of Outer Padnia, the long broad dark greenish-blue inlet of the shallow Sea of Cymbaline twisted into the inner reaches of the landmass. Smooth brown plains on its southern border gave way to the complex intermix of bright green river valleys, broad expanses of plateau and intermittent mountain ranges that constituted the vast majority of the fertile region. To the west stretched the jagged coastline of Novo Salzar, strings off yellow-brown islands lay offshore in its coastal waters, and along its southern reaches spanned the vast green delta created by the entry of the great River Salzarance into the western seas. Between the two southern regions rose the vast almost never-ending wastelands of the central plateau region, a patchwork of olives and sage greens, intermixed with the occasional paler brown that represented the very highest zones of the region. Finally, he noted the enormous deep blue semi-circular shape that he knew to be the mysterious Lake Magnu, lost in the far realms of the barren southern polar region.

Vartin gazed long and hard at the landmass before the stasis ship finally passed over its western shores and out across the deep blue ocean that spanned the rest of the globe's circumference. All that lay before him was under his complete and absolute political and military control. He returned his thoughts to the Ur-Tokar mission, and his further plans for domination within the Nexus Cluster. For a brief moment he felt like he was the master of the universe. Finally, he mused to himself, the wind of time was blowing through him. His time had come, his destiny awaited him, the world was now moving relative to him and to him alone. He would shape the future like no other individual in history before.

Slowly he came consciously back to the reality of the moment, and became aware that his officers were waiting attentively for his orders. Vartin then duly gave a short morale-boosting speech to all those present, one that concluded with a demand for complete obedience to the Zeleyanian nation and the need for total victory. He saluted Rosson, and he and his officers returned to the transporter shuttle and a short time later were all landing safely at the spaceport of Gombos where they were met by various officials and his motorcade.

His thoughts dwelt for a while on recent events. He had harboured certain misgivings about Rosson's promotion to Space Fleet Commander, but he was beginning to believe he had, in fact, made the correct decision. His opinion of Rosson had improved in recent months and he was feeling increasingly confident about the mission's nature and the likelihood of success. Vartin wasted no further time at the spaceport, and headed back immediately to his residence in Zeleyan City. He had pressing matters to deal with, not least of which was the second stage of the plan that he believed would see him going down in the history books as Zeleyan's greatest ever leader.

At the same time, on board The Crusader, Rosson was concluding last minute details before the departure of the starship from Zeleyan. His skeleton crew had been issued with the appropriate orders and once all systems had been checked and designated as fully functioning, the plasma engines accelerated the spaceship out of orbit and out into inter-planetary space. Coordinates for the journey to Ur-Tokar had been keyed in and the ship accelerated with great force as it escaped the gravitational pull of Zeleyan. Rosson had, not surprisingly, once again plotted a course that would take him past the two gas giants of the planetary system so that he might once again enjoy the opportunity of admiring their vast size and beauty. He was still convinced he might gain further mystical insights into their existence and his own newfound purpose in life.

Eventually, a few hours later, having finally passed the gas giant of Keitzel, and still accelerating as they passed through the space dust of the Oort cloud – the zone which marked the full transition into inter-stellar space - they departed from the entire Hedillan star system, and were finally on their way to their destination of Ur-Tokar. A further few hours later, with all ships systems still indicating they were functioning at maximum performance, Rosson ordered the skeleton crew into their stasis pods, locked down the ship and headed for his own stasis pod, leaving the AI units to pilot the ship for the duration of the journey to their designated planetary destination.

Arrival in Utopia

For eight long relentless months the spaceship made its long lonely journey through the endless black corridor of space. The occupants of the sleek silver machine, immersed in the wastelands of sleep, sped through interstellar space, oblivious to the bleak neutrality of its harsh cold darkness, through the visible infinity of galaxies - the constellations of billions of stars grouped together as if to take comfort from the dark harshness of its infinite deepness. The spacecraft travelled through time and space, ever onwards across the lonely forbidding void of darkness, oblivious to the unfolding events on the many scintillating points of light that punctuated that bleak black coldness. But slowly, and almost imperceptibly, it bridged that long cold darkness, and as the months passed by it began to close in on the one particular scintillating point of burning white light it had designated as its destination.

Zeleyan – stasis ships arrive from Rorque 4

Whilst the Crusader made its lonely journey across interstellar space, developments continued apace on Zeleyan in preparation for the second stage of the mission. However, despite the carefully laid plans of Supreme Commander Vartin, he was frequently forced to deal with the disaffected and rebellious masses of the Zeleyanian population. Whilst Outer Padnia had been successfully pacified by Davila – for which he was rewarded with promotion - serious unrest later spread into the more prosperous region of Novo Salzar, where his personal intervention eventually required.

Nevertheless, approximately four months after the departure of The Crusader, he was finally able to take a break from trouble-shooting rebellions and deal with what he considered to be far more appropriate matters, those he believed he should actually be dealing with, not unwanted potential insurrections. The array of satellites circulating high above the planet's surface had informed party headquarters that the fleet of spaceships bought from the Rorque Corporation were currently decelerating past the gas giant Keitzel and would be arriving in orbit around Zeleyan in the early hours of the following morning. Vartin ordered a senior officer to head immediately for the spaceport at Gombos in order to undertake a thorough inspection of the three starships.

Three days later, a senior officer within High Command arrived in Zeleyan City and made his way along the city's wide boulevards to party headquarters late that morning. With him he possessed a fully comprehensive report drawn up following the inspection of the three ships. Upon arrival at the building, it was relayed immediately to Vartin, who read through the summary of the report and made brief notes concerning certain features he considered to be of significant interest within its pages. Despite one or two minor misgivings, he was pleasantly surprised that the Rorque Corporation appeared to have proven to be a fully reliable business partner, for the specific details he had laid down in the contract had been carried out almost to the letter. He briefly wondered if Rosson's performance had played any part in this success, but soon followed a different line of thought.

Despite this welcome piece of good news – and in significant contrast to much of what he had recently been experiencing in Novo Salzar - this actually left Vartin with something of a dilemma. Cautious and somewhat pessimistic by nature, he had believed he would probably need a few extra weeks or even a month or so to fully prepare the stasis ships for their departure to Ur-Tokar. Now he found he was in a position where he could launch them much sooner than he had expected, if he so desired.

He had, of course, not heard any word from Rosson, other than the standard pre-programmed automated emissions transmitted from The Crusader at regular intervals, stating that it was still on course for its original destination and that the ship was proceeding without mishap. It would be another six and a half months before he would hear of the successful arrival of the stasis ship at Ur-Tokar, and probably another two before he knew the first stage of the mission had been successfully completed. Vartin unexpectedly found himself in a situation where he could considerably fast forward his carefully prepared plans, something that was very much out of character for the highly cautious leader. He suddenly found himself feeling very impatient.

Arrival in Utopia

Earth - exodus

The exodus from Earth in the late twenty-first century, though initially slow and somewhat hesitant, gradually gathered pace and over the space of about a decade or more, a wide range of ships of differing sizes had departed for the dark unknown depths of outer space. Many of these had departed in relatively large fleets, others in smaller groupings, whilst some had left in solitary ships – the reasons for doing so typically being dictated by the particular priorities and theoretical understandings of those constituting the passengers on board. At one point in the early 2090s several starships were departing on an almost daily basis, though this was not typical of the wider period - it was far more common for launches to be spread across weeks or even months.

The actual number of departures depended on the speed with which the starships could be supplied, and thus the existing state of a global economy that was facing an ever changing range of new challenges and difficulties, as the impact of runaway climate change strengthened its inexorable grip on the planet. As one major tipping point was invariably followed by a further related one, major deteriorations in regional climatic conditions and the flooding of highly populated coastal areas inevitably forced slowdowns in the economy, whilst at the same time precipitating increasingly large spikes in demand for space travel from populations desperately seeking some viable path out of a visibly increasingly apocalyptic scenario for those remaining inhabitants of Earth. Unsurprisingly, what commenced as a reasonably ordered mass departure into space, ended as an increasingly chaotic and erratic free-for-all, as desperate populations sought to escape the rapidly deteriorating situation on hothouse Earth.

Whatever the size of the ship, its particular date of departure, its exact purpose or its final destination, an exceedingly long voyage awaited its dormant passengers, as they crossed the immense stretches of the galaxy needed to arrive at their sought-after destinations. Vast stretches of icy cold, potentially dangerous cosmic darkness needed to be safely traversed. In order to achieve this successfully, the stasis ships were equipped with a significant range of protection devices, not just to shield the sleeping humans from the cancer-inducing dangers of cosmic radiation, but to protect the ships from possible collisions with cosmic debris, randomly-flighted meteorites or any other form of possibly dangerous object that might damage them. At the speeds reached by the spacecraft – typically a third of the speed of light – even small pieces of cosmic detritus posed a potential threat to the structural integrity of the starships.

If any one individual or organisation had kept a detailed and precise record of the number of stasis ships which were launched into the depths of space, their date of departure and the numbers of sleeping colonists on board each ship, such a chronicle had long been lost in the mists of time. Almost certainly a large number of ships were lost in the icy depths of the cosmos. Faulty engineering doubtless accounted for a certain percentage of these losses, as did collisions with meteor storms or dense fields of cosmic debris. Amongst the space travellers and their newly created settlements, though, there eventually emerged persistent tales of malfunctioning AI units, or of passengers and crew emerging prematurely from stasis and aborting a mission they no longer believed in. Legends were legion of missing and lost ships, encounters with unexplained phenomena, unimaginable tragedies and disasters, of whole ships and fleets mysteriously disappearing without trace, of lost civilisations and failed colonisations.

Without doubt, any chronicler recording the exodus would have expected a certain percentage of losses and disasters, and the space legends and folklore indicated that this had been the unfortunate reality. The lost chronicles, if ever found, would have made for sober reading. But despite all the difficulties, a significant percentage – again unknown – of the starship exodus proved to be ultimately successful. Planetary destinations, almost always long and lonely decades later, were eventually attained. For most of the human diaspora, the vast distances and aeons of space were traversed safely and successfully. Given the different departures, destinations and speeds of the stasis ships this was a process that continued to unfold over a period of several decades, indeed, some legends claimed it even continued further out across the galaxy for centuries afterwards.

Information from the successful 'genesis pods' had been beamed back constantly in an Earth-bound direction, so that the growing exodus of stasis ships knew which destinations held the most promising planets as they searched for their new home in space. Where life looked feasible and habitation distinctly possible, a skeleton crew on the ship could be woken, and decisions made concerning the finer details of whether to colonise a promising planet or not. Upon reaching its destination, the arriving stasis ship would start its deceleration far from their intended stellar system so that it slowed sufficiently to catch the gravitational field of the destination star. Upon arrival, further information could be relayed from the AI units on the planetary surface to the newly orbiting ship informing it of the progress made in making the planet suitably habitable. On many occasions, though, planets proved – for a wide diversity of reasons - to be unsuitable or failed to meet the occupants expectations, and so the stasis ship would depart for yet another long haul across interstellar space, usually following a more promising and recent update from a 'genesis pod' in the search for their own particular utopia.

Where the decision was taken to remain and settle the planet, the waking occupants emerging from stasis were most likely to be underwhelmed by their new planetary home. Whilst the planet had been made suitable for human life and rudimentary settlements created for those achieving first arrival, what all the initial settlers would invariably discover was their newfound planet could not possibly hope to compete with Earth in terms of richness of biodiversity and suitability for human life and all its different needs and desires – at least the Earth as it had been before its experience of devastation by human over-exploitation.

None of the planets discovered and settled proved to be exactly Earth-like in nature. The colonised planets varied in size, gravitational force, orbital distance from their star, degree of stellar brightness, length of day and year, chemical composition of atmosphere, relative percentages of land and ocean, available mineral resources, number of moons, number and size of neighbouring planets and a whole host of other salient features. Their newly settled homes necessitated a considerable degree of adaptation and adjustment, and exactly how humans – and the other Earth-originating life forms introduced to the planet – coped with their new environments varied significantly – from outright failure and rapid extinction to many centuries of peace and prosperity.

But all of this underscored what everyone had known right from the very beginning of the exodus. This was, to all intents and purposes, the greatest 'push migration' in all of human history. People were actively fleeing from a rapidly deteriorating and catastrophic situation, not being pulled towards a bright new promising and better destination. Not a single person who fled from Earth knew exactly what awaited them - it was the greatest leap into the unknown ever undertaken in the history of humanity. Humans had evolved over millions of years to meet the specific requirements of Earth's numerous, varied and ever changing environments, but they were always Earth environments.

It was extremely unlikely that a planet better suited to humans was ever likely to be discovered – indeed, no such claim had yet been made - no matter how lucky the settlers might get with their new planetary home. As such, the colonists would have little choice but to make the most of their newfound, but almost certainly inferior situation – at least in terms of planetary environment – and start to implement as best as they possibly could, the new life and civilisation they had envisioned creating before their departure from planet Earth. All of this only served to underscore the huge error the human race had managed to achieve back on Earth, but whether the space colonists recognised this error varied enormously from one new civilisation to the next.

PART 2

The Wrong Destination

Rorque 4 – arrival of the two stasis ships

Approximately three long years after the initial departure of the diaspora from Alpha Fraczan, the two stasis ships, The Avante and The Spirit of The Age, finally approached their newly designated destination of Rorque 4, both within a few short days of each other. As they approached the stellar system of Eleutheria they reversed their engines so they could perform the long, slow deceleration needed to arrive safely within the system. The skeleton crews of the two starships were woken – according to standard practice – a few days out from their arrival at the planet, and oversaw the final stage of the voyage. Decelerating strongly, the two ships made their way through the assorted debris fields, asteroid belts and dwarf planets of the outer system, and then they finally dropped into orbit around the fourth planet of the system, Rorque 4.

From their orbit, the skeleton crews were able to view a largely brownish-red planet, though occasionally tinted with the green of vegetation, particularly on the seaboard edges of the various continents. Many of the continents possessed occasional high plateaus and massifs, but there was little in the way of significant high mountain ranges. Equally notable was the lack of any large river systems, though the plateaus were interspersed with deep dry canyons, which they presumed were the relic of previous geological ages. Interspersed amongst the extensive continental masses were several shallow light blue oceans, but a notable lack of large islands. There were no polar ice caps, just further shallow seas at the poles of the planet. The initial thoughts of the observing scientists were that they had swapped a cold dry planet, for what appeared to be a significantly hotter dry planet.

It was also something of a considerable shock for most of the members of the two skeleton crews that they had not arrived at their originally designated destination of Zeta Kotlin, but at the entirely new one of Rorque 4 instead. Alex Kim and Anna Dubois had both needed to use their status, charm and some fairly dubious excuses to explain why their respective ships had arrived at the wrong planet. There were some puzzled and irritated exchanges once the realisation of what had occurred finally permeated through their still somewhat hazy mental states. Ultimately, though, there was little they could do to alter the situation and, as both Anna and Alex had calculated, once their initial surprise had dissipated, they turned their attentions towards dealing with their newfound situation. They would have to settle matters with the respective Commanding Officers at a later date.

On Rorque 4 meanwhile, there had been some initial confusion as to how many stasis ships were actually heading towards the planet. It had taken some time for those interested in the matter to discover that Cosmic Solutions and the Rorque Corporation were in communication with two different ships – initially it was assumed it was the one single ship – but as the two ships closed in on their destination it became increasingly apparent that this was not the case. This had left the authorities feeling somewhat better about the whole episode - a feeling that was further enhanced when transmissions later arrived indicating that a third ship was also heading in their direction, having decided to not remain on Zeta Kotlin. For those in power, this was more in line with what they believed should have been happening all along. Surely, they thought, Rorque 4 offered greater opportunities for personal advancement and enhanced prestige and status than the dismal egalitarianism of Zeta Kotlin. There was also the little matter of the corporations on Rorque 4 being in dire need of some new ideas and expertise in the fields of space technology and flight engineering.

Both corporations had arranged for teams of senior executives and media crews to be transported to the respective stasis ships to greet the new arrivals and welcome them to their new planetary home. The executives, on arrival at the stasis ships, welcomed the new arrivals in front of the cameras and explained the procedures they had put into place to Alex and Anna and their respective skeleton crews, a process that further angered some members of the skeleton crews, as the degree of collusion that had been occurring beforehand became increasingly apparent - though others seemed more relieved by the fact that concrete plans had already been put in place. The corporations had already arranged for accommodation to be organised for the thousands of scientists arriving at their universities, which had proven to be a considerable undertaking. Additionally, they had both made preliminary arrangements for the construction of new departmental buildings, in the event of these being needed.

Arrival in Utopia

Over a period of several days - to ensure that the exercise operated smoothly and with as little waiting around as possible - the thousands of academics and scientists on board the two ships were gradually brought out of stasis and transported to their new accommodation. Unsurprisingly, the reaction of the waking passengers to the news that they had arrived at Rorque 4, rather than Zeta Kotlin, was an extremely mixed one, ranging all the way from outright rebellious anger to a quietly assured appreciation for the new arrangements that had been organised. Those of the former were extremely dismayed at the thought of working under a system driven entirely by a system of corporate profit, whilst those of the latter were quietly pleased to have avoided what they considered to be the stifling egalitarianism of Zeta Kotlin.

Whatever their opinions, though, there was initially little they could do to alter their newfound situation – as Alex and Anna had calculated. Once recovered from the effects of stasis, and - at least temporarily - reconciled to this new reality, their thoughts turned to their new lives and careers; to where they would live, their prospects for employment, possible promotions, the size of their departments and their budgets, and how employable their particular field of research would make them. Whatever their exact thoughts on these matters, within a matter of days they were all soon housed within temporary university accommodation. Over the course of the following weeks, interviews were conducted with each individual in order to ascertain their employment prospects, and the exact positions, roles and salaries they would receive within the two corporations.

The situation with regards to the six Margallans who had accompanied their stasis ship into space in order to return it to Margalla – and deliberately woken from stasis late in the disembarking process - went distinctly less well. All six had volunteered for the journey since they possessed a range of personal reasons for wanting to visit Zeta Kotlin or experience space travel. Their plan had been to spend some months on the socialist planet pursuing their respective interests, and then return the ship safely to Margalla once these had been completed. The discovery that they had instead arrived at Rorque 4 was met with utter dismay and then anger towards Anna Dubois, once the reality of their situation became fully apparent. The fact that they had been forced to journey to a planet they held in complete disdain and with no prior consultation whatsoever, was particularly annoying. Little did they realise that matters would actually significantly deteriorate even further for them.

Anna Dubois had, of course, anticipated all this and was long gone by the time they were woken from stasis. She had hurriedly left the starship - determined to negotiate for a senior position with her new employer – several days before they had been finally woken from stasis. Their dark mood only worsened when they additionally discovered that Rorque 4 had – as they had always hoped – been unaware of the Margallan's existence, though this was clearly now no longer the case. To make matters worse, their ship was also in need of some significant maintenance and in need of refueling, and they discovered they were expected to pay for any assistance or materials they received from the Rorque Corporation. For a people that hailed from a civilisation with a non-money economy and with no direct experience of employment, this was a significant problem. The corporation did, however, offer them some form of temporary accommodation and loaned them a small amount of credit, albeit begrudgingly, and only after the intervention of the Alphan scientists. The six Margallans now needed to decide what their next move would be.

Ur-Tokar – the semi-frozen planet

Of the assorted planetary systems in the Nexus Cluster, the one surrounding the diminutive red dwarf star of Rogan was clearly one of the more interesting. Considering the relatively small size of the star, it had, nevertheless, still managed to acquire a varied and eclectic array of orbiting bodies. In addition to a range of asteroid belts of different size and densities, it contained something in the region of fifteen different planets and dwarf planets, though with the exception of a couple of moderately-sized gaseous globes, all of these were relatively small in size – mostly small rocky affairs or ice dwarves.

Equally, the system was one of the more challenging of the cluster when it came to the matter of establishing human habitation. The inner-most planets were very close to Rogan and tidally locked, with one side of the planet always facing the diminutive star. In terms of habitation for humans these were clearly non-starters - one side of the planet being far too hot, and the other side being far too cold to exist upon. This was also likewise for the more distant rocky and ice planets towards the outer regions of the stellar system, which were far too icebound and frozen for any serious consideration to be made with regards to establishing a planetary residence upon them.

This left three closely spaced and moderately sized rocky planets, all verging towards the outer edge of the Goldilocks zone. All three possessed water and showed recent signs of volcanic activity; it was just that on the outer two the water was almost permanently frozen within massive sprawling ice caps that spread equator-wards smothering their mountainous land-surfaces. With more advanced technology and masochistic levels of determination, they might have sustained small populations, albeit in semi-permanently freezing conditions. This left Ur-Tokar, the inner-most of the three; cold but only permanently frozen at the poles and the higher temperate latitudes. The 'genesis pod' arriving at Rogan had deemed it potentially habitable - though not its two sister planets - and had carried out the standard procedures for terra-forming the planet as best it could - then announcing this achievement to the approaching tide of humanity.

Ur-Tokar had clearly experienced considerably lengthy periods of glaciation in both its recent and distant past, though in the present period it was experiencing a relatively warmer interglacial interregnum. It was perhaps for this reason, that tree growth had proven particularly vigorous, in contrast to many of the planets encountered by the 'genesis pods'. The glacial moraines deposited by the retreating glaciers readily mixed with the organic matter brought by the 'genesis pod', and in the planet's wet, cool and semi-mountainous equatorial zones, great swathes of the land were slowly but steadily covered by a mixture of spruce, fir, pine, rowan, oak and silver birch. In the drier more tundra-like climes of the mid-latitudes, goat willow and dwarf hazel formed the predominant shrub-type.

When the first stasis ship speculatively arrived in the stellar system, whole regions of Ur-Tokar already resembled vast tracts of northern Canada, Siberia and Scandinavia before runaway climate change had utterly changed these landscapes in the second half of the twenty-first century. In the following years, a number of ships arrived, though few chose to stay. For some arrivees, the cold and mountainous planet offered poor prospects or did not meet their specific requirements, and so they moved on to search for destinations that looked significantly more promising. For others, the stasis ships that had first colonised Ur-Tokar had brought a strange combination of settlers, who appeared to be developing a distinctly unpromising civilisation. This in itself proved sufficient for the awakened skeleton crews to opt for a further destination and another prolonged period of stasis journeying across space.

Ur-Tokar – history

The known history of Ur-Tokar was far from a precise affair, and the main features it focused upon, differed considerably within its two disparate communities. Amongst the Mountain People, the accounts of its unfolding constituted a significant section of their folklore, and much had been incorporated into their varied and rich cultural traditions and heritage. There were, additionally, learned figures within their community who kept an account or chronicle of events as they unfolded, but these were very much a personal affair, and their contents may or may not have been more widely known amongst the wider population.

History was not an important subject for their people, and neither was it for their schoolchildren – ranking far behind ecologism in the amount of time dedicated to the subject in the schoolroom. This was perhaps unsurprising given that the history of the planet was a relatively short one; and since the break with the monarchists there had been little in the way of significant developments, until the recent outbreak of unrest between the two peoples. More importantly, though, the Mountain People placed far greater import on the cyclical variations of the seasons and the flora and fauna that existed within them, than – in their opinion - the dubious importance of any possible linear chronicle that might have been experienced by their people.

By contrast, for the Monarchists, their official history – carefully and precisely written down in the royal chronicles – was that of the writings of scholars working directly for the monarch of the day. These were subject to regular revision as each different monarch attained the throne, overseeing a reworking of historical accounts that would show them in a much better historical light, whilst their erstwhile competitors and adversaries were treated in the opposite manner. Whilst certain important monarchist traditions had lasted throughout the entire period and delivered a sense of continuity within the chronicles, these intermittent revisions had meant a somewhat disjointed and uneven picture of their past had been established. Those children who were schooled – from the wealthiest sections of the population – received only a version of history officially approved by the present monarch and thus one that was far from historically accurate.

The following account is an amalgamation drawn together from both traditions, and pieced together by the visiting crews of the Opa-Loka, established during their unexpectedly prolonged visits to the planet.

The original settlers of Ur-Tokar - all part of the later waves that constituted the mass exodus from Earth - derived from a widely diverse range of political and religious beliefs. Nevertheless, they did all share one feature in common – a general dislike of modern civilisation, and, in particular, a specific disdain for modern technology. In the latter parts of twenty-first century Earth, it had become increasingly obvious to many that modern civilisation had little hope of surviving in its then present guise. A proliferation of anti-modernist movements had been launched - often led by charismatic leaders promising their disenfranchised followers untold rewards on both heaven and Earth - and a number of these had temporarily flourished during the period of the great exodus into space.

These prophets of doom invariably, and unsurprisingly, blamed the climate catastrophe on a range of features associated with twentieth and twenty first century economies and their associated institutions, processes and products. Chief amongst these was what they coined 'the iron dream' - the process of industrialisation, mass production and the development of modern technology. These, they strongly believed, had brought widespread devastation to the many varied ecosystems and habitats that had so enriched the planet for nearly half a billion years. Mixed in with such beliefs were added an eclectic dislike of urbanisation, secularism, godlessness and overpopulation amongst others - all of which had contributed in some way to the armageddon faced by non-human life on the doomed planet.

Whatever their particular and exact theoretical or theological approach, they all believed that humanity would need to return to a more simplified way of living, and each particular movement developed its own specific strategy as to how they would put this primitivism into actual practice. For the majority, this simply meant finding locations on planet Earth that might escape the worst of the floods, droughts, fires and heat-waves, establishing themselves in these safe refuges and reverting back to their chosen more primitive lifestyle. In practice, this tended to mean locations where they could escape the increasing heat – northerly latitudes or high altitude mountain valleys.

However, occupying land on a planet on which it was in increasingly short supply – and thus increasingly expensive or fiercely fought over - was far from straightforward or easy, and a belief that life on Earth in the short term was simply doomed, meant that breakaway sections of some of these movements often opted for the 'stellar alternative'. The irony of using advanced space technology to transport them to their non-technological utopias was, of course, not lost on their detractors, but expedient excuses could always be found, and so - as with so many other social movements of that time – the anti-technologists, frequently led by someone they believed to be the last messiah on Earth, joined the mass exodus into space.

Whether it was pure coincidence that a number of these ships - having travelled many light years across inter-stellar space - all homed in on Ur-Tokar, or whether its distinctive properties somehow displayed a particular appeal to this type of departee, was still a matter of continuing speculation. For the religious groups it was, of course, divine providence that had led them to their promised land; for the other settlers there were usually more pressing matters for them to consider than worrying about such esoteric concerns.

Whatever the exact reasons were that had brought them collectively together on Ur-Tokar, the initial process of colonising their newly-found world had progressed reasonably smoothly. The eclectic mix of groupings had all set about implementing their pre-modern blueprints in their own specific manner. The predominant settlement-type of the settlers was small village communities, though in some of the more favourable locations small towns were eventually established. Others - typically of a Deep Green ideological leaning - had headed to some of the remoter parts of the equatorial regions and established more isolated settlements – an eclectic array of log cabins, homesteads, hamlets and small villages set amongst the forested mountains. The religious communities – whether pantheist or monotheist – had almost invariably established semi-isolated monastic orders and settlements, devoting themselves to a life of keeping domestic animals, growing crops, fruit and vegetables and worshipping their particular god or set of gods.

In the beginning - and indeed ever since - there had been an explicit agreement amongst the entirety of the settlers that it was essential – if they were to avoid repeating the damaging mistakes carried out on Earth – that their newfound communities must rely on only low-level technologies. The exact way in which this idea was implemented varied from community to community, and ranged from the fairly pragmatic to quite extreme levels of technological rejection. And, with the timber of the widespread forests plentifully available to them, together with the natural rocks and ores of the planet, a low technology existence was not a particular difficult one to establish. Houses could be built from stone and wood and any other readily available materials. The landing craft that had brought them to Ur-Tokar's surface were effectively recycled - stripped of all useful materials, particularly the metal ones, which were initially difficult to acquire. This also had the added advantage of removing any temptation that might arise to use the stasis ships, which had all been left in continuous orbit around the planet. In addition, all AI units had been left behind on the orbiting ships.

Most of the communities quickly settled into some form of existence based on small-scale farming, typically a mixture of arable and livestock farming interspersed with fruit orchards and vegetable plots. This was especially the case for those communities located in the valley lowlands. In this respect, the settlers of Ur-Tokar were almost unique amongst the vast numbers of stasis ships partaking in the exodus from Earth, in that they deliberately transported large domestic animals with them with the intention of making them a key part their new existence. Almost all the other stasis ships had rejected this option – preferring to rely on the mini-fabs, ultra-modern ferming units, and plant-based sources of nutrition.

Space on the starships had often been at a premium – and in some cases very expensive - and many of the departing organisations had only allowed humans to enter stasis. Additionally, the science of placing non-human animals into stasis was not yet fully proven – research had been overwhelmingly devoted to the requirements of humans – raising both ethical and viability concerns. Finally, given that twenty first century advances in technology had rendered domestic animals largely surplus to requirements – no longer needed for food, clothing or as beasts of burden – there seemed little reason to add an additional layer of complexity to an already complicated array of difficulties facing Earth's departees. Large domestic animals were generally not taken on the starships. For those starships that did transport non-human life-forms, the animals chosen were usually selected on the basis of durability, amenability to humans and on the basis that they would be needed to form viable ecosystems.

Two of the stasis ships arriving at Ur-Tokar had taken a distinctly different approach to the rest of the arriving settlers on the planet. Although determined to break with the technology of the modern Earth era, their particular philosophy also envisaged a return to pre-capitalist forms of economy, and thus anticipated the need to farm large domestic animals to meet their various needs and requirements. Accordingly, they had placed a range of young domestic animals into specially adapted stasis pods, and those that had survived the rigours of the journey and stasis were to form a key part of their agrarian livelihoods. These people were the feudalist settlers who were not only opposed to modern technology, but also to the various political and social structures that had accompanied it.

For these backward-looking groups, humanity had taken a disastrously wrong turn when the transition from feudalism to capitalism had been effected on Earth from the seventeenth century onwards. Until this point in time - as far as they were concerned -the human race had lived in relative peace with nature and the planet. It had been the invention of steam power, factories, modern transport, large cities, robot culture and democratic and secular regimes that had ultimately led to climate catastrophe. They deplored the abandonment of the traditional structures and ways of life – the decline of religion, aristocracy, monarchy and patriarchy. These latter they considered to be natural and fully sustainable, and thus essential for any society seeking to avoid a further catastrophic climate breakdown.

It had always been their intention to effect a full return to these feudal structures, and the rudimentary beginnings of such a feudal system had been established right from the earliest colonisation. However, after first landing, there had been a host of other more pressing - largely economic - priorities and early developments in the political realm had been implemented with a light touch. Those with very different political persuasions, such as the Deep Ecologists and some of the pantheist religious groupings, had eyed the monarchists with some degree of caution, but in the very earliest days of planetary settlement had seen little that readily alarmed them, certainly nothing of the dangerous vision that was to later blight their communities.

For these more esoteric groupings, it was the modern technology and mass production associated with an anthropomorphic set of philosophies placing humans before nature, that had caused the eventual destruction of life on planet Earth. The essential feature, for these groups, was to work with nature and not against it; and so for them the social and political structures of modernity were not necessarily a problem. They had no particular attachments to a secular, democratic and egalitarian society, but neither did they have any particular problems with it wither. For these groupings, the all-important criteria was to apply an ecocentric philosophy to whatever undertakings they pursued. Some of these groups, nevertheless, anticipated future political problems with the feudalists and headed for remoter areas in the forested mountains.

As the years passed by though, and the planet's differing communities increasingly consolidated themselves beyond what had initially been a tenuous existence, the monarchist forces began to assert themselves in a far more aggressive manner. Strict feudal hierarchies were devised as the leaders of the various exodus groupings established themselves as ruling aristocrats, and eventually a monarch emerged from amongst these self-appointed leaders, capable of commanding the loyalty of these ruling families, and of ruling this particular world of tiers. It was this first monarch, King Gustav, who, relatively early in his reign, decided to stamp his authority on all the peoples of the planet. Believing himself to have been chosen by divine providence, he saw no reason as to why he should not expect the loyalty and servility of all the planet's inhabitants, and irrespective of their previous loyalties. After all, he announced to all around him, he was of royal blood and they were mere commoners.

The issue he chose to enforce this act of loyalty was, not surprisingly, one concerning the issue of technology – close to the hearts of all of Ur-Tokar's colonists. The monarchists had dogmatically banned the complete use of electricity in all its various forms within their own communities, but some of the other groupings had maintained a low level usage of the phenomena. As long as the means by which it was generated was renewable and sustainable, and did not damage nature in any significant way, then it was considered acceptable for use in heating, lighting and for any other purposes they felt were appropriate. King Gustav decreed the use of electricity completely outlawed upon the pain of death. His reasons for doing so were largely political and for the purposes of seizing power - though there was always the possibility that the other planetary groupings might use it for subversive communication purposes, both amongst themselves and even possibly to connect with other planets through the use of the satellite system that still orbited the planet. There were thus beneficial security side effects.

The enforcement of the decree was seen for what it really was by the other groupings, and a series of conflicts broke out between the different civilisations. After only a few weeks of fighting though, the monarchists proved to be the better organised and stronger of the competing forces, and the other disparate groupings increasingly found themselves forced into the mountains or remoter regions of the landscape if they wanted to preserve their freedoms. Those failing to do so entered an undesired life of serfdom and servitude. The monarchists lacked the numbers, resources and, of course, the technology to fully control all the sparsely inhabited areas of Ur-Tokar, but they maintained dominion over much of the lowlands and the relatively more densely populated sections of the land – in reality, a few dozen small towns and scores of scattered villages.

These events all occurred during the first twenty five years of the planet's inhabited history, and little of substance was to change in the nature of society on Ur-Tokar in the intervening years. The monarchist system had established its superior position on the planet and – using ancient chronicles they had brought with them from Earth – attempted to replicate medieval feudal society as closely as physically possible. Strict hierarchical structures were constructed and maintained, adhering tightly to the traditional customs and practices historically established. The aristocratic families dominated in all areas - militarily, politically, culturally, socially and economically. They kept the best lands for themselves, with a bonded peasantry forced to labour for them in the fields, whilst the more compliant religious communities were brought under the control of the monarch to offer a spiritual dimension to their existence. However, despite these efforts – or perhaps because of them - the population of these areas barely increased. In the absence of scientific knowledge and modern technology, famines were frequent and occasional epidemics spread rapidly through the towns and villages, leaving widespread death in their wake.

Meanwhile, the Mountain People, as they became to be known, scattered across the more disparate parts of the continent. Despite their marginalised status, they were still eventually able to achieve a settled and reasonably affluent existence, largely homed in scattered mountain hamlets and assorted homesteads. Theirs was a more profound attachment to the land and environment; a concerted attempt to live sustainably in conjunction with nature, imparting only a minimal impact on the lands upon which they settled. Their loosely scattered societies were more pluralistic and egalitarian than the monarchies of the lowlands, often infused with a pantheist spiritualism and reverence for the land and nature. Whilst adhering to a low technology existence, they were somewhat more adaptable, flexible and inventive than the lowland-living monarchists, since their communities did not share an attachment to the suffocating traditional customs that so inflicted the monarchist society.

Nevertheless, despite these differences, what both communities did share was a way of life that effectively saw their societies become frozen in time. Neither was willing or able to substantially change in any significant direction; both because of their dislike of advanced technology, but one because of its reverence for nature, and the other because of its reverence for hierarchy and its feudal possession of the land. Because of these limitations, neither society was able to substantially increase its population, and so their relative impacts on the one large continent of Ur-Tokar that was actually habitable, remained peripheral at best. Most of the Ur-Tokar created by the 'genesis pods' remained as a pristine wilderness – unaffected by the actual physical arrival of humans.

At least, that was the case until recent times, as the relationship between the two very different communities becoming increasingly fraught, and with one very simple explanation for this increased tension and conflict. The venerated customs and traditions so beloved of the monarchists required an assorted variety of metals – iron, copper, gold and silver amongst various others – but these had always been subject to shortages of supply. Attempts to locate mineral-rich lodes in the mountains had never been particularly successful – especially as they had dispensed with any form of modern technology. And, once the two communities effectively parted, it had become even more difficult for the monarchists to prospect for and mine ore-laden rock seams in the mountainous areas of the continent, domains in which their presence was generally undesired and unwanted.

From the earliest of days, the monarchists – aware of these resource deficiencies - had reluctantly struck up an uneasy relationship with a Zetan trading starship to acquire certain desired raw materials, even though it jarred with their anti-technology beliefs. The relationship had never been a particularly amenable one, and in recent years, it had also become increasingly difficult and fractious. The monarchists had increasingly come to the belief that the ship was deceiving them in some manner - though they were not sure exactly how this was being done – and were looking for ways to end the trading relationship. In order to achieve this, they had set about prospecting for metals in the mountains with renewed vigour, and had decided to remove any of the Mountain People who happened to be unfortunate enough to get in their way. This was the source of the recent conflict between the two peoples.

Arrival in Utopia

Rorque 4 – Margallans initial arrival

The six Margallans who had volunteered to accompany The Spirit of the Age to Zeta Kotlin, but who now found themselves orbiting the entirely different planet of Rorque 4 instead, spent their first few days after being woken from stasis aboard the starship deciding on how next to proceed. They had deliberately been the last people on the spacecraft to be brought out of stasis, and as such, Anna Dubois and the rest of her skeleton crew were long gone by the time they were awoken.

Once recovered from stasis, they engaged in a series of slightly bewildered discussions in order to assess their unexpected and unwanted situation, and with the intention of deciding collectively what their next moves should be. This was accompanied by the crew members also getting to know each other significantly better, since most of them actually knew little of each other, since they hailed from three different islands; though given the nature and size of the small population on the Margallan Archipelago they had all occasionally encountered each other at social or other occasions, so were not complete strangers. They also became more familiar with the reasons as to why each one of them had volunteered for the journey.

Akiko had joined the group largely because of her desire to meet up with environmental scientists on Zeta Kotlin and to exchange ideas and theories with them. She knew their work was far in advance of her own and she hoped to garner ideas from both the people and the ecosystems of that planet. Her aim had been to carry out fieldwork on the planet that might help her understand the problems she was encountering of understanding life systems on Margalla. Her discovery that they had instead arrived at Rorque 4 was a major shock and disappointment, and she was struggling to see how she could salvage anything from this unfortunate turn of events. She had already scanned Rorque 4 and discovered it consisted mostly of land with only a few shallow seas – quite unlike the oceans on Margalla and Zeta Kotlin – and so of limited use for her studies.

Zhavia and Zek were sometimes mistaken for brothers, but to the best of their knowledge this was not actually the case – at least biologically speaking. Both of them, though, had curly brown hair, were of a similar height and were quite thin and rangy in stature. They had spent much of their childhood growing up together in the same communes, moving locations at the same time, and sharing the same interests and mutual friends; and it was also for this reason that they often seemed so alike. As with all other Margallans, they had been left free to develop their own interests and shape their own education once the educational basics had been learnt. Together they had both developed a keen interest in computers, gaming, science fiction and anything and everything relating to space travel and foreign worlds, in fact, the more exotic the better. They were thus both keen astronomers and cosmologists, though in the amateurish way that was the norm for all personal interests on Margalla.

At their commune in Maknon, where they had resided until very recently, there had been few others who shared their specific interests, and, though they enjoyed relationships with many of their community, they had always gravitated back towards each other, spending large amounts of time indulging in their shared passions. When the opportunity to actually travel into space had arisen they had unsurprisingly jumped at the prospect. Given that few other Margallans shared their interests, or a desire to leave their utopian existence, they had little trouble becoming part of the crew on The Spirit of The Age.

They had made occasional visits to The Spirit of the Age before this journey, and had often dreamed of travelling through space with the aim of seeing its many wonders, but probably more to simply just get a feel for the actual experience of being deep within space itself, than for any other specific reason. Thus, arrival at Rorque 4 was not too much of a problem for them initially, for they had taken the opportunity to have a good look at Eleutheria's whole planetary system whilst they were orbiting Rorque 4, an experience that had resulted in more questions than answers as far as they were concerned.

Kiyona had joined the group as she had felt guilty about giving away the existence of the Margallan people's existence to the scientists on board the Web Weaver. Slightly darker skinned than most Margallans, with a largely innocent looking face, a quirky sense of humour and a broad range of changing hairstyles and dress senses, Kiyona had enjoyed the typical carefree childhood of any Margallan child. She barely knew her parents - only through their occasional fleeting visits to the commune she was residing in – though this was not unusual on Margalla. Slightly more unusually, she had remained largely at the same commune throughout, with only occasional stays in a small number of others. Her friends had come and gone over the years as they chose to move around, but she had chosen not to do so.

Typically for a young person on Margalla, she had enjoyed a number of relationships with both sexes, though none had lasted for particularly long. Equally, she moved regularly between interests, none seeming to hold her attention for long either. Her place of abode seemed to be the only major continuity in her life. She had thus acquired a reputation, amongst her fellow communards, for being somewhat skittish – lacking any profound or long-term engagement in her activities - and for taking only a passing interest in most subjects. On a world like Margalla, with its live and let live ethos, this was not particularly problematic, but she frequently found she could not contribute much to the long and intense conversations that were common at Margallan social gatherings.

As she had moved into her twenties, she became increasingly self-aware of these perceived shortcomings, and a desire to change for the better had developed within her. The only problem was, she had discovered, was that she was unsure as to what subjects to become more interested and engaged in, or even how to go about effecting such a profound change. In this respect, the incident with the Web Weaver thus threw her something of a life-line. Suddenly she had a project she could immerse herself in. She felt she needed to make amends for her error, and helping the rest of the crew return their ship back to Margalla seemed as good as anything else she could think of doing. Arrival at Rorque 4, she initially believed, did not effectively alter her plans in any significant way, and might actually offer additional opportunities to redeem herself.

In contrast to Kiyona, Xander was tall and slim with a shock of ginger hair, blue eyes and pale skin. As such, he was not particularly suited to the sub-tropical climate of Margalla and tended to mainly socialise in the early mornings and evenings. This meant he spent far more times inside than the average Margallan and he had developed a penchant for all things electronic. He was particularly adept at helping to repair and improve AI units when this became necessary, was a keen gamer, excellent with computers and a big fan of old Earth entertainment emissions. He had watched all the old classics and considered himself to be pretty familiar with its ancient culture. He had decided to join the crew because he was something of an expert with computers and communication systems, and whilst the ship and the AI units were entirely automated and self-functioning, he believed there was always the possibility that his skills might be needed if the unexpected was to occur.

Even by the relaxed standards of Margalla, Arlo was considered by his fellows as easy going, care-free and open-minded and a bit of a space cadet, in the more metaphorical sense. He was well-liked and often popular, but enjoyed few deep-seated relationships, whilst most of those he did engage in were with other young men of a similar age. He found it supremely easy to mix with others - of almost any sort - and was highly sociable. His main interest was other people and he frequently travelled around the archipelago making new friends and acquaintances.

Over the years, Arlo had also become attracted to various esoteric philosophies and beliefs, many of which related to astronomy, the inter-stellar exodus of the human race and a firm belief that intelligent alien life would eventually be found somewhere in the galaxy. Arlo had frequently combined his love of space and use of hallucinogenic drugs - the use of mind-altering drugs was a common feature of Margallan culture, though, unlike Arlo, most used them in moderation and for largely social purposes - in combination and the chance of flying across space whilst stoned in order to meet new friends on Zeta Kotlin had particularly appealed to him, though the long periods spent in stasis meant this was not something he had actually managed to achieve yet in any significant way.

Arlo was basically something of a dreamer and was of the opinion that there was nothing as fantastical and romantic as travelling in deep space. As the discussions involving their newly discovered dilemma developed, Kiyona thought he was one of the most charming people she had ever met, but could not help feeling he would not be much use in an emergency, or if they encountered any significant difficulties on Rorque 4.

Thrown together in unexpected circumstances, the six Margallans not only needed to make sense of their newfound situation, but to also forge friendships with each other and make assessments of who possessed which useful skills and talents that might help them resolve their difficult situation. Fortunately, this was something the islanders spent much of their lifetimes engaged in, frequently travelling around the islands, establishing and exploring new relationships and engaging in any activities that arose during the course of these wanderings. As such, they initially felt confident they would quickly resolve their newfound dilemma and soon be on their way home.

A short while after recovering from stasis, the crew was strapped into reclining black padded chairs seated around a small conference table they had recently shifted into the viewing deck. Scattered around the table were an array of drinking and eating devices designed for use in low gravity situations. The viewing decks of the stasis ships had been designed to offer a panoramic view of what lay around the starships, and so the backdrop to their discussion, as they repeatedly orbited the planet, were the slowly shifting clouds, continents and shallow seas of Rorque 4. The room itself was a largely steel-grey and black affair, containing little in the way of fixtures, simply a large number of chairs and small tables, designed in order to maximize viewing conditions for crew and passengers who wished to pass their time star and planet gazing.

'So I assume Anna Dubois simply took control of the ship's computer and reprogrammed a new destination, and the AI units were given instructions to comply accordingly. After all, we only ever use open access systems – we all had general access to them - so it was supremely easy for her to take control of the ship. It never even occurred to me that anyone would do something like that,' stated Akiko, smoothing back her silky black hair, and still trying to come to terms with what had actually occurred to them. 'Do you think she even consulted with anyone? She certainly never asked us. Surely we have the right to decide where we travel to. It's not her decision.'
'Well, we've never had any reason to mistrust anyone on Margalla before – not on that kind of scale anyway - so we all enjoy complete rights of access to all computer systems, which are all effectively communal anyway. Basically we trust each other, and had no reason to believe they were any different,' added Xander, also trying to make sense of the situation. 'When we depart from this place, we need to strengthen the security protocols to make sure

the same occurrence doesn't happen again. I can sort all that out when we've finished here, and provide you all with the access codes,' he added helpfully.

'I really think she should know what we think about her. It's totally unacceptable what she did to us,' stated Kiyona, after finishing a long drink from one of the liquid-containing canisters. 'Is there any chance of us catching up with Anna and letting her know what we think about her behaviour?'

'Probably not; where would we find her . . . what good would it do? I can't imagine what she would do to rectify the situation,' replied Zhavia. 'We need to concentrate more on how we're going to get away from this place. What's the present condition of the ship? How long will it take to make it ready for the return journey?'

'Well, it's not as bad as it was when we first arrived. The AI units are pre-programmed to inspect and repair the starship after long voyages. They're already working on the maintenance and repair routines and it's looking like two to three weeks for these to be fully completed', answered Xander, who had earlier spent several hours working his way through the ship's latest data reports. 'Our main problem is a significant shortage of rocket fuel; we need to acquire more to be sure of a safe return to Margalla.'

'But we didn't actually come very far – compared with the ship's initial journey across the galaxy from Earth, I mean – so how come we've used up so much fuel?' asked Akiko, somewhat puzzled and suddenly aware that their departure might be considerably delayed. She stared out at the planet they were orbiting and wondered what the world below was actually like. So far, it looked as though it would be of little use to her, and the prospect of a prolonged stay was not particularly appealing.

'Most fuel is used in the acceleration away from the planet and then reversing the engines on arrival. The actual journey uses relatively limited amounts of fuel. In addition, on long galactic journeys, the starships have supplementary systems to boost their energy levels. I suspect Anna Dubois never gave this issue any thought, and fuel levels have been allowed to run low,' explained Zek, as he munched his way through one of the protein bars left behind by the Alphan scientists. 'That's probably why we have a problem now.'

'So what does the ship actually run on, what do we need?' asked Akiko, her attention now returned to the rest of the crew.

'It's a hydrogen-based plasma propulsion system. It's the standard one used by all the stasis ships that left Earth, as far as I am aware. We should be able to obtain supplies from Rorque 4. The ship's computers have registered the existence of active stasis ships in orbit around the planet, so they must have the necessary fuel supplies at hand,' answered Xander. 'We've already received some strange looking messages from the Rorque Corporation offering to sell us the fuel.'

'They want us to pay for the fuel! How are we going to do that? We don't have any money! That's not a fair way of doing things,' stated Kiyona, completely perplexed as to how they would go about achieving this, and beginning to realise that their situation was more complex than she had originally thought. Any thought of rapidly returning home to Margalla was beginning to dissipate.

'Anyone got any ideas on how we could go about achieving that?' Arlo struck up a few moments later, making his first contribution to the discussion.

The crew looked blank, and made various exasperated noises. Paying for goods was not an idea they were particularly familiar with, Margalla enjoying a moneyless economy where production and consumption were largely a collectivist affair. They were vaguely familiar with the concept from watching old Earth entertainment emissions, and were aware that some other planets used such systems, but they were not sure of the finer details of how such an economic system actually worked in practice.

'Maybe we could get Anna Dubois to pay for it – she sought of owes us one, really,' Kiyona interjected a couple of minutes later, believing she'd had something of a brainstorm. 'She's presumably at a Rorque Corporation university right now, probably being paid large amounts of money. She must be feeling at least slightly guilty about what she's done to us. We could land on the planet with an aim to visiting her and see if we can persuade her to help us. She really ought to. After all, it's her fault we are in this predicament in the first place,' she added optimistically.

Margallan culture tended not to place great amounts of blame on individuals for the mistakes and errors they made – or indeed their achievements - seeing each and every person as a product of their collective culture - their actions and behaviour resulting from a shared upbringing and the product of a collective community endeavor. In general, it was seen as the responsibility of the whole community to fix the errors made by individuals. However, in this particular case, the crew was entirely in agreement with Kiyona, and made various noises of agreement.

'Well anyway, I'm bored of being on this ship, I'm sure we all are, and I'm really struggling with low gravity. Nothing works the way it ought to,' added Kiyona. 'I know Rorque 4 has a poor reputation, but it can't be as bad as people say, surely. We could descend to the planet and see what we can sort out and have a look around at the same time. We can't actually come all this way and not visit the planet guys,' she offered optimistically. 'Anyone against this idea . . .' she looked around the faces of the crew, 'no . . . well let's see what we can manage then? Maybe we can find Anna and sort something out.'

Once the decision had been made, the crew then made enquiries about how they could go about effecting it. In the end, it took the best part of a day to locate someone sufficiently senior within the Rorque Corporation to deal with their situation, and even longer for them to agree to an arrangement that even partially suited their needs. Eventually the corporation agreed to accommodate the Margallans in a hotel somewhere on the outskirts of Rorque City whilst they organised their refuelling issue. During the process, though, they gained the distinct perception that the corporation was only acting very begrudgingly and seemed almost completely uninterested in their predicament. They all knew decisions and actions on Margalla, at times, could move quite slowly – since often the collective community needed to arrive at an agreement together – but decision-making on Rorque 4 seemed to be particularly slow. They assumed that the corporation must be a very large one, so needed more time to agree upon important or unfamiliar matters.

Once organised, they flew their landing craft to the spaceport at Mirivan and arrived on a very warm sultry evening, just as Eleutheria was setting in a pinkish-yellow sky. They had been loaned a small amount of credit by the corporation, and collected the devices needed to activate this at the spaceport. Once they had been instructed on how to use these, they were able to board and pay for the autocar waiting for them, which would then transport them to the hotel they had been placed in. As the vehicle passed smoothly but silently at a steadily maintained speed through the darkening

218

streets on the outskirts of the city, they could not help but notice and remark upon just how shabby, run-down and dilapidated almost every house, street, and amenity area they passed actually looked. None of them had ever seen anything like it. They wondered how any community could actually allow their environment to descend into such a poor state. It was at this point that the crew began to wonder what they had allowed themselves to get into.

Arrival in Utopia

Rorque 4 – dealing with the scientists

Shortly before this, Ralph Parker had been sat - fortunately for him - in a comfy chair on the top floor of the Rorque Corporation's impressive city headquarters, listening to a lengthy list of instructions from the chief executive, Colin Jamieson. Jamieson was explaining at great length how he expected Parker to deal with the scientists who had arrived on the Margallan spaceship. In reality, Jamieson could simply have transmitted a voicemail to his subordinate, but issuing orders in person - as Parker himself well knew - gave an impression of authority that speaking to a computer could never hope to replicate. Parker also knew he would receive a recorded version of the instructions at some point in the near future, and was beginning to lose the ability to concentrate much further, though safe in the knowledge that this was unlikely to prove to be a problem for him.

Instead, his attention drifted to Jamieson's appearance and demeanour. Several years younger than Parker, he was a member of the sharp-suited ultra-free-market brigade that had entered the business world, perhaps fifteen years or so after Parker's own generation had done so. He was clearly ultra-ambitious and highly competitive and this, combined with his acerbic and easily irritated personality, meant he never suffered fools gladly. Parker somewhat resented the younger man's seniority over him, but was aware enough to realise that Jamieson was a far more driven man than himself, and was thus more likely to have been selected for rapid promotion, even if it was also true that he had been to a far more expensive Liberty School than the one Parker had attended. His mind drifted back to Jamieson's lengthy exposition.

'Now that the scientists are all safely ensconced at our universities, though I'm using the word 'scientist' in the loosest sense of the term here - as some of them just seem to be dreamers lost in obscure and useless theoretical science, whilst others are clearly cloud nine philosophers or left-wing social scientists engaged in all manner of academic gobbledygook. We need to establish which ones are actually useful to the corporation. We don't want anyone involved in all that quark, strangeness and charm nonsense; what we need are people who can actually contribute to inventing new innovative products that will sell profitably on the markets. We need scientists who are engaged in proper practical science, engineering and technology – useful science. Who knows, we might even find one who can invent an orgone accumulator that actually works,' he added sarcastically, 'now that would be a revelation!'

Jamieson had spent his whole working life dealing with a wide range of technicians and experts, and he had arrived at the conclusion that they were all inclined to use their supposedly more-learned status to indicate how indispensable they were to the corporation, at the same time indicating just how essential it was that they retained their positions, whilst also expecting better pay and working conditions. Equally, he had spent much of his working career replacing them with AI units wherever possible, in an attempt to prove them completely wrong. Jamieson had not been the most able of students at school, and had carried a grudge against the class of student who performed more highly than himself, long into his adult years.

'They all need to be interviewed thoroughly and at considerable length,' he continued. 'Those that are clearly useful to the company should be put on short-term contracts, assigned to a particular university and department, and commence work as soon as logistically possible. We will review their progress after six months, and those that have demonstrated their utility to the corporation should be retained on longer-term contracts, which we will determine at the time.'

He paused for a moment, walked around the room briefly, spent a while looking out the window and then returned to his desk. Parker was not sure why he had actually engaged in this short performance, but figured, that by keeping him waiting, it was probably some exercise in demonstrating his seniority. Parker tended to hold as much disdain for those above him, as he did for those below him, but was wise enough to know he needed to keep on the better side of his superiors. He simply said nothing, looked attentive and waited.

'Those we do not want to keep – and unfortunately I think this will prove to be a great many - should be offered short-term loans at a medium rate of interest to tide them over for the near future. We can offer them accommodation in some of our cheaper residences – for which they will have to pay rent, of course – and once they have secured some other form of

221

employment, they can start paying the loans back immediately to the corporation.'

Parker had wondered exactly what the plan would be for those failing to make the grade, and was slightly surprised by what, he considered, was actually quite a generous offer by the corporation's recent standards of employment. The Rorque Corporation owned many subsidiary companies, so maybe Jamieson thought they could secure employment in any one of these, and eventually prove to be of some use to the corporation, he figured.

'Make sure the senior officials amongst the scientists receive contracts. There's bound to be some form of rebellion by those who are refused contracts, but without any leaders it should amount to nothing once the fuss has died down. If the senior officials eventually prove to be inadequate, we can simply let them go later. By that point, I'm sure any trouble will have died down. You'll need to deal closely with that Dubois woman – I believe you've already had some dealings with her – but keep an eye on her. Apparently she hijacked the starship without consulting a single person. Someone capable of pulling off a stunt like that might prove very useful, though equally she might prove to be highly problematic. Whichever it turns out to be, we need to be sure we've judged her correctly.'

Parker had, indeed, already met Anna Dubois on two or three occasions, and considered her to be attractive, but perhaps holding too high an opinion of herself – though Parker thought this of a great many people he encountered. His first dealings with her, he believed, had been satisfactorily successful, and the idea of spending time working with her – now officially sanctioned – was something he found particularly appealing.

'The university authorities have already been informed of the procedures I want followed, and it is your role to make sure they are implemented effectively, thoroughly and at the lowest cost feasible. Remember the company can ill-afford to employ the unnecessary and unprofitable - despite our recent endeavours - so make sure you operate within the projected budgets. I expect all this to be completed within a few short weeks.' Jamieson stopped and appeared to have concluded. 'And remember, as I said right from the beginning, it is essential that we locate these rocket scientists as a priority. I believe they have yet to be identified, but once we do so, they need to be assigned to our space programme immediately. Our future probably relies on this. Once you have achieved this, report back to me directly. I want to meet them in person.'

Jamieson finally came to a conclusion, much to Parker's relief, and indicated it was time the subordinate left his office. Parker returned to his own considerably smaller work-station and set about instructing the relevant AI units in initiating the instructions just related to him by Jamieson.

Ralph Parker was slightly on the tall side, well-built with short spiky black hair and a thin moustache and beard. Schooled at one of the semi-privileged medium-ranking all boys Liberty Schools, he had developed a general disdain for those from the upper echelons, whilst also despising and abusing those from lower down the social hierarchy. His father – and his friends - had been boorish, whilst his mother was extremely strict, straight-laced and highly ambitious for him. She had overseen his upbringing and education and placed strict and confining limits on his behaviour to ensure he would do well later in life. Living in an otherwise male-dominated culture, though, he had deeply resented these restrictions, but lacked the courage to directly rebel against his mother, who he generally feared – though an almost pathological fear of ridicule meant he would never have admitted this to anyone.

As such, almost invariably his rebellion against his mother's restrictions had been directed at others, in a classic form of displacement activity. Any other person or social group he took a disliking to – which was much of the population - could become the target of his suppressed frustrations. Despite this, an almost schizophrenic desire to feel both superior, but also to be popular at the same time, meant that he had a tendency to blow both hot and cold – one moment he could be buying you drinks, the next he could turn particularly nasty if his thin-skinned nature left him feeling that that he was being slighted or insulted. As such, many people found him a difficult character to read and most simply avoided him.

He was, however, reasonably intelligent, sometimes hardworking and quite fit and strong - though he had gained a considerable amount of weight as he aged. These qualities, and the connections made at his school, ensured he had found managerial employment in the Rorque Corporation and had –

despite his many personality defects – proven to be a useful character to Colin Jamieson in a number of roles and for several recent purposes.

Over the following weeks, Parker ensured that the process outlined by Jamieson was strictly followed. However, try as he might, he could not locate a single Alphan scientist specialising in rocket science or, indeed, space flight technology of any kind. This failure had slightly worried him in the early days of the process, but he had initially presumed that it must have been the result of some form of oversight. But as the days passed, and more and more interviews were conducted, he started to believe – and become increasingly concerned - that the space flight technologists must have been on the other ship, the Avante, and that they would be working for their great corporate rival, Cosmic Solutions.

Throughout the course of the operation, he had also developed an awareness that Jamieson was becoming increasingly impatient with him, since missives enquiring about the space flight technologists had started arriving on an increasingly frequent basis. Informing Jamieson of the conclusion he had arrived at was not going to be pleasant, and so Parker delayed sending his thoughts on the subject and also started looking for possible scapegoats. When the interview process had finally been concluded – on time and within budget he was pleased to note - Parker mailed through a full report of the entire procedures to Jamieson.

Ultimately, only about forty percent of the academics and scientists interviewed had been considered to be of use to the corporation. Given that the Rorque Corporation had involvements in virtually every major economic activity on the planet – over the decades they had found numerous means of absorbing, neutralising or destroying their competitors – this was considered to be a very disappointing return. Far too many of the academics engaged in highly theoretical or over-specialised fields of research, in subjects that were of no practical or economic usefulness to the corporation. These had not been offered employment.

Despite the low return for their efforts, Parker quietly considered this to be something of a vindication for a personal belief he had always held, for, like Jamieson, he also held a low opinion of the academic community. If academics were left to their own devices, he had always assumed, they would simply engage in some form of intellectual self-indulgence, studying subjects that were simply an exercise in personal gratification, with no consideration as to whether they were useful to the economy or individuals in general. The autonomy which the Alpha Fraczan universities had given to their academics had fully proven his point.

Despite this, his report, he considered, still needed to make sure that he could be seen as blameless in this partial failure, and so it was interspersed with frequent comments indicating that the corporation had been deliberately deceived by the Alphan scientists. His dealings with Anna Dubois had not been as successful as he had originally envisaged – his original opinion of her as too uppity had been proven correct, he had concluded. As such, he had implicated her in the deceptions. Given that he had few subordinates working for him – AI units carried out the vast majority of roles performed within the corporation – there were few other scapegoats he could implicate for what was originally his own error, and so she became the main scapegoat for his failings.

He was hoping that Jamieson – who clearly shared his own view that the highly academic were also highly duplicitous – would arrive at the same conclusion. The failure to find any space flight technologists or rocket scientists amongst the academics was a major blow for the corporation, and Parker feared Jamieson's wrath over this particular issue. He had no desire to feel the iron boot, the kiss of the velvet whip, or whatever kind of punishment Jamieson might devise, and was determined to emerge from this episode with his reputation intact, and as little scathed as humanly possible.

Finally, there had been significantly more resistance to the outcomes of the process than he and the corporation had anticipated. Sixty percent of the academics and scientists had been refused positions, and were instead offered loans to help them to settle on the planet over the next few months. This had provoked outright outbursts of anger and a great feeling of injustice. The academics had quickly established committees to deal with the situation, and, to his great surprise, even some of the senior officials and those securing positions had shown support and solidarity for those without contracts. Protests were currently being held, followed by demands for meetings with the corporation's leadership.

Parker had definitely not expected this. On Rorque 4 they were used to dealing with individuals who were far more compliant. Since its inception, the planet had instituted laws, plans and procedures to effectively suppress any radical forms of opposition to the system, whilst rewarding conformity. These and the prolonged period of economic deterioration had created a supine population. Parker was thus unsure of how exactly to proceed with this development – dealing with inhabitants from another planet was something he had no previous experience of. He was unsure if the same rules applied to them as to the citizens of Rorque 4, so for the moment he did nothing that might jeopardise his own position. All this, he figured, would need to be taken to a higher level. Nevertheless, he knew what he would really like to do to them.

Halfway round the planet, in the sprawling city of New Galtsville, a similar process had been conducted from the headquarters of Cosmic Solutions. However, Christine Sanchez was in a considerably better mood than the senior executives at the Rorque Corporation, mainly because Alex Kim and his fellow space flight technicians had been aboard the Avante and were all signed up on five-year contracts – just about the longest you could possibly expect to receive from the corporation, or indeed any other. They were now settling into their new faculty at one of the corporation's universities, that of Diana Park - the university the corporation was increasingly devoting to the project of terra-forming the neighbouring planet of Morpheus, the fifth planet of their stellar system.

They had also offered shorter contracts to a whole range of other scientists, particularly ones specialising in the planetary sciences, but also a range of engineers and technicians in any field that might prove useful in developing a whole new planetary biosphere and economy. This amounted to a considerable number of those who had been working on Alpha Fraczan, and, as such, they had offered contracts to over fifty-five percent of those on board the Avante. This meant that Cosmic solutions, too, was attempting to find a way of dealing with disgruntled Alphan academics.

Those who were not given contracts received similar treatment to that dished out by the Rorque Corporation; and so Cosmic Solutions were also faced with thousands of angry academics currently protesting and organising against the decisions made by the corporation. There were even rumours of revenge being meted out on Alex Kim, so security had been strengthened at Diana Park University, just in case anyone really did try to harm him. Despite these latest problems, Sanchez was in a better mood than she had been for some time now. The Morpheus Project was an enormous undertaking and they had experienced far more setbacks than successes. Finally, she now believed, they might be able to make some substantial progress and move the project along at a considerably faster rate. The future of her corporation was looking significantly brighter.

Ur-Tokar – the Zeleyanian military forces arrive

Approximately one month later, the Zeleyanian Space Fleet Commander Vice-Admiral Rosson plotted a course through the Rogan star system that ensured it would take in a tour of its more interesting outer planets during its entry into the system. Two days previously he had been woken by the AI units as they had begun their approach to the outer limits of the star system. He and his skeleton crew had checked over the ships most important systems, but finding little to be concerned about – since the AI units had successfully performed their routine tasks during the eight month journey – turned their attention to other matters. Rosson, since first leaving Zeleyan for the Necron star system, had developed an unexpected predilection for space tourism - taking in a view of the planets as he entered and departed star systems - and so he made sure the starship passed as many of the outer planets as was logistically possible. It would add several hours to their journey as they manouevred their way around the planetary system, but this was of little relevance, and, once again, he was not to regret his decision in doing so.

Rogan's star system contained two large gaseous planets, though it would have been something of a stretch to describe them as giants, since by galactic standards they were at the relatively small end of the spectrum. However, what they lacked in size, they made up for in their uniqueness. The first one they encountered was that of Corusa, a fairly unremarkable mass of mostly swirling and tightly circulating cloud bands coloured mustard, orange and brown, except that, from a distance, the planet seemed to be bathed in a pale yellow shimmering and sparkling, almost glitter-like light. As the space craft approached more closely it became apparent that the coruscating sparkle was caused by billions of small firework-like explosions just above the surface of the outer gaseous cloud layer – the planet seemed to be constantly emitting a fiery yellow substance across the entirety of its surface, making it appear as though it was on fire.

Corusa lacked the splendour and majesty of the gas and ice giants Rosson had enjoyed marveling at on his recent journeys, but he was intrigued by a planet that appeared - at least to him - to be constantly trying to divest itself of an unwanted substance, to be cleansing itself of some noxious material. If this was intriguing, then that of the slightly larger Lapiz, he found even more perplexing. Closer to the centre of the star system than Corusa, it was clearly a planet experiencing some form of serious long-term decay. Even from a significant distance, long swathes of gaseous material could be seen streaming away from the planet, as if it were being slowly stripped of its outer layers.

As the spacecraft followed its curved trajectory closer to the giant planet, Rosson could discern whole areas of the sphere which appeared to have been stripped of their outer bluish-grey gaseous layers, allowing him a view into a lower glowing burnished-yellow under-layer of intensely swirling gases that were clearly rotating in the opposite direction to the upper layer. Within the golden void he was able to observe vast churning vortices and enormous electrical storms, whilst out of the void emerged intense bursts of electrical activity, huge lightning strikes that lit up whole swathes of the outer bluish-grey layer. At the void's end the swirling golden gases dived down like a huge cascade of falling clouds to ever deeper layers within the planet's core. It appeared to Rosson that the void of golden light, and its tumultuous storm-driven activity, was in some strange manner driving the destruction of the outer layers of the strange bluish-grey giant. How and why this was occurring, though, was a complete mystery to him.

Rosson was still wondering over the two mysterious planets and their hidden secrets when his stasis ship The Crusader finally made its decent into orbit around the small rocky planet of Ur-Tokar, a short time later. As the ship approached the small sphere, Rosson was able to appreciate the deep indigo blues of its oceans, the shimmering white ice-caps of the extensive polar regions stretching far into the sub-tropics, and the dark lush greens of the forests that now covered the mountainous equatorial zone. This was a pristine world, primitive and largely untouched – unlike the extensive grassy plains of his home planet - except, he had to remind himself - it was actually human intervention that had forested the planet and made it habitable in the first place.

Once the ship was safely in orbit, an immediate transmission was sent back to Zeleyan informing Vartin of their arrival, and the ship's computers then set about scanning the surface of the planet. They also attempted to key into the planet's satellite system, but although the satellites were clearly functioning, they were unable to gain access, despite attempting several different command systems. This was a puzzling development, but Rosson was eventually forced to assume that some form of locking procedure had been carried out by the planet's original inhabitants, as part of their desire to dispense with all forms of advanced technology. Rosson also noticed there were no stasis ships circling the planet – and surmised that after several decades of orbiting they had probably finally lost orbital traction and experienced a fiery death in their descent down towards the planet below. The planet very much had an abandoned air about it, he concluded.

The mission's main task was to find a suitable area to construct a military base on the planet's surface. It needed to be relatively near to the key major settlement, but far enough away to remain undetected by the local population. Once it was established, Rosson was under strict orders to make a detailed analysis of the planet's society, particularly its military capabilities, and to draw up a plan for a military takeover of the entire world. It was well-known that the inhabitants of Ur-Tokar were anti-technology, but at what level they had drawn their dislike of technology the Zeleyanians were unsure. Vartin had assumed that whatever level it was, they would be no match for his own forces, but it was still important to know what level of resistance they were likely to encounter.

Rosson's first problem was actually finding a settlement of any particular significance. There seemed to be nothing anywhere on the planet of any considerable size, though they eventually found one that possessed a fort and a greater degree of activity than elsewhere, and which they presumed passed for what could be considered as a regime capital, that of Meridin – later confirmed to be the seat of the monarch by reconnaissance missions. The next problem was that the military base had to be constructed somewhat further from the town than they had would have originally desired. The agricultural lowlands around Meridin offered nothing that was useful to them, and they were forced to clear an area of deep forest behind low hills several kilometers away, in order to remain hidden from sight.

Despite these initial difficulties, approximately two months later the base had been successfully constructed, a suitably large detachment of soldiers established within its confines, and reconnaissance missions undertaken to assess the military strength of the monarchist regime. All the indications were that it was extremely low, particularly as the population of the planet also appeared to be so small – Meridin itself would barely count as a medium-sized town on Zeleyan. Clearly their society had not flourished particularly well. Rosson was not surprised, he could not fathom why anyone would want to dispense with advanced technology and its numerous benefits. However, he was forced to admit that the planet, on the whole, enjoyed a certain pristine and primeval beauty, that was almost completely absent on Zeleyan. Maybe, a lack of technology had its compensations, he also conceded.

Great care had been taken to make sure the military base remained fully secret and out of sight. Communications with the stasis ship - and the Zeleyan spy satellite installed a few years previously - were kept to an absolute minimum. Landings and departures were always carried out under the cover of darkness. After two months of construction, Rosson was fully satisfied that he had completed the initial stage of the mission. The military base was completed and the necessary routines had been established – effectively, everything had gone to plan without any significant mishap. Rosson ordered the transmission of a communication to Vartin back on Zeleyan informing him of their initial success. He had been given strict instructions that once this part of the plan had been completed, he was to do absolutely nothing else but wait for the arrival of the main invasion force.

So, all he needed to do now was lie low and wait for the arrival of the main invasion force. Vartin had not informed him of why the invasion was planned in this way, nor exactly when this would occur, but he had made his own rough calculations and figured it might be several months before the rest of the starships arrived. This left him with two main problems. How would he maintain morale amongst the troops on the base over the coming months, but more importantly how was he going to pass the time himself? Three possibilities occurred to him; he could go into stasis for several months, but that might be construed as a neglect of his duties, he could explore the wider realms of Ur-Tokar, though this had arguably been forbidden, or he could indulge in a little more space tourism and enjoy another tour or two of Rogan's many and varied planets.

Rorque 4 – the semi-arid planet; early history

The official history of Rorque 4 had been largely established under the auspices of its ruling class, though it was not an uncontested one. Although there were competing versions with regards to the exact historical details and degree of importance of certain significant leaders, its general nature had largely been settled upon, and was disseminated widely through the society's educational system and media outlets. The established narrative perfectly suited the purposes of the Rorquean ruling class, and effectively lauded the progress and achievements of the neo-liberal economic system, whilst almost entirely ignoring the plight of the oppressed, exploited, impoverished and marginalised peoples of the planet. Neither was there any meaningful mention of the damage inflicted upon the ecology of their world.

For knowledge of the latter issues, it was necessary to resort to alternative versions of the planet's history written by the few historians able to emerge from the lower echelons of the class system, or from disillusioned or disaffected historians deriving from the privileged classes, some of whom had lost complete faith in the official discourse of the official polity, even from an early age. The following account is drawn from both orthodox and alternative histories of the planet.

Rorque 4 was the fourth planet of a large and bright yellow-white G class sun the colonists had decided to name Eleutheria. Somewhat closer to the star were two other planets of a similar size to Rorque 4, but both possessed thick extremely hot gaseous atmospheres - similar to that of Venus - due to their proximity to their mother star, and were thus entirely uninhabitable for humans. Closer still was the large, barren and intensely sun-baked planet of Thar, which was equally uninhabitable, and also of little economic use.

A short distance – in astronomical terms - beyond Rorque 4 lay Morpheus, slightly smaller and even less mountainous than Rorque 4. Geological surveys of Morpheus conducted by the settlers of Rorque 4 indicated that it was highly likely that until recently it had been a geologically active planet with an atmosphere, magnetic field, oceans and possibly even extra-terrestrial life-forms. It was believed by some of the surveyors, that with a helping hand from humans it could be brought back to life, thus Morpheus was widely considered to be a dormant rather than a dead planet.

Arrival in Utopia

The 'genesis pod' that had arrived over a century beforehand, had little reason not to identify Rorque 4 as potentially habitable for humans. In most conventional respects it possessed all the characteristics considered necessary for human colonisation. The largely ochre-brown disc had proven to be a very warm and dry planet – at least in comparison with Earth. It had one large moon - that would offer long-term stability to any life established on its surface - in addition to two much smaller satellites. Further out in the stellar system were three gas giants which had undoubtedly hoovered up much of the space debris of Eleutheria's planetary system over the eons – there were relatively few discernible craters on either Rorque 4 or Morpheus. However, its oceans were somewhat limited in extent – the planet was over sixty five percent land surface – consisting mostly of extensive shallow seas, and there was a distinct scarcity of fresh water. The planet, whilst not perfect, had distinct colonisation possibilities, and so the standard terra-forming process had been implemented, and was widely considered to have been a successful one.

Rorque 4 contained little in the way of significant uplands – just the occasional range of low-lying hills and a few areas of highish plateau landscape. The relatively hot, dry and flat nature of the planet meant that only the more xerophytic plants and trees were able to flourish, and only in particular regions of the large continents that constituted so much of the planet's surface. The acacia tree, in particular, flourished, helping to create the large areas of open savannah that predominated along the coastal areas of the various continents. Much of the rest of the planet consisted of desert or semi-desert, especially the vast continental centres, which remained largely barren, with little else than occasional scrubby bushes and cacti.

The oceans, by contrast, witnessed a relative flourishing of marine life as the extensive mix of organisms constituting the 'primordial soup' took easily to the shallow warm seas, though those preferring more saline environments tended to be the life-forms that prospered and multiplied most abundantly. The shallow nature of the seas, however, meant that the ecosystems that evolved were of a fragile nature, and easily subject to disruption. In addition, the lack of any deep oceans and a paucity of islands meant that the range of ecosystems that developed was also limited somewhat in scope. In sum total, Rorque 4 was a habitable planet, but not exactly an environmental paradise.

This ecological poverty was not, however, of any significant concern to the first settlers arriving at the planet. The stasis ships that commenced first landfall on Rorque 4 were predominantly 'corporation ships'. A short time into the great exodus from Earth, a considerable percentage of the wealthier and larger corporations had decided to effectively place almost the entirety of their finances, transferable resources and personnel onto their own stasis ships, and launch them it into space with the aim of reestablishing their business activities elsewhere in the galaxy. They figured that if enough companies chose to follow the same course, then a viable and advanced capitalist economy could be constructed reasonably quickly and easily, and the corporate leaders could once again enjoy the prestige, status and lavish lifestyles they had been accustomed to – lifestyles that had latterly appeared doomed across most of Earth's surface.

The early years of Rorque 4's colonisation and habitation had appeared to prove them largely correct. The standard teething problems that accompanied the colonisation of any planet had occurred, but the level of technology, expertise and organisation brought on the starships ensured that such problems were effectively overcome, and a successfully functioning capitalist economy and society were established after a relatively short duration of time. The economy was, of course, subject to the standard periodic cycles of prosperity and stagnation found in any market system, but this had been expected and even welcomed by the neo-liberal ideologues who had dreamed up the whole planetary venture.

The corporations had brought with them large numbers of mini-fabs on their spacecraft and there were sufficient local building materials to ensure the construction of many large towns and cities, all connected through an extensive and highly modern road network. This in turn had allowed extensive industrial, service and information sectors to flourish - these providing the vast majority of the employment opportunities. By contrast, Rorque 4's problematic climate and landscape provided little in the way of farming, forestry or mining opportunities, and its new inhabitants thus relied quite heavily on the ferming units they had brought with them - and then later mass produced - for much of their food production.

Arrival in Utopia

For nearly a century afterwards the economy and society had prospered and flourished, notwithstanding the standard periodic downswings that impacted cyclically on economic activity. However, of late though, the population of Rorque 4 had begun to experience a series of protracted problems – effectively the consequences of the particular pattern of economic development they had chosen to pursue - ones that were now leaving them exposed and ill-equipped to deal with the particular difficulties that had arisen because of both the frailties of this particular economic arrangement and those of the planet they had colonised.

From the very beginning, the overriding priority of the settlers had been to rapidly grow an economy that would satisfy their never-ending desire for greater material prosperity, wider consumer choice and increased individual freedoms. However, the economic, political and social structures they believed were most conducive to this process were now showing serious signs of cracking under the various strains placed upon them. In a civilisation that placed corporate profitability before absolutely everything else, it had not been long before low-priority issues had begun to impact negatively on the planet, the economy and thus the lifestyles of the wider population.

In particular, the relatively fragile Rorquean environment had become severely degraded as economic activity rapidly expanded, and the population quickly increased in the early decades. Most of the trees - never plentiful in the first place on Rorque – had been harvested but had rarely been sustainably replaced. The shallow seas had been severely over-fished to the extent that many species were now considered to be commercially extinct – in an almost depressing replication of what had occurred on Earth so many years before. What little farmland actually existed was often overexploited and denuded, soils turning to dust and then abandoned. Pollution had spoilt the few rivers that flowed across the continents, marshes were drained and coastlines degraded as cities spread along their shores. Many of the precious shallow water bodies of the planet were now effectively dying seas.

The corporations had ensured - from the very start of colonisation - that environmental regulations were kept to an absolute minimum; certainly none were permitted that might interfere with the activities of the free market. This had remained the case ever since, despite growing concerns from the population over environmental and related issues. In addition, taxation levels had been maintained at extremely low levels, so there were effectively no public bodies capable of stepping in and resolving or reversing the environmental degradation. Unless a corporate entity could make a profit from clearing up or addressing a particular problem, it was effectively left to fester and become gradually worse and worse.

A further problem for the Rorquean civilisation had been the dramatic increases in social inequality - always present in Rorque 4's economy - but now reaching chronic proportions. The old adage that 'money goes to money' existed in spades in the Rorquean economy, but of even more pertinence was the lack of any countervailing agencies to reverse or offset this general truism. Those at the wrong end of this increasing inequality had few means at their disposal to turn their personal situation around. Unions and strike activity, - which might have been able to increase wages and working conditions - had effectively been outlawed, and there was no form of welfare state, schooling, housing or healthcare to help those facing this relative deprivation. All economic and social activities were run by the private sector and were prohibitively expensive for those at the bottom end of the economy.

To compound these matters, a standard response of the corporate leaders during long-wave downswings in the economy had been the increasing implementation of AI units to perform an ever-expanding variety of functions within its various sectors, leading to chronic underemployment for an ever expanding underclass. AI units were now performing almost all the routine tasks undertaken within the corporations, leaving little in the way of employment for the former workers of Rorque 4. Contrary to the propaganda of the neo-liberal ideologues, the economy of Rorque 4 had not proven self-regulating – the rich got richer and the poor got poorer, and there was no internal mechanism that seemed capable of reversing this process.

The structural nature of this process had led to a further protracted problem that had originally gone unnoticed, but was now beginning to worry those in power. As each generation became more and more exposed to inequality and underemployment, so the number of people surviving to bring up children was steadily declining. Alcoholism, drug-abuse, self-harm and suicide were rife within the underclass and premature death rates rising steeply. Those consigned to a life of suffering severe social inequality chose not to have children or died prematurely before they could even start considering a family. The population of the planet was now experiencing a noticeable decline in its numbers. For an economy based on a need for ever-expanding markets this was a chronically important issue, and other than changing the fundamental principals upon which the economy was built, no viable solutions had, so far, been forthcoming.

The latest difficulty to be faced by the people of Rorque 4 in this long line of problems was now a climate related one. As with all planets, Rorque 4 experienced long-term wobbles in the orbit around its star, and had recently entered a medium-length phase which brought it in closer proximity to its star, Eleutheria. Astronomers had first noticed this beginning to occur approximately 25 years before – and unfortunately coinciding with the start of a long-wave downswing in the economy – and the planet had been gradually heating and drying ever since. Given the planet was already a relatively hot and dry one, and that the industrial activities of the economy and its damage to the environment had been contributing to increased warming for some time beforehand, this was now showing all the makings of a potentially major catastrophe.

Yet – 25 years on - an economy based on delivering material wealth and consumer choice, and with little in the way of collectivist public bodies capable of making a meaningful intervention, had produced few answers to the enduring crisis. It could sell more air conditioning units, fire-fighting apparatus, desalinated water and gas masks to cope with the pollution, but in the long run, these only made matters worse. The corporations were all looking to their latest economic ventures – often ones of an increasingly desperate nature – as a means of emerging from the protracted crisis, but to date none had delivered on their promises or lived up to the inflated expectations made of them.

Rorque 4 – Alex Kim

Alex Kim could not quite believe his good luck and from time to time simply started laughing to himself. He could still not quite believe that his dubious gamble of effectively hijacking an entire stasis ship had actually paid off, and in such a successful manner. He was now one of the leading figures in the Space Flight Faculty at Diana Park University and was being treated as something of a VIP member of the Cosmic Solutions Corporation workforce. He now effectively had at his entire disposal a complete and newly-equipped faculty with a budget he could only have dreamed about on Alpha Fraczan. Compounding his recent good fortune, his preliminary conversations with the existing faculty staff had pleasantly surprised him - the advances made in both space flight theory and engineering technology had been minimal since the inhabitants of Rorque 4 had arrived over a century beforehand. He considered his own theories and engineering know-how in the discipline to be way ahead of anything he had yet encountered in the university faculty, and so it should be extremely easy for him to make significant advances to the corporation's space flight programme.

He was currently showing Christine Sanchez around the ultra-hi-tech laboratories and rocket testing grounds adjacent to the university. She had made a special flying visit to the university with the express reason of meeting the increasingly famous rocket scientist in person, and to gauge the level of progress being achieved in her all important project of reviving the planet Morpheus. She was also keen to impress upon Alex Kim just how crucial his engineering advances would be in ensuring the project remained economically feasible and thus a potential success. She had been pleasantly pleased with both his level of enthusiasm and self-confidence, and was now beginning to believe that the project might actually come to fruition after so many protracted setbacks.

Alex's initial engineering project was simply to scale up the size of those laboratory tests he had previously considered promising back on Alpha Fraczan - over three years previously now, he reminded himself. This would allow him to better identify the advantages and drawbacks of the particular propulsion systems he had designed, and to then gradually refine the processes until he had developed engines that were significantly more efficient and powerful than the standard ones used on the stasis ships. Effectively, the latter were still extremely similar to those designed, built and installed on Earth at the back end of the twenty-first century - since there had been no pressing need to improve them until recently. He had previously experimented with a variety of flow processes, new combinations of gaseous mixtures, and an improved range of structural materials and some of these, he considered, had appeared highly promising.

Alex looked across the compound in which he was accompanying Christine Sanchez, and noticed the extra security personnel that had been implemented in recent days, in addition to those accompanying the leader of the corporation. The corporate leadership had informed him that this was to deal with the risk of espionage from rival companies, but he was also aware that threats had been made against his person by some of his embittered fellow academics, and so was unsure of the exact reason for their presence. Personally, he thought he had little to worry about – it was unlikely any of them would actually physically attack him, he believed - but he was keen to avoid any unpleasant verbal exchanges, not to mention actual physical assaults, and so had started to be a little wary of who he actually met with.

He had initially acted out of a sense of hopelessness, but was becoming aware that his actions could also be seen as motivated by a sense of selfishness, and to some degree through wanting to effect a form of revenge. His research efforts on Alpha Fraczan, he strongly believed, had been underappreciated, marginalised and unjustly ignored. He had also been pleasantly surprised when he had discovered that Anna Dubois – someone he believed had been partially responsible for his own lack of advancement on Alpha Fraczan – had performed an extremely similar manouevre to his own. There was an ironic degree of institutional symmetry in their actions, which he found quite pleasing. He could quite imagine why she had reached a similar conclusion to that of his own, with regard to where their destination really ought to be. It was also ironic that on his home planet he had been regarded as an irrelevant dreamer, but here, on an alien world, he was seen as something of a hero, whilst his endeavour to achieve faster and more efficient space flight was being hailed as an enormous benefit to everyone concerned.

Nevertheless, he did feel some growing sense of responsibility and guilt for those fellow academics who had failed to secure contracts. He knew only too well what it was like to be unwanted and marginalised, though he had – perhaps naively – assumed this was simply because the Alphan university leadership lacked the right vision. He had been surprised by just how ruthless the corporation on Rorque 4 was in singling out the academics it had no use for – quite unlike the institutional behaviour of the universities on Alpha Fraczan. There, a place could be found for even the least respected fields of research – which he reluctantly admitted had included his own. Somewhat grudgingly, he now recognised that approach had allowed him to be where he was now. The unwanted academics on Rorque 4 would receive no such munificent treatment, and this struck him as extremely unfair and a major waste of potential talent.

He tried to reconcile his contrasting feelings through a belief that justice had perhaps been finally served – that the worth of his practical-based research had ultimately been recognised, in contrast to the more obscure and esoteric endeavours of some of his academic contemporaries, which were now considered of little or no use. It was becoming very clear to him that academia on Rorque 4 was entirely dominated by quantitative-based research - if it was not measurable, it was not worth knowing about. Given that the universities were all run by private enterprise this was of no great surprise. Corporations were, at the end of the day, all about numbers; entirely concerned with shifting a specified number of units, meeting numeric targets and efficiency ratings whilst achieving identified profit margins – their operations were ultimately controlled by the bean counters in the finance departments. Grand theorising, blue sky thinking, discursive conceptualisation and qualitative-based research were considered as valueless and of little use to profit-hungry corporations. Rorque 4 civilisation was all about quantities and numbers – here it truly was the age of the micro man and woman.

He also reminded himself that he and thousands of other scientists were now involved in a whole range of new scientific endeavours, including the exciting prospect of being involved in the mammoth task of returning a whole dormant planet back to life. Such a venture entailed a huge number of theoretical and engineering challenges being faced and duly overcome; it would not only guarantee employment but also intellectual engagement for several decades to come. This was the type of venture a handful of his fellow scientists had discussed and dreamed about for years; now they were actually involved in such a venture for real. His deception, in the long run, he believed, would prove to have been the correct decision. Hopefully, the academics who had failed to secure contracts could work something else out over time. From what he had seen of Rorque 4 so far, it seemed to be a highly prosperous planet with a highly advanced economy. There must be plenty of opportunities out there for highly educated people, he figured optimistically.

With this more positive thought in his mind, his attention returned to his dealings with Christine Sanchez. She had been occupied for several minutes conversing with certain of his colleagues, but she now turned her attention fully to Alex Kim and indicated she would like a private conversation with him. They left the laboratory and headed into his plush new office, where she spent a moment considering her thoughts. Unbeknown to Alex, she had spent a considerable amount of time attempting to second guess Alex's motivations, and now that he stood before her she figured she had worked him out correctly. She also liked the way he looked. Alex was more than a decade younger than her, in his mid-twenties, slightly stocky, but in good physical shape. He had a slightly broad face with dark eyes and silky black hair combed heavily to one side. She briefly wondered what he was like as a lover, but quickly decided that any developments in that direction should wait until later.

'Well, Alex, welcome to the future. You are now at the centre of the greatest project this world has ever experienced. For some time now I have dreamed of terra-forming our sister planet of Morpheus,' she commenced, in the manner she frequently used in order to maintain her slightly off-beat reputation. 'We've enjoyed some great successes, but also some major setbacks. There have been technical and financial difficulties, sometimes of an immense nature. Only recently, I was being asked if the dream has ended, but with you and your colleague's arrival together with your advanced levels of technical expertise, I now believe that the dream goes on. I believe you have the right stuff, exactly what we need to make this future a success. As the seasons pass, I'm sure we will now move rapidly towards the goal of bringing our sister planet back to life. Faster space travel is exactly what we need to bring this project to fruition, and on time and within budget.'

She paused a while for effect. 'I simply want you to be yourself, to know that you have the full backing of the corporation, and that we can provide you with everything that you could possibly need to achieve success. We can turn things upside down if necessary to help you achieve that success.' She smoothed back her curly ginger hair and smiled at him. 'Remember, we can achieve great things together, we are depending on you – the future is depending on you, make sure you repay our faith in you,' and with that she turned and exited the office, followed swiftly by her security retinue, and then out of the building towards her waiting autocar.

Alex was momentarily dumbfounded; this was not the kind of welcome he was used to; he had not expected anything of that nature from a corporate leader. He wondered briefly whether he was hallucinating, but his surroundings appeared totally normal. No one else on Rorque 4 had talked to him in this manner, so it was clearly not a cultural thing. The very one-sided conversation had confused, worried, concerned and encouraged him all at the same time. He wondered if he had missed some profound underlying meaning to her strange welcome. In fact, he spent much of the next day or two mulling over the meaning of her words. The more he thought about them, the more he wondered whether he was out of his depth. He ultimately decided he needed to prove to the corporation and all those around him that this was definitely not the case.

Earth – the space pioneers

If the engineering side of leaving Earth had proven particularly problematic, this was nothing compared with the protracted political and social complexities that were eventually played out during the length of the entire process. Whilst it was true that scientists and private entrepreneurs had made most of the running in terms of interplanetary exploration, its study, and its commercialisation during the first half of the twenty-first century, the nation-states - and their associated regional associations such as the European, African and Eurasian Unions - had never fully retreated from the theatre of space, and had continued to pursue their own aims, particularly ones related to the issues of security and economic development. As such, both private and public institutions had developed a degree of expertise in space travel, and both were in a position to embark on its pursuit across a much broader front.

Initially, it was the nation-states that made the first moves with regards to seriously considering an interstellar exodus. Wealthier states looking in the future, and increasingly faced with the imminent prospect of millions of climate refugees fleeing from worsening episodes of coastal flooding and other climate-related disasters, began to consider the 'stellar alternative', as it came to be known. If there was limited space in the country's interior and no realistic prospect of transporting citizens to vacant land within other nations, then the wider cosmos came to be seen as an increasingly attractive and realistic option.

Some of these states had initially looked at the possibility of encouraging emigration to the increasingly unfrozen lands within the Arctic Circle, and with some cooperation from the likes of Canada, Russia and the Scandinavian countries this had worked to a limited degree with the opening up of new mining, shipping and agrarian frontiers. However, the possibilities engendered by this process had ultimately proven insufficient and frequently impractical, and as each new damaging episode of climate breakdown occurred, so even this development came to be seen as simply another temporary stop-gap.

Whilst it was true that the space corporations had occasionally flirted with the idea of sending paying passengers, or even settlers, deep into space, the

243

economics were largely untested and it was highly uncertain as to whether such ventures could prove profitable. Would sufficiently large numbers of shareholders be inclined to invest - possibly enormous sums – in a venture with a highly dubious likelihood of actually seeing any return on their investments, they wondered. Slickly produced promotions suggesting possibly massive returns on mineral wealth or the discovery of fantastically productive planets, had occasionally been floated, but more in hope than in expectation. Ultimately, sufficient funds had never been accumulated. Joint ventures between the mining behemoths and the newly emerging space corporations had tentatively been established in mid-century, and some small-scale experimental mining of asteroids had occurred, but technological advances in this field had remained limited. The vast distances that needed travelling to cross interstellar space meant that any thoughts of similar ventures in even the closest of stellar systems to Earth were effectively considered a non-starter. The costs, it was presumed, would far outweigh any likely and largely unknowable returns.

For the nation-states, the most immediate problem was how to market 'the stellar alternative' without appearing as though they were ducking their responsibilities to their citizens. Amongst politicians, party advisers and civil servants there were enormous doubts as to the viability of such a vast and potentially politically calamitous undertaking. But, with each new coastal inundation and climate emergency and associated following wave of refugees, minds were concentrated, and the attractiveness of such a project began to look increasingly appealing. Invariably, ways were eventually found to portray the space exodus as a positive and bright new start in life, rather than an escape from a rapidly deteriorating situation. Appeals to national pride and patriotic sentiments were interspersed with a largely progressive message of opening up the space frontier and pushing back the boundaries of human knowledge.

As the stasis ships began to roll off the production lines, so states acquired a growing list of 'patriotic volunteers' willing to take their chances on projecting their nation's interests and patriotic pride out into the depths of space and on yet undiscovered planets. It was soon discovered, though, that many of the volunteers might not prove to be the best material for these new national colonies. Indeed, many of the most enthusiastic volunteers were deemed to be the last kind of people you would want recreating your nation on a new and probably problematic destination – a motley assortment of chancers, time-wasters, fanatics, fantasists and escapists seemed to be significantly over-represented amongst the volunteers. States thus switched to a more conservative and cautious approach to selecting settlers. They worked on the assumption that the new planetary society would broadly reproduce the existing one on Earth. Selection by status, vocation and life experience became the de rigueur requirements, rather than any particular enthusiasm for space travel or patriotic fervour.

The first stasis ship to be actually launched was by the Chinese state in 2083, against the backdrop of a recent protracted demise in the global economy and the heightened political tension between the left and right that resulted from this development. Not to be outdone, launches by India, the USA, Japan and the European and Eurasian Unions followed shortly afterwards, and the race into interstellar space was finally on. The fanfare and national pomp that accompanied these departures seemed to suddenly jolt wide sections of the human population into an awareness of what was actually occurring. The tide of the century was abruptly turning. Originally believing 'the space alternative' to be just some new media hype, they could suddenly see that it was genuinely real and actually happening, and increasingly they wanted to be part of the movement. But not in exactly the same way as was being organised; for the thought of starting a new colony with several thousand other people simply based on the fact that they happened to be from the same nation, proved to be far from an attractive proposition for many. Increasingly, those leaving for space wanted to leave with people who believed and shared in similar ideas to themselves.

The long economic upswing expansion of the 2060s and 2070s had given rise to a renewed upsurge of optimism about progress and the possibility of creating a better world, not just in the developed world, but particularly in the strongly developing nations of Africa, southern Asia and the remoter parts of Latin America that were able to escape the worst of the climate breakdown. This was particularly the case amongst the younger generation and a plethora of progressive, radical and revolutionary movements and organisations had emerged seeking to change the world in a left-wing direction. The pressing problem of climate change had made their desires and demands all the more urgent, and their efforts had been devoted to effecting some form of last minute dramatic economic alterations in the hope of finally addressing the environmental crises impacting upon humanity and the rest of the planet.

However, as one climatic catastrophe followed another and the economic expansion stalled and then stagnated into a downswing from the early-2080s onwards, so this mélange of left-wing political, social and religious groupings began to look at the 'stellar alternative'. If they could not implement their utopian vision on Earth, they figured, then why not start anew on a completely different planet and create it somewhere else, where there would be no resistance to their dreams from conservative political and economic forces. Increasingly these groups sought to convince any state or non-state organisation that would listen to them to loan, sell or grant them access to their own stasis ships. As the planet descended further into climate catastrophe, ships occasionally became available, and through a combination of begging, borrowing or stealing, a number of these groups were able to launch their ship of dreams, with the aim of transporting them to a freer, more peaceful and more equal future.

At the same time as the 'utopia ships' were departing, some of the more outlandish entrepreneurs and capitalist organisations were coming to similar conclusions, though for entirely different reasons. The climate catastrophe was now combined with a protracted economic slowdown and an almost persistent decline in profit margins, with the prospect of ever seeing a return to some form of more profitable scenario looking increasingly remote. Insurance claims were now being measured in the trillions of dollars, euros and renminbi, whole cities and their industrial zones were disappearing under the sea, whilst less profitable sectors of the economy were in freefall or total collapse. Ultimately, a number of corporate leaders decided that their lavish lifestyles could only be continued if their operations were translocated to another more promising planet. The Trans Planetary Corporations were only too willing to oblige, and soon corporations were informing their entire workforce that they either entered into stasis and joined the exodus on one of the 'corporate ships', or faced instant dismissal as the company closed down its operations on Earth.

Arrival in Utopia

When a number of climate tipping points were breached and it became obvious that the human race was no longer in control of its future on Earth, the trickle of ships departing in the exodus eventually became a flood. The production lines for the stasis ships at this point went into overdrive. For a while it seemed to be the only burgeoning industry; some economists even predicting that 'the space expansion' was characterising a new wave of technological innovation, and would frame the entire technological and structural nature of the next economic upswing – assuming there was one! Production lines sprang up across the globe, and ships rolled off them at a surprisingly fast rate to meet the varying needs and desires of states, private corporations, universities, religious groups, political organisations and any other groupings that felt their future and destiny now lay out somewhere in deepest space.

Throughout the whole process, though, the basic original stasis ship design never fundamentally changed, only their size and the different variety of materials and resources taken with the passengers on board each ship. Unsurprisingly, the wealthier organisations were able to build larger ships and transport a much greater variety of resources with them, whilst the poorer ones often had to make do with whatever they could find or manage, but by hook or by crook the numbers of ships and the large numbers of people leaving continued to expand at an almost exponential rate.

From a fairly ordered beginning, it was not long before the exodus turned into a chaotic free-for-all, as an ever-increasing multitude of increasingly diverse groups – gripped by what seemed like a form of global psychosis - sought to depart from the planet whilst it was still actually possible to do so. Capital poured in as the space industry seemed to be the only investment game in town. And where the money went, so there followed the workers and consumers - especially during a prolonged economic downturn. Ever greater numbers of spacecraft were built, whilst more and more - sometimes even paying - passengers entered into stasis and the search for a new and more stable planetary home. Spaceports, and the infrastructure required to service them, quickly sprang up across the entire planet. So great was the concentration on spaceship construction that it had the effect of creating a shortage of resources, materials and skilled and unskilled labour for other sectors of the economy, a process that only served to further funnel capital and labour into 'the space expansion'.

It was a classic bubble economy, and as demand increasingly outstripped supply, so prices rose until the point where a severe shortage of necessary construction materials halted further significant production. About a dozen years after the first ship had departed, the bubble burst and another severe recession ensued, severely impacting on the exodus. Production did later recommence, but at a slower more moderate pace - never approaching the dizzying heights of the earlier phase - and ultimately fizzled out as runaway climate change pushed the economy into an ever downwards spiral amidst a series of unstoppable climatic disasters. The climate refugees had got out just in time.

For the millions of passengers that were firmly ensconced in stasis - as they sped silently towards the stars - the fate of Earth was now neither of relevance nor of any great importance. They were now hurtling their way through interstellar space towards a new future; their destination the myriad of stars that stretched across vast swathes of the near galaxy. They were to spend the next few decades hibernating within their protective spaceship homes, oblivious to the array of stars, gas nebula, galaxies and other fantastic stellar formations that would have been visible from the viewing decks of the ships if they had been woken from their prolonged torpor.

Communication between the numerous ships was a straightforward process, once the lengthy times between sending and receiving emissions was factored in. And many of the ships sought to remain in communication with each other for a whole variety of reasons. Following ships could be forewarned of potential hazards, solutions to engineering and technical problems shared, and potentially suitable destinations suggested for exploration and mass settlement. There were others, though, that maintained complete radio silence, holding no desire for any others within the great departure to know of their chosen destination. For a whole range of different reasons they had no desire to associate with the rest of humanity; especially with the groups they held responsible for making such a gigantic mess of living on Earth. This next time they were going to get it right, and the last thing they needed was a bunch of unbelievers messing with their new utopia.

But, if they had really thought the whole process through extremely carefully, they would have realised that this was a venture that was unlikely to end well for all. The deep, dark, vast coldness of space was a hostile environment for humans, and many of the ships - for a whole host of reasons - were to meet their fate in its frozen wastes. Some of the ships disappeared without trace, communications suddenly ceasing, lost forever. Others put out emergency calls for help, but travelling at a third of the speed of light, there was little realistic prospect of being saved by another ship - more often than not, only advice, rather than physical rescue, could ever be offered. Yet more seemed to simply malfunction and just drift ever onwards, further out into the inky depths of the far galaxy. Nevertheless, with such a vast array of ships departing from planet Earth, invariably some - possibly the majority - succeeded in reaching promising new planetary homes. New homes, new lives and new experiences awaited them at the planets deemed suitable by the 'genesis pods'. However, for the lucky ones who made planetfall, their experiment with destiny was only just about to begin.

Rorque 4 – contemporary political and economic situation

Purely by coincidence, the two stasis ships arriving on Rorque 4 had landed on the planet during the most important election campaign anyone could remember for more than a generation, with some commentators even claiming the whole future of the planet might be at stake - depending on the actual outcome of the election. Whilst hanging around in their hotel room and the main lobby area, the Margallans had noted a number of emissions relating to the subject, mixed in with a plethora of adverts, game shows, social media clips and various reality TV shows. They had, however, shown little interest in the emissions since they possessed only the vaguest idea of how representative democracy functioned, and thus failed to recognise them for what they actually were.

On Margalla, what passed for political decisions were largely the result of community discussions arriving at some form of consensus, or occasionally the use of direct voting when matters could not be resolved without an actual vote. With no class system and no group-based forms of discrimination, Margalla knew nothing of political parties, ideological schisms or professional political practice. On Margalla everyone was a politician – or alternatively, no one was a politician. As such, they were completely oblivious to the idea of election campaigns, and it was some time before they became aware that an event of significant importance was occurring during their time on the planet.

The original colonists who had made Rorque 4 their new home and who laid down the foundations of its presently existing civilisation, had decided to dispense entirely with the system of nation-states. They believed that back on Earth, on far too many occasions, sensible and right-minded business decisions had been, stalled, thwarted, distorted or simply abandoned because of misguided national sentiment or unthinking patriotic idiocy. As Thorsten Friedenman put the matter at the inaugural opening of the first session of the World Assembly, 'there's nonsense, complete and utter nonsense, and then there's nationalism. Never in the field of human affairs has so much drivel been devoted to one singular subject.'

Far too often, the original colonists believed, national considerations had been placed before sound and sensible economic or financial decision-making, and the majority of the newly-arrived settlers strongly maintained that this had been the real reason Earth had undergone its catastrophic climactic breakdown. It was not the shortcomings of capitalism that had destroyed the planet - as many in the exodus from the planet had maintained - rather it was its inability to function as it truly should have done. Nations had done much to hamper the true workings of capitalism, and were now regarded as surplus to requirement; a major hindrance, rather than any form of help to the economic system.

The early settlers had, instead, instituted a form of world government so that national rivalries and misguided patriotic loyalties would not upset the smooth running of Rorque 4's laissez-faire economy. This decision had been broadly popular with those of first origin, though had not quite achieved a complete consensus, since a small dissenting minority felt that absolutely all activities should be left to the private sector, and there should be no form of government whatsoever. Such objections were readily dismissed, though, as most of the new arrivees believed that some form of state was needed as an arbiter for when major disputes broke out between the rival corporations and that a small number of activities were best left to state institutions – largely because they created little, if anything, in the way of profit. The world government was thus constructed as a minimalist one, and the planetary economy was almost completely left in the hands of the consumers and producers of Rorque 4.

The state they established was, in accordance with their beliefs, democratic and constitutional. The state passed the laws, oversaw justice, imposed law and order and kept security across the planet. It did very little, if anything, else. The political system remained a democratic one, and had eventually evolved to be dominated by three large political parties, though there also existed a plethora of much smaller ones that, despite much effort, continued to exercise almost no influence on the political situation whatsoever. The reason for this was quite straightforward. The three main parties all enjoyed extremely close institutional links to the largest and most prosperous corporations on the planet. With no restrictions on party financing, this meant a political oligopoly had effectively been able to establish control of Rorque 4's world polity, one that very much matched the economic oligopoly that dominated across great swathes of the business world.

Arrival in Utopia

As with all democratic political systems, the precise areas of policy importance on which the parties campaigned had varied over time, but in the last two decades the economy had been struggling with what seemed like a never-ending crisis of profitability and recurrent bouts of economic stagnation. Initially, the standard procedures and policies had been implemented to boost economic activity – workers were laid off, companies were merged, surplus activities closed down, interest rates lowered, money was printed, credit made more easily available, increasingly large loans distributed, and a search for new markets had been embarked upon. The problem, however, was that most of this had been standard practice within the economy ever since Rorque 4 had been established over a century beforehand. Even in total all these amounted to very little in practice, and the economy remained mired in semi-continuous recession, debts continued to amass and employment stagnated badly.

In recent years, the three large corporations and their political mouthpieces had started to engage in a search for more and more outlandish strategies to end the economic depression. They had effectively arrived at the conclusion that the reason the planet's economy was struggling was the fact that it needed to create highly original and vibrant new markets if it was to return to profitability. The existing markets – now pretty much all dominated by the big three corporations - had driven prices as low as they possibly could. The markets had been milked for all they were possibly worth; to the extent that profit margins these days were thin to non-existent. The corporations were too large to eliminate each other, and they had all come to the reluctant conclusion that there was a distinct lack of new and profitable economic activities to move into.

They had already sold everything they could possibly think of to the population of Rorque 4. The scientists and technicians at their private universities and research departments were increasingly at a loss when it came to developing new technologies that could be profitably exploited. Additionally, the entire planet had developed as one large integral economy; all parts of the planet possessed an advanced economy, so there were no undeveloped geographical areas to move into and develop for the first time. The planet had a mature, even ageing economy, and now appeared to be incapable of reinvigoration. In a nutshell, it needed new and profitable markets to survive but was struggling to discover what and where these might be.

The leading executives, shareholders and political representatives of the three large corporations were though, unsurprisingly, not about to let their luxurious, privileged and opulent lifestyles become a thing of the past for a second time in history. They were determined to not go down without a fight and each corporation had arrived at a significantly different solution to the prolonged economic malaise they were experiencing and failing to overcome.

The Rorque Corporation, its associate businesses and their political party mouthpiece, the Liberty Party, had arrived at a position where they believed that the only means to create new markets and restore profitability was to look outwards, away from Rorque 4. This in itself, however, was problematic and beset with significant and protracted problems. The nearest known inhabited planets were Zeleyan, Ur-Tokar and Zeta Kotlin. Ur-Tokar's tiny anti-technology population offered no realistic prospects. Zeleyan was currently controlled by fascists but it did appear to possess a strengthening economy, and so offered potential new markets for the corporation.

The final alternative was the socialist planet of Zeta Kotlin. It possessed a well-developed economy and a considerable population, but access at the moment, for obvious political reasons, was completely blocked. However, recent contact with the authorities on Zeleyan had led them to believe that Zeleyan was drawing up plans to invade Zeta Kotlin, and if the Rorque Corporation could somehow be involved in this process then there was scope for making vast profits from the whole process through the provision of ships and other resources and manufactured materials. In addition, they might ultimately gain access to the potentially lucrative markets of both Zeleyan and Zeta Kotlin. However, there were also numerous technological difficulties involved in this outward looking strategy. Present levels of space technology had barely changed since the exodus from Earth, and space flight remained frustratingly slow.

The recent departure of the scientists from Alpha Fraczan, though, appeared to offer new hopes and promises in this and other areas. It was hoped they might be able to offer new technologies and thus new marketable products to be sold. Equally, the original message had indicated that the Alphan scientists had developed new space flight technologies and improved rocket science, ones that might be utilised for the connections that needed to be made with Zeleyan and ultimately Zeta Kotlin. Thus, the Rorque Corporation had made offers of an almost unlimited science budget, positions at the top universities and access to well-funded and equipped laboratories in the hope that they could entice these scientists into their plans. The fact that they had ultimately been employed by one of their rivals was a bitter blow, though the corporation was currently formulating plans to deal with this setback.

Their main corporate rival, Cosmic Solutions and its associated political grouping of the Justice and Order Party, had previously considered the plan being pursued by the Rorque Corporation, but had ultimately decided it to be unrealisable and even potentially dangerous for their civilisation. Zeta Kotlin was a socialist planet and would never allow capitalist corporations access to their economy. Dealing with Zeleyan offered greater possibilities, but it was run by a potentially dangerous and militaristic regime that might turn its aggressive attentions towards Rorque 4, the corporation feared.

Since Rorque 4 effectively possessed no military forces of its own – only extensive and very well-armed private security forces to maintain internal control – taking control of the planet might not prove to be a problem for the far more experienced military forces of Zeleyan. For these reasons, the corporation had opted for a different means of escaping the prolonged economic stagnation - that of terra-forming their neighbouring planet of Morpheus, a development that if realised could open up a whole new swathe of virgin markets and thus a return to healthy profit margins and extensive dividend payouts for their shareholders.

The prospect of gaining advanced knowledge of planetary systems from the Alpha Fraczan scientists, and the further possibility of also obtaining advanced space flight technology, would mark a major boost and advance for their plans, and their deal with Alpha Fraczan's leading rocket scientist was considered a major fillip for the corporation. As a result of this, they now held great expectations for a project that had recently stalled in several areas. The corporation was beginning to believe they had stolen a significant march on their competitors – one that would see them win the race to create profitable new markets.

The third of the significant corporate and political factions, was United Rorque Technologies – the product of numerous major corporate mergers in preceding decades – and its closely associated political appendage, the Democracy Party. Their solution to the prolonged crisis of profitability was less outlandish than the other two factions, and sought a more traditional and endogenous approach to returning the global economy to profitability. Their plan was simply to intensify and extend all the current features of the existing economic system; the foundations of the economy were ultimately sound and the correct ones to use, they believed, they simply needed to do more of the same to recover profitability.

Taxes might be very low, but they could be still further reduced. Although effectively little was actually banned from being bought and sold, laws could be passed to help new technologies come more quickly to the market. The corporation also desired laws that would allow workers to be deployed more effectively, whilst AI units should be extended into the small number of areas they were still restricted from being used within. There were calls for even greater sections of the legal and security systems to be privatised. Effectively, they were calling for even greater levels of neo-liberalism. Their two corporate rivals were highly disparaging of such a programme – it had all been done before, on numerous occasions, and had produced no discernible improvement to the economy. Currently, this programme was also proving to be the least popular with the voters – grandiose space projects, by contrast, had captured the imaginations of the electorate.

And so, purely by chance, the stasis ships from Alpha Fraczan had arrived in the midst of this global election campaign; one that most political observers were touting as one of the defining democratic moments in the history of the planet. Everything was currently at stake; this was a make-or-break election and would determine the future direction of the planet, its economy, and its status within the Nexus Cluster for decades to come. There was everything to play for and the corporations were typically throwing large sums of money at their respective campaigns. Slick advertising was dominating the airwaves whilst endless media emissions, sites and programmes praised or damned the relative merits and demerits of the different politico-corporate strategies, as each sought to gain the upper hand.

Arrival in Utopia

The six Margallans had quickly bored of residing in the fairly shabby hotel the Rorque Corporation had provided for their accommodation in a semi-dilapidated part of the city known as Shade Gate. Equally, they had made no initial progress with finding a solution to their rocket fuel problem. All their attempts to contact Anna Dubois had been firmly rebuffed by the corporation. They had visited the university where they believed she had been employed, but had been quickly marched off site, since they possessed no security clearance. And since that episode they had devised no further plans for resolving their dilemma. Bored, one day they had wandered into the local neighbourhood and entered one of its many bars, a retro-jazz outfit known as the Honky Dorky. The Rorque Corporation had provided them with a small amount of credit - which was also time-limited - after they had kicked up a fuss about having nothing to live on. The corporation had informed them they had devised a possible means by which this could be paid back, but the Margallans were still not fully sure of what was desired of them, or even how such arrangements actually worked. Nevertheless, they were now able to engage – if only marginally – in Rorque 4's economy and social life.

They were presently sat in the bar of the Honky Dorky trying to make sense of the electoral debate that was being played out on the large bluescreen on the wall before them. With no state, no political parties and no elections on Margalla, their politics were conducted in a completely different manner. It was not often they needed to make key political decisions, but when they did so it was done through a system of direct democracy at extraordinary community meetings. There were also few administrative positions, and those that did exist were filled through sortition, whereby the position holders were chosen randomly to carry out the role for one year only. This meant that in the course of a lifetime, each Margallan could expect to be chosen for a small number of short-lived administrative roles, and so their understanding of how Margallan society functioned was generally quite a good one, as they had to engage with it on an irregular basis in several different social areas.

The politics being played out before them did bear a passing resemblance to their own community meetings, but, here, only three individuals were engaged in the conversation, and they eventually worked out it was so that one of these individuals could be elected to an important position of power, and make all the key decisions in government for the next five years. This struck them as an entirely unfair system and one that was wide open to potential abuse. What on earth possessed anyone to think this was a good way of running a planet, they all agreed.

The bar was not particularly busy, and a fairly tall and thin young man with curly blonde hair and a tanned complexion, who had clearly been listening to their conversation, approached what he considered to be one of the oddest looking groups he had ever seen in the local neighbourhood.

'Hey are you those guys from that new planet they've found out about . . . err. . . what's it called?'

'Margalla', responded Akiko, slightly surprised that someone had actually started to converse with them. She had begun to wonder if everyone in the city was completely unfriendly or was avoiding them for some reason.

'Yeh, that's the one. I couldn't help overhearing your conversation about the election. It's all a farce you know. Only these three parties have any real chance of winning and they all believe in roughly the same things, they just differ on minor details. The party that spends the most money usually wins. Most people don't bother to vote you know, that's assuming you can vote in the first place,' the young man glanced around and seemed a bit nervous and hurried, and Akiko wondered if he was anxious about something in particular.

'Why can't some people vote?' asked Xander, genuinely oblivious to why this might be the case.

'If you have a criminal record, and that's most people round here, then you're barred from voting. It stops the more radical parties from getting elected,' he paused for a moment, 'added to which they have virtually no money to campaign with anyway.'

'What's a criminal record?' asked Zhavia. 'Why do people have criminal records?' asked Kiyona at almost exactly the same time. Margalla possessed few laws – just those in their original constitution, which were so firmly embedded in society they were rarely, if ever, breached. For acts considered by members of the local community to have been anti-social, community gatherings could be called which would then attempt to resolve the differences between the two individuals or groups involved. There were no prisons and no police force, so the concept of criminality barely existed, and Kiyona and the others effectively had no working knowledge of the concept.

'Mainly for stealing or some other form of theft – fraud is very common. Often, you can't get what you need round here, especially, when there's so little work. Stealing food is often the only way you can obtain anything to eat,' said the young man, who later in the conversation they discovered was called Mark.

'Can't you just get your AI units to do it for you?' asked Xander, though he assumed the answer was going to be in the negative.

The young man burst out laughing, 'your planet's obviously completely different from ours. You need to be very wealthy here to own an AI unit. Mostly their used by the corporations for purely employment purposes; though the wealthy also use them for their own personal purposes. They are far too expensive to buy for most people, especially the people round here,' he retorted, and now seeming less nervous.

All the Margallans had watched old Earth movies and other emissions at some point or another in their lives, especially when they were younger, so they had previously believed they had a reasonable idea as to how capitalist societies worked. However, even after a few days on Rorque 4 they were beginning to realise there was no substitute for experience, and were already feeling somewhat out of their depth.

'So you need employment here to get money and then buy goods,' stated Kiyona, increasingly uncertain of her knowledge on the subject, 'but once you've done that for a while, can't you buy an AI unit to work for you?'

'Employment is difficult to find these days. In the early days of the planet I think it was a bit easier. Nowadays the AI units carry out nearly all the economic roles and functions. The only employment humans can find is either highly skilled, creatively-minded or psychological-type stuff that is beyond the scope of the AI units – they're generally better at more routine tasks. You need a good education for those jobs though; only the rich can afford that. Otherwise, there's the low order, largely menial stuff that the corporations can't be bothered with, as it makes so little profit. That's what most people around here do, but the work is intermittent, doesn't pay well and you need to do long hours or several lines of work even to make enough to feed yourself. Basically, in that situation you're part of the underclass and have no hope of ever becoming wealthy. If it's cheaper to use an AI unit than a human, the corporations choose an AI unit every time,' Mark explained, sounding angry but also somewhat defeated at the same time.

Arrival in Utopia

The crew pondered this statement for a while, but could not fathom why anyone would want to run a society in such a way, never mind the finer points of how it actually functioned.

'So it's very difficult to get a good education and obtain one of these better jobs in order to become wealthy. And the reason for that is you need to be wealthy in the first place. Isn't that like a never-ending circle of non-opportunity?' asked Akiko, not fully sure if she had grasped the nature of the problem.

'Yes, all schooling costs money; some schools are just about affordable, but only the rich can afford the top schools – the Freedom Schools – so only their children have any hope of obtaining the best employment. The cheaper schools aren't that good; you only get a basic education, so you can't pass the tests and get into university, unless you go to one of the relatively cheap universities, but there seem to be less and less of them nowadays - a few have closed recently, I've heard. Some children just don't get educated at all, their parents can't afford it – they have no hope of achieving anything,' he responded, and Akiko noted he seemed to be becoming even less nervous, as though this was proving to be a cathartic experience for him.

For Kiyona, listening carefully to this answer, something suddenly clicked inside her brain. She remembered when she was much younger that she had asked why they needed to learn literacy at school, since you could simply verbally instruct computers, machines and AI units to do what you wanted, and to be informed of what you wanted to know. She had been told that literacy and education were essential to keep society from falling into ignorance, superstition and adopting beliefs that were incorrect and harmful for herself and others. Without an education she would be at a disadvantage compared with others, and might believe in any ridiculous idea or theory she was told. Knowledge was power, and everyone should possess it. She had always been quite sceptical about this answer, and had continued to place little importance on learning. Now, however, faced with a world with such a stark disparity between the well-educated and the poorly educated, she felt her earlier disdain for knowledge and learning was beginning to seem embarrassingly naïve.

She was about to ask Mark a further question, when the debate between the political leaders on the large bluescreen suddenly stopped and a long series of adverts played out on the screen. The crew watched in puzzlement. They had not been on the planet very long, but they all agreed they had not seen a single person who looked like any of the people in the adverts. They were all extremely happy, very attractive, very smartly dressed and smiling all the time – almost the opposite to the people they had met so far on Rorque 4. They also seemed to be informing the viewers that without buying such and such a product, their lives would be so much worse than those who did buy the product. Could buying a simple product really make your life better than that of other people, they wondered? After some discussion they decided that maybe on Rorque 4 it might be true, but it seemed very depressing if that was the case.

After the adverts, there were suddenly four politicians in the debate on the screen. Kiyona enquired of Mark as to why this was the case.
'They received the fourth most votes in the last three elections, so they get less airtime than the others. They're actually the best party in my opinion – the Equality Party – but they have no chance of winning. They have very little money to spend and don't own any big media outlets, so their media output gets swamped by the big three.'
'Is that who you vote for then?' she asked.
'No, they have no chance of winning, it's a wasted vote. I'll probably vote for the Justice and Order Party – they have the best chance of keeping the Democracy Party out of power, who just want to make the present situation even worse than it already is. The polls indicate the Justice Party might just clinch it this time, and their plan to terra-form Morpheus looks promising to me, especially now that they have all those scientists that came with you lot. It sounds like it actually might work now.'
Kiyona was fairly sure the scientists in question were actually on the other stasis ship that had arrived, but turned back to the screen, curious to know how this fourth party might be better than the others.

The leader of the Equality Party – an information strip along the bottom of the screen identified her as Katie Altair - was making a case for improving the lives of ordinary working people. She emphasised the importance of repealing something called the Impediment of Business Activities Statute – apparently a major component of Rorque 4's Constitution. It effectively outlawed any activity that was deemed a hindrance to the business activities of the banks, companies and corporations, and had led to trade unions, strikes and many forms of protest activity being effectively outlawed. She claimed that if ordinary people were able to organise and protest then they could drive up wages, rather than relying on endless loans that mired them forever in debt. They would have more money to spend and this would increase demand in the economy and lead to an economic revival.

The three other party leaders reacted with fury at this proposal and gave it very short shrift. A series of political and personal attacks ensued, denigrating some of her past activities and accompanied by accusations that she was a communist and probably in league with terrorists from Zeta Kotlin. Very little was actually said about the actual policy proposal itself though, other than some clearly well-rehearsed lines concerning attacks on individual liberties and the right of business leaders to decide how they ran their business and which products they could create and sell.

'All these leaders keep mentioning the importance of freedom, but it doesn't sound to me like people actually have very much freedom here. If you have to find employment to buy the things you need, but mostly can't find employment, what freedoms do people actually have here?' Kiyona enquired.

'If you have large amounts of money you do actually have unlimited freedoms here, you can do almost whatever you want, live where you want, consume anything you desire and travel anywhere on the planet. But you're right, people living round here – with minimal amounts of money – have very few freedoms; they are highly restricted in what they can do, in fact they have very few real freedoms,' answered Mark.

'So what do these people actually do with their time if they have so little money, work or freedom?' asked Kiyona, beginning to get a feel that she was actually understanding something of Rorquean society.

'Some people turn to charities or to religion, but there's only so much they can do for you. Gambling's popular, but only tiny numbers ever get rich that way. More and more, people are just drinking themselves to death or taking drugs to escape reality. It's so easy to fall into despair. There's been a whole spate of suicides recently. For most people, these are the only ways to escape underemployment. And the reality of poverty is that many turn to crime, but if you do that the penalties are severe and you really don't want to end up in the prisons here – they are absolutely horrendous.'

If the crew members had not watched old Earth emissions they would have possessed only the vaguest knowledge of what Mark was talking about. Most of these concepts were completely unknown on Margalla, and the idea of taking drink and drugs for negative reasons was particularly surprising – on Margalla this was always done to enjoy yourself!

'Do people rebel against this? If the election system is as bad as you say, are there other ways to change the system?' asked Arlo, unsure as to whether this was an intelligent question or not.

Mark hesitated a moment, 'decades ago there was a movement aimed at destroying the AI units in the hope that more employment could be created for humans, but the response from the authorities was highly draconian. The ringleaders were tried and executed. Others received extremely long prison sentences and languished in prison for decades or simply died there. The laws concerning AI units were strengthened – destroying, damaging, stealing or interfering with an AI unit owned by another person or institution in any way at all, holds very severe repercussions. The repression that followed the rebellion seemed to leave the population here demoralised and defeated. There's only been occasional protests since then, it's very difficult to organise anything, everyone is so isolated and individualist. I participated in one or two when I was younger, but they didn't achieve much and I soon lost interest.'

'What do you do for employment, anyway?' asked Akiko, deciding this all sounded a bit depressing and wanting to hear something a bit more cheerful.

'I'm an artist. I create proper art, not like that soulless, mass produced unimaginative crap the AI units churn out. My work has imagination, originality and feeling put into it. Here have a look at these,' and he showed them some of his designs on an electronic device he was carrying, which they had noticed virtually everyone on Rorque 4 spent a huge amount of their time looking at. 'What do you think about them?'

After a brief discussion as to what his images were about and what they were trying to say to the observer, Akiko asked if he was able to make a living being an artist, beginning to feel she had some understanding now of what employment actually meant.

'Occasionally I sell my work, but there's a great deal of competition. It's one of the few things the AI units do badly, so lots of people try to make a go of it. I've been trying to create images that will appeal to the senior executive market. Some of them buy large amounts of artwork. If I can sell my work to at least one of them, then my name will become better known and I've a chance of making it big', he replied, sounding slightly more upbeat and hopeful for almost the first time in their conversation

'So what would that allow you to do?' asked Arlo, who was still struggling to understand how Rorquean society worked.

'I'd get out of this dump as fast as possible, and move over to Gaynor Park on the smart side of town. I could get my kids into a top Freedom School then and they'd have much better prospects for the future. We might actually be able to afford a decent holiday and some other good things. Most of all, I could enter the higher echelons of the art world, afford to create better quality pieces and start to see my work properly appreciated.'

This, for the Margallans seemed something of a clouded vision, and was not quite the answer the crew had expected from someone who had spent most of the evening berating and criticising everything about life on Rorque 4, particularly the higher end of society.

Mark seemed to second guess what they were thinking, 'you can't beat the system, there's no other way out. If you can't beat them, you have to join them,' he said, almost apologetically. 'Follow the voice inside your head, not in your heart.' At this point he wished them good luck and wandered off to buy another drink.

The crew had not found their time in the bar particularly productive, and the music was not really to their taste either, though the conversation with Mark had cleared up a number of features of life on Rorque 4 they had found puzzling, whilst also highlighting how little they understood the society they suddenly found themselves stranded within. All in all, though, it had added to a depressing picture of the planetary civilisation, and after a few more drinks, they decided to call it a night and went back to their hotel for the rest of the evening.

Arrival in Utopia

Rorque 4 – Margallans visit Phetamine Street

During their first few days on Rorque 4, during their initial encounters with the folk of Shade Gate, the name Phetamine Street had been mentioned on a number of occasions, and eventually Kiyona decided to ask one of the casual acquaintances they had made exactly where this place happened to be and what went on there that was of such great interest. It turned out to be an old and abandoned amusement park further east towards the outskirts of the city and had originally been - and officially still was - known as Rose Wilder Park. However, a series of fatalities had occurred on the rides due to lax health and safety procedures and the prolonged and expensive lawsuits that followed, combined with falling visitor numbers, meant that the park had been temporarily mothballed until its legal situation had been fully resolved in the courts.

This situation had occurred several years into the economic downswing that was still inflicting its misery on the planet, and it had not been long before the long-term unemployed, the homeless, black market traders and various other marginal groups had spotted an opportunity that addressed their different and varying needs. Security at the location was limited – to keep down costs – and on such a large site it had proven effectively impossible to prevent its gradual occupation – first by the homeless and then by a variety of small time entrepreneurs, lifestyle alternativists, rebel groupings and various other marginalised sub-groups amongst the local population.

Fairly rapidly, the park had become a large-scale squatter site and the centre for a whole range of illicit activities. However, with the ownership of the site effectively suspended and contested until a variety of complex and long-running court cases had been finally resolved, any form of eviction was legally problematic and of doubtful financial benefit. The local security forces made occasional sweeps, raids and arrests at the site but the scale of the venture and the intractable nature of the problems that had led to its rise meant that they were always fighting a losing battle. Ultimately, they turned a blind eye to all but the most flagrant abuses of the law, whilst also deciding it was quite convenient for concentrating illicit activities into one manageable location.

Arrival in Utopia

The site had soon become known to the locals as Phetamine Street as it quickly became the source of all manner of black-market goods. Very few products were actually illegal in Rorque 4's free-market economy, but many were far too expensive for the average citizen. As such, there was a thriving black market in goods that had either been stolen, adulterated, pirated, damaged or simply sold onwards because they were ageing and worn out. In a nutshell, if you wanted something dodgy, Phetamine Street was the place to go. It was suggested to the Margallans that there might be an outside chance of finding someone there who could put them in touch with a contact who might be able to acquire rocket fuel for them on the cheap.

The Margallans had no means by which to know how realistic a prospect this might be and decided to give it a try – after all, they had plenty of time on their hands and little to lose. They were accompanied on the visit by a young man called Harvey who they had met in one of the clubs they frequented. He had long curly brown hair – far longer than most of the men they met in Rorque City – and a slightly bemused smile, and he seemed quite interested in their predicament, and had offered to help them out if he could. He was clearly very familiar with the site and had plenty of useful contacts there.

After a short journey, they arrived at the location and were somewhat taken aback by the sight that met them. The Margallans had never seen anything like Phetamine Street before – it seemed a strange combination of poverty and squalor intermixed with the bizarre, the fascinating and the vibrant.

'Why are all these people sleeping out here in the park when there is so much housing nearby?' asked Kiyona. 'I've seen plenty of empty properties around here. Why don't they live in them?'
'They've fallen on hard times and it's almost impossible for them to escape,' replied Harvey, slightly bemused by Kiyona's naivety. 'It's not called the poverty trap for nothing, you know. It only takes a prolonged period of illness, a redundancy at the wrong time, a death in the family or some other unfortunate or unforeseen event for someone to fall on difficult times. And if you have little or no money and limited education and your contacts can't put you in touch with anyone useful, then it's effectively impossible to work your way out of the poverty trap. You're stuck here if you're without good contacts, useful skills or with no money. The only way out really is if others

help you out in some way,' he paused, 'but you're very much reliant on generous individuals for that. There are very few agencies or organisations that will or can help . . . sometimes some of the charities will, but even they are very selective about who they offer welfare to.'

'I thought there were people on this planet with huge amounts of money, can't they share some of it with these people - given they don't have any of their own?' Kiyona asked in reply.

Harvey laughed. 'The extremely rich – they won't part with their money, though they easily could. They have enough to last several lifetimes.' He paused for a moment, 'in fact, once you're that wealthy it's more difficult to become poor than to remain wealthy. Money goes to money, as they say. They have billions in high interest bank accounts, invested in stocks and shares, property and the like. They get richer just by sitting around doing nothing. And then they pass the whole lot on to their children who repeat the cycle all over again,' he stated with some confidence, since this was clearly a subject he had clearly discussed at some length before and on numerous occasions. 'They *could* use it to help the poor, but they tend to think it will most likely be wasted and squandered. They would rather keep their wealth to themselves and use it to out-compete their fellow billionaires – a bigger mansion, more prestigious private plane or luxurious yacht or whatever takes their fancy. It's always been like that, and I see little reason for it to change anytime soon.'

The group moved past the abandoned amusement park buildings which now acted as a source of shelter and accommodation, and on towards an old enclosure whose present function was to act as a market for almost anything and everything you could conceivably want or need – as long as it wasn't too expensive.

'This is the thriving heart of Phetamine Street,' Harvey explained, 'you can buy almost anything here and all at knock-down prices. These people will sell you anything, they would offer time for sale if they could work out how to do it. If you're going to find rocket fuel that's affordable, this is probably as good a place as any to find it.'

The crew duly made enquiries with a small number of traders recommended by Harvey, but none had any idea of how they could obtain such an unusual product, although one or two said they would make enquiries and see what they could come up with. Ultimately, though, they made no tangible progress with the main element of their quest, although they did make some new acquaintances and contacts, and engaged in some interesting conversations, so there time there, they felt, was not entirely unproductive.

Kiyona, though, almost from the moment they arrived at the site, had not found the place to her liking. It smelt unpleasant, was noisy, dirty and crowded and the air of destitution was everywhere. She also quickly realised she didn't really understand what was actually occurring at the site, so – despite her misgivings – had decided to make a point of observing the behaviour of the many people at the market, in order to gain some idea of what the whole place was all about. By the time they were about to depart, she reckoned she had figured out the basics, but some aspects still puzzled her. She turned to Harvey for help.

'So basically people come here with money or credit and they exchange that for the goods that are being sold here. But what happens if someone has more money than you, do they get better deals and greater preferences?'
'They certainly do,' replied Harvey. 'All markets work on that basis; the more money you have the more deals you can make. You can drive harder bargains, acquire more expensive and better quality goods, buy goods cheaply in bulk and sell them on at a higher price – all sorts of advantages really. The people with the least money benefit the least from the market. Some think they might get lucky, or find a trader who's not that bright and get a great deal, but it rarely happens. Almost always, the wealthiest benefit the most from the markets. As everyone says, 'the more money you have, the more freedom you have.' Those with very little money, can't do much and have very little choice or freedom.'
From what she had seen of Rorque 4, this did not surprise her, but Kiyona was slightly surprised by one of his comments, 'So you can buy something and then sell it on to someone else, and for a higher price. Isn't that sort of unfair or cheating?'
Harvey laughed, 'that's how the whole system works! All these traders here bought their goods from someone somewhere, and now they're selling them at a higher price so they can make a living.'

'So these people didn't make all these goods at the mini-fabs so they could sell them, they bought them cheap from someone else so they can sell them here for more money. Why don't the customers just go to the mini-fabs in the first place, where it's cheaper, or get their own?'

'The mini-fabs – and, in fact, all the other forms of production and manufacturing – are all owned by the corporations. They're far too expensive for ordinary people to own themselves and they charge high prices for some of that stuff. Most of this gear has been acquired second-hand, is stolen, adulterated, slightly damaged or of lower quality for some reason. If you know the right people and have the right connections it can be acquired cheaply and sold on at a profit,' replied Harvey.

'Mmm, I keep hearing this word 'profit' everywhere we go, and how important it is to make a good profit. What does that mean?' asked Kiyona.

Harvey scratched his head, and thought for a moment. He was not entirely sure how to explain the concept. 'Most people – those with jobs anyway – work for a corporation for a certain amount of money each week or month, but the goods and services they create are sold by the corporation for a higher amount, and the difference between how much it cost the corporation to make it, and how much they sell it for, is called profit.'

Kiyona thought for a moment. 'And I guess they try to make that difference as large as possible, so they try to pay the workers less, or charge the customers more, or both,' Kiyona offered, believing she had at least understood this part of the process.

'I guess that's about right.'

'So, the whole system is based on some sort of theft or exploitation,' she surmised.

'Well, the corporations do make the investments and own the land, buildings and machinery,' he offered, almost apologetically.

'Which they could afford – and others couldn't - because they had more money in the first place.'

'Well, yes . . .' and at this point Harvey seemed as though he was becoming tired of the questioning, as he started looking around for something or someone. However, Kiyona had a couple of more questions she wanted answering.

'If you want to acquire more money – and as you say, gain more freedom – then how do go about this?'

'Well, for most people round here, that involves finding employment, if you don't already have a job, or if you do, working longer hours or gaining promotion or doing a better paid job – which usually means extra time spent training and working longer hours as well.'

This was more or less what she had already figured from what she had seen. 'But I've heard people frequently grumbling and complaining about how badly they are treated at their workplace – badly paid, long hours, bossed around by superiors and doing pointless activities and various other complaints.'

'Well, that is largely true,' he conceded. 'We are meant to live in a completely free and open society, but once you enter a workplace that all seems to come to an abrupt end. Workplaces are more like dictatorships – you simply have to do what the boss tells you, otherwise you lose your job. And it's not like it's any different anywhere else – they're all pretty much the same!'

'So this all means giving up your own time – and the freedom to choose what you want to do in that time – to be somewhere that's unpleasant and where you don't really want to be, in order to make more money, which people believe gives them more freedom. So, effectively you are giving up one form of freedom – time - to gain more of another one - wealth. Does that mean people here think that money is much more important than time?'

Harvey had to think hard about that one. 'Well I guess they generally do, the way you put it. Normally people say 'time is money' because the longer it takes to do a job, the more you need to pay someone. Though the people right at the top – with so much money in the bank they don't need to work – have all the time in the world to do exactly whatever they want. They have lots of time and clearly value it, and they have no intention of giving up their privileged position. So time *is* important to them.' He wasn't sure where else to go with this line of thinking, so asked, 'I guess your society sees time as more important than money, then?'

'We don't have money. If we need something we get it made at the mini-fab, obtain it from the general community store, where unneeded or unwanted items are kept, or just get the AI units to sort it out. We get most of our food from the fields and gardens. So, we have lots of time to do whatever we want – a bit like the people at the very top of your society, I guess. Except, on Margalla, everyone lives like that, not just a lucky few who need the rest of society to work hard to keep them there.'

Harvey looked surprised. He had no idea Margallan society functioned that way, but did suddenly realise why Kiyona seemed so unfamiliar with market economics, though, on reflection, she did seem to be learning very quickly.

'It sounds like your planet is much better than ours, then,' he said, though with a hint of sarcasm. He was vaguely aware of more egalitarian political thinking, but had always assumed it was unlikely to actually work.

'So why don't people here do the same as we do,' she replied, ignoring the sarcasm.

Harvey was clearly growing tired of the conversation, and simply offered, 'well, I don't think most people think it would work, and they're not about to take the first step on their own. If no one followed, they would just look a fool. You would need everyone to do it at the same time, and on a planet as obsessed with individualism as ours, I can't really see that happening. I'd be amazed if it ever happened here!' he concluded.

Kiyona decided she had run out of questions to ask.

Whilst this conversation was occurring, the rest of the crew had been discussing what to do next, but were still undecided as to what that should actually be. With so little credit, there options were very limited. They came over to where Kiyona and Harvey were standing, and Harvey could see they were looking slightly disappointed.

'Well they have got your number, so if anyone hears anything promising, they can contact you and let you know about it. You never know, one of them might come up with the goods. I guess it's not too surprising though, knocked-off rocket fuel is probably not the easiest of products to acquire, I would have thought. However, we do have a free market economy – supposedly – and he glanced at Kiyona, so someone out there might be selling it somewhere. You never know, you might just get lucky!'

Zeleyan – news arrives from Rorque 4

Supreme Commander Vartin was, as was the case each working day, seated at his desk at party headquarters in the centre of Zeleyan City. Of average height, stocky, with short dark hair and in the latter years of middle age, he was of fairly unremarkable appearance. However, Marcus Vartin had been born into to one of the wealthiest and longest lasting of the established elite families on the planet of Zeleyan. As such, he had been born into a life of power and privilege and his family had always expected great things of him, to which the young Marcus had not proved disappointing. Whilst passage through his elite school and military academy training had been largely effortless it had, nevertheless, not all been plain sailing. In his mid-twenties he had become entangled in a long drawn out and bitter power struggle between his father and various other members of the elite, who had previously been considered as close allies of the family, over the issue of land ownership.

His family had come out second best in the dispute, and he had received much of the blame for their defeat, though the setback had ultimately proved to be a temporary one, as the family successfully sought and enacted revenge at a later date. Nevertheless, the lesson he had drawn from the dispute was that absolutely no one could be trusted, and set in stone a suspicious and untrusting mindset that had lasted until the present day. At the same time, he had felt the blame apportioned to him for the defeat had been wholly unjustified and he still bore a certain level of resentment towards his own family as a result of the incident.

Nevertheless, this problematic episode had proven to be only a rare setback on his long march towards becoming the supreme leader of the planet, and in hindsight he believed it had taught him some valuable lessons concerning power, people, allies and his fellow elite members. He had currently been the Supreme Commander of the supercontinent for nearly two decades now, and he had spent some considerable amount of time in the preceding years searching for ways to mark his twentieth anniversary in power in an appropriately spectacular fashion. Eventually, he had decided that the invasion of Ur-Tokar was to be the great event that would remind the world of his pre-eminent importance.

As such, Vartin had been impatient to launch the next phase of his grand plan, but was still playing safe – as usual - and wanted to make sure each stage of the plan fell neatly into place before proceeding with the next. He was currently waiting for confirmation of Rosson's arrival at Ur-Tokar without mishap, though given the communication time lag and that all previous communications had indicated that the mission was proceeding as planned, he cautiously assumed that Rosson had almost certainly already made successful landfall on Ur-Tokar by now. If all went to plan, he was working on the assumption that the military base would probably be fully established within six to eight weeks, presuming his forces there met no military resistance or significant operational difficulties. He was also beginning to believe he might actually start to have more in trust Rosson, but also reminded himself that it was actually the starship's AI units that would be responsible for the safe arrival of The Crusader, rather than the vice-admiral himself.

With all this in mind, Vartin was sorely tempted to move ahead with stage two of the mission but still prevaricated. The three stasis ships that made up the invasion fleet were all fully prepared and ready for departure. All his regular troops were in stasis aboard the starships and the necessary supplies, materials and resources had been methodically stored away on board. However, his shock troops were back on the streets quelling a further outbreak of political unrest in the eastern sector of Outer Padnia once again and he was reluctant to leave before this had been fully suppressed, and also before he had final confirmation of the military base at Ur-Tokar being fully established. As normal, caution had got the better of him.

In addition, the delay was now further compounded since his spy satellite orbiting Rorque 4 had recently relayed news of an entirely unexpected nature. Apparently, he had just discovered, two of the stasis ships that had departed from Alpha Fraczan had not continued to Zeta Kotlin, but had diverted to Rorque 4 and had recently arrived at the capitalist planet. Vartin launched an immediate investigation into why the regime's communication monitoring stations had not discovered the changed trajectories of the two spaceships at a much earlier date. This latter detail though, was the least of his worries. Some of the information the satellite was picking up from local media sources, although partially speculative, indicated that the Rorque

Corporation were now employing scientists from the ship that contained Alpha Fraczan's leading rocket scientists and space flight engineers.

For Vartin, this posed several possible dilemmas, and became yet another cause for further prevarication. He decided he needed to discuss the matter with Varela, his Science Officer, and issued orders for an autocar to be sent to collect Varela and deliver him to the party headquarters immediately. Vartin arranged for the meeting to take place in one of the conference rooms further down the main corridor from his office on the top floor, and ensured that the meeting would remain an entirely private one between the two senior figures.

A short while later, he was informed of Varela's arrival and he made his way to the conference room, where Varela was already seated waiting for him. Dispending with any form of familiarities, Vartin informed Varela of the news from the spy satellite and launched into an immediate discussion of the matter with his Science Officer.

'If the Rorque Corporation - and perhaps Rorque 4 in general - gains knowledge of advanced rocket technology, faster space flight and the more sophisticated engineering needed to accompany it, we need access to that technology. If the Rorquean corporations can travel more quickly through space than we can – and who knows who else they might sell this technology to – then we are at a severe disadvantage, both militarily and economically. I'm growing tired of waiting - these damned space flights between planets are taking forever. If we can get hold of that technology, we can end all this waiting around, our missions can move far much faster and we will also possess the element of surprise. At the moment we're relying on stealth to achieve our aims, but we can't rely on that forever.'

Varela did not particularly want to be the bearer of bad news, but felt the need to introduce an element of caution into the conversation. 'It will probably take the Rorque Corporation years to build spacecraft equipped with any completely new technology they acquire, and at least several months to retrofit it to their existing starships. I don't think this is going to be of any immediate use in our mission to Ur-Tokar, though equally it's highly unlikely it will be of any immediate threat to us either. I think our plans can proceed as currently scheduled.'

Vartin was not particularly pleased with the response from his most trusted aid, and since he had already convinced himself this matter was a serious one, he was expecting Varela to be more supportive of his belief that decisive action needed to be taken quickly. 'But If Rorque 4 has this technology, then it is still essential that we obtain it, and as quickly as possible. That bunch of bean counters will undoubtedly want to make money out of it, and they won't be too fussy about who they sell it to either. We need to make sure we are at the head of the queue, that we acquire that technology first.' He paced up and down the long room, glancing at the long line of portraits of previous Zeleyanian leaders hanging on its wooden panel walls. He stopped at a particular chair and leaned on its wooden frame.

'And further to my point, we still don't know what technology Zeta Kotlin has acquired from these scientists – since our spy satellite there stopped functioning some time ago. If we are to have any realistic chance of invading that planet, then I'm increasingly of the belief that faster space flight will be essential to our success. With current technology, it's a sixteen month flight between Ur-Tokar and Zeta Kotlin. At those slow rates of travel, they would see us coming months before our arrival. If we can even half that time, then we might have some chance of taking them unawares and unprepared, especially if we can keep our presence on Ur-Tokar top secret.'

Varela was as keen as Vartin was to see an end to the socialist society on the planet once and for all, and had worried that the Supreme Commander might be using the news from Rorque 4 to further delay his plans for their conquests in space. Now that he realised this was not the case, he changed tack. 'Zeta Kotlin appears to have no military forces of any sort – at least that was the case when we were last able to monitor their planet – and, given their pacifist sensibilities, it's highly unlikely they have developed any since, I would imagine. I suspect they believe that their relative isolation keeps them safe from outside forces. If they were to face an external threat, they probably believe that they have sufficient time to prepare and mount some form of effective defensive campaign - given the slow nature of space travel. Personally, I doubt that would be the case against our military superiority, and a successful invasion is still the most likely outcome, by my calculations. But, nevertheless, you are correct, with faster space travel and the element of surprise, the odds shift even more heavily in our favour.'

Pleased that Varela now appeared to be supporting his desire to move quickly, Vartin felt he, himself, could now add a note of caution to the discussion. 'Of course, we need to see how matters develop on Ur-Tokar before we make any final decision, but I have every reason to expect complete success there. It's imperative, of course, that our presence there remains secret to the outside world, but if we soon have the option of faster space travel available to us, then our plans can advance as previously decided, but even more rapidly. We need to acquire this technology and this knowledge and have it sent to us as soon as is humanly possible.'

'If we want to use it to invade Zeta Kotlin, I suggest we will need to have it dispatched straight to Ur-Tokar – the delay of sending it here and then to Ur-Tokar will add several unwanted months to our plans. Given we want to move far more quickly, that would seem to be by far and away the best option.'

Vartin started pacing the room again, pondering this idea. 'Do we have technicians on Ur-Tokar who are sufficiently competent to implement this new technology? I would be extremely reluctant to use scientists or technicians from the Rorque Corporation for any retrofitting procedures. That would add even further delays and hold all manner of security implications.'

'We have a range of AI units on the mission to Ur-Tokar which can presumably be programmed to carry out whatever procedures prove to be necessary – be it the introduction of new technology or retrofitting the existing ones,' replied Varela. 'I don't see that as a problem.'

'And, whichever procedure happens to be the case, it does, of course, mean that Rorque 4 will know that we are on Ur-Tokar, and they could probably figure out for themselves what we are planning to do next.'

'Yes, that is definitely a concern, but it's as much in their interest as it is ours to see the destruction of socialism on Zeta Kotlin. If we arrive at certain agreements, I suspect we can rely on them to keep quiet about our plans, especially if they are able to envisage making significant profits from our future plans.'

'So we will make immediate enquiries about the technology, indicate our willingness to pay for the relevant knowledge or new technology, or both, and once this is agreed upon we will arrange for it to be sent immediately to Ur-Tokar. I myself will be there in less than twelve months time, so there is a strong possibility it could arrive whilst we are consolidating our planetary position, and making arrangements for our next great victorious venture into space. I will, of course, oversee its successful implementation. As such, I think the matter is settled and we can leave it there.' With this, Vartin concluded the meeting and indicated to Varela he could now leave.

Vartin called for his Communications Officer and issued orders for contact to be made with the Rorque Corporation, and the preliminary arrangements for a deal to be made to acquire the advanced space flight technology were set in motion. Once this had been completed, he sat back in the chair at the head of the table and once again looked around at the portraits that lined the long length of the room. For Vartin, the wheels were now all set in motion. The prospects for his grand plan were looking increasingly promising. He wondered what the great men – who included his all-time hero, Commander Charles Rocco, and the various other generals who had ruled the planet – looking down at him from the wall would think of his plans. He was reminded that it was in this room, and as a result of looking at these portraits, that he had first conceived his plans for conquering the Nexus Cluster. Vartin reflected for a while on the history of Zeleyanian civilisation and his place within it.

Zeleyan - history

Zeleyan City sat right at the heart of the Zeleyanian supercontinent – the only landmass of any consequence on the planet - and other than a few scattered islands at various disparate points of the compass, the vast supercontinent was the only habitable land of any significance on the planet. The city itself was a recent creation, located and constructed by Vartin at the centre of the supercontinent to impart complete control across its extensive landmass. The exact location of the city – on a small area of grassy steppe almost completely encircled by mountains - had been chosen entirely for security reasons. A surprise attack on the capital was inconceivable since watchtowers had been placed at regular intervals along the entirety of the surrounding mountains. It was impossible for any advancing force to take the city by surprise. The only passes between the mountains through which transport and troops could move were heavily guarded and fortified with an array of forts, watchtowers and guardhouses.

Vartin had abandoned the previous capital, Kantor, a smaller and much older city close to the western shores of the landmass in Novo Salzar, several years previously. He had come to believe that it was too difficult to defend and too associated with previous party leaders. It was also a major centre of manufacturing and his relationship with the captains of industry was sometimes a problematic one. A brand new city – a political centre at the geographical centre – allowed him to stamp his authority across the entire planet once and for all, whilst offering an opportunity to impress the masses with a grandiose structure and his own glorious personal vision of the future. Power was concentrated entirely in his - and only his - political and military leadership; he was head of the party, the government, the state, the armed forces and any other organisation that mattered. Nevertheless, this had not been achieved without difficulty and neither by Vartin alone. He was only the latest of several military commanders to take upon themselves the task of imposing security and law and order across the entire planet.

The official history of the planet of Zeleyan was a highly inaccurate and wholly manufactured affair, established to show the present fascist regime in the best of possible lights. Effectively, it portrayed the existing regime as having originally attained full political control, having come to the rescue of a planet damaged and half-destroyed by degenerate left-wing political forces, in an act of great moral and national reawakening after years of degeneracy, division and despair. Since attaining power, this official history had painted a picture of a land enjoying almost unbroken peace, prosperity and harmonious development by effectively writing out the intermittent periods of unrest and rebellion, and glossing over the numerous incompetency's and economic disasters, whilst selectively cherry-picking the more successful parts of its historical civilisational development.

Fortunately, for any more neutral onlooker, the early chaotic period of the planet's history was fully documented by contemporary observers of the time, and the numerous media broadcasts remained permanently available to later historians, though far more easily available on the other planets of the Nexus Cluster. More objective historians were thus able to picture together a far more accurate and truthful account of Zeleyan's early historical perturbations and troubled development, and the following account is drawn from one such source, that of the esteemed historian, Leroy Chirawa, based originally at Sienna Pools University on Alpha Fraczan.

Zeleyan had originally been a continent of disparate nations scattered across its vast plains, mountains, plateaus and hilly coastlines. Wars and hostilities had broken out on a highly frequent basis. Ostensibly, these had been fought over access to valued resources such as farmland, minerals, timber and productive fishing areas, but also to achieve strategic goals – access to the sea, rivers, certain offshore islands and defensible highlands. Each nation had proclaimed its inalienable right to possess whatever it deemed necessary to secure its culture and its survival, and all too often, though, these demands had ended in outright conflict. An objective observer would have noted that these chaotic developments very much resulted from the nature of the original stasis ships that arrived at the planet, nearly one hundred and fifty years before present.

Zeleyan possessed two standard-sized moons, orbited a fairly standard G class star named Hedilla, and was situated almost centrally in the centre of 'the Goldilocks zone'. Around it there existed a useful array of other rocky planets in the star system - besides the two gas giants of Keitzel and Muisson towards the outer limits - orbiting Hedilla, all of which offered potential mining and resource opportunities. As such, it came as close to the Solar system as anything that had been found by the 'genesis pods' in the near galaxy so far. Admittedly, Zeleyan had a day that was twenty six Earth hours long and an annual orbit of 416 days, but this did not significantly detract from its attractiveness as a new home and planetary destination.

Not surprisingly - given its promising features - a good number of stasis ships homed in on the planet, amongst them some of the earlier 'nation-based' ships that had departed from Earth in the original wave of departures. Some years behind them, they were joined by a number of 'corporation' ships, and finally by a couple of 'patriot ships' as they liked to call themselves, but essentially an assortment of far right nationalists, authoritarians and fascists that had departed Earth in one of the later waves of the exodus, finally abandoning the fight for a more aggressive nationalism in their respective countries, after an ungrateful Earth had refused to recognise the wisdom of their unpalatable ideas, even when faced with imminent self-destruction.

For the freshly arrived colonists of Zeleyan, it had not taken too long for political matters to degenerate into conflict. As with all newly inhabited planets there had been an initial burst of enthusiasm as the usual necessities of colonisation – political, economic and social – were established and then consolidated by the first settlers. Unsurprisingly, the earliest arriving starships occupied the regions and lands of the supercontinent that appeared the most promising for the purposes of creating a prosperous society. For these nations, matters tended to initially work out promisingly. Towns and cities were built, farming was established, factories created and transport systems established. However, some of the later arriving ships had derived from nations or social groups that had seen themselves as high ranking in the pecking order on Earth, and resented their allocation of the poorer territories and lands that the earlier settlers had passed over as unsuitable. For these late arrivals, there was considerably less scope for creating a prosperous future.

By the time the 'patriot ships' arrived, local rivalries and jealousies had already spilled over into low level conflict. It was not difficult to turn a border dispute on a newly inhabited - and thus newly demarcated - continent into a full-scale political and military incident. During the next few decades, the various nations found themselves sizing up potential rivals and allies as it became increasingly obvious that the originally established borders were not going to hold. Conferences were held in an attempt to avert a major conflagration, but the 'deprived nations' were unable to achieve the terms they were looking for, in what was effectively a zero-sum game, and low level conflicts continued. When thousands of ideologically-driven far-right nationalists were inserted - into what was already a combustible situation - it was not surprising that all-out war was the eventual result. This particular set of colonists seemed to have learnt nothing from the lessons of Earth's recent history.

All the 'nation ships' had brought military units with them for defensive purposes, so weaponry was widely available to the new colonists. In addition, sufficient manufacturing capability had arrived with the settlers from Earth, and the mining of local minerals and other materials meant additional weaponry could easily be added to the existing military arsenals. The wars that followed were not particularly bloody, but they were highly demoralising for the inhabitants involved. The settlers had recently left one major catastrophe behind only to find themselves now embroiled in yet another one, when they were actually meant to be establishing and building a brave new world.

A considerable degree of destruction followed - not just on the surface of the planet, but also to the stasis ships and satellites orbiting the planet, nearly all of which were destroyed to prevent their military use by rival nations. As the troubles rumbled on, many colonists decided to look for quick fixes to end the conflict, and a distinctive trend developed in which nations opted for mergers with other compatible nations under the aegis of a strong and decisive nationalist leader who they believed were capable of delivering future security. Ultimately, the various disparate nations found themselves forming three super-nations – the Northern Alliance, Novo Salzar and Outer Padnia. These stronger super-nations, it was thought, would be more durable, bring stability to the deteriorating situation, and were less likely to be invaded, since their collective defensive capabilities were considerably greater than those previously available to the smaller nations.

However, this scenario ultimately proved to be equally unstable. The newly-formed Northern Alliance – probably the weakest of the three super-nations - largely encompassed territory composed of the vast and extensive northern plains, but regarded its existing position as effectively indefensible, and so it sought to gain control of a strategic central mountain range which offered a much better chance of defending its lands from any potential invasion from the south. Novo Salzar and Outer Padnia simply saw this as a land grab, and these two super-nations formed a – supposedly temporary - military alliance, launching a joint offensive that entirely crushed the forces of the Northern Alliance and seized its not inconsiderable territories.

Martial law was imposed by the invading forces in order to maintain control over the vanquished lands and its discontented communities. However, events took an unexpected turn when the citizens of New Europe – one of the more urban and industrialised regions of Outer Padnia - launched a general strike demanding an end to martial law in the lands of the Northern Alliance. Progressive elements amongst the population there feared the extension of martial law into their own super-nation, and were attempting to pre-empt any such development. In the confusion and political tension that followed, a high-ranking colonel with strong fascist leanings named Tarafel saw this as a perfect opportunity to remove the political leadership of Outer Padnia, which he had long believed was too weak and insufficiently right-wing.

Tarafel immediately extended martial law across Outer Padnia, but concerted levels of resistance from the populace ultimately demonstrated that Tarafel had over-reached his position. His security forces, despite repeated clampdowns, proved incapable of establishing full military and political control. Faced with the immanent prospect of his own removal from office, Tarafel turned to the superior forces of his erstwhile allies Novo Salzar for help in reestablishing political order, a desperate and potentially risky move, but effectively his only remaining choice. The forces of Novo Salzar did indeed come to the successful rescue of Colonel Tarafel, but the leader of Novo Salzar, Commander Charles Rocco, also of extreme right political leanings, considered Tarafel to be a liability and once he had established full control in Outer Padnia, had Tarafel summarily executed.

Now effectively in control of the entire super-continent, Rocco took the opportunity to extend martial law across the entire planet, once he had established alliances with the necessary political, economic and military groupings, all of which were rapidly brought under his own personal control. Rocco moved quickly to eliminate any potential rivals and crush all forms of dissent. All parties except his own United National Patriotic Party (UNPP) were banned, the few popular assemblies that still existed were closed down, and civil liberties were permanently suspended for the entire population. All sections of society were effectively placed under the control of the United National Patriotic Party – business organisations, religious movements, trade unions and any other significant institutions within Zeleyanian society. According to party propaganda, they were permitted to carry on with their normal everyday activities, but with UNPP officials stationed in every single organisation and making sure the policies of the Supreme Commander were followed at all times, their level of autonomy was, in reality, limited to non-existent.

Rule of law – where all citizens were considered equal before the law and enjoyed equal rights and protections – was replaced by rule by decree. The judiciary was placed firmly under the control of the UNPP so that all trials, convictions and legal rulings accorded with the wishes of the party. The trade unions could continue to enhance the lives of their members but with UNPP officials leading and controlling the unions and their branches, this needed to accord closely with party policy. Strikes, or any other form of industrial action, were, of course, completely outlawed. Essential sections of the economy – notably those concerning security and infrastructure – were brought under the direct control of the state, but the majority of business activity was left in the hands of private entrepreneurs. UNPP officials, however, were placed on the boards of all leading corporations and companies to ensure that the drive for profit did not in any form or manner undermine national unity or the wider interests of the super-nation-state.

The laws concerning AI units were particularly strict, and punishment for contravening them was swift and severe. All AI units were to be held in the possession of the state, the UNPP or private business, no other individual, group or organisation was allowed to own an automaton or be permitted to alter their programming. Those under the control of the private corporations were to remain so, only as long as national law was fully complied with. Contravention would lead to their confiscation by the state. In the case of national emergencies, the state could commandeer all AI units it required, until the emergency had been satisfactorily dealt with. This meant that, whereas many other settled planets had used their AI units to save humans from the most boring, tedious and difficult forms of employment, Zeleyan prioritised national security and protection of the nation-state; most AI units worked for the military or security services. As a result, the working people of Zeleyan could be subjected to any form of employment no matter how degrading, health destroying or mind-numbingly dull.

Under the rule of Supreme Commander Rocco, the planet did experience a lengthy period of political stability, but also one of intense repression and an almost complete lack of freedom. Rocco eventually died of a heart attack in his early fifties and had since been replaced by a line of six further Supreme Commanders, each in turn maintaining high levels of repression, though fortunately not preventing the planet from attaining a significant level of economic development. The latest in this line of dictatorial leaders was Supreme Commander Vartin. Vartin had initially planned to simply maintain the existing social status quo – much like his immediate predecessors had done - but several years after being promoted into the highest position in the land he had grown restless and become distinctly more ambitious.

Whilst he admired the previous line of Zeleyanian commanders he had succeeded – the portraits of which adorned the walls of the conference room he had held his meeting with Varela in - over the years he had come to think of them as having been too conservative, too concerned with simply maintaining security and law and order, whilst failing to think on a bigger scale. Vartin was worried that, whilst the lives of great men might be remembered for many years beyond their deaths, he too would eventually be seen in this conservative light. He wanted to stand out from the elite crowd, to be seen as a leader of particularly special note, and to go down in the history books as one of the great Supreme Commanders, if not the greatest ever.

His problem was, though, that his regime already ruled the entire planet, from the grassy plains of the northern reaches, through the mountains and plateaus of the centre, to the coastal communities of the south-western and eastern seaboards. There was nowhere left to conquer, unless, of course, he considered the other planets in the Nexus Cluster, and given his then lack of spaceships and the painstakingly slow nature of space flight and communication this initially seemed an unlikely prospect. Additionally, he was unsure of the exact political situation on the other planets, and of their economic and military capabilities. Certain features were well-known, but there was much that was largely speculation. He considered sending spies to observe the other planets, but given that ships rarely travelled between the different star systems this was logistically improbable. Ultimately, he had opted for placing spy satellites into the orbits of the four other worlds of the Cluster known to be inhabited. This though had delivered mixed results.

The satellite placed in the orbit of Ur-Tokar had confirmed pretty much everything they thought they already knew about the society on this particular planet. The one sent into orbit around Rorque 4 ultimately proved extremely useful, allowing him an extremely advantageous position in his dealings with the planet's corporations. By contrast, the satellite sent to orbit Alpha Fraczan simply ceased transmitting several days after arriving. That sent to Zeta Kotlin lasted slightly longer, though not before it had confirmed that the planet's society was still as depraved and degenerate as his predecessors had always believed it to be. In both cases he assumed the local inhabitants had destroyed the satellites; he had no way of being able to confirm this, but for the suspicious Vartin that was clearly the obvious explanation.

Nevertheless, now armed with a range of information that seemed to confirm most of what were previously only regarded as given-truths, Vartin began to set about engineering his place and destiny in history. Initially, he had felt no great need for urgency. Ur-Tokar was not about to change anytime soon, and there were no discernible threats to his leadership on Zeleyan, and so his plans moved forward at an unhurried pace. However, two unexpected developments had recently changed matters. The first was the highly unexpected departure of the diaspora starships for the socialist planet of Zeta Kotlin. The second was continued outbreaks of political unrest amongst the people and workers of highly urbanised and relatively prosperous regions within both Outer Padnia and Novo Salzar.

Vartin, by nature, was a highly suspicious person and was naturally inclined to link the two events. He suspected local socialist elements amongst the rebellious provinces were in contact with Zeta Kotlin; the arrival of the diaspora ships at the socialist planet would be a huge propaganda coup for their ideology and might have spurred local agitators into initiating action. Alternatively, it was possible the Zetans themselves had somehow placed their own agents amongst the workers; there were some indications that Zeta Kotlin had maintained a presence in space, albeit limited in nature, but perhaps capable of delivering personnel to the planet secretly. His efforts to verify such a strategy, however, had come to nothing and the planet's satellite system had detected no suspicious extra-terrestrial activity in the local area of space. As such, he favoured the first explanation for the political unrest, but it was always prudent to bear alternatives in mind, he believed.

His secret police were under orders to locate and identify the origins of the unrest. Political agitators were, of course, dealt with in the usual manner – exile, imprisonment or execution invariably followed, subject to the actual severity of the particular crime the perpetrator had engaged in. Equally, the media were under orders to increase the number of reports vilifying unpopular minorities whilst also linking the unrest to conveniently disliked scapegoats. Despite all this, Vartin was increasingly of the mind that in addition to using divide and rule strategies and harsh repression to maintain order, what the inhabitants of Zeleyan really needed was something to feel proud of, a new glorious military victory to arouse the patriotic fervor of the masses. This, he believed, could put an end to the political unrest. Such a victory would also openly and clearly proclaim to the planets of the Nexus Cluster the superiority of the Zeleyan political system and hopefully inspire like-minded citizens on the different planets to copy their successful example.

Additionally, the leading members of the business section of the UNPP had been trying to impress upon him - and for some time now - the fact that they believed a number of negative structural problems had persisted within the economy for far too long, and that these were beginning to reach the point where the economy was in critical danger of stagnating, and with all the negative repercussions that followed from such a development. They were pressing him to create a more open and freer economy in order to open up new and thus profitable markets.

Vartin had persistently stonewalled these demands; a more open and freer economy would be much more difficult to police and to control. Economic freedoms, personal choices and an end to travel restrictions would invariably lead to demands for political and social freedoms, and all the disorder and degeneracy that went with such a social system. Additionally, Vartin suspected that the real concern of the business leaders was actually more about lining their own pockets, rather than any great concern for the health of his regime. Vartin wanted to maintain the closed and controlled economy that allowed him to retain a high level of centralised control, and he saw no good reason to dispense with a system that had worked so effectively for so many decades.

However, if they wanted expanded markets then he would give them expanded markets, just not in the form they were pressing for. His invasion of Ur-Tokar would thus kill several birds with one stone; quell the unrest in the provinces, satisfy the business leaders, impress the rest of the Nexus Cluster and cement his place in history on the twentieth anniversary of his attaining power. It was for these reasons that he had dispatched Rosson and a military force in The Crusader to Ur-Tokar, and it was for these reasons he had acquired further stasis ships from Rorque 4; which even now sat ready and waiting for a full-scale invasion of the technophobic planet. But, this he hoped, would only be the start of his endeavours in space. Much more would follow. It would soon be time for his date with destiny.

Vartin looked once more at the seven portraits of the military commanders hanging on the wood paneled wall. He had already decided where his own portrait would be placed and, indeed, the portrait had already been commissioned. There were, of course, numerous portraits of Vartin displayed across the supercontinent, but this one, in his opinion, would be an extra special likeness. In addition, the backdrop to his portrait was an image of space and the Nexus Cluster constellation within which a prominent Zeleyan loomed large behind him, thus portraying him as both a planetary and an interstellar ruler. It was also considerably larger than the other seven. Vartin allowed himself a rare smile, rose from his chair and returned to his office for the rest of the afternoon.

Rorque 4 – Margallans attend a concert

It was more than two months since the Margallan crew had arrived in Rorque City, and they were still no closer to working out the means by which they could successfully effect their departure from the planet. Somewhat in desperation, they had asked random strangers they happened to meet for help, but none of these, unsurprisingly, had a clue as to where you bought rocket fuel from, often looking at them like this was the most stupid question they had ever been asked. One particularly insecure individual took great offence, becoming quite violent towards them, as he thought they were trying to make a fool of him. As the days passed - often very slowly - their likelihood of actually leaving Rorque 4, they began to think, was looking more and more remote, whilst their desire to depart was becoming ever greater; the more they saw of its society, the less they liked of it.

None of the crew had ever experienced sexism, racism or homophobia back on Margalla, but on Rorque 4 these all seemed to be a widespread and persistent problem. Given that they were from an entirely different culture, they were largely oblivious to the more nuanced elements of this abuse, but its more blatant manifestations they found dispiriting and depressingly unfair. On a range of occasions, they were refused access to certain establishments, subjected to verbal abuse from members of the public and occasionally stopped and searched by the security forces. Initially, they had wondered if all these episodes were simply routine experiences for the inhabitants of Rorque 4, but slowly they became aware they were being discriminated against on the basis of who they actually were, rather than anything they had done.

A further major problem for the crew were the issues of security and trust. They very quickly discovered that Rorque 4 had huge amounts of the former and very little of the latter. Almost everywhere there were locks, alarms, security doors, surveillance cameras, security checks and identity devices. None of these existed in any form whatsoever on Margalla. Not being citizens of Rorque 4, they could not initially prove who they were, which quickly became a frequent problem, and they were forced early on to obtain ID from the Rorque Corporation. The degree to which they were mistrusted - particularly by establishment and property owners, and for no apparent reason - was particularly mystifying for people from a planet where everyone tended to implicitly trust each other, unless given a very good reason to do otherwise.

Equally, deriving from a planet where private property related to a few personal possessions and little else, whilst everything else was shared collectively by the whole community, the crew experienced endless problems adapting to the idea that they could not just use resources, facilities, property, land and whatever else, as and when they desired or needed. There were frequent disputes with property owners, numerous misunderstandings and occasional arrests for theft by the security forces, which again entailed interventions from friendly acquaintances - and occasionally the Rorque Corporation - in order to explain their unique situation.

But what they found most dispiriting was their general and persistent lack of freedom. On a planet where they could visibly see and hear a whole range of different entertainments, experiences and resources - and when advertising constantly encouraged them to partake and indulge in such activities - they found that their lack of credit meant they were actually able to experience almost none of this so-called freedom. Instead they found themselves left at the mercy of the cheapest establishments and their poor quality produce, charities with their strict rules and regulations, and a few well-meaning neighbourhood community projects attempting to provide something worthwhile but with very few resources. To add insult to injury, they often witnessed a small percentage of the population visibly over-indulging, whilst they and those around them were left with very little or nothing.

Upon arrival on the planet, they had been loaned a small amount of credit by the Rorque Corporation, but this they soon discovered was insufficient for their needs, and so they spent much of their time at the hotel or engaging in the few activities they had discovered were actually very cheap or free – which were not actually that many. Despite this problem, a combination of boredom and a morbid curiosity frequently got the better of them, and so they explored the local area, occasionally frequenting the cheaper bars, cafes and retail outlets which were spread haphazardly around the neighbourhood of Shade Gate. One evening they found themselves in yet another fairly rundown and ramshackle retro-music venue, this one specialising in alternative rock music and psychedelia, with a poorly lit sign over its peeling front doors identifying itself as The Aubergine that Ate Rangoon.

It seemed to the Margallans that many of the inhabitants of Rorque City had decided – possibly en masse – to hark back to previous eras and ages, presumably on the basis that belief in a more certain past was preferable to the highly uncertain difficulties of the present period. There appeared to be a popular belief that past generations had enjoyed better times and thus better music. The Margallans were still somewhat puzzled as to how entertainment was provided on Rorque 4, and were intrigued as to why at different points throughout the evening, a variety of different-sounding bands came on stage to play a combination of their own songs, but also selected cover versions, some of which they were told were first played by bands on Earth over two hundred years ago. They were currently watching a band known as the Psychedelic Warlords who commenced their set with a very strange electronic intro and then launched into a stream of songs that all ran one into another. Certain songs seemed to be held in an almost reverential regard by the on-lookers and the whole audience sang vociferously along to the words and then cheered loudly at the end of the song.

The clientele of the venue were dressed in a very different manner to the majority of the people whom they had met previously – who mostly seemed to wear what were clearly mass produced garments of a fairly uniform design and nature – and they also discovered during the evening that those attending the venue tended to think differently as well. They were clearly far more willing to question the social system they were living under, than the rest of the inhabitants of Rorque City they had met so far. They were also friendlier than most of the individuals they had met elsewhere, and it was much easier to strike up meaningful conversations with them. In addition, word had now spread around the district that the Margallans were staying in their area, and some of the locals were curious to meet them and know everything about the planet they hailed from.

Not too long after they entered the venue, they were approached by a small group of men and women who were mostly slightly younger than themselves. They seemed to be wearing odd-looking clothes and sporting hairstyles that all looked somewhat similar in nature but also somehow slightly individual – something the Margallans had noticed was a frequent feature of Rorquean society. The group was clearly eager to know about their lives on Margalla and everything they could tell them about Margallan society. Over an increasing number of alcoholic drinks – which they all agreed were far inferior to the ones they brewed on Margalla - the crew explained to the group at some length the nature of their lives, their living arrangements, how they made decisions on the planet, their leisure activities and almost anything else they cared to mention. Many of the group looked distinctly impressed, as they told the Margallans that they too were socialists and anarchists, and had been agitating for a similar way of life on their own planet. They had frequently encouraged the people of Rorque 4 to rebel against the oppressive capitalist system and to replace it with an egalitarian utopia, though unfortunately, so far they had made little in the way of any substantial progress.

From time to time their attention was drawn back to The Psychedelic Warlords as they continued to play their set amidst a backdrop of swirling lasers, thick plumes of dry ice smoke rising from the stage, contorting dancers and a constantly changing light projection. Eventually, the band finished their set, the audience applauded loudly and they watched the Psychedelic Warlords disappear in smoke, as they made their exit to the rear of the stage. Suddenly, the visual bluescreens - that seemed to be so ubiquitous across Rorque City – sprang into life all around them across the walls of the venue, to offer their standard daily mixture of almost endless advertising, sports news, celebrity gossip, video clips and short current affairs programmes.

As they continued the conversation with their new found acquaintances, they suddenly became aware that a number of people had turned their attention towards the multitude of screens, because a new news story was breaking across them. The screens were showing a city called Libertyville, on the far side of the planet, engulfed in ferocious flames, and informed the viewers that tens of thousands of people had been forced to flee from their homes. Prior to this, bush fires had raged for several days in the adjacent rural areas, but unseasonably strong winds had pushed them towards the city, and the flames were now sweeping across the outlying districts of the city. The authorities were apparently investigating the possibility that the fires may have been started deliberately by arsonists.

'Who would do such a thing as that? Surely they must have known that it's highly dangerous?' commented Kiyona, somewhat naively.

'It's far more likely to be an accident, if you ask me.' replied Mik, a young man sporting a large bushy blond beard, and wearing a multi-coloured tie-dyed psychedelic shirt, light green flared trousers and a red bandana with his hair tied back in a ponytail. He seemed to be more confident and approachable than some other members of the group. 'Our planet is clearly getting hotter and hotter; fires like this one are breaking out more and more frequently. I can't say I'm surprised that a large city has eventually become engulfed by one of them, and now they're trying to blame individuals rather than accept it's the fault of an economic system that had done precisely nothing to deal with this climate crisis.'

'Whatever the cause, it must be dreadful losing your home like that, all your possessions . . . and I bet most of them aren't even insured – it's so expensive to get insurance,' added his girlfriend Órfhlaith. She looked to be slightly younger than Mik, somewhat thinner, and wearing a brightly coloured psychedelic dress and a long black velvet jacket, with her long copper-red hair cascading over her shoulders and down the back of the jacket.

'Where will the homeless people go – are there community places they can stay in?' asked Akiko, wondering how such large numbers of people could be catered for.

'If they're lucky they might be housed in a hotel or sports centre or some large building of that nature,' suggested Mik, 'but they'll be expected to pay for the time they spend there, or take out a loan if they are unable to pay immediately. They won't let them stay there for free, that's for sure. Even when you're in desperate need of help, you're still expected to pay. You don't get anything for free here,' he added caustically.

'Your planet is getting hotter then. And the reason is?' asked Zek.

'The official reason – the one that's put across by the corporate media - is that we are for some reason or other closer to our star Eleutheria than usual, so the warming is therefore natural. There's other theories knocking about that it's actually the corporation's economic activities that are warming the planet, which wouldn't surprise me, at all. It could be both, I guess, there's not really that much on the media about it, so I'm not really sure exactly why this is happening. It seems to be becoming a big problem though. There's not just fires these days, there's also been droughts – occasionally whole city districts have lost their water supply for several days and a couple of cities have experienced intense heatwaves where hundreds of people died – mostly older people admittedly – but it still looked dreadful,' explained Ben, who was clearly a close friend of Mik and also one of the more politically radical members of the group. 'It's probably not happened here yet because we're in the capital city, so it receives preferential treatment to prevent these kind of things, but if you live in some of the smaller cities there have been some huge problems recently,' he added.

At this point, the breaking news item ended and was replaced with a short entertainment programme across all the bluescreens involving a group of very conventional-looking young people, all of whom appeared to be residing on a large ship together. During the short emission they each in turn engaged in performing various strange and bizarre tasks, all of which were either highly degrading or embarrassing. The presenter of the programme seemed to take great delight in the humiliation they suffered, particularly in respect to anyone on the ship who performed poorly at their task or fell overboard during their period of humiliation. Clips of these failures were then repeated over and over again as the presenter reveled in their discomfort and embarrassment.

The Margallans had noticed that a very high proportion of the entertainment emissions shown on the bluescreens over the last two months had involved similar-type scenarios; small groups of people on Rorque 4 seemed to do the most strange, bizarre, embarrassing, degrading and dangerous activities imaginable across a very wide range of scenarios on these media emissions. In fact, this appeared to be one of the most popular forms of entertainment with the locals, which for the crew was highly puzzling and sometimes disturbing.

'I don't understand. Why do these people engage in activities that are so clearly degrading and humiliating to them? Is it just some form of acting?' asked Akiko clearly confused, and hoping there must be some form of rational explanation for such bizarre behaviour.

'They get paid for it; it's as simple as that. Employment is so difficult to find round here, people are desperate for money. They'll do anything if the alternative is either starvation or resorting to criminal activity. It doesn't matter how degrading, unhealthy or dangerous the activity they're doing is, if it means an electronic transfer, then some people are willing to do anything for credit. Yeh, the media here is just one gigantic freak show full of performing monkeys. It's all lies and it's all brainbox pollution,' Mik uttered in a combination of exasperation and disgust. 'And if you think these ones are bad, you want to see some of the emissions on the premium subscription channels. In some of their activities, people actually die. It's unbelievable what some companies will do to make money, and some people will do to avoid poverty!'

'I think some of these people just like the attention,' chipped in a slightly younger and darker haired woman called Sophie, whose costume was considerably more subdued than the rest of the group. 'They're attention seekers and narcissists; they just want to be noticed. They can't bear to think they're unknown nobodies. They're all shallow and vain and just want to be the centre of attention. I bet they all have major insecurity problems. They like to claim that somehow they're being individuals and doing something special or unique or different, but it's all completely artificial. They're just being used by the corporations to make large amounts of money.'

'There seems to be a great deal of importance placed on individualism on this planet, I've noticed,' remarked Kiyona, 'the media emissions and the adverts are frequently telling people to be themselves, to be independent-thinking and to do their own thing. But I've noticed most of the people actually look quite similar, and think and behave in the same way. There seems to be something of a contradiction, or have I misunderstood something.'

'Yeh, we're always being told how important it is to be yourself, to make choices for yourself, to work hard as an individual and not be dependent upon others, so you're not a burden on society. It's a bad joke really given how little work there is. If they ran the planet differently – more collectively, for instance - then I guess someone would have to pay for it . . . the rich would have to pay more taxes and they hate that idea, they want to keep all their money for themselves. That's why they tell us all to be individuals and do everything for ourselves,' Órfhlaith opined, as Mik passed her another drink after a visit to the bar.

Arrival in Utopia

'But people here don't actually seem to be that different from each other, they all seem to do everything in a similar way – dress the same, think like each other, eat the same mass-produced foods, visit the same places – it all seems quite uniform, in reality. On Margalla, we have much more emphasis on community but people are far more varied and individualistic than here - in our society people really do just do their own thing,' observed Kiyona, who had made a decision to make a concerted attempt to understand the society she had accidentally found herself stranded in, and figured this was most easily achieved through comparisons with her own society – unsurprisingly, given it was the only one she actually knew.

'People conform to the norm here because they want to find employment, to not be harassed by the security services, to keep their jobs or achieve promotions, so they can climb higher in society,' Órfhlaith laughed. 'Yeh, I guess it's ironic that on a world devoted to individualism people conform all the time, and on a world devoted to community, it sounds like people can really be themselves because they have far more security. That sounds like poetic irony to me.'

'I think you're actually talking about two different concepts here,' interjected Ben, seeing an opportunity to express one of his more recently thought-through ideas. 'Individualism is where people put themselves before others and the collective, and act out of selfish interest, whereas individuality is where you remain true to yourself and behave as you really are. We have individualism, whereas your world seems to have individuality. The two don't always go together - which is clearly the case in our world.'

Kiyona reflected upon this for a while, considered the two societies, and decided this seemed to make a considerable amount of sense, though she was still not fully sure why this would be the case. She wondered if it was possible for everyone to enjoy both individualism and individuality at the same time, but figured that this would probably only work if somehow everyone was economically equal – a highly unlikely outcome in a society devoted to individualism. In an unequal world, by contrast, it seemed that only those with wealth and in positions of control could probably enjoy true individuality, though she was not sure even this would always be the case, as their might be organisational expectations placed on them. It seemed a very complicated subject, so she made a note to consider the subject at greater length at a later time, and returned her attention to the conversation.

'The Rorque Corporation wants us to do something called a photo encounter and appear on a chat show hosted by someone called Tricia Toyota. What's a chat show?' asked Akiko, suddenly changing the conversation after remembering something she had been meaning to ask about for some time now.

'Normally it's just a media interviewer asking famous people fairly anodyne questions – never anything challenging or embarrassing - or that might show them in a bad light - otherwise they wouldn't go on the show in the first place. Dull as ditch water usually,' replied Mik disparagingly.

'You shouldn't do that!' interjected Órfhlaith at almost the same time, 'the media have recently started portraying you as a bunch of primitives from a backward and simplistic civilisation. She'll treat you as simpletons, make you look innocent and stupid - encourage the audience to laugh at how naïve you are by seeing it as you really are, and misunderstanding our supposedly more sophisticated civilisation. Basically, you'll be treated like dumb animals or naïve children. She has previous on this. It's not a good move, if you ask me. I'd tell the corporation where to stuff it, if I was you. It will be TV suicide if you do it,' she concluded with considerable certainty.

The Margallans could not say they fully understand the point she was making, but it was no surprise to hear that the Rorque Corporation was expecting them to engage in some form of unpleasant encounter, and, already doubtful about this request by the corporation, they made a collective decision there and then to turn down the request. At this point, the freak show on the ship came to an end on the bluescreens, and the usual blitz of what seemed like never-ending adverts began, once again attempting to convince those watching, that their lives were hardly worth living unless they started to consume the various products on offer - everything from deodorant to cosmetic surgery to life insurance.

The Margallans, after some initial puzzlement and amusement during their first days on the planet, had already become inured to these emissions, but one in particular intrigued Kiyona. It was an advert for a highly attractive-looking sex robot called Angela Android, who could apparently satisfy men by providing far better sex than any real women could. Its tagline was 'we serve mankind'. On Margalla, the population was generally quite promiscuous – sharing bodies was simply another aspect to a society that believed in sharing pretty much everything else. Sex was largely a means to become better acquainted with the other members of the community and for reinforcing solidarity within the group.

It had never occurred to Kiyona that sexual performance was particularly important, other than ensuring that those engaged in the activity benefitted mutually together. However, the crew's time spent in Rorque City – which included a number of sexual encounters with the locals – had demonstrated to them that sex was regarded in a very different way on Rorque 4. It seemed to be pursued for one of two extremes – either as an almost entirely dispassionate and mechanical sexual act that seemed to hold virtually no personal significance whatsoever, or else the gateway for engaging in a long, possessive and quite obsessive relationship with a single other person. For the Margallans, both approaches were problematic; the first was deeply unsatisfying and the second was simply not a part of their collectivist mindset. Kiyona wondered if Angela Android was designed to address the first of these two problems, though she had not noticed any adverts for a male equivalent.

She wondered if a sex robot delivered electric orgasms, electric tears and electric sighs. And then, for a while, she wondered what it must be like to love a machine, and had concluded that it must actually be deeply unsatisfying. She could not imagine an AI unit ever delivering the satisfaction that was obtainable from a close and intimate association with another human. Most of the adverts she had seen were almost instantly forgettable, but for some reason she could not get this one out of her head. Somehow it seemed to sum up the whole of Rorquean society – offering the exact opposite of what you actually got. Rorquean society was like a mirror of illusion - nothing here was actually what it seemed, she eventually concluded.

One of the group standing next to her, a guy called Max, noticing her interest in the advert, suddenly said, 'One of my friends bought one of those. Apparently it was rubbish; when she came, it kept moaning another man's name, and the company wouldn't give him his money back.'

Kiyona was not exactly surprised and she switched her attention away from the annoying advert and back to the conversation.

Arrival in Utopia

'You said people on Margalla live in communes. Isn't that a bit oppressive though; no privacy, everybody else knowing your business, no space of your own. It sounds a bit restricted. Don't you lose your individual freedoms living like that?' asked Mik, who wanted to believe that the Margallans really did live in a utopia and that such a society could actually exist, but could still not quite believe it was actually as positive as the picture they were painting.

'Not really. We have our own bedrooms; they're quite spacious in reality, and so are the communal buildings. You choose who you want to live with mostly – there's never a shortage of places to go round, so it's fairly easy to pick and choose. I like the fact that there's always someone around to talk to, play games with, eat with, or watch visual emissions,' noted Akiko, who had never given this subject much thought before.

'When you're a child, it's great – there were always plenty of other kids around to play with. I also liked the fact that I could talk to so many different adults. They all had different opinions to my parents – my parents were a bit odd – so I could hear plenty of other viewpoints,' offered Zek more enthusiastically.

'It's also good for parents; if you want to go anywhere it's not a problem as there's so many people around to look after all the children,' added Akiko. 'Old people also get looked after when everything becomes a bit of a struggle for them. I think it benefits everyone, now that I think about it.'

'But what about issues like child abuse, isn't that a problem in communes,' asked Sophie, vaguely remembering some drama she had watched a few years ago.

Kiyona wasn't too sure what she was actually asking about but suggested helpfully, 'I've not heard that's a problem anywhere. I would imagine if it occurred we would all find out about it very soon and put a stop to it very quickly. I would have thought it would be more of a problem here on Rorque 4. Surely it could secretly last for ages behind the closed doors of one of you individualist houses. Why do you ask, is it a big problem here?' she asked, suddenly wondering if this was a common problem in Rorquean society.

'Abuse is almost endemic in our society – the whole economic system is based on exploitation, so it just cascades down throughout the whole of society. Sometimes it seems like everyone's doing it to someone in some manner or other,' answered Ben, suddenly sounding more jaded than before.

'And I guess your communally-owned AI units do all the clearing up, cleaning, washing and maintenance work,' enquired Sophie somewhat jealously, and who was also beginning to sound a little drunk.

'Yes, I can't believe your world doesn't use AI units in the same way that we do. The more I think about the difference between our two worlds, the more I'm beginning to think it's actually the crucial difference between them – it's why the two worlds have ended up so differently,' Zek informed them. 'It looks like our collective control of them has given rise to an entirely different type of civilisation.'

'I'm sure you're right, we took the wrong step years ago,' remarked Ben, 'we should have started with an approach like yours, except our world, of course, was started by 'corporation ships' and it's remained neo-liberal ever since. We really do need to desperately change this world; maybe one day the people here will rise up and create a utopia like you did. You never know, it might actually happen one day.'

'Come off it,' exclaimed Sophie, 'you know you're only dreaming, people won't do that, at least not in our life time – they're far too selfish, greedy and competitive. We've had years and years of prolonged economic difficulties, and they still haven't rebelled. The only way out of this hellhole, is to leave it, to get away from it as far as you possibly can. It's beyond hope this place.'

Kiyona, who had been listening attentively, recognised Sophie's comments as a variation on a very common theme in Rorque City – the system was dreadful, but there was nothing that could effectively be done about it. The Rorqueans seemed to be a people without hope of a better future. She wondered for a while just how dispiriting that actually was on a personal level – to live somewhere you hated, but believe that it could never be improved. She was about to ask about this, but when she returned her attention to the conversation, Ben was once again offering his radical opinions, and she also noticed an older guy had quietly joined the group.

'But, you wouldn't expect left-wing rebellion in difficult economic times. It's difficult enough just to find employment and make ends meet. People's expectations are far too low; establishing a new utopian society is way beyond most people's ambitions. Revolutions occur when the economy and society are improving, when people have high expectations, when the future looks promising and seems to be getting better, except the existing regime – for whatever reason – cannot meet the expectations, and then people take matters into their own hands and take control through a social revolution,' Ben explained.

Akiko opened her mouth to say something, and then thought better of it. As with Kiyona, she was also keen to improve her understanding of this new world, but more because she wanted to work out where it had all gone wrong. She tended to be slightly more anxious and more of a worrier than the average Margallan - though given their largely free and easy way of living, this wasn't actually saying much. During her time on Rorque 4 she had started to wonder whether Margalla could ever descend into the nightmarish society that was Rorque 4, and, keen to hope it never would, she was attempting to work out the crucial differences between her own world and the one she now found herself trapped on. She mulled over Ben's ideas for a while. These were matters the Margallans had never needed to think about, so she had no real opinion on the subject, and Ben's ideas seemed sort of counter-intuitive, she thought; surely when everyone's situation was worsening, they would be more inclined to do something about it, not the other way round. She conceded he probably knew more about the matter than she did, and returned her attention to the conversation to learn more.

'In some ways both Ben and Sophie are both right, people's ideas change as the economy changes', stated the older man who had just joined the group, and who they later discovered was named Dave. He looked somewhat grizzled in appearance – Kiyona assumed he must have experienced a difficult life – with long sandy-blonde hair and a drooping moustache. His scruffy boots, loose trousers and a long, worn and battered old sandy-coloured hippy overcoat gave him the air of a refugee. 'There's so much competition for employment at the moment, some people will do literally anything to undercut each other – it's a real dog-eat-dog world out there; there's little chance of achieving any meaningful solidarity. People who want to find a job, or keep the one they have, are too scared to rock the boat and cause trouble. And whilst the situation's like that, people only care about getting on in the rat race; most people think the only way out of poverty and oppression is to achieve promotion and move upwards – to support the system even more than before. Whilst people are thinking along those lines, there's little hope of revolution. But Ben's right, when I was younger, the economy was in better shape; we had more work and more money. We could shop around and find the best places to work, tell fascist bosses where to stick it, rebel against stupid rules and regulations - we were able to organise more activities, get underground unions going and the like – people were more optimistic about the future, they would help each other fight against the system - but that all fell apart after the mass lay-offs were implemented, and they started using AI units on an even wider basis than they had before.'

After this long explanation, Dave moved onto other matters. Dave Shevecke, they soon discovered, had been a member of a generation that had entered into an economy that, thirty to forty years ago, had been considerably more vibrant. Initially they had been a lucky generation; the economy flourished for a considerable period of time and employment levels remained high. There were numerous opportunities for even the partially educated, plenty of money to go around, and a vibrant, forward thinking and progressive culture developed amongst an age cohort that had known nothing but continuing improvement and gradually rising expectations. After two previous decades of conservatism and conformity on the planet, their generation had instigated political rebellion, cultural iconoclasm and progressive social change.

But all that now seemed a lifetime away for his generation. The Centennial Depression had taken everyone by surprise and wiped out jobs in their millions. Profits had plunged and whole industries disappeared. The use of AI units by the corporations was now more widespread than ever; AI employment – not human – now seemed to be the norm. The economy, according to Dave, had yet to properly recover – attempts to invigorate it just seemed to create yet another economic difficulty to be overcome. And with years of economic stagnation, everything else had changed – society, culture and the political situation – all now seemed so much more regressive, authoritarian, diminished and culturally impoverished.

Dave's generation was now effectively cut adrift – strangers in their own land, no longer able to orientate in a landscape that had changed beyond recognition. Political, social and cultural vibrancy had been replaced by a desperate competitive struggle to navigate through an unfamiliar socio-economic situation. But Dave and a dwindling band of revolutionaries soldiered on, keeping the struggle alive and waiting for better times. The younger members amongst the group weren't sure whether to regard this grizzled old political warrior with respect or as a relic of a gone-bye age. His behavior could sometimes be quite odd - he seemed to have a touch of the reefer madness about him - and they were also aware of the fact that he had been involved in some fairly dubious activities in the past – and maybe still was, given his semi-secretive lifestyle. He had, they knew, spent several periods in prison, with convictions for fraud and assault and battery, amongst other things.

Nevertheless, he was always good for some interesting stories and seemed to have endless useful contacts and information. He was able to offer them advice on political campaigning, tips on organisation, how to protest effectively and how to use the mass media for their own ends. Additionally, he was able to procure a whole variety of goods and materials which were usually well out of their price range, though the Margallans, upon enquiring, discovered that rocket fuel was somewhat beyond his capabilities.

'In addition, political apathy has come at the worst time possible,' continued Dave. 'This city – in fact, everywhere on this planet – is sleepwalking into disaster. Not only do we have an economic crisis, but we also have an environmental one now, and it wouldn't surprise me if the two are intimately connected. It's already impacted heavily in other parts of the world – some other cities have been impacted really badly. I've spent years trying to raise awareness about this, but hardly anyone seems to care. They just think it won't happen here – they're all dreamers, this is a dreaming city detached from reality, but soon it's going to experience a rude awakening. If it doesn't do so, it will soon become a void city – the same as happened to Randville in the deep south of the continent. There's not much of that place left either after the fires they experienced. Maybe if they'd had a better spirit of community and a sense of solidarity they could have saved the city, but instead, they all just did their own thing and now it's just a pile of smouldering ashes.'

Órfhlaith and one or two other members of group looked somewhat depressed at Dave's final point. If he and Ben were correct, there was little immediate prospect of achieving a better world; the citizens of Rorque 4 were not about to turn to the radicalism they were hoping they would.

Therefore, Órfhlaith changed the subject, 'so what do you think about the bands?' she asked the Margallans, keen to know about their musical tastes.

'They all sound a bit weird, I guess they're probably an acquired taste,' Xander offered diplomatically, 'some of the songs were good though. One or two sounded familiar, I think I've heard them on some old Earth collections people play back on Margalla.'

'So what bands do you have on Margalla?' asked Mik, who had been expecting a more enthusiastic endorsement.

'We don't really do entertainment this way. It's more of a collective effort. We don't have your distinction between the performers and the audience. Everyone just joins in instead - the best musicians do the most, admittedly, but it's mostly about everyone participating together. They're always good fun – lots of dancing, drinking and eating, joining up with partners . . . now that I mention it, I suddenly miss them,' said Arlo, experiencing a sudden bout of homesickness.

The group continued the meandering conversation throughout the rest of the evening, consuming a range of drinks and recreational drugs, listening to the various bands that came on stage and watching the irritating but somehow morbidly fascinating bluescreens. Eventually, the final band of the night concluded their set and the bluescreens around the walls buzzed back into life for one last time. They were running a breaking news story concerning the Alphan scientists. The reporter sounded distinctly uncomplimentary about them, indicating that the scientists had been deceiving the corporations as to their level of expertise, damaging the accommodation they had been housed in, and trying to abuse the goodwill shown to them by the people of Rorque 4, whilst behind him the whole time, the screen showed some brief news clips of the scientists protesting about something, though exactly what, was left unclear.

'That's surprising', declared Mik, 'we've heard nothing but praise for them so far; how brilliant they are, and the fact that they will prove to be a major benefit to our economy. Now they're claiming they're a problem.'

'All that is solid melts into the air,' declared Ben.

'What?' asked Kiyona.

'This is typical of our society. For ages they insist on the supreme importance of some matter or other and how everyone must move heaven and earth to achieve it, and then suddenly it's all completely irrelevant and of no interest anymore, and the focus shifts to some other new and ultra-important matter. It's like we're in some gigantic never-ending game, but the rules just keep changing. It's difficult to take anything seriously when they keep doing this to you – you just feel like you're an actor in a play you have no control over,' explained Ben. 'I suspect it's because of some change in economic priorities; maybe they don't need the scientists anymore,' he added, hoping this made sense to the Margallans, especially as he had noticed they seemed to be struggling to understand even the most basic aspects of Rorquean society.

This did, however, remind the Margallans they needed to sort out their own specific situation with regards to their spaceship, but enquiries amongst the new friends they had just made, yet again came to naught. As with everyone else they had met so far, there was little idea of how you went about acquiring rocket fuel. A few well-meaning suggestions were made, but none were very practical or legal. Despite this - wholly expected - setback, the people they had met at the music venue were by far the most interesting and sociable they had encountered so far on Rorque 4, and so they made a point of getting to know them much better over the next few days and weeks. Several of them were involved with radical underground political movements and they promised to attend some of their up-and-coming meetings so that their comrades could hear all about life and society on Margalla.

A short while later, the group spilled out onto the dilapidated pavements outside the club with the rest of the concert-goers, except those who had decided to carry on drinking into the small hours of the night. Back on the dimly-lit streets they were once again reminded of the poverty, squalor and deprivation that characterised so much of this sector of the city – rubbish piles were strewn across the decrepit alleyways, the deteriorating roads were badly in need of repair, and most of the street lights were no longer working. Homeless people, wrapped in moth-eaten threads, sat huddled in decrepit doorways hoping for even the most meagre of food and drink donations from the passers-by. Occasional groups of dodgy-looking characters associated loosely outside the various eateries and bars.

Inside the venue the songs, drinks, drugs and convivial atmosphere had enabled them to forget about the ramshackle neighbourhood, but it all suddenly came spilling back as they made their way drunkenly along the squalid streets of fear back to their shabby hotel – back to the reality of Rorque City. As they approached their temporary place of residence, a kerb crawler cruised slowly past them, making suggestive and lewd comments, only to be followed by a stream of abuse once the females within the Margallan group had told him what he could do with his unwanted comments. The crew looked at each other and they all knew what each other was thinking – we gotta get out of this place, and as fast as possible!

Rorque 4 – scientist rebellion

Earlier that day, outside the headquarters of both the Rorque Corporation and Cosmic Solutions, hundreds of angry Alphan scientists had launched noisy protests, waving placards and chanting slogans in an attempt to gain as much media attention as possible. Protests were not particularly common on Rorque 4. They were often outlawed under the Impediment of Business Activity statutes, and their organisers summarily arrested. In this case, however, the security forces initially held back, waiting for instructions from the corporations, as they were unsure of what type of exact response was expected of them.

The fact that several thousand academics had failed to secure positions and employment in the universities of Rorque 4, had been met by those involved with a mixture of anger, despair and incredulity. On Alpha Fraczan, knowledge had been valued for knowledge's sake, and once an individual had commenced their life of research and teaching in the universities they typically remained there for life, even into their gradually phased-in retirement programme. Admittedly, there were very few other professional career options on the planet, but the dominant ethos of their society had clearly been one based almost solely around knowledge, learning and intellectual enquiry. These were all held up as worthy of pursuit in their own right, and valued above all other aspects in society. Those involved in these pursuits had always taken it for granted that they were valued and respected members of their community, and would remain so for life; so to be unceremoniously dumped on the scrap-heap so rapidly by the two corporations was a huge shock to their personal and group well-being.

The offer of short-term loans to help them adjust to their new world had simply added insult to injury for the rejected academics, especially once they had started looking into the realities of alternative housing and employment on Rorque 4. The universities they had initially been accommodated in were all located in the wealthiest urban districts or pleasant and prosperous areas of the countryside. Their scans of the planet now showed them that these were wholly untypical of Rorque 4; around ninety percent of the towns and cities were in some way either impoverished, dilapidated, insalubrious or run-down, or a combination of all of these put together, and yet still not even cheap to live in. Not a single one of these areas looked attractive to a group of people were used to enjoying a comfortably high standard of living and quality of life.

The overwhelming feeling amongst the community now was that they were better off leaving the planet and trying their luck elsewhere. For those that had arrived on the Margallan ship, The Spirit of the Age, this was initially thought to be somewhat problematic as they did not own that particular stasis ship, and they assumed it would have departed from the planet by now, anyway. Scans of sub-space showed, however, that, strangely, the ship was still in orbit around the planet, though they could only guess as to why the crew had not already departed. Nevertheless, attempts to locate the Margallans proved fruitless once they had discovered this fact – the Rorque Corporation proving to be particularly uncooperative in respect to this particular matter.

Ultimately, though, this might not have mattered, as even the two groups of rejected scientists combined together were still sufficiently limited in number to be able to comfortably fit on the Avante, given the number of stasis pods it was carrying. This was until - to their great shock and horror - they discovered that the Cosmic Solutions Corporation had already taken ownership of the spacecraft in a previous legal agreement. This had been signed by some of the leading officials of the Alpha Fraczan universities upon arriving at Rorque 4, ones who had, of course, easily secured employment in CSC universities. This arrangement had, apparently, been concluded to help offset the costs of transporting and accommodating the new arrivals. Further appalled and angered by this news, the rejected scientists demanded to know why they had not received a share of the proceeds, and were duly told that indeed they had, and it had been factored into the loans they had been offered, and even now was paying for their temporary accommodation.

As the knowledge of these developments emerged, the scientists had been organising a continuous stream of meetings and had also elected organising committees to liaise with the corporate leaderships. At the later meetings - following their discovery of the changed ownership of the Avante - it had been suggested that they should fight the unfair legal agreement through the courts on Rorque 4. However, the organising committee explained they had already consulted on this, and it was widely believed that they had no hope of defeating the CSC and their army of expensive lawyers in the courts - that this particular avenue would most likely prove to be a dead end. With little in the way of other viable options, the rejected academics had eventually - though somewhat reluctantly - opted for a series of high profile protests which were now culminating in the coordinated demonstrations outside the headquarters of Cosmic Solutions and the Rorque Corporation. A small number of the academics were also engaged in a concerted search attempt in hope of finding the Margallans, who now appeared to be their only hope of leaving the planet.

On the respective top floors of the Rorque Corporation and Cosmic Solutions headquarters – in their different cities and located on different continents - Colin Jamieson and Christine Sanchez had both been pondering their next moves. For both, there was the continuing and unanticipated problem of dealing with the protesting academics and scientists. Ordinarily, the security forces would have been called in and arrests made under the Impediment of Business Activities statute. Their media outlets would have reported the unruly unrest, whilst showing their respective corporations in a favourable light, and the matter would have ended with the courts handing down punitive rulings to those involved. There would be grumblings from the usual suspects – those who complained about everything the corporations did - but a largely compliant populace would have ultimately accepted the situation without much fuss.

However, this particular scenario was considerably different from those they were used to dealing with. They were faced with thousands of very angry, highly determined and well-educated people, who possessed a strong sense of self-esteem, and who were not about to meekly accept the directives handed down from on high, as the majority of Rorquean people tended to do. Both leaders also knew that people tend to fight harder when they have something existing to lose, rather than when seeking a new and hitherto unrealised gain. In addition, the scientists were from another planet, and the law was unclear on how much jurisdiction existed over such people. A situation such as this had not arisen on the planet before, and the lawyers were unsure as to how it would play out in the courts.

Sanchez and Jamieson were also growing weary of the meetings and protests, ones which were slowly being ramped up, and were beginning to attract the attention of known subversives and troublemakers and their dangerous vision of a better world. They had both ordered their respective media outlets to start broadcasting negative stories about the protesting scientists, whilst taking care not to alienate those who had been given employment and contracts - not always an easy task. Corporation journalists had been dispatched to uncover unsavoury details of their past lives or their present beliefs, and to search for examples of unacceptable behavior in their new residences. This would make it easier to undermine the position of the protestors, and reduce any sympathy for their cause that might have developed amongst the population. Previously, the media had been all aglow with the accomplishments and brilliance of the Alphans, but this was now beginning to change. Sections of the media were suggesting that the rejected scientists were simply ungrateful, lazy foreigners and thus unworthy of any sympathy.

To add further to his problems, Jamieson had been passed unconfirmed reports that the Margallans were stirring up trouble in the district they had been placed in, and were now associating with known subversives and possibly even suspected terrorists. He was beginning to regret having had them accommodated in a semi-bohemian district like Shade Gate, and was now contemplating on whether to move them to a different hotel or simply to terminate their arrangement entirely. He was doubly minded to do this once the Head of Media had informed him that they had failed to show up for their scheduled media and talk show appearances - appearances that were effectively meant to cover the costs of the credit they had been loaned by the corporation.

Initially, he had wondered whether he might be able to make money out of the odd-looking group, but slowly, as the AI unit charged with looking after them relayed more and more demands from the crew back to senior management, he began to tire of their dependence. They seemed to think he was some sort of dream worker, he thought to himself, who could just fix their every problem and meet their every need. As he discovered more and more about Margalla, he began to picture a world that looked more like a holiday resort than any proper civilisation. No one there seemed to do any work, so it was no wonder they wanted the Rorque Corporation to do everything for them. It did sound quite idyllic though – he wondered if he could open it up as a tourist resort when the corporation acquired faster space craft and had dealt with other more pressing matters.

And Jamieson, unlike Sanchez, had the additional problem of having not secured the services of the rocket scientists and space flight technicians, even after Parker had led him to believe that this would be the case. This failure, he believed, could have highly negative implications for his dealings with the Zeleyanian government, and he needed to turn all his attention to rectifying this particular matter, rather than dealing with irritating protestors and lazy anarchists. Failure in this section of his ongoing operation could mean a wider breakdown for their entire space project, with all the appalling implications that held.

Finally, the opinion polls were now putting the ruling Liberty Party – closely associated with the Rorque Corporation - behind their great political rivals, the Justice and Order Party. If the party associated with Cosmic Solutions Corporation gained control of the World Parliament they were bound to introduce legal impediments to the Rorque Corporation's dealings with Zeleyan. He would probably still be able to overturn these through the courts – the constitution should help him in that respect - but that could constitute years of legal wrangling between the two teams of expensive corporate lawyers, and significant delays were the last thing Jamieson wanted right now.

At this moment in time, he had now decided he needed the Margallan and protesting scientist problems like he needed a hole in the head. Previously, he had toyed with the idea of using them for electoral purposes - offering them certain deals that would play well with the voters - but he considered both groups to be unreliable and unpredictable, and could not be sure of their compliance and gratitude. He was also concerned that the scientists who had been given contracts might now reject them in some misguided and futile demonstration of solidarity with their rejected colleagues, and also seek to depart the planet out of spite. That afternoon, therefore, he had arrived at an entirely different decision, one that he believed would both portray the corporation in a magnanimous light to the voters, and rid him of the whole scientist-Margallan problem.

He had decided to provide the Margallan ship with the rocket fuel they needed for free, and offer all the rejected academics free passage on the starship to wherever they wanted to go – or at least that's how the media would sell it to the electorate. There was the slight problem of individuals being seen to get something for nothing, but given that they had been portrayed - until recently - as special visitors from another planet this could be passed off as a unique situation. The media outlets were, even now, in the process of receiving new orders to run stories the next day that this was what the two different groups wanted, and would therefore be highly grateful for the corporation's munificence.

There was, he admitted though, the additional problem that the two groups might decide to head for their original destination – the socialist planet of Zeta Kotlin – with all the negative propaganda connotations this entailed for his planet and it ideological outlook. It was obviously not what he wanted, but it might just have to be the price he had to pay for a short term political fix. And anyway, he mused, if his arrangements with the Zeleyanian regime ultimately came to fruition, the Zetan problem would all be dealt with in a satisfactory way in the fullness of time - fleeing to the socialist planet might in the end prove utterly pointless.

When Sanchez later heard of Jamieson's decision – plastered all over the Rorque Corporation's media outlets – she correctly deduced what her rival was scheming, and decided her best option was to simply jump on the bandwagon. The Justice and Order Party could also be seen to be magnanimous – at the very least this should neutralise any advantage the Liberty Party might gain from this affair. She too would be rid of a protracted problem and could also concentrate on matters of far greater importance. To date, her corporation had emerged more successfully from the developments that had resulted from the Alphan diaspora, and she was keen to maintain her lead over her corporate and political rivals. She was beginning to believe that fortune was definitely on her side, and she was not about to let a few protesting scientists blow her off course.

Zeleyan – the invasion of Ur-Tokar is announced and the space fleet departs

Six weeks before word was due from Rosson that he had successfully arrived at the planet of Ur-Tokar, Vartin had finally thrown caution to the wind – by his own standards – and decided to launch his full-scale invasion of the semi-frozen, technophobic planet. Vartin had originally drawn up an invasion plan that could only be described as measured, methodical and highly cautious. However, the diaspora from Alpha Fraczan, the recent news from Rorque 4, and the periodic bouts of unrest on Zeleyan had all served to significantly disrupt his carefully laid plans. In recent weeks, he had been torn between alternating bouts of caution and impatience, but the impatience had finally got the better of him – he had grown tired of waiting for tomorrow, and had finally reached a point where he believed he needed to act decisively.

The recent information from Rorque 4, he had decided, meant that he needed to move far more quickly. In addition, his shock troops had ended the political unrest in Outer Padnia – once and for all he was hoping – and so he considered he was now able to make his next big move. The regiment was used to brutally quell the worst outbreaks of unrest, and as part of this process it was typically flown in to trouble spots by means of the few aircraft the planet actually possessed and operated - an absence of fossil fuels on Zeleyan meaning that air travel was kept strictly for military and elite purposes only, and the general public was thus not used to seeing actual aircraft in action. Due to the manner of their arrival, therefore, the regiment had become known as the Angels of Death, particularly by those who caught at the wrong end of their brutal activities, and were feared across the planet. Vartin was particularly keen to take the regiment with him, partly to ensure complete military victory on Ur-Tokar, but also to ensure his own security. Their recent success in the eastern region meant that he was now able to finally embark on the mission he had been planning, for what now seemed like an eternity.

Vartin was currently standing on the balcony of the first floor of the party headquarters, where he was engaging in a long appreciative appraisal of the city that spread out before him. Everything looked in perfect order. The streets were clean, the flower beds were neatly ordered and the grass had been freshly mowed. Even the autocars were parked in neat orderly rows. Uniformed officers stood purposefully at regular intervals along the sides of each path and roadway down below him. Above him stretched the clear blue sky – save for a few fluffy white cumulus clouds over the mountains in the distant background - and a bird sang somewhere below and to the right of him amongst the long rows of magnolia trees that bordered the pathways that criss-crossed the plaza in front of the grandiose building. Beyond the neatly-arranged grounds of the party headquarters, the city stretched outwards in all directions in a neat, even and orderly fashion. Somewhere in the sun-baked distance he could just about discern the outskirts of the city which then gave way to the short grassy plain that in turn buttressed up against the mountains that almost completely circled Zeleyan City and its environs.

He could not have picked a better day for his monthly speech, he thought, and he paused for a few moments whilst the masses below him waited patiently in expectation. Stood out here on the balcony, supreme commander of all before him, he once again felt like he was the king of the world, and any doubts he might have held about what he was about to proclaim to those below him, were now swept completely away. If Vartin had been completely honest with himself - and this was something he would never admit to others – those doubts had been recurrently surfacing far too often in recent weeks. The political and social unrest in the eastern sector had proved far more persistent than he had expected, and, although his favoured troops had now quelled the disorder, the level of violence that had proven necessary to do so had slightly unnerved him. The speech would be cathartic – both for him and for the nation – he believed.

And so Supreme Commander Vartin launched into the speech that he believed would change the course of history for ever. 'Loyal citizens we have much to be grateful for. We live in a prosperous and peaceful society, free from crime and degeneracy. We enjoy lives of safety, security and predictability. Our nation has worked tirelessly to achieve this greatness, this prosperity and this security. We all of us have much to be grateful for . . . ,' and he carried on in this vein at some length and for some time, outlining a history of the regime's great achievements, and the many advantages of their particular approach to civilisation.

'But, all this may be in danger, for we have recently discovered hostile forces plotting against our prosperous society. Even as I speak, foreign agitators are actively attempting to undermine our peace-loving society, to blacken our good name and spread lies and untruths. There are plans afoot to send agitators and terrorists to our beloved homeland, with the aim of undoing all our hard work and endeavour, to spread dissent, to stir up unrest and to create all manner of chaos, disorder and disaster. Rest assured, my people, for we will never allow such occurrences to develop. Your munificent regime will strain every muscle and every sinew to ensure your complete safety and security. We will not let these subversives stand in the way of our greatness and our historical destiny.' He paused for a few moments gauging the reaction of the crowd, and savouring the moment when he would proclaim his great venture to the world.

'However, the period of tolerating such despicable plotting is now over. No longer we will sit back and passively accept such unwarranted behaviour towards our great civilisation. No longer will our name be besmirched and blackened in such an unacceptable manner. We expect the other worlds of the Nexus Cluster to recognise the glorious nature of our regime, to appreciate the great things we have achieved here, and to inspire others to the greatness we have achieved. It is for this reason that your glorious leader has made the glorious decision to launch a fleet of starships to take complete control of the planet of Ur-Tokar. Our loyal agents have informed us that the enemies of our planet plan to use Ur-Tokar to undermine the great and glorious civilisation of Zeleyan. It is for this reason that we must thwart the plans of these enemies and secure control of the planet ourselves. Through our strength, dedication, loyalty and endeavour we will ensure total victory and open another glorious chapter in the great history of our nation.'

With this Vartin concluded his speech; for a moment there was a pause, but when the masses below realised this was the culmination of his speech they broke into rapturous applause – the overseeing soldiers made sure they had little choice in this matter – and after soaking up the adulation for several minutes, Vartin saluted the crowd and retired from the balcony. Back in his office, with his senior officers around him, Vartin felt a sense of pride, but also one of relief – the decision had been made and there was no going back now. He was pleased with the delivery of his speech and the crowd's reaction, though it was, of course, a foregone conclusion that the speech would be accepted adoringly, given the authoritarian nature of their society. Vartin was already ranking it as one of his better speeches, though if truth were to be told it was actually a pretty standard one – Vartin was not the most imaginative of leaders.

He had, however, taken a calculated risk in announcing the invasion publically, for there was the danger that news of the invasion plans could eventually become known elsewhere in the Cluster. For this reason he had implemented strict media directives aimed at ensuring that the other planets in the Nexus Cluster remained oblivious to the on-going invasion of Ur-Tokar. Measures were being taken to ensure that none of the publicity surrounding the speech would make it onto the inter-stellar airwaves. In the event that this were to actually fail, though, he figured that by the time the other planets received news of the speech, the invasion fleet would be well on its way to Ur-Tokar and there was effectively nothing anyone could do about it anyway. Ur-Tokar, of course, would have absolutely no idea of what was about to hit it whatever precautions he did or did not take.

Vartin had arranged for a full-scale military send-off for himself and the departing troops at the spaceport of Gombos. This was to be a truly historic occasion and needed an appropriately important looking ceremony. Therefore, two days after the speech, rows of smartly dressed soldiers in ceremonial dress lined the driveway between the main building of the spaceport and the transporter craft which Vartin and his senior officers were soon to depart on. Rows of flags representing the various districts of Zeleyan fluttered in the breeze and a brass band played stirring military songs as those assembled waited for the arrival of the Supreme Commander.

When Vartin and his officers arrived, the band struck up the national anthem and all present stiffly saluted their Supreme Commander. Once the anthem was completed, a number of lengthy speeches were given by senior members of the party praising the attributes of their great leader and the glorious mission he was soon to embark on. Normally, Vartin listened to such speeches quite carefully, attempting to assess the degree of sincerity expressed within them – it was always useful to know who was genuinely supportive of his rule – but on this occasion he left such concerns behind him; he felt he could just bask in the adulation of the occasion and soak up the praise. When they had concluded, he too gave his address to the expectant crowd, one that consisted entirely of the most significant and important figures on the planet. The crowd applauded enthusiastically once he had concluded his speech, and so his cortege made its way to the special transporter craft that had been constructed for this particular occasion.

A few minutes later, and the shuttle craft was accelerating hard towards the outer limits of the atmosphere, through sub-space and into orbit. Vartin finally felt he could afford to relax for a while now; the whole ceremony had gone exactly to plan, and he very much felt that this was a good omen for the future. Security, of course, had been extremely tight, given the pockets of unrest that had continued until recently on various parts of the continent, but nothing untoward or unfortunate had occurred throughout. His security detail had feared the rebels might switch their tactics from open rebellion to one of assassination. In the event, though, no assassins had marred his great moment in history, and he was now all set for a successful departure into space and for military conquest.

He now took a moment to look around him at the senior officers that accompanied him on the shuttle craft. General Neumann and Lieutenant-General Tarrafel – a descendant of one of the earlier rulers of Zeleyan - had been chosen for their unswerving loyalty and were known entities to him. The recently promoted General Davila, to the left of him, however, was a bit of an unknown quantity since he had apparently worked his way up from a humble background. This slightly concerned Vartin, for it indicated he probably had genuine talent, ambition and ability, unlike so many of his senior command who had been born into privilege, and thus enjoyed the necessary contacts to ease their way into senior positions of authority at some point during their careers, irrespective of their actual talents and ability.

Vartin also hailed from such a privileged background, so knew these people well, but he also knew their sense of entitlement and the readiness with which they would replace him, if they saw the opportunity and thought they could find the support for such a move. Fortunately, he also knew all the skeletons in their closets and exactly where the bodies lay – and they knew that he knew this. He also knew their strengths and weaknesses, and they had invariably been placed in positions that ensured Vartin's complete control over the regime, and ones that minimised their ability to do anything about this. Davila, on the other hand, would have a very different mindset, though there were still methods by which he could be controlled. He was undoubtedly ambitious, and he probably harboured grudges against the senior officers from a more privileged background. These could both be used to ensure his loyalty.

He had spent several hours discussing with Varela who should accompany him on the invasion of Ur-Tokar. Senior generals might be needed on Zeleyan to deal with any further troublesome outbreaks of unrest that occurred across the various sectors of the continent. However, of far more importance, he would be away for well over a year on the mission to Ur-Tokar and he could not take the risk of leaving behind a significant senior military figure who might successfully usurp his position. Only the totally loyal generals had been left behind, though unfortunately – in the event of further unrest - these individuals were often the least militarily competent, being incapable of making decisive decisions on the ground. As such, the security of the planet might be compromised, though he was hoping the brutal crushing of the rebels in Outer Padnia would prove to be the final fight in this particular period of unrest, and that no further problems would actually ensue.

It had thus been decided that those he did not fully trust, but who he still considered to be able and competent, had to be taken with him on the invasion fleet. It was for this reason that General Davila had been chosen to command the third stasis ship, The Destroyer, and a Lieutenant-General Nemev was commanding the second ship, The Invincible. They had both proven effective in dealing with the recent troubles, and were therefore likely to prove to be able commanders in the suppression of any resistance on Ur-Tokar. Zeleyan had not experienced any full-scale military conflicts for several decades now, so Vartin had little else to judge his potential commanders upon. In the unlikely event of the mission actually failing, they would also make suitable scapegoats for the defeat.

This he still believed, though, was not an outcome that could be realistically expected. Ur-Tokar, he was sure would possess only poorly armed military forces – no match for his own well-equipped forces. He had chosen to place himself at the head of the mission to ensure that he, and he alone, would enter the history books as the Zeleyan Supreme Commander who had invaded Ur-Tokar successfully, and had thus set in place the first chapter in the planet's glorious conquest of the whole Nexus Cluster. There could be no confusion as to who was responsible for such a great epoch-changing achievement; not, for instance Rosson, or any other commander who he might have appointed to lead the invasion fleet. Vartin had made the all-important decisions, he had drawn up the plans and he would lead the invasion fleet to victory. He knew this was all a calculated risk, but with the careful planning and selection of personnel he had undertaken, combined with his own strategic genius, he was sure the mission could only end in outright success and personal glory.

Once safely on board the lead stasis ship, The Patriot IV, and with familiar figures from the High Command at his side, he took the opportunity to fully brief his officers with regards to what was expected from them on this all-important mission, whilst the transporter craft further relayed Davila, Nemev and rest of the senior officers to the two remaining starships of the invasion fleet. Once this had been achieved and Vartin had received the information that all the ships were ready and fully-prepared for departure, he gave the order to commence the mission, and the military starships moved out of orbit one by one, as they followed Vartin's lead ship on the eight month flight to Ur-Tokar.

Vartin looked back at his home planet as the stasis ship accelerated out of orbit. The continental side of the planet was in full view and in full daylight, and he once again studied the flat verdant plains of the Northern Alliance and the more varied topography of the two southern regions. And once again, he reminded himself, he was the lord and master of all that he surveyed below him, his word was final, he alone decided its fate and future. He too was beginning to acquire a taste for space travel – though for very different reasons to his Vice-Admiral, Rosson. Soon he would be able to look over the planet of Ur-Tokar and feel the same sense of power – soon he would be the master of two worlds. And, he was not about to stop at two, either.

Arrival in Utopia

The space-fleet accelerated rapidly in convoy across the stellar system, passed the outer gas giants of Keitzel and Muisson, then the various dwarf planets, through the various asteroid belts of Hedilla's system, across the dust clouds at its outer limits, and eventually out in the deep black darkness of interstellar space. The convoy gathered pace as it streaked unerringly through the night sky. Observers on the planetary surface watched as the small fuzzy silver-white light that marked the tightly knit group of spacecraft gradually but discernibly shrank in size, a diminishing point of light that eventually diminished into the depths of the night sky, until eventually it was no longer visible, replaced only by an inky darkness and the quiet of the night sky.

Rorque 4 – departure of The Spirit of the Age from Rorque 4

By no stretch of the imagination was the Margallan crew disappointed to be leaving Rorque 4. Their undesired stay, on a planet they had never wanted to be on in the first place, had long since become a form of prolonged mental torture, especially as they developed an intense and growing dislike of the bizarre society that characterised the neo-liberal world. Only the solidarity within the group, and the friendship with their newfound comrades, had allowed them to endure and survive what was a largely demoralising and dispiriting experience. Most of what they had experienced had either been alarming, confusing or profoundly depressing.

On frequent occasions, the members of the crew had been subject to highly personalised racist and sexist abuse, both from those in authority and from ordinary members of the public; a phenomenon that never occurred on Margalla, and for which they thus had little idea of how to deal with. Margallan society, from its very inception, had been a cosmopolitan society - its original inhabitants hailed from all the continents and many of the nations existing back on Earth, and freely mixed to create a society of all ethnicities, but effectively one of none. On Rorque 4, by contrast, this was clearly not the case; they had observed from very early on how common it was for people to identify and socialise on the basis of gender, age, ethnic group or some other form of social division. Additionally - as with all other aspects of Rorquean society - hierarchies clearly existed between the different social groups, through which they treated each other differently, and frequently abusively. Such a divided society was clearly full of tensions and hatreds, and the Margallan crew had frequently been on the receiving end of the abuse that came with such a fragmented culture.

In the same vein, Margallan society had always been a strongly androgynous one; males and females within all the communities made their own personal choices – within the context of their specific society - as to how they lived their lives, rather than choices and decisions being expected to be based upon their sex. Other than the bearing of children, the lives of males and females were effectively very similar, with no particular expectations placed on individuals and how they should behave with regards to the sex they were born into. Appearance, education, leisure, child-rearing and all other aspects of life on Margalla were effectively very similar or identical for both sexes, and this was so ingrained within their culture that they barely gave it a second thought.

On Rorque 4, this was clearly not the case, and the Margallans were frequently insulted or denigrated for not adhering to the gender stereotypes that predominated across the planet. In particular, they had no real conception of why men and women were expected to dress and use cosmetics differently, to frequent separate social activities and to engage in different economic and domestic roles. All this was a complete mystery to them and completely unfathomable. Initially, they believed that the society they found themselves in must have engaged in some massive collective act of self-delusion, but this made little real sense. However, in a desperate attempt to impart some form of rational explanation for the division, they ultimately decided it must in some way serve the purposes of the corporations and their compliant state, and to somehow be coercively maintained, though this theory seemed to suffer from the fact that there appeared to be little significant opposition to the division.

In addition to their ever present problems with the strange nature of Rorquean society, they had also made no progress whatsoever with their original aim of acquiring rocket fuel for their stasis ship. Not a single individual person they had encountered during their four months on the planet had been able to help them in any substantive way towards this goal. Ultimately, the most helpful suggestion had been to search the spaceport for fuel supplies and to simply steal them, though they had quickly discounted this plan once they discovered that being caught would result in several years in one of the brutal and soulless prisons to be found in the remote and forgotten corners of Rorque 4's less populated continents.

With such little credit available to them, they were unable to buy the fuel and - with no desirable employment skills or relevant qualifications - the possibility of earning sufficient funds was also effectively closed to them, especially once discovered that rocket fuel was prohibitively expensive and that they would probably need to work for several years before they could afford sufficient quantities anyway. Manufacture of the fuel was way beyond their technical skills, and neither did they have access to the necessary equipment – unlike on Margalla. As a last resort, they had tried something recommended to them known as crowd-funding – but very few members of the population seemed to want to help them and contribute to their fund, and so ultimately they had effectively run out of possible solutions to their problem.

So, when an AI unit from the Rorque Corporation came to their hotel one day and informed them of the recent decision made by Jamieson, they jumped at the offer. They knew from regular contact with their own AI units on The Spirit of the Age that their ship was now in good repair and ready for immediate departure. All routine maintenance and necessary repairs had been completed, and once refuelled it would be fully ready for its following voyage. They decided to stay one final day more to socialise with their comrades from the local area, and inform them of their imminent departure, and then took an autocar the following day to the spaceport at Mirivan, met the Rorque Corporation AI units there, and organised the process of transporting the requisite rocket fuel supplies to their spacecraft. They flew their transporter craft back up to the stasis ship, settled into their quarters and then discussed what they should do next.

They had been made aware that they needed to meet with the departing scientists who were to accompany them on their journey, as this was an essential part of the deal that had secured their departure. Their personal preference was to make the return journey immediately back to Margalla - always part of their original plan - but they were acutely aware that the scientists might not share their desire to make Margalla their first port of call. Even if they did, it was doubtful that Margalla could absorb such a large and sudden influx of people, especially ones that possessed a significantly different social outlook to their own, and with different ambitions in life. If they were to initially head to Margalla, the scientists did then have the option of boarding The Web Weaver and flying it to wherever they wanted, but their journey would then prove to be an extremely long one, and they had only just recently spent nearly three years travelling across interstellar space.

They discussed the alternatives to an immediate return journey to Margalla. During their time spent on Rorque 4 they had learnt a great deal more about the other planets of the Nexus Cluster, but they considered their options to be pretty limited. The nearest two inhabited worlds were Ur-Tokar and Zeleyan. They had discovered Ur-Tokar was an anti-technology civilisation, so they could not imagine thousands of hi-tech scientists wanting to reside and work there. Zeleyan was ruled by a fascist dictatorship and, additionally, the Rorque 4 media had been broadcasting occasional newscasts concerning political and economic unrest on the planet. They had quickly learnt that the corporate newscasts were less than reliable - and almost always driven by political and economic considerations rather than factual accuracy - so these might not actually be accurate, but, nevertheless, they assumed the scientists would hold a similar opinion to themselves with regards to living in a highly repressive and restrictively authoritarian society.

This, in effect, only left Zeta Kotlin, which had, of course, been the scientist's original destination. According to sympathetic sites on various forms of social media, the socialist communities there had built a host of new settlements and universities for the scientist ships that had arrived there originally, so there appeared to be plenty of habitation and opportunities for the scientists if they chose this as their destination. However, it was something in the region of a twenty-three month journey to the socialist world, and then a further twelve months back to their own planet. Admittedly, they would spend most of this time in stasis, but it still meant a further three years away from their friends and community – people who were already beginning to seem like a distant memory. Despite this, they felt the scientists had the right to decide where they would eventually reside, especially as they were effectively refugees who had recently experienced the entire destruction of their own civilisation - the Margallans might arrive back late to their own, but at least they had one to return to. Zeta Kotlin was thus looking highly likely as though it would be their next destination.

Their meeting the next day with the scientist's representatives went pretty much according to how they had anticipated. They too were aware of recent developments on Zeleyan and Zeta Kotlin and had decided the latter was their only viable destination, though they were very diplomatic as to why they thought Margalla was perhaps not the most suitable of places for their future lives. During the meeting they also worked out the number of passengers that were coming with them, and made sure there were enough stasis pods for everyone coming aboard The Spirit of The Age. A tally of the numbers wanting to leave – almost everyone who had not received a contract, plus a small number who had received one but wanted to leave anyway – showed that the ship would be at about ninety-five percent carrying capacity, in terms of stasis pod occupancy.

With this number now known, Kiyona initiated a conversation amongst the Margallans as to whether they should take any of their new found friends and acquaintances from Shade Gate. They all seemed so profoundly disillusioned with their situation and the society they were living in on Rorque 4, and with few of them believing there was any real prospect of political and social developments moving in the direction they desired. It had appeared to the crew that if they were able to put their political ideas into practice, they would be creating a world very similar to that of Margalla or Zeta Kotlin, so they should easily be able to make new lives on either of these planets, if they chose to come along for the journey. Their lives, the crew assumed, would be much better than on the depressing and quite alarming planet of Rorque 4. The crew was in entire agreement with Kiyona's suggestion, and so they messaged all the people they could think of with an invitation to join them on their journey to Zeta Kotlin - or later to Margalla, if that was their choice.

Within a week of the deal agreed between Jamieson, Sanchez and the protesting scientists, the Spirit of the Age was fully ready for immediate departure. The thousands of scientists had been quickly transported to the ship from the two spaceports of Mirivan and Stratostan, and had once again gone been placed in suspended animation. Fuel levels were now at maximum, and the corporate media outlets had reported the whole grand departure as a magnanimous gesture generously organised by the two giant corporations. This time, the Margallan crew made sure they were fully in control of the departure process, and had introduced a series of security protocols to ensure that their orders could not be overridden - the ship's computer would inform them of any such attempts to do so. They were not about to make the same mistake for a second time.

Many of their new acquaintances from Shade Gate had decided to join them on the starship. In fact, it turned out to be a few dozen more than they had expected coming aboard the vessel; their comrades had told a range of other friends of the invitation, and many had jumped at the chance of being able to leave Rorque 4 and make a new life in a utopian society. Fortunately, they still possessed sufficient stasis pods to accommodate the additional numbers, and the extra passengers were now in the torpor of stasis, fully ensconced in the wastelands of sleep, and oblivious to the long journey that would take them to their new life on another planet.

Once this had been effected, the Margallans then made the final technical and operational arrangements that would oversee the departure of their stasis ship on its next long voyage into the depths of interstellar space. They also dispatched a lengthy communication message into space, organised by a delegation of the scientists before they entered stasis, explaining their experiences on Rorque 4 and why they were now headed towards Zeta Kotlin.

'Well, I can't say I'm sorry to be leaving that place. It was like a living nightmare – it's hard to believe that such an appalling society can even actually exist. What we see as a psychopathy, they see as rational behaviour. I'm half expecting to wake up and discover the whole episode was just some awful dream,' reflected Akiko.

The others all nodded knowingly in agreement. They had initially attempted to engage positively with their newfound and unexpected situation, but a long series of misunderstandings, restrictions on their actions and behaviour, and several abusive and depressing experiences and episodes meant they had all come to the same conclusion a significant time ago - it was by far and away the worst experience of their lives.

'It's quite frightening really,' agreed Zhavia, 'it's only by an accident of birth that we were born on Margalla and not here on Rorque 4. Imagine if you had been born here instead - and it could have been any of us. It makes me shudder just to think about it.'

'What a depressing thought, and I feel sorry for those still down there,' stated Arlo. 'All that misery and squalor, poverty and ignorance, it was such a sad place. I wish we could do something to help the Rorqueans, they were suffering so badly. There seemed to be no end of depression and anxiety, not to mention the high self-harm and suicide rates we kept hearing about.'

'Given that most of the population had such a negative view of human nature, it's hardly surprising though,' said Zhavia. 'Imagine if you thought that pretty much everyone else was selfish, greedy, untrustworthy and even potentially dangerous. You would be paranoid about all the people around you, as well. And, what would there be to look forward to – just more of the same – and forever. What a depressing thought! No wonder they have so many mental health problems and so much despair and dismay.'

'Yes, sadness runs deep amongst their people; but I'm at a loss as to know what we could actually do to alleviate it,' stated Arlo, who had seemed, at times, to take some of their experiences far too personally, to the point where his fellow Margallans had occasionally feared for his mental health too.

'Same here, and I can't think what it would be either. I think most of the people we met would just refuse our help. They seemed inured to all the misery, exploitation and oppression; it was like they had no hope for a better future other than the one being constantly pushed in their faces - that of seeking promotion, acquiring greater wealth and buying yet more material goods,' added Kiyona.

Nevertheless, whilst she shared the crew's opinions of the planet and how depressing their experience there had been, she was also aware that for her, at least, some benefits had accrued from their time spent in such a difficult society. Her decision back on Margalla to make something more of her life had now made some significant progress, she believed. Their period of difficulty and adversity on Rorque 4 had been a particularly educational one for Kiyona, and she felt she was beginning to mature and grow as a person, though she was still unsure as to how exactly this might benefit her in the future.

'I guess they just see their world as normal and that no other realistic options actually exist. It's all they've ever known; in the same way that we've always seen Margalla as completely normal,' Xander offered. 'I'm also beginning to see why we've kept our existence secret for so long now, as well; we really don't want the corporations of Rorque 4 invading, and destroying our culture. Imagine if they took control of our islands – it would be a complete nightmare, the destruction of our entire way of life.'

'But our society is a far more utopian one, whereas theirs is so dystopian,' stated Akiko. 'Surely they can see that . . . and secretly I think they can, but they're just afraid to admit it – the implications of doing so would be so vast and so difficult, that they're unwilling to face up to the implications. It's just easier to do nothing and to conform.' Like Kiyona, Akiko had also engaged in some long periods of reflection and a considerable amount of time comparing the two societies, and felt that she too had arrived at some important realisations, but was struggling to apply them to her previous concerns about Margalla's environment – despite much effort to do so.

'And, I never really felt like I fully understood what was going on down there,' added Akiko. 'Nothing ever seemed quite real; it was all so ephemeral, like their society was not quite rooted in reality. The people didn't seem to truly be themselves. It was like they'd chosen an identity and put on a mask, one that was needed to get them through the travails of daily life, but it was not really them. And then the wider situation just kept changing, and sometimes so quickly. As Ben said, 'all that is sold melts into the air' - it was like one day something was ultra-important and the next it was simply irrelevant. It must be very difficult to maintain any genuine values and beliefs in such a society. It was as though you were just expected to change your values at the drop of a hat, and just move onto completely new ones, whether you wanted to or not.'

'And judging by their media reports – which were admittedly far from always being a reliable source of information - that's how their whole economy seems to work. It just moves into a new location, extracts what it wants, makes a profit and then leaves when the situation is no longer productive – usually leaving a mess behind to compound problems. It seemed to happen over and over again,' explained Xander. 'It has no tangible connection with the locality or the people living there – it's not rooted in anything substantive, just a desire to extract profit, and then move onto the next profitable location. It is all very ephemeral and unreal. I'm not surprised people seemed so confused and unsure of what to do.'

'And if they did rebel they would face the immense challenge of defeating the security forces, which always looked so aggressive and militarised. To me, that looked like an enormously difficult task,' said Akiko, and paused as if she was trying to picture such a development.

'Yes, for a society supposedly ultra-committed to all forms of freedom, there seemed to be a great deal of effort going into preventing it – endless laws, highly armed security forces, brutal prisons, harassment of anyone who opposed their system – and all well financed and organised for maximum effectiveness,' stated Xander.

'There's certainly little or nothing we could do to help them in that respect. When Dave said you can only liberate yourself, that others can't do it for you, that was so true. I can't imagine anything we could do would make a great deal of difference for the people down there. At best we could tell them about our society and show them that a better world is possible, but ultimately they would still need to do it for themselves, and at the moment I can see little sign of any real change in that direction.'

'Maybe that theory of Ben's needs to come true. He reckoned that radical change most readily occurs when the economy is growing very strongly. People see that their world is improving so they believe that even further improvements are possible and can be achieved. It seems sort of counter-intuitive that you would change a system when it's doing so well, but it does have a sort of logic to it. They certainly haven't changed it after decades of it performing so badly, so there might be something to his theory.'

'Well, however it's done, it's going to be a massive task – they've got a long way to go to sort that place out. I don't envy them that job, at all,' concluded Zek.

'How are we doing for departure preparations?' asked Kiyona, as keen as any of the others to depart as soon as they possibly could. They were all slightly concerned that some mishap or other might cause a further unwanted stay on Rorque 4. She looked out through the viewing screen down towards the largely dry-brown planet. She could make out some of the shallow blue-green seas, but the rest of the sphere was largely a patchwork of browns and yellows. In the blue-black darkness above the planet she caught site of the sparkling moon of Scintilla, glinting in the sunlight of Eleutheria – apparently its barren surface was quite literally littered with billions of quartz crystals. Somehow, the presence of the sparkling moon in such close proximity to the depressingly dull brown planet seemed completely and utterly incongruous, Kiyona thought. 'I really think it's time we left,' she suggested strongly.

'Fine, everything looks to be in order, except the ship's computer is indicating we are missing a landing craft. That's odd, where did that go?' asked Xander, more to himself than any of the others.

There was a pause for a few seconds. 'Ah, that must be the one Anna Dubois took down to the spaceport. It must still be at Mirivan,' he replied to his own question.

'Well, I for one vote we do not go back to retrieve it,' Akiko chipped in. 'The last thing we need is any more time on that hellhole. Anyway, we can always replace it with one from the Web Weaver,' and paused to think. 'I wonder if anyone is actually planning to come back and collect it. I assume Anna Dubois isn't!' They all laughed and made various comments of agreement.

Xander instructed the ship's computer to ignore the missing landing craft, and with confirmation that all the ship's systems were now fully engaged and ready for departure, he programmed in the final protocols and they readied themselves for the next chapter in their unexpected odyssey.

'Time we left this world today,' declared Xander, and he gave the order for the ship's computer to commence acceleration. Soon they were moving out of Rorque 4's orbit and way beyond the planets and asteroids of Eleutheria's outer regions.

The crew remained out of stasis for a couple of days; now that they had left the problem world of Rorque 4 way behind them, they could finally relax and start to become themselves again. They took the opportunity to socialise together and to come to terms with what they had experienced, reflecting on their experiences, on what they had learnt and how it had shaped their thinking. They also spent considerable periods of time looking out across the universe, at its stark majestic beauty, at its millions of stars and galaxies, its strange but beautiful gas clouds, and then, just contemplating the cold frozen darkness of that vast inky vacuum. It was simply too large and too infinite to fully comprehend. Finally, once they had experienced their fill of reflection and space gazing, they locked down their ship, placed themselves into stasis, and left the AI units to mind the ship as they sped their way silently across the vast darkness of interstellar space and on towards the distant world of Zeta Kotlin. Or so they thought.

Earth – is there Anybody out There?

In the more than a century that had passed since the great exodus from planet Earth, humans had travelled far and wide across the nearest regions of inter-stellar space; the numerous starships traversing vast distances across those sections of the galaxy most proximate to the Solar system. As years and decades passed, the starships had journeyed ever onwards, and as each further decade passed, encountered phenomena both expected but also inconceivable to generations of Earth-bound observers. Distant exploding supernova briefly bursting into dazzling magnificence, only to return once more to the vast darkness of the cosmos. Spectacular gas nebulae, twisted and contorted, their amazing multi-coloured contortions sprawling majestically across the darkness. Spiral galaxies studding the cosmic spacescape, indiscernibly rotating about the super black-holes that lay at their core. Comets speeding across the skies, blazing a trail of icy-cold vapour as they hurtled through the vacuum of space and its frozen temperatures, whilst asteroids shot past them like bullets travelling at the speed of light. Space dust proved to be virtually ubiquitous, spread thinly around and between the stars, whilst the icy rings of Oort clouds circled the distant dark depths of virtually all the star systems they encountered. These were just a fraction of the wondrous experiences that awaited those travelling into the deepness of space.

As they ventured out across the cosmos, as the exodus spread ever onwards, the starfarers had encountered a vast array of different star-types. Most numerous were the red dwarfs that populated whole regions of the galaxy, with their dark orange light and diminished planetary systems. Bright yellow-white G class stars, like that of the Sun were scarcer, but the most sought after by the multitudes of the exodus, as they searched for a planet that bore some approximation to the conditions for life on Earth. Occasionally, a much rarer, but highly stable, orange dwarf K star system was encountered – often touted as the most likely planets for the existence of extra-terrestrial life. A few desperate ships had even found their way into the systems of the much scarcer and less promising red giants, blue giants and supergiants, and finally the brown dwarfs – though rarely did any of these provide the suitable planets they were searching for.

Whilst the variety of different star types encountered had been significant, those of the planets had been immense. Planets came in a vast variety of forms, sizes and configurations. Dwarf planets, small metallic planets, large rocky planets, gas giants with rings, gas giants without rings, huge ice giants and tiny ice dwarves, binary planets, planets with no moon, and planets with dozens of moons, planets with no atmosphere and planets with atmospheres constituted by a whole range of complex gaseous mixtures. Some star systems possessed a single planet, whilst others enjoyed the orbits of dozens of satellites. Planets they discovered in their thousands – a vast number of types and configurations - often beautiful and intriguing, but almost invariably lifeless. For, only a small fraction of the many planets they encountered actually contained liquid water and were thus capable of being terra-formed.

And what they did not discover out in the vastness of space, amongst this immense diversity of planetary entities - except perhaps in a tiny number of contested cases - was the existence of any extra-terrestrial life. Not with any certainty anyway. There were numerous rumours of discoveries - claims by a whole host of explorers to having discovered basic forms of primitive life. These claims usually involved the detection of unicellular life-forms, primeval slimes, extremophiles, crypto-bacteria and a myriad of extremely basic alien life-types. Some assertions were considered to be more accurate and acceptable than others. But transmitting data and physical evidence across the vast times and even vaster distances of space meant that such claims could rarely, if ever, be verified for certain by third parties. Frequently, contamination by Earth-based sources proved to be the provenance for such claims of indigenous life. In sum, there appeared to be little or no alien life out there.

Those who wanted to believe that a whole array of alien life-forms were out there waiting to be discovered, needed plausible explanations for this barren sterility. The most popular theory was to blame the 'genesis pods'. Their arrival at a liquid water planet was invariably followed by the rapid introduction of the 'primal soup' needed to prepare the way for terra-forming the planet. When the astro-biologists back on Earth had first heard that this was the planned way of proceeding, they had been appalled. Local life-forms would not only be left undiscovered, but would very likely be destroyed by the mass introduction of Earth-originating life forms. Such objections went largely unheeded though; humans were already in the process of destroying their own unique biosphere, and they showed little interest in protecting the existence of life-forms they were completely unaware of, and that might not even exist.

Once, though, it became clear that the exodus into space was about to begin in earnest, the astro-biologists had managed to ensure that the 'genesis pods' at least conducted initial tests for indigenous life-forms, before the introduction of 'the primal soup' from Earth. This small concession, they believed, would at least allow them to know that such alien life-forms existed, even if they might soon be subject to rapid extinction. The pods could gather samples and preserve them for posterity. Yet, in the fullness of time, very few of these tests were considered to have actually ever encountered locally originating life-forms, if indeed any of them had. Those expecting to encounter a whole array of exotic extra-terrestrial life made their excuses; the tests were not extensive enough, they were too brief and insufficiently analysed. Nevertheless, nothing much beyond basic unicellular life-forms was thought to have ever been encountered, and even this somewhat disappointing result was still contested.

Occasionally, there were stories of little green men, bug-eyed monsters, beautiful creatures with blue skin, strange and bizarre entities with telepathic powers, sentient gas clouds and the like, but they only ever proved to be stories or space yarns - the fantasies of space explorers with over active imaginations, suffering from space sickness or with far too much time on their hands. Throughout the entirety of the great inter-stellar exodus, no intelligent alien life form had ever been reliably encountered, nor had any made contact with humanity's ever expanding exodus.

For some, this was an immense disappointment. Aliens had often been suggested as the saviours of the human race – their enlightened ways or advanced technologies capable of helping humans to create the utopias that so many of their number were seeking and searching for. Others hoped for the cosmopolitan mixing so beloved of science fiction movies – thus forcing humans to dispense with their damaging anthropomorphism and parochial self-obsessions. For scientists, genuinely existing aliens would offer opportunities to better understand the origins of life on Earth and the mystery of life in general.

For others, though, it was a genuine relief. No starship had ever been caught in the nets of space, its crew turned into flesh fondue for carnivorous space hunters. The absence of intelligent extra-terrestrial life forms meant there was no danger of being abducted by aliens, of becoming the lunch for some horrendous acid-dripping xenomorph or a meal for a blood-thirsty star cannibal. The new planetary civilisations were not about to face invasion and subjugation from the forces of hostile extra-terrestrials - only humans posed that form of threat. Space had its many dangers, perils and pitfalls, but menacing and hostile extra-terrestrials was not one of them.

Competing arguments for this apparent absence of intelligent alien life - for the eerie silence encountered by the voyagers - had drawn heavily on the dispute between the Drake Equation and Fermi's Paradox. Drake had believed that once Earth could support life, evolution would inevitably produce intelligent life-forms that were ultimately capable of organising space travel. But, there were literally billions of planets out there - and as Fermi asked - why had no alien life form ever contacted the human race? The failure by the exodus to encounter any form of intelligent aliens appeared to support Fermi's assertions. The resolution of the dispute appeared to revolve around the mistaken belief that evolution would gradually and inevitably produce more and more complex organisms, until it eventually produced an intelligent life-form, capable of achieving space travel - one that would ultimately travel to the stars.

The evidence from the exodus was that it appeared to have done no such thing! At best, planets might simply produce primitive organisms that gradually became better and better adapted to their disparate ecosystems. Invariably, during the life of a planet those ecosystems would change and alter, occasionally dramatically. But when the ecosystems changed, evolution would simply adapt the life-forms for suitability to the new conditions. There was no guarantee of increasingly complex and increasingly intelligent life-forms evolving, just continual change in random directions. There was no teleological destination for evolution – it was simply a random set of sequences that may or may not produce any given particular form of life — intelligent or otherwise.

On the tiny number of planets where life might possibly become established it would face frequent major setbacks - collisions from asteroids or other cosmic phenomena, the eruption of super-volcanoes, runaway greenhouse gas events or a mass freezing over of the planet. Major extinctions would have followed, discontinuing the evolutionary paths that had previously been developing. On occasions, life would have ended entirely, long before the arrival of the human exodus.

Where life did survive, there was no inherent reason to believe that newly emerging life-forms would be more complex or more intelligent than those before. Even when humans had eventually evolved — in the fortuitous space vacated by the dinosaurs 65 million years ago, following their own unfortunate and unlucky demise — there was no guarantee that they would spread across the entirety of the planet, move from a foraging existence to an agrarian one, develop science and industry, or indeed follow any other particular pattern of development. None of this was inevitable - all these developments could have easily not occurred.

The evidence from the experience of the exodus was that few planets could possess life, and those few that could, would struggle to hold onto that life, and even fewer were likely to produce complex life forms. Only a small numbers of planets had sufficient warmth and water to achieve this, and where life was thought to have been encountered it had not moved beyond the most primitive of stages. The development of intelligent life-forms had, so far as was known, only occurred on Earth — there were simply too many adverse factors preventing the rise of life-forms intelligent enough to be capable of advanced technology and space travel, for this to be a common, or even infrequent, event.

Planets needed to be relatively safe and stable — to be protected from cosmic bombardments and collisions, destabilising planetary wobbles, damaging solar radiations and a myriad of other challenges capable of destroying life. Equally, they could not be so static and unchanging so as to create conditions where adaptation and further complexity were not even likely to occur in the first place. Earth was lucky enough to have fallen between these two extremes, to have enjoyed sufficient levels of both stability and change, and had thus been capable of eventually giving rise to intelligent space-faring organisms. This was why - despite the exodus across so many light years of space - humans continued to find themselves alone in the universe. Earth was special in a unique way they had never fully appreciated.

Arrival in Utopia

Interstellar Space - the Opa-Loka arrives at Ur-Tokar

Jiaying was carefully observing the large bank of digital displays arrayed before her. She had checked the light specific data, adjusted the D-Rider stabilisation systems and compensated for the fluctuating E.M.C. emissions. Now, following the calculations imparted to her by the ship's computer, she could put the powerful plasma-engines of the Opa-Loka fully into reverse. And so began the long deceleration that would take them into the heart of the Rogan star system, cruise past the two gaseous planets of Corusa and Lapiz, and finally slow them smoothly along the black corridor and place them into orbit around the fifth planet of the stellar system - the small rocky semi-frozen world of Ur-Tokar. She had tracked this course before and had named it 'the chronoglide skyway' – it was just like taking a journey back through time.

In the days since she had emerged from stasis, she had been keeping a close eye on the diminutive red dwarf. At first, the small orange-red dot, whilst easy to discern, had not been particularly distinctive amongst the vast array of white, yellow and orange points of shimmering light that covered the dark canvas of space, despite its relative proximity. As she did so, she wondered at the marvels of the cosmos. Interspersed amongst those stars, she had spent prolonged periods wondering at the coloured marvels of the various gas clouds; the fantastically pale electric blue of the Helix Nebula and its bloodshot-like eye, the slightly spooky eeriness of the Ghost Nebula, the stunning crimson flower-like structure of the Carina Nebula and a number of others she could not even name, but which looked like distant phosphorescent jellyfish, indiscernibly floating their way through the darkness of the cosmos. She knew how they formed – stellar explosions - but why did they all appear so vastly different, she wondered.

The spiral galaxies, almost hidden amongst the stellar array, whilst more uniform in shape and design, were equally beautiful, she thought to herself, with their tightly swirling arms of pink, white, blue or golden light, intensely circling their glowing bright white centres. Each spiral looked as though it was engaged in some incomprehensibly eternal struggle to break loose from its centre, whilst at the same time coiling ever inwards, making itself incapable of ever actually escaping. Consisting of billions of stars and an immense number of light years far away across vast dark voids of inter-galactic space, she wondered if humanity would ever traverse such vast distances, and if they were to do so, what they would discover there.

Presumably, she thought, they would not be so very different from our own galaxy, after all, the laws of physics remained constant across the universe. But, nevertheless, ever since she had commenced her journeys and travels across the frozen wilderness of inter-stellar space she had wondered whether there might not be more to space than simply the laws of physics. Its wondrous spacescapes, its never-ending darkness and its eerie quietness all seemed to hold out the promise of something intangibly more. She wasn't the first to wonder if there was some extra-planetary answer to the mysteries of life out there – whole generations before her had pontificated at great length over this matter – and she would not be the last, but she could not help feeling that there was more to space than meets the eye.

Fairly quickly though, as the starship hurtled its way through space and started to close in on the planetary system, Rogan transformed from being a smallish orange dot to becoming more and more discernible as an actual star. A short time later, and they passed the first of Rogan's two gaseous outer planets, Corusa, initially an unremarkable-looking mass of swirling mustard, orange and brown gaseous clouds, albeit in distinctive bands; but she quickly remembered the distinct pale-yellow, shimmering, glitter-like light that surrounded the globe –giving it, to all intents, the appearance of a sparkling glitterball in the deep dark blackness of space.

As the space craft cruised past, she remembered the first time she had discovered that the coruscating sparkle was caused by billions of small firework-like explosions emanating from slightly below the surface of its upper atmosphere – giving the distinct appearance that the planet was on fire. As Rosson had done so two months earlier, Jiaying could not help but be impressed by the cosmic firework display, but unlike Rosson, she assumed that this was the result of some underlying clash of incompatible chemical elements in the higher layers of its thick atmosphere - that the planet was probably burning up immense quantities of one of its more volatile elements, and then ejecting them violently and spectacularly into its cold dark surroundings.

Next, was the intriguing bluish-grey globe of Lapiz, clearly being stripped of its outer gaseous layers, as they could be seen to be visibly streaming into the emptiness of space. The golden void that had opened up across parts of the sphere clearly indicated that this was the result of massively violent internal electrical forces, rather than that of some external gravitational influence – not that there were any large or dense enough within the stellar system to achieve this anyway – and Jiaying wondered for how long the planet could sustain such a massive loss of material. She wondered whether it would eventually be stripped down to some inner rocky core, or was the entire planet composed of gas only to eventually shrink to nothing. She made a mental note to check the ship's data banks for an answer some time - her knowledge of planetary science was still a work in progress.

Finally, Ur-Tokar became visible on the viewing screen as they powered down the black corridor towards the planet, and eventually swung into a high orbit around its northern hemisphere. Jiaying studied the small white and blue disc intently and remembered – with mixed emotions - her previous visits to the planet. This was her third trade mission to the ice and forest world, and neither of the previous two visits had been particularly enjoyable. This time, though, she had planned for matters to be different; they were simply aiming to arrive and depart in the shortest amount of time possible and with the minimum of fuss. This, she was hoping, would avoid the dramatic problems and errors of their previous visits.

Jiaying was now in her late thirties, and had been a member of the ship's crew on and off for nearly fifteen years now. She was still not quite sure why she had opted for a life aboard a spaceship – it had never even been a remote ambition when she was much younger. As a teenager she had been somewhat less sociable and gregarious than many of her contemporaries, and whilst never a loner, had tended to prefer the company of smaller groups. Early on in her life, she had grown bored of the small settlement of Kapal she had grown up in, had travelled for a couple of years around Xestronia - the continent of Zeta Kotlin she originated from - and found she quite liked the semi-nomadic life of a traveller.

Whilst on her travels and staying in Zeta Kotlin's only still functioning spaceport - the small equatorial city that had half-jokingly renamed itself

Earth City, once the decision to consolidate all spaceport activities there had been made - and hanging around in the local community centres, she had become aware of the possibility of joining the crew of the Opa-Loka, Zeta Kotlin's only inter-stellar trading ship.

For most citizens of Zeta Kotlin, there was little incentive in living the life of a space trader. It was widely considered to be boring and uninteresting, subject to all the myriad dangers that existed in space, it kept you away from your community for months or years on end, and finally you might even end up lost in space forever more. In addition, the socialistic economy of Zeta Kotlin relied heavily on AI units for much of its economic activity. These performed the routine, difficult or dangerous tasks that the various communities considered unsuitable for humans. This meant that humans were free to engage in the activities they found most preferable – and these tended to be the more intellectually and socially satisfying ones, not ones perceived to be uninteresting and potentially dangerous.

Employment by private individuals and companies – in keeping with socialist thinking - had been outlawed from the very first days of settlement of the planet - though a form of communal employment did supposedly exist, but remained something of a nebulous concept, since the distinction between work and leisure was effectively a blurred one. The structure of this society did, however, ensure that all individuals saw their material needs met at all times. Effectively, therefore, there was little to incentivise or coerce anyone into any activity they considered undesirable, so, all in all, there were few incentives – either positive or negative – to attract any of its population into space. Yet, it had discovered that it needed to do so.

Since the first 'genesis pod' had arrived and transformed Zeta Kotlin into a highly pleasant and largely prosperous planet, the planet's ecosystems had effectively flourished. Across the vast majority of the planet - its citizens had collectively decided - these natural ecosystems should be kept for the benefit of the limited wildlife that had been brought on either the original genesis pod or the 'utopian ships' that arrived later. This was to avoid repeating the same drastic mistake made previously on Earth of destroying virtually all the world's natural ecosystems, and thus contributing significantly to the climate catastrophe of the twenty-first century. It was also hoped that a wider range of life-forms would gradually evolve to populate these fertile regions.

These 'utopian ships' had brought numerous ferming units with them; so much of the food on the planet could be created artificially. Nevertheless, about thirty percent of the planets vast lands had still been given over to agriculture, and a wide range of fruit and vegetable crops together with some cereals were grown across its plains and lowland valleys. The vast majority of the planet's population populated these areas, predominantly in medium-sized settlements, though a number of small open-plan and environmentally friendly cities had been built on the shores of the freshwater lakes that dotted the plains and along the shores of the numerous continental coastlines.

Unfortunately, whilst there was much to commend the planet of Zeta Kotlin, its lands were also relatively flat, and mountains were notable by their almost complete absence, consisting, other than the Cascade Mountains, of only a few clearly ageing minor ranges, most of which were inland and distant from the coast. As such, the plains of Zeta Kotlin's continents experienced fairly low levels of rainfall, not low enough to cause significant economic or habitation problems, but they did mean a general lack of densely forested areas – wooded regions tending to consist of only very open and large savannah-like areas on the extensive lowland plains and plateaus.

Of more concern to Zeta's citizens, though, was the dearth of metal and mineral ores that resulted from their continents being so relatively flat. The Zetans had quickly located and mined what little existed, and had then attempted to extract the metals and minerals they needed from the sea-beds – though with limited success. In addition, they had also recycled the limited number of rare metals that had been brought from Earth with them. Acutely aware that their free and easy lifestyles were heavily dependent on keeping a plentiful supply of AI units, and although they possessed the manufacturing ability to keep producing new ones - and recycling contributed to this continued production up to a certain point - ultimately they realised they were in need of new supplies of scarce rare earth metals and other mineral resources that they were unable to extract from their own planet, or able to artificially generate through chemical processes.

It was for this reason that the Zetans had eventually decided to consolidate the spaceport of Earth City – the other ports established early in the colonisation period having all been closed down once they fell into disuse – in order to launch their space trading activity. As the world already possessed several stasis ships, it was not difficult to convert one of them – The Skylark - into a trading ship suited to carrying bulk loads of mineral resources. The problem they quickly encountered, though, was finding people to crew the ship. Long - probably very boring - periods spent travelling across the vastness of space, the process of entering and emerging from stasis, and being away from friends and communities for long periods offered little appeal to the planet's inhabitants, who were invariably already engaged in pursuits they had decided were far more worthwhile and meaningful. Additionally, their egalitarian socialist economy precluded the use of any financial inducements or status rewards.

Early in the programme, they toyed with the idea of simply crewing the ship entirely with AI android units, though they harboured major doubts about the wisdom of such an idea, particularly their ability to successfully program the units to conclude suitable trade deals with the planets they were dealing with. However, they quickly abandoned this approach when the ship - and all aboard The Skylark - simply vanished into space without a trace on its maiden voyage, never to return or to be heard of ever again. No reliable explanations for its disappearance had ever been established, though there were still occasional unsuccessful attempts to discover its whereabouts. As a result, the space trading programme ultimately came to rely on the recruitment of mavericks or misfits who considered the experience of travelling through space to be an interesting one, or capable of satisfying their own personal ambitions, whilst they also performed a vital service for their planetary community. It was never a very reliable solution, but there were effectively no viable alternatives.

Nevertheless, the concept of human-crewed ships – given the limitations of existing technology – had posed the community numerous protracted and mostly unsolvable problems. They had attempted as best they could to reduce the impact of low gravitation, cosmic radiation and other health-related issues that resulted from travelling in space over long periods of time, but none of these had ever been fully and satisfactorily dealt with. Possibly for this reason, and no doubt for numerous other ones, crew turnover always remained high; the majority only engaging in one or two voyages at most. Jiaying was unusual in this respect, in that she had now carried out several trade missions, to a number of different destinations, though admittedly with some significant time gaps in between.

This was despite the fact that Jiaying had fallen pregnant on two occasions – at different communes and with different lovers - and had decided to take the pregnancies to term. On both occasions, though, she had chosen to stay with the child for only two or three years, knowing their communities would provide all the love and support they needed as they grew older. With one, she knew the father was still in regular contact, but was unsure with regards to the other. This was far from unusual on Zeta Kotlin. Growing up in a commune, children spent large amounts of time with their contemporaries and there were always adults and AI units on hand somewhere nearby to address their needs and desires – at least, those deemed appropriate or practical. Material circumstances were always provided for and no child was allowed to go without.

As such, parents could easily engage in their chosen activities without needing to worry about childcare, and this had allowed Jiaying to spend several long periods in space as a result. For these reasons, Jiaying had found no difficulty in recently rejoining the space programme and once again becoming a member of the latest manifestation of the Opa-Loka crew. On this particular voyage she found herself with four other slightly eccentric fellow crew-members, about the same number as was usual on these ventures. These were Savverio, Janicka, Neema and Kahlil, all of whom were somewhat younger than herself, and all were less experienced in space travel.

She had travelled with Savverio before and she liked him a great deal. Children growing up on Zeta Kotlin invariably grew up in largely carefree conditions amidst material plenty, a range of available carers – both human and android – and a set of ready-made companions in their commune. Long days were spent exploring the neighbourhood and all its various nooks and crannies, hidden secrets and wide open spaces. Interspersed with this were shortish periods in the education centres acquiring the basics of a Zetan education and pursuing their chosen projects. For Savverio, though, this was not quite the case. Born with an initially severe disability, he had been more limited in terms of the adventures he could pursue with his fellow communards. Unsurprisingly, therefore, he had gravitated towards more indoor activities, computer games and associated activities and developed something of an expertise in these areas.

He was, she had decided on their previous mission, dependable, great with computers and possessed a very ironic sense of humour. She knew that he had originally been born with two deformed legs and, despite numerous operations and the fitting of artificial supports, walking remained a slow, difficult and sometimes painful process for him. He had admitted to her that he had chosen to join the space trade mission because he figured – largely correctly – that in a low gravity atmosphere his disability would be significantly diminished, and as such he had generally flourished, often taking charge of dealing with the ship's technical problems and working innovatively with its powerful computer systems.

Janicka, Neema and Kahlil were, by contrast, all unknown quantities and she knew little of them. From what they had told her so far, though, she had gained the impression that their previous lives and endeavours on Zeta Kotlin had run their due course, and they were now looking for something new and different in their lives. Like Jiaying, they had no strong attachments to any particular community, but were probably just passing time before they discovered some newfound purpose in life. They all seemed friendly enough, if perhaps a little naïve, she thought. They did, though, seem to possess their own particular eccentricities, and Jiaying was looking forward to seeing how these played out once they arrived at the destination of Ur-Tokar.

She had met them briefly on several occasions during the course of their basic space training back at Earth City and given them a tour of the starship whilst it was still in orbit around Zeta Kotlin. Here, she had managed to discern something of their backgrounds.

Untypically for most children on Zeta Kotlin, Janicka's parents had actually remained with her in the same commune well into her teenage years. Eventually she felt that they were interfering far too much in her life – it was quite noticeable to her that her peers received much less advice on how they should be behaving – and she decided to move to another commune, a standard procedure for those feeling they were in need of a change. Unlike most though, she did not move to one nearby, but to one on an entirely different continent, that of South Kestronia. This turned out to be a wise move on her part, as her different cultural upbringing meant she was often the centre of attraction and considered almost exotic in her new location, allowing her to easily make friends and engage in numerous sexual relationships with relative ease.

However, with no real roots in her new location and after several years of greater autonomy, she felt she was now very much her own person and could afford to move on once again. She had believed that a further move and a new location could further enhance her sense of freedom and newfound confidence, and whilst staying over temporarily in Earth City had become aware that the Opa-Loka was looking for crew members. She figured a bit of space exploration could be exactly what she was looking for and – once basic training had been completed – enthusiastically joined the crew on the trade mission to Ur-Tokar.

Serious, and seemingly more down to earth than Janicka, as a small child Neema had actually been far more outgoing, exuberant and extroverted. For the most part, this was not a problem on a planet like Zeta Kotlin, but Neema had often pushed her luck too far when it came to what was considered acceptable within her community. Initially, a number of fairly minor incidents had simply led to mild rebukes or, more often, long explanations as to why she should be more considerate and careful of others. However, when a prank went badly wrong and she burnt several apartments down within the commune – though fortunately without loss of life or limb to any of the residents – she was forced to explain herself to the entire community at the standard hearing into such an incident.

Unlike in a capitalist society where you might be judged on the basis of material wealth, family connections, employability or social status, in a socialist society you were regarded almost entirely on the basis of your behaviour and your relationship to others within that community. Although the community cleared her of any malign intent, and realised her action was effectively the result of stupidity, so embarrassed and ashamed had she been over the entire episode – especially the realisation that she might have actually killed someone - that soon after the tribunal and her designated involvement in the reconstruction of the apartments, she had moved location and decided on an entirely new approach to life, one that now entailed being a valuable member of any community in any way possible.

A series of projects and studies that met this requirement duly followed, including an investigation into the Zeleyanian spy satellite enigma, which she had played a major part in uncovering and explaining. When she later heard that the Opa-Loka was in need of crew members for its next trading mission, she had decided she should volunteer, believing that out in space she would be further helping her society, not only through acquiring much-needed resources, but also in the fact that she might be able to discover if Zeleyan had further hostile intentions towards her home planet.

Like Janicka, Kahlil had joined the mission largely to develop his individuality. On Zeta Kotlin, just as resources were not owned by individuals, nor were other individuals. Zetans tended to enter and leave sexual relationships in an entirely consensual manner as free individuals. Given that few stayed in very long-term ones, it was usually easy for those leaving a relationship to find new partners – of either sex – relatively easily, and so sexual jealousies were usually short-lived, if they existed at all. Unfortunately, this had taken Kahlil a little longer to learn than for his peers, and he had become entangled in a relatively long, damaging and drawn-out – by Zetan standards – affair, until he had eventually realised the emotional distress he was causing the others in the relationship.

The community he was living in at the time was not far from Earth City and he had moved to the spaceport city, partly out of embarrassment, but also to significantly reevaluate his life. Whilst there, he had met Neema who was planning to travel with the Opa-Loka and had decided to join her, though he wasn't totally sure as to whether this was to escape from his previous life for a further period of reflection – where better than outer space, he thought - or because he was attracted to Neema, though possibly it might be both.

Despite all this, Jiaying had not spent much initial time with them, so it was not until the first few days of the voyage – during the period in which they departed from the star system of Aequitas, and before they entered stasis for the sixteen month journey to Ur-Tokar – that any real opportunity had arisen to become more fully acquainted with her new crew members.

The original conversations on board had proven to be fairly predictable and revolved around the subjects that most new crew members wanted to know about – the effects of space travel on their health, the potential for serious problems to occur, and what would happen if they became stranded in space for one reason or another. Once out of orbit and clear of any difficulties within the outer limits of the stellar system, one of their first had been as they had gathered on the forward deck, regarding the spacescape before them.

As the most experienced crew member, Jiaying felt as though she was required to open the initial semi-formal meeting on board. 'So everyone, welcome to the dream machine,' she said, and Savverio sniggered, and the others looked slightly worried.
'Oh, it's not that bad,' she reassured them, 'you'll eventually get used to its various quirks and peculiarities and whilst there are problems associated with travelling long-distance in space, I'm sure you'll get used to them.'
'So long journeys such as this don't have long-term impacts on our health, as some people claim?' asked Janicka, somewhat earnestly.
'Well, we shouldn't have any significant problems as we are in stasis for over ninety percent of the time, and when we're in orbit around our destination we can spend most of the time down on the planet. However, those old spacefarer tales of space ship blues and prolonged periods of psychosis are not completely the stuff of fiction, they really do occur,' answered Jiaying, warming to one of her favourite subjects. 'Space travellers who spend far too long awake and conscious in high speed, low gravity situations soon begin to lose their bearings and experience mental health problems. It's not unusual to suffer mild psychosis or even severe disorientation – our brains did not evolve to work in that kind an environment. In severe cases, they can suffer lucid and powerful hallucinations – even stronger than with the best LSD. It's not uncommon for them to even start thinking they have magical powers – psi power, radio telepathy, powers of levitation, or such like. They can suffer from tormented inner visions, can start hearing angel voices or seeing galactic angels, or begin thinking they're the lord of light or the master of the universe, or some other supernatural all-powerful being. I heard of one

character who thought their ship was under some form of sonic space attack and blacked out all the communication systems in order to hide from their imagined enemy - the ship seriously overshot their destination as a result. Once you're that far down the psychosis track you become a danger to yourself, the crew, the ship and everything around you. It's not hard to see why a number of the stasis ships that left Earth disappeared without trace, never to be seen again and their disappearance never adequately explained for. That's why they normally had androids running the ships.'

'And do many starships simply vanish into the ether, disappear into the void?' asked Janicka, wondering if some of the old tales and sagas of lost space ships were actually true, and not just stories for small children.

'Who knows, space is deep, its endless, its vast, its dark and its relentless – there's no way of knowing just how many ships have met a cold, silent, icy demise out in that immense dark blackness. I would guess quite a few. There's much that can go wrong – not just technical difficulties or crew members becoming suicidal, there's also random space debris, the gravitational destruction of stars and large planets, unknown cosmic phenomena – all sorts of stuff.' Jiaying noticed Neema was looking a little concerned, so changed tack. 'We'll be OK though, we know this terrain, we've travelled it several times and we know what we're doing. As long as we all follow standard procedures, we'll be fine. We know what we're doing.'

'And what if we do end up stranded in space – the engines fail or something such as that. What actually happens to us then?' asked Neema, still slightly concerned. Now that she was out in space, surrounded by its immense blackness, she was suddenly aware of just how lost, stranded and isolated it was possible to be out here in its vast desolation.

'Fortunately, it's never happened, so far - the AI units have managed to fix everything that's malfunctioned. I guess we would send out an emergency call for help and then go into stasis while we wait for the rescue ship. Zeta has several functioning stasis ships in orbit, so we should be rescued sooner or later – it would just take a considerable amount of time, I guess. Again, I'm not expecting to experience such a problem,' she thought for a moment, 'and I particularly don't want to be stranded on Ur-Tokar.'

Ur-Tokar was definitely the least favourite of the destinations she had visited; unfortunately it was also one that was visited fairly frequently. The planet itself was not the problem; it held a certain timeless beauty – its extensive mountainous polar ice-caps were particularly stunning, and possessed a pristine and primitive beauty. The vast, never-ending pine-forested mountains that circled the equatorial region were like nothing that existed on Zeta Kotlin, and reminded her of scenes in some of the Earth movies she had watched as a child. The seas were a deep dark indigo blue, strewn with craggy islands and beautiful icebergs that glowed white and neon-blue as they drifted across the mirror-like surfaces of the oceans. Ur-Tokar also seemed to have little in the way of violent weather, just an almost semi-permanent state of calm frozen winteriness.

No, the problem she had with Ur-Tokar was the social regime she had to deal with. Earlier, as they were making their approach towards the Rogan star system, she had returned to the subject and tried to describe to Kahlil, Janicka and Neema – experiencing their first visit to the planet – just how dreadful the civilisation there really was.

'It's difficult to know where to actually start, it's that bad. Their society is ruled by an arrogant, pompous individual who calls himself King Alfonso and who thinks he knows everything, but it's so obvious he is a complete and utter moron. How could he not be in a society that rejects all the benefits of modern technology? He treats the people around him – they call themselves aristocrats – with utter disdain, and they, in turn, treat the rest of the people – who they call commoners – with the same contempt. Alfonso became the king because he was the eldest male child of the previous king – they don't allow women to become rulers! He has absolute power, including the right to execute people, and to run any element of their lives he believes he has the right to meddle in – which is everything! What's worse, though, is that the people around him believe this is actually an extremely good way to run their civilisation. They pay him complete obedience; despite the fact that they must know he is as fallible and ignorant as anyone else on their world.' She stopped for a moment, remembering her previous, often unpleasant, experiences on the planet.
'How could a people be so stupid as to allow such a state of affairs to occur?' she muttered more to herself than those listening. They all looked at her. 'It means that absolutely any idiot could have total control over their society. They could be entirely ignorant – like King Alfonso – malicious, sadistic,

mentally-deranged or just plain psychotic but they are allowed – even encouraged - to shape and totally dominate the entire affairs of all their so-called 'subjects'. In the past, apparently, a king died young and left a small child to run the planet, with disastrous consequences – a power struggle broke out amongst the aristocrats who murdered the child and replaced him with someone called a Duke. On another occasion the eldest child suffered from significant mental-impairments – apparently they have an in-breeding problem because the king will only marry aristocrats, and there are therefore only a few very closely related women to choose from – became king, and was utterly incapable of ruling in any coherent manner. Apparently, their society was utterly chaotic for several years, until the throne was usurped by another aristocrat. Alfonso's father suffered from severe old-age dementia, but was allowed and expected to continue ruling the planet, despite having only the barest idea of what was actually occurring around him.' She paused once again, and then concluded, 'I've spent long years travelling across space and have had more than enough time to think about this issue - and believe me I've thought about it at some considerable length - but personally I cannot think of a more stupid system of government than that of monarchy. I've tried hard, but I've yet to come up with it. It's just such a patently stupid system, and on so many different levels.'

Savverio laughed out loud, he knew she had encountered significant problems with Ur-Tokar's system of government and its individuals on previous trips - especially the last visit - though he had not personally experienced the difficulties himself, as he had remained on the starship for much of the mission. Undoubtedly, her own personal experience had unduly coloured her view of the regime, and placed it in such a negative light, but for anyone growing up in an egalitarian, classless and freedom-loving socialist system such as their own, it was almost impossible to fathom why any intelligent human would establish and endure such an obviously ridiculous system of governance. Savverio assumed it could only be the threat of violence and a high degree of social coercion that had allowed it to last as long as it had done. Unfortunately, they had discovered they needed to deal with this ridiculous system.

The original aim of Zeta Kotlin's space trading mission was to acquire resources that were in short supply on their own planet but were essential for the smooth running of their economy. Chief amongst these were a range of rare elements and metals, particularly the rare earth metals, which were needed for their electronics industries, and especially for the construction of further AI units, in addition to the maintenance of those already manufactured. The Opa-Loka had, over the decades, travelled to all the closest star systems, but with mixed success. In the earliest years, the planets around Gannexon - which included Alpha Fraczan - had yielded some of the metals they were looking for, but only in small quantities. However, the scientists on Alpha Fraczan, although polite and diplomatic, had seemed disapproving of their mission, giving the distinct impression that the sooner they left the star system the better. As such, they had done so.

Missions to Sazhina's planets had also yielded little of what they were looking for. It had, though, resulted in the fortuitous discovery that one of its planets, Margalla, was actually inhabited, contrary to what had previously been thought. Jiaying liked visiting Margalla - she treated it as something of a holiday destination - its inhabitants were largely friendly, fun-loving, strictly egalitarian and had proved very welcoming once she got to know them. They knew how to party and she enjoyed socialising and partying with them - and the nights that then followed. As on Zeta Kotlin, it wasn't difficult to find someone worthwhile to spend the night with there and with relative ease. She tried to extend her stays there for as long as was possibly feasible, but would reluctantly have to leave, once the planet's orbital position was suitable for a more rapid return to her home planet. Unfortunately, Margalla had very little that was of material use to Zeta Kotlin – though the opposite was not the case - so her visits there were less frequent than she would have liked.

This effectively left the star system of the red dwarf Rogan, and Ur-Tokar's ore-laden mountains had proven to be particularly rich in mineral deposits. When the Opa-Loka had first arrived in the Rogan star system several decades before, the ship's crew had seen the wide range of planets orbiting the dwarf star as a promising sign, but ultimately they had been forced to opt for mining operations only on Ur-Tokar. Mining on its uninhabited sister planets held several problems. Firstly, they needed to initially place scanning satellites in orbit around the planets, and then wait for the results of the geological scans to be produced. This could be a very time-consuming process. Secondly, the frozen and inhospitable nature of these worlds meant that their mining equipment was only barely adequate; only the AI units could actually operate on the planetary surfaces - an issue that created a significant range of difficulties - and again a great deal of waiting around would be necessary. Theoretically, the crew could have entered the stasis pods that had been left on board until the ore-mining and loading of the ship had been completed, but dealing with Ur-Tokar had ultimately proven to hold significant advantages over these fully frozen worlds.

Upon arrival in Ur-Tokar's orbit, the original crew of the Opa-Loka had quickly realised that any inhabitants of Ur-Tokar were not using their orbital satellites. Because of this they had no problems logging into their data banks and using the planetary information – especially geological - that already existed. Whilst engaging in this task, they also carried out some running repairs, updates and repositioning of the satellites as they were clearly suffering from years of neglect. Their non-use was initially puzzling, because they could soon see from the data banks that the planet was clearly inhabited, though it appeared quite sparsely so. Additionally, the pre-existing geological scans clearly showed the planet to be rich in mineral ores – particularly the rare earth metals they were searching for. The deposits most easily accessible appeared to be in an area of the world where there were no significant settlements, in fact, possibly none at all.

This left the crew with a conundrum. They had assumed the planet's inhabitants would make contact with them as they approached, but there had been complete communications silence. A debate then ensued amongst the crew as to whether they even needed to contact the local inhabitants with regards to trading, or whether they should simply send AI units down to carry out the mining operations and depart once the ship was loaded. Whilst the latter might be the most expedient course of action, there was always the danger of being discovered and thus jeopardising future expeditions to the planet. In addition, it was felt that simply taking – or stealing – the resources of the planet without permission, amounted to a form of exploitation and imperialism, and was, at the end of the day, morally unjustifiable. Admittedly, no one was actually mining the metals at the moment, but the locals might choose to do so at some point in the future. After some deliberation the crew took a vote and it was unanimously decided that they should contact the local inhabitants.

Their arrival on the planet's surface, though, was met with much consternation and a huge degree of suspicion. Initial contact had been fraught with problems and misunderstandings, and it was very clear that some individuals wanted them to depart as quickly as was humanly possible. Fortunately for the Zetans, though, they had arrived in the period shortly before the monarchists had established full control of the equatorial regions, and after considerable negotiating efforts, they had eventually come to some form of arrangement with the local population – albeit a population that was clearly divided about how to go about dealing with the visitors from space. Complicating matters even further, though, the local inhabitants had shown no real interest in the various goods the Opa-Loka had brought along for trading purposes, but it had become apparent during the negotiating process that they were interested in acquiring certain metals – though fairly basic ones like copper, iron, gold and silver. Zeta Kotlin had no significant deposits of these, but the geological scans had shown them to be abundant on remoter parts of Ur-Tokar.

It also become extremely obvious during the course of the negotiations as to why the planet's satellite system high above them was not being used; the entire civilisation had completely abandoned all use of modern technology. Equally, there was no sign of any AI units in use anywhere; so the Opa-Loka's crew had assumed that this was why the mining of metal and mineral ores on the planet had proven impossible for the locals to carry out themselves. The crew thus decided that they could mine both the minerals they wanted and those that the Ur-Tokarans desired, deliver the latter to them, and then head back to Zeta Kotlin with their own cargo of precious rare earth metals and whatever other useful minerals they could load aboard the ship. The crew – again after some deliberation - considered this an acceptable compromise between expediency and acting in the correct ethical manner.

After all, they were not obtaining something for nothing and depriving the locals of their rightful resources. In addition, the Ur-Tokarans were proving to be a strange people; driven by priorities the Zetans could not fully comprehend – ones that seemed to be dominated by superstition, strange rituals and matters of strict hierarchy. They did not seem to be a very rational people, and their dealings with them were being dominated by matters that were clearly not based on economics or rational common sense. The Zetans – on their home world – had no experience of such behavior and were at something of a loss as to how exactly they should proceed, but ultimately decided to keep contact to a minimum – especially as it was obvious that they were not really welcome there anyway.

As such, the crew ultimately spent nearly three months either on the planet exploring its spectacular mountainous terrain, its rocky sea islets and its beautiful coastlines, or else orbiting on their starship, whilst the AI units mined the minerals and ores in the mountains and transported them back to the ship, using their converted shuttle craft. Once they had acquired all they could transport, they duly delivered the cargo of metal ores desired by the local people, and then commenced the long journey back to Zeta Kotlin, after what they eventually decided to have been a highly successful trip, notwithstanding their inability to engage meaningfully with the local inhabitants.

Whilst on the planet, they had made additional enquiries concerning the planet's satellite system and the three stasis ships which were still orbiting around the planet. The satellites were clearly not wanted, so they locked them into a variation of a security system that had recently been established back on Zeta Kotlin – one created following the discovery of a hostile spy satellite, which years later had eventually been traced back to a corporation on Rorque 4. The stasis ships had sunk to a fairly low orbit, and the Zetans correctly guessed why this was the case. Their maintenance AI units were in need of maintenance themselves, and the ships were all running on low-level back-up power systems. They were all imminently in danger of sinking further from their less than fully safe orbit and burning up in a fiery descent to the planet below.

The Zetans asked if the locals still wanted the stasis ships and were told they were more than happy for them to be removed. The crew had then initially attempted to re-program the ships for a journey back to Zeta Kotlin, but scans showed the ships were in need of considerable repair and maintenance before they could perform such an undertaking. Eventually, they had managed to re-boot some of the AI units, boost the ships into a higher orbit and initiate some of the most essential repair procedures. However, they would need to return with a crew possessing greater technical know-how and some extra AI units before they could be safely and securely delivered to Zeta Kotlin.

This indeed did eventually happen successfully, though about five years later – as it took some considerable time to find people with sufficient technical expertise in Earth City and its environs, and acquire sufficient numbers willing to help pilot three extra ships from Ur-Tokar back to their planet. This next visit of the Opa-Loka - mindful of the experiences of the first expedition - engaged in even less contact with the locals, and this had proven to be a wise decision as a monarchist despot had seized control of the planet in the intervening five years. Eventually, they returned with three extra stasis ships, numerous additional AI units and an ample supply of scarce minerals, precious stones and metals. In fact, this expedition proved to be so bountiful that it was fully sixty years later before a third trip was undertaken to Ur-Tokar to acquire more metal ores – Jiaying's first voyage to the planet and not a trip she looked back on favourably.

The Zetans felt that after a sixty year hiatus, they would need to re-establish their acquaintanceship with the inhabitants of Ur-Tokar, since it was unlikely that anyone living during the first two visits would actually still be alive and remember them. The arriving crew and its intentions would probably be a complete unknown after the passing of two generations. The Zetans - though they had constant access to the planet's satellite communications system - were ignorant of any social or political developments on the planet below, since no electronic messaging derived from the few settlements that actually existed, and they could only surmise from this silence - and the fact that few new settlements had been established - that there had probably been little notable change in Ur-Tokaran society in the intervening years. As such, they had no current knowledge as to whether the absolutist monarchy, which had previously seized control, was still firmly established and had become firmly embedded within the social structures of most of the planet's inhabitants, or whether further changes had occurred.

Arrival in Utopia

Upon arrival in Rogan's planetary system, the Opa-Loka's now completely new crew had descended in their landing craft and landed close to its capital, Meridin - though still only a small town by the standards of most planets - and had very quickly been taken prisoner by a detachment of horse-mounted guards. The crew had been warned that the planet engaged in primitive authoritarian behaviours, but had assumed these warnings had been exaggerated, and with no experience of such behaviour – other than occasionally watching old Earth movies – had no idea as to what to do, other than accept being taken captive. Jiaying had never been so scared in her entire life, and basically just wanted to get out as fast as possible – preferably with her life intact. On the whole - like her people in general - she was an optimist by nature and tended to believe things usually worked out for the best, but the Ur-Tokaran monarchists, she quickly realised, were far from rational people and a favourable outcome was definitely not guaranteed.

After several hours of being held against their will – for the first time ever in their lives - and the subject of much interrogation, they were eventually paraded before the king, Olaf the Second. Fortunately for the crew, he was familiar with the stories of their previous trade mission – the first one had indirectly led to one of his ancestors seizing power – and he was vaguely aware of the previous trading relationship. Equally fortunate was the fact that basic metals were once again in short-supply on Ur-Tokar, and so he agreed to a similar arrangement to the one the original crew had settled on. In addition though, Olaf demanded a range of precious and semi-precious stones to be delivered alongside the metal ores. Olaf had developed a taste for magnificence and splendour and was increasingly set on surrounding himself with beautiful objects as a means of establishing in the minds of his people just what a splendid monarch he was.

He also regarded himself as a munificent sovereign and used their arrival as an excuse to throw a spectacular banquet. The crew had been the guests of honour, but unfamiliar with the customs and practices of the feudal court, not to mention the food – they still ate dead animals they found, to their disgust – they had stumbled their way through a series of courtly faux-pas's that provoked considerable disapproval amongst the assembled aristocrats. If it had not been for ample supplies of beer and whisky keeping the king in an amiable mood, they might well have jeopardized the whole trading arrangement. Nevertheless, over the next few weeks, they duly delivered their side of the bargain – though took care to deliver the ores and precious stones in such a way as to ensure they could not be taken captive again – and headed back to Zeta Kotlin with their precious cargo of rare metals, semi-precious stones and minerals, as fast as they could get out of the place.

Upon the Opa-Loka's return, and made aware of the difficulties in collecting these much-needed resources from Ur-Tokar, the General Council of Zeta Kotlin had eventually, after much deliberation, decided to engage in a stock-piling operation; to obtain as much mineral material as they possibly could whilst inter-planetary relations allowed trade to continue, and then take stock of the situation accordingly. Decisions made at the planetary level of government tended to be few and far between and were invariably long-winded affairs. Democratic approval was needed from the lower levels of community government – where most decisions were made through a system of direct democracy - and after proceeding through all the relevant stages of democratic consultation, a final planetary decision was ultimately agreed and put into action.

And so Jiaying had found herself - several years later - back at the dusty windswept spaceport on the outer margins of Earth City about to embark on a second journey to Ur-Tokar. In the intervening years, she had made two enjoyable visits to Margalla, and had semi-convinced herself that a life in space was not such a bad one, after all. The spaceport, however, had clearly seen better days and lacked the AI unit maintenance it really needed. Its ageing buildings had seen better days and there was a general lack of activity around the place that gave it an air of disuse. For some citizens, interstellar trade was not a priority activity, as they believed such activities were an unwarranted distraction - though on the rare occasions this matter actually went to a vote, they found themselves in a minority. However, aware of its contested existence, community resources in the region were typically prioritised elsewhere, leaving the spaceport with a distinct air of neglect.

Unfortunately, if Jiaying thought the first trip to Ur-Tokar had gone badly, then her second had been an almost complete and utter disaster. The mostly-new crew, which now included Savverio, had voted to make the initial descent accompanied by AI units, in case problems similar to those experienced by the previous expedition arose. Jiaying had argued against this – being more familiar with Ur-Tokaran thinking - but had been outvoted. Upon descent, they discovered there was a new king, King Alfonso – a far more despotic monarch, who had apparently had Olaf the Second murdered a few years previously - and who took great offence at discovering the presence of AI units within his kingdom. From that point onwards, the delegated visit had descended from bad to worse.

Alfonso had been one of the aristocrats at the banquet who had severely rebuked the behaviour of the previous crew and soon recognised Jiaying. At various points in the negotiations, he took every opportunity to make his disapproving opinions of her previous conduct known, and typically attributed these to her gender and ethnicity. Eventually, Jiaying lost her patience and blew her top after yet another sexist invective had been heaped upon her. She was already beginning to feel angry with herself for not having more vehemently opposed the use of the AIs for their initial visit, but this stream of royal abuse was more than she could cope with, and was totally unlike anything she had ever experienced in her entire life.

In the ensuing melee, the crew had, without a doubt, needed the AI units to whisk them out and back to their ship alive – the guard's swords being largely useless against their advanced material exteriors. That had proven to be the final dealing with the monarchists. The crew had returned to the Opa-Loka and, after a heated discussion, voted by a majority to pursue the mining mission as originally planned and intended. Despite the previous fracas, they delivered metal ores to Meridin under the cover of darkness and at a safe distance from the town, as they felt this was still the appropriate – and safe - decision to take. On the return journey to Zeta Kotlin, before entering stasis, they had deliberated at great length as to what they should tell the people of Zeta Kotlin upon their return.

One of their crew mates, a young woman named Katie from the central part of the continent of New Republica, had argued strongly in favour of reporting the whole incident to the General Council. She believed that they had acted without permission from the inhabitants of Ur-Tokar, and that their mining of minerals and ores on the planet had effectively been an act of exploitation and imperialism. Savverio and Jiaying – who had previously discussed the matter at considerable length and who knew they were on very shaky ground – had argued that by keeping to previous agreements and delivering the requisite metal ores to the monarchists, they had not in fact behaved in an imperialistic manner, but kept to a reasonable trading agreement.

A completely honest report to the General Council, they maintained, would jeopardise the whole space trading programme – Savverio was keen to pursue further missions, so was particularly concerned in this regard – and could easily lead to the closure of the spaceport and the end of Earth City as a space hub. They also argued that the trade was vital to the economy of Zeta Kotlin, and should not be jeopardised by a single dispute with an arrogant and unreasonable demagogue. They believed that future trade missions to Ur-Tokar could deal with non-monarchist inhabitants on the planet, and so should be continued if deemed economically necessary.

Katie was far from convinced by these arguments and the dispute continued for some considerable time, as the two sides attempted to convince each other of the correctness of their argument. Ultimately, they had not been able to reach any form of agreement or compromise and so the decision went to a vote of the nine crew members that were on that particular mission. Jiaying and Savverio just managed to win a knife-edge vote with a five to four winning margin. Though Katie accepted the majority decision, she was clearly not happy and immediately resigned from the space programme once they had returned to Zeta Kotlin.

As they had voted for, upon their return, they had been somewhat economical with the truth. Embarrassed about their near-fatal mistakes, and not wanting to be responsible for the fall of Earth City as a spaceport – they were aware a previous generation had considered closing it down entirely - they had simply reported the fact that the mission had been completed successfully. Factually speaking this was correct, but it meant future crews – unaware of the breakdown in relations between the two planets - could possibly be placed in significant danger of losing their lives. Partly because of this fact – following a break of missions to Ur-Tokar for a period of eight years - Jiaying had found herself once again back at the spaceport, agreeing to participate in the follow-up mission and then on her way to Ur-Tokar – something she had previously sworn she would never do again.

Arrival in Utopia

The spaceport had been in considerably better repair, though – mainly because the arrival of so many transporter craft from the Alphan stasis ships had warranted a major overhaul of its condition and facilities. There were also AI units and Alphan scientists busily working around the facility dealing with the delayed departure of The Star Chaser. The spaceport community was still, however, unaware of what had actually occurred on the previous visit to Ur-Tokar, so that when she had heard of the planned trade mission, she had felt a sense of guilt and responsibility to those going, and a pressing need to be on that mission. She believed that the new crew should know of the near disaster that had occurred on the previous visit, and that appropriate alternative plans could be put into place accordingly. This had particularly been the case, when she had been informed – incorrectly as it turned out - that Savverio would not be travelling on the mission, because of health issues.

This voyage, however, she swore to herself, would definitely be her last mission into space. She had already experienced one alarming cancer scare, and she had also developed new interests in art and literature that she wanted to pursue on Zeta Kotlin. Additionally, she thought it might be good to spend more time with her two kids. She saw them occasionally between missions, and she knew they were well looked after in their respective communities, but felt she wanted to get to know them better as they developed into young adults. They were turning into well-rounded outgoing adolescents and she wanted to join in with some of their activities and experiences and become better acquainted with their friends and companions.

With regards to the actual mission itself, she and Savverio had - many years ago - devised a plan for avoiding the difficulties experienced on the previous mission. For, on their last visit, they had discovered that the monarchists were not entirely in control of the whole planet. There were other societies on the anti-technology world, and ones which they thought might be populated by a more reasonable community of people; it was with these people they were planning to liaise and work with. Jiaying now just needed to find a way to explain this to the rest of the crew, wholly aware that this could be a potentially fractious subject. She was banking on Savverio backing her up if and when necessary.

Shortly before their arrival into the Rogan star system, she had broached the subject when all the crew had collected together for a meal sometime after recovering from stasis.

'There's something I've been meaning to tell you about our previous mission to Ur-Tokar, something that means we need to conduct our operations in a different manner to the plan you have been informed of,' she started, slightly hesitantly, once the meal was coming to an end.

She glanced at Savverio, who gave her a reassuring look, indicating that he fully supported what she was about to say. She explained to the three new crew members what had happened on their previous trade mission, going into some considerable detail, and making sure she painted a particularly negative view of the monarchist regime. Finally, she came to the end of her account. 'Whilst we were waiting for the AI units to finish the last of the mining operations, we did a bit of exploration in some forested mountainous areas somewhere to the north-east of Meridin. We happened to notice a scattering of small settlements deep within the forest; some were simply single dwellings, but there were also some slightly larger, village-type communities. Initially, we kept our distance, assuming they were part of the monarchist civilisation, but the more we observed the people of these communities, the more we became convinced that they appeared to have no connection with the monarchist regime. They appeared to be living a much freer, more autonomous, non-feudal way of life, though they have also clearly eschewed the use of modern technology.'

She paused, but the others continued listening. 'We were debating whether to make contact with them when the AI units reported they had completed their mining operations, and given we were all very keen to depart the planet quickly and without further mishap, we simply decided to leave there and then, before making any actual contact with them.'

She stopped again for a moment, finished her drink, and then continued. 'I propose that we approach these mountain people and make some form of trading agreement with them. We saw no signs of weaponry or indeed anything that looked particularly militaristic in general, so hopefully, they're a more reasonable and peaceful people than the monarchists. If we can do some form of deal with them, we can mine all the stuff we need, deliver to them whatever they want, and then return quickly to Zeta Kotlin. If the approach proves successful, later missions can follow the same plan and we're sorted for the future. The best part about it, is that it has the major bonus of not needing to deal with the moronic monarchists.'

Neema, Kahlil and Janicka were slightly taken aback by this news. During their training for the mission back in Earth City they had been informed that the voyage would follow the established approach of dealing with the monarchist regime. They might not be overly happy about dealing with – and thus aiding - a class-based feudal regime, but they were at least mining with local consent. They were slightly shocked that Jiaying and Savverio had not been fully honest with the spaceport community back on Earth City.

Neema stated what they were all thinking, 'but if you hadn't been on this mission, the crew would have had no idea of the danger they faced when returning to Meridin. We would have walked into a death trap, by the sounds of things.'

'We know and we argued about this on the way back to Zeta Kotlin, but we were worried that the General Council might decide to end missions to Ur-Tokar, and that could be the end of Earth City as a spaceport – there'd been endless rumours about closing it down, and we thought this matter might actually turn those rumours into a reality,' Savverio chipped in, feeling that Jiaying was in need of some moral support.

'It's ultimately why I decided to come on this mission; the previous one was going to be my last, but I felt I had to do this one – partly to make amends, but also to avoid the issue you have just mentioned. This one will definitely be my last voyage - though I always say that,' Jiaying laughed.

'Why do you think these mountain people are more reasonable than the monarchists?' asked Janicka.

Jiaying looked at Savverio, 'they just seem to live an isolated and peaceful existence in the mountains. There was no sign of any real centralised form of organisation as such, their dwellings were very varied and there was no sign of any aggressive or military type activity. We watched some of them engaging in some form of ceremony that looked like moon worship or something similar, so it's possible they live some type of foraging existence, and are probably just easier to work with.'

Savverio agreed, 'it all looked very decentralised, no central authority as far as we could see, they're probably living some form of deep ecologist-type existence. Incidentally, the planet has two moons, but they were probably worshipping the much larger purple one known as Arioch.'

'So, why didn't you contact them, if they looked so friendly?' asked Kahlil.

'We'd already had the traumatic experience with the monarchists, and we were all still suffering a degree of paranoia - we simply didn't want to risk engaging in any more negative experiences,' replied Jiaying, 'though on reflection, I think we were probably too cautious. When we discussed it later, we agreed that contact with them would probably have gone well.'

'Anyway, we need to make a joint decision about whether to go with this idea – preferably a unanimous one - so have a think about it,' concluded Savverio. 'We can vote on it after sleeping if you like, after you've had more time to reflect on our alternative plan.' After a period of discussion and reflection, the crew did indeed later vote in favour of this alternative approach, since the three new members could think of no other viable options, and were also keen to avoid the monarchist regime, especially after all the negative comments they had heard about it from Jiaying and Savverio.

Sometime after this, they eventually approached the planet of Ur-Tokar, the crew all expectantly observing the gradual largening of the planet as they homed in on their target destination. Shortly after the ship's computer had brought the Opa-Loka into orbit around the planet above its northern hemisphere, and as they were circling Ur-Tokar for the first time, Jiaying was thinking through exactly how they should play out the new approach they had agreed upon. She was wondering exactly how they would descend to the planet and greet the mountain people without alarming them, when suddenly she spotted something strange on the ship's scanners.

'Fuck, where did that come from?' she suddenly exclaimed.

The others, slightly alarmed, stopped looking at the blue, white and green planet below them and turned their attention to the electronic screen.

'It's a fucking stasis ship. Where did that come from? There shouldn't be any ships here; we took them all back to Zeta Kotlin years ago. It must be from one of the other planets! Fuck, this could be a big problem!' Various thoughts whizzed through Jiaying's mind and she thought out aloud, 'Margalla has a ship, but they never take it anywhere. Maybe it's one of the Alpha Fraczan ships, with all the scientists on board, but I thought they had both headed straight to Rorque 4.'

'The one that left Zeta Kotlin was heading there but it's impossible for it to have arrived here ahead of us. Our scanners showed it's still somewhere between here and Zeta – it's about one month behind us. We've picked up news broadcasts from Rorque 4 stating that the other two stasis ships arrived safely at their planet four months ago, so it can't be any of the Alphan ships,' Kahlil - who had been monitoring the ship's communications - informed the crew.

'Why would they come here, anyway – there's nothing for them on this planet,' Janicka added, further indicating this was an unlikely development.

'Well it can't be them, we know that from the communications we've received,' Savverio reaffirmed. 'That only leaves the possibility of ships from Rorque 4, or even worse, Zeleyan - unless it's arrived from completely outside the Cluster. I'm not aware that Rorque 4 or Zeleyan have any active space programme.'

'Given how slow news travels round here - and the fact that our monitoring system could be considerably better, to say the least - if either of them had started a programme recently, we probably wouldn't know about it anyway,' suggested Jiaying, looking at the monitors puzzled and increasingly perplexed.

'Have they seen us?' asked Neema.

'Don't think so, they're thousands of kilometers ahead of us. I've already slowed the ship and we're moving into a slightly lower orbit to avoid detection, just in case. I'm going to put the planet between us and them, and stay in its scanning shadow,' stated Jiaying. 'Long ago, the ship was painted a deep indigo blue and fitted with stealth technology to make it harder to detect. Apparently, they were worried that our trading activities within the Cluster might be misinterpreted, so they decided that keeping them secret was a good idea. I doubt the technology fully works, but I guess we're about to find out. This might be a big problem! We need to work out exactly who it is and why they're here', she added, realising at the same time she was stating the glaringly obvious. 'Let's log into the satellite system here and find out what's going on,' she stated, commencing the process as she said this.

She quickly checked the data banks on the planet's satellite system and was soon much better informed of their current situation. The unknown stasis ship had been orbiting around the planet for the previous forty-five days and had originated from the direction of Zeleyan. Its landing craft had made a number of trips to and from one particular site, not too far from Meridin. On zooming in on the site they discovered what was obviously a new structure – clearly unlike anything else on Ur-Tokar – and one with a distinctly military look to its appearance.

'What are they doing down there, are they planning to invade the planet?' asked Kahlil, already concerned by Jiaying's recent revelations, and now beginning to wonder if matters were about to become even more complicated.

'Looks like it, there's no indication of links with the locals – it looks well hidden in that dense forest,' replied Jiaying. 'They're using minimal communications as well, and with only what appears to be their own satellite. They're clearly trying to remain hidden. If they're here for the same reason as us – mineral wealth – this doesn't make a great deal of sense. Why would they remain isolated and hidden? It must be some covert military operation.'

'The Zeleyanians are fascists - they're clearly planning to seize the whole place for themselves. It's the logic of their political system to invade other lands and establish imperial regimes over them. Their leaders need to do this to perpetuate their own political legitimacy, to justify high levels of military spending, and to sustain their highly authoritarian and martial social system. And in the long-term, their closed economy stagnates if it doesn't acquire new markets and resources from elsewhere', stated Neema.

They all looked at her, slightly surprised by this sudden revelation of significant ideological knowledge.

'I've studied political history. After the Zeleyanian spy satellite was discovered, I did a research project on fascism. I wanted to know what the Zeleyanians were up to. Their system is totally unlike ours; its authoritarian, there's no freedom or democracy and it's highly centralised. Their leaders are vicious and cruel. They don't care about anything but their own power and glory. They're also obsessed with achieving military victories against other peoples. They hold a very low and pessimistic opinion of human nature, so they believe that if they don't invade first, then others will invade them – it's a dog-eat-dog universe, in their opinion, and only the most aggressive and most powerful survive.' Neema continued, slightly defensively, as she was not wishing to sound too intellectual. 'I suspect this development and the spy satellite they placed around Zeta – and the one they've obviously placed here as well – are all part of some plan to expand their presence across the Cluster. I suspected this might be the case during my research, and this just seems to confirm it. I did inform my community council and the General Council of my suspicions, but they thought I was being too alarmist.'

'Exactly how sure are you about this? It does seem a bit cloak and dagger – like something from a movie or an old story book,' asked Savverio, suddenly wondering whether Neema's presence on the mission, was not all it seemed. 'We've not seen any sign of this before anywhere; there could be a simpler answer. . . though I'm really struggling to think of one.'

'Well if Neema is correct, we really do need to be careful. I wonder if that ship has weapons systems – it's probably the kind of thing fascists would do with their ships,' Jiaying wondered out aloud. 'We need to keep well out of sight, and discover what communications capacity its spy satellite possesses. We also need to see if they've cracked the security system we placed on Ur-Tokar's satellite system. I'll get the ship's computer to check on all of this immediately.'

'Definitely, and if their ship possesses weaponry adapted for use in space, we really do need to keep out of their way. We also need to keep a landing craft permanently on standby, in the event of them firing on us. We've got nothing that would defend us against a missile attack!' added Savverio.

'But before we do all that, the first thing we need to do is to inform Earth City and the General Council on Zeta Kotlin as to exactly what we have discovered here. It's just suddenly occurred to me. What if they're using this as a forward base for an attack on Zeta Kotlin?' asked Jiaying. The crew looked even more worried than they had a few moments earlier.

Ur-Tokar – Opa-Loka crew descend to the planet

The sighting of the Zeleyan stasis ship orbiting Ur-Tokar had thrown a potentially huge spanner into the workings of Jiaying's plan, as far as she was concerned, but after discussing the alternatives – of which they all agreed there were basically none - she still felt determined to follow it through to as close a degree as originally intended and as practically possible. She also figured that the people living in the forested mountains would need to know about the military base constructed by the Zeleyanian forces, as it was unlikely they were aware of this planetary incursion themselves, and it would almost certainly pose them a grave threat in the future. The priority now was to warn them of what was occurring and to explore possibilities for undermining the invasion. She also toyed with the idea of informing the monarchist regime of the Zeleyanian incursion, but decided to put that particular thought on the backburner for now, and deal with them later, if indeed that proved to be necessary.

Savverio had instructed the planet's satellite system to monitor the Zeleyan spacecraft and to scan it for information with regards to weaponry and any other hostile capabilities. The scan had come back negative with regards to weapons, so they had no need to worry about being taken by surprise or unawares and shot down in the night - or anything suchlike - which was something of a relief. He had instructed the planetary satellites to keep them informed of exactly where the Zeleyan ship was located at all times, so they were able to keep it at a safe distance and thus from being discovered. The planet's satellite system also informed him that the Zeleyan spy satellite - which had been orbiting the planet for several years now - was not keyed into any wider communications network within the star system, so evading its scanners would prove relatively straightforward. As such, he implemented the additional measures needed to ensure that the hostile satellite would be unable to detect their presence.

On the previous trade mission to Ur-Tokar, the crew had located the presence of the Mountain People – as they came to know them as - in the heavily forested Kauai river valley area, way to the north-east of the monarchist lowlands. They were located in one of the most northerly forested areas, and not a huge distance away from the extensive northern ice-caps that actually extended well into the sub-tropical zone. Savverio concentrated his efforts on searching the area with the help of the satellites, and was eventually rewarded for his efforts with the location of a number of small settlements along the northern edge of the river valley. The crew decided it would be best to descend to the planet in person – they were not about to make the same mistake of using AI units as previously – but that two of them should also stay on the Opa-Loka in case of any emergency involving the Zeleyanian forces. After some discussion, they decided a daytime arrival would be best, but they needed to ensure a time when they would not be visible from either the Meridin region, or by the Zeleyanian ship and its spy satellite.

Once this was all calculated and the appropriate time decided upon, Jiaying, Kahlil and Neema headed for the landing craft. Strapped securely in their seats and with the final system check signifying positive, they opened the cargo doors of the stasis ship and powered out into the sky below them. Neema, piloting the craft manually, rather than using the ship's computer, took them on a tight downward spiral, losing height as fast as was physically possible without actually harming themselves or the craft, and had soon descended to a level where they could power through to a low altitude approach. This took them to a height where they were able to admire the pristine beauty of the mountains, the dark green forests and the canyons that covered this particular region of the planet. To the distant north they could easily trace the white glimmering edge of the vast northern ice-cap that reached far into the lower latitudes of Ur-Tokar. To their south ran an extremely impressive range of snow-capped purple-hued mountains that stretched unbroken towards far and distant horizons.

Neema pursued a course that took them along the deep canyon for a short while, and which eventually brought the landing craft down into an area of montane meadows adjacent to the Kauai River, and close to a settlement they would soon discover was known as Lato. They had decided that their entrance into the settlement should be as open and unthreatening as possible, and that it was clearly obvious they were not carrying any weapons. They were also careful to dress in clothes that would mean they would not be mistaken for the monarchists, on the assumption that the two communities were probably not on particularly good terms.

After leaving the shuttle craft, they simply walked into the middle of the settlement and Jiaying asked someone on the main street if there was a village council or community grouping of some form they could talk to, resisting the temptation to go with the cliché of asking someone 'to take me to your leader'. It was not long before a small crowd gathered around them, since one or two of the locals immediately suspected they were off-worlders – their vocabulary, costumes and general appearance clearly marking them out as something very different from anything they had ever seen before.

Fortunately for the crew, the crowd proved to be far more curious than hostile, and they were soon led to the Hall of the Mountain Grill and supplied with food and drink from the tavern. The crew was more than happy to accept; after living on food that had been designed largely on the basis that it would survive the rigours of space travel, they were now more than able to tuck into a real meal with real food. Various introductions were made and the crew set about explaining why they had decided to visit the settlement.

Previous to their departure from the Opa-Loka, they had provisionally devised a plan they thought might be capable of dealing with the Zeleyanian forces, but without cooperation from the Mountain People it had considerably less chance of proving successful, so they very much needed to make a good first impression. With this in mind, and also wanting to complete a successful trading arrangement, the crew was unsure as to how honest they should be about their previous visits and dealings with the monarchists, so initially decided to remain silent on this particular matter, as they were unsure as to how exactly the two communities regarded each other.

'We are from the planet Zeta Kotlin', commenced Kahlil, thinking he sounded like someone in a movie, 'and crew a trading ship known as the Opa-Loka. We have arrived here in the hope of acquiring various minerals, metal ores and perhaps other natural resources. We operate on the basis that hopefully we can provide you with resources you might need, and in return you allow us to take what we need. It should only take a matter of a few weeks or so, and then we will return back to our planet. Is there anything that you might need that we can trade or supply you with?'

At this point Jiaying noted a slight change in the mood of those gathered around them, but she could not be certain as to its exact nature. However, she did gain the distinct sense that some of those present were in some sense disappointed by this opening statement, though she chose not to ask why.

'It's unlikely, we have everything we need thanks, we pursue a highly sustainable lifestyle on this world. We only take what we need from the land, and in such a way that it will repair itself naturally. I'm not sure I like the sound of the idea of you removing resources – do you mean timber and the like,' asked a fairly surly looking, dark-haired young man, they later discovered was called Raven.

'We're mainly interested in mining operations. We will make sure we do minimal damage to your environment; we only use non-polluting methods and would never knowingly degrade any of your ecosystems. Our planetary society also works on a need-only basis; we're not driven by profit or a desire for power. We have no intention of repeating the mistakes that were made long ago back on Earth. We would ensure at all times that we were extremely careful with your environment and avoid causing any long-term damage,' replied Jiaying, quickly realising the people here were living up to the pre-conceived ideas she had formulated about them.

'Some extra metal and minerals wouldn't go amiss though; we're not exactly awash with them. If you're operations are not damaging to the environment and limited in scope and time, I believe that could be compatible with our way of life. Where are you planning to do this?' asked a young girl with pale skin and long auburn hair, and appropriately known as Autumn.

'It's some way from here, to the south in the foothills of the purple-mountain range,' replied Neema.

'The Zarozinian mountains – there are sacred places amongst those mountains. They cannot be damaged in anyway. They must be protected to preserve their sacred and sacrosanct character,' interjected a young woman known as Amethyst, who happened to be the younger sister of Topaz.

'Well, that's not everyone's opinion. We don't all believe in that spiritual stuff. But we certainly won't tolerate any operations that damage the environment. Ecosystems need to be protected from unsustainable activities at all costs. How long does it take to return to your planet. I mean are you likely to come back and repeat this again and again?' asked Raven, still not fully liking the sound of their plan, but accepting Autumn's point that the community could well do with some extra metals to work with, now that he thought about it.

'About sixteen months each way – so nearly three years, and it's a long time to spend on a spaceship. We don't do this very often,' replied Jiaying.

'And, are you planning on coming back?' asked Amethyst.

'We're not sure, it will depend on what our community council decides and how our economy develops. We might have less need for these metals in the future. We can't be sure. As I said, it's a long distance there and back – we only do trips like this very rarely. There's no likelihood of us returning and stripping the place bare on a regular basis, if that's what you're worried about' interjected Neema, anticipating where the conversation was going. 'We only need relatively small quantities of ore and minerals, compared with what your planet possesses.'

'I'm still not happy about this idea,' stated Amethyst. 'We would need a whole community decision before allowing anything as potentially damaging and disruptive to our way of life as this. I can't see the community accepting this, quite frankly.'

Jiaying wasn't sure the conversation was moving in the direction she wanted and so decided to take a risk.

'How do you get on with the lowlanders – we noticed there are some larger settlements down there, but they didn't look like people we could work with. That's why we decided to come here first.'

Before anyone could say anything different, Raven suddenly blurted out, 'we hate those bastards; they've been moving in on our lands and killing our people. For years we tried to have nothing to do with them, but then they attacked us and now we're at war with them. In reality, we would like them to just leave us alone so we could have absolutely nothing to do with them . . .' and then he tailed off, suddenly aware that this was probably not the wisest of statements to make to complete strangers.

The crew later discovered why he had made this untoward remark. Raven was one of a small number of health practitioners in the community, and like all the others specialised in herbal and holistic methods of healing. The health of the Mountain People was generally good – fresh air, clean water, low population density, exercise and natural foods ensured that this was mostly the case. Health problems tended to relate largely to the hard physical activities they often engaged in, the close proximity of some of the community to domesticated animals, and the occasional periods of cold weather.

Fortunately for the community, a sufficiently wide range of plant seeds had been brought on the original 'genesis pod' for a good variety of medicinal plants to be found growing across the planet. Amongst those considered of particular importance were natural contraceptives and abortifacients which allowed the communities to control their population levels, and to faithfully follow their widespread belief that populations should be kept to limits that were compatible with environmental sustainability. However, in recent years, the practitioners had spent an increasing amount of time treating injuries, sometimes very serious ones, resulting from their conflict with the lowlanders, and Raven and the other healers had found this increasingly distressing – being called on again and again to treat life changing wounds that they believed really should not be occurring. It seemed that for Raven, at least, the pressure was becoming too great.

Given the looks and murmurings from some of the others, it was clear they too were far from sure that Raven's remark was actually a wise thing to say to complete strangers. The Zetans might be in collusion with the monarchists, for all they knew, or simply depart and work with them instead. Such comments were potentially dangerous.

But Jiaying had quickly figured this statement offered an opening, and she decided to come clean at this point and recounted their previous visits to the planet, their dealings with the monarchists, of how they had broken down so badly, and of how much she despised the feudalists as well. At the end, she apologised for not being fully truthful with them originally, but hoped they could understand their caution. As she did so, she began to feel their position was actually quite embarrassing and a bit pathetic, now that she thought about it. In reality, all they were doing was getting a second opinion, because they didn't like the one they received from the first group of people they had dealt with.

Fortunately, their mutual dislike of the monarchists played stronger than the fact they had not been entirely honest, and were now coming across like a bunch of opportunists.

'We've effectively been at war with them ever since they massacred everyone at Greenback. We've tried to prevent them from making any further incursions into our territory. We've had to fight a defensive guerilla insurgency ever since the massacre, picking off small isolated groups and individuals and retreating into remoter territory when they send armed cohorts after us. We're really not much of a match for their weaponry, though. They also have superiority in numbers and organisation over us. So far, we've managed to cause them intermittent problems, but they seem determined to keep penetrating into our territory, and so the conflict just continues,' explained Raven.

'Why, what exactly are they doing here, in your area and your lands?' asked Jiaying.

'They're definitely looking for places to mine metallic ores, but we think they are also looking to occupy additional territory as well,' replied Amethyst.

'How long has all this been going on then, when did it all start?' asked Kahlil.

'Since the massacre at Greenback; about eight or nine years ago,' answered Topaz, remembering her dreadful experience that night.

Jiaying did some quick mental arithmetic – that was around the time of her last visit, which might not be a coincidence. Had she and her fellow crew members unwittingly contributed to the outbreak of this conflict, she wondered?

'That's a long time, have you not tried talking . . .' Jiaying stopped, realising the stupidity of the question she was about to ask. Trying to reason with someone as arrogant, stubborn and vainglorious as King Alfonso was, she knew, an utter waste of time.

'There's something else we think you ought to know, as well,' Kahlil interjected, thinking it was about time they dealt with the issue they had really come to address.

Kahlil explained all about their discovery of the Zeleyanian military base close to Meridin, why they thought it had been constructed, and what they thought the implications of all this were likely to be. The inhabitants of Lato had no knowledge of the world of Zeleyan, and only the vaguest understanding of what fascist ideas were about. The crew tried to impress upon them the seriousness of the situation, and that this development was likely to lead to an all-out invasion of their planet. The fascists would utterly destroy their entire way of life, so it was imperative that their plans for conquest should be halted. After impressing upon them the ruthless nature of fascism, its ingrained xenophobia, and its complete disregard for liberty, the inhabitants of Lato seemed to finally understand the peril they were potentially in, though some looked sceptical, wondering if their standard tactic of holding out in the hills might allow them to escape Zeleyanian rule.

'We have no way of surviving against that level of weaponry; we would have to hide like scared animals in the remotest parts of the forests and mountains to just survive. We clearly need to destroy that base before they have the opportunity to mount any offensive against us; then we might have a chance of succeeding, but how can we match their firepower? It would be impossible for us to defeat them in any sort of attack on their base,' remarked Raven somewhat despondently, but it was also clear he recognised the need to do something decisive.

'What we also don't understand is why only one starship has arrived and in a highly secretive manner. Our monitoring has shown no sign of any other warships on their way - from Zeleyan or anywhere else - though communications between here and their planet take nearly three months, so it's possible others are already on their way, but we just don't know about it yet. It seems to make no sense; especially as it has all the appearance of being a forward base. Additionally, we believe the monarchists are oblivious to their presence. But, whatever the reason, clearly being hidden is part of their plan, so we need to put an end to their invisibility. We have a plan to do this, though we're not sure exactly what will happen after our intervention – it involves making the monarchists aware of their existence,' explained Neema.

'We suspect Alfonso will be outraged at their presence within his realm and attack them. I can't see that he'll enjoy a great deal success, but who knows? Stranger things happen in space! What he lacks in social skills, maybe he makes up for in military acumen. I haven't a clue; but the fascists will no longer have their cloak of invisibility, and if it's the advantage of surprise they're hoping for, that will no longer be the case either,' added Jiaying, who at that moment was beginning to feel that the Mountain People might actually be warming to their plan, judging from the knowing nods and murmurs coming from the assembled gathering.

'With any luck they'll both destroy each other and do us all a massive favour,' interjected Topaz, and those around her nodded their heads and made a variety of approving comments.

'That would be a best case scenario, but unfortunately, in my experience, they virtually never occur,' opined Jiaying. 'But whatever happens, we need your help. We need someone to take us through the forests, to take us as close to the military base as is humanly possible – but without being detected - and then we can put our plan into action. Is there anyone here who would want to help us do that?' asked Jiaying.

'I will, I know those woods like the back of my hand. It's a forest trek of about two to three days. We need to avoid Meridin, but other than that it's reasonably straightforward when you know the terrain and various key marker points along the way,' struck up Topaz confidently.

'That's great, but it's best if we have two or three more, if possible. Are there any other volunteers?' asked Kahlil, observing that whilst the gathering seemed generally supportive of their plan, there was something of a reluctance to actually become involved in its implementation. He figured that perhaps that was not fully surprising, given that they were complete strangers, had not been fully truthful about why they were there in the first place, and were engaged in a trade mission about which they had serious misgivings.

'I know two others who will come - Rowan and Indigo - I'm sure they will want to help. I'll sort everything out and we can make a start in the morning when we've gathered sufficient supplies for the journey,' Topaz offered helpfully. Once decided, Jiaying indicated to Topaz just how much she appreciated her help, since she knew that without her assistance the crew of the Opa-Loka really would have been on their own, and probably without any form of viable plan.

'Sounds great, we have everything we already need, so effectively we're ready when you are. We just need to retrieve our gear from our landing craft,' stated Neema, relieved that for the first time something on their mission to Ur-Tokar was actually going to plan. 'We'll sort out the mining issue at a later date,' she suggested.

Whilst Topaz was away organising everything she needed, the crew spent a few hours getting to know the people of Lato much better, their lives, their beliefs and something of their history. They discovered that most of the people in this part of Ur-Tokar were influenced by ideas that back on Earth were closely associated with pantheism, paganism, deep ecology or an eclectic mixture of these various beliefs. They believed that humans had ultimately destroyed the environment back on Earth because they had placed themselves above nature and could therefore then justify its denigration, destruction and neglect. To escape this, their people had fled into space.

On Ur-Tokar, they were not about to repeat the same anthropogenic mistake again. Their society only engaged in behaviours and actions that worked closely with nature; they took only what they needed, and in such a way that any ecosystem remained vibrant, undamaged and sustainable. The key to achieving this, they believed, was to use only low-level forms of technology, ones that had not been mass produced, but to also keep their population levels at a sustainably low level. Having more than two or three children was heavily discouraged by their community, though exceptions were made where it occurred for natural reasons, such as giving birth to twins or if a small child had died at a young age. In general, though, they attempted to minimise their impact on the landscape to as little as was practically possible.

Jiaying seemed to vaguely recollect hearing about such ideas from someone she had met years ago, but couldn't place where and with whom. She could see how it might work here on Ur-Tokar, but with Zeta Kotlin's much larger population it was totally impractical, she thought. In addition, she didn't like the idea of giving up on advanced technology – it was far too useful. AI units - in particular - meant a life of relative ease and comfort, not to mention all the other benefits they brought. She had no great desire to give up on all the benefits of her civilisation.

Not wanting to be disrespectful of the beliefs of the people she was depending on for help, she explained, somewhat diplomatically, her own people's approach. 'We also try to work with the environment, but our main means of doing that is to run an economy based on need - not based on profit - so there is no excessive use of land, extraction of resources or exploitation of the environment on our planet either. To ensure that continues, we maintain a political egalitarianism in which communities retain complete control over the environment around them. Given their unlikely to want to live within a despoiled, denuded or polluted environment, we believe they can be trusted to protect their local ecosystems. So far it seems to have worked very well, the environment is generally very healthy and in good shape on Zeta Kotlin. I've been told our ecosystems are still evolving - we haven't been there that long – and I understand they are developing greater complexity and diversity, which it's assumed is a good thing.' She stopped for a moment, and decided she should find out more about the society she was dealing with, rather than explaining her own.

'What political structures do you use in your society?' Jiaying asked. 'Ours are strictly decentralised, egalitarian and democratic. I thought most primitive . . . err . . . low technology cultures were patriarchal and very hierarchical, like the monarchists. It looks to me as though you're not like that.'

There was something of a silence from those assembled, so Autumn offered, 'well, it's actually quite difficult to define how they work. Your system sounds a little like ours, but perhaps more formal and better organised. We don't have many formal structures; it's often done on an ad hoc basis. For some issues, the most outspoken characters take charge, for others, it's the spiritual guides that have the greatest influence. Sometimes we have community gatherings, and sometimes individuals just do what they want. Our settlements are very dispersed, so it's difficult to organise in the same way all the time. There's quite a lot of loners in the forests and higher up the mountains as well - they tend to keep to themselves. I'm not sure if you can really sum up our system in one word or sentence,' Autumn concluded almost apologetically, unsure as to whether she had said anything Jiaying might actually find intelligible.

Jiaying simply nodded and smiled – this was sort of what she had assumed, and she didn't press the point any further. However, Raven then decided to add to Autumn's explanation, 'that's probably less true nowadays though. Our long running confrontation with the monarchists has forced us to become more organised, and also more secretive in certain matters. We've kept things decentralised for security purposes, but I'd say we've seen some subtle changes in the way our society organises in recent years, and it's the conflict with the monarchists that had driven this – probably for the worst, as well.'

Arrival in Utopia

Jiaying was about to ask Raven for more information about the conflict with the monarchists, but at that point Topaz returned slightly out of breath, and informed them that everything was sorted. She would have all her gear and supplies ready shortly, and would meet them where their shuttle craft had landed. With confirmation that their plan could now proceed, the crew returned to the landing craft to make preparations for the adventure that would follow the next day. A couple of hours later, and Topaz and her two companions, Indigo and Rowan, also arrived at the meadow. They spent what was left of the evening eating, drinking and socialising – getting to know each other better for the expedition which soon lay ahead. As the evening air cooled, they made a small fire and sat around its warming flames conversing. The conversation soon turned to the rudimentary plan that the crew had hastily conjured up.

'We decided on this plan, simply because we have so few other options. We lack weapons and numbers and we don't want to risk using anything like dynamite or any other high explosive – so it's effectively the best we could come up with. We're very much relying on disruption rather destruction to achieve our aims. With any luck the monarchists will cause them more problems than we ever could – hopefully they will try to evict them or even destroy the settlement. We're effectively dependent on them for doing most of the disruption,' explained Neema, whilst thinking to herself that the plan was actually not that convincing.

'How long exactly will it take us to reach their base?' asked Kahlil.

'My best guess would be two and a half days; the terrain is heavily forested. We need to cross a couple of medium-sized rivers and traverse three different low-lying mountain ridges. We're basically taking the back route into the lowlands. If we travelled by the main tracks along the valley floor it would be easier but quite a significant distance longer, and, of course, we'd also be seen,' explained Topaz, who had already mentally worked out how the whole trek would be covered. 'It's going to be tiring, but once you know the route it's fairly straightforward. It's too dark and difficult to pursue it at night, especially as there's no howling moon tonight, so basically we're just waiting for tomorrow, for when Rogan rises in the morning,' she added.

'Once it's dark, we should bed down; we need as much sleep as we can get. Tomorrow's going to be a long gruelling day, especially if we are to make the progress we need to,' added Indigo.

'Right, so hurry on sundown, let's see what tomorrow brings,' said Jiaying, more to herself than anyone else, and cautiously impatient to get started the next morning.

Before too long, Rogan dipped behind the distant low lying tree-covered mountains to the west, spilling its orange-red light across their ridges. The last vestiges of light finally disappeared and the gloaming gave way to the blackness of night hanging heavy over the silent forest. High above them the stars twinkled, and the lonely moon of Arioch began its nightly journey across the heavens, its dim purple light shining weakly through the noctilucent clouds spread thinly across the upper reaches of Ur-Tokar's cold, clean and pristine atmosphere. Down on the forest floor all around them lay still and silent.

Arrival in Utopia

Earth – the space settlers

For those who departed from Earth in the great exodus of the late twenty-first century, surviving the journey across the vast frozen wastes of interstellar space was only half the battle in respect to what lay ahead of these desperate departees. For having once finally made landfall on their newfound planetary home, light years from Earth and in realms as yet unknown and unexplored, a whole new host of challenges and problems lay ahead for these settlers, for the pioneers of a new planetary way of life.

First and foremost, was the fact that they found themselves on a world possessing geo-planetary conditions for which humans had not evolved over millions of years in order to be perfectly suited to. Varying levels of gravity, different types of daylight, differing lengths of day and year, unfamiliar atmospheric and climatic conditions, and a whole host of other factors, all produced a range of difficulties and problems which would challenge the ingenuity and stamina of the new settlers. Humans had evolved to suit a specific set of planetary conditions, and, faced with a set of entirely new ones, frequently suffered from a wide range of physical and mental health difficulties, sometimes only subtle, but sometimes entirely debilitating. It would take decades and future generations to become better adapted to the lower levels of gravity, extremely long daylight hours, or whatever other debilitating features the planet happened to possess.

Second, was the decision concerning which type of civilisation they would opt to construct. For some, this was highly straightforward. Many of the stasis ships, particularly the earlier 'nation ships', were set on recreating a culture – usually a national one - as near as was practically possible to the one they had left behind on Earth – or at least when it had been enjoying better times. Political, economic and social systems were closely replicated, as much for a sense of familiarity as for ease of construction. The newly emerging towns and settlements were typically named after those they had departed from. The names of the continents, mountains, oceans, seas, plains and deserts were all chosen to remind them of the planet they had departed from, and to impart a sense of tradition, security and belonging. All in all, the aim was that the new should simply be seen as an extension of the old; though frequently this was simply a means of legitimising the reconstruction of the unfair and unequal social structures that had existed back on Earth.

For those, by contrast, seeking to make a clean break with the ruinous approach left behind on Earth – typically the 'utopian ships' of the later waves – nothing could be more different. A dogged determination to create new political and economic structures, new forms of society and a brand new civilisational approach was their highest and most important priority. The complete absence of any conservative political forces resisting their ambitions made such attempts far easier and smoother than had been the case back on Earth, and a whole proliferation of new societies were launched - from the weird and wonderful to the more practical and mundane, from the simply pragmatic to the highly ambitious.

Some proved highly successful, creating flourishing utopias on their newly found planetary homes. Others endured and survived, whilst a few ended in horrendous disaster, their numbers dwindling rapidly, desperately seeking escape to anywhere they could possibly find or reach. But whatever their particular approach, they all sought desperately to break completely with the old destructive ways on Earth – and new homes needed new names, new societies needed new concepts, and new cultures needed new approaches, though occasionally grateful nods were given to old and venerated heroes or to the pioneers of their own particular way of thinking.

Whichever of these approaches was taken, though, all faced the issue of dealing with a different set of resources to those that had existed on Earth; ones that were unique to each planet. All the new civilisations needed to commence construction almost entirely from scratch. The exact nature of construction depended on the availability of the differing local resources – sometimes abundant, sometimes much less so. All had taken mini-fabs on board their ships with them, so manufacturing expertise was not a problem, only acquiring the materials needed for the productive process was a pressing matter. Energy requirements, by contrast, could usually be addressed quickly and wholly adequately. None of the new worlds contained fossil fuels, of course – and most lacked deposits of uranium – but renewable technologies were well advanced and usually proved sufficient to meet all but the most energy intensive of their needs.

Arrival in Utopia

The natural resources available to them also varied according to how well Earth life had taken to its strange new planetary environment. The seas and oceans were often already teeming with life, spreading out quickly and successfully from the 'primordial soup' brought by the 'genesis pods'; rapidly taking to what was effectively a large empty ecological niche just waiting to be populated. On land, by contrast, plant growth varied enormously according to the climactic conditions, length of day and gravitational pressures. Some settlers were far unluckier than others in this respect, and needed to adapt accordingly. Animal life on the land tended to be sparse – mostly consisting of smaller creatures or those that certain groups or individuals had made a point of taking with them. Space on the stasis ships was usually at a premium and, normally, few large animals had been transported to the new worlds. This in turn could give rise to temporary explosions of the smaller life forms, or the near demise of others. Only evolution and time could eventually resolve these imbalances.

Food production was not usually problematic, since ferming units – extracting water, bacteria and gases from the atmosphere to create foods rich in protein, fat and carbohydrates – were invariably put to maximum usage. However, they were unable to supply all dietary needs and some form of farming needed to be established fairly rapidly. In the absence of most or all of the domestic animals familiar back on Earth, fruit, vegetable and nut production – much of which had been initiated by the genesis pods - was invariably favoured by the settlers in order to provide the necessary minerals, vitamins and fibre. Some of the new civilisations chose to utilise the ocean resources for food production, others – mindful of the marine disaster that had unfolded on Earth during the twentieth and twenty-first centuries – chose to do otherwise and to leave the sea-life in peace and to its own devices.

Even once these basics had been sorted successfully, the level of civilisational development achieved on the new worlds tended to be quite limited, and not just because of a scarcity of available resources or because social systems had been chosen which did not prioritise material wealth. There were also the standard limiting factors; populations were initially low, and the existing level of construction when they arrived usually close to minimal. Housing, transport and mining would invariably be commenced from first arrival onwards, and certain basic industries and services became commonplace, but some of the old industries and services that had existed back on Earth required economies of scale or levels of energy usage that were just not viable for the smaller, developing economies on the discovered planets. Aviation, particularly in the absence of fossil fuels, remained something of a niche activity on the new worlds.

Busy creating a new civilisation almost from scratch, adapting to a new and unknown world, and with small populations and sometimes limited resource bases, few planets were able to make significant technological advances beyond those that had existed on Earth, particularly in the first decades and early centuries. New inventions, patents, technologies, processes, and working practices might become commonplace, but tended to be small-scale in both their scope and their implementation. Those needed to effect a qualitative leap to a higher level of systemic advancement - major advances in space travel, energy from nuclear fusion or massively improved cyber-engineering, for instance – proved to be unforthcoming and the stage of development remained within the parameters of what had been familiar for Earthbound populations.

Nevertheless, what did change over time, though, was that the people of all these civilisations – sooner or later – needed to face the question of who exactly they were. Were they the descendants of Earth or were they a new people with a new planetary identity? Gradually, but very unevenly, across all the planets, as the passage of time progressed, civilisations typically began to depart from the old Earth ways – particularly where contact with their space age neighbours was limited or non-existent. Cultures and languages developed that owed increasingly less and less to their Earthean heritage, and more and more to the planetary, geological and climactic conditions of their new home. Social structures dramatically diverged and with relative ease, whilst, slowly and more uncertainly, certain biological features were selected for according to factors such as gravitational pressure, distance from their star and the length of the day.

Scientists and academics were faced with a particularly intractable problem. Initially, standard Earth measurements and units had been retained on many of the new worlds, especially in the more conservative civilisations. But the use of many of these standard units – of length, weight, pressure, age and time – were highly problematic on a world where they now made little rational sense. Scientists, historians and various other intellectuals, everywhere, agonised over the continued use of standard units and measurements established back on Earth, in finding a means of maintaining continuity within the traditions of their academic discipline, whilst also using units of measurement that were of relevance on their newly established world. Some broke quickly from the ancient conventions - particularly on the utopian worlds adopting measurements and units that related to the physical features of their new world. On others, rearguard actions were fought to retain the traditional norms and customs of old, with wide-ranging disputes breaking out between the young and the old as to which systems should prevail – generational battles over a disputed human identity.

Slowly, the peoples of each respective world took on a distinctive appearance – both culturally and physically – to the extent that they could be readily identified – at least by those in the know - as being a member of a particular civilisation. New stereotypes arose, new understandings and alliances, new prejudices and new concerns. But in a galaxy where space travel and inter-planetary communications remained relatively slow, and where the civilisations typically remained far from one another – so that interactions with the other worlds remained the exception rather than the norm – any newly acquired characteristics or differences were rarely of any great significance, or imparted much in the way of long-term impacts upon other peoples. Amidst the vastness of inter-stellar space, the new planetary civilisations were like small distant islands, autonomous and isolated, floating in a sea of darkness, simply going their own way and doing their own particular thing, largely oblivious to life in the rest of the galaxy.

Ur-Tokar – through the forests

The group rose early in the morning as an orange glow peeked over the eastern mountains. A light dew lay across the alpine meadow, and the thin mist that had developed overnight began to slowly lift as Rogan's ascent into the cool wintry sky warmed the early morning air. The occasional bird called from the forest, but otherwise the montane meadow was steeped in silence, save for the distant murmur of the Kauai River flowing ever downward through its ancient canyon. Once they had consumed their early morning meal, they finished off packing their supplies, crossed the slowly flowing river, and headed up the incline into the woods. Before them lay the extensive pine and fir forest that would take them up and across the first of the mountain ridges they needed to traverse.

Apart from the generally upward nature of the trek, the going was fairly easy for most of the initial climb. The trees were widely spaced and the pine needles that littered the ground cushioned their steps as they made their way through the forest. Nevertheless, the trees appeared endless and all very similar and the Opa-Loka crew quickly realised they had no real idea of where they were actually heading, and even the occasional clearing did nothing to help them find their bearings. They were now entirely reliant on Topaz and her friends to guide them in the correct direction.

By the time they reached the first ridge, Jiaying, Kahlil and Neema were more fatigued than they had expected. Sixteen months in a starship – even if much of it had been spent in stasis – had weakened their bodies and they were not used to dealing with this strength of gravitational force, though fortunately Ur-Tokar was slightly smaller than Zeta Kotlin and thus enjoyed lighter gravity. Unused to such exertions, they needed a prolonged break when they finally reached the crest of the first ridge. At first, all they could do was soak up the magnificent mountainous vistas and slowly recover their breath.

The scenery, as they had noted almost everywhere on Ur-Tokar, was simply spectacular. The unbelievably high purple Zarozinian Mountains were now behind them, but still stretched across the entirety of the southern horizon. Distantly to the north, they could now easily discern the shimmering white of the glaciers emerging from the extensive mass of the northern polar ice-cap. And between these two outstanding features was simply a series of long parallel mountain ridges, an endless blanket of pine forest, and, snaking slowly between them, the occasional silvery glimpse of meandering rivers shining in the winter sunlight. The air was still, quiet and refreshingly cool.

When the three Zetans had finally started to breathe more normally, they brought out their food rations and ate a light meal, whilst taking in the awe-inspiring scene before them. The two groups were both keen to know more about each other and soon struck up a conversation.

'When we first arrived in the tavern in Lato, I couldn't help but get the sense that some of the people we first met there were looking at us in a highly expectant way, scrutinising us, almost as though we were something they had been waiting for. I got the impression they were hoping we had arrived to deliver something important to them. But once we explained who we were, that expectation sort of dissipated and they looked slightly disappointed. What was that all about, or was I just imagining the whole thing?' asked Jiaying, remembering the slightly puzzling incident.

'No you didn't imagine it,' replied Topaz. 'Some of them thought you might be fulfilling an old prophecy that exists amongst our people. There's an ancient legend within our culture, shrouded in myth and long forgotten memories, that tells of a group of space explorers from a previous time and age.' She paused a while trying to remember the final details of the legend, as it had been recounted to her whilst still a child.

'The PXR5 was not a standard stasis class starship, but a nova drive model. Its small crew held revolutionary ideas that were at odds with the machine society they emerged from. They eschewed the use of robots and computer technology and so they departed from their world to become outlaws in space. They believed that the human race derived from life sown beyond the stars, and its demise had resulted from knowledge lost to humans as they travelled across those stars.' She paused again so she could remember the story correctly.

'So the crew went in search of the knowledge that had been left behind in the cosmos, travelling from star to star in search of the answer that could save the human race. Their dream was to travel across time and space to discover an ancient and forgotten past. But, the engines on their nova drive repeatedly failed, their life support systems failed to take the strain of such an odyssey, crew members died and long years were spent drifting in the depths of space. To this day, no one knows if they still continue their journey into space, or whether their quest succeeded and they found the lost knowledge they were searching for - to once again became the seed of life.' Topaz concluded the mythic legend, fairly sure she had remembered it correctly.

'Some of the more mystical members of our people thought you might be the ancient questors returning with the lost knowledge that could save the human race. Since our quarrel with the monarchists began, the legend has made something of a comeback. Some of our people are hoping that their return might bring some form of salvation for us.'

'Wow, that's really weird. There's a similar story within our culture about a starship called the PXR5, though the details are slightly different. I'd always assumed it was just some old spacefarers tale created to make space travel sound more romantic, but maybe it actually has some truth in it. Maybe it was some unorthodox grouping in the time of the exodus from Earth. It must have occurred very early on in the exodus, if we know some of the details of what actually happened to the ship. If the story is true, I wonder what did happen to it, though I very much doubt it was successful in its quest,' pondered Jiaying.

'Why do you say that?' Topaz asked, though she thought she probably knew the answer.

Neema butted into the conversation at this point. 'All the evidence shows humans – and all the other lifeforms we know of - evolved entirely on Earth. There's no good evidence for any advanced life from elsewhere. We weren't descended from space-faring aliens, so there's basically nothing out there to find.'

'The evidence could be misleading, though, or there might be gaps in their knowledge still to be filled,' suggested Topaz.

'Well, that's always a possibility with anything, but the evidence in this case is pretty overwhelming. All the biological, geological and cosmological evidence points in the same direction,' replied Neema. 'So far, none of the new planetary civilisations has discovered anything remotely close to advanced life-forms.'

'So you think their quest was a waste of time?' Topaz asked sounding slightly disappointed. She had been secretly hoping this particular legend might turn out to be a real one, especially if it helped sort out their problem with the monarchists.

'Well, it's possible they just wanted to escape from an oppressive society or start a new and better one, or pursue some other objective, so it might not have been a complete waste of time. But I don't believe they will ever find some long-lost hidden knowledge on the far side of the galaxy that will prove to be our salvation,' replied Neema.

'Personally, I would say we have already liberated ourselves through our own efforts; we've certainly done that on our own planet, in any respect,' offered Jiaying. 'Admittedly, some of the others have been distinctly less successful in that regard. I suppose in that respect, space travel did prove to be our salvation, but we already possessed the knowledge of how to do this. We brought it with us; we just needed to find somewhere to implement it.'

They all paused for a while, Jiaying's comments being something of a conservation stopper. 'What exactly did Amethyst mean when she said the mountains were sacred?' asked Neema suddenly, deciding to change the conversation, and who, like most Zetans, possessed only a very sketchy knowledge of spiritual ideas and practices.

Topaz considered the question for a moment. 'It's not a view I particularly share, though I admit you only need to look at the beauty of the mountains to see that they are something extra special. Some of our people - like Amethyst - believe that spirits live in the forests, the rivers and the mountains – and not just in living beings like the forest animals and the trees – but also in the rocks, the waters and the sky and that they imbue these inanimate objects with life. They believe that spirits dwell in all the ecosystems and help to keep them in a healthy and natural state. These spirits, though, need to be respected and looked after. They should never be harmed - for if that was to happen, these natural habitats would degenerate and die without them to nurture and protect them. And as the natural habitats die, then so we all do as well.'

'Have you seen them? These spirits, I mean,' asked Neema, highly sceptical that such metaphysical beings might actually exist.

'I'm not really sure they are visible. The believers are a bit vague about how they are perceived. Occasionally, people claim they catch glimpses of them, disappearing into the shadows or shimmering under the waters of the lakes and rivers. Some of the believers claim that taking hallucinogenic drugs under certain ritualistic conditions allows them to meet and mentally converse with them. They talk about concepts such as ritual breathing, the secret knowledge of water and the wisdom of the air. They just seem to know that the spirits are there and that they should be protected - if you can't see them, it doesn't necessarily mean they don't exist, they always say,' Topaz replied.

'An absence of evidence, is not evidence of absence – as the conspiracy theorists always like to claim. But I always think, if you believe in something you should really be able to provide evidence of its existence. If you can't, why should any reasonable person take you seriously? The onus is on the believer to provide evidence, not on the sceptic to prove non-existence - after all, it's usually impossible to prove a negative. The believer can just say you looked in the wrong place at the wrong time, for whatever it is you're trying to prove doesn't exist,' explained Kahlil, expressing a view that was commonplace amongst the Zetan population, given their rationally-based education system.

'And if you think otherwise, then people can believe in any old religious or superstitious nonsense, and you just have to accept they might be right – no matter how ludicrous their fictitious entity might be,' added Neema.

'It sounds to me like it might be an additional way to convince people to protect the environment. Just supplying an extra layer of protection above those that already exist, but adding what seems like a more moral or profound reason for safeguarding natural habitats,' stated Jiaying, who was now beginning to worry that her mining plan could be jeopardised by the Mountain People's spiritual beliefs. She was wondering how she had managed to forget that pre-socialist societies were often steeped in religious and superstitious folklore, especially after experiencing similar problems with the monarchists on her previous visits to the planet.

'You don't believe in such things then?' asked Topaz.

'There's no religion on our planet. We have no need for such beliefs. Our legal and educational systems are constructed democratically through our communities, not based on religion. Knowledge is based on rational enquiry, discussion, evidence-based science and proving and disproving theories – not from dubious texts handed down from on high. We live in supportive egalitarian communes – people help you through the difficult times; they help you to come to terms with illness, accidents, death or other tragedies, so we don't need to turn to some higher metaphysical power. Our world is based on equality, so there is no ruling class using religion to perpetuate their control over an oppressed society. All the reasons for religion existing are absent on our planet,' explained Jiaying. She remembered learning about this when she was much younger, but had never expected it to actually be of much relevance to her own life, until she had the misfortune to engage with the strange religious beliefs of the monarchists.

'We learn that on Earth religion caused divisions, conflict and war. It stopped people from discovering how the world really worked. In the end it led to humans destroying their environment because religion told them that humans were in dominion over nature and could treat it as they pleased, and with all the damaging results that ensued from that belief,' added Neema.

'Yes, I've heard similar views from some of our people, the ones who dislike the spiritualist beliefs, and I know some hold very similar views to yours, but I think the religions on Earth were very different to the ones that are believed in here,' replied Topaz.

'Do you think we'll be able to come to an arrangement with your people so we can mine for ores in the mountains? We'll make sure no damage is done to the environment, we can give you a complete guarantee on that,' Jiaying offered, still concerned, and still wondering whether her mining plan would be derailed at some point by superstitious beliefs, ones that she ultimately thought were complete nonsense.

'Well, I doubt we could actually stop you if you went ahead with it, anyway,' replied Topaz.

'But we like to gain agreement with the local people. We're not a bunch of imperialists, barging in and just taking whatever we want – not like the Zeleyanians are probably planning to do.'

'Speaking of which, we really need to get moving, said Topaz, who was not entirely comfortable with this conversation. 'I want to reach a particular location by nightfall, and we've been travelling quite slowly. We need to make good progress this afternoon,' she added. With this, their lunch came to an end, and now refreshed and strengthened, they were soon making their way down the other side of the ridge, once more to be led through the dark and seemingly endless forest.

For two more days they made their way steadily through the forest, across the rivers and over the mountain ridges. Along the way they had many more conversations and the crew discovered a great deal more about their companions and the type of life the Mountain People led.

Like many in and around the settlement of Lato, Topaz followed no particular profession or calling. She frequently taught in the settlement's small primary school and helped out regularly with the boats used for fishing or moving goods along the river. Like most, she also maintained her own smallholding to supply much of her dietary and other living requirements. The economy of the Mountain People was a generally mixed one involving small-scale farming, a small amount of herding, but also some trading and foraging. All economic activities were expected to impact minimally on the environment and a range of cultural, political and legal conventions had been established to ensure this was not broken with. It was true, she said, that the boundaries between what was and was not permitted could be uncertain, and there were occasional disputes between the different economic activities, but overall the conventions were largely adhered to.

Topaz was never happier, apparently, than when she was foraging for food and other resources in the forests and mountains. In this she was far from alone, and given the fixed status of the settlement at Lato, this often meant travelling for days at a time, often far into the wilderness, and away from the settlement where the population size was too great for there to be much of use in terms of foraging potential. As such, she had developed and possessed an intimate knowledge of the local terrain, its notable features, its varied geography and changing weather conditions.

Indigo they discovered was a very close friend of Topaz, despite living some distance away from each other. The settlement of Lato, though thinly populated, covered a surprisingly large area given how few people actually lived there. This was so that each household possessed sufficient land for their smallholdings, and as a result, many had needed to build log cabins or similar structures on the adjacent wooded hillsides as the settlement spread away from the relatively flat area that ran alongside the River Kauai.

Indigo was one of those living in the hillside log cabins and was thus less involved in farming than those in a more favourable location. As such, she had become one of the many artisans of the area, creating wooden artefacts – both practical and decorative – from the plentiful supplies of wood available to them, though the small scale of her and other woodworkers operations meant a strict practice of sustainability was easily achievable and pursued at all times. Mass production methods were strictly forbidden within their culture and any artisan who looked like they might be moving in this direction was warned of the consequences. However, with such a small population, she said this was rarely necessary, and the artisans knew that their livelihood depending on acting in this way anyway.

Rowan, another close friend of Topaz, turned out to be one of a small number of councillors who had been elected to the settlement's administrative body, to ensure that the long-term sustainability of the settlement was always considered. The politics of their culture seemed to be fairly ill-defined and tended to work very much on an ad hoc basis. With a disparate range of beliefs and economic practices, their political system was appropriately decentralised to match this reality. Most laws related to preserving environmental sustainability, but also attempted to sustain a mixed system of semi-private and semi-public land ownership, and the largely peaceful, and mostly egalitarian, social structure that had been arrived at organically, rather than through the implementation of any particular ideological blueprint.

As such, Rowan's role largely involved ensuring environmental practices were adhered to, and also with trying to mediate disputes within the community. On rare occasions, a household or family would try to merge land holdings that then breached the maximum permitted size and this would need to be rectified, usually with the involvement of the wider community, who were keen to prevent such developments from occurring. He had been keen to join the group's mission as he was sure he would be heavily involved in the fall-out that resulted from the action they were planning to take, irrespective of whether it proved to be successful or not.

Topaz and her friends clearly knew the terrain extremely well and never once lost their way, though did occasionally pause to take their bearings. The crew could not help but be impressed by their ability to find their way in a terrain that seemed to offer few obvious landmarks and that seemed to contain no distinct pathways. The endless forest appeared to be pretty much the same to them in whichever direction they looked. The crew also began to feel the strength slowly coming back into their bodies as they acclimatised to normal gravity combined with the arduous exercise, though by nightfall each evening they were shattered and fell into a deep sleep, until Topaz once more raised them at daybreak the following morning for yet another days trekking.

On the third day, they began to close in on their target. They were working on the assumption that there would be military guards patrolling the perimeter of the base, so began to approach much more stealthily, keeping noise to an absolute minimum, proceeding slowly and pausing regularly to ensure there was no one ahead of them. They possessed no weaponry of their own, so it was crucial that they should remain completely undetected. Having, arced round in a large semi-circle, the base was now between them and the town of Meridin and the plan was a simple one, though the crew was still highly uncertain as to what would actually happen following their intervention.

As they neared the base, they traversed a small stream, climbed its bank, and were making their way through the dense scrub that flanked the stream when they suddenly spotted two guards ahead of them, even though the base was still a good two hundred metres ahead of them. The guards clearly heard something, as they turned and looked towards the group. Topaz and the crew had already crouched down quickly in the thick undergrowth and froze still and silent. The guards probably only looked in their direction for a matter of about ten seconds, but for Jiaying – not used to such precarious situations – it seemed like ten seconds of forever. An eternity seemed to pass, but nothing happened. There was no noise and there was no abrupt reaction from the soldiers. Then, they turned away and simply continued with their routine.

Maybe the guards just assumed they would simply not encounter anyone on their perimeter walk, or that they had just heard a wild boar foraging for food, or one of the deer released into the forests for hunting purposes by the king. Zeleyan had no dense forests like the ones that dominated Ur-Tokar, so they were out of their comfort zone anyway. Whatever the reason, when no further noise followed, they simply continued with their perimeter walk and soon disappeared into the thickness of the forest.

Jiaying, concerned by this brush with danger, made it clear that this was the last scare she wanted to encounter, and so the group decided to commence their plan in an adjacent clearing, rather than advance any closer to the base, which was still not fully discernible through the thickness of the trees. They had brought a large caseload of exploding flares with them - ones that could be connected to a timer and fired on a delayed basis. They spent a few minutes quietly connecting them up in the clearing and then the group retreated back the way they had come from through the trees.

Thirty minutes later, and they had put a good amount of distance between themselves, the flares and the military base. By now, it was nearing the middle of the day and suddenly the flares zoomed into the sky and a bright and extremely loud cacophony of reds, blues and greens exploded noisily high above the forest canopy. The show only lasted for a few minutes but they were sure the people of Meridin must have both seen and heard such a display. The group retreated further back up the slope, and about an hour later they had returned to the crest of the ridge they had descended from earlier that morning. From here, they could enjoy reasonably adequate views of the lowlands below, though the tree cover remained a problem with regard to viewing purposes. They waited and listened for some time and then, sure enough, they soon heard the sound of raised voices, horns blowing and the thunder of hooves – a sure sign that the king's troops were on the move. The group settled in for a protracted wait – the plan appeared to be working.

Ur-Tokar – the Battle of Meridin

That morning, the day had broken pretty much the same as any other in Meridin. Rogan's red-orange glow emerged from behind the mountains to the east, a thin mist hung over the lowlands, dew glistened on the fields, early birds moved from their roosts to their feeding grounds, and the people of Meridin emerged to slowly go about their daily tasks. By mid-morning the mists of Meridin had lifted and the sun had risen higher into the watery blue sky warming the wintry air; it had all the makings of an ordinary pleasant sunny morning. The peasants were out working in the fields tending their animals, the townspeople made their way to market or whatever other activity they had in mind, and the royal guards kept watch at the town's gates and other strategic positions around the town. There was absolutely no reason to believe that this day would be unlike any other day in the short history of Meridin.

So, when loud explosions suddenly sounded from the forest to the south-west of the town, accompanied by a fusillade of brightly multi-coloured lights bursting across the sky, the townspeople could only stand and stare in incomprehension. By chance, King Alfonso was, at that particular moment, in the grounds surrounding his castle, engaged in mounted sword practice with his fellow knights, and thus witnessed the entire event. The entirety of the royal court simply stopped dead and gazed in awe at the brief but puzzling event. And when the strange light-and-sound show had finished, they turned to the king for an explanation, for which, of course, he had none readily at hand.

The king immediately ordered scouts to be sent out in the direction of the incident to discover the source of this wholly unexpected event. He was inclined to believe that he would discover that the Mountain People were somehow responsible for this incident, though something running through the back brain of his mind bothered him. Although their shared and largely negative approach towards modern technology was more flexible than that allowed under his monarchical rule, this stunt was not like anything they had pulled before, and did not really bear their hallmark. He was concerned that there might be a more worrying explanation for the event.

He sent orders out for the royal army to be readied and for all soldiers to be prepared for immediate action. Whatever underhand scheme the Mountain People might be engaged in – if it was indeed them - this would prove an opportune moment to diminish their numbers. Their long running campaign of guerilla warfare against his regime had scored some notable successes, whilst his attempts to destroy their homes and villages had simply pushed them further back into the forested mountains. They were proving to be like the biting insects that buzzed around you, but could never be fully swatted away, never mind eliminated. Whilst waiting for the army to be readied he consulted with his astrologer as to whether action would be auspicious this particular day. The astrologer, readily able to read the king's mood and his desire for quick action, assured him that the heavens were indeed favourable for the monarch on this particular day, and so approved the course of action that the king was already set upon.

The scouts returned after an hour or so, and reported the presence of movement in the woods by people unknown and unfamiliar to them, and possibly in some significant numbers. They also claimed to have seen some form of large wooden structure amongst the trees, but could offer no specific details other than it appeared to be a high and very long wall. King Alfonso quickly assumed the worst, convinced that the Mountain People were engaged in some form of trickery that was aimed at harming or even bringing down his regime, and so he concluded that a swift and harsh response to their provocation was duly warranted. The royal army immediately set out hurriedly towards the source of the explosions, and a short ride later the king and his troops arrived at the outskirts of the mysterious wooden-looking construction.

Alfonso halted the army in a forest clearing some distance before the strange structure in front of them. It appeared to be wooden in construction, but was unusually uniform in appearance. In places along the structure, on what looked like slightly raised look-out towers, there appeared to be strangely dressed guard-like figures. King Alfonso had never fought a proper pitched battle before – his was the only properly armed regime on the planet – and so he had little direct experience of military warfare. He had, however, heard the songs sung and the stories told of medieval battles fought on Earth, and he had trained and drilled his army in standard military manoeuvres, gleaned from ancient writings. With nothing else to guide him in this strange and unexpected situation, he simply reverted to standard battle formation and tactics. His archers were ordered to move forward and rain arrows down upon the fort. As this tactic came towards its conclusion, he gave the order for the rest of his army to surge forward in a standard cavalry and infantry formation. Screaming and shouting, with banners held high and drums beating loudly, both sections of the army surged forward, charging as fast as they were possibly able through the forested clearing towards the fortified structure.

The outcome of the battle was, of course, something of a foregone conclusion. The Zeleyan soldiers were armed with heavy modern artillery and hi-tech assault weapons. The sound of loud explosions and the crackle of intense gunfire spattered across the wooded area in front of the fort for several minutes as the charging royal forces were soon cut down with relative ease. Only the presence of the few trees in the forest clearing prevented an even higher casualty rate than the one they suffered. Those forces that reached the perimeter wall found their weapons were useless against the fortified structure, which was not made of wood as they had thought but the advanced material corbalite used by so many of the settlers across the galaxy – tough, versatile, light, hard-wearing and almost entirely fireproof. The king watched on with growing dismay as his forces were cut to the ground and faced near annihilation, and was soon forced to issue the order to retreat.

The remnants of the royal army fell back behind the original clearing in the forest, beyond the range of the artillery fire and resumed formation. The king was at a loss as to what his next move should be, until one of his knights suggested they should burn the structure down instead. With no other viable options or suggestions, a small detachment of soldiers was ordered to return to Meridin to collect barrels of pitch and return forthwith. Soldiers were ordered to gather deadwood from the forest floor and to furtively place it into large piles as close to the fort as they could possibly manage. Somewhat surprisingly, this activity met with no resistance from the Zeleyanian forces, and Alfonso noted that the military base had suddenly fallen particularly quiet.

Ur-Tokar - inside the base

The flares launched by the crew of the Opa-Loka had taken the Zeleyan forces by as much surprise as they had the royal court of Meridin. Guards had been sent hurriedly into the forest to the rear of the fort to discover the source of the explosions, but had failed to find any persons present or the origin of the explosions. Whilst they were doing so, the officer in charge of the garrison, Captain Peran, had hurriedly sought to contact Vice-Admiral Rosson, who had previously returned to the stasis ship The Crusader orbiting above the planet, and inform him of the unexpected incident and await further orders. Unbeknown to the Captain, however, Rosson had left the orbit of Ur-Tokar several hours beforehand and was currently enjoying a tour of the outer planets of Rogan's star system.

After successfully establishing the military base and sending a communication to the Zeleyanian High Command confirming his achievement, Rosson had decided to return to the stasis ship and contemplate his next move. Vartin had not indicated any precise date for the arrival of his forces – he presumed this related to Vartin's untrusting and cautious nature – but was well aware that he was likely to be left waiting for several months before the rest of the fleet arrived to implement the full invasion of the planet. Rosson had briefly wondered about returning to stasis to avoid the boredom that awaited him over the next few months, but had decided that, as the commanding officer of the operation, this was probably not a wise option. He had also considered exploring some of the remoter parts of the planet below him, but was concerned that this might give away their presence to the local inhabitants, so he had decided this could wait for a later time.

He had initially attempted to resist the temptation of indulging in his new found interest of space tourism, but after several days of growing tedium he had been able to resist no longer. After all, he figured, he was the commanding officer of the operation and he had successfully completed the first part of the mission. If he needed to take a well-earned break then he deserved it, and anyway, it was highly unlikely that anything untoward would occur on the planet's surface whilst he was gone. It was a very quiet and uneventful planet. And so he had ordered the ship to lift out of orbit for a pleasant and leisurely tour of the gaseous planets and ice dwarves that constituted the outer reaches of Rogan's planetary system.

Back on the planet, Captain Peran could not understand why his initial attempts to contact Rosson were not being answered. He was not aware of any technical issues or similar such problems aboard the ship, but he was totally unaware of Rosson's predilection for space tourism. By the time he did finally receive a reply from Rosson, the base was already under attack from King Alfonso's royal army and he had already ordered his troops to return fire, since he had assumed this was the obvious response required. There was no question now, of course, of remaining hidden and undiscovered, so he now prioritised the survival of the garrison in the face of hostile enemy forces. The outcome of the initial battle was a huge relief for the captain – as he had taken personal control of the situation and knew he would be held fully responsible for whatever outcome ensued – but he could not help but being dumbfounded by the sheer stupidity of the battle tactics used by the monarchist forces. The battle was utter one-sided carnage.

There then followed a break in the fighting and period of relative calm, during which he thought the monarchist forces might have entirely retreated. He had continued his efforts to receive some form of coherent plan from Rosson, but whilst waiting for orders, had suddenly been taken by surprise by a deluge of flaming arrows that rained down on the base. Wave upon wave fell upon them like fiery demons descending from the sky; though after several minutes of bombardment it looked as though their impact was going to prove minimal, as only isolated small-scale fires had broken out across the base. He ordered his troops to fire upon the archers, but the presence of so much forest between the two forces made only a limited impact on their numbers. And then suddenly, a flaming arrow finally got lucky and hit home inside one of the armouries. A huge explosion followed which ripped through one whole half of the base. Burning debris flew out in all directions and whole sections of the base finally caught fire. Casualties were high, troops scattered in all directions and it took the whole of the captain's authority to regain control of the situation.

The base was clearly in danger of being completely destroyed, as whole sections of the perimeter wall had been blown away by the blast. Trying to save it would have left the reduced Zeleyanian forces at the mercy of any oncoming onslaught from the royal army. So instead, the captain had ordered a controlled but offensively-aimed evacuation of what was left of the base, and had decided to take the fight to the enemy. They had overwhelmingly superior firepower, he figured, so should be able to overpower the enemy if they could hold their formation long enough. Captain Peran had seen action in several of the urban uprisings that had beset the fascist regime on Zeleyan, and was something of a veteran when it came to the art of taking control of cities seized by rebellious forces. In the event, his experience served the Zeleyan forces extremely well.

The royal army was preparing for a second attack on the destroyed side of the base, when they were caught by an unexpected counter-attack from the Zeleyanian forces breaking out of the section of the military base that remained intact. Alfonso's forces were caught completely by surprise as the Zeleyanian forces emerged through the trees spraying them heavily with rocket launchers and automatic gunfire. Once again, the ill-equipped monarchist forces were utterly decimated, and amongst the many casualties they suffered this time, was King Alfonso himself. In only a short matter of time the battle was effectively over and the tiny remnants of the royal forces turned tail and fled back towards Meridin.

The captain, however, had already calculated he still had sufficient forces intact to take control of Meridin, whilst also leaving a small detail behind, tasked with saving what was left of the military base. The captain's calculations proved to be correct, heavily armed and with what proved to be sufficient numbers, his forces met little resistance from the remnants of the army and the people of Meridin as they entered the town. Within a few hours, despite relying on diminished military forces, he was fully in control of the town. Even when faced by a limited Zeleyanian force, the locals simply had no answer to their far superior technology and firepower. With their monarch dead and the army completely routed, Meridin and the monarchist territories were now effectively under the full control of the invading Zeleyanian forces.

PART 3

Rendez-vous at Ur-Tokar

Ur-Tokar – Vice-Admiral Rosson visits Rogan's outer planetary system

Vice-Admiral Rosson's second tour of Rogan's varied array of planets had, initially, gone even better than he had anticipated. After the boredom of routine procedures at the somewhat spartan military base close to Meridin, it was a pleasant change to once again be viewing the wonders of the cosmos. It was true that Rogan lacked any genuine gas or ice giants, but the strange natures of Corusa and Lapiz made up for this lacuna, and Rosson had made a number of course deviations with the intention of viewing what proved to be an interesting and varied array of smaller rocky planets and medium-sized ice worlds permanently locked in a state of frozen suspension.

Like most party members on Zeleyan, Rosson's belief system was composed of a jumbled concoction of established science, pseudo-science, conspiracy theories, mysticism and semi-mythical beliefs which made little coherent sense. Effectively, the dominant ideology of the party used any ideas that were deemed useful for demonstrating the superiority of fascism, often in a blatantly contradictory manner. Rosson had never been much of a thinker - though at times he had been forced to reflect at length on the undesired positions his family had decided he should experience - but his recent planetary encounters in space had initiated a thought process within the Vice-Admiral's mind that was attempting to link the ideological beliefs he held to his own personal journey through life, through the prism of his recent planetary experiences.

Rosson surmised that the heat from the small red dwarf star at the centre of this particular system was insufficient to produce any significantly large gaseous body within its environs. It was also the reason for why so many of the smaller planets were permanently frozen. As such, he made a point of visiting several of those frozen planets and dwarf planets with a view to understanding what it meant to lack sufficient warmth to remain alive, and to experience a state of frozen torpor. He was toying with the idea that this corresponded to long periods of his own life – estranged from the person he really wanted to be. He was also wondering, though, whether this represented some form of metaphysical punishment; for Rogan was a weak sun, and he too, for long periods of his life, had displayed a mental weakness that he was now beginning to look back on with a growing sense of disappointment.

Whilst the gas planets offered spectacular images of majesty and greatness, the icy dwarf planets were simply small pinpoints of white, lost in a vast cosmic sea of utter blackness. To Rosson, they gave off a distinct air of loneliness, of everlasting frozen coldness in an inhospitable and unforgiving darkness. And yet they survived, tough lumps of frozen rock that had endured everything the cosmos could throw at them. He saw connections to his own life and to those of many others he knew, only furthering his growing belief that his appointment as Vice-Admiral of the Space Fleet was more than simply a career promotion, but had been deigned by some form of mysterious power or life-force with important implications in mind, both for him personally, and possibly for his civilisation more generally.

After viewing the stark loneliness of the diminutive ice planets, Rosson could not resist a return to the strange gaseous worlds of Lapiz and Corusa. Once again he wondered if they were subject to some form of cosmic punishment – locked in a violent and endless conflict with themselves, or some mysterious, yet powerful and unknown, entity. Both planets gave the distinct appearance of enduring suffering, of experiencing everlasting damage and even possible eventual destruction. Was this another metaphor for his own life and perhaps that of humanity in general, he wondered. His mind was racing with all forms of connections and possibilities.

And yet, despite their violent internal struggles, he was still struck by the sheer size, complexity and strange compelling beauty of the two worlds. In fact, so transfixed had Rosson been by the glitterball-like effect of Corusa, that when the communication arrived from Captain Peran informing him of the attack on the military garrison on Ur-Tokar, it had taken several seconds to permeate his consciousness, for it to even register with his mind that there was a problem, in fact, a problem so enormous it had the potential to destroy his entire career.

A sudden wave of anxiety swept through him as the enormity of the situation became apparent. He was out here on the outer limits of the planetary system indulging himself in an extravagant form of space tourism, whilst the base he commanded was under serious attack from hostile forces. For a moment he panicked, and a short period of time and confusion followed in which he attempted to calculate a way out of his difficulties, unsure of what course of action he should take. Gradually, though, he gathered his composure, and unable to conceive of anything more sophisticated than a reciprocal response, he simply issued orders to Peran to resist and destroy the enemy. He then ordered the ship's computer to effect a hasty exit from the orbit of Corusa and return to Ur-Tokar on the fastest trajectory possible.

The ship's computer used the gas planet's gravity to accelerate the spacecraft back towards Ur-Tokar, but it would still be several hours before they were able to descend once again into orbit around the small partially forested, partially frozen planet. As they did so, though, Rosson was relieved to receive an encrypted communication from Peran informing him that the Zeleyanian forces had triumphed and routed the monarchist enemy, though he was much less pleased to discover that the military base had been half-destroyed. Peran's seizure of Meridin was not what he had been expecting, but he immediately began to wonder how this unexpected development could be worked to his own advantage.

The major problem Rosson now faced, though, was that he was almost certain that amongst his senior officers there would be a regime spy; at the very least, one of them would be a confidante of Vartin's, with close links to High Command, and who would now relate the whole precise detail of the episode to the Supreme Commander. Yet he had no idea which officer might be the secret agent, though, admittedly, before this episode he had given the matter little serious consideration. Vartin, he had discovered over time, trusted precisely no one and left nothing to chance. Rosson's forces might have been victorious at Meridin, Peran might have saved him from disaster, but he was still a long way from being out of the woods just yet.

Rosson started to obsess with his personal position, becoming increasingly paranoid about which of his fellow officers might be Vartin's stooge. As The Crusader resumed its planetary orbit around Ur-Tokar, he had still not settled upon any particular candidate, and had arrived at no concrete decision as to how he could now proceed in discovering exactly who it was. Short of devising increasingly elaborate ways to eliminate his entire officer class, he was at a loss as to how to extricate himself from this particular predicament –

as he looked down towards the planet, he was still hoping for some form of divine inspiration.

Once established in orbit, they immediately descended in a shuttle craft to Meridin and Rosson took stock of the newfound situation. On the upside, the monarchist forces had been entirely vanquished by his troops and appeared to offer no form of threat to their position either in Meridin or at the military garrison now. The garrison itself could probably be salvaged and rebuilt, though they would need some local materials to help complete the project. He was still ignorant of the expected arrival date of the main invasion fleet, but it had to be several months yet, so the reconstruction of the base, he believed, was probably the least of his worries.

On the downside though, the Zeleyanian existence on the planet had now been discovered, and he had also lost a significant proportion of the military detachment that had arrived with him at Ur-Tokar. Vartin had allowed him to take only one regiment to Ur-Tokar – he was still not fully sure why this was the case – even though the ship had several thousand stasis pods. There was also the question of who had launched the flare explosions that had given away their position. He was under the distinct impression that the whole planet had a very low-tech economy, so was unsure as to how such an event was even possible. He issued orders to his junior officers to commence interrogation of the local townspeople in order to obtain information on the subject, to discover if they knew anything of use. He also instructed the ship's computer to locate the position of the invasion fleet – for surely it was on its way by now, he thought - and calculate an exact arrival date for it, even though he knew this action would be regarded with suspicion by Vartin once his actions were discovered.

Rosson then made the decision to base himself in the town of Meridin henceforth. The king's palace was considerably more comfortable and luxurious than his quarters in the military garrison, and, from a strategic point of view, he would be better able to command the townspeople and effect control of the immediate countryside from this location. The local inhabitants were clearly unsure as to what to make of the recent turn of events, but for the moment Rosson was taking no risks, and imposed a strict curfew on the entire area. He had also ordered The Crusader to make a more detailed scan of the immediate area – he was increasingly curious as to who had set off the flare explosions, though he was fairly sure he knew why it had been done. He suspected some form of sabotage, and those responsible would not be getting off lightly. He wanted retribution for the extremely awkward position he now found himself in.

Arrival in Utopia

Interstellar Space - The Star Chaser arrives at Ur Tokar

After its much delayed departure from Zeta Kotlin, The Star Chaser had made its way steadily across the central - largely empty - sector of the Nexus Cluster for a period of nearly sixteen months. It contained the group of scientists and their children that had chosen not to make their new home on Zeta Kotlin, and was now on a direct flight path to Rorque 4 in the hope that the capitalist planet could better meet their expectations than the socialist one they had left behind. The entire body of passengers on board was in stasis, as was standard practice for such a lengthy journey, immersed in the wastelands of sleep that engulfed all those that entered the stasis experience, and oblivious to the starry realm the ship passed silently and undeviatingly. The starship hurtled on, ever forwards, on its two year journey to Rorque 4.

Whilst the starship's passengers slept, it was standard practice for the ship's AI units to log all incoming communications the ship registered, and to remain alert to those that might have either positive or negative consequences for the ship, its passengers and its journey. For the AI units, operating on pre-set algorithms, this was not a process they always managed to engage in correctly, but for one such message logged by The Star Chaser, there were no such difficulties for the AI unit tasked with dealing with in-coming messages. It was the communication emitted by The Spirit of the Age as it had departed from Rorque 4, and The Star Chaser was, of course, one of the desired recipients of the message. Upon receiving the communication, the AI unit duly woke the designated skeleton crew who, as per standard routine, were given time to become fully conscious and renourished and then informed of the contents of the in-coming missive.

The skeleton crew was largely comprised of scientists who had held senior positions at the universities on Alpha Fraczan, and were, of course, generally more favourable to the social system that they believed existed on Rorque 4, than the one they had departed from on Zeta Kotlin. Unsurprisingly, therefore, they listened to the emission with growing dismay and an increasing sense of disbelief and exasperation.

'So the two other stasis ships did definitely divert to Rorque 4 after all and arrive safely; I thought that would probably be the case, but it's nice to have it all confirmed,' stated Petra Xi, previously a senior professor in the computer science department of Cliff Bay University, one of the smaller university establishments on Alpha Fraczan.

'Have we really just spent an extra sixteen months in stasis for nothing, and now, even worse, we need to turn around and head straight back to Zeta Kotlin?' asked Xandra Gomez wearily, looking at the others in disbelief. She had been a leading figure in the science of construction materials at Sienna Pools University and an associate of Mila Lustrom, and had been working on the assumption that her knowledge and engineering skills would be highly regarded and desired by the Rorquean universities.

Mila glanced at her. 'Wait a moment; we need to be sure this is actually correct, there's always the possibility this is not fully accurate, or that it might even be some sort of fake. Have we even verified it as an authentic account?'

'Look at the names of the people who sent it, I recognise Jack Peters and Kate Milstrom – they're reliable people. I worked with them for several years and never had any reason to doubt their abilities or their devotion to their studies and research. Why would you have doubts about the veracity of the message? Why would anyone fake such a message, anyway?' asked Petra.

'Well they failed to receive work contracts with the Rorquean universities, whilst their colleagues were far more successful. They are bound to feel embittered and negative about the whole experience. They are also bound to dissuade us from going there, since their own experiences were such negative ones,' offered Mila, though as she did so, she could already see the problems with this line of thought herself, and had the distinct feeling the others were planning for a halt in the journey whatever she might say.

'But that could happen to any of us. It also states that the planetary economy is performing badly and has been doing so over a prolonged period of time, something like 25 years – that's a long time for an economy to stagnate. If that's the case, I can't see that they'll be looking to take on even more of us, they probably have everyone they want and can afford, if the economy is doing that badly. It doesn't sound like we're heading towards a promising situation,' argued Xandra.

'But they have taken on some of our colleagues, maybe those of us who have the requisite skills and knowledge will be fine, it's possible they may still be looking for additional expertise and personnel,' replied Mila.

'And what about all the others, those that fail to gain contracts - what will happen to them? Presumably the same as happened to those on the other two ships,' offered Petra, who was as dismayed as the others at what they had just learnt, and was mentally trying to calculate her own chances of employment, but was also struggling to decide what criteria she should be using to do so.

'Yes, and what if those without contracts are unable to leave the planet, with no means of departure – it sounds as though they will experience years and years of poverty and underemployment,' interjected Simon Kamenev, formerly a senior figure in chemistry at Red Mountain University. 'That's not something any of us would want to experience, I certainly wouldn't want to. I'm not sure I want to take my chances with such a precarious arrangement. If we can't be guaranteed positions, we need to thoroughly reevaluate our position.'

'They could leave on the Avante . . .' started Mila.

'Unless it was sold to the corporations in payment,' finished Xandra. 'I'm not sure I thought this all through properly either. I'd sort of assumed that Rorque 4 would be similar to our set-up on Alpha, but just more connected to business and revolving more around competition. We would all be valued and all guaranteed a similar lifestyle to that on our home planet. It sounds as though, in reality, it's totally dominated by business interests and run extremely ruthlessly. To be brutally honest, I'm not sure I could cope with that type of system – I want something more civilised.'

The conversation continued in this vein for some time and it became increasingly apparent that they were not all about to agree on any particular position. Mila could also see she was clearly in a minority position – the others all harboured severe doubts about continuing with the journey - and she was even struggling to convince herself of the need to proceed further. The picture of the planet painted by those who had recently departed from Rorque 4 was not at all like the one she had envisaged. She hated to admit it, but Zeta Kotlin now seemed to compare quite favourably – possibly very favourably - with the planet she had only recently chosen as her new destination and home.

'In my opinion, we will need to wake everyone relevant and take a vote. I think it would be unfair to continue the journey knowing what we know now, and that we could be taking large numbers of people into what amounts to a career dead-end, and possibly a lengthy period of living in poverty. I would feel extremely guilty about doing that to anyone,' stated Petra.

'I agree, it clearly needs to go to a democratic vote. We can't, in all honesty, make a decision that big, purely by ourselves. It would be unfair and there could be serious repercussions for all of us if matters went badly wrong on Rorque 4,' added Simon, suddenly wondering what exactly had happened to Alex Kim and Anna Dubois and how they were feeling about developments on Rorque 4.

'Do we have the resources on board in order to keep several thousand people awake, healthy and renourished? Especially if it's for a prolonged period,' asked Mila, still not happy with the turn of events. 'I'm not sure we do.'

'We need to check the inventories, but I would also be surprised if we do; there was an assumption that the journey would be continuous and uninterrupted. Zeta Kotlin didn't supply us with very much – just the essentials I believe, and to be fair they were more than generous whilst we were stuck there temporarily,' answered Xandra. 'We would need to make a fairly quick decision and then re-enter stasis, I doubt we could manage much more than that.'

At this point an AI unit asked permission to speak to those assembled. It had been in contact with the ship's computer and informed the skeleton crew that the spacecraft would soon be passing the red dwarf star Rogan and that one of its orbiting planets, Ur-Tokar, was habitable. Rogan's star system was also highly isolated, being the only one in the central zone of the Nexus Cluster. If they needed supplies, resources, fuel or any other form of planetary help, this was the only opportunity for several months to come.

'Ah, that's the planet with a civilisation that rejects technology, isn't it?' asked Petra.

'What all technology? How is that even possible?' asked Simon.

'I suspect it's above a certain technical level. I would guess anything electrical or more advanced. That's how certain anti-technology cults operated back on Earth – they probably derive from groups such as those,' Mila interjected. As an astrobiologist she had acquired a reasonably good working knowledge of the inhabitants of the planet they had all originated from, and was also familiar with some of the civilisations and ecosystems that existed on different planets across various sectors of near space.

'And they used a space ship to get there!' quizzed Simon.

'Sorry to interrupt your discussion,' interjected Xandra, 'but I think it's more important to know if there will be resources on the planet that we can use. If its low technology, there's unlikely to be much in the way of surplus food. On the other hand, there should be water, we can set up a ferming unit and there might be food we could gather in addition, and possibly other useful resources,' she offered.

'It doesn't sound very promising though,' interjected Mila, 'I'm not convinced this plan will work.'

'I'm not sure we have any other choices,' stated Petra. 'I really think we need to pause this journey and have a major rethink about where we are planning to proceed to. We will just have to make the best of a bad situation and see what Ur-Tokar can offer us.'

The skeleton crew was largely supportive of Petra's suggestion and did not even need a vote to be taken, for even Mila could see that they needed to reevaluate their position, consult the sleeping passengers on board the spaceship, and then make an informed decision as to what they should do next. The starship was placed on a course towards Rogan's stellar system, where it would arrive a few days later, with the aim of settling into orbit around Ur-Tokar, scanning the planet for possible useful resources and waking the passengers on board the ship for an onboard democratic consultation. They would need a major conference to reevaluate their situation, but the exact nature and duration of their visit would depend on what they found on Ur-Tokar.

Ur-Tokar – the Opa-Loka makes several interesting discoveries

Savverio and Janicka had remained on the Opa-Loka throughout the entire period in which the other three Zetans had successfully carried out the plan that had eventually led to the battle of Meridin, and the complete routing of the monarchist army and destruction of its feudal leadership. During this time, they had been keeping a close eye on the strange comings and goings of the Zeleyan stasis ship, The Crusader, and were still largely at a loss as to why it had suddenly departed on a tour of Rogan's planetary system, though it had been far more obvious why the great silver machine had zoomed back with such inordinate haste.

The task of keeping their presence above the planet a secret had been made slightly more problematic by the temporary departure of The Crusader – it was far more difficult to remain in a scanning shadow, whilst they had also needed to keep a close eye on its hurried return. This had in turn made it more difficult to monitor the movements of the crew down below, though ultimately there had been no real concerns about their presence being discovered. Despite all of this, they were fairly certain the Zeleyanian ship was still oblivious to their presence around Ur-Tokar. Nevertheless, at all times, they had kept their second landing craft ready for any imminent rescue that might need to be rapidly undertaken, though exactly how they would have undertaken such a task in a densely forested region, they were not fully sure.

It was routine procedure for the ship's computer on the Opa-Loka to monitor electronic emissions and inter-planetary communications, in their various forms and coded languages, as the trading ship went about its various missions travelling between the planets. In more normal times this simply entailed receiving large amounts of media output and routine communications data emitted from the various planets for their own domestic purposes, and little of any significance was ever logged. However, these were not normal times and over the course of the next few weeks it became apparent to the watcher in the sky above Ur-Tokar, that there was an unusually high amount of space traffic moving around the Nexus Cluster at this point in time. Somewhat ironically, it seemed that most of this hi-tech space transport was heading in the direction of the extremely low-tech planet of Ur-Tokar, or at the very least to the isolated star system of Rogan, which - from a stellar perspective at least - was located in the largely empty central section of the Nexus Cluster.

Firstly, they were already familiar with the fact that an Alpha Fraczan ship known as The Star Chaser had departed from Zeta Kotlin for Rorque 4 sixteen months earlier, and was soon due to skirt past Rogan's stellar system as it headed for the capitalist planet, still approximately another seven months flight away. When this ship duly changed course, slowed and started heading towards Ur-Tokar they had a reasonably good idea as to why this was occurring, since slightly earlier they too had received the transmission from the scientists aboard The Spirit of the Age. However, they immediately identified potential dangers for both themselves and The Star Chaser itself, and Savverio and Janicka made it an immediate priority to contact the approaching ship and bring to its attention the presence of the Zeleyanian military vessel, which by this point had resumed its orbit of Ur-Tokar.

Secondly, they had been aware for some time that two stasis ships containing Alphan scientists had arrived at Rorque 4 about five months earlier, but the message from the scientists had alerted them to the fact that one of these spaceships had departed approximately three months later. Computer records had recognised that ship as the Margallan's The Spirit of the Age, a craft the Opa-Loka had encountered on its occasional visits to Margalla. They were also able to confirm that its initial trajectory was taking it straight towards Zeta Kotlin, with an approximate arrival date of just over two years time – since the ship seemed to be travelling at a slightly slower speed than was standard for stasis ships. The reason for this trajectory had been included in the message sent by the Alpha Fraczan scientists aboard the starship. Savverio and Janicka assumed – correctly - it had also been sent with the intention of informing those left on Zeta Kotlin what exactly they had recently experienced. They also presumed it was to ward off any of their colleagues from making the same mistake they had just made themselves. Janicka duly returned an encrypted message to The Spirit of the Age, informing the vessel of the present situation around Ur-Tokar.

Thirdly and a little later, the Opa-Loka discovered the presence of the Zeleyan invasion fleet heading directly towards Ur-Tokar, on the shortest trajectory possible between the two star systems. They had already assumed that such a fleet was likely to be on its way sooner or later, and this simply proved to be confirmation of their expectations. The ship's computer estimated that the fleet's likely arrival date at the semi-frozen world would be in a little over five months time. This knowledge was relayed to the crew members still below on the planet, and allowed the whole crew to start making plans for their immediate future, both down on the planet below and up above in orbit around Ur-Tokar. The Opa-Loka also kept the spaceport at Earth City on Zeta Kotlin fully informed of all the developments in their region of space with regular updates and appraisals of the situation. In addition, they contacted The Spirit of the Age a further time, to warn them that within a few months they would be in close proximity to the Zeleyanian invasion fleet.

During the course of these discoveries, they had received a brief and encrypted response from The Star Chaser, with a request for guidance and the Opa-Loka's assessment of the present situation on and above Ur-Tokar. It also indicated that its current aim was to pause its journey to Rorque 4, with the intention of acquiring resources and reassessing its destination in the light of the information it had recently received from The Spirit of the Age. This largely confirmed what Savverio and Janicka had already figured out for themselves, and they advised The Star Chaser to perform the same manouevre they were following, in order to evade detection by the Zeleyanian ship and any monitoring capabilities that might still exist at their military base on the planet.

Once The Star Chaser had dropped into the same parking orbit around Ur-Tokar as that of the Opa-Loka, its skeleton crew decided they needed to meet up with the Zetans in order to become better acquainted and fully informed of the situation on the planet beneath them. Petra Xi and Mila Lustrom volunteered for the visit and made the short trip in one of their transporter craft, whilst Simon Kamenev and Xandra Gomez stayed with The Star Chaser. They were welcomed on board, offered refreshments and were soon strapped into their seats around the small conference table in the forward deck ready to hear all about the predicament they found themselves in. After Savverio and Janicka had informed them of the recent events at Meridin, the two scientists fired off a barrage of questions, concerned for their future safety both on and above the planet, and still unsettled by the news from Rorque 4.

'What do you actually know about the Zeleyanian military forces? How large are they? Are they only based around Meridin?' asked Mila. 'They don't seem particularly competent judging by the number of mistakes they've made. Do you know much about their commander, for instance?'

'We know his name is Vice-Admiral Rosson, but obviously we know little about him other than through the communications we've intercepted, which have been largely procedural in nature. He departed on some jaunt around the star system, but we're not sure why he did this. Possibly, he was checking out potential resources or locations for strategic bases, but he hasn't been placing any new communications devices, which is a bit odd. We think they are overly-obsessed with secrecy, which might explain the latter,' answered Savverio. 'His forces were clearly caught unawares whilst he was away, so he was obviously not present for the duration of the battle. His forces – which we think were numbered in the low hundreds - might have been victorious, but given their superior technology and firepower, that was pretty much a foregone conclusion anyway. We don't know what losses they have incurred. We have not detected any Zeleyanian presence anywhere other than at Meridin.'

'Are they aware of your presence here, have they discovered your starship?' asked Petra, apparently satisfied with the previous response.

'We are fairly certain they have not – there is no indication of that, anyway. However, they must know of your departure from Zeta Kotlin, and your intended destination - we've been aware of your position all along. Hopefully, they have been rather preoccupied with other matters recently, so it's possible your arrival in the star system has not yet been registered. Judging from their behaviour, they were clearly not expecting the presence of any other starships in this region of space - their communication equipment looks fairly basic, and so their monitoring systems may not be operating at a high alert level,' answered Janicka.

'Is their ship armed? Do they pose a military threat to us?' asked Mila.

'Their ship is not armed as far as we can tell, it appears to have undergone no major modifications – it looks like a very standard Earth-type stasis ship, so we think we're safe in that respect,' answered Janicka. 'With regards to being an immediate threat - that would seem highly likely. We think their plan is to militarily occupy Ur-Tokar, but after that it's anyone's guess as to what they will do next. We're concerned they might have their sights set on Zeta Kotlin. They are bound to regard us as a major problem if they discover us. Remember, they possess a highly authoritarian and extremely repressive political system – they are very likely to seize us and our ships for their own regime purposes. In our opinion, they are definitely very dangerous,' she concluded.

'What about the level of their technology, the sophistication of their computer systems and such like,' asked Petra, who was already beginning to assess potential means of protecting The Star Chaser, and possibly how she could cause problems for the Zeleyanians.

'It appears to be somewhat below our own levels. There have been technological advances on our own planet over the decades, but no really significant leaps and bounds since we arrived over a century ago. Our main concern and priority has always been to ensure that access to all technology is freely available to the entire population, and so most advances have been made with this purpose in mind,' Savverio stated with some degree of certainty, though he wasn't sure of the exact details. 'That was highly unlikely to be the main priority on Zeleyan – more likely their main priority was the security of the regime – but their level of technology does not seem to be fundamentally different from when they departed from Earth, as far as we can tell – it looks fairly standard, slightly basic even,' he surmised.

'That's interesting to know, replied Petra, 'computer science and electronic communications happen to be my area of expertise, and we have made major and significant advances in that field during our time on Alpha Fraczan. It would be worth investigating just how easy it is to break their security codes and gain access to the ship's computer without their knowledge. If you have no objections, I would definitely be interested in giving that a go.'

Janicka suddenly looked very interested, 'that could tip the balance of forces strongly in our direction. If we could control their ship, that offers us a whole range of possible scenarios. We could send it back to Zeleyan . . . though on second thoughts, out into deep space might be a much better option.'

'Would you have any use for it at Zeta Kotlin?' offered Mila, helpfully.

'That's probably not a good idea. Stealing another planet's stasis ship could provoke an interstellar incident – even if it is here for hostile or illicit purposes. It's not the type of attention our planet needs or wants. Deep space would be a better option, but we'd still need to manage the whole situation carefully and correctly. We could inform the approaching Zeleyanian military fleet that its presence here was an act of war, so its ejection from Rogan's system was an entirely legitimate act, and not one that should have repercussions for our planet,' offered Janicka. After a moment's thought though, she added, 'though I suspect a regime such as theirs would still see that as a reason to attack us anyway.'

'Would you be able to lock them permanently out of their ship's communication systems, so they have no means of retrieving the ship? Is that a possibility?' asked Savverio.

'It should definitely be a possibility. It depends how sophisticated their de-encryption programmes are, but if ours are far more advanced - as I suspect is the case - I doubt they would be able to regain access to the system,' replied Petra. 'I need to work out the finer details of how we would actually carry this all out, but theoretically it should all be entirely possible.'

'We'll still have the problem of the invasion fleet coming, but it would be one problem out of the way, at least, and it must weaken their forces down on the planet,' suggested Savverio, somewhat optimistically.

'Sorry to change the conversation, but there is another matter we need to know about,' interjected Mila. 'Do you know if there are sufficient resources on the planet to sustain a few thousand passengers for several days? We need to wake all our people from stasis and consult them on the subject of where we should journey next. Our original plans might not be as popular as we had previously thought,' stated Mila, who upon further reflection, had also started to question the wisdom of heading to Rorque 4. At Sienna Pools University, as a senior academic, she had always enjoyed a high degree of autonomy and control over her work and her research, and thus a level of independence she had very much become accustomed to. She had initially assumed that this could be continued on Rorque 4, but the recent news from her former colleagues aboard The Spirit of The Age had now made her question this - what now seemed highly speculative – assumption.

'Yes, we figured that might be the case; we intercepted the communication from The Spirit of the Age. Their experience accords with everything we've ever heard about Rorque 4,' noted Janicka. She was about to question the wisdom of The Star Chaser's original decision to leave her home planet for a capitalist one at this point, but then thought better of it - a prolonged political argument at this moment in time was probably not what either crew needed, especially as they were intent on joint collaboration.

'With regards to resources on Ur-Tokar, I think you might have difficulties in that respect. They have very basic farming technology so very limited surpluses, if any at all. The locals will definitely not be able to supply food for that many people. We know the oceans and forests have edible resources - especially if you still eat animals - and there are nuts, fruits and vegetables, of course, in the vegetated zones if you forage for them, but again, for thousands, that might be difficult. The logistics make that problematic. How are you equipped for AI units and ferming labs?' she asked.

'We do have some of those, so it sounds as though we might just manage, if that's the case. I assume there are plenty of sites we can descend to safely that are sufficiently far from the Zeleyanian forces,' Mila enquired.

'The planet is very sparsely populated, especially the interiors of the continents, it's mostly terra mystica as far as we are concerned. It appears that some areas have no habitations at all, or certainly not ones large enough to show up on our scans. Other than the monarchists in the lowlands, there are also some forest dwellers that live in very low population densities in the numerous forested mountains. The majority of the coastlines are constituted by steep cliffs and fjords, though there are a small number of coastal fishing villages in a few scattered sheltered bays and inlets. The planet has few major rivers systems, so there are no deltas, and little in the way of freshwater marshes. You do have a variety of options, but in terms of gathering food, there's nowhere that looks substantially more promising than anywhere else, as far as I can see,' explained Janicka, at some length.

Despite Janicka's caution, the boarding party from The Star Chaser was reasonably assured by the information they had obtained from the two Zetans. The situation down on Ur-Tokar appeared to be one they would be able to work within, at least for the foreseeable future. Mila decided to return to The Star Chaser, where Xandra and Simon had made more detailed scans of the planet with a view to identifying suitable landing and foraging locations. The ferming labs could be located almost anywhere, so sources of berries, nuts, fruit and vegetables were their main priority. Petra, however, remained on the Opa-Loka with Savverio and Janicka with the intention of further devising and finalising a plan for dealing with the Zeleyanian stasis ship.

Whilst they were engaged in this task, their ship's monitoring system also became aware of occasional messaging between Rorque Corporation satellites and the Zeleyanian invasion fleet, and, after some deliberation on the matter, the crew figured they had a pretty good idea of why this was occurring. They made the decision to contact The Spirit of the Age again, though this time to acquire more information with regards to specific elements of the situation on Rorque 4, and what they knew of the dealings between the Rorque Corporation and the scientists who had arrived from Alpha Fraczan. They were already aware - from corporate media emissions - of the unfolding political situation on Rorque 4 and the changing positions of the various corporations and political parties. Confirmation of their theory from the Margallans might prove very useful for the future plans they were developing.

Amidst all this monitoring of space communications conducted by Savverio and Janicka, they also remained in continuous contact with their fellow crew members down below on Ur-Tokar, who had by now returned to Lato and decided to remain within the community there a little longer. Naturally, they kept them abreast of the latest developments in space and the plans they were now working on with the Alphan scientists, whilst also enquiring of developments on the planet's surface. It was during the course of one of these dialogues that they discovered matters down below on the planet had taken a turn for the unexpected.

Ur-Tokar – rebel conference at Lato

Jiaying, Neema, Kahlil, Topaz, Rowan and Indigo had all been able to watch the battle of Meridin play out in its two separate acts. At the point when they realised the Zeleyanian forces were seizing full control of Meridin, they had decided to effect a quick departure from the area, just in case the soldiers sent out search parties looking for those responsible for the flare explosions that had initiated the whole episode. They made the long trek through the forested domain on foot back to Lato without any significant incidents, their minds focused largely on the possibilities that the battle's outcome might engender. The two groups did, however, take the opportunity to further enhance their knowledge of each other and the communities they lived in, and discovered they had more in common than perhaps they first thought. Whilst their distinct approaches to technology were clearly a major difference, they did find common areas of agreement such as a dislike of hierarchal social systems and arbitrary rule, respect for the natural environment, and a love of freedom, though always one that should be enjoyed equally by all, rather than based on a narrow and selfish individualism.

When they arrived back at Lato early one calm still evening, the dimly lit main street through the settlement was deserted, save for one small boy playing with a wooden horse on the street in front of his house. Nevertheless, their arrival back in Lato had been eagerly and anxiously anticipated, and once news of their return had spread, a small crowd gathered in the Hall of the Mountain Grill to hear the details of their adventure. Topaz, in particular, took great delight in retelling the misfortunes of the monarchist forces – despite the long years, she had not forgotten the massacre at Greenback, and was always keen to cause problems for their erstwhile enemy. Upon finishing their tale, a series of discussions broke out amongst the assembled group, all speculating on how they could take advantage of this fortunate turn of events.

The Zetan crew had also been kept informed of the unfolding developments around the planet's orbit by Savverio and Janicka of the Opa-Loka and, after some discussion, decided they had no choice but to fully trust the people of Lato with their newfound information. Jiaying informed those gathered in the tavern of the plan to effectively strand the Zeleyanian forces on the planet by means of seizing their stasis ship and sending it out into the infinity of deep space. They were also informed that the main Zeleyanian invasion fleet was due in slightly less than five months time, and there was a general agreement that they needed to rout Rosson's forces on the planet before this eventuality actually occurred. This would hopefully create difficulties for the arriving forces, and it might even make them think twice before carrying their invasion plan through to the full.

Jiaying related some of the information they were receiving from their ship. 'The Zeleyanians might now control Meridin, but they still aren't fully in control of the situation. Our scans indicate they are currently rebuilding their military base, and we also know they are sending scouting parties out into the areas around Meridin, presumably to discover the source of the flares we exploded,' she explained. 'We need to find ways to harass their forces and disrupt their activities, whilst they are still underprepared and disorganised and uncertain as to exactly what occurred and why.'

'But even if we were successful in that endeavour, how can we stop a heavily armed invasion force from landing on the planet and seizing control? We don't have the forces or the firepower to prevent that,' asked Autumn, who had earlier been delighted to see the return of her friends. Like all those gathered in the tavern, she was delighted by news of the complete demise of the monarchist forces, and was as keen as everyone else to press ahead against their enemies, but at the same time was well aware that their military capabilities were pretty limited.

'Our crew on the Opa-Loka is working on a plan; we have some ideas on how we might discourage the invasion fleet - to put them back in the box they came from. We're also hoping our planet's governing body can offer some advice and help, though that's probably a long shot,' explained Kahlil. 'It's probably best if we deal with one problem at a time. We need to deal with the Zeleyanians that are here first, and then worry about those coming later.'

'And, the fascist troops might have superior firepower and technology at the moment, but if they're cut off from their ship, they will have finite amounts of ammunition, resources and energy. Half their base and armoury are already destroyed, so if we can find ways of destroying or damaging the rest of their forces, their position here will become that much more precarious,' added Neema.

'I think it is now essential that we do indeed make every effort possible to destroy their army and as quickly as possible,' stated a middle-aged man called Dettmar, who had previously been very quiet, and who Topaz identified to the group as one of those who lived in the remoter cabins further out in the mountain forests. 'I think we can all rejoice in the fact that the monarchist forces have been thoroughly decimated, but we need to press ahead whilst we have the advantage, and take this opportunity to completely eradicate the appalling feudal regime the monarchists have imposed on this planet. If we can encourage the peasants and townspeople to rise up against the Zeleyanians, rebel against their oppression and then adopt our way of life, we can then preempt any attempt to resurrect an alternative aristocratic hierarchy. We could finally be rid of their menace forever whilst also removing the Zeleyanians, and live a truly peaceful and prosperous existence on this planet, for once.'

'They're a pretty docile lot though; they might just accept the Zeleyanians as their new overlords – still subservient but with new masters,' suggested Raven, reflecting a widespread opinion of the feudal peasantry held by the Mountain People. 'Are you sure we should rely on the support of an unreliable group like that?'

'I think it's unfair to call them docile, they've never known anything other than complete subservience,' Topaz intervened. 'If we can show them a better way of life exists, I'm sure they will be able to change their ways. If there's no set of people to oppress and exploit them – new or old - they must be able to see the advantages of switching to our way to living,' she argued. 'They are human after all; they can't be totally stupid, surely.'

'Well even if that does turn out to be the case, it's more essential than ever that we devise a strategy for eliminating the Zeleyanian forces, before they have a chance to bed in as their new masters. We'll have to hope the Opa-Loka's plan to thwart the invasion force is successful. If not . . . well, I guess we'll just have to cross that bridge when we come to it,' responded Dettmar. 'In the meantime, we need to start organising and as quickly as possible.'

'Any plan we devise needs to play to our strengths and to their weaknesses,' stated Jiaying, who was starting to revel in their newfound situation, and beginning to feel as though she was some form of revolutionary guerilla fighter. 'We have a much better knowledge of the planet and its terrain than the Zeleyanians. We have a better knowledge of the local people – whether they are likely to help us or not, and other relevant matters. They're main weakness is that they have a very rigid and hierarchal command structure – if we can eliminate or remove the leadership, then the base is much easier to deal with. Their troops are habituated to following orders; they have limited experience of acting autonomously and thinking for themselves – possibly none at all. With no issuing orders to follow, they won't know what to do. That is then our greatest opportunity – we can encourage them to disarm if we can convince them their lives are not in danger.'

'I would also imagine that some of their troops will be conscripts, others will only be in the army because they performed poorly in the educational system. They'll probably have no great desire to actually be on a half-frozen planet they are completely unfamiliar with. I bet they'd rather be back on warm, sunny Zeleyan,' added Kahlil. 'That could help us as well. If we can make their lives as miserable as possible here, that might increase their desire to pack up and leave.'

'Right, so we need to harass and undermine the morale of the soldiers - we know how to do that, we've been doing it for years to the monarchist forces. But what we need most of all is a plan that separates the head from the body,' summarised Raven and paused for a moment. 'Any ideas anyone?' he asked.

There then followed several suggestions as to how they might take on the Zeleyanian forces. Their self-sufficiency in food and resources eliminated some of these possible plans, and the Mountain People's own lack of advanced military technology precluded a range of other options. Eventually, however, the informal conference at Lato finally opted for a plan that Jiaying, Kahlil and Neema all considered to be extremely risky and harboured major doubts about. The Mountain People – despite their long-running conflict with the monarchist lowlanders – still had a number of contacts and associates amongst the townspeople of Meridin, and they planned to use these contacts to infiltrate the town and the castle, seize the military leadership and then remove them physically from the town. They would then hold them ransom and demand the disarming and disbanding of the military in exchange for their safe return.

Jiaying, in particular, thought the whole operation sounded risky and fraught with problems; at so many junctures it could all go disastrously wrong. However, in the absence of any better strategy she kept her silence; the people of Lato and its environs had been involved with a long-running, albeit low-level, conflict with the monarchists, and had scored several successes over the years. Maybe they had reasons to be optimistic about this approach. And after all, they understood many aspects of the situation far better than she did, she figured. Nevertheless, given the Zetans had been partially responsible for the present situation, she also felt they needed to volunteer to help with the success of the mission - despite her misgivings about its likelihood of success.

'We'd like to offer as much help as we possibly can with the operation,' offered Jiaying, after consulting briefly with Kahlil and Neema. 'We can use our constant contact with our starship to help monitor the developing situation in the town, and use our advanced communications to keep everyone informed of what is occurring as the mission progresses.'
She had not expected the response that came from Rowan though. 'I don't think you and your people should be involved in the mission, not on the ground anyway,' he stated in a very considered manner. 'It's a high risk operation and if you are captured they will hold you ransom with the aim of gaining control of your starship. That would substantially improve their strategic position. We cannot afford to take that risk,' and he paused to gauge the reaction of the gathering. When no one raised any objections, he continued. 'I think you should concentrate on your plan to seize their spaceship and leave the ground-level operations to us. It will be safer that way. We appreciate what you have done so far, but we need to fight our own battles. It's crucial that we improve our relations with the lowlanders that are left now. The monarchist leadership – the aristocrats - always used us as a means of retaining control over the lowlanders. They claimed we were a threat and a danger to their way of life, and that their rule was essential for the security of the lowlanders and a means of countering the threat we supposedly portrayed. We need to pursue this operation in such a way that we can break down the barriers between our two peoples and unite our forces against the Zeleyanians. If we are successful in that endeavour, then it will be so much easier to pave the way for a new and more peaceful society

for all of us,' he concluded. Those around him nodded with approval, and he received a few appreciative pats on the back.

The Zetans were slightly taken aback for a moment by this statement, but after a short period of reflection they realised that the long-running conflict between the two peoples must have provoked a whole range of ideas about how to reshape society on their planet, so it was perhaps not surprising that the people of Lato had decided to pursue this particular strategy. It sounded like some of them had been considering this for some time now. And at the end of the day, it was their planet, so they had a right to decide how they should conduct their own affairs.

'That's fine by us,' Jiaying stated, glancing at the other two for approval, 'we will fight them up in space and you will fight them on the ground. With a two-pronged attack we have a much better chance of success.'

The others nodded their agreement, and the local inhabitants and the various Mountain People assembled in the tavern seemed remarkably pleased with this outcome. Their reaction was as if this was the day when the wall could come down – one that had been separating different peoples for far too long, but was now due for imminent destruction. Jiaying wondered if there was something else she didn't know about, and concluded that there was probably a great deal - but now was not the time to ask about it. She still wanted to raise the matter of their mining operations in the area - she was concerned that if they needed to make a hurried departure from the star system, they would be returning to Zeta Kotlin with an empty ship - but felt that too was an inappropriate subject for the present moment.

With their plans and impromptu conference concluded though, it was time for some celebrations and the ever increasing crowd that had developed during the course of the evening dispersed across the tavern. Soon flagons of ale were being quaffed and the local produce – of which the Zetans frequently remarked upon its excellent quality - consumed in large quantities. The people at Lato had much to celebrate, the return of their fellow inhabitants from a successful mission, the destruction of the hated monarchist leadership and a plan formulated to defeat the Zeleyanian forces and bring peace to their planet. They had not had much good news of late, but to the Zetans it looked as though they were determined to make the most of this particular success, and the crew joined in wholeheartedly.

As the night developed and the celebrations continued, though, Jiaying began to feel weary from her recent exertions and retired momentarily to a wooden bench towards the end of the tavern, and sat quietly for a while taking in the atmosphere in the Hall of the Mountain Grill. It had been a long and tiring day. She looked around at the grey stone walls, the colourful tapestries on the wall, the wooden furnishings, the fire burning in the great hearth, the loud and mirthful conversations of the tavern goers and the tables covered in flagons of ale and great piles of food. There was nothing quite like this on Zeta Kotlin and she was suddenly caught, almost schizophrenically, between two moods – an appreciation for the warmth and bonhomie of her present convivial surroundings, but a sudden longing for the modern familiarity of her home planet. She spent a few minutes absently thinking about her life back on Zeta Kotlin, her recent problems and her future plans, but a loud burst of laughter suddenly brought her back to her surroundings.

She looked around the tavern once again and suddenly felt far more positive about their whole situation – maybe it was the contagious optimism of the taverners, she figured. She had some major misgivings about the plan the locals had formulated, but perhaps they had their own good reasons to be optimistic, she mused. She then made a conscious decision that now was not the time to engage in personal self-reflection or dwell on her doubts, and so she joined Kahlil, Neema and the others at one of the large wooden tables covered in food and drink in the centre of the tavern. With renewed vigour, she decided to make the most of the celebrations, - it might be their last opportunity for some time - and spent the rest of the night partying, as the settlement of Lato celebrated long and hard into the small hours of the cold dark night.

Arrival in Utopia

Ur-Tokar – the Zeleyanian space ship is seized

Back on The Opa-Loka, Savverio, Janicka and Petra had, after some deliberation, arrived at an agreed plan for attempting to seize control of the Zeleyanian ship, The Crusader, and then projecting it out far into the depths of space. Petra, with her vastly superior knowledge of computer systems, had quickly become the leading protagonist in the endeavour. Young, bright and enthusiastic, with long wavy brown hair, large glasses and an equally large smile, she proved to be remarkably easy to work with. Savverio and Janicka quickly discovered she was highly confident and competent, and someone who could take quick and decisive actions.

Untypically - for a computer scientist - it turned out she was also particularly accomplished at sports and other demanding physical activities. On Alpha Fraczan, her somewhat diametrically opposed interests meant she had tended not to fit in too well with any one particular group, and she had ultimately been a bit of a social misfit. It was for this reason that she had made the decision to head for Rorque 4, because she felt their individualist society would better suit her unorthodox personality, and feared she might not fit in well with Zeta Kotlin's far more communalist approach. Despite these misgivings, though, they noted she had no particular difficulties working with them on the Opa-Loka.

Equally importantly, she was always keen to try out new experiences and take on new challenges, and with regards to devising a plan to seize The Crusader, the two Zetans figured that she turned out to be almost the perfect person for the job. For the most part, the plan relied on Petra's advanced knowledge of computer communications systems, but still involved taking a number of risks with some fine margins of error. Petra had initially considered using the planet's satellite system to implement their plan, but, upon further investigation, discovered this would be technologically problematic, and the scheme therefore necessitated the Opa-Loka being in direct communications contact with the Zeleyanian ship. She had, nevertheless, been able to use the satellite system to gain what she considered to be a sufficiently good knowledge of The Crusader's operating systems for her scheme to succeed.

In order to effect the plan successfully, they had calculated the optimum orbital position for their strategy – one that involved careful positioning of their own spacecraft in relation to both The Crusader and the Zeleyanian military base at Meridin – in order to avoid detection, and then moved their craft into the pre-calculated position. The Opa-Loka waited until it had just entered the far side of the planet from the base at Meridin – and thus in its communication shadow – and accelerated rapidly towards the shadow zone behind the Zeleyanian ship so that, whilst still distant from the vessel, it was now possible for the Opa-Loka to be detected electronically.

Petra rapidly set about hacking into the ship's computer on The Crusader, fairly certain she could take it by surprise and without alerting any of its warning systems. At the same time, she also took control of the operating system controlling the AI units. The relatively basic operating systems – by Alphan standards - being used on the Zeleyanian ship meant she was able to achieve this without any great deal of difficulty. For her highly elevated level of expertise, the security protocols, protections and other warning devices on The Crusader were pretty simplistic devices that she was easily able to dismantle or even bypass altogether. Once inside the system, she launched a range of protocols to hide the fact that she was now operating within the ship's computer system, and set about dismantling all the relevant alarm systems and other warning devises.

Once sure that she was in effective control, she then set about manipulating the ventilation and life support systems on the ship. The Crusader only had a skeleton crew left aboard and Petra was able to slowly diminish the oxygen supply to the point where she believed the crew would lapse into unconsciousness. Holding the oxygen level at this point, she waited a while and then checked the life support analysis systems, which did indeed indicate the crew was now unconscious. The Opa-Loka then very quickly launched one of its transporter craft and flew Mila, Janicka and the rest of their team to the Zeleyanian ship. Petra was able to remotely open the cargo doors with little difficulty and allow its entry onto the stasis ship.

Wearing protective space suits, the team members made their way carefully and methodically around the stasis ship to make sure they found each and every one of the unconscious crew members. Whilst still unconscious they were placed securely into stasis pods, and once in the tube each was immersed into the deep sleep of suspended animation. The team members then departed hastily from the ship. Whilst this had been occurring, Petra had taken full control of the ship's computer, reprogrammed the controls and protocols governing the ship and – once the others had departed from the ship - sent it rapidly and immediately out of Rogan's star system and deep out into interstellar space. She also programmed the ship's computer to send regular messages to the military base below informing it that the ship's systems would be down for a short period of time, in order to repair a major fault it had recently detected within the communications system.

Despite an awareness of the extremely unpleasant nature of the Zeleyanian military regime, neither the Zetan space traders nor the Alphan scientists had wanted to actually kill or badly harm any of the soldiers aboard the ship. As such, there had been a long conversation as to where they should actually send the ship once it was captured. Mila had joked that they should send it in the same direction as the three stasis ships following Itzel's plan to colonise a new planet far out across the near galaxy several light years away. Itzel had not actually informed them of her planned destination, but the scientists had, nevertheless, subsequently calculated the destination of the ships from their initial trajectory, and they were almost certainly headed for the star system of Alchemy.

In the absence of any better ideas, Petra had decided to actually implement this idea, though with some slight modifications. Once she had keyed in this trajectory for The Crusader, she also locked in her own control protocols across the ship's systems for the duration of its starflight over the next seven years. After this period, control would be rescinded back to the AI units stationed on the ship. Once this was effected, the AI units would then be able to carry out all of their designated standard ship routines. They would return to making relevant semi-autonomous judgements defined within their preset programming system; judgements such as to whether the ship should continue onwards towards its destination, or, if necessary, slow or deviate to deal with any potential hazards identified by the ship – as per standard stasis ship procedure.

Later, feeling a touch guilty about their joke, they had sent a message to Itzel's section of the diaspora to explain their actions and the fact that they were not based on any form of malice, just a matter of expediency. They wondered what Itzel would make of it all, and burst out laughing hysterically for several minutes. Would they want the Zeleyanian ship and its occupants? Would the Zeleyanians – perhaps woken by the AI units to make a decision they themselves were incapable of taking - want to continue with their voyage and join the Alphan scientists? The answer to both questions was likely to be in the negative, but that would all be a very long time in the future, and of little immediate import.

More importantly though, they waited until the stasis ship had departed some considerable distance from Rogan's system, and then sent an open message to both the military base at Meridin on the planet and to the Zeleyanian invasion fleet informing them of the action they had just undertaken. They also made it clear to both military groups that the whole of the Nexus Cluster now knew of their presence on Ur-Tokar – a move they hoped would make the invasion fleet reconsider their planned imperial occupation. They were increasingly convinced that Ur-Tokar's occupation was only the first stage in a Zeleyanian plan to establish an inter-planetary empire across the whole sector, and not just a one-off incident. They also informed the spaceport at Earth City on Zeta Kotlin and The Spirit of the Age of their recent action and its successful completion.

Interstellar Space – the Zeleyanian invasion fleet receives a message from Ur-Tokar

The ships of the Zeleyanian invasion fleet sped through the deep dark coldness of empty space, three small points of white light steadily powering their way through the immense distance that separated the bright star of Hedilla on the outer edge of the Nexus Cluster from the red dwarf, Rogan, towards its near-empty centre. Throughout the entirety of the voyage, the three ships retained a fixed formation, almost as though they were physically attracted to each other in some strange but invisible manner, whilst also maintaining a steady travelling velocity and remaining steadfastly on their fixed trajectory, in the highly regimented manner that was typical of all matters Zeleyanian.

For The Patriot IV and its companion ships, The Destroyer and The Invincible, the planned journey to Ur-Tokar would take the best part of eight months. For the first three of these months nothing of any consequence occurred. The ship's computers navigated their way through the dark bleakness of space and implemented minor course adjustments when and where necessary, avoiding rogue pieces of space debris and any other potential dangers to the fleet. On board the ships, the AI units went about their business quietly and methodically performing routine maintenance tasks and repairs. Within the stasis pods, thousands of soldiers lay comatose, deep in sleep, too unconscious to even dream. The ship's computer monitored their vital signs and adjusted conditions as and when their support systems indicated was necessary. All in all, the ships made good progress towards their intended destination.

After three months of uninterrupted travel, an encrypted message arrived at the Patriot IV. The ship's computer logged the message and noted its status. Instructions were sent out to an AI unit to awaken the Supreme Commander and his two most senior ranking officers, General Neumann and Lieutenant-General Tarrafel. The procedures for bringing them out of stasis were implemented, and several hours later the three senior officers were sat strapped into seats on the forward deck being attended to by AI units plying them with the required renourishment drinks and food. When the ship's computer judged sufficient time had lapsed for them to effect a full and sufficient recovery from stasis, it identified the code status of the communication it had received and asked permission to relay the message to the officers. Vartin, recognising the code name attached to the message, ordered immediate transmission of the message.

Military base on Ur-Tokar attacked and damaged by enemy forces. Vice-Admiral Rosson touring outer planets and not present at time of incursion. Captain Peran successfully defended base, destroyed enemy forces and seized enemy capital. Significant casualties suffered. Rosson now returned and commanding depleted forces from enemy capital. Awaiting further instructions.

Vartin was still slightly groggy from the effects of stasis, and his mind was still only slowly working its way back to a full stage of consciousness. It took a while for the full implications of the message to dawn on Vartin, but when they finally registered he blew his top. Containers, books and any other object within his reach were hurled towards the walls – though in a low gravity environment this did not quite achieve its desired effect - and a string of expletives and abuse launched in Rosson's metaphorical direction.

'That fucking bungling idiotic moron Rosson! How dare he conquer the planet? What unbelievable incompetence. How can the man be so fucking useless? I give him one simple task to perform and he cocks up on a monumental scale like this. Unbelievable! Who the hell does he think he is? He's finished, he's a dead man. I'm not standing for this level of treason and incompetence,' ranted Vartin almost apoplectically, and carried on ranting in the same vein for several minutes more.

Still seething with fury several minutes later, Vartin ordered the ship's computer to issue a return communication to the source of the message, authorised using his own highly personal security code.

Arrest Rosson and detain for court martial upon my arrival. Assume command of forces through implementation of Directive 5, Variation 3. Reply when successfully implemented and maintain contact. Supply details of present position and of enemy forces.

General Neumann and Lieutenant-General Tarrafel nodded approvingly. For a considerable time now they had both considered Rosson to have been significantly over-promoted and unworthy of the position he held. A far more junior role would have suited him, in their opinion; one where he could cause significantly fewer problems. They had, of course, known him at Military Academy, and whilst he was pleasant enough as an individual, in their opinion he lacked the necessary leadership abilities of a senior commander. They were under no illusions that his considerable family connections explained much of his rise through the ranks, though additionally they had also calculated that Vartin had presumably regarded him as offering no personal threat to his authority. Promoting such people, though, had its drawbacks as was now glaringly obvious. Rosson had - as far as High Command was concerned - been on probation these last few months, and he had now failed to secure long-term tenure in the most spectacular of ways. His future as a senior commander – possibly as a human being – was now completely over.

Several hours later, Vartin had still not fully calmed down, but he then informed the two senior officers – to their surprise - that they would be remaining out of stasis for the rest of the journey. If there were further unexpected and unfortunate developments, they needed to be ready and awake to deal with any ongoing situations. Vartin, henceforth, would need to be fully in command of events and in complete control of the situation. They glanced at each other and wondered what five months on board a spaceship with an angry Vartin would be like. Neither officer could imagine the time passing quickly or particularly pleasantly.

Ur-Tokar – Vice-Admiral Rosson reconsiders his position

It was late afternoon in Meridin and Vice-Admiral Rosson was seated in one of King Alfonso's favourite chairs in what had previously been the royal banquet hall, but had now been converted into the military operations room of the Zeleyanian forces on Ur-Tokar. Rosson gazed round the stone walls of the building, taking in the various banners, tapestries and animal trophy heads displayed upon its high vaulted walls. The former banquet hall was very similar to the ones he had seen portrayed on old Earth movies set in the medieval periods; so much so, in fact, that whoever had designed this particular room seemed to have been deliberately replicating an exact scene from of one of these ancient films. He wondered at the mentality of those who had travelled light years across space with the sole purpose of recreating an ancient period of Earth's history. They must have been either misty-eyed romantics or complete fools - he wasn't sure which – possibly both.

He was paying a visit to the military operations room after an unproductive day in his office, but his thoughts had quickly returned to his own precarious position. For a short period of time he was probably safe enough, he considered, but once the invasion fleet arrived, or Vartin's spy initiated communication with the invasion fleet, matters could change abruptly. He was sure Vartin would regard his recent conduct as reckless and unacceptable – he might even face a court martial. However, if he could quickly discover who Vartin's spy was and find some way of eliminating him, he would then be in a position to alter the facts of the story in order to show himself in a much better light – that he himself had been personally responsible for routing the monarchist troops, despite being taken by surprise – and then he might be seen as the hero of the hour, rather than the commander who had bungled the mission. His officers could be expected to confirm his version of the story. This, he figured, was probably his best course of action.

At least their presence on the planet was still not known to the rest of the planets in the Nexus Cluster - especially Zeta Kotlin - he assumed, though there was still the question of who had launched the explosive flares. Interrogation of the townspeople had drawn a complete blank with regards to that particular issue. He was still awaiting reports from his scouting parties in the forest, though worryingly two of them appeared to have lost contact with both the base and the stasis ship. The stasis ship itself - upon completing further scans of their immediate vicinity - had discovered some remote and isolated villages in the forests and mountains, but nothing that looked like the source of a higher level of technology. All this both puzzled and worried Rosson. He remembered that when they first arrived at Ur-Tokar they had found the planet's satellite system to be locked down to keep out intruders. Maybe this was not the doing of the planet's founders as part of their anti-technology drive, as he had assumed, but the action of more recently arrived visitors.

His mind turned once again to who might be Vartin's spy, or even whether there might be more than one. He considered which of the various senior officers was most likely to be the secret agent from High Command. There was Major Pushkov, a very orthodox straight-down-the-line sort of officer who always played strictly by the rules and never set a foot wrong. He had always thought that any successful undercover agent would take on such a persona; their chief aim would be to not attract any untoward attention, to fit into any particular team perfectly, and thus remain above notice and suspicion.

But maybe everyone thought that way, so possibly Lieutenant Walker was the spy – more of a braggart and a boaster than Pushkov, a somewhat vain character with a gambling problem, though often considered by the junior officers to be good for entertainment purposes and drinking sessions. Walker was popular with many of the soldiers and some of the officers – maybe that was a better approach for a spy – to be popular and unexpectedly unorthodox. Rosson thought this to be unlikely though; Walker was a somewhat ineffectual character.

Or could it be the slightly irritating Colonel Normanton, who frequently demanded better of everyone, presumably indicating to all and sundry that he was an entirely devoted supporter of Supreme Commander Vartin and his regime, and thus somewhat superior to those around him. Or was an ultra-loyalist too obvious a choice? It could be a double bluff, of course – to choose the most obvious officer as your secret agent. And these three were not the only possible choices - he could imagine reasons as to why any of the officers might be the spy, or any of them might not be the spy. Rosson reluctantly admitted he was not a particularly great judge of character, and was entirely unsure of who he should be focusing on.

He decided he needed a plan to flush out and uncover who exactly the agent was, but so far he was at a loss as to how to go about this. He had imagined all sorts of scenarios, but had rejected each in turn as either unworkable, too obvious, or as making his already tenuous position even more untenable. He had even briefly considered whether it could be arranged for the entire senior officer class – presumably including the spy - to be disposed of in an 'accident' – a transporter ship crash, or something of that nature. He wondered if this was way too outlandish, or could he justify it as a case of the ends justifying the means. What reason could he concoct for the entire officer class to all be together – possibly a high-level meeting? He would need to promote junior officers if this was to occur, but that was not too much of a problem. Would his own position remain secure under such circumstances, though, he wondered? He had decided not to run with this idea, but as the invasion fleet neared he might need to reconsider this option.

He then began to wonder whether his position at this very moment was as genuinely safe as he first thought. The official reason he had given as to why he had been unable to offer immediate help to the garrison when it fell under attack, was that he had been touring the planetary system for reconnaissance purposes – to ascertain the possibility of securing further bases, locating supplementary communications stations and identifying useful resources. This reason had been disseminated to the ranks and junior officers, but those with him on The Crusader – and this included some of the senior officers - knew this to be almost entirely untrue, and he wondered if the real reason had, in fact, become common knowledge amongst the lower ranks. If this was the case, then should one of his senior officers - the spy, for instance - seek to depose him in the near future, his loss of prestige would probably count against him in any power struggle. It was surely better if he moved quickly, before anyone moved against him. But what exactly should his move be?

It was whilst Rosson was lost in these solitary mind games, that the Communications Officer Sub-Lieutenant Schultz suddenly announced he had received an unusual message from The Crusader. He had been concerned about the status of the ship for much of the day now - receiving only a routine and repeated communication from the starship, even after making requests for specific information - and had been wondering why his requests were being delayed by the crew on the stasis ship. He was further hampered by the fact that his communications equipment on the planet was technically limited – for the purposes of secrecy - and he was thus working with inferior resources anyway. The repair work to the communications system seemed to be taking much longer than the message from the stasis ship was repeatedly indicating, and so a suddenly very different message arriving had taken him completely by surprise.

Rosson was still lost deep in thought, considering his personal position and his various options, and had only a half a mind on what was actually occurring around him, and just instructed Sub-Lieutenant Schultz to broadcast the message within the room. The message was the one Petra had logged into the ship's computer and was now being beamed back to the planet, but also in the direction of Vartin's invasion fleet.

We have taken control of your stasis ship, The Crusader. It is now beyond Rogan's star system and at this very minute is accelerating rapidly along a trajectory to the distant star of Alchemy, located in the sector of the celestial sky dominated by Spiral Galaxy 28948 and within the Kadu Flyer constellation. The star is a distance of 7.8 light years away and so the ship will arrive there approximately twenty-two years from now. None of the crew on board was harmed. This is an open message being transmitted to all Zeleyanian forces. We have also informed all the planets of the Nexus Cluster of your military actions. We strongly advise you to call off your invasion of Ur-Tokar and return to Zeleyan.

Rosson had initially leapt to his feet in surprise when the message had commenced, but he now slumped back, almost in resignation, into the former king's large, leather-padded, comfy chair. He was too stunned to be angry, and too shocked to find someone to blame. He sunk into the chair and suddenly felt incredibly tired and weary, as though the weight of the world was entirely upon his shoulders. He could not believe his recent run of bad luck. Previous to his mission to Ur-Tokar, his career had been moving along at a promising pace. His promotion, voyages, meetings and personal experiences all seemed to be moving him inexorably in a positive direction. Since then, though, it had been one disaster after another. Was this just bad luck, or were there greater forces at work here, were mysterious forces working against him – had fate dealt him a deceptive hand, he wondered. Was he now finished, or was this a new challenge for him, or was this part of some greater mysterious grand plan? None of it made any sense.

He came out of his self-absorption to realise Colonel Normanton had ordered the Communications Officer to verify the veracity of the message. The latter's attempts to communicate with the ship continued to fail though, so he initiated a scan of the space quadrant indicated in the message. After a few minutes, the computer confirmed there was indeed a starship accelerating away from the stellar system in that quadrant of space and it matched the systems details of The Crusader. Further and repeated attempts at communication with the ship continued to fail. A further scan of near space also brought to their attention the disappearance of the Alpha Fraczan starship Star Chaser, which until recently had been heading steadily on a trajectory towards Rorque 4. It was now no longer doing so, but equally there was no sign of it anywhere in the immediate vicinity of space.

All eyes in the room turned to Rosson. He half expected one of the senior officers to draw their pistol and arrest him there and then. But nothing happened. If there was a spy in their midst, he must be under orders to do nothing to give his position away, thought Rosson. The agent might wait until Vartin arrived at the planet, before giving a detailed account of events to the Supreme Commander. If this was the case, this would give Rosson a certain amount of time to consider his next move, but he was now certain his overall position was completely lost. No amount of lying, evidence-fixing, finger-pointing and general deception could now save his situation. It was now a case of damage limitation, and getting out of this feudal hell-hole alive and in one piece. He ordered his staff to return to normal duties and informed Pushkov and Normanton that they would be meeting in the next room - the former throne room - but now converted into his own personal office.

Rosson established with his officers that the absence of the stasis ship had no immediate impact on their present situation; the garrison possessed sufficient AI units, ferming units and min-fabs to be largely self-sufficient. In addition, they now had full access to the produce of the local area and any other materials or resources they might need. He ordered Pushkov and Normanton to make sure standard routines were followed amongst the soldiery, and that the theft of the stasis ship should not be divulged to anyone outside of senior command. They were under strict orders to keep this matter fully secret. He ordered the guards to be doubled and the base to be put on high alert for possible intruders. There was a possibility that the theft of the ship might be followed by an attack on their position on the actual planet, though he somehow doubted this was likely to be the case. The message sounded to Rosson as though it was aimed more to demoralise them, rather than to foreshadow an attack on the town, but it might be a double bluff – so it was better to be safe rather than sorry.

The senior officers were then dismissed and he turned his thoughts once again to his own personal situation. He poured himself a large glass of the local beer. He was now under no illusions that Vartin would have him court-martialled, and that execution was the most likely outcome of the trial. He would be tried for dereliction of duty and he knew what the standard punishment for this heinous crime was. He considered whether he should simply do the decent thing and accept his fate – after all, he was partially responsible for his current predicament - but this was not in Rosson's nature. He came from a privileged family, had been raised with a certain sense of entitlement, an expectation of the good life, and to enjoy greater levels of freedom than the average inhabitant of Zeleyan. In addition, he believed he had plenty of good years left in him; he was too young to die just yet. He needed a way out.

If given the choice, he would have preferably liked to return to Zeleyan – to the society and life he was familiar with – but he could see no viable means of return. He might somehow be able to seize a starship from his unknown foes and return home, but on Zeleyan he would be a disgraced figure and would need to remain in hiding for the rest of his life. This could never work. In a moment of far-flung fancy he even imagined deposing Vartin as Supreme Commander upon his arrival at Ur-Tokar, and taking full control of the military so he could then return to his home planet, but he knew this idea was a complete non-starter – Vartin's position was far too strong and secure.

A second option would be to head to another planet – Rorque 4 might be a possibility – but he would still need a starship and he had no idea of how to contact his enemy, never mind tricking his way onto their ship and seizing control of it. They would surely suspect any advances he made towards them as highly suspicious, and must already consider the Zeleyanian forces to be completely untrustworthy. Whilst not impossible, this also seemed to be another unlikely solution, he thought to himself.

He considered the situation further and poured himself another beer. The disappearance of the scientist's spaceship, The Star Chaser, puzzled him. He assumed the scientists might have the technical know-how to seize The Crusader and spirit it away unnoticed. But why would they do this, and how had they known about the military base in the first place? All communications had indicated they were planning to journey to Rorque 4. The message from the ship departing from Rorque 4, The Spirit of the Age – which the Zeleyanians had also picked up - may have affected their plans, he thought. But why had they suddenly stopped at Ur-Tokar and then kidnapped his ship? This made no sense at all.

Maybe they were not on their way to Rorque 4 after all, he wondered. Maybe it was all a ruse and The Star Chaser was now a socialist Zeta Kotlin ship that had somehow acquired knowledge of their presence on Ur-Tokar. Maybe the scientists and Zetans had been in league with each other all along, and had planned to stop the invasion through some form of combined effort. Was the departure from Alpha Fraczan a false story to cover up the real intentions of the two peoples? But this still left unanswered the question of how they knew of the base's existence in the first place. Or, maybe, this was just one paranoid conspiracy theory too far – too many of its elements did not seem to add up.

The perceived absence of The Star Chaser meant it was almost certainly hiding in the communication shadow of either Ur-Tokar or one of the other planets in Rogan's planetary system, avoiding detection from their somewhat limited communications ability. If he could discover its position and enter into dialogue with the crew he might actually be able to trick his way on board by some means or other. Or did the ship hold an army that was about to invade the planet, he wondered? He dismissed this thought as unlikely, since the Zetans were famously anti-militarist. In that respect at least, he was probably safe.

He poured another beer. A further option was to stay on Ur-Tokar and go native. Maybe he could become the new king - but he would need to find a way of turning the invasion fleet around and ensure it headed back to Zeleyan. This would be a tall order – Vartin was set on conquering the whole of the Nexus Cluster; how could Rosson stymie his dreams of glory. It would need an extremely good reason for the fleet to turn around and head back to Zeleyan. Vartin would soon know of his own blunders, and, with his highly suspicious nature, would surely see that any attempt to dissuade him from completing his mission to Ur-Tokar was likely to be Rosson scheming against him. This plan also looked like a non-starter.

He had been intrigued by the tales he had recently heard of people living in the forested mountains of Ur-Tokar – the so-called Mountain People. What form of lifestyle did they lead, he wondered? Back on Zeleyan he had once been a young and ultra-keen party cadet – living out in the wild, camping in the outback, climbing mountains, rafting down the rivers and tracking the few wild animals that actually inhabited the planet. He poured himself another beer, and mused on his childhood adventures. He remembered trekking through the mountains of the Central Belt, kayaking along the upper reaches of the great River Salzarance, and camping on the shores of Lake Magnu in the barren, semi-frozen, southern reaches of the supercontinent. These had been enjoyable, much simpler times, with no real responsibilities or expectations of him, other than to actually complete the outdoor activity in one piece. Life back then had been full of new experiences and new possibilities, future adventures and honest optimistic relationships with his fellow cadets.

And now? He poured another beer. Now, his life was full of irrelevant responsibilities, second-guessing Vartin, overseeing dreary routines and keeping order - or it would be, until he was executed. Rosson suddenly felt very depressed and caught hopelessly in a web of emptiness. His thoughts repeatedly spiraled upwards and downwards. He was asking so many questions of himself and of his life, but he never seemed to know any of the answers. His thought processes took him around in endless darkened circles, unsure of which way to go and of which way to turn. Occasionally, he thought he glimpsed the prospect of light at the end of the tunnel, a way out - smiling faces and helping hands seemed to offer him a possible path out of the darkness. But then the doubts re-emerged, and he feared he would just return to the world of emptiness. Voices in his head kept asking him which way he should go, but he just felt like the demented man, lost, beleaguered and unknowing which way he should turn for help.

He poured another beer and tried to lift the depression, to be more optimistic and feel less sorry for himself. Maybe a life up here in the mountains could be a good one, he thought to himself. Maybe he could return to a simpler and more honest way of life – a genuinely meaningful way of life. Away from Supreme Commander Vartin, away from the pressures of leadership, away from the fear of failure, from the ridiculous stuffiness of the military and its obsession with orders and shiny uniforms. And, most importantly, away from the prospect of execution. He began to imagine how he might live out his life in the forests and the mountains, and how much simpler and easier his life would be. It would be just like his early cadet days.

When his personal orderly arrived later that evening to clear up after the Vice-Admiral, he found Rosson slumped across the table completely drunk and fast asleep.

Rorque 4 – Anna Dubois

Anna Dubois had initially considered her decision to redirect The Spirit of the Age to Rorque 4, rather than continue onwards to the designated designation of Zeta Kotlin, as very much one her better ideas. She had been warmly welcomed by the Rorque Corporation, and as the stasis ship's designated leader and a formerly high-ranking member of the Seven Mountains University on Alpha Fraczan, the corporation had treated her as a welcome guest, whilst securing a reasonably high position at Altair University for her. She was also fortunate in that her specialist field was pharmaceuticals, for the Rorque Corporation had a whole division devoted to the production of drugs and medicines for the planet's inhabitants. In these difficult economic times, it remained one of their few really profitable areas of business.

It was equally true, though, that deep down she continued to feel a certain level of nervousness with regards to the course of action she had taken. Her decision had been largely motivated by personal ambition, though she was hoping that in the fullness of time the whole scientific community would eventually benefit from her decision, as they secured employment in well funded and highly provisioned centres of learning. Nevertheless, she tended to avoid some of the initial gatherings of the various scientists and academics from her home planet, aware that many were distinctly unhappy at not being consulted in her decision to divert the starship to a different planet from the one collectively decided upon when they departed from Alpha Fraczan.

Increasingly, therefore, she sought out those who approved of her decision and tended to only socialise with those supportive of her new choice of world. She was, of course, extremely pleased for those who secured positions in the various universities owned and managed by the Rorque Corporation, but she had not anticipated the large numbers that were eventually rejected for employment; nor had she realised that finding decent employment and accommodation on Rorque 4 would prove to be quite so difficult. Almost everywhere she looked, employment was dominated by AI units. Effectively, if a reliable algorithm could be constructed for any particular task, job or career then that task was given to an AI unit. This was not something she had bargained for; her previous visions of what life would be like on Rorque 4 were almost immediately beginning to unravel, and some doubts began to creep in with regards to the wisdom of her decision back in Margalla's orbit.

When the scientists who had failed to secure employment began their committee meetings and protests, she had become even more concerned with their plight, though she ensured she remained away from their gatherings, in case they turned their wrath against her. At the same time, she became aware that personal relationships were being damaged and even destroyed by the highly selective employment and non-employment decisions taken by the Rorque Corporation, and that the children of these relationships were suffering as a result. She had attempted to use her influence within the university to suggest more employment contracts should be offered, and to highlight certain individuals who she considered to be worthy of recruitment. However, initially polite rebuffs to her suggestions eventually turned to firm put-downs, and it soon became apparent to her that many of the Rorquean staff were actively trying to prevent the employment of Alphan scientists.

Whilst those at the top of the corporation might view the arrival of the scientists as an unexpected opportunity, many of those lower down the hierarchy simply saw them as a potential threat. On a planet that placed individualism above all else - and where employment was an increasingly scarce commodity - a dog-eat-dog culture of ruthless personal competition had become widely prevalent. When the Alphans had first arrived at their temporary accommodation, the existing university staff had provided them with a great deal of information concerning the difficulties of living and working on the planet. At first, she had assumed they were offering the newcomers useful warnings and friendly advice, but gradually she had come to realise that they were actually attempting to dissuade them from staying on Rorque 4; that they were actively trying to persuade them to depart for somewhere elsewhere in the cosmos.

These initial difficulties had genuinely concerned and troubled her, so she was somewhat relived when the rejected scientists departed aboard The Spirit of the Age for Zeta Kotlin. Nevertheless, she felt emotionally bruised by the whole experience, and realised she had also become something of a partial recluse. To avoid the mental trauma of the whole episode she had thrown herself into her work at the university. The faculty was developing a new class of drugs to help with mental health issues, particularly anxiety and depression, which were apparently widespread amongst the Rorquean population. She was told that there had been an increase in suicide rates recently and the corporation was seeking to help the situation with a range of drugs that could lessen anxiety rates and thus lower the suicide rate. She felt pleased to be part of a project that was helping some of the more unfortunate people on Rorque 4, and in some respects this helped alleviate the guilt she was now feeling about the plight of her fellow Alphans.

However, it had not been long before further problems began to develop even within her new employment role. Back on Alpha Fraczan, AI units had mainly been used for the more basic and menial tasks that no human had wanted to perform. As such, she had somewhat limited contact with the machines and any instructions issued to them were relatively simple and straightforward for them to perform. Here on Rorque 4, the robots were used for such a wide and varied range of tasks that she found it necessary to be in contact with them on a day-to-day basis, and had become increasingly frustrated with their poor performance levels and inability to act beyond their pre-set programming. Errors, misunderstandings and communication breakdowns were frequent and she spent much of her time compensating for their failings. Frequently she found herself wondering why people feared intelligent machines - surely it was the stupid ones you really needed to be worried about!

Contact with the human staff was often not much better, since their highly competitive individualism made them suspicious, narcissistic and often rude and insulting. She had initially assumed they were all working for the greater collective good, advancing understanding and pushing back the frontiers of scientific knowledge. Slowly but surely she was disabused of these notions. The real priorities turned out to be meeting targets, satisfying demands from on high, affirming pre-designated decisions, maintaining a high ranking departmental position and - for much of the staff anyway - seeking promotion at every available opportunity. And to add to all these difficulties, there seemed to be a growing number of incidences of prejudice towards anyone from her home planet. The working conditions were quite unlike anything she had experienced on Alpha Fraczan.

She also came increasingly into conflict with those in authority above her. On occasions, she had made various suggestions, which to her seemed little more than common sense – means of improving the performance of the laboratories, for instance, or the investigation of new interesting compounds and biochemical procedures. Initially, she had been fobbed off with a variety of polite excuses and meaningless platitudes as to why this could not happen, but eventually senior management lost patience with her and pointed out that unless a drug, procedure or work practice was profitable it was not worthy of any consideration. Those in authority had already made the appropriate decisions – with all the widespread knowledge and experience available to them – and these decisions would be faithfully followed by all involved, including herself!

She had noticed how those at the very top often quickly closed ranks in the face of any criticism, often in an almost tribal manner. She had once mentioned that she had noticed that those in charge had all been educated in the same expensive schools, and asked whether this was the reason as to why they were all so successful. The reaction she had received had bordered on the threatening. They had all earned their place through merit and hard work, she was told in no uncertain terms, and it was in no way related to a privileged or advantaged upbringing. However, she noticed that the differing merits they discussed and talked about were all in relation to one another – with those from exactly the same background, one which they seemed to assume was a typically normal one. Comparisons with those from different, invariably less advantaged, backgrounds were not even considered. She began to understand their defensiveness, but also the exclusive nature of the world she was now living in, and why she was faring so badly.

Over time she began to feel underappreciated, overworked and – given the long hours she worked and the high price of living in the city – underpaid. She frequently compared the overall organisation of the society on her new home with that on Alpha Fraczan, and found the former very much lacking. Frequently, she reflected on how much better they had managed their working and personal lives on the small, cold, reddish windswept planet. When she occasionally pointed this out to the inhabitants of Rorque 4, they mistook her well-intentioned advice for arrogance and superiority and a lack of respect for their own society and then suggested that she might want to return to her home planet if it was so much better there. She began to feel a certain tinge of nostalgia for her home planet and for her time at Seven Mountains University, and her thoughts eventually turned to wondering what had actually happened on the planet since their departure nearly four years previously.

She knew that one of her close colleagues at Seven Mountains University, an astrophysicist named Phil Jacobs, had secured a position working for Cosmic Solutions on their terra-forming project based at Diana Park University. Knowing him fairly well, she also figured he would be following developments on Alpha Fraczan, at least in his spare time, if not actually whilst he was at work. She made the decision to contact him, and over a series of conversations she discovered that their initial predictions had largely been accurate. Their world had, indeed, experienced a considerable tilting process and a subsequent period of intense volcanic activity, earthquakes, tidal waves and intense flooding episodes. Satellite data showed that the oceans had shifted, coastal plains had become inundated, rivers had dramatically altered their course, and it was also safe to assume that the vegetation zones would be altering dramatically over the coming years. Recently, though, there were signs of conditions settling down and a new period of stabilisation – a sort of planetary homeostasis was becoming established. She wondered nostalgically if she would ever see her home planet ever again.

A few days later, she was suddenly hauled in front of a disciplinary panel wanting to know why she had been collaborating with an employee of a rival company. The reasons she gave were not considered sufficiently exculpatory, but as she was new to the planet she was only given a disciplinary warning, but told that if it happened again she could be dismissed by the corporation. Ralph Parker - still the main liaison person between the corporation and the scientists – took a considerable amount of pleasure in informing her that her card was now marked, and that she had no hope of promotion from here on. Confused and feeling belittled, Anna retreated further into her work over the following weeks, often working long hours and staying late into the evening in the laboratory. Here at least, she could console herself and find some familiarity with the life she had once lived and enjoyed.

Arrival in Utopia

It was for this reason that one Thursday evening she was typically working late and alone on an unexpectedly damp day in August. So rare was rain on Rorque 4 – especially at this time of year - that she had taken a short break from her work to watch the raindrops from the brief summer storm spatter on the window pane of an annex to the side of the laboratory she undertook the majority of her work in. As she watched the big fat drops of water bounce off the glass panes, she noticed the reflection of a man behind her. She turned to see the unmistakable figure of Ralph Parker standing in the doorway, middle-aged, dark haired, tall but also considerably overweight.

Anna had never taken to Parker. He seemed something of a braggart and he showed no regard for her opinions or for those of her other female colleagues. He clearly held a high opinion of himself, but she could not figure out the basis upon which he thought this actually rested. He seemed to hold an equally low and dismissive opinion of others, brusquely rejecting opinions he disagreed with and belittling the honest endeavours of others, especially if he thought they might show them in a better light than he himself. He also had the irritating habit of laughing at his own remarks, despite the fact they were singularly unfunny. Anna could only guess at his reasons for doing so.

'Good evening', he declared and paused for a moment 'working late like a busy bee are we?' he added somewhat patronisingly.
Over the previous months, Anna had grown used to his irritating and often insulting remarks, but on this occasion she felt something was different. Often he was just bluff and bluster and clearly playing to the gallery for laughs, but here they were alone and there was a hint of seriousness in his tone. She felt something was wrong.
'I'm just doing my job, preparing the experiments in my room for tomorrow's work,' she answered non-committedly.
Parker glanced around for a moment and then said slowly, 'it's not the only way to get back into the corporation's good books, you know. There are other ways of achieving promotion. I could always put in a good word for you, do things for you, if you were to do certain things for me. I have very good connections in very high places, you know.'
Anna had a pretty good idea of where this was going, but was unsure of just how serious Parker was going to treat the matter. He could frequently blow hot and cold, and was often a difficult character to judge. Initially, she tried to

make light of his comments, but after several further remarks from Parker in the same vein, she began to become exasperated. 'Are you losing your mind? We have nothing in common, we're completely incompatible. There's no chance of us getting together, not now or any other time. Stop fooling around!'

'You burn me up, Dubois! Am I fooling? Really? Is that what you think this is? I think you really need to consider this far more seriously. Otherwise, it might be the last good offer you get,' he stated quite seriously and with a hint of menace. 'Now, do you want this body or not?'

The idea of having sex with Parker filled her with disgust. She had experienced a couple of sexual encounters with men on Rorque 4 already, but they had both been fairly unsatisfactory. Both men had been attractive and were senior figures within the university. They had paid for lavish meals at up-market restaurants, designer clothes and visits to expensive visitor attractions, and there seemed to have been the unstated understanding that as they had spent a considerable amount of money on her, so they should have automatic access to sex, and, as it turned out, not even sex that was attentive to her desires and needs. Neither affair had lasted particularly long. She could not imagine sex with Parker would be any better, in fact, it was likely to be considerably worse.

Several thoughts went through her mind as to how she could escape from her present situation, but ultimately she simply told him that she was uninterested and that she wanted to leave now. Parker refused to move out of her way, so she made for the doorway and tried to push past him. Unfortunately for Anna, he was considerably larger and heavier than she was and grabbed hold of her and pushed her against one of the side tables. As she struggled to release his grip, she stamped as hard as possible on one of his feet and as he pulled his leg away in pain, they both went tumbling down towards the floor. Fortunately for Anna, although she ended up down on her knees, she was also closer to the doorway than Parker, and before he could fully recover from the fall and make another lunge for her, she stumbled to her feet, ran through to the adjacent laboratory and then made the fastest exit she possibly could from the building, occasionally glancing behind her, though as she did so, she noticed he was now nowhere to be seen.

Anna lodged an official complaint against Parker with the Rorque Corporation with regards to the incident the next day. The subsequent inquiry lasted significantly longer than she had expected, but, as meetings were held with various investigatory figures, she began to develop the distinct impression that far from achieving justice, matters appeared to actually be moving against her. Parker had provided an alibi for the time of the assault. In addition, there were no witnesses, no CCTV footage and there were no bruises on her body. In fact, there was no proof that the incident had ever even occurred, other than her testimony. It slowly dawned on her that Parker had chosen the place and time very carefully – that he understood the system far better than she did. He was also personally appointed by Jamieson and enjoyed certain protections as a result. Ultimately, she was found guilty of wasting company time and bringing false allegations against a fellow employee. Even worse, she had to witness Parker's gloating in the final hearing. The corporation put her on a final warning.

For Anna, this marked a final turning point in her opinion of her new world. She had always considered herself to be a reasonable, intelligent and hard-working person. On Alpha Fraczan, she had been treated with respect, her positive attributes appreciated allowing her to work her way up to higher positions of authority and prestige. But here on Rorque 4 she had been treated as some form of naïve, insubordinate inferior. She wondered if this was an approach unique to the Rorque Corporation or whether it was common to all the other corporations. She made discrete enquiries amongst some of her former colleagues and discovered it was effectively no different at Cosmic Solutions, URT or any of the smaller companies. For a world that claimed it was founded on the basis of maximising individual freedom, she was really struggling to see exactly where any of that freedom actually existed.

It had not taken her long - nor for many of her fellow Alphans - to discover that this was also a world of extreme economic inequality. For the relatively small numbers at the top, there may well have been a certain degree of freedom to choose from a range of careers, places to live, personal services, leisure activities, holiday destinations, consumer goods and various other facilities. But for those like her in the middle, there seemed to be few meaningful choices – simply choosing which corporation was going to order you around and treat you like an idiot, was about as good as it seemed to get. This was not her idea of what freedom was all about. And as for the great morass of the swelling underclass at the bottom of society, their only freedom seemed to be choosing which charity they were going to become dependent upon, or the method by which they chose to escape from the bleak reality of life on Rorque 4 – drink, drugs or suicide.

As such, she realised her situation here was now a highly precarious one and it was difficult to see what alternatives were available to her. She felt trapped and her choices seemed highly limited. On the one hand, she could simply do as she was told, accept the idea that the system was right and she was wrong, conform to all the behaviours and procedures she so-disliked and accept her current position - but this was a highly unsatisfactory option for someone with her upbringing. Alternatively, she could grovel and suck up to those in authority in the hope that a promotion would make her life considerably better - but she had too much integrity for that option, and feared that she might just find herself at a higher level but with the same old problems. She even briefly considered finding a highly wealthy man to marry so she could escape her present predicament, until she pictured the humiliations she would need to experience to achieve that particular escape route.

Despairing of her own personal position, she started to take a greater interest in the political situation on the planet – perhaps, she thought, political change could offer some solution to her predicament. She had only very cursorily followed the recent elections on the planet, but from what she had seen, none of the political parties seemed to show any serious desire to fundamentally change the economic system on Rorque 4 – at least none that had any hope of winning the elections. Greater interest and investigation of the subject only seemed to reaffirm her initial thoughts on this matter, but certain features puzzled her, so one day, whilst at work, she broached the subject with one of her university colleagues.

Since starting work at the university, she had gained the distinct impression that a number of her co-workers treated her in a fairly patronising way and untrusting manner, simply because she was from Alpha Fraczan, rather than a native Rorquean. Hasani Gowon, however, was unlike these others and treated her more as an equal, so it was to him that she turned to, in her attempt to find out more about Rorquean politics.

'We had representative democracy in the universities back on Alpha Fraczan, so I know how it all works, but it's seems somewhat different here. It appears to be more about personalities and party positions, whereas we concentrated more on ideas and policy planning,' she commenced. She knew she needed to be diplomatic about the subject and not give the impression that she believed her own system was superior in any way – the Rorqueans seemed to particularly dislike this - so she chose her wording carefully. 'But, the parties here don't appear to be very different from each other on ideas and policies. Have I got that right, and if so, what do people think about that?'

'Ah yes, that's definitely correct,' Hasani replied, slightly to her surprise. 'Yes, you're right, the differences between the parties are wafer thin. They all believe in basically the same economic system and have no real plans to change that in any significant way. Equally, they are all closely linked to one of the big corporations, so it's the corporate bosses who call all the shots, anyway. That's why it's all about personalities and party image. As to what people think, well, I think people just generally accept this, they just know they are all similar.'

'But wouldn't people like more choice?' Anna asked. 'I thought choice was an extremely important feature of Rorquean culture.'

'Well, it is, but not so much in the political sphere. Most people don't vote - they don't care much about politics as they know the parties are all quite similar. They know that real democracy lies in the market, anyway,' Hasani replied.

'What do you mean?' asked Anna, slightly puzzled.

'Well, that's where you get the choices that really matter. As the great twenty-second century economist Kavinda Lopez said, we have a market democracy – you can buy anything you want, wherever you want and whenever you want it. If you want something enough, someone will produce it and then sell it to you. As a result, there's an unlimited choice and you have the freedom to choose whatever you want. That's real democracy! They deliver on whatever it is you want to buy. When you have that, you don't really need to worry about politics.'

Anna had not come across this idea before and had to think about it for a while.

'But in a democracy,' she eventually replied, 'you have one person one vote, and the voters all have an equal say - in theory at least. But in a market, some people have far more money than others, so it's not really a level playing field, is it. The rich have a much greater say than the poor.'

'Well, that's why you need to get on, get promoted and make more money. Then you have more of a say,' suggested Hasani.

Anna was about to say something in reply, but thought better of it. She knew that the Rorqueans often became very touchy when she criticised aspects of their culture, so she decided to keep quiet instead. However, it was obvious to her now that their political system was constructed largely to benefit the corporations, rather than the people, whilst the strange idea of a market democracy clearly favoured the wealthy to an even greater degree. As such, this potential avenue of escape from her difficulties looked like a distinctly closed one; liberation through a collective solution looked as unlikely as through an individual one.

Whilst taking a greater interest in contemporary political affairs, though, she had also noted a number of news reports on the planet's global warming problem, and with a growing level of concern. There were increasingly intense and prolonged heatwaves, and the water shortages seemed to be more frequent of late and to last longer than previously, whilst wildfires were now raging across several different parts of all the continents. The significance of these events was frequently downplayed by the media, and the explanations for them were disjointed and often unconvincing. She was not particularly familiar with climate science but she could not help but feel there was far more occurring here than they were being told about. She was already a refugee from one planetary disaster, and now she was beginning to wonder if she had walked straight into another one.

With this in mind she arranged to meet an old colleague, Kristin Lampang, who she knew was now working for the Rorque Corporation as a hydrologist in one of their many subsidiary companies. Kristin was middle-aged with short dark hair, pale skin and an impish smile that resulted in an almost elfin look about her. Anna had always found her quite captivating, and their rendez-vous once again reminded her of good times back on Alpha Fraczan. After exchanging news of their current situations, and some reminiscing about their times on their home planet, Anna addressed the main reason for their get together.

'How bad exactly is the climate situation here?' she asked. 'I'm beginning to wonder if we're in the middle of yet another planetary disaster, and I might become a refugee for a second time.'

'Rorque 4 is going through a warming phase due to its slightly irregular elliptical planetary orbit. This takes it slightly closer to its star Eleutheria for a duration of about three decades, as far as I can see. Even without this, it is already a warm planet and the warming is putting the whole environmental system under great strain. In the initial years of the warming, the effects were not that noticeable, but of late, its manifestations have become more and more intense. Normally, I would have said it would survive this warming and we would come out the other side – depleted in respect to certain resources – but largely intact.' She paused, 'the main problem is the manner in which the Rorquean corporations have treated their planet. The seas and lakes are all shallow and far from extensive, but they have already been heavily polluted and massively overfished; some of them are now effectively dying seas. The artesian basins we know of are all exhausted – I'm part of a team currently searching for newer deeper ones, but with no success so far. They've allowed the woodland – which was open savannah and never extensive in the first place - to effectively be destroyed, either through logging or to make way for development. The only significant stands of trees left now are the highly cultivated orchards used for fruit production. Any ecosystems that might have helped the planet to cool has been damaged or destroyed. All this just exacerbates the warming, and has stretched the planet's coping mechanisms to breaking point. Much of the planet is arid and semi-desert at the best of times, so it's no surprise that fires are spreading through the scrub and reaching the cities, as the desert extends and the aridity increases.'

'How low exactly are the freshwater supplies?' asked Anna, now even more concerned than before.

'The natural known ones are either finished or unusable because of pollution; the only viable supplies now are from the desalination plants. It's an expensive and energy-intensive way of supplying water but theoretically they should be able last through the crisis, though the pollution in the seas is making this far from easy,' Kristin answered.

'That's assuming you can afford it though. The problem for most people is the price of water. It's rising, and whole swathes of the population can no longer pay for it. There are already widespread droughts, and disease is rampant in some of the poorest sectors. If this is the case, it's just going to get worse, isn't it?' Anna enquired, and Kristin suddenly realised that life was not going well for Anna on Rorque 4.

'Yes, and their ideological system sees this as just another problem that requires a market solution. But as far as I can see, in the absence of increases in supply - which looks unlikely - the price will only carry on rising. It's only likely to fall when demand falls and that's probably only going to happen after huge numbers of people have died. There are no alternatives to water, and there are limits to how much any individual can actually cut back their needs. I can't see that there is actually a market solution,' observed Kristen pessimistically.

'And the state is so weak here - it has an institutional incapability of dealing with any such major crisis. They would need to considerably extend its scope, financing, powers and capabilities to be even partially effective in dealing with this problem. That would entail changing the constitution, the law and the whole mentality of how this planet works. I cannot see that happening any time soon, even in an emergency like this one,' Anna added with a note of exasperation. 'Are we actually at or close to a tipping point?' she finally asked.

'The recent droughts, heatwaves, pollution incidents and fires, I think, are beyond a market solution. I cannot see how their already recessionary economy can solve these. Additionally, as you said, there is no political will to effect the changes needed to solve the crisis. I can only see matters getting worse, so I guess we probably have already passed the tipping point,' she answered, suddenly clarifying her own thoughts on the issue.

'So, how do we get out of here? Do you have any plans? We don't really belong here anyway! Is there any way off this planet?' The questions came tumbling out of Anna, but Kirstin had few answers.

'I've been too busy – working long hours – to really think about it. Now that you mention the subject, though, I was told by a colleague that security at the spaceport at Mirivan had been strengthened considerably in the last few weeks. Large numbers of AI units have been deployed there by the corporation. I didn't think much about it, but, maybe you're not the only one thinking about departing from the planet,' Kristin offered.

Anna thought for a while. 'Would the corporations just up and leave for another planet?'

'And leave this disaster behind them - yeh, why not, they've done it before!' quipped Kristin, 'and we did it as well, remember,' she added reflectively.

Ur-Tokar – Opa-Loka and Star Chaser crews work together

Although the Zetan crew members took turns in descending to the planet, aboard the Opa-Loka, it was Savverio and Janicka who spent the greatest amount of time engaged in analysing communications data, monitoring developments on the planet, liaising with the crew of The Star Chaser and making further preparations for a new approach to their mining operations. Despite all this, they still experienced the standard problem of so many orbiting crews – that of preventing the long hours spent on their spaceship from turning into endless boredom. Whilst they also spent a significant amount of leisure time gaming, watching movies, reading books, star-gazing, eating, drinking and conversing, Janicka had been particularly keen to discover if space sex was all it was cracked up to be, and so she and Savverio had spent significant amounts of time together trying out the various positions and sex acts that only a low gravity environment permitted.

Savverio, who had taken an instant attraction to Janicka's infectious enthusiasm, was only too happy to help her act out the various sex dreams she had fantasised about. As they did so, he remembered his own curiosity with regards to this matter on his first space flight several years before, at which time he discovered it was standard practice for all first-time crew members to explore and investigate free-floating sexual practices. Love in space, he had discovered, was not quite all it was cracked up to be. Whilst he no longer needed to worry about his poorly functioning legs, bouncing around in a low gravity environment brought with it its own particular physical issues, and gaining sufficient bodily traction during intercourse was far more difficult than he had anticipated.

After several intermittent weeks together, Janicka eventually admitted that she too had arrived at a similar conclusion. Whilst it was fun to act out your fantasy floating through the air, lying on the ceiling, or pressed against the ship's viewing windows with the entire cosmos as your lovemaking backdrop, she had to admit that space love was far from straightforward, required considerable care and constant physical adjustments involving strange and awkward contortions. Eventually they had opted for simply strapping themselves onto chairs, beds or couches in order to make their sex life more manageable and simplistic – the standard space approach!

Arrival in Utopia

It was after one such session that they found themselves together, gazing out through the huge windows of the viewing deck, and yet again speculating idly about the myriad stars that filled the blackness of space that lay before them.

'Can you adjust me,' asked Janicka, 'I seem to have become too tightly strapped to the couch, but I can't see where the problem is.'
Savverio spent a few minutes locating the problem and altered the strap length behind her once he located the source of the problem. 'Sorted, that should be more comfortable now,' he declared confidently, and she eased back into the comfort of the couch and took a long sip from the drink container lodged in its arm section.
'I wonder how many of those stars have planets with human habitation on them now?' mused Janicka absent-mindedly.
'Probably still only a small percentage, I suspect. I know thousands of stasis ships departed from Earth, but even if they were all successful – and we know some met unfortunately premature ends – that's still only a small percentage of what we can see before us,' answered Savverio, in his usual methodical way.
'And some of the civilisations failed as well, I understand,' commented Janicka, 'and not just for the standard geo-planetary reasons. I've heard some went spectacularly wrong. Is it true what they say about the Medusa planet?' she asked, remembering a story that one of her childhood friends had tried to frighten her with many years ago.
'You mean the planet Perseon 2, orbiting Cygnun IX in the following star cluster from ours – that was its official name, anyway. Yes, I wondered about that story too, it looked intriguing and I wondered if any technology had been developed that might sort out my legs. So, I looked it up in the ship's data banks on my first voyage. It was colonised by several stasis ships that were amongst the earliest waves to depart from Earth, some time before the Opa-Loka itself. As such, we have all their transmissions; from the first landing on Medusa, right up to its eventual evacuation - not that there were many people left to evacuate.'
'So the stories are true then,' Janicka exclaimed, slightly surprised, but keen to know more.
'Well, I'm not sure which ones you've heard, but some *were* particularly grisly and disturbing. In the earlier years of their civilisation they really went for it.

The stasis ships that arrived there were full of tech enthusiasts. They were heavily into biological and cyber-engineering, brain implants, psycho-alteration, cosmetic manipulation, indefinitely extending human life spans and suchlike. Basically, they were keen to experiment on all aspects of the human body and mind, and with the aim of dramatically improving the human experience, or creating some form of superhuman perfection – most likely part-human and part-machine, I believe. There seems to have been nothing they were unwilling to try out in order to create a more perfect human race - some of it looked way over the top, in my opinion.'

'So it's true that they did cross people with animals, like snakes and wolves and such like,' Janicka interrupted. 'Well, that's what I was told,' she added, when she saw Savverio's disbelieving look.

'I couldn't find any actual evidence for that in the ship's data bank, but they did use DNA from various animals in their genome experiments and sometimes with horrendous results – some form of xenomorph-type disaster was the usual outcome, I believe. I think that's where the Medusa tag derives from, but they tried all sorts of other stuff out as well.'

'Such as what?' she asked, keen to know more.

'Bioengineering procedures were very common, and varied across the whole spectrum, but many just ended in crippling injuries and premature death. Then there was the more bizarre stuff. One group attempted to download their minds into AI units with disastrous results – they all suffered severe mental disorders, and then premature death from the madness that followed once the mind cut had been initiated. Another group decided they would do something similar, and attempted to meld their minds – or possibly their bodies, the records are not too clear on this - with the computer's that controlled the stasis ships. Apparently they wanted to fly around the universe like giant metallic birds.'

'And did it work?' asked Janicka, almost not believing what she was hearing.

'It doesn't look like it, though again the records are not fully clear. The ships seemed to either end up lost in the depths of space, or subject to some form of major communications breakdown, though it's not clear if that was on the ships themselves or back on the planet. Given all the weird attempts going on to meld minds and machines there was a great deal of confusion, so anything could have gone wrong, I guess.'

Arrival in Utopia

He paused for a moment, 'And if you think that's weird, there were even attempts to cyber-engineer people back from the dead – a bit like the Dream of Isis - though with distinctly less successful results. I think this was linked to their desire for everlasting life. Transdimensional man was another popular experimental format, as they sought to create superhumans - or some form of master race - that could defy the parameters of time, space and the universe. As far as I'm aware there's still no evidence for a multiverse, but that didn't stop them trying to find it through a whole range of cyber-engineering processes inside their brains and minds. Severe mental trauma was the usual result, according to the reports.'

'But after a while, didn't they realise that it was all going badly wrong and just give up on it?' Janicka asked, now beginning to wonder just how stupid humans could actually be. 'You can't really perfect humans – and perfection is such a subjective concept, anyway.'

'The leading exponents were billionaires back on Earth. They were so-filled with their own self-importance and so used to dominion over others, that they couldn't bear to think that their lives would actually come to an end one day. They wanted to live forever – basically turn themselves into gods – just like the really ancient rulers on Earth. I think they had also been heavily ridiculed on Earth and many of their practices outlawed, so they were ultra-determined to prove their detractors wrong. And they couldn't accept the thought of failure, so just kept experimenting, believing that the next outlandish attempt might prove to be the one that successfully created super powers, time travel, everlasting life or whatever perfection it was they desired. But it all went so badly wrong in the end - effectively, they travelled across space in search of Shangrila, but just ended up creating some hideous mutation zone. Having said all that, though, I'm not really sure why so many of their attempts didn't actually work, or often actually made their lives worse.'

'I think I know why that was,' Janicka offered, 'I recently read Darva Torvack's classic work on this subject. It's easy to find on the spaceweb. According to his theory, life spent billions of years evolving on Earth. The only organisms and biological processes that flourished successfully were the ones that could survive all of the worst physical, chemical and biological harms that the universe could possibly throw at them. The hostile environments, the chemical warfare and the damage of life, in all its myriad varieties, was never ending; so life-forms developed complex, internalised, overlapping and highly interlinked systems to survive – a bit like highly advanced natural ecosystems. When you try to significantly alter one part of the system it cascades through the rest creating all manner of unexpected consequences and strange behaviours and responses. At the same time, the system resists and fights back in order to maintain its homeostatic state, to return it to its familiar position. To achieve that state, it can create all sorts of internal damage, or even destroy the organism itself in its attempt to restore normality to the whole body. Tampering with such a system is always likely to end in failure; and the greater the alteration, the more you are likely to create an equally major disaster.'

'Mmm, sounds about right to me,' agreed Savverio. 'That could well be the reason there was such a high failure rate on Medusa. I never came across any technology that might significantly improve my legs; at best it sounded like there might possibly be some procedures that could make them similar to an averagely able-bodied person. Unfortunately, I have no idea where their data banks are located, or how I could access them, so I lost interest in the planet.'

'And, so in the end, very few of the tech colonists succeeded or survived – I assume that's what happened,' enquired Janicka.

'Basically yes, as the engineering became more extreme, so the casualty rate – both in terms of life and sanity – rose exponentially. But additionally, it sounds as though there was something of a major rethink towards the end of their civilisation. A section of the settlers seem to have rethought their situation entirely. They appear to have lamented for simpler and far more authentic times. In the few areas where their technology had actually worked, this grouping came round to believe that their time-held dreams of devising some form of human superiority, had actually created a human race characterised by uniformity - effectively a world of clone-like humans with very similar identities. Effectively, they came to believe that in their search for human perfection, they had lost their individual uniqueness and anything special and distinctive they could call their own. Towards the end, these individuals seem to have abandoned their techno-dream altogether. For them, the cyber world had completely lost its animus as the spirit of the age – and they ended up believing that imperfection was not actually as bad as they had originally perceived. As a result, some of them even mooted a return back to Earth – I think they wanted to go back to basics or something -

or some other desperate flight to freedom. Eventually, someone put out an inter-stellar distress call, but by the time a passing stasis ship arrived, there were very few of them left to rescue by the sounds of things.'

'Mmm, seems a bit sad in a way, and a very costly way to discover the truth,' suggested Janicka.

'I guess so. Maybe, they should have just followed our approach of changing the social environment to improve the human condition, that would have produced much better results,' added Savverio, slightly smugly.

'Yeh, I'd never thought of it like that,' agreed Janicka. 'If you want more freedom and control, there's not much point in improving your mind or body, if you're society is an oppressive one, and you still have to live in it.'

Down below on Ur-Tokar, following the battle at Meridin, the decisions made at the conference in Lato, and the successful seizure of The Crusader, Jiaying, Kahlil and Neema had all decided they needed a period of time back on the Opa-Loka to discuss matters with the other two crew members. They had made occasional short-natured returns to the starship for a variety of reasons, but they all agreed it was now time to take stock of their current position and take some serious decisions about what they should do next. Before doing so, they informed Topaz and her friends at Lato that the Zeleyanian forces were now without their spaceship, and thus more vulnerable until the rest of the invasion fleet arrived, which would be in a matter of approximately four months time. Any plans they had for dealing with the fascists would be best pursued before the rest of their fellow troops arrived, they suggested.

Once back aboard the Opa-Loka, and seated around the improvised conference table in the forward deck, Savverio and Janicka brought them up to date with all the most recent developments in near space and from the neighbouring planets of the Nexus Cluster. This included a slightly updated expected time of arrival for the Zeleyanian invasion fleet, various pieces of news they were receiving from Rorque 4, and their recent communication attempt with The Spirit of the Age, from which they were hoping for a reply within the next couple of months.

'I think we need to consider exactly what we are doing here, now that developments have quietened down,' Jiaying stated. 'We originally came to the planet to simply collect mineral resources and various metal ores we needed, but somehow we've ended up in the middle of a war. What do people think should be our next move? Should we just pursue our original mission and then head for home, or should we stay and help the Mountain People with their struggle against the Zeleyanians down below?' she Jiaying, worried about the situation they had unwittingly found themselves in, but genuinely unsure of what their next move should be.

'There's also the issue of The Star Chaser,' mentioned Savverio. 'Some of their crew are currently down on the planet at the moment, near a prominent coastal headland on the far eastern side of the continent known as Turner Point. They're stocking up on food supplies so they can hold a conference on their ship and discuss where they will go next. I think we should encourage them to return to Zeta Kotlin. We could talk to them, see what their initial issues were about living on Zeta, and try and persuade them that they will be better off on our planet than on Rorque 4 – especially at the moment with all the problems it's experiencing. It really shouldn't be too difficult to convince them, I would have thought,' he added optimistically.

'With regards to the minerals and metallic ores we came for, extensive scanning of the planet has indicated alternative sources, some of which are not far from where The Star Chaser crew is currently located. It's partly the reason I recommended the site to them. It's sufficiently far from any human habitation and it's easily accessible. We should be able to put the AI units to work there, and be ready to leave long before the invasion fleet arrives. I know it's part of our belief system that we should only work with the consent of the local inhabitants, but given the present unique situation, I don't think we can afford to be too ethical about the matter at this precise moment in time,' added Janicka suggestively. 'It's not the perfect solution, but it saves us a great deal of trouble, and we have done them some favours in other ways.'

'Well, I think we could extract the ores and minerals we need, and offer some of them to the people at Lato. You never know, they might be more positive about the resources, when they actually see them. Even if they refuse, well, at least we've tried,' suggested Jiaying.

The rest of the crew nodded and made various noises of agreement. They were not fully happy with such a decision, but there was a general consensus that this was probably their most realistic option given the situation they found themselves in.

'I agree, we can still ask Topaz, Rowan, Raven and the others if they would like some of the metals, minerals and precious stones we mine. It won't hurt to ask, and if they say yes, then we've sorted the imperialism problem,' Neema added. 'But, what about the situation at Meridin, is there anything we can do to help there? None of us have any experience of warfare or anything military, so I don't believe there is much we can do in any actual conflict that breaks out, but there must be other ways we can help, given we have far superior technology to those down below,' she enquired of the others.

'We're monitoring the communications arriving and leaving Meridin, but quite frankly there's not that much going on, and what little there is, is encrypted. We can monitor troop movements around the base reasonably well. If there is anything of significance, we could return to the planet and inform the Mountain People at Lato. Other than that, I'm not sure we can do a great deal. It's a pity they don't have any electronic communications systems to make life easier – did you offer them any?' asked Savverio.

'Yes, but they refused. It's against their principles,' answered Kahlil. 'It certainly would make life easier if they used our technology, but I guess that's not going to happen any time soon. If it's quiet at the moment at Meridin, I think we can delay any decision with regards to our continued involvement with the conflict. Let's sort out the minerals and The Star Chaser issues first, and then see where we are after that. We seem to have plenty of time at the moment, so we're not exactly in a hurry,' he added.

The others nodded in agreement.

'But, we do need someone down there fairly quickly to talk to the Alphan scientists,' said Jiaying, 'whose call is it anyway?'

'Ah, it's definitely our turn to descend to the planet,' stated Janicka enthusiastically. 'I could do with some more time off the ship, it seems like we've been here for years – yet we came out of stasis less than three months ago.'

'Yeh, that's right, it's amazing how much has happened since we arrived,' observed Jiaying. 'Ok, so that's fine, we can take over the monitoring of Meridin and the army base - just let us know what to look out for. I'm also looking forward to talking with the crew on The Spirit of the Age; you never know, with a bit of luck there might actually be someone on board I know. That would be a turn-up for the books.'

Not long after their discussion concluded - and once the starship was over the relevant section of the planet and well out of reach of Zeleyanian communications systems - Savverio and Janicka collected together a group of AI units, gathered a few possessions and made their way to one of the landing craft. A few minutes later they were making the rapid descent out of sub-space into the upper reaches of the atmosphere of the planet below. After a short while, Janicka put the craft into a form of freefall so they could almost glide their way down through the latter part of the descent, and admire the view below at a more leisurely pace. Having lived all her life on the relatively flat Zeta Kotlin, Ur-Tokar was unlike anything she had seen before, and she was keen to once more gaze in awe at the towering snow-capped purple mountain ranges, the deep chasms and canyons, endless dark green forests and the jagged coastlines hugging the indigo blue ocean, as they made their downward descent once again. Each time she descended she found even more to be impressed by.

Janicka landed the shuttle craft in a cliff-top clearing close to the coastal promontory of Turner Point where the crew of The Star Chaser was currently based. The AI units on board the craft were first issued instructions on where and how to reconnoiter the prospective mining sites, and once this all looked to be in hand, Savverio and Janicka then wandered slowly along the cliff sward over to where the Star Chaser crew had set up camp.

They were based along a section of mountainous coastline, inset with a series of small sandy bays and occasional fjords that each stretched several kilometers inland. The sea there was a magnificent deep dark indigo blue, with turquoise-blue and white icebergs drifting almost imperceptibly slowly across its mirror-like calmness. Further north along the coast, jutting out into the calm stillness of the ocean, a series of high jagged island peaks stretched out southwards from the mountain range that towered before them. Bright blue-green waterfalls cascaded down their vertically sheer steel-grey cliffs into the sea far below. To the east the ocean waters stretched distantly to the horizon, eventually lost in a thin narrow band of low haze-like cloud floating just above the sea's surface.

Arrival in Utopia

Towards the west, cloaking the mountain sides for as far as they could see, was a blanket of blue, green and purple fir and pine trees, forming a thick layer of forest that stretched distantly inland, verdant and unbroken, save for the occasional bare rocky ridge. The air was cool and crystal clear to breathe and the strong smell of pine wafted down from the mountainside and into the clearing. The whole picture before them seemed primitive yet pristine at the same time. It looked - almost literally - as though no human hand had ever touched the place; yet ironically, they both knew that the forest only existed in the first place because of human intervention over a century beforehand.

Janicka stopped and stood still for a while. She looked around in awe at the landscape, taking in the salty sea air, the pungent smell of the nearby pine forests, and soaked up the breathtaking sea and mountain views that stretched in all directions before her. She had quite literally never seen anything, in all her life, quite as spectacular and so staggeringly beautiful as the scene that lay before her, she thought. It suddenly dawned on her why the Ur-Tokarans so adamantly refused to use modern technology.

They ambled slowly over to The Star Chaser crew members who had been forewarned of their arrival, just in case they became alarmed that their arrival might be that of Zeleyanian forces. Close to their landing craft, several ferming units were working flat out and the crew and their AI units had been busy foraging amongst the trees and bushes gathering large quantities of fruit, berries, mushrooms, nuts and other foods. They showed Savverio and Janicka the large quantity of food they had already amassed and packed into their cooling cases, and it was quite clear they were close to completion of their task.

'We just need enough food for one or two days really, though it's still a tall order as there are several thousand people on the ship. It's a far from ideal scenario, but we need to make a quick decision for practical reasons more than anything else,' explained Mila Lustrom stopping her work for a while. She looked unusually rosy-cheeked, was sweating profusely and was clearly becoming exhausted by the whole endeavour.
'What are your own personal thoughts on the subject? Have you decided to return to Zeta Kotlin or do you want to continue to Rorque 4?' asked Janicka.

'We've been studying the media reports arriving from Rorque 4 and the economic and climate situation there look to be deteriorating quite badly. Personally, I now think that realistically we have no real choice but to return to your planet, but the waking passengers will not be familiar with these reports. Of course, we will relay our knowledge of events to them, but it's possible they might take some persuading,' Mila answered, but also trying to sound optimistic at the same time.

'Why did you decide to leave Zeta Kotlin in the first place, I mean, why would you find the capitalist system of Rorque 4 more attractive than our system?' asked Savverio. 'It's not a choice anyone from Zeta Kotlin has ever made before, at least as far as I know,' he added, genuinely puzzled as to why anyone would prefer to live on a planet that he believed was run on a far inferior socio-economic model.

Mila paused and thought about the matter for a while. She wanted to give a diplomatic but truthful answer. 'I think there were several reasons. Our planet's first dealings with Zeta Kotlin were during a period of political crisis, and I think we always retained this image of your world as being a politically unstable one. I think there were also many of us who believed your political system was a repressive and authoritarian one, though our time on your planet clearly indicated otherwise. We believed that we would lack academic freedoms and that our teaching and research would be closely controlled by the state or less educated people – we would be forced to engage in studies that held no interest to us, and that our work might be used for purposes we did not approve of.' She paused a moment, and then continued, 'in addition, a number of people, including myself, who held senior positions in the universities at Alpha Fraczan were unhappy at the idea of losing our status. We didn't like the idea of being considered completely equal with everyone else – especially those with less education and probably holding more ignorant views. We've enjoyed positions of status, respect and privilege – it's difficult to give those up and just be part of the crowd.'

She looked at Savverio and was fairly sure she knew what he was thinking, 'I have to admit, it all looks a bit childish now. After our recent experience here on Ur-Tokar, and then discovering how badly our colleagues were treated on Rorque 4, it seems quite petty to be worrying about where you should be sitting in the pecking order. At the time, though, it somehow seemed crucially important, but I've had time to reflect here, and I can now see there are clearly more important issues to be concerned about.'

She stopped again for a while. 'And, personally, if I'm really honest, I just didn't think human nature allowed such a society to exist. I just didn't think people were cooperative and altruistic enough to create any form of utopia that actually worked. But, it just looks like I was wrong on that account, at least, it's not what I observed when I was there.'

Janicka smiled, she was proud of the society she lived in and wanted others to share in her good fortune. 'Our approach to science is a very positive one, as well, you know. Like you, we believe in a rationally ordered universe, one that can only be understood through proper method and enquiry. It's just that we believe that all science needs to be conducted so that the entire population benefits equally from its successes. It would be unfair if it only benefitted a privileged few, or if it developed processes or products that were harmful to society.'

'And how does your society actually ensure that science works in this manner?' asked Mila, though she suspected she knew the answer, given what she had seen whilst she was on Zeta Kotlin.

'Well, firstly, I guess we are just brought up with this idea from an early age, so it's almost like second nature to us. Also, the universities are open to anyone who would like to participate in them, and they are self-governing with open democratic forums for when disputes occur. It can get a bit chaotic at times - there's often lots of debate and argument - but mostly they just rumble along happily enough and people generally research what they want to. If it produces something useful and people like it, then it gets voted into use.'

'Mmm, it sounds a bit disorderly, though. What if someone is engaged in research that others find completely unacceptable and they want it stopped?' Mila asked, wanting to know more about the system that she had now decided she would soon be trying to persuade her colleagues to join with.

'I don't think it happens much – we're a fairly open and tolerant people, after all – but if it did, they would be asked to defend their research project publically, and if people were still not convinced and it met further disapproval, there would be a vote by the university or local community on whether it should be halted or allowed to continue,' answered Janicka.

'And if they refused to comply?'

'Well, they could always try elsewhere, I suppose, but usually if a majority of the community dislike something and have explained clearly why they do so, then most people are socially responsible enough to abide by the community decision. We have a strong sense of community, and pretty much everyone wants to remain a valued part of that society,' explained Savverio.

'If it's an open system, what is there to stop lots of weird and strange ideas and projects being pursued. Won't they just hold up the better thought-through ideas and projects?' Mila asked, believing she still needed to know more.

'Most people work in teams, so it's unlikely there will be too many completely eccentric projects in the first place, but sometimes ideas that sound wacky at first, turn out to be good ones. Also, most people tend not to work long hours – we like socialising on our world – so there's usually lots of time, space and resources to go around in your average department or faculty, so I don't think this ever becomes a major problem,' answered Janicka.

'What about allocation of resources and access to materials, how is that organised?' asked Mila, continuing with the questioning.

'There's a common inventory, listing all materials and how much of each is available. Everyone can see if you take more than your fair share, so generally people don't. Most projects are collaborative anyway, so when a material is genuinely scarce there are probably only one or two groups opting to pursue projects that require it - so there are few issues in this respect, anyway. Resources, machinery and the like are all shared. All the AI units and mini-fabs are collectively owned and controlled, so we can make most of what we need, usually. A few materials are scarce, like the ores and minerals we've come to collect from Ur-Tokar, but generally we have few problems with material scarcity.'

This aspect of the university system on Zeta Kotlin had some similarities to that on Alpha Fraczan, so Mila did not consider this would be difficult to explain to her colleagues. It was the lack of hierarchy that was probably going to be the biggest stumbling block, she thought. She was concerned her colleagues would find it too anarchic and disorganised. However, she was intending to play them the message sent from The Spirit of the Age that explained the deteriorating situation on Rorque 4. This, she considered, would probably be the most influential part of the conference, whilst the rest act as supplementary arguments.

Mila had one final thought which concerned the wider political aspect of Zeta Kotlin. 'Your world's not how I'd always imagined it being. I thought it would be more centralised and authoritarian, with the state controlling people's behaviour, and deciding exactly what was and what was not permitted. Why is it so different to that popular image?'
'That's right, there has always been a huge emphasis on keeping everything decentralised on Zeta. I believe this had something to do with previous efforts on Earth to create socialism, where centralised approaches were used and which went badly wrong. The first settlers on our planet were determined to make sure that mistake was not repeated again, though I believe it took a while to convince absolutely everyone of this,' explained Savverio, correctly guessing as to why Mila thought the way she did. 'In addition, centralisation of power hardly seems compatible with creating a politically egalitarian society; it's more likely to produce the opposite.'
'After all, it fits with human nature,' added Janicka. 'We're all pretty reasonable, rational and intelligent people. We're sociable and we trust others to make sensible decisions. Once you trust others to do the right thing, then you can allow decentralised decision-making. Additionally, we keep it that way by ensuring that all major decisions are based on direct democracy; office-holders are chosen by sortition and only keep their positions for relatively short periods of time. We try wherever possible to keep everything transparent and accountable, and ensure there are no conflicts of interest when it comes to office-holders implementing democratic decisions. It's worked very well so far,' she explained, with her usual enthusiasm.

Mila was quite impressed with the mini-political lecture, but said nothing. Her dealings with the crew of the Opa-Loka over the last few weeks had all been very positive ones. The crew all seemed to be very well adjusted individuals, and she was starting to believe that any society producing people like Janicka, Savverio and the others must have some considerable merits. The only real issue she still had, was that they rarely seemed in a hurry, and that their decision-making and implementation process had, at times, taken considerably longer than she would have liked. Their approach to life seemed to be quite chaotic, though she also admitted that it did seem to work – just, perhaps, not quickly enough.

She was still not entirely convinced that open access to a university was a fully workable concept, it would depend on the general standard of education on the planet in question, she figured, but in many respects the crew of the Opa-Loka had put to rest some of her main concerns. Loss of status might just be something she had to live with, especially as the few alternatives still existing now, might deliver a considerably worse outcome. And after all, she thought, she could spend more time on her actual research and less on administrative tasks. She was particularly interested in further developing her theory concerning how differential gravitational forces impacted on the development of terrestrial life on different planets. She was thinking about throwing all her energy into this particular project. She had, however, been slightly concerned as to whether the universities on Zeta Kotlin would be sufficiently interested in such a project, but it sounded from their conversation as though it was actually unlikely to meet any significant opposition.

At this point, Mila was joined by Simon Kamenev who informed her that he now estimated they had gathered and manufactured sufficient food supplies to feed all the passengers on their starship. As this was the case, the AI units could presently load the ferming units back onto their landing craft, and they would soon be ready to return to The Star Chaser. They gave Savverio and Janicka a quick update on their immediate plans and assured them they would keep them abreast of all up and coming developments.

'Well, enjoy your time spent down here, the views are fantastic and the air is so clean and so clear. It's an amazing place to relax. What are you planning to do?' asked Mila.
'Mmm, not too sure, just relax, chill out . . . spend some time watching the grass grow, staring at the clouds and the sea. Other stuff. Not really sure. I'm sure we'll find something,' replied Janicka, whilst looking knowingly at Savverio.
'Yeh, we just need some planetary reality after so much time on the ship,' Savverio added. 'I hope your conference goes well, remember we'll be

rooting for a return to Zeta. Oh, and enjoy your vegan lunch, after weeks spent consuming space rations it looks great.'

'Yeh, yum yum, and good luck with the conference! I'm sure you can persuade them that socialism's the way forward,' added Janicka, with a smile and a sparkle in her eyes.

'Well, I'll do my best. Good luck, and see you later,' and Mila headed back to their transporter craft.

A short time later, with their landing craft fully loaded, they waved farewell, and soon they were speeding rapidly upwards into near space and back to their spacecraft. Janicka and Savverio watched until the craft disappeared high above into the stratosphere.

Savverio and Janicka were in no particular hurry to do anything - they had spent an untypically long period of time out of stasis and on the starship, and simply wanted to enjoy some time on an actual planet, even if their bodies were still struggling slightly with a normal gravity environment. Savverio had the additional problem of his poorly functioning legs, so they often spent long periods of time simply lying in the long grass along the cliff-tops watching the ice-bergs float past, or staring at the numerous cumulus clouds above them and commenting on the unbelievably wide variety of shapes they could form.

They were simply planning to take things easy for a few days. Janicka remained constantly fascinated by the scintillating beauty of the whole place. She frequently stopped and lay down on her back in the long blue-green grass, listening to the constant hum of the insects in the trees on the mountain slope, and staring at the fluffy cumulus clouds that appeared to hang motionless above her in the pale cerulean blue sky. The sun shone warmly, the air was still and it frequently reminded her of her childhood.

She thought back to the long lazy days spent outdoors in the summer sun, to the sublime sense of freedom, never knowing what time it was, or exactly where she was. She thought of her childhood friends and the fabulously intricate games they had created and acted out, frequently imagining they were on the run from all manner of dangerous forces, or floating free above the clouds, or exploring ever more difficult terrain on some outlandish adventure. Long enjoyable hours spent playing ever more complicated games, like dragon rider, in which their fortunes were controlled by the ever shifting nature of the constellations and the tides. She tried to remember the rules of the game, ones which were forever being made yet more complicated. She closed her eyes and thought for a while. Without realising it she dozed off in the warmth of the midday sun.

Several hours later, she woke to find Savverio busy on his personal electronic device. He smiled as he saw her wake, made a sarcastic comment about how tiring their work was, and informed her that the AI units had started to make good progress with preparing the mining operation. Their scans had proven correct and they had found the rich veins of the ores and minerals they needed, but it would be several days, or even longer, before the first of their mining operations would be completed and several cargo-loads could be transported back to the spaceship.

This was the news Janicka had been hoping for, since it meant they could spend some extra quality time together enjoying the fresh air, the mountain scenery and exploring the local woods and the coastline. Ur-Tokar was a very different planet from Zeta Kotlin and it was unlikely, she thought, that she would ever enjoy another chance to experience such pristine beauty.

Sometime later on The Star Chaser, however, Mila Lustrom was finding she needed to work a bit harder than Janicka and Savverio. The process of bringing around several thousand passengers out of stasis at approximately the same time had been difficult enough - though thankfully the AI units and the ship's computer were able to perform the bulk of that particular task. Once fed and sufficiently recovered from the torpor of stasis, though, Mila had then needed to explain where the ship was presently located and why they had temporarily halted their journey.

She had transmitted in full the message from The Spirit of the Age and had watched her audience intently to gauge their reaction to the information it contained. She could soon discern worried faces, looks of concern, sighs of disappointment, people shaking their heads and negative mutterings. She interpreted this as meaning it might be reasonably straightforward to make the case for a return to Zeta Kotlin, but there were then numerous questions that needed fielding, and she had ultimately needed to engage in a great deal of persuasive argument.

She had also prevaricated over whether to mention the fact that a Zeleyanian war fleet would be arriving in the sector in approximately four months time – for fear of creating alarm - but ultimately thought it would be unethical not to do so. Its mention did heighten the sense of unease though, and concentrated minds to the fact that any decision they made needed to be quick one. She outlined the news they were receiving from Rorque 4, of its climate deterioration and its longstanding economic recession. This, together with hints of political unrest on Zeleyan and a potential invasion of Ur-Tokar were making - what their people called - the Far Sector of the Nexus Cluster appear distinctly unstable. It looked a much better prospect to return to the Near Sector and the stability of Zeta Kotlin, Margalla and their own home planet which they now knew was beginning to stabilise.

Ultimately, she related news of their good working relationship with the crew of the Opa-Loka and Janicka's description of the academic situation on Zeta Kotlin. Even after this, she could discern that there was still some resistance to returning to the socialist planet – largely for similar reasons to those which had originally convinced her that it was best to head for Rorque 4 – but when the decision finally went to a vote, the majority opting to turn around and head back to Zeta Kotlin was a pretty comfortable one. There was, however, and unexpectedly, a call for a second vote on when this should actually occur.

A very small minority thought they might be able to help the people down on Ur-Tokar in their struggle against the Zeleyanians, whilst significantly more suggested that tourist-type visits to the semi-frozen, heavily forested world would be an interesting visitor experience. However, the majority believed there was actually little they could do to help a people who rejected modern technology in such an outright way, and with an imminent invasion fleet arriving soon, it was probably too dangerous to remain in the area for too long. The vote was heavily in favour of an imminent departure.

Mila had not given this latter aspect of their situation much thought – concentrating on why they should return to Zeta Kotlin, rather than when – and suddenly discovered that she didn't actually want to leave Ur-Tokar quite yet. She wanted to see how the situation developed at Meridin and whether the Zeleyanians could be defeated. She too had been enraptured by the beauty of Ur-Tokar and was developing good working relationships with the crew of the Opa-Loka. Whilst she told none of this to her fellow crew members on The Star Chaser, she resolved to look into the matter of switching to the other starship; they were both ultimately heading back to Zeta Kotlin now, and exactly when she arrived there seemed of no pressing importance.

Interstellar Space – The Spirit of the Age is awakened

The Spirit of the Age was four and a half months into what was supposed to be its two year journey across the Nexus Cluster to Zeta Kotlin, when an encrypted message from the Opa-Loka was logged by the ship's computer. Until this point in time, its progress had been unhindered and uninterrupted, albeit a little on the slow side, but pursuing the preplanned trajectory programmed before leaving the orbit of Rorque 4. The message was given a high priority code by the AI unit that reviewed the message. The AI unit then duly made its way to the huge, dimly-lit stasis chamber, and worked its way along the endless corridors of the vast but eerily quiet construction, until it located the relevant stasis pods and slowly brought the Margallan skeleton crew out of stasis one by one.

Several hours later, the six Margallans were sat in the forward deck sipping from containers of nourishing soup and various mineral salt drinks to replenish their energy levels. Slowly, as they recovered from the torpor of suspended animation and began to feel like their old selves, they became fully conscious of their wakened surroundings. When the ship's computers finally indicated that the vital signs of the crew had stabilised at standard pre-determined levels, one of the AI units responded to this information, and displayed the message from the Opa-Loka on the large bluescreen that spread across the majority of the wall in front of them.

Greetings from the Opa-Loka. We are currently in the Rogan star system on what was a routine trade mission that has become distinctly non-routine. Zeleyanian military forces have established a military base on Ur-Tokar, but it has been half-destroyed, partly thanks to our intervention. They have a larger invasion fleet heading for the planet due to arrive on Star Date 2335.12.09. The invasion fleet is in frequent communication with the Rorque Corporation on Rorque 4; we believe this is probably with a view to acquiring advanced space flight technology, but might also be for other reasons. We are aware of the deteriorating climactic situation on Rorque 4. Are the authorities there planning to depart with the intention of settling on Ur-Tokar? In short, can you supply us with information that would be useful in helping us assess the Rorque 4-Zeleyanian relationship better? If you know anything that might deter the Zeleyanians from invading Ur-Tokar, we would strongly advise you to send a message to them directly. Your comrades, Jiaying, Savverio, Janicka, Kahlil and Neema.

'Wow, Jiaying is still flying round the universe in that old rust bucket - I haven't seen her for years. I thought she'd have retired by now,' exclaimed Akiko, surprised by news from her old friend. 'It would be great to see her again. We had some great times together back on Margalla.'

'So, you know her as well. I didn't know that. I met her on their last trip to Margalla. Yeh, she told me then that she was going to retire to Margalla after one more mission – I wonder what happened to that plan?' remarked Kiyona, who had spent time with one of the previous Opa-Loka crews, sharing the delights of Margalla's islands, culture and people with them. 'I think I've also met Savverio, the name rings a bell, I'm sure.'

'You've met her as well, I had no idea, how was she when you met her?' asked Akiko, and the two of them started reminiscing at some length about their previous encounters with the Zetan crew members.

A few minutes later, though, Xander stated, 'sorry to interrupt your trip down memory lane, but I really think we have more pressing matters to deal with; in particular, we need to discuss how we respond to their plea for help,' he interjected, after a few minutes of listening to tales of who slept with who, and how much partying and drinking they had indulged in with Jiaying and her various crew mates.

'From their message, it sounds as though the situation on Rorque 4 has deteriorated even further whilst we've been in stasis. I suggest that we ask the computer to give us a summarised appraisal of recent events there, before we make any decision about any message we might transmit,' indicated Zhavia, aware that any intervention they made could be a crucial one, but would also entail giving the appearance that they were fully on top of events and aware of all the latest developments.

The ship's computer was thus instructed to relay them details of the most significant news events arriving from Rorque 4 in the last four and a half months, and a few minutes later it delivered a summary that largely consisted of further outbreaks of widespread and intense droughts, extensive fires, searing heatwaves and various unsuccessful attempts by the major corporations to kick-start the economy back into life. As they watched the scenes and listened to the serious of back-to-back newscasts on the developing economic and climatic disasters, it slowly dawned upon them that they were watching the demise of a planet that seemed to be entering the initial death-throws of some form of fiery, semi-apocalyptic, climate-induced disaster, and for which there was little hope of impeding its impending doom. 'It's such a shame they've made a complete mess of what was quite an attractive planet. It had far more going for it than Margalla - all that land, the beautiful shallow seas, the rolling hills and plateaus. In many respects it was a beautiful planet,' opined Kiyona, 'and so completely unlike the dreadful society they created,' she quickly added, not wishing anyone to mistakenly think she had actually liked Rorquean society.

'The corporations have done nothing to look after the place; they've just exploited the whole planet and let it deteriorate, and then deteriorate even further. It wouldn't surprise me if they did decide to up sticks, and just leave for another planet once they've decided the place has become unprofitable . . . and uninhabitable, by the looks of things. After all, that's what they did on Earth,' Zhavia pointed out. 'I don't remember anyone ever mentioning Ur-Tokar, though, never mind setting up a new society there. If that was their plan, they kept it very quiet.'

'Seems unlikely to me as well! They were forever bragging about their achievements – no matter how dubious they were. I suspect they would have done the same concerning any plans to settle on Ur-Tokar,' agreed Akiko. 'Rather than leaving the planet - like rats departing a sinking ship - it would be far better if someone actually did something about the situation. It's a pity the people haven't decided to take collective control of the situation; I'm sure they could reverse much of the damage and actually sort out the problems they have, if they put their minds to it. It might be a long and difficult process, but I'm sure the planet could be rescued, it didn't look like a completely lost cause to me,' she added.

'But the average Rorquean seemed either oblivious to their predicament, too engrossed in their own personal ambitions, or so defeated and apathetic that none of them believed that anything could actually be done to rescue the situation from any sort of disintegration. It's difficult to see how people like that could save themselves, never mind a whole planet,' Zek said somewhat gloomily. 'It's a pity they can't come up with a better society. Then it might be a great planet to live on – all that space and so many places to travel to. Then it might be worth a prolonged visit.'

'I still think it's all down to the AI units,' chipped in Zhavia, returning to one of his favourite subjects. 'On Margalla, we have collective control of them, and so we decide what happens and we do it in the interests of everyone. It means production is collectively organised and for the entire people. It also means we're freed up to live our lives in any meaningful way we think is suitable. We have freedom and prosperity and it's organised on the basis of equality. On Rorque 4, the AI units are mainly controlled privately by the corporate elites. The corporations use them to pursue individual prosperity and freedom but only for a small and highly privileged elite. The rest of the population is simply left at the mercy of the system. It creates massive inequality and the lower classes have no real control over their own lives. If they followed our approach and controlled the AI units collectively, then everything else would fall into place; they could create a better society and resolve their climate crisis,' he concluded. 'If they want to sort the planet out, basically that's what they need to do.'

'Are you sure it's actually that straightforward. The people we met held all sorts of negative and unhelpful ideas; they were divisive, selfish, greedy, uncaring and often very ignorant. Are you sure collectively controlling the AI units could transform all that,' asked Kiyona, somewhat sceptical that such a huge transformation could be achieved through one basic economic alteration. 'Don't get me wrong, I agree our approach is way better, but won't they first need to change a whole range of other elements of their society, in particular the way they think, surely?'

But before Zhavia could reply, Akiko quickly intervened, 'we've become sidetracked again, we need to decide what goes in this message that we need to send. Jiaying and the others want us to send a message to the Zeleyanians which will deter them from invading Ur-Tokar. What do we know that might upset their plans, or confuse and demoralise them?'

'Why was the Zeleyanian government talking with the Rorque Corporation about advanced space flight, I though the rocket scientists were on the other starship and ended up working for Cosmic Solutions?' asked Arlo, making a rare contribution to their discussion.

'That's right, they were, so the Zeleyanians should have been working with Cosmic Solutions, not the Rorque Corporation. That doesn't make any sense! The Rorque Corporation did sell them some stasis ships though, which are presumably now the invasion fleet heading to Ur-Tokar, but they were all old ships,' answered Akiko. She thought for a while. 'Maybe the Rorque Corporation lied to the Zeleyanians, to keep them from dealing with Cosmic Solutions, but they never had any intention of helping them any further.'

'That wouldn't surprise me – they're all obsessed with competing against each other. It's all they seemed to do. If they'd spent as much time cooperating with each other to save the planet as they did competing against each other, they'd probably be living in the perfect utopia by now,' added Zhavia, unable to comprehend why supposedly intelligent people were incapable of following a more enlightened approach. 'The Rorque Corporation could be playing all sorts of games, but I remember being told they did have some long-term plan to work with the Zeleyanians to revive Rorque 4's economy. Maybe they were working together and planning to exploit Ur-Tokar for its natural wealth and resources.'

'I thought Zeleyan was a largely self-contained society. I thought fascists liked their economy to be an autarky and self-sufficient so they were not dependent on foreign planets. Surely they should just keep to themselves and stay where they are – they always have in the past. If they're like that, why do you think they are invading Ur-Tokar in the first place?' Akiko asked, it suddenly dawning on her that this might be of some importance.

'They believe in social Darwinism, that we all live in a highly competitive universe, and if you don't dominate the others, the others will come and dominate you, sooner or later. For them, we live in a dog-eat-dog cosmos! It's inherent within their ideology to invade and conquer others before they are conquered themselves. It's based on a highly negative view of human nature. In addition, their political system is so repressive that they ban a wide range of economic activities; so when the economy needs to expand, often it's simply unable to do so, as they are worried that the new economic freedoms will undermine their political control. The alternative is to expand externally, to invade new territories and acquire new markets and resources, and impose a similar political situation there s well,' answered Zhavia with a great deal of authority. 'I guess that's why they're invading Ur-Tokar, probably for those two reasons. But logically they won't stop there; they will continue conquering further planets until . . . well, probably until they experience imperial overstretch.'

They all looked at him slightly surprised.

'I found this on the space web, in the Xenon Codex by a recent thinker called Astron Z, when I was researching the subject of fascism, whilst completing a social studies project. At the time, I was interested in how a society like Zeleyan could actually function. I couldn't understand why anyone would work for a system when they had no freedom, so I read up on it,' he stated, slightly defensively. 'I hadn't realised they were given no choice, and were punished severely for not cooperating.'

'I noticed from our ship's planned flight trajectory, that we will be passing Rogan's star system at approximately the same time as the invasion fleet arrives. We might want to think about altering our course,' Zek suddenly stated, once again changing the direction of the conversation.

'Shouldn't we be arriving there more quickly, has something delayed us?' asked Akiko, suddenly remembering a 3-D space chart she had been looking at earlier, as they were recovering from stasis.

'We've not been delayed, we're travelling at a slower than recommended speed. I wondered about that as well. According to the ship's computer the rocket fuel is not burning as efficiently as should be expected. Diagnostic checks show all engine systems to be functioning effectively and efficiently, so it must be the quality of the rocket fuel,' explained Zhavia, who had previously been checking their progress through space.

'So the Rorque Corporation supplied us with some dodgy rocket fuel . . . now who is surprised by that,' quipped Kiyona.

'Probably just a slightly inferior batch they were happy to get rid of,' Zhavia offered.

'Will it make a difference?'

'Probably not, we're just travelling a little slowly. It might mean more maintenance work on the engines at a later date, that's all,' answered Zhavia.

'Zek, did you mean we should change course to head towards Ur-Tokar to go and offer help, or to avoid the area entirely?' Kiyona asked, returning the conversation to the previous issue. 'Because, it doesn't sound to me like we're exactly the kings of speed at the moment, so I doubt we can come charging to their rescue,' she pointed out.

'I was thinking of detouring away from the area. The invasion fleet might attack us, or try and capture the ship. Remember we have thousands of space travellers on this ship. We should avoid putting them and ourselves in danger. If we went to Ur-Tokar, how could we help, anyway? Is there much we could actually do there? We have no weapons or military know-how, or the ability to wage war,' replied Zek. 'Not that I would want to do anything like that, anyway.'

'Err, I'm not sure, we might be able to help with evacuating people or with supplying communications expertise or something like that,' said Kiyona, unsure of what they could actually do. 'But if Jiaying is in any sort of danger, we should definitely try and help her out, and her crew mates. We can't leave them there on their own.'

The others offered various nods of agreement or approving comments

'Are you all really sure that's a good idea?' asked Zek, still concerned that they might be blasted out of the sky or something similar. 'It sounds potentially reckless, maybe even dangerous and highly risky. I know some people might find that exciting, but we really should consider this carefully.'

'Well, I'm not suggesting that we like to be frightened, or want to deliberately put our lives in jeopardy; it's just that we could be of use to our comrades,' Kiyona replied. 'I just think that if we are needed, we should go and help them if we possibly can.'

Before, the argument could continue, Akiko decided to intervene at this point. 'We need to find out more about their precise situation. I suggest we don't go back into stasis just yet and that we remain in communication with the Opa-Loka. We need more information from them, and we might also need to act on it quickly, as well. At the moment, we can keep our options open and make a more definitive decision later, once we know what exactly is occurring at Ur-Tokar,' she stated. She looked at the others and they all indicated agreement.

'I've also been thinking about the Rorque Corporation, and have just remembered some comments made by our friends in Shade Gate. I have an idea about the message that we should send to the Zeleyanian starship fleet, and it just might encourage them to call off their invasion.'

The others all looked at her in surprise.

Interstellar Space - Zeleyanian invasion fleet receives a further message

Aboard the Patriot IV, if General Neumann and Lieutenant-General Tarrafel had thought that time might drag when they first considered the predicament of travelling on a spacecraft in deep space for several months with an angry and irritated Vartin, they had not been unduly pessimistic. Partly to deal with this particular problem, but also out of sheer curiosity, the two had sought ways to pass the time that involved avoiding the Supreme Commander. As a result, they had spent a considerable amount of time space-gazing and both found the view of the starscape that the ship sped past endlessly fascinating; its sheer immensity, vast darkness and an almost endless array of red and white stars, distant spiral galaxies, gas nebulae and whizzing comets had all been truly transfixing. They had thus initially spent long hours frequently mesmerised by the stunning starscape their ship travelled through. But overtime, it changed so imperceptibly slowly, as the ship traversed through the same sector of space, that its captivating beauty soon became an expected and accustomed backdrop to their regular routine of tasks.

But, what the two generals did find almost impossibly difficult to become accustomed to, was life aboard a starship hurtling through deepest space. Their daily routine, by necessity, consisted of several hours of exercise to compensate for the loss of bone and muscle mass suffered in a low gravity environment. For two ageing, overweight men, this was a particularly arduous task, and one that frequently delivered long-lasting niggling strains and injuries to parts of their body long unused to vigorous exercise. Additionally, for longstanding members of High Command born into the pampered Zeleyanian elite, and used to the finest food, wine and cigars the planet could offer, a diet of prepackaged space rations was impossible to appreciate or become enamoured with.

Add all this to the constant low hum of the ventilation systems, the stark metallic brutalism of the mass-produced stasis ship, and a lighting system that had no realistic hope of mimicking the diurnal changes of a real planetary lightscape, and the two elite military commanders found themselves in an environment that was not only entirely alien, but also one in which they felt as though they had been demoted to the equivalent of working on a factory floor. Their cabins had been partially personalised before the mission had commenced, but there had been no expectation of spending long hours ensconced within them, so even these offered few home comforts, nor any real sanctuary from the otherwise industrial nature of the huge silver space machine. Both men, as a result of these travails, suffered frequent bouts of the space ship blues – and they saw no reason to believe matters were any different for their leader.

With little else of use to do, Vartin had ordered them to sift through the vast mountain of communications data that the ship had logged since departing from Zeleyan. Most of this amounted to routine media emissions from the various planets at the different ends of the Nexus Cluster. They became intimately familiar with the nature of Rorque 4's ultra-competitive society and its almost god-like worship of commerce, but also its seemingly never-ending economic crisis and the developing problems associated with the climate catastrophe that was unfolding on the planet. Zeta Kotlin, by contrast, appeared as a beacon of calm and stability; indeed, they were unable to register any major incidents of any note occurring on the planet. There appeared – unsurprisingly – to be an increased interest in science, and of the other planets in the Cluster, but little else of any great interest. Margalla, remained silent, and they were oblivious to the existence of its small utopian island society, anyway. Ur-Tokar, was equally silent, but for very different reasons. The emissions from Zeleyan were, of course, carefully controlled by their own regime.

Vartin, meanwhile, had taken to concentrating his attention on the information sent from the spy satellite that he had put in orbit around Ur-Tokar several years ago. He was building up a detailed picture of its various continents, deep blue oceans, extensive ice-caps, jagged mountain ranges, cascading white rivers and deep rocky canyons. It was a world unlike Zeleyan, he thought; a cold, untamed and primitive planet, one that lent itself to wildness, anarchy and rebellion. Zeleyan by contrast, with its vast plains and single supercontinent, was a world that could easily be mastered and controlled, a world that could be civilised with relative ease. He decided he would need to find different methods to tame Ur-Tokar from those used on Zeleyan.

He had always known Ur-Tokar was sparsely inhabited, but the detailed scans from the satellite showed it to be barely inhabited at all. There were certainly no cities nor even large towns; at best he could find isolated small towns, occasional villages and hamlets, but little else of note. The lack of electronic activity meant that detecting settlements was problematic and subject to error, so there might still be others, he assumed. He also presumed that their rejection of advanced technology had left the inhabitants at the mercy of famine and disease, and had thus prevented any significant growth in population numbers and the creation of habitations of any significant size. Why anyone would willingly choose to live such a backwards existence was beyond him, though, he frequently thought.

In some respects, it was also all slightly disappointing for Vartin – after the capture of Meridin, there appeared little else for him to conquer; and what remained of the isolated settlements would prove easy enough for his forces to secure. There was clearly sufficient coastline and suitable river valleys to build new settlements and grow the population in size. In addition, the clearance of the lower-lying forests would also free up land for new habitation. But there were clear limitations to what could be achieved; in totality, the semi-frozen world clearly had limited scope for development and would never be an equal to Zeleyan. Nevertheless, it would still be able to serve his original purpose, as a step into space, and as a suitable base for further imperial expansion, he consoled himself with.

The three officers also became aware of the movement of various starships around the Nexus Cluster. Media reports, in addition to communications scans, allowed them to know of the departures of The Star Chaser and The Spirit of the Age - in directly opposite directions - and the reasons given for their respective journeys. The fact that neither had even considered travelling to Zeleyan they attributed to pernicious propaganda being disseminated by their enemies, particularly the socialists of Zeta Kotlin. Vartin almost felt tempted to send out invitations to the scientists outlining the attractions of working on Zeleyan, but he knew this would attract undue attention to the invasion fleet and so resisted any such urges in this direction.

It was whilst they were working through the communications logs one day that the open message from The Star Chaser suddenly appeared on the ship's computer.

We have taken control of your stasis ship, The Crusader. It is now beyond Rogan's star system and at this very minute is accelerating rapidly along a trajectory to the distant star of Alchemy, located in the sector of the celestial sky dominated by Spiral Galaxy 28948 and within the Kadu Flyer constellation. The star is a distance of 7.8 light years away and so the ship will arrive there approximately twenty-two years from now. None of the crew on board was harmed. This is an open message being transmitted to all Zeleyanian forces. We have also informed all the planets of the Nexus Cluster of your military actions. We strongly advise you to call off your invasion of Ur-Tokar and return to Zeleyan.

Vartin and the two generals could only stare in disbelief at the message on the screen in front of them. Vartin hoped against hope that the message was untrue, that it might be some ruse concocted by Rosson to save his own skin. It had been approximately one month since he had ordered his secret agent to arrest Rosson, but a quick calculation indicated that this mysterious message must have been sent before any arrest of Rosson could have been effected by his spy. The ship's computer confirmed such a calculation and that his missive to the regime spy would still not, even now, have reached Ur-Tokar. At the present point in time, Rosson was probably still in command on Ur-Tokar. Vartin ordered the ship's computer to check in-coming data from the spy satellite orbiting the planet. A few minutes later it confirmed that the satellite had indeed registered the departure of the spaceship from the star system and towards the space coordinates indicated. The satellite had not registered the starship's presence since.

The enormity of the implications of the message only slowly became apparent to those aboard The Patriot IV. Another major disaster had occurred under Rosson's command – a further reason to have him court-martialed; but this time, in Vartin's mind, it would be for treason. His neglect or incompetence had actively undermined the regime. To make matters worse, there was no in-coming message from Rosson on this subject, just complete silence. Routine communications were continuing, but not a single word on his one and only starship being captured. It was abundantly clear that Rosson was hiding information from his Supreme Commander – a completely unsatisfactory state of affairs. He even wondered momentarily whether Rosson had gone completely rogue.

But, more importantly, their invasion plan would now be known across the disparate planets of the Nexus Cluster. Given that none of them had any known form of military space capability, there was nothing any of the other planets could actually do to prevent the invasion, but it did mean that they would be forewarned of any further Zeleyanian incursions into space. As such, any further imperial conquests would be significantly more difficult from this point onward. This, thought Vartin, made the acquisition of more advanced space flight technology and improved rocket engines from Rorque 4 all the more imperative. The element of surprise was now gone, but speed and rapid attack forces could compensate for this tactical lacuna.

However, this latter concern reminded Vartin that all his private communications with the Rorque Corporation had, so far, been answered with fairly bland corporate statements assuring him that the corporation was working on the situation as best as it possibly could, that it had his best interests at heart, and that the satisfaction of the customer was always paramount, but had so far not promised him anything of any real substance. Vartin was beginning to believe that the Rorque Corporation was either making no progress at all with the deal, or that it had decided to stall or even renege on their previous dealings. The deteriorating political, economic and climate situation on the planet made him wonder whether his deal was either becoming irrelevant to the corporation, or that conditions on the planet were making it impossible to actually complete. He had pressed the Rorque Corporation for greater clarity on the matter, but to no effect.

As Rosson had done a month earlier, Vartin also pondered on whom exactly might have seized his starship. The only people capable of achieving such a feat and with a presence in the area were the scientists on The Star Chaser. He was less sure as to why they would do this - assuming they had - though. As with Rosson, he concluded that they must be in league with the socialists on Zeta Kotlin - their previous point of departure - but how they had discovered the military base and how had they been able to communicate its presence to others so rapidly, he was entirely unsure of. None of what occurred made any sense. He suspected there must therefore be other forces in the vicinity of Ur-Tokar, and instructed the ship's computer to alter the spy satellite's settings so it focused on a wider area within Rogan's system, in addition to its current monitoring of the surface and near orbit of Ur-Tokar. He also strengthened the security protocols on the three invasion ships to ensure no remote and hostile takeover occurred of his own ship. Finally, he sent a further message to his secret agent on the planet, stressing the importance of keeping Rosson under arrest, and to use the planet's satellite system to search for hostile forces in their immediate vicinity. He himself should, naturally, be kept abreast of all ongoing developments.

Against his better judgement, but in the absence of the presence of his usual advisor Varela, he decided to consult his generals on the present situation. They had - as with all his senior officials - been chosen on the basis that their total loyalty and devotion to Vartin could be assured at all times, so he was not anticipating a particularly thought-provoking conversation. However, Vartin felt the need to think out aloud, because doubts were beginning to creep in to his mind as to whether he should now complete the mission he had embarked upon only a few months beforehand. His usual caution was beginning to get the better of him. He needed to convince himself it was worth proceeding further with the invasion, and that his glorious incursion into space should remain an ongoing consideration.

Both of the senior officers had originally presumed they would be spending eight months in stasis, leading a successful invasion force that had no realistic prospect of losing, celebrating a swift and decisive victory and then returning to Zeleyan to be feted as heroes. The prospect of spending long months or years away on a backward planet like Ur-Tokar offered no attraction to them whatsoever. As such, a premature return to Zeleyan would not necessarily be an unfortunate turn of events. There would be no military victory, of course, but at least they would be back to the comforts of civilisation. However, they also knew they could not afford to show open disloyalty to their Supreme Commander, and that they needed to engage with their leader with considerable caution.

Arrival in Utopia

The three officers met in the control room of the starship. Vartin saluted them in and the two men strapped themselves into the waiting chairs. Without further ado, Vartin immediately launched into one of his usual lengthy and pompous appraisals of the situation. 'Our national forces already control the chief settlement on Ur-Tokar, and we have sufficient forces to take control of all major habitations, and thus the entire inhabited planet. With our overwhelming military superiority, securing this part of the mission is still a given. The loss of The Crusader makes no actual material difference to the situation, since our forces on the planet are secure and fully in control of events. The only negative here is the continued command of Vice-Admiral Rosson, but I have put steps in motion to address that unfortunate matter.' His two officers nodded knowingly upon hearing this.

'Upon arrival at the planet,' he continued, 'I will assume full control of all military operations both in orbit and on the planetary surface. It is my patriotic duty to do so. Rosson will be dealt with swiftly and accordingly. The planet clearly has some colonisation potential for our people, and the economy of Zeleyan will undoubtedly benefit from our permanent presence on Ur-Tokar. There appear to be useful resources and potential living space for many of our citizens wanting to start a new life.' He paused for a brief moment. 'But, gentlemen, the big question is whether we should continue with further plans for conquest across the Nexus Cluster. We have now lost the element of surprise – thanks to that bungling idiot Rosson – so further conquests will entail the use of larger and battle-hardened forces and a much higher degree of strategic planning. We will undoubtedly meet determined resistance and invariably suffer casualties and losses, though that is the nature of war. There will be glorious victories to be won, and to die in battle is an honourable death. I am sure the regime will have many heroes to honour, but, I believe all this is still within the capability of our magnificent forces. What do you think gentlemen?'

This was not what either senior officer had particularly wanted to hear, though they were half expecting such an analysis. They had heard numerous vainglorious speeches over the years from their Supreme Commander and were well used to such a tone. But somehow they had both expected a somewhat more considered approach given recent developments, and were somewhat caught off guard. Vartin seemed set on this imperial project of his to a degree they had not, until now, fully appreciated. Both, though, were highly uncertain about openly challenging Vartin, but equally neither believed Vartin held a fully accurate appraisal of the situation. Lieutenant-General Tarrafel knew he could not be seen to be at odds with both Vartin and with General Neumann and initially said nothing.

General Neumann started hesitantly and diplomatically, 'the conquest of Ur-Tokar, I agree, will undoubtedly be a great patriotic success. Colonisation of the planet should also follow immediately. Once we have returned to our great nation of Zeleyan we can organise the transportation of volunteer settlers and the appropriate resources needed. We should have no trouble consolidating our position and civilising the planet.' He paused and glanced at Tarrafel, who almost imperceptibly nodded. With a little more confidence, he then continued, 'a period of consolidation on Ur-Tokar, I believe, would be useful before we embark on further conquests. As you said, we have lost the element of surprise. We might need to take stock of our new situation, let the situation settle for a while and then consider our next moves. We can assess the response and behaviours of our enemies and then prepare for further conquests. There are still security issues on Zeleyan that need dealing with, diverting troops for major engagements on Zeta Kotlin or elsewhere might be more appropriate at a later date. I have some concerns on the issue of overstretching our forces.' He stopped again in case of some response, but as none occurred, he continued with his diplomatically constructed answer. 'If we were to receive the advanced space flight technology promised to us by the Rorque Corporation, however, then that might significantly alter the situation. We would then be able to move much more quickly, invade with speed and still have some element of surprise, even if in a diminished form. I agree with your general appraisal of the situation, but we might want to reflect on some of the finer details.'

The General had wanted to end on a positive note and felt he had managed to do so, but was wondering whether he had overstepped the mark with his deviations from Vartin's original plan. He had never openly disagreed with Vartin before, but he was in largely unknown military territory now, and this fact, together with his concern over recent negative developments and his desire to return to Zeleyan left him, he believed, with no option but to offer a more cautious approach than Vartin might actually like.

Arrival in Utopia

Vartin had expected a more ringing endorsement for his plans, and was slightly surprised by even this token level of dissent. He knew, as no doubt the General did, that the arrival of technology from Rorque 4 was looking increasingly doubtful, so the General appeared to be attaching any delay in further conquests to the failures of the Rorque Corporation – a convenient scapegoat. He also gained the distinct impression that Neumann was hoping for a reasonably quick return to the comforts of Zeleyan. Nevertheless, the General's caution had chimed with some of his own doubts and so he sought the further opinion of Lieutenant-General Tarrafel. To no great surprise, he offered a very similar appraisal of the situation as that already delivered by his senior, and as Vartin had pretty much expected.

Vartin considered the situation for a few moments, keeping his senior officers on tenterhooks. Vartin could see no immediate reason for calling off the invasion of Ur-Tokar, but he conceded that there were reasonable doubts about further incursions deeper into space. However, his detection of a distinct desire to return to Zeleyan from the two officers was extremely useful to know; in the event of needing to do so, he now knew he would suffer no loss of face or any form of resistance. He was not about to actually do this anytime soon, but if circumstances changed it made any such decision considerably easier.

'Then it's agreed, gentlemen', he finally commenced. 'Our patriotic duty is to complete the invasion of Ur-Tokar as originally planned. We will rapidly build up our forces on the planet with a view to further missions. In the meantime, we need to redouble our efforts with the Rorque Corporation. We need to know what technology is being made available to us and when it will be delivered. You are now dismissed.'

All three military officers clearly understood the situation as it stood.

Ur-Tokar – the second Battle of Meridin

Whilst Vartin and his officers narrowed the distance between themselves and their destination of Ur-Tokar, at Meridin on the planet itself, Vice-Admiral Rosson had overseen something of a return to normal over the previous four weeks. The military garrison had been reconstructed, and whilst it was less impressive than the original construction, it was now capable of housing a full regiment once again - not that this was immediately necessary for his currently depleted forces. His military control over the town and the immediate vicinity remained intact; though at no point did he feel he had gained the genuine support of the local villagers and townspeople. They had become habituated, he believed, to a longstanding set of local traditions and customs and the present situation was far outside their traditional comfort zone. Maybe eventually, over time, they would become accommodated to their new leaders – after all, did it make much difference as to exactly who was issuing the orders, if the orders remained much the same as they always had been?

His Communications Officer, Sub-Lieutenant Schultz continued to monitor the general situation in the Nexus Cluster. Rosson was detecting – despite the carefully managed control implemented by the state media – an increased level of political rebellion and unrest on Zeleyan. He knew the coded messages they used, the carefully chosen words selected by the media authorities and their true hidden meanings. In rare moments of optimism, he wondered if Vartin and the invasion fleet might turn their ships around and return to deal with the political unrest, leaving him in a position to determine his own future on Ur-Tokar. However, constant monitoring showed the fleet to be steadily continuing towards their destined target and they were now due to arrive in approximately three and a half months time.

More specifically they were still keeping a close eye on their own local quadrant of space. This monitoring had allowed them to become aware of the degenerating climactic situation on Rorque 4 and the departure of The Spirit of the Age from the neoliberal planet, as well as its newly chosen destination. They had also discovered that it was heading roughly in their direction, and that it was clearly communicating with a starship within Rogan's star system – presumably The Star Chaser. There was still no actual

491

sign of The Star Chaser − or indeed of any other stasis ship − in their immediate area of space, though. However, they knew it had not departed from Rogan's star system, so he figured it must be using evasive manouevres to avoid their communication scans.

They had sent messages to the spaceship requesting to talk, but there had only been complete silence in return. He wondered why they still remained in orbit − for surely they were still there − but could think of no plausible reason, without resorting to some unlikely conspiracy theory involving an intra-stellar alliance organised against the Zeleyanian invasion of Ur-Tokar. Possibly their ship was in need of repair or supplies from the planet, but neither of these explanations was particularly convincing. Maybe they were in contact with people on the other side of the planet, he thought, but those regions were extremely sparsely inhabited, so this would seem to serve little practical purpose.

He still wondered about the possibility of tricking his way onto the ship, but had yet to devise a plan that seemed likely to actually work. He wondered about luring The Spirit of the Age to the planet with some phony call for help, but they were still several months away and most likely in contact with The Star Chaser − this seemed an even less viable means of acquiring a ship to escape on. And anyway, where would he go − he had no desire to live on Zeta Kotlin with a bunch of do-gooder, starry-eyed lefties, and Rorque 4 seemed to be in terminal decline. It looked as though his future lay on Ur-Tokar − be it for better, or for worse.

As such, with his own problematic personal position in mind, he had sent out feelers into the local community, and hopefully to the Mountain People, with the aim of finding out far more about the local inhabitants, and with the aim of making useful personal contacts. His efforts had initially been unsuccessful − it was difficult to know how to tempt a people uninterested in overt material wealth and advanced technology - but there had been some recent signs of progress, though his go-betweens were still working on the exact nature of how this would all work out in practice. In the event of the invasion fleet arriving, he now believed his only viable approach of avoiding execution, or, at the very least long years rotting in a military prison, was to head for the hills and take his chances with the locals.

Given the inexorably slow nature of space travel and communication, Rosson knew he still enjoyed a significant amount of time to consider his options, but with one important caveat. With the latter in mind, he had made a point of spending considerably more time with both his officers and the regular soldiers than had been the case in the past. He was carefully making assessments of who the spy in his entourage might be, of who he could rely on if he discovered the identity of Vartin's secret agent and then moved against him, and of who he might be able to trust in aiding him in the event of needing to head for the mountains at an unexpectedly early date. One thing he knew for certain was that the spy would only move against him following direct orders issued by Vartin. As such, he had ordered Sub-Lieutenant Schultz to immediately inform him of absolutely all messages of an encrypted nature arriving at Meridin or the military garrison, especially ones emanating from the invasion fleet.

Two weeks later, his scheming paid off as such an eventuality came to occur. One mid-morning, Sub-Lieutenant Schultz had reported hurriedly to Rosson that an encrypted message had indeed arrived via the Zeleyanian spy satellite orbiting above the planet. The encryption was one he was unfamiliar with and he had no means of deciphering the message. Rosson, resisting the urge to panic and over-react, decided to circulate more widely amongst his troops and carefully observed their comings and goings throughout the course of the morning. Despite this, he noticed nothing untoward as the day developed and spent an uncomfortable and paranoid period of time scrutinising every last detail occurring around him. Later that evening, though, Major Pushkov informed the Vice-Admiral that he needed to retire to the military garrison for the evening to urgently attend to some resource issues that had recently been brought to his attention. This was out of character for the Major - who always followed a strict and orderly schedule - and was effectively all Rosson needed to know to understand that the coup against him was about to be launched.

He gave permission for the Major to depart and dismissed him as normal. Once the Major was out of sight of the town, though, Rosson immediately mobilised the troops in the medieval settlement, tripled the guards, and issued orders stating that they had received information relating to an imminent attack, so should remain on full alert at all times. Rosson had previously worked his way through various possible scenarios that he might be faced with, and an attack from the garrison was one he had previously 'war-gamed'. He had also discovered that this would be one of the easier scenarios from which he could emerge victorious. Approximately two hours later, his advanced look-outs reported the near-silent movement of troops heading towards the town, stealthily moving through the thick forest under the cover of darkness. Pushkov had clearly opted for a standard covert operations approach. Rosson waited until they were close to the edge of the town and then ordered his troops to open fire and to show the enemy no mercy whatsoever. Even when it became apparent that they were firing on fellow Zeleyanians his guards were instructed to continue until their opponents had been thoroughly routed.

The battle that ensued did not quite follow the pattern assumed by Rosson. Pushkov also had small pockets of support within the town, and supplementary troops had entered via unexpected routes on the far side of the settlement. Whilst the main attacking forces were severely depleted in the early stages of the battle, Rosson's forces underwent a significant and concerted rearguard attack – and considerably greater than his preparations had anticipated. Gunfire frequently crackled around the town and occasional explosions shattered the stillness of the night air. Small bands of soldiers shadowed each other as they engaged in a game of cat-and-mouse through the narrow cobbled streets of the town's central districts.

The troops and guards loyal to Rosson took heavy casualties in the street-to-street fighting that ensued, which lasted several hours longer than he had anticipated. A prolonged street battle close to the church in the town's square was particularly deadly for both sets of Zeleyanian soldiers. However, as Rosson knew full well, defending a position was typically far easier than attacking one, and his forces gradually gained the upper hand, and what little remained of Pushkov's rapidly dwindling forces eventually surrendered. Major Pushkov himself died during the course of the fighting.

Whilst Rosson emerged victorious and still in control of the town and its immediate vicinity, victory had come at a very high price. Compared with the original complement of soldiers he had arrived with on the planet, his overall forces were now severely depleted. The wounded were tended to, and

Rosson ordered that an enquiry into the events of the night should begin first thing the following morning. Any officer associating with Pushkov was arrested, with a view to being tried in due course and executed if found guilty.

Early the next day, a count was made of the troops still available to Rosson and when completed he quickly realised that - despite their overwhelmingly superior firepower - if the local townspeople turned against the Zeleyanians en masse, it was unlikely he now had sufficient forces to hold the town. Even if he added the available AI units to his depleted numbers – neither side had used them in the recent battle as their reliability in an internecine dispute was known from previous experience to be worse than useless – he was well short of what he considered to be an effective defence unit. No longer did his forces resemble a disciplined, fully equipped and confident invasion force at the forefront of an imperial expansion - they now looked more like a disparate group of beleaguered and ill-equipped soldiers at the edge of time, lost in space and devoid of any real purpose. He had successfully eliminated one long-running problem, but in so doing, he had now created an entirely new and different one.

Once the dust had settled from the battle, he also faced the vexing question of whether he should inform Vartin of the recent episode. He had successfully eliminated the spy as had long been his aim, but the option of relating a version of events to Vartin to show himself in a suitable light was now long gone. Vartin had clearly given the orders to Pushkov to effect his arrest, and Vartin's arrival would still undoubtedly mark the end of his own career and more likely his life as well – on this matter, he was now unable to envisage any other scenario.

As far as he could calculate, he now had only two viable options left open to him. Firstly, to somehow dissuade Vartin from invading the planet and return to Zeleyan. If this was possible, he could avoid likely execution, remain as commander-in-chief, and become the new ruler of the town and its surroundings. However, if this dissuasion proved impossible he would clearly be unable to defend the town from Vartin's overwhelmingly superior forces once they arrived. He would then have no option but to flee and join the Mountain People.

The first option he considered to be the preferred one, but he needed to devise a message to send to Vartin that would somehow encourage him into returning to Zeleyan. The most obvious way was to recount to Vartin that all was lost, that the cause was hopeless and he should thus call off the invasion. But would Vartin buy such a warning – almost certainly not! Maybe reverse psychology would be more effective, he wondered, or maybe even give Vartin the impression he was walking into a trap. He was a highly suspicious person by nature – maybe he could play on his paranoia. This sounded a more promising approach and he decided to give such a plan some serious thought once he had returned Meridin to some semblance of order.

Zeleyan – further political and economic unrest

The relatively short history of the planet of Zeleyan had frequently been one of intermittent rebellions and uprisings, invariably followed by periods of concerted repression until the opposition had been suppressed and quietened by the regime forces, and leading to the emergence of periods of relative quiet and continuity. This had particularly been the case in the earliest years of the fascist dictatorship. Under the first leader of the supercontinent, Commander Charles Rocco, an initially brutal period of repression had eventually given rise to a lengthy, if somewhat reluctant, compliance with his dictatorial rule. Ultimately this had paved the way for three decades of political conformity and regime stability – a period in which the supercontinent's economy had been able to develop at a steady, albeit unspectacular, level of growth.

Over the decades, this particular pattern of political action and reaction had been played out again and again, though usually in a much less dramatic manner than under the early years of Rocco. Down through the years, the rebellions had become more localised and of diminished intensity, and thus dealt with more quickly by the highly repressive security forces. Eventually, over time, a relative calm had settled across the planet within which the brutal repression of the regime appeared to no longer actually be needed any further. The economy developed slowly and a degree of relative prosperity spread from region to region. Within this apparent calm, there developed a tacit agreement between the regime and the people - that as long as their living standards were gradually improving, the people of Zeleyan would accept that they enjoyed no political voice; a form of social contract – though unlike that formulated by Locke or Hobbes - and one that had been common to many of the authoritarian regimes back on Earth.

The greatest beneficiary of this economic development and slowly rising prosperity had been the province of Novo Salzar, centred around its old capital of Kantor on the shores of the Western Sea. Kantor, with its mixture of pale pink sandstone and whitewashed buildings sat astride the banks of the mighty River Salzarance, by far the largest of the rivers that flowed across the plains of Novo Salzar and into the Western Sea. The old city had been a centre of prosperity from the very beginning of the colonisation process, with a developing service sector economy at the heart of its crowded centre, and sprawling industrial zones that stretched outwards from the city's heart, out across to the plains that formed its rural hinterland.

Across those plains stretched extensive fields of wheat and other grains, vineyards, olive groves and orchards of citrus and other fruits. Employment levels in the area were high by the standards of the planet, especially since the economy of Zeleyan made significantly less use of AI units than that of Rorque 4, for instance. Additionally, the fascist regime regarded the unemployed as a source of disruption, crime and disorder and a possible source of rebellion, so they had essentially outlawed unemployment by forcing all citizens – especially men - to be in employment, wherever possible. For this reason, it was humans who were still used to perform the vast majority of employment tasks.

In recent years, however, the social contract between the people and the regime had experienced an increased level of strain, and nowhere more so than in Kantor. Under the rule of Vartin and his immediate predecessor, a new generation of Zeleyanians had emerged, one that had not experienced the economic scarcities and difficulties of their parents and the political rebellions of their grand-parents; one for whom the social contract made little immediate sense. Years of improving prosperity and a healthy economy were taken for granted by this new generation – they had never known anything otherwise – and they just simply expected their material circumstances to continue improving. In addition, they had no direct personal understanding and experience of why the widespread political and economic restrictions existed as they presently did – no genuine knowledge of the tacit compromises, agreements and sacrifices that had been made by their forebearers many decades beforehand.

Ever since Vartin's regime had instituted the new universal working arrangements - over two years ago now - there had been simmering or outright discontent in the province. The immediate reaction to its implementation had been a one day spontaneous general strike across the city leading to a large but peaceful protest in Kantor's main square – its citizens having reacted in a mixture of shock and disbelief to this highly unexpected and unwanted imposition. The local regime responded with a mobilisation of troops – both human and AI - and the announcement that the new measures would only prove to be temporary in nature. The clamour had died down, but it later emerged that they had not been informed as such by the officials at Zeleyan City, and that this had been a deceit perpetrated by local officials with the sole intention of restoring order.

The local business elites within Kantor held mixed opinions with regards to Vartin's plans for imperialist extra-terrestrial conquests – and for which the new working arrangements were paying for. The long-term aim of eliminating socialism on Zeta Kotlin was one they could all, of course, approve of. Their, sometimes less than wholehearted, support for the fascist regime had always been based on its ability to maintain law and order and stability, and to stave off socialist rebellion. Whilst socialism on Zeta Kotlin continued to exist, it could always act as an inspiration and rallying point for the working people of Novo Salzar. They believed that if its elimination was successful and the threat of socialism declined, then the regime might be more inclined to open up the economy and the opportunity for making greater profits. On the other hand, the short-term pain and rebellion the decision had caused alarmed some of the business owners. Some also suspected that the imperialist adventure was an alternative to opening up the economy, not a prelude to it.

When the initial protests had broken out they were therefore unsure as to how exactly they should respond. Fortunately for them, though, the initial response of the local party officials seemed to be successful, and whilst discontent had continued to simmer amongst the citizenry, there had initially been no repeat of the one day general strike. There had, however, been an increase in alternative displays of rebellion by the younger generation, more cultural and social in nature – a shift to new and more innovative forms of fashion, music and sport. The local regime had tried to deter such changes and emphasized the importance of traditional culture and society, though some of the capitalist class had spotted new business opportunities - assuming the regime allowed such cultural developments to continue.

As time passed though, the second anniversary of the implementation of the new working conditions approached and the new working arrangements still remained in place. Tension in the city and the wider countryside increased and minor strikes, disorder and rebellions began to surface with increasing frequency. The intermittent, localised, spontaneous and widespread nature of the protests made it difficult for the local regime to implement any effective clampdown, and its continued hold over Kantor and the wider province was now beginning to looking distinctly shaky. The local rebels knew that a significant number of regiments - including the most hated ones - had flown to Ur-Tokar with Vartin, and they calculated that this made the regime particularly more vulnerable at the present moment – a situation that would not last forever – and should therefore be acted upon whilst it continued.

The authorities in Zeleyan City also regarded the increasing and persistent unrest in Novo Salzar with growing unease. They had traditionally held something of a schizophrenic attitude to the prosperous province. On the one hand, it delivered much needed resources and wealth for the regime, but on the other, it had never been fully cooperative with the regimes demands, often maintaining a slightly different cultural and administrative approach to that demanded by the centre. They had attempted to cultivate rival centres of wealth in the other two provinces, to offset its importance, but none had achieved quite the same level of wealth and confidence as that focused around Kantor. Of late, they had grown impatient with the local authorities there, but were unsure as and how to react, for fear of alienating elites within their most prosperous province. At this particular point in time, with Supreme Commander Vartin billions of kilometres away in space, they also lacked decisive and authoritative leadership.

General Plenge - a longstanding member of High Command - was nominally in charge of the Zeleyanian government whilst Vartin was absent conquering Ur-Tokar. At the time of Vartin's departure, all political unrest had previously been subdued and the supercontinent appeared to have returned to a more typical normality. Plenge had believed that his time in power would simply be that of a caretaker and little else. He had not expected to be making any crucial decisions, never mind regime-deciding ones, and was unsure of exactly what his next move in Novo Salzar should be. If he made any huge errors of judgement, his position once Vartin returned would be an extremely precarious one. Discussions with other senior military officials, party leaders and business representatives had not been hugely useful, except for confirming what he already knew – everyone wanted the unrest dealt with. None, however, were willing to stick their head above the parapet and offer a definitive solution. As far as they were concerned, if it all went wrong it was Plenge who should take the blame.

General Plenge ultimately made the decision to do what Vartin usually did when he was unsure of political matters and consulted Vartin's Science Officer, Varela. Plenge was supremely aware that he needed to emanate an air of effective control whilst head of government, but without actually usurping the position of the Supreme Commander – not much of a dilemma when little needed to be done, but in times of crisis a balancing act fraught with difficulties. As such, he decided, he needed to be seen to be doing something.

The General arranged to meet Varela in his office on the second floor of the party headquarters. Varela, as was so often the case, arrived a few minutes later than had been arranged, and gave the appearance of someone who would rather be elsewhere. Plenge approached the conversation with Varela with his usual caution and in his own typically clipped manner. He was not the most loquacious of people, rarely bothered with small talk, and tended to go straight to the heart of any matter immediately. As such, he commenced the conversation with an overall appraisal of his dilemma.

'The situation in Novo Salzar, as I am sure you are aware and agree, is increasingly unacceptable. Such unrest cannot, of course, be tolerated. That would be wholly unpatriotic. I have ordered the military garrisons to be put on stand-by across the entire region. This is all currently in hand. What I am unsure of, though, is the degree of support to which we can rely on amongst the local elites in Kantor. We are detecting signs of resistance from certain sectors, with regards to implementing a military solution to the present difficulties. In addition, we cannot rely on our usual elite regiments to quell the unrest since they are accompanying the Supreme Commander in the invasion of Ur-Tokar. It has unfortunately become necessary therefore to rely on the use of locally stationed regiments in the event of outright rebellion. For this reason, I would prefer a political solution to the troubles before embarking upon a military one. I would therefore be interested in your appraisal of the political situation in Novo Salzar before moving ahead with any major decision.'

Varela looked at the General carefully without wishing to give too much away. His view of Plenge had never been a particularly high one – he regarded him as more of a military bureaucrat than a true supporter of the fascist regime – but he never held any doubts as to what advice he would recommend to the general.

'There have always been elements within the Kantor business class who think they know how to administer the regime better than we do ourselves; individuals who have never wholeheartedly and patriotically supported our form of rule and governance. These people have never been one hundred percent reliable. I think the present crisis offers us an ideal opportunity to demonstrate to them exactly who rules the roost, and to the nature of the regime that really should be in existence, despite what other else they might happen to believe. They are a minority tendency, in my opinion, and can be dealt with appropriately at a later date, and as and when we deem necessary. As you said yourself, we cannot tolerate any degree of unrest and insubordination in the region. The protestors should be taught a lesson they will never forget. Novo Salzar is our wealthiest region, it is crucial to our national economy and cannot be allowed to go its own way or receive special treatment. We might even use it as an opportunity to settle some old differences.'

Varela paused and thought for a moment. Plenge was familiar with these arguments, but he was not sure they were actually helping him to devise any specific strategy, but said nothing.

'With regards to the regiment issue,' Varela continued, 'put Colonel Musson in charge of the local troops. As a trusted confidante of the Supreme Commander he can be fully relied upon. Make sure there are sufficient AI units under his control – they will certainly hold no qualms with regards to who they shoot, and we don't need to worry about collateral damage in these particular circumstances. If necessary, mobilise national troops from the other regions – they've been politically quiet for some months now, so should not be missed. The media in these two regions have been working overtime recently to portray the Kantorans as ungrateful, overpaid and selfish. That should ensure support for their cause does not spread elsewhere, and will help troop mobilisations to be . . . more determined in their efforts, shall we say.'

Finally, Varela finished with what seemed to the General like a veiled threat. 'It is essential that the regime continues and flourishes, whatever the cost, but I'm sure you will manage that General. After all, it is your patriotic duty to ensure this,' and then paused again. 'Failure, of course, would come at a very high price.' He stopped for a moment. 'If that is all, then I will return to my work,' and departed abruptly from the room, without waiting for agreement from the General.

General Plenge was a military man and not much of a politician. His consultation with Varela had not proved to be a particularly useful one to him in political terms, and the conversation had been much shorter than the general had been expecting. It did, nevertheless, seem to scotch any thoughts of a political solution. But, if so, he was still unsure on whether to rely on local troops in the Kantor region to deal with the rebellion, or whether he should use the forces stationed near to Zeleyan City. Both options held their own particular risks. He was, however, under no illusions that he needed to act, but as for the precise nature and timing of how he should act he was still undecided. Ultimately, after some considerable prevarication, he eventually decided to follow Varela's recommendations, but held back from using troops from regions beyond Novo Salzar. He was not fully convinced they would be needed, or that it was safe to move them away from the other important cities of the continent. If they were truly needed, he could always mobilise them at a later date, he decided.

It was only a few days later before the decisions made by Plenge were put decisively to the test. Left-wing groups and movements in the Novo Salzar province had called for a demonstration in the main square of Kantor to mark the second anniversary of the imposition of the new and hated working regulations. The regime authorities had automatically banned the demonstration and immediately stationed troops in the main square. They had assumed this would suffice when dealing with the matter, but had completely underestimated the level of support that ultimately emerged for the protest. When the day of the demonstration came, workplaces simply did not open as usual, because instead hundreds of thousands of working people marched through the streets and main avenues from all directions with the aim of converging on the central square of the city.

As they began their advance into the square in their tens of thousands, chanting anti-regime slogans, banners and flags waving amidst their crowded ranks, Colonel Musson, a hard-line supporter of the fascist regime normally based in Zeleyan City, gave the order for the troops to fire into the front rows of the advancing crowds. However, the troops were members of a local regiment and were aware that in amongst the rapidly swelling crowd were their own close friends and relatives. They had not joined the military to massacre unarmed civilians – particularly not their own people - and hesitated.

As far as the local troops were concerned, as the Colonel had not even issued a preliminary warning to the crowd or ordered them to fire over the protestor's heads, under such circumstances they were able to convince themselves that refusing to fire on unarmed civilians was an acceptable decision. Unknown to the Colonel, and aware that such an eventuality might arise, they had previously discussed such a scenario whilst back in barracks and had collectively agreed that they would refuse to fire. The troops glanced sideways nervously at each other, almost surprised that the decision they had agreed upon had actually been adhered to. They half expected someone to break ranks with the decision, but the first shots were not forthcoming.

Musson had never personally experienced such disobedience before, but he had been taught how to deal with such a situation in officer training, back at military school many years previously. Standard procedure was to fall back on the AI units, which possessed no such misgivings about firing into an unarmed crowd. As anger and disbelief rose within him, he gave the automated soldiers the order to fire; they duly moved forward and the sound of gunfire immediately crackled around the square. A number of protestors immediately fell to the ground and suddenly the shrieking and shouting from the front pierced the calm warm summer air and echoed all around the closed walls of the square. The entering crowd, unsure of what was occurring, panicked, but was still arriving in its thousands and from all directions. Those further behind in the closely packed ranks of the crowds surged forwards, completely misunderstanding the situation. At the same time, the column arriving from the eastern quarter of the city, and which had not initially been fired upon, suddenly made a headlong surge towards the troops. Thousands of protestors poured rapidly and tightly into the square, whilst the casualties caused by the AI units continued to accumulate.

The AI units continued firing into the crowd, but the human troops panicked; some threw down their weapons and rushed to join the crowd, others, appalled at the carnage, began to fire on the AI units. One soldier turning towards his left, looked across and saw Colonel Musson firing enthusiastically into the crowd. Utterly appalled, he raised his assault weapon and put a round of bullets into the Colonel. The Colonel slumped heavily to the floor. The AI units continued firing in their methodical fashion but it was not long before they were overrun, no longer able to fire as the huge press of the crowd surged over them, whilst others were dispatched from behind by their own troops. Before long the crowd was in full control of the main square and the regime troops were effectively disarmed and defeated.

The fallout from the events surrounding the protest was immediate, as news of the massacre and the defeat of the troops spread rapidly across the region. The whole of Novo Salzar was soon paralysed by a spontaneous general strike. Protestors took control of every major town and city. Whole sections of the rank-and-file within the military and security forces rebelled and joined the uprising. All the key buildings of the regime – party headquarters, military garrisons, police stations, media outlets and elite clubs – were seized by the rebels. The AI units employed within the security systems were seized, deprogrammed and rendered inert. At almost lightning speed, the entire region fell rapidly to the insurrection.

By the following day, unrest had spread to Zeleyan City itself, geographically in the far north-east of the Novo Salazar region, though politically self-governing. The speed with which events moved took General Plenge entirely by surprise. He was a man who typically took his time in making a decision, after considering his options at some considerable length. He prided himself on never making rash or hasty decisions he would later regret. On occasions, it could even take him several days before his course of action was finally decided upon, though, once the decision was made, he stuck rigidly and unswervingly to his carefully chosen course of action. On this particular occasion, such an approach proved worse than useless.

At the time the unrest spread quickly towards Zeleyan City, he had been busily working in party headquarters in the city centre, and so his carefully prepared plans were soon rapidly overwhelmed by the speed with which events moved. With his preferred plan of operation no longer available to him, and also as a military man, his gut instinct was to be with his troops. Isolated from his regiment in party headquarters, he believed, was not the place to be when dealing with a rebellion. He resolved to head to the military barracks at Hexagone just beyond the outer limits of the city, originally established at this location in order to defend the capital from possible attacks through the Etchanaty Pass, the south-western route into the city's environs. From such a position he had the option of dealing with both the capital city and spreading out southwards across the plains that stretched across the northern regions of Novo Salzar. This would have to be his fallback plan and position.

Rorque 4 – the Rorque Corporation makes a historic decision

Colin Jamieson was seated at his impressively large desk in the centre of his spacious office on the top floor of the Rorque Corporation's headquarters in the centre of Rorque City. The whole room had been laid out largely with the purpose of allowing him to make optimum use of the tower's slowly rotating disc structure. At any time of the day he could gaze out across the slowly changing vista before him and to all directions of the compass, as the flattened dome structure continued slowly on its never ending rotation. To the south and south-west he could see the shallow Ricardian Sea, its turquoise blue waters sparkling in the intense sunlight. To all other geographical points, beyond the city's limits, laid the vast expanses of scrub and semi-desert that stretched further than the eye could visibly see, continuing well beyond the horizon for yet more hundreds of kilometres in an inland direction.

He was currently seated viewing the eastern quarter, where far in the distance the orange-red remnants of the previous day's fire continued to sweep their way through the tinder-dry brush, leaving only ashes and a blackened landscape behind them. It was only the latest in a long series of fires that appeared to be turning the already dry landscape into genuinely true desert, and leaving nothing living in their wake. The city had been shrouded in a thick crimson twilight for much of the previous day, as though a reddened glass lid had been placed over the thick drifting clouds of smoke that had been pushed in by a steady easterly breeze that had lasted the best part of the whole day. The atmosphere was somewhat clearer today, though a strange smell like burnt sand remained hanging slightly noxiously in the air.

Jamieson drew his attention away from the vista and returned his thoughts to business matters. He was an increasingly frustrated man. He had believed at the time of signing, that his groundbreaking deal with the Zeleyanian government would mark the beginning of a great turnaround in both the fortunes of the corporation he had latterly devoted so much of his life to, and to his own closely intertwined career. Ever since that momentous event, though, on far too many occasions he had felt like he was wading his way through particularly thick treacle. There had been the continuous problems with the scientists from Alpha Fraczan and the anarchists from Margalla, and then a whole host of business and climate related issues that had hampered, or even halted, entire sections of the corporate monolith's operations. He was now facing yet further business complications and political difficulties.

Following the completion of his deal, he had remained in contact with the Zeleyanian regime, though the slow nature of space communications – a return communication from Zeleyan spanned a period of over five months - meant that further progress was painfully slow. Their government had notified him of a strong interest in acquiring rocket engines for their newly launched space fleet, and ones of a significantly advanced technological nature. He knew, of course, why they believed he had access to such technology, and he had not discouraged them from continuing to believe this inaccuracy. However, the absence of any rocket scientists on The Spirit of The Age meant he was currently in no position to immediately proceed any further with his business dealings vis-à-vis Zeleyan. He had, though, spent a great deal of time attempting to resolve his difficulties concerning this particular matter, various options having been considered by his calculating opportunistic mind.

He had worked his way through various plans by which he might secure employment contracts with the rocket scientists working for Cosmic Solutions, but none had eventually proven to be plausible. The inescapable fact was that his great corporate rivals were fully aware of his disadvantaged position, and would make every effort possible to ensure that the present situation continued to remain in their favour. On occasions, he had even found himself pondering on the sheer bad luck of contacting the wrong one of the two spacecraft, and whether this was some form of ill-fated bad luck he was being forced to endure. More usually, though, he spent his time devising methods by which he might be able to head-hunt the rocket scientists, or to engage in industrial espionage and furtively acquire the technology they were developing. He figured that if the worst came to the worst, he might simply have to pay Cosmic Solutions for the technological know-how; but the humiliation of doing so, meant he would be paying a very heavy price, both literally and figuratively.

Whilst this particularly vexing problem had been preoccupying him, the latest quarterly figures for the corporation had also made for dismal reading. Most of their divisions were still heavily ensconced in debt, failing to generate profits of any great significance, and in some areas actually losing turnover and suffering declining revenue. Without the deal with Zeleyan, some of the figures would have looked catastrophic. After twenty-five years of economic malaise he was increasingly at a loss as to how to turn the corporation's fortunes around. They had long ago laid off all the surplus workers and replaced them with AI units wherever applicable, pared back on working terms and conditions and lengthened working hours. Unprofitable sections of the corporation had been hived off, mergers effected to reduce the competition, and research conducted into potentially profitable new markets. In reality, only increasingly large loans from the banks were still keeping the corporation afloat.

On numerous occasions he had felt like Prometheus, forever striving to achieve a goal that just seemed to remain tantalisingly out of reach. He had long ago concluded that the economic malaise was more than just cyclical, and that long-term structural factors in the economy were blocking a sustained recovery. This was the reason he had brokered the deal with Zeleyan – to open up promising new markets and launch into as-yet-untried ventures, but had now run into profound problems, which were currently proving irresolvable. This venture too was beginning to look like yet another failed strategy, one that initially offered so much promise, but ultimately failed to deliver. He would need to respond to the quarterly figures with some new initiative – the shareholders would demand as much - but he was now seriously beginning to wonder if the Rorquean economy was coming to a natural end.

And today, Jamieson was facing an even more pressing crisis. The corporation's political rival in the World Assembly, the Justice and Order Party, had been the outright victor in the recent planetary elections, and had wasted no time in putting a bill before the assembly; one that halted all dealings between Rorque 4 and Zeleyan, on the basis that the fascist regime on Zeleyan represented a clear and present security threat to the inhabitants of Rorque 4. The Rorque Corporation had, of course, anticipated such a move and had already mobilised its team of extremely well paid lawyers to ensure that any newly passed law would be declared unconstitutional, on the grounds that it was an interference with legitimate business activity.

However, they had not anticipated the passing of an emergency powers clause by the assembly, one that immediately halted all communications between the two planets. Any non-compliance with the clause would result in immediate arrest of those breaching its orders. Justice and Order had needed the extra votes of the Democracy Party to achieve such a result, and he wondered what price Cosmic Solutions had paid to buy the support of their erstwhile rivals. It meant, therefore, that until his lawyers could have this additional legislation too declared as unconstitutional – a somewhat more complicated and lengthy procedure - he was effectively barred from contacting the regime on Zeleyan and pursuing any further business dealings. Jamieson felt distinctly outmanoeuvred, and a number of his subordinates had felt the wrath of his temper that day.

Even before all this, the corporation had already scaled back its business operations in a number of economic areas, once the dealings with Zeleyan had begun to look problematic. With its future cash flows uncertain, the banks had been reluctant to offer even higher amounts of credit – the corporation was already operating with extremely high levels of debt - and had instead recommended a consolidation into core areas that were still returning at least some basic level of profit. The recent news meant that even this might not be sufficient, and Jamieson, uncharacteristically for someone usually so sure of himself, had decided he needed to take a break from the office and spend a significant amount of time considering the latest data concerning the current situation. Certain figures had him particularly perplexed, and thus uncertain as to how to proceed next.

As such, he had unexpectedly decided to take a rest from the city and spend several days at his coastal villa consulting a range of important corporate figures; there they would be able to reflect on the current critical situation in total privacy, and without bothersome interruptions and unwanted distractions. The appropriate communications had been issued and suitable arrangements had then been organised, and following a brief lunch, he took the elevator down to the underground car park, where his motorcade was ready and awaiting him.

The journey to his villa further along the coast was a largely straightforward one, given it stood on the cliffs overlooking Spencer Bay, only fifty minutes drive from the heart of Rorque City. As was always the case, his autocar travelled in convoy, with security to the front and rear of his own vehicle. Jamieson had made a significant number of enemies during his long career in business, and these days one of his major concerns was to avoid being kidnapped and held to ransom - a crime that was becoming increasingly and alarmingly popular amongst the more hardened elements of the criminal fraternity. A few minutes after leaving party headquarters, the convoy breezed through the outskirts of the city – the roads seemed emptier these days Jamieson noted – and hit the coastal section of the journey, approximately twenty minutes later.

The convoy had initially made good progress along the coastal section of the motorway when the autocar suddenly alerted Jamieson and his security detail of an incident further ahead, one which they would soon be approaching. The security AI units automatically switched into alert mode and his human bodyguards also readied their weapons. Most members of the elite only employed AI units for security, but Jamieson - who could afford to pay for such indulgences - preferred the doubled security of an automated and human-based approach, just to add an extra level of protection that might be needed in unexpected eventualities. The armour-plated, bullet-proof autocars of the convoy slowed and the screen in Jamieson's vehicle switched to a local satellite transmission.

According to the transmission, a significant armed confrontation had taken place in a small town close to the motorway. Two of the occupied vehicles involved, had ultimately ended up finishing their dispute on the motorway, as their respective occupants sought to murderously finish each other off. The confrontation had been over access to increasingly scarce water supplies; one group of householders accusing another of hijacking access to the supply they had already paid over the odds for. The dispute had quickly escalated and the various individuals involved had resorted to their deadly assault rifles to settle their differences. By the time the security forces had arrived, more than a dozen lay dead, and the few survivors had been taken into custody. Jamieson was aware that this was a far from isolated incident – disputes amongst criminal gangs over access to water supplies were increasingly common, but now seemed to be spreading to sections of the population who had traditionally been considered as firmly law-abiding.

Arrival in Utopia

As he sat in the autocar waiting impatiently, Jamieson reflected on the social deterioration of recent times; there were sections of the major cities that were now effectively no-go areas for any respectable citizen. Only heavily armoured security detachments could safely enter these areas. Underemployment in these zones had been a chronic reality for over two decades now, leaving criminal gangs effectively controlling access to local employment markets. To add to this, with householders no longer able to afford the upkeep of their roads, refuse services and street lighting, nor always able to afford to pay for water and electricity services, these zones had descended into chaos, disrepair and ruin. Rubbish was left uncollected, disease was spreading, shootings were common and crime was rife. Normally, he would have wondered why the populace was not working harder to find or create employment and business opportunities, but in these desperate times he had begun to wonder if some form of population cleansing might not be the best solution. There would be complaints about the loss of individual liberty, of course, but at least life would be better for the respectable law-abiding members of the population that remained afterwards.

Whilst lost in these thoughts, the security services suddenly issued an all-clear alert to Jamieson's convoy, and they were immediately waved through without any further delays. The convoy continued its journey along the coast without encountering any further difficulties, whilst Jamieson looked out over the blue-green waters of the shallow Ricardian Sea to the south. A small number of speed boats and a single fishing boat were ploughing their way forwards in one direction or another, scattering occasional small groups of seabirds as they did so. Other than this, though, the sea looked uncharacteristically empty and devoid of activity. The convoy followed the route along the coastal cliff-tops, and at certain points he noted large frothy blue-green slicks of some unpleasant looking material washed up onto the small sandy cove beaches that were so characteristic of this stretch of the coastline. He wondered what exactly it was.

A short while later, the convoy passed through a sophisticated gated security system, travelled up and along an impressive driveway, and finally arrived at his grand coastal villa. A few minutes later he was greeted by Maria, his third wife, though his two teenage children were nowhere to be seen. He assumed they would be otherwise occupied in their bedrooms – probably gaming or on social media. He discussed his plans for the next few days with Maria, who then issued appropriate instructions to their personal AI units, so that all necessary preparations would be in place for when their esteemed guests eventually arrived. Maria then went back to sunbathing next to the impressive infinity pool, whilst Jamieson changed, poured himself a large scotch and immediately set about pouring through the latest economic data yet again.

Over the next couple of days, Jamieson was visited by the best economists and accountants money could buy. The corporate data was checked and rechecked and analysed from a number of different angles and perspectives. However they looked at the figures, though, they could not avoid one particular and inescapable conclusion. Once they had definitely agreed it was, nevertheless, absolutely correct, they then took time to look through a range of other data concerning a wide range of other extraneous issues on Rorque 4. By the end of the second day, Jamieson had finally arrived at the not wholly unexpected conclusion that the situation was far worse than even he had initially assumed; something that finally explained his earlier perplexion and puzzlement.

On the third day of the sojourn, his distinguished guests began to arrive one by one throughout the course of the morning, and initially spent their time socialising in the impressive garden terrace that fronted the luxury villa. The terraced garden sat on a high sandstone sea-cliff, and from their lofty vantage point they could look over the shallow sandy waters of the Ricardian Sea below. As on most days, the sea lay very still in the hot summer sun, and its pale blue-green waters stretched calmly to the horizon. A thin haze was beginning to form as the strengthening heat of the sun commenced its usual daily evaporation. There was, however, a notable lack of activity on the calm sea – either in the form of human activity or from the increasingly scarce wildlife that existed within its waters – a feature which the various guests commented upon.

At midday, the small party adjourned to the ultra-modern dining room, where an eight course meal that spared no expense was served to the gathered guests. Most inhabitants of Rorque 4 lived on a staple diet of food manufactured by the ferming units – a wide range of foodstuffs created from a mixture of water, gases and bacteria present in the atmosphere. This provided adequate levels of fats, protein and carbohydrate and was essentially healthy and nutritious. However, it could also be adulterated in an almost unlimited number of ways, with a whole range of differing additives, preservatives and flavourings made available, leaving it in a far less healthy and nutritious state. This was what most of the population consumed, but what they really lacked access to, though, was genuinely fresh food.

By contrast, Jamieson's guests were treated to an array of freshly produced and expensive products that was well beyond the price limits of all but the planet's wealthiest inhabitants. A variety of exotic fresh fruits and vegetables, grown in the continent's dwindling orchards and market gardens, were washed down with a large selection of fine wines and soft fruit drinks. These were supplemented by a variety of sea foods – fish, prawns and crustaceans – from the planet's shallow seas, though these too were now extremely scarce due to the extensive overfishing of the planet's seas.

In the early days of Rorque 4's colonisation, the planet's initially abundant seas had been parceled up into private commercial zones, each one exploited by its owner until their stocks became commercially extinct. At this point they would move to a new zone and engage in a similar operation, whilst expecting the abandoned ones to recover and restock. However, the rate of exploitation had proven to be far too rapid, seabeds were often irreparably damaged, and the fallow zones simply failed to recover – typically they were hired out to smaller commercial interests – and over time the stocks of marine life had rapidly dwindled. Now only the wealthiest of the planet's inhabitants could afford to pay for the meagre catches landed by the few boats that continued to ply the fishing trade.

Once his guests had been suitably fed and watered, they were duly able to commence the real purpose for which they had gathered at Jamieson's villa that day. By the middle of the afternoon, the small assembly had gathered comfortably around the extensive dark cherrywood table that dominated the centre of his personal conference room. Amongst his elite guests figured the highest ranking management figures of the Rorque Corporation and its banking division, the major shareholders of the corporation, and leading figures of the Liberty Party – a small grouping that constituted some of the wealthiest and most powerful people on the planet.

Jamieson thanked them for all for their presence at the gathering, and then proceeded to outline his appraisal of the many and varied problems they were facing, and that those assembled were only too familiar with. The difficulties of the deal with the Zeleyanian government, the unfortunate political situation, the protracted economic crisis, the deteriorating climate of the planet, rising crime and the increasing social unrest were all outlined and explained in considered detail. He could see from their studied attention and occasional nods and expressions of support, that none present were in general disagreement with his highly detailed appraisal of the contemporary situation.

Having established a picture of the planet that appeared to be the consensus of those present, he turned to the issue of what the appropriate response should be from those gathered at his villa that day.

'I have spent the last few days poring over the data with the corporation's top economists and accountants, and we have arrived at some startling conclusions and are now in the position to make some imminent and instant predictions. The population of the planet is declining, important natural resources are either exhausted or close to being so, and the present climactic heating can only worsen this situation. Productivity amongst the workforce shows no sign of recovery, the rate of profit is in terminal decline and there are no realistic prospects of opening up new markets. The various data sets all agree that the economy is effectively dying.'

Jamieson took stock of the situation for a moment, looking at the various faces around the room, most of whom he had worked with for years, if not decades now, and with whom he had typically maintained good working relationships over that period of time. He could see from their muted reaction that most, if not all, had instinctively arrived at the same or similar conclusions to his own in recent weeks. Jamieson was simply confirming with data and figures what they had already been noting with their intuition and senses.

Jamieson continued, 'the big question we need to ask ourselves is whether we have arrived at a natural conclusion to our time spent on Rorque 4. Our forefathers before us departed from Earth when they calculated it was no longer a suitable place for pursuing profitable business, and we now need to ask ourselves the same question. Is it now time for us too to move on? After all, humans have always been a semi-nomadic species. Throughout the whole of history we have ventured to a new location, used its resources, and then moved onto fresh pastures, once those resources have been exhausted. Ancient foragers did this on the savannah, fishermen in the oceans, miners underneath the mountains, and now, we too, follow the ancient pattern, but simply on a larger, planetary-wide scale. From this inescapable logic, we were born to go beyond the stars – again and again. Are the resources on Rorque 4 now exhausted to the point where we need to once more journey across space to find fresh pastures anew,' he asked more rhetorically, than in the expectation of any actual reply. 'My own personal analysis of the situation has arrived at the belief that we have now definitively reached that point.'

The president of the Liberty Party, George Minoche, was an old ally of Jamieson's, and the two regularly consulted each other with regard to aligning the strategy and tactics of their two organisations. He had been aware for some time now of the direction in which thinking had been developing within the upper echelons of the corporation, and was the first to comment on Jamieson's thoughts. 'Let's, for a moment, assume that your analysis of Rorque 4 is correct – and I've also been developing a similar line of thinking myself recently. Firstly, do we have a preferred destination lined up that appears suitably promising, and, secondly, do we still have the ready means of journeying there safely?'

'The answer to both questions is effectively 'yes',' answered Jamieson. 'I think we've always known that this eventuality might one day arrive, and the astronomy department at Rose Wilder University has, from the very earliest days of our existence on this world, been gathering and collating data from the transponders left by the genesis pods sent out to explore the galaxy, all those many years ago. Given the immense spatial and temporal distances involved, we can never be one hundred percent certain of the accuracy of the data, but they have duly identified a small number of planets that have been deemed suitable for habitation, and also appear suitable for our own more specific purposes. To the best of our knowledge these planets remain unoccupied. We have identified one planet, in particular, that appears to be more appropriate than the rest. It is orbiting the star Zarak 2, approximately twelve light years from our own system, and I suggest this should be our chosen destination.'

He paused for a moment, half expecting further comments, but none were forthcoming. 'With regard to the second question, again 'yes', we still have four fully functioning premium class stasis ships at our disposal, even after the sale of the more basic models to the Zeleyanian government. These will be sufficient to transport all our AI units, a sufficient proportion of our current employees, and all the other resources we will need, to successfully commence the colonisation of our future home.'

'Have we really completely run out of other options?' asked an elderly shareholder named Venetia Ludlow, who was not quite as enamoured by the idea of leaving the only planetary home she had ever known, as some of the others in the room seemed to be.

'Well, I'm sure those on the political left would suggest some form of social or political intervention, but as I'm sure everyone here will fully agree, we all know that they simply do not work. If we go down that misguided path, we are accepting a major loss of our freedoms and some form of invidious authoritarianism. It will just be the slippery slope to communism. No, there is no other viable solution, unless you want to live in some form of slavery and enforced poverty,' he concluded.

A further question followed from the head of their banking division, Naomi Whitlow. 'From your previous answer, I assume that we will only be taking a certain percentage of our productive workers with us, the rest will stay behind I presume, is that a correct assumption?' she asked.

'It certainly is. Yes, there is no question of taking the whole planetary population with us. I'm sure you'll agree, there are a large number of characters we are much better off without,' and Jamieson waited for the knowing nods and smirks of amusement that he knew would result from this comment. 'No, we are only taking the most useful and productive with us. The planetary population may well be declining, but we only have room for those who deserve to be on board. And, even if we possessed a larger number of stasis ships, I would still recommend that we only transport limited numbers. Let's face it, most of the productive work is achieved by our AI units these days, anyway – so, yes, there will be many humans who prove surplus to our requirements. I understand from our contacts in Cosmic Solutions and United Rorque Technologies, that their respective leaderships look as though they too are arriving at a similar conclusion to ourselves. No doubt they will come to a similar decision, with regards to numbers . . . so, yes, many will be left behind. I'm sure they will enjoy each other's company,' and paused, as he waited for the laughter to subside. 'Yes, there are distinct indications that our competitors are, indeed, considering a departure from the planet – we are clearly not the only ones considering this option. We do not know their chosen destination yet, but if they too choose Zarak 2 it will not hurt us to be ahead of the game, in that respect.'

Jamieson looked around his audience. They had all been aware of the deteriorating situation for several months - or even years – now, and their last throw of the dice – the deal with Zeleyan – had fallen far short of their expectations. He could see that for some of those gathered, his talk had been an almost cathartic experience – no longer did they need to grapple with turning around a deteriorating economy. Some looked almost relieved by the news he had delivered. They could now plan anew for the future, on a fresh and blank canvas. A lengthy discussion then ensued amongst the group ranging over details such as who would accompany the departure, the necessary resources to be taken with them, a provisional timetable for the exodus, the logistics of its organisation, various security considerations and the perceived advantages of the proposed destination.

Having discussed all these issues and explored a number of promising scenarios, Jamieson eventually decided to bring the discussion to a conclusion and put the matter to a formal vote. He had taken soundings previous to the meeting, and from the atmosphere in the room he could see that there was unlikely to be any serious dissent to his proposal. Clearly no one in the room believed there was any serious option other than that laid before them, and he recommended they support his proposal. The decision in the room to leave Rorque 4 was unanimous, as he had expected.

Rorque 4 – Cosmic Solutions joins the exodus

A few days later, across Rorque 4 on the adjacent continent of Eastern Shala, Christine Sanchez was seated in her office in the headquarters of Cosmic Solutions located at the heart of New Galtsville. Her office, not surprisingly, enjoyed all the latest technology money could buy. The floor-to-ceiling windows that ran the length of her room tinted automatically, and to any shade or colour she desired, usually in accordance with the strength and colour of the sunlight as it altered during the course of the day. Additionally, she was able to instantly activate surround-screen, so that her office appeared in any imaginary environment she so desired. The environmental controls, as usual, were set to suit her exact requirements. Today, however, she was completely unconcerned by the hi-tech paraphernalia at her disposal.

Sanchez was studying the corporation's quarterly results. In recent times, she had seen similar trends in company reports on several occasions, and was now increasingly worried about the distinct lack of progress being made in the Space Flight Faculty at Diana Park University. There had been some reasonably promising progress from other departments working on terra-forming Morpheus, but the two she really needed to see advances from were stalling badly. She could see quite clearly from the charts and figures before her that a significant break-through in faster and more efficient space flight was not occurring; a Rorquean aerospace age was not about to happen anytime soon.

She wondered fleetingly if she had been the victim of some major hoax played out by the scientists from Alpha Fraczan, or whether Alex Kim and his colleagues had simply overestimated their own abilities. She suspected the latter - she was not gullible enough to fall for a hoax on that kind of scale - but whatever the exact reason for their shortcomings, she was facing persistent and prolonged problems with the huge gamble the corporation had embarked upon, and ones which were now looking intractable and unsolvable.

Aside from the problem of achieving faster space travel, their other major technological headache facing the corporation was the plan to reheat the inner core of Morpheus. Their long-term aim was to wake the sleeping planet and provide the dynamic geological processes needed to then keep the planet alive, and thus habitable on a sustainable basis. Their scientists had explored the possibility of using nuclear explosions to reignite the core, despite the fact that Rorque 4 currently possessed little in the way of nuclear technology. A number of them had enthused over the possibility of developing nuclear weapons capable of delivering suitably large amounts of concentrated energy and explosive warming. These, they believed, could be delivered down the deep vents of Morpheus's dormant volcanoes in order to reignite the core. The science was unproven, but they considered it was definitely worth a try.

In the absence of any uranium deposits on the planet, though, only fusion explosions were considered as a viable option, but the calculations the corporation's engineers had ultimately arrived at showed that the number of explosions they would need was way beyond anything they were currently able to manufacture. Additionally, further calculations indicated that the nuclear radiation resulting from such explosions would probably lead to an uninhabitable planet for many years or decades to come. After considerable investigation into the matter, the corporation had concluded that the scientists were not about to get the nuclear toy they so desired to play with – it was simply too expensive and far too unpredictable.

The only other viable option was to create some form of super-massive reflecting device, suitably placed in orbit around Morpheus in such a manner that it was able to collect solar radiation from Eleutheria and redirect a concentrated beam of light into the dormant volcanoes on the surface of Morpheus. This might be an array of reflecting mirrors – an orbiting necklace around the entire planet – or one giant reflector dish. However, they soon discovered that whichever of the systems they used, not only was the price literally astronomical, but the time period for achieving success was far longer than anything they had envisaged. The beam they were capable of creating would need to be transmitted for decades before it delivered an appropriate amount of heat and energy - time the corporation simply did not possess.

Cosmic Solutions had been aware of such potential problems from the very beginning of the Morpheus project, but had hoped that a combination of entrepreneurial vigour and a large dose of serendipity would help them proceed along the path to corporate success. To date, no such luck had fallen their way and the prophecy of awakening a sleeping planet was clearly not coming true anytime soon. The corporate elite of Cosmic Solutions was now arriving at a position that the fortunes of the project were likely to remain this way, and as such the whole project should be abandoned before their already high debt levels became astronomical.

This would lead to a number of subsidiary decisions for Sanchez. With specific regards to Alex Kim, whilst he might not have been the dream worker she had been hoping for, she had no intention of letting either him or his any of his close colleagues leave for their great rivals, the Rorque Corporation. There was always the danger that their work there might suddenly take an unexpected upward upturn in fortunes. As such, she had decided to maintain his university department in its current form but slowly wind down their funding and operations there, until she believed it was safe to finally terminate the programme completely, whenever that might prove to be. The commercial side of the operation, though – Trans Air Trucking – was due for imminent termination and the employees and AI units would be redeployed to more useful projects.

Sanchez paused in her thinking for a while, and gazed out through the huge tinted windows that spanned the entire length of her penthouse office. Below her, spread a variety of high rise offices that constituted the business district of the city. Beyond these sprawled the variously shabby outer suburbs of New Galtsville, the far edges of which morphed into the extensive dry and dusty plain - dotted with its isolated towns and villages - that formed the hinterland of New Galtsville. It was the colour of burnt ochre, which Sanchez thought was particularly apposite as she noted plumes of smoke rising from a number of isolated fires that punctuated the far reaches of the plain. They had increased in number of late she noted - not surprisingly, she thought, since the planet had always lacked much in the way of freshwater as a means of extinguishing them. She knew there had been suggestions of late to use seawater instead, but as of yet no one had shown willing to shoulder the expense.

This led her to consider the situation with the ongoing drought, one that appeared to be deteriorating badly by the day. A whole suburb in the northern section of New Galtsville had seen its water supply halted for several days earlier that month. The south-eastern zone of the city had outbid the suburb for the latest batch of water pumped from the now almost empty artesian wells, and so the latter had seen its water supply abruptly terminated. It had now secured a payment for desalinated water from the shallow salty waters of the Havekyian Sea, but the price of this was also escalating rapidly as demand inexorably soared, and the prices being offered to householders were increasingly exorbitant. It was unlikely they would be able to afford this particular solution for much longer, she calculated, though the corporation had, nevertheless, made some quick profits whilst they were still able to do so.

For the majority of the continents inhabitants, the water situation was an increasingly desperate one. There had been calls from house-owners for the state to intervene to address the increasingly dire situation. This had been met with a barrage of abuse from the various corporate media commentators and warnings of higher taxes and the loss of individual liberties. The truth was, thought Sanchez, that even if funding for state intervention to deal with the drought could be found, the state lacked the institutional capacity to save the situation anyway - so ingrained was the idea that the private sector performed all important functions within their society. No one within the state apparatus would know how to organise such an operation, let alone fund and implement it. The state was so weak and underfunded it was institutionally incapable of dealing with any significant crisis. In any event, she thought, it was the role of the corporations to perform such functions anyway - if someone was willing to pay, then they would be provided with the service. That was the law of supply and demand.

She looked at the time on the bluescreen in front of her and suddenly realised she should have been attending a meeting in the conference room next door. She secured her computer account, rose from her chair and made her way into the large airy room that lay adjacent to her own spacious office. Already seated around the table were Nisha Tanaka, the president of Cosmic Solutions, Edward Hawley, the chair of the Justice and Order Party and Mehana Boucher, Head of Security for the corporation. They exchanged greetings and she apologised for her late arrival, though the others indicated this was not a problem as they had only been present a few short minutes.

'So you have closed down the World Assembly in Paterson Bay I hear – the pollution must have been dreadful,' Sanchez commented, looking in the direction of Hawley.

'Yes, the stench had been dreadful for several days, but when a persistent south-easterly blew in from the Havekyian Sea, the air became literally unbreathable. Some form of toxic sulphurous mix deriving from the rotting algae in the coastal waters of the sea I've been informed. Whatever it was, it was near-lethal to anyone who failed to buy an oxygenator mask. We've closed the building temporarily until the situation improves. The capital has been semi-evacuated - those that have somewhere to go, anyway. I don't envy those left behind.' He stopped for a moment, 'though I'm guessing from the fact that we are all seated here together now, that the closure of the assembly is perhaps the least of our concerns.'

'Your guess is a correct one, I'm afraid,' stated Tanaka, 'we need to agree on whether it is now time to launch Project Freefall, as previously discussed. The Morpheus Project, as I'm sure you are all aware, has stalled badly, and the latest quarterly figures demonstrate there is no imminent prospect of a concerted economic upswing anywhere on the near horizon. In fact, far from it; we are still mired in economic stagnation, declining profitability and decreasing turnovers. In addition, the planet – as we've just intimated to - is becoming an increasingly unpleasant place to inhabit. We have reached the undeniable conclusion that we have now exhausted the possibilities available to us here on Rorque 4, and that our time on this world appears to have arrived at a natural conclusion. The figures clearly bear us out on this. In my opinion, it is simply a case of deciding exactly when it is that we depart, not whether we depart.'

'It's even worse than I thought, then,' commented Sanchez, though she was far from surprised.

Hawley nodded, 'Yes, indeed, it is, and I concur entirely with Tanaka's analysis. A selected destination was identified some time ago, one that will meet all our requirements, I believe, and is considered to still be uninhabited.' He turned to Boucher, 'I assume that once the decision has been authorised, it is simply a case of following all the designated procedures and guidelines and we can be ready for departure within the calendar month. Are we likely to meet much resistance to the plan?'

'The Project protocols have always anticipated that at least a proportion of the employees will show a degree of reluctance to the idea of leaving their home planet.' Boucher replied. 'However, the media department has already created a number of news bulletins, emission clips and short documentaries for our subscribers, describing the manner in which society will collapse once we have departed. As a result, I suspect there will be very few who will actually want to remain behind. We have sufficient room on the stasis ships for all our employees, and they will each be able to take one container full of possessions with them. I have been informed that the contracts of anyone we believe is not worth taking will be terminated, so we may even have some spare capacity. Those chosen for departure will simply be transported to the spaceport at Stratostan on a prearranged timetable and placed immediately into stasis. Security at the spaceport has already been increased – we anticipate that there could be trouble, since we are sure certain undesirables will also be wanting to depart from the planet. The stasis ships themselves, of course, are fully repaired, maintained and fuelled as has always been the case. Everything is set in place for a scheduled departure. We simply need authorisation to commence the procedure.'

'Excellent, just as it should be,' stated Hawley. 'If that is the case, and we are all agreed . . .' he looked around the room, waited for objections, and when none were forthcoming continued, '. . . then I suggest we authorise the agreed departure, and that we are ready to leave orbit at the end of the month. Thank you all for attending the meeting.'

The atmosphere in the room had been slightly sombre – after all, they were leaving the only planet that they had ever known, and great hopes had been pinned on Project Morpheus, which would now clearly be abandoned unfinished. However, there was now also a perceived air of relief, as though a great weight had been taken off their shoulders, for they had all suspected for some time now that this decision would need to be taken sooner rather than later.

Before they left though, Christine Sanchez decided to formalise an ending to the proceedings, 'I think we all knew this day would arrive one day. Just as our ancestors found it necessary to join the exodus from Earth once their planet no longer met their needs, so we have found the need to act likewise. Rorque 4 has been a good home to us, but it is no longer suitable for our purposes, and we need to depart for the next stepping stone on our great journey across the galaxy. I am sure we will be equally prosperous at our next destination. Welcome to the future colleagues.' They all nodded in agreement and congratulated each other. Shortly afterwards, they made their separate ways out the building, now knowing what destiny held for them.

Arrival in Utopia

Ur-Tokar – Jiaying attends a festival

Whilst waiting for their AI units to carry out and complete the various mining operations they had decided upon, the crew of the Opa-Loka spent several largely peaceful weeks exploring various regions of Ur-Tokar, though remained ever mindful to keep well away from any possibility of encountering Zeleyanian military forces. None of the crew was fully able to acclimatise – at least to their own personal satisfaction - to life out of stasis on the spaceship – though Savverio tended to deal with the particular problems it presented somewhat better than the others. The low gravity environment and lack of a diurnal cycle were particularly problematic, and there existed the ever present worries concerning cosmic radiation and the quality of the processed space rations. As such, they were always keen to spend some extra time on the planet below.

The crew had therefore decided to take it in turns to descend to the planet's surface, where daily life was considerably more amenable. Typically, three of them would descend to Ur-Tokar, whilst the other two kept an eye on matters up above whilst still on their starship. Time spent down below had proven to offer a whole variety of possibilities - spending time with its inhabitants, but also exploring and experiencing the unique features of the planet.

They had flown over the extensive ice sheets of the higher latitudes, but, other than the occasional group of rocky peaks poking their way through the vast depths of solid ice, they had proven to simply be vast expanses of frozen bleakness; a white zone of icy coldness and constant biting winds. The ice sheets were so thick and embedded that they extended far into what would be considered temperate zones on the majority of planets. It was not until they reached the sub-tropical latitudes that the air temperature was sufficiently high to precipitate the melting of the great glaciers that stretched their long sinuous way down through extensive deep gorges, valleys and canyons towards the central equatorial zone.

Here the glacial melting gave rise to a number of high altitude rivers which made their graceful meandering way through the deep U-shaped canyons carved out between the mountains by previous, more intense, periods of glaciation. This latitudinal zone of the planet was clearly highly fertile, for the lower slopes of the mountains were blanketed with fir, spruce and pine forests, though the higher peaks remained bare and craggy, or even snow-capped in the colder months of the year. The rivers invariably made their eventual way to the calm deep indigo blue oceans that constituted so much of the equatorial latitudes. Some had carved out broad lowland valleys as they approached sea level, but many simply poured over the towering sea-cliffs of hardened igneous rock, great gushing waterfalls of never ending glacial meltwater pounding relentlessly into the deep blue sea.

It was these coastal areas that offered the greatest attraction to the crew members of the Opa-Loka and it was here that they typically made touchdown in the shuttle craft. The coastal zones were more open and less heavily forested, and thus more easily explored. There were endless bays, strands and coves to venture around, or they could simply sit and watch the blue-white icebergs drift slowly and serenely by on their almost imperceptible voyage towards the central equatorial zone, where Rogan's heat was finally sufficient to see their eventual melting into the green-blue waters of the wider ocean.

On occasions, Mila Lustrom, who had now switched to their ship from The Star Chaser, joined them in their explorations. As an astrobiologist she had spent much of her time on Alpha Fraczan studying how life originating on Earth had adapted to her home world. She now wanted to spend some time on Ur-Tokar studying how Earth-originating life had adapted to this planet, so she could make comparisons between the two worlds. Such comparative knowledge she believed would help her to refine her theories on the subject, particularly ones concerning the impact of gravity, and develop a more generalised theory that could apply to all the newly colonised worlds. She had been joined by three of her colleagues from The Star Chaser, and they had set about undertaking as detailed a study of the vegetation zones and marine life in the seas as possibly they could in the short time available to them.

Between these expeditions, they also spent considerable periods of time based at Lato. The crew informed the inhabitants of Lato that their scans of the planet during this period had registered some form of battle or fracas between Zeleyanian forces at Meridin. They were, of course, unable to identify what the dispute actually concerned, nor what the outcome was, but it seemed to indicate that hostile rival factions had developed within the garrison. They offered the - admittedly obvious - assumption that opposing a divided enemy force would offer a significantly greater chance of victory, when they chose to launch their action. They also informed the villagers that, unfortunately, the Zeleyanian invasion fleet was still en route for their world, but they were still looking for ways to encourage it to turn around. They also indicated that their mining operations were progressing nicely, and that they were now working out a final date for their own departure back to Zeta Kotlin.

Before they did so, though, Jiaying had decided she wanted to find out more about certain aspects of their culture, particularly some of its philosophical and spiritual beliefs. There was no equivalent of the Mountain People on Zeta Kotlin and what she had learnt of their beliefs so far, had both intrigued and bemused her. Her attention had been drawn to the particular fact that there was soon to be a major spiritual festival and social gathering at a sacred site in the foothills of the Zarozinian Mountains. Her friends in Lato, particularly Amethyst, told her she was more than welcome to participate in the festivities, and this looked as good an opportunity as any to discover more about the anti-technology community before she departed from their world.

Amethyst had told her that the festival marked the beginning of their new astrological year, a concept Jiaying was largely unfamiliar with. On Zeta Kotlin no such belief systems existed. Education there was founded on a rational and scientific basis and few Zetans believed in supernatural or meta-physical beliefs, although it was possible to study why oppressed and impoverished societies did follow such superstitious and religious belief systems, though Jiaying herself had not actually done so herself. Amethyst was keen that Jiaying should find out more about her society's spiritual beliefs, and so she invited her along to the festival with her and all her friends.

Jiaying had discovered that, from an early age, Amethyst had been drawn strongly to the spiritual side of their culture. She had become convinced - by a Gaian-type philosophy - that the whole planet was in some undefined way a complete and living entity, with all its myriad aspects interlinked and mutually supporting each other. She was convinced that the mountains, streams, forests and seas were inhabited by living spirits that furthered these connections, and was sure that, on occasions, she had even caught glimpses of them. She was also convinced that all aspects of the natural world held some form of intrinsic value, and that every effort should therefore be made to preserve their existence and thus their value to the wider biotic community.

A strong believer in all aspects of spirituality, she was a keen astrologer and followed events in the heavens closely, again believing that events within the cosmos somehow affected those on her planet in an intimate, but as yet not fully understood, manner. The predictability of the movement of the stars, galaxies and planets in the heavens above matched, in some sense, the predictability of the seasons and the well-known changes of nature on the planet below. In a unified cosmos, it was not too hard to believe that the two were in some manner connected. It was also therefore quite believable that anomalies in the night skies – comets, supernova and unusual alignments of the planets - foretold or matched some unexpected or strange occurrence on the planetary surface. For her, in the grand scheme of the wider cosmos, such an alignment seemed highly plausible and fitting for a society that believed in a holistic universe, planet and way of life.

For Amethyst and her fellow believers, there was no end and no beginning, only the eternal circle of life, the wholeness of nature, the completeness of the never-ending cosmos. The believers had built sacred stone circles at strategic sites to map the astral movements in the heavens; sites they now treated with holy reverence and in which periodic nocturnal worships had become a regular feature of their lives. On a calm still moonless night, as Amethyst stood in awed reverence, transfixed within her circular temple of love, gazing at the mass of stars illuminating the night sky – the myriad shapes, patterns and configurations of multi-coloured light twinkling in a night sky of endless indigo-purple darkness – it was impossible for her not to believe that they were, in some cosmic way, an integral part of an eternal and unified cosmic sense of wonderness.

Amethyst had shown her an astrological map of the heavens above Ur-Tokar that divided the sky into twelve equal segments, each segment depicted by a particular creature or cipher that had been drawn by linking up certain prominent stars within that segment. Jiaying was already very familiar with the densely star-studded skies above Ur-Tokar, and could not help but think, that with so many stars present in the night sky, they could probably have drawn absolutely any creature they had felt inclined to do so. She did admit to herself, though, that some of the brighter or more colourful stars did sort of lend themselves to such a depiction, but as for the rest, to her mind, it looked more like wishful thinking than anything else.

Amethyst explained that the star chart could help predict your future, though was unable to offer any rational reason as to why this might be the case, when pressed on the issue by Jiaying; it just seemed to work, she said. She also claimed that people born whilst a particular section of the chart was in the ascendant in the sky displayed certain typical personality characteristics. When younger, Jiaying had noticed on Zeta Kotlin that people born at similar times of the year sometimes seemed to share certain characteristics, but had assumed this was something to do with seasonal changes in the climate or some other annual cycle caused by the planets rotation. It had never occurred to her that this might be astronomically linked, and mentioned to Amethysts that she could think of no rational reason as to why it should be either.

Amethyst, however, seemed convinced by the belief system and she was clearly not alone amongst the Mountain People, as their festival was clearly attracting a significant proportion of the local population. Despite - or perhaps because of - her scepticism, Jiaying still decided to join in the procession that set out one morning through the mountain foothills, up along the narrow rocky paths that eventually ascended to the festival site high amongst the mountains. The journey lasted the best part of a day, but towards late afternoon they eventually arrived at a curiously large concave clearing at the base of one of the higher mountain slopes. It had all the appearance of a natural amphitheatre, with quite steeply sloping sides, but an extensive, largely level, expanse at the base of the slopes.

Into the sloping sides, though, Jiaying noticed that some form of terracing had clearly been created, allowing large numbers of people to be seated on the slopes. At the centre of the flat lower expanse, she spotted what looked like a series of constructed stone shelters, interspersed with platforms and shallow runways to form what was clearly some type of theatrical arena. When she looked out over the arena and across the south-eastern edge of the clearing, it was possible to see way into the distance, down the long U-shaped valley, and she thought she might even be able to discern a distant dark blue ocean on the very furthest reaches of the horizon.

Within the clearing and dotted around its slopes, there were already several hundred people milling around the periphery, gathered around an array of brightly coloured tents and various stalls offering food, drink, clothing and a variety of spiritual artefacts. Everywhere, small groups and knots of people were socialising, merrymaking, eating and drinking. A few of those present she recognised and greeted, but the vast majority of the figures there were completely unknown to her – presumably they had travelled far and wide to be present at what was clearly a significant social occasion.

Jiaying stopped for a while on the edge of the clearing to take in the view, soak up the atmosphere and try to make some sense of what appeared before her. Festivals and other social gatherings were popular on Zeta Kotlin, but they tended to be more organised than the one that sprawled somewhat haphazardly before her. It seemed a quite chaotic affair and, of course, there was the complete absence of the advanced technology she was so used to. However, it had a pleasant and quite relaxed atmosphere about it, she thought, even if it did seem a little on the quaint side.

As she scanned across the clearing, she noted that its centre was marked by a number of brightly coloured stones arranged in the shape of an eagle. Amethyst had previously informed her that this was the first symbol of the zodiac, and that its soaring upward flight marked the end of the old year and the birth of a new one. Jiaying recalled that she had noticed a number of eagles soaring above the forests in recent days but could not remember this being the case earlier in her stay at Lato. She wondered if it was the beginning of their breeding season, and whether an increase in their aerial activity occurred at this particular time of year.

This reminded her of a conversation she had been involved in a few weeks earlier. During her time on Ur-Tokar she had noted that the planet - despite its colder climate - seemed to possess a significantly wider range of fauna than that of Zeta Kotlin, especially that of larger animals. Upon enquiry, she had been told that the original settlers here had made a point of bringing a wider array of birds and animals to the planet than was normal on other stasis ships, because they knew they would be dependent upon these creatures for a whole variety of resources and activities. However, she could not work out where an eagle would fit into this particular plan, and made a mental note to ask someone about their presence.

As she thought about the signs of the astrological chart that Amethyst had described to her earlier - many of which were represented by animals and plants - she could easily imagine a number of them corresponding to peaks in natural animal and plant behaviour throughout the year – the arrival of salmon in the rivers, beavers emerging in the early spring, the flowering of the rose, and nuts appearing on the trees in the autumn. Their astrological calendar was probably more a celebration of the natural world and the wonders that lay around them, rather than some dubious link to the cosmos, she thought. So why bother making an astral link at all, she wondered.

Whilst lost in these thoughts, Indigo, Raven and Rowan suddenly appeared on the scene, and after receiving a warm welcome, she was invited over to one of the tables covered in food and drink, where she tucked in hungrily and at some length - having built up a considerable appetite trekking up the mountain. As she did so, late afternoon passed into evening, and she noted that the groupings began to gradually disperse to the point when the scene was clearly being set for the commencement of far more formal procedures. A number of people had donned strange and elaborate costumes and were gathering towards the centre of the clearing; she noted several figures she recognised from the local folklore, including a wizard, a wood nymph, an alien, some dark-looking lords of chaos and a demon, but also a variety of costumed dancers, musicians and some other oddly dressed figures she was much less certain about.

The crowds were beginning to move up the slopes and gather on the terraces, so that soon there was barely a spare place left amongst them. Jiaying, along with Indigo, squeezed into the seated crowd somewhere on the higher reaches of the slope that looked westward, just as plates of hash cake and bowls of a tea made from magic mushrooms were being passed around the gathering. Jiaying felt it would be rude to turn them down, and indulged in the mind-altering substances just as everyone else seemed to be doing. Then, just as Rogan finally set behind the western mountains, and day turned quickly to night, a hush fell across the clearing and Jiaying waited silently and expectantly with the rest of the gathered assembly. Fires had been lit at strategic points across the clearing for illumination and the costumed figures took up their places, strategically placed within the natural amphitheatre.

Figuring that Jiaying might not understand what was about to follow, Indigo carefully explained the initial scene to her - that the whole episode was meant to represent a dream - and as the performance unfurled before them, she offered further occasional excerpts of narration, whenever she thought Jiaying might struggle to understand aspects of the performance.

Initially, and very suddenly, from the side of the clearing the wizard blew his horn - a twisted affair shaped from an animal Jiaying was unfamiliar with - and the costumed dream dancers, led by some form of green-finned demon, entered the eagle-shaped stones, performing what Jiaying assumed to be some form of snake dance; the dancers firstly twisting and turning their way across the open clearing, and then moving in and around the yellow, blue and orange stones in a monotonously hypnotic fashion for some considerable time.

Accompanied by rhythmic drumming and dancing flutists, the prolonged and repetitive dance had a mesmorising quality which so transfixed Jiaying that she only slowly became aware of a tall dark and imposing figure watching over the whole affair. Then, the wood nymph, she had noted earlier, gracefully entered the arena, dancing its way to the centre of the clearing, at which point the demon and its attendant snake dancers moved menacingly around it, cavorting and twisting alarmingly in some form of demonic reptoid vision. The snake dancers were then slowly and gradually joined by the dark lords and a group of haloed figures wearing long dark heavy robes, and indicated by Indigo as representing angels of death. Together, these dark forces chased the wood nymph threateningly around the centre of the clearing, creating scenes of chaos as they whirled and twirled around and around, and then finally seized the wood nymph and held it captive against the eagle stones at the centre.

After what then seemed like an eternity of further repetitive and mesmorising drumming, the wizard reappeared, and Indigo indicated that he was now blowing the horn of fate - what to Jiaying's eyes simply appeared to be a bull's horn. A few moments later the watcher figure slowly, but confidently, made its way to the centre of the spectacle followed by the alien and some haloed figures wearing long diaphanous white robes, which Indigo indicated represented angels of life. A dramatically acted fight and skirmish then ensued for several minutes between the two differently robed sets of angels, with the angels of death ultimately suffering defeat. As the final fight sequence came to an end, the watcher waved his arms aloft above him, dramatically struck his twisted staff against the standing stones, and banished the chaos army of the dark lords from the clearing.

The watcher then set about protecting the wood nymph through an elaborate series of dance moves that first held back the green-finned demon, and then united the three together in unison. United together, and holding hands, the three then strode into the centre of the clearing.
'I am the reptoid,' declared the green-finned demon, 'I am nature.'
The wood nymph moved forward and declared, 'I too am nature, and together we two are one.'
Then finally the watcher strode forward and declared, 'I am the watcher. I am the eye that looks within. I see all.'
Then all three together declared, 'in nature we are one, and in one we are nature.'
Once this was completed, the alien then advanced to the centre of the clearing and recited a lengthy poem in a language Jiaying was completely unfamiliar with. At the conclusion of the alien poem, the small figure stepped forward and declared, 'alien, I am, but I do not reject your human touch.'
With this, the wizard once more appeared, and loudly blew a different horn this time - the original twisted one - which Indigo indicated was the horn of destiny. This seemed to mark the end of the performance, for the whole dance troupe then gathered together at the front of the clearing, accompanied by an upsurge in the drumming and assorted wind instruments, and a huge and prolonged cheer followed, accompanied by fervent clapping from the whole of the assembly gathered on the terraced slopes.

Arrival in Utopia

As the performance ended, Jiaying slowly looked up and around her. Her lofty position allowed an uninterrupted vision across the clearing, and one that overlooked the valley which was now entirely darkened, with soft shadows cast by the purple moon of Arioch and the host of stars that lit the night sky. She thought about the magic scenes she had just witnessed, and assumed the dance represented some form of symbolic unity between humans and the beneficial and harmful aspects of nature, but one that had only been achieved through the defeat of dark forces, and by travelling to alien worlds across the infinite depths of space. Nevertheless, she had to admit to herself that the performance - set in the natural mountain clearing above the forests, and under the purple moon and a star-lit sky overlooking the impressive valley and jagged mountains in the far distance - had a distinctly magical and mystical aura about it, that she could not help but be impressed by, though she figured the hallucinogenic substances she had consumed earlier were also adding pleasantly to the whole experience.

The lengthy and elaborate performance apparently marked the highpoint of the proceedings and was then followed by a series of far less formal dances and musical and artistic performances all of which, as far as Jiaying could discern, seemed to represent certain signs of their zodiac or other significant elements of the local folklore. These included a quite genuinely spooky ghost dance, a very loud and impressive dragon song, a song of the swords type fable accompanied by clashing costumed warriors, a very long and sad ballad about a dead god's homecoming, a bewitchingly beautiful ode to a timeflower, and an exciting devilish dirge led by a manic violin player. All were enthusiastically appreciated by the assembled crowd who sang or danced along to the various performances in a manner which indicated they were clearly familiar with the whole proceedings.

And gradually, as the night progressed and the small hours of the morning passed, the crowd became more and more involved, and more and more integrated into the dances and the musical performances. The proceedings seemed to continually develop until eventually becoming a truly unified social gathering of the entire community. And then, suddenly, the music and the dancing ended and the proceedings came to an abrupt halt. Jiaying looked around her to see if she had missed something, but could see nothing of any particular note. A quiet hush of expectation had fallen across the crowd and they all started looking eastwards towards the mountains.

The sound of a lone guitar began to jangle in the background. Slowly a drum roll began, one that seemed to build a sense of anticipation amongst the crowd, followed by a warming flute-like call which only added to the growing expectation. The fluting song of a lone oriole suddenly lifted out of the woods, out across the clearing. The slow drum beat continued building in anticipation, the flute added its occasional wistful tune, cymbals shimmered in the background, the flute warbled once again and then suddenly the first red rays of Rogan's light broke across the mountains. The drums slowly rolled once more. The music began to quicken in tempo and the crowd began to dance. The morning sky began to lighten orange-red, the dance quickened, Rogan climbed higher, and the weak sunlight grew stronger. Slowly, Rogan fully emerged from behind the mountains, its light spreading across the morning sky, and the dancing crowd quickened in time to the rhythmic drumming and guitar beat.

The slowly building crescendo of music, dance, and morning sun built and built until the Cajun Jinx was danced ceremoniously and triumphantly to a final grand flourish, one that involved the entire assembled gathering stomping joyously together around the eagle stones to the rhythm of the drums and guitars. When Rogan finally broke fully above the eastern horizon, the entire community ended their rhythmic dancing, and together, in complete unison, sang a hymn to the sun. With this completed, the crowd slowly dispersed, tired but elated, and under the mask of morning, Jiaying, along with all the other festival-goers, made her way slowly and half-dazed to one of the tents, where she collapsed and spent most of the ensuing day in a deep sleep.

Jiaying remained for a couple more days of dragons and fables, but as the festival began to wind down, she eventually made her way back down the mountain with Indigo and the others, and once more found herself in The Hall of the Mountain Grill in Lato. Whilst there, she received a message from Savverio who happened to be minding the starship on that particular day. The AI units had effectively completed the final mining operation, since they had now secured all the ores and minerals they had originally sought, plus a few unexpected bonus ones. They had calculated that access to any further deposits would be difficult and time-consuming and had questioned whether this was worth pursuing, requesting a decision on the matter from the crew. Savverio had checked the data and arrived at the same conclusion as the AI units. The mining operation he felt should be concluded as a result.

As such, Savverio had started to run a series of diagnostic checks on the ship's main systems to ensure they were fully prepared and ready for their imminent departure. Unfortunately, the checks had discovered that a long-running drive issue with one of their engines had now developed into a major fault. They would still be able to journey to Zeta Kotlin using the remaining engines - which were all working at a sufficiently high level of capacity - but this would add several months to the journey and create unwanted stresses to the main structures of the ship. He suggested that the whole crew needed to meet up and make a decision regarding their next move.

Later that evening, the various groups made their way back to the starship and then from the shuttle hanger, through the long grey metallic corridors, to their reasonably spacious quarters – the stasis ship having been retrofitted to meet the requirements of a crew that would spend several weeks at a time out of stasis. They then dropped off their various items and possessions, though none needed to wash or change as this had been previously done down on Ur-Tokar – they all knew by now that this was a far more sensible way of arranging matters. Once ready, they took the elevator tubes to the highest floor of the space ship and made their way to the forward deck.

As they entered the room, most instinctively gazed out of the viewing gallery at the star-filled blackness of space and took in the view before them. Ur-Tokar's curved circumference took up much of the vista and Rogan's orange-red rays were breaking over the horizon of the planet's long curved surface somewhere in the far distance, since the starship was currently heading towards Ur-Tokar's early morning sunrise.

Once they were all finally seated again around the makeshift conference table on the forward deck, the crew, Mila, and her associates started listening to Savverio's appraisal of the situation.
'We're looking at three weeks work minimum according to the ship's computer. We have all the replacement parts and necessary tools and

machinery we need on board, but dismantling and then reassembling the damaged sections of the engine whilst the ship continues to orbit around Ur-Tokar will be a slow and complicated procedure. It's just about within the capacity of the AI units, but I expect they will need to proceed carefully, slowly and with considerable mechanical precision. Basically, it's not going to be a quick fix, some of those parts can be very tricky to extract and then reinsert and position in exactly the correct manner,' he explained.

He paused for a moment, 'the alternative is that we head for home using the three existing engines. The problem with that, though, is that we will possess significantly lower levels of initial thrust on departure, and the power imbalance is also likely to deliver major stresses to the internal structures of the ship throughout the entire journey. The computer indicates a high percentage safety level for the journey, but it does mean arriving home much later than if we were using full power, and we've already been here two months longer than we originally intended,' and he stopped, and looked around at the others to see what they thought.

'So is it possible we could come home to Zeta quicker if we actually wait another three weeks for the repairs to be completed?' asked Kahlil.

'Yes, the journey time with only three functioning engines will be a little over five months longer than with full power,' Savverio replied.

'Right, so it clearly works to wait for the repairs if we do it that particular way. How long before the Zeleyanian invasion fleet is due to arrive? Where are they now?' asked Neema.

'They are still a minimum of two months away, possibly a little more. Even if we're delayed – which is definitely possible – we shouldn't have to worry about encountering that lot. In reality, we can depart whenever we want to, even with the repairs unfinished – we can just suspend the process if need be - so the invasion fleet should never actually be a problem for us,' Savverio answered.

'Obviously, it's your decision,' stated Mila looking around the crew, 'but any extra time for us on the planet would be a major bonus. Additional data can only ever be useful, and there are still some marine areas we'd particularly like to study, so time spent there would be very useful from our point of view,' she explained. Her colleagues made various supporting comments of approval, presumably so her position carried greater weight in the discussion.

For a few moments no one said anything, so Jiaying took the opportunity to offer her opinion. 'Personally, I also have no problem with spending some extra time on Ur-Tokar if that's what people want to do. I've really come to love the place, and I'd quite like to know what's going to happen at Meridin. I received the distinct impression from Topaz that it's all going to kick off there pretty soon,' she said, hoping the others would be equally enthusiastic. 'And anyway,' she added, 'we can provide Zeta with better information if we know the result of the conflict.'

'Yeh – who's gonna win the war down there? That's quite important for us to know,' added Kahlil. 'If the fascists at Meridin are completely defeated, then the main invasion might yet be called off, or at the very least have less chance of succeeding. Information like that could be very useful back on Zeta.'

'Is there any word from Earth City yet in relation to our message about the Zeleyanian base being established on Ur-Tokar?' asked Janicka. 'Are they preparing for the worst?'

'The message won't even have arrived there yet – that's about another two weeks away. We'll be long gone from this place before we receive any news from Earth City. I've been sending them regular updates and news of any significant developments, but I'm not expecting much in the way of return traffic.'

'Everything's so slow in space, it all seems to take so long. It's almost like we're time captives, just waiting endlessly for everything to happen elsewhere,' commented Janicka.

'Well, we are talking vast spatial distances, but you sort of get used to it after a while,' Jiaying offered. 'Assuming the invasion fleet continues on its current flightpath and carries out its original mission, the ship's computer is already programmed to message Zeta when it discovers the actual invasion has taken place. They should be fully informed of all the developments taking place here, whatever we do. We still have full control of the satellite system as well, so we can follow their eventual progress even after we have departed – unless the Zeleyanians destroy the system, of course,' Savverio suggested as an afterthought, 'which I guess is always a possibility,' and he shrugged. 'Well, anyway, with regards to helping Zeta, it doesn't really matter if we leave now or depart in three weeks time.'

'We also promised not to get involved in any actual conflict down below,' added Neema, 'so we can't make much material difference down there either. It doesn't seem to matter too much whether we stay or go, only that - somewhat bizarrely - we arrive quicker if we actually wait longer.'

'I'm detecting a desire to go with repairs and delayed departure, so we stay a while longer, rather than leave immediately. Is that correct?' asked Jiaying, hoping to speed up the decision process.

'Jiaying wants to get bombed out her skull and visit the wood nymphs again,' Kahlil joked, and they all started laughing.

'Ah, yes, I heard about your trip in the mountains. What was that all about?' asked Janicka, genuinely intrigued by what the others had told her.

Jiaying looked a bit pained. 'It's difficult to say exactly . . . it's difficult to know what was just theatre, and how much was actually part of their belief system. It was all a bit weird, strange folklore creatures, outlandish dances and, yes, hallucinogenic drugs all mixed together. It was a weird trip,' and they all laughed. 'But, ultimately, I think it's a means to help them stay true to their ecological value system. They don't seem to have much in the way of political or legal structures to ensure their way of life is maintained, so I guess they rely heavily on cultural influences instead.'

'Their way of life and philosophy is clearly based on a singular and particular interpretation of why civilisation on Earth failed — that mass produced technology led to humans becoming divorced from their natural environment, and through their own ignorance, unknowingly became the destroyers of the life support system that had previously kept them alive,' Savverio added. 'But as each generation on Ur-Tokar grows old and dies, an increasing temporal distance is put between this perception of reality and their present existence. They need to find ways of reminding each generation of why they live the way they do. That's why they do these things.'

'Yeh, that sounds about right to me, as well,' added Kahlil. 'To me, their society looks like a fairly fragile one, and it must be easily prone to disruption. I would have thought they rely on these types of activity a great deal, from what I've seen of their society.'

The discussions of the Opa-Loka on most topics had a habit of meandering in different directions to ensure that everyone who wanted to have a say did so, and so that all possible considerations were covered — in this respect they were very much a product of the culture they came from. However, on this occasion most of them, one way or another, had experienced a long day on or off the planet, and were once again beginning to feel the debilitating effects of space flight. Aware of this, Jiaying wanted to wind matters up more quickly than usual.

'OK, come on everyone, let's not worry about why they hold festivals, let's make a decision about the ship,' she announced, suddenly feeling very weary and ready for a concerted period of sleep.

With all present also feeling it was time to reach a conclusion, and with no one raising any major objections to a delayed departure, it was agreed that the damaged engine should firstly be fixed before making their return to Zeta Kotlin. With this, the meeting thus came to an abrupt end. Savverio issued instructions to the AI units to commence the engine repair process, whilst all the others made their way to their quarters to get some much needed sleep.

The following day, most of the crew, together with Mila and her colleagues, made a swift return back down to the planet. They all had their own particular purposes for doing so in mind, and there was a general expectation that this would be their last period of extended time on the planet, and so any last ventures or unfinished activities needed to be completed or concluded. However, none of them anticipated that their last touchdown on Ur-Tokar would prove to be a considerably problematic, and even potentially dangerous, one.

Ur-Tokar – Vice-Admiral Rosson waits for news

Approximately one week later, Vice-Admiral Rosson was seated in the former banquet hall of Meridin Castle surrounded as usual by his closest members of staff. He had previously ordered the removal of the old, hideous animal trophy heads and ridiculously pompous tapestries from the high stone walls of the castle. These had been replaced by banners celebrating the glories of Zeleyan, intermixed with pictures of notable Zeleyanian landmarks and the more notable planets that constituted Hedilla's star system. The mini-fabs had been working overtime recently, mass producing an array of propaganda materials that were now displayed at appropriate places in the town, and throughout the public buildings the military forces now occupied.

Rosson looked around at the replacement banners and wondered whether there had even been much point in displaying them. A few days previously he had ordered his Communications Officer, Sub-Lieutenant Schultz, to deliver a daily update on the progress being made by the Zeleyanian invasion fleet – ostensibly so he would know their exact day of arrival, and so appropriate preparations could be made in anticipation of the expected landing of the Supreme Commander and his invasion forces. However, this was not the real purpose behind Rosson's instructions.

By his own calculations, enough time had now passed for his encrypted message to Supreme Commander Vartin to have been received by the invasion fleet. What he really wanted to know was whether the fleet had turned tail and was now heading back to Zeleyan. Much to Rosson's chagrin, however, the report each day continued to indicate that the invasion force was still on its way and due to arrive in exactly two months time. His communications operation had, so far, registered no change at all in its direction of travel nor in its estimated time of arrival. He had been hoping this might simply be due to a time delay in the transmissions, but was now beginning to believe his message had simply not achieved its desired objective.

However, during the course of his duties, Schultz had also relayed to him an open transmission from The Spirit of the Age, about a week earlier, one which he had initially assumed was meant for The Star Chaser, but possibly also directed towards Zeta Kotlin. The message from The Spirit of the Age had intrigued him, though. It was mostly an update of developments on Rorque 4, but he got the distinct feeling that sections of the message might actually be aimed surreptitiously at Zeleyanian forces. The more he read through the message, the more he became sure that the section of the message relating to the Rorque Corporation was actually intended for himself and Vartin. He could also imagine Vartin's mood when he received this particular information, which surely he had by now. For the first time in weeks Rosson burst into laughter as he imagined Vartin's livid reaction.

Schultz had also previously notified him of the departure of The Star Chaser for Zeta Kotlin approximately a month ago. They had closely tracked the starship ever since, but its projected destination had remained unchanged and they had largely lost interest in the vessel now. The message from The Spirit of the Age would have arrived at the starship sometime after its departure from Ur-Tokar – with the crew presumably in stasis - and he wondered if this was down to a communications mix-up, or was there, as he had sometimes suspected, still another starship in their vicinity with which it was in contact with. There were certain developments on and above the planet that still didn't add up, he believed, and the presence of a second ship seemed to make increasing sense to him.

Despite all this, the invasion force – irrespective of the recent messages – appeared to be still making steady progress towards his position, and so he was rapidly running out of time. It now seemed obvious that he needed to make a decisive decision about his own future and the quicker the better. The option of crowning himself king now seemed completely out of the question and somewhat risible – a particularly stupid idea! Effectively, he only had one viable option left, and in a bizarre sort of way he was beginning to look forward to it.

For, he had tired of being a commander, of daily telling himself, 'to get yourself together man or you're going to fall apart'. Behind the face of steady control and calm that he portrayed to his men throughout the working day, the secrecy, the worry and the paranoia of his present situation were all slowly eating away at him. He longed for some form of release and freedom from this mental captivity, but he also knew he could not act rashly or too soon. He had been biding his time and was waiting for the right moment and for certain connections to be established before he could make his next move. And finally, his latest intelligence gathering exercise indicated that his waiting could soon be over.

Interstellar Space – the Zeleyanian invasion fleet receives further messages

Aboard the Patriot IV, time had passed painfully slowly over the previous six weeks. Vartin, Neumann and Tarrafel had all experienced considerable difficulties coping with prolonged space flight. Poor quality food, a low gravity environment and the lack of any diurnal cycle had all taken their toll on their mental faculties and physical health – despite the fact that after a few days of travel, Vartin had ordered the ship's computer to alternate the lighting to mimic night and day, with the intention of eliminating at least one of these problems. However, there was little he could do in terms of blocking out the constant irritating hum of the ventilation and life support systems, or the frequent metallic creakings and moanings of the starship as it powered its way through the darkened cosmos.

On occasions, the three men realised just how isolated and how far from any inhabited planet their current position actually was. The sense of isolation and loneliness, far out into the deep depths of space, was occasionally more than their minds could bear. If the three invasion ships ran into any serious problems, there was no place and no one they could turn to. They were completely on their own and subject to the cold hard vicissitudes of inter-stellar space. Disaster would mean instant death. As such, the three military officers were rarely in a positive mood and tended to avoid each other as much as physically possible. They spent most of their time assessing communications from the various planets, or working their way through the bank of classic literature, old movies and other entertainment emissions held on the ship's database.

Keeping track of time had initially proven difficult and had ultimately seemed pointless. At this point in time, there was still a further eight weeks of travel until they finally reached Ur-Tokar, and all three had developed reasons to wonder whether they could continue to cope with the situation, and even whether it was worth the actual effort. Only a combination of patriotic duty and a fear of being seen to fail kept the three military leaders motivated. For Vartin, there was still the tantalising prospect of historic glory, though too often it all seemed a long way into the future now. For Neumann and Tarrafel it was simply a desire to keep their commissions. They kept their doubts and their darker thoughts to themselves, but this too only added to the mental stress of their situation.

Monitoring communications from the various planets of the Nexus Cluster brought some alleviation from the tedium and boredom of space flight, though most of these emanated from Rorque 4, with a lesser amount from both Zeta Kotlin and their own home planet. These eventually achieved a degree of sameness and familiarity that they too became part of the endless ennui and routine. Little else of importance was noted, though communications from the Zeleyanian spy satellite circling Ur-Tokar had eventually confirmed that The Star Crusader had departed from Ur-Tokar's orbit and was heading in the direction of Zeta Kotlin. This they agreed was highly suspicious and offered proof that Zeta Kotlin had almost certainly been responsible for the abduction of their stasis ship, The Crusader.

It was during a typically uneventful period of waking that the ship's computer suddenly brought to Vartin's attention the fact that an encrypted message had been received bearing Vice-Admiral Rosson's security code. Before opening it though, Vartin checked with the computer as to whether his message for Major Pushkov would have arrived at Ur-Tokar before this message was transmitted, and the computer replied in the affirmative, stating it would have reached Pushkov two days earlier. Vartin opened the message fearing the worst, and indeed his fears were duly confirmed.

Our military forces have suffered a major defeat at the hands of local insurgents who proved to be far more numerous than first thought. We have suffered major casualties, including both officers and the ranks. Major Pushkov and Captain Peran are amongst the officers who were killed by the insurgents. We have dispersed into the countryside and are in desperate need of rescue. Winter is closing in fast, so rescue is urgent.

Vartin stared at the message and a whirl of thoughts went through his brain. Could the message actually be true, he wondered. Was this even further evidence of Rosson's complete incompetence? Over recent weeks he had completely convinced himself that Rosson was an outright traitor and a threat to his continued rule. But maybe he had been wrong, maybe Rosson was simply incompetent and a fool. Only his stupidity was actually dangerous.

However, the reference to Pushkov, he felt, was highly suspicious. Was this a way of telling him that Pushkov had been discovered and executed; that his attempt to oust Rosson from his position as commander had failed. Was this, in fact, a double bluff by Rosson, and by begging for rescue he was hoping that Vartin would do the opposite? Was Rosson at this very moment planning to become the new ruler of Ur-Tokar? His opinion of Rosson had sunk so low that he seriously wondered if the whole message was actually a complete pack of lies. But, if on the other hand it was true, his forces might face a long guerilla campaign whilst trying to hold onto the planet in the middle of winter.

It was impossible for Vartin to know for sure which of his thoughts were correct, but his suspicious nature told him there was something untoward about this message. Something really did not add up. He debated whether to inform his two generals and after some prevarication, resolved to do so. They both knew Rosson through the various officers' clubs and they might possess some extra insight into his personality. He summoned them to the control deck, and they were informed of the transmission from Rosson. Once they had read the message he waited for their thoughts

General Neumann read the message carefully several times. He too went through several mental permutations as he read the message. He had already mentally decided he had no great desire to continue with the conquest of Ur-Tokar, but he could not admit this openly, for fear of displeasing the Supreme Commander. He had been waiting for some way of deterring Vartin from continuing with the mission and this seemed to offer an opportunity, though without directly saying so.

He chose his words very carefully, 'I've never thought Rosson was a first-rate commander, but it appears that their armed forces must be considerably stronger than we originally conceived, for even Rosson to suffer two major defeats at their hands. I see no great reason to rush to his rescue . . . he's a traitor and a military failure. We could leave him to be finished off by the insurgents; after all, it's all he deserves. I see no reason why we should still not be able to conquer Ur-Tokar, though. However, a mid-winter occupation accompanied by a determined guerilla insurgency is not something our troops have ever experienced, nor are they trained for such an eventuality. It will not be easy, but we should still prevail if that is what you are still planning.'

Vartin already knew his generals had major doubts about the invasion, and he saw straight through the thoughts of Neumann, but chose to say nothing. He assumed Tarrafel would simply repeat the senior officer's thoughts. At least he knew exactly where they stood on this matter though. On second thoughts, he decided not to pursue the matter of Rosson's personality and traits, but he was not yet ready to abandon his plans. His starships contained thousands of well-armed troops; he would still be able to take control of the planet even if there was an insurgency – and he was far from convinced that there actually was one. And if Rosson had proclaimed himself the new ruler of the planet, he would take great pleasure in deposing him. Vartin informed the generals of his decision to continue, and the need to deal appropriately with Rosson. He dismissed them and they returned to their monitoring of communications.

It was only a few hours after this short conversation that the open transmission from The Spirit of the Age arrived at the Patriot IV, and thus Vartin had no means of hiding it from his generals, which, retrospectively, he very much wished could have been the case. The transmission was quite lengthy and was clearly being sent to some sympathetic contact – though Vartin could only speculate as to who exactly this was, probably Zeta Kotlin, he thought. It mostly contained an appraisal of the situation on Rorque 4, in particular the economic and political deterioration, but also sections on the climate catastrophe that was unfolding. Amongst the many sections of the message Vartin noted the following part in particular:

The situation on Rorque 4 has deteriorated dramatically in recent months and it has entered a period of severe economic stagnation. The space flight engineers from Alpha Fraczan and aboard the Avante have been employed by the Cosmic Solutions Corporation since their arrival. Cosmic Solutions are currently using their expertise to terra-form their sister planet Morpheus. The Rorque Corporation and United Rorque Technologies have been unable to gain access to any of their ideas and technology, and are pursuing other solutions to the economic crisis.

Arrival in Utopia

For Vartin, the endless delays and procrastinations by the Rorque Corporation had eventually become highly suspicious. Some of the news bulletins from Rorque 4 had shown rocket engineers working for Cosmic Solutions, but it was much harder to discern what exactly was happening in terms of his erstwhile business partners. He knew there were numerous problems on Rorque 4, but he had long suspected there were other issues the Rorque Corporation were keeping from him, and this message clearly confirmed this suspicion. His business partners had been double-crossing him; they possessed no advanced space flight technology and neither had they ever done so. They had been stringing him along all this time for some nefarious purpose, probably something to do with money - the only thing they cared about - knowing the Rorque Corporation.

The wider implications of the transmission slowly began to dawn on him; he would not be gaining access to advanced and faster space flight technology. His plans to conquer planets beyond Ur-Tokar were in tatters now. He had been banking on using speed and the element of surprise to achieve further conquests, but this strategy was now a complete non-starter. And, if Rosson's message somehow turned out to be true, even the conquest of Ur-Tokar might now be in doubt.

Even worse, the two generals suddenly appeared at his door informing him of the message that had just arrived from The Spirit of the Age. They would know that he had been double-crossed by the Rorque Corporation, that he had been fooled by a bunch of money-grabbers and that his plans for conquest beyond Ur-Tokar lay in disarray. He suddenly felt too tired and too angry to explain matters to them and summarily dismissed them. Vartin began a long period of serious reflection.

Rorque 4 - Alex Kim visits Motorway City

It was nearly nine months now since the Avante had conveyed Alex Kim and his colleagues into orbit around Rorque 4; for Alex Kim it had been nine months of increasing frustration and concern. The source of his frustration centred round the scaled-up tests of the prototype rocket engines he had been conducting at the university test site. The computer simulations and laboratory tests he had run back on Alpha Fraczan had been extremely promising, but here on Rorque 4, with the opportunity to scale them up to a much larger non-laboratory level, a whole array of engineering difficulties had become glaringly apparent.

It had also been increasingly apparent that the technical difficulties were all closely inter-linked and effectively inseparable. As soon as he improved matters in one area – for instance, flow conductivity – associated problems manifested themselves in interlinked areas, such as pressure expansion. An adjustment in one part of the engine system almost invariably led to an additional complication or deterioration in performance elsewhere in the system. After nine months of continuous adjustments, fixes and compromises, his engines were effectively little better than the ones currently in service on a standard stasis ship. In addition, lengthy meetings and conferences with his colleagues devoted to brainstorming the problems had failed to break the impasse, and Alex had become a worried man.

He knew full well that the corporations on Rorque 4 were results-driven businesses and that they would not tolerate such failure indefinitely. What he had not been so sure about, though, was how much time he would be allowed before they reduced or even terminated his funding. He knew he was important to their plans, but also knew he was not indispensable. He had also regretted the fact he had been so optimistic at their initial meetings, and had raised expectations within the corporation to such a high level. This had now come back to haunt him.

He ultimately realised he might be looking at years of hard work before he made any significant progress, and even that was far from guaranteed. On particularly bad days he had started to look around for excuses; if he had received greater support and backing on Alpha Fraczan he might not have been in such a situation, he had frequently thought. The authorities there should have shown greater confidence in him – then he would have been further along the path towards an engineering breakthrough. But ultimately, he had realised, he had only himself to blame for his predicament, and only he too could resolve it.

Alex was currently making his way to Motorway City. He had been travelling asleep in the overnight autocar, but as he neared his destination the autocar's computer had woken him in preparation for his arrival. He peered ahead through the night sky, and there in the distance before him he perceived the silhouetted black cityscape of Motorway City, outlined by the orange glow of the neon skyline above the city. The autocar sped down the motorway – passing the small number of vehicles which were travelling at such an early time in the morning - the orange street lights lighting up the night sky above him and flickering monotonously across the windscreen as the vehicle passed smoothly and silently beneath them. Alex gazed sleepily out the window into the darkness of the night.

He returned to his thoughts. The world here was a considerably lonelier one than he had expected, though beforehand, in actual fact, he had not given this aspect of his future life much thought. On Alpha Fraczan he had existed within a fairly tight-knit collegiate atmosphere; one that he was only now beginning to appreciate and, just recently, to even miss. On his home planet there had been no real external pressures other than to develop his theories, advance his research and conduct his testing - at whatever pace he deemed to be appropriate. In reality, this had really been no pressure at all, as space flight and rocket engineering were the greatest loves of his life. Typically he had immersed himself in his life's work and he was more than happy to do so.

Here, on Rorque 4, though, the pressures emanating from the corporation were of an extremely short-term nature – effectively dictated by quarterly business reports. His life and career were now driven by targets, league tables, performance observations and circumscribed by strict budgets. He felt like he was under constant scrutiny and endless pressure to deliver. He had started to cut corners, exaggerate success in his reports, omit errors and failures, blame others for his own failures, create less ambitious targets and downgrade expectations. On occasions, he had felt like giving up on the whole project and just quitting in protest. He had not felt good about any of this – he had never felt the need to do this before - but he had slowly become aware that his fellow senior colleagues were all playing the same game; though, like him, they were all keeping it very quiet.

He had also becoming alarmed, like many of his colleagues, by the rapidly deteriorating climate situation on the planet. Enquiries amongst his university colleagues had elicited the information that the problem had been around for several years now – possibly longer – but the deterioration was accelerating at an alarming rate. He had just escaped one planetary disaster, and he had begun to wonder whether he would need to repeat the exercise all over again.

Then suddenly, his worst fears were actually confirmed; the corporation had made it discreetly known that they were intending to leave the planet imminently, and head for some far-flung star further along the Orion-Cygnus arm of the near galaxy. He was far from sure that he wanted to be involved in the start-up of another civilisation – what he really wanted was to develop his rocket engines, but he needed much more time, and new ideas. On the other hand, though, his life on Rorque 4 was not living up to expectations and so something needed to change.

Motorway City lay at the heart of a highly complex major road network system – hence its name - and could thus be reached from all the other major conurbations with relative rapidity, though the network had clearly become over-complex, as each competing company had felt the need to add its own additional private routes to the sprawling web-like system. The autocar navigated its way through the spaghetti-like array of roads - the ubiquitous neon orange street lamps above the roads lighting the night sky up like an orange flame - and made its methodical, almost seamless, way towards the destination keyed into the satellite-controlled navigation system.

As the autocar reached the outer suburbs, Alex looked on with increasing dismay as he took in the dilapidated, rubbish-strewn impoverished outskirts of the city. The drive by was simply one set of burnt out cars, wrecked furniture and shanty houses sprawled across an area of wasteland, after another. Paint peeled off the graffiti-covered external walls of semi-demolished buildings, pavements had been liberated of their flagstones, whilst doors and window frames had been stripped out to be used for firewood to keep the inhabitants warm during the cold desert nights. He wondered how such misery could even be tolerated.

Alex had been in two minds about making the journey to Motorway City, and such scenes only made him even more unsure about the wisdom of his decision to do so. It had not been his idea, and he had harboured doubts from the beginning about the whole exercise, but he had ultimately felt that, at a time when his personality seemed to have taken a distinct turn for the worse, it was about time he did something helpful for others for a change.

He had known Anna Dubois reasonably well during his brief time at Seven Mountains University, before he went to Sienna Pools, and he also knew she had engineered the arrival of the second scientist ship to arrive at Rorque 4 – though apparently not the same one they had set out on at Alpha Fraczan. Having this much in common, he had originally wanted to meet up with her, but Cosmic Solutions had discouraged any such meeting, and he had soon been absorbed by his work at the university and forgotten all about the idea. Thus, when he had received a somewhat cryptic message from her asking for a meeting he had been intrigued by the request. His present plan was simply to see exactly what it was she wanted, and then to finish his preparations for his departure on the stasis ship, which he had now decided was better than staying on a dying planet.

Anna had arrived from the neighbouring continent of Northern Thule – a fairly short ferry journey across the Straits of Nozike, followed by a long, but very straight and rapid, journey along a series of motorways that ultimately lead into the heart of Motorway City. The landscape along the route was mostly treeless, monotonously flat and effectively endless parched desert for most of the journey, and she had spent the journey reading her autobook rather than watching the tiresome media emissions on the autocar screen. She arrived in the heart of the city slightly tired, somewhat nervous and in need of a long cool drink.

She had recently been refused a position on the departing Rorque Corporation stasis ships, a decision that had initially angered her, but had not come as any great surprise, given some of the enemies she had made, together with her recent rebellious phase. Once her anger had subsided, though, she still knew she desperately wanted to leave the planet – there was very little here she found enjoyable anymore, she disliked the person she had been forced to become, and she disliked the society she was living in. She was less sure about travelling so far across the galaxy, but there appeared to be no other route out of Rorque 4, so she had asked the corporation to reconsider - only for her appeal to subsequently fail.

After this setback, though, she then hit upon the idea of asking Alex Kim to help her secure a place on a Cosmic Solutions ship; she was hoping Alex – with his esteemed status – might carry some influence within the rival corporation. She had wanted a personal meeting with Alex for various reasons; she no longer trusted the electronic communications network on the planet and she believed that a face-to-face meeting with Alex would make it harder for him to say 'no'. In the event of him agreeing to her request, she was also now fairly close to the spaceport at Stratostan, which had a relatively quick and direct link to Motorway City.

They had agreed to meet at a small restaurant for breakfast near the city centre around mid-morning. The wide open dusty streets of the centre were not what either of them had expected, and it very much had the feel of being a transport hub and very little else. There was little in the way of amusements, eateries or retail and the whole place had a distinctly utilitarian feel about it. They greeted each other in the foyer of the eatery, and after ordering food and drink from the serving AI units, they sat in the corner away from the windows and told each other of their relative experiences since landing on the planet.

Alex was surprised Anna had fared so badly on Rorque 4. He had always regarded her as an ambitious person, but one who he could trust, since she had always played by the rules as she attempted to enhance her status and achieve promotion to higher positions. The fact that her career here on Rorque 4 had fallen apart so quickly, further enhanced his opinion that the world he was on was organised in a profoundly mistaken way. Anna was equally disappointed that Alex was also struggling with his projects. She had always felt he had unrealised potential and, given the right support, that his theories and projects could be a great success. She also wondered if this now meant he lacked sufficient status to secure her a place on a departing stasis ship, but said nothing of this.

Anna had hoped there would be some form of indirect or diplomatic way in which she could ask Alex to help her leave Rorque 4, but after discovering that he too was vulnerable and struggling on the planet, she now perceived him as a more approachable person, and simply went for the more direct route, 'I really want to leave this planet, I can't tell you how much I dislike this place. Its priorities are all wrong – it's obsessed with materialism, individual selfishness, trite entertainment, pandering to popular ignorance ... almost everything is superficial; none of it has anything to do with genuine integrity,' she related to him, almost in desperation. 'It's a fake, false and shallow world, but the Rorque Corporation won't let me leave, it's refused me a place on their stasis ships. But I really do want to leave. I was hoping you might be able to secure me a place on The Avante or some other Cosmic Solutions ship. Do you have enough influence to manage that?'

Alex now suddenly realised the reason for a face-to-face meeting, and felt a little cornered, but he could see she was genuinely desperate and made a split second decision that he ought to help her. He inhaled sharply through his teeth and then let out a long breath, 'I'm not sure I have enough influence to swing anything like that, I'm only a mid-level employee, in reality, but I'll see what I can do. The preparations are already at a very late stage as far as I am aware; I believe they've loaded most of the passengers onto the stasis ships already. I'm scheduled for a departure tomorrow – I think I'm in the last cohort to be evacuated.'

He paused, 'I would suggest smuggling you on board, but the security systems they're using are very tight. Without authorised recognition, I suspect you'll simply be turned back at the security checkpoints. I would really like to help you and I'll give it a go, but I can't promise anything,' he smiled apologetically at her, wishing he could do more. Anna smiled back, knowing this had always been a long shot and thanked him for any efforts he could make.

A thought then crossed Alex's mind, 'but if you hate the society here so much, what makes you think the new civilisation they create on their next planet will be any better? Surely it's likely to be very similar to this one, so you'll probably dislike it just as much, won't you?'

'Mmm, you're probably right, but I just need to leave this place as soon as I can. I've thought about that as well. I don't know really. I guess I'm just an optimist. OK I've failed here, but I was a success on Alpha Fraczan, so theoretically I can do it again. A new start on a new planet might somehow just work out better. You just have to make what you can of what presents itself to you. Some of my problems here have been with particular personnel. With any luck I might get to work with better people, there might be more opportunities and . . . Cosmic Solutions, might somehow be different. If not, maybe just move on to another planet, if the opportunity arises. Who knows?'

Alex was not particularly convinced by her response, but said nothing. It crossed his mind that she might be suffering from depression. He guessed she must have just become stuck in a rut and was looking for the quickest way out; and the only choices available to her were either a departure on a corporate stasis ship, or to take her chances on a dying planet that looked as though it might soon descend into chaos and mayhem.

'Where are Cosmic Solutions going to, anyway,' Anna asked, as an afterthought.
'Ahh, they're being very secretive and not telling us. Everyone just calls it Planet X. I'm not sure why the high levels of secrecy are needed, but I guess it has something to do with competition with the Rorque Corporation. They're heading for Zarak 2 - is that correct? That's light years away, I believe,' Alex enquired.
'I think so; it looked very distant on the space maps. Maybe Cosmic Solutions have found somewhere better and closer, and want to keep it secret,' Anna suggested.
'Might be? Nothing would surprise me with that lot, anymore. I guess we'll just have to wait and see.'

He then said once again he would do what he could, and apologised for not being more helpful. She shrugged, and said she would appreciate any effort he could make, but if it wasn't possible, well there wasn't much they could do then. She then informed him that she had already arranged to stay overnight in a local hotel, so if he was successful, she could be at Stratostan spaceport as soon as was necessary. Alex apologised again that he could not do much more, and stressed that he would make enquiries whilst on his journey back to Diana Park University, and if anything positive turned up, he would let her know immediately. They hugged and kissed and then went in their separate directions.

Alex had never visited Motorway City before and decided to have a look around the city before he departed; after all, it was his last full day on the planet. Outside the restaurant he ordered an autocar, and a few minutes later it slowed to a halt in front of him. He climbed into the vehicle, the autocar authorised his payment, and he then sat back in his seat and attempted to relax, as the vehicle made its way through the streets of the city on a tour of recommended sites and locations. However, the city soon proved to be as disappointing as it had originally appeared, and after yet another mediocre landmark, he ordered the autocar to commence the journey back to his university. A short while later he was back on the open road.

During the return journey to his university, Alex went about trying to organise what he had promised Anna, and attempted to find a place for her on one of the stasis ships. He went through several contacts he thought might carry some weight, and most had indicated they would see what they could do, but they all thought at this late stage there was likely to be very little in the way of places left available for her. They believed that all the places on the stasis ships had been allocated, and, following further enquiries, indicated that there appeared to be absolutely no spare capacity, as they had originally thought.

In addition, they saw no good reason as to why they should help save a Rorque Corporation reject, and with security systems at such a high level of alert, non-corporation personnel would be regarded with an extremely high degree of suspicion. They were aware that terrorists and saboteurs had already made several unsuccessful attempts to delay, disrupt and even halt the evacuation process. It also became apparent to Alex, as he made his efforts to help Anna, that the administrative process was largely under the direction of AI units and they were simply following their programming. Effectively, there was no flexibility in the system.

Arrival in Utopia

Alex, increasingly frustrated with the level of bureaucracy, nevertheless kept trying, and towards the end of his journey was finally informed by a senior security official of a possible solution. If Anna arrived at the spaceport with all appropriate documentation, there might be a possibility of a place on one of the ships if he could fully vouch for her, and if a designated passenger failed to arrive by departure time, as she would be able to effectively replace the non-attender. Alex immediately contacted Anna with the information and she thanked him repeatedly for his efforts. She would definitely be at the spaceport early the next morning in the hope of securing a place.

After this, Alex began to relax and was working his way through the latest media emissions when the autocar suddenly slowed, and the wheels screeched as it braked long and hard on the hot dusty road. Alex noticed that the cars alongside were also all rapidly coming to a halt. He looked forwards towards the horizon and all the autocars had now stopped in long lines in front on him, where he could also see thick smoke billowing across the motorway. The scrub to the north of the trunk road was ablaze and the wind was sweeping the fiery smoke across all six lanes of the motorway. An alert flashed up in the autocar and warned Alex to remain inside the vehicle as it would be dangerous to leave. It also informed him that the fire ahead was being dealt with. He peered into the distance, and through the haze he could just make out AI units from the company that owned the road moving through the smoke, presumably attempting to put out the flames.

His wait on the motorway proved to be an extremely long one. The intense and extensive fire was only slowly subdued by the AI units, but after what seemed like an era, the traffic started moving, slowly at first, but eventually it flowed freely to his eventual destination. By the time Alex arrived back at his university accommodation it was already late, the night was dark and Alex was several hours behind schedule.

Ur-Tokar – rebel uprising in Meridin

Nearly three months had passed since the conference at Lato, and in that time the Mountain People had been busily working away on the plan they had devised that memorable night – one that would later pass into local folklore. They had spent much of the intervening time working with known contacts in Meridin, as well as initiating some new ones. Some of the foresters and trappers who worked in the extensive forests were well-known to them, and whilst relationships with them were not always on the best of terms, they shared certain common interests, and occasionally encountered each other in the forests and mountains as they frequented the same locations and sought the same resources.

These contacts allowed them to gain access to the town – despite the presence of the Zeleyanian guards – and to ascertain the strength of the enemy forces. They were also able to assess possible access routes into the town and to identify how heavily they were guarded and at what times of day and night. The process was often a slow one, but they slowly built up a comprehensive picture of the town's security system and where the strong and the weak points of the Zeleyanian occupation forces were situated.

They were also able to gauge the level of support, amongst the townspeople and the adjacent farmsteads, that any uprising they launched might attract. Initially, this seemed to be quite low. The Lowlanders had been in a state of disarray following the collapse of the monarchist regime – the only system of government they had ever known – and were unsure about their new leaders, of whom they knew little or nothing. Over the weeks, though, they had become gradually disillusioned with the Zeleyanian forces – largely due to their lack of respect for their long held local traditions and customs, for which the fascist forces showed little or no respect. The armed conflict between the forces of Rosson and Pushkov only served to exacerbate this disillusion, adding an extra layer of disenchantment, and the belief that the new regime lacked stability, in addition to a lack of respect for their cherished customs.

Ironically, the conflict had also set back the launch date of the uprising. It had quickly become apparent to the Zeleyanian forces that their defences were significantly weakened as a result of the fratricidal conflict. To address this issue, they had initiated a campaign of recruiting locals into a new Town Guard, though recruitment had been fairly slow. Nevertheless, this development led to recriminations and divisions amongst the locals, as some argued that those joining were helping to establish a new safer regime, whilst others regarded them as traitors. It also meant the Mountain People needed to completely reassess their intelligence on the security situation, though they had eventually concluded that the newly established arrangements were actually more favourable to an uprising occurring.

Their plan was a fairly straightforward one, though fraught with potential difficulties. The Zeleyanians had high-powered assault weapons and computer-level technology – the Mountain People only their spears, axes and bows and arrows. However, they did have the advantage of local knowledge and surprise on their side. Once they believed they had sufficient support in the town and infiltrated enough of their own people into Meridin, they commenced their operation. They chose a dark moonless evening when their intelligence sources had told them Rosson would be holding a meeting of what was left of the High Command in the former banquet hall of the castle. They knew which routes were lightly guarded and which ones to avoid. Moving stealthily through the shadows, they avoided the more heavily guarded points and silently dispatched any guards they encountered along their designated route.

Meridin Castle was situated on a hilly area towards the rear of the town but was not a particularly grand affair. Whilst it contained the standard moat and drawbridge arrangement of any medieval castle, the defences of the castle were not capable of withstanding any significant invasion force – mainly because they had never needed to - the kings of Meridin having never faced any major adversary before the arrival of the Zeleyanians. It had been built more for show and status purposes, than defensive ones, and served no real functional purpose. As such, Topaz, Raven, Indigo and a force of about thirty others had little trouble in breaching the guarded positions, and quietly and swiftly arriving at the side entrance used mainly by traders and servants, and where they had planned to effect their entry.

Once assembled at this point, one of the servants - an inside contact that supported their cause - unlocked the large wooden gate from within, and they filed silently through the darkened doorway and along the narrow arched corridor that led to the rear of the castle kitchens and then through to the banquet hall. The first part of the operation had been thoroughly planned and rehearsed and they had expected this to pass without any significant problems, as indeed it did. However, they knew the more difficult part of the operation now lay ahead; seizing the High Command, they believed, was the most dangerous part of the plan and held the greatest likelihood of failure.

The raiding party passed through the extensive kitchens, which at this late hour were now completely deserted. Topaz glanced nervously to her sides across the huge tables, towards the alcoves with their stores of food, arrays of pots and pans, and to the large earthen ovens and fire pits, and the spits that straddled them. Other than a few glowing orange embers, though, there was no sign of life anywhere in the vast room. The group made its way silently and stealthily to the other end of the kitchens, through the large wooden doors that led into a highly vaulted and poorly-lit stone-walled anteroom, and then finally towards the doors that led into the banquet hall. They amassed around the doors, silent and in a hushed sense of apprehensive expectation. Furtive and nervous glances went round the group as they waited for everyone to ready their weapons and take up position.

Once ready, Raven gave the order to advance. The large wooden doors were unceremoniously and dramatically barged open, and the thirty strong group made a headlong charge en masse into the cavernous room, with the aim of eliminating any guards that blocked their way, and then taking High Command captive, who they assumed would be sat around the table and taken completely by surprise. Topaz was at the head of the advancing group, but as she charged through the doors the scene was not the one she had been expecting. The room was brightly lit but almost empty, save for a small group of figures gathered at the far end of a large wooden table.

As she advanced across the room, her heart beating louder and faster than she ever thought possible, she could see the group was waiting in expectation for them, and she recognised at least three of the seated figures. One of them was Hagan, the forest cabin dweller who had done so much to resist monarchist incursions over the years, whilst the two others - with whom she was less familiar - were known to her as Juniper and Wolf.

Accompanying these three, were a small number of seated Zeleyanian soldiers and a grandly dressed, middle-aged man who she assumed was Vice-Admiral Rosson. She could also see that Hagan and his two accomplices were indicating to them to slow down and stop, and as no weapons were being pointed in their general direction, so she and the rest of the group all came to a gradual and confused halt, looking around the room suspiciously half expecting some form of trap to be sprung.

Hagan stepped forward, and stated quietly, 'nice to see you all, and just at the right time. We've been in contact with the Vice-Admiral for some time now, and we've arranged for him to come and live with us in the mountains. The rest of the High Command are already disarmed and tied up in the room adjacent to this one. You can proceed with the rest of the plan as scheduled, but we are going to spirit Rosson away under cover of your uprising.'

Topaz and the others all looked slightly sceptical, but whilst Hagan had a reputation for being something of a maverick, he was also trusted as someone who would fight to the death to preserve the Mountain People's way of life. Rosson presumably also noted their caution. 'I've come to realise our invasion of your planet is an unacceptable use of force,' he announced. 'We have no right to be here, and I have advised our Supreme Commander to turn round and return to Zeleyan. As such, I have no future on my home planet of Zeleyan and wish to live out the rest of my days here on your beautiful planet,' he continued, not quite truthfully. 'You should be able to disarm the remainder of my forces as you follow through with your plan, and they can then choose the type of life they want to live here. I have deactivated all the AI units, and only I have the security codes to reactivate them. I have assumed you will want to destroy them, along with my soldier's weaponry. I hope it all goes well for you.'

In reality, Rosson had made the calculation that this was probably his only viable way of getting out of Meridin alive and in one piece. He had been on the planet for seven months now, and for most of that time he knew that he was in deep trouble. He had, therefore, spent a considerable amount of that period getting to know his troops better, whilst also developing contacts with the Mountain People, and discovering more about their way of life. He had liked what he heard - though he was less sure about living a low technology lifestyle, but thought he could still give it a try. He now knew which of his troops shared his love of the outdoors and enjoyed the spirit of adventure, and these were the soldiers currently gathered around him. When his spies had discovered the plot to seize his High Command and launch the uprising, he had seen this as the perfect opportunity to disappear quietly and successfully. None of his forces would be in a position to hunt him down now, and by the time Vartin arrived, he would be almost untraceable.

He did not want to field any questions, since his story was far from watertight and he had told different lies to different groups of people, and knew it was best to depart whilst saying as little as possible. He signaled something to Hogan, and the small group of Zeleyanians and mountain dwellers made a hushed exit through the large wooden doors at the far end of the hall.

The largish group of would-be insurgents looked around at each other, almost stunned to silence.
'Well, I wasn't expecting that, but if it's true what they said, they've done us a massive favour,' exclaimed a relieved Indigo.
'Right, and if that's the case, let's see if it's all true. Let's find these officers and execute the rest of the plan,' added Raven, still not quite believing that the uprising was proceeding even better than planned.

They soon found the officers gagged and bound in the throne room next door and marched them out to the front of the castle. The highest ranking officer left after the various battles was now Lieutenant Walker, who was instructed by the raiding party to issue orders to the rest of the troops in the town to surrender immediately, or else all the officers would be executed in turn, one by one. At around this time – as previously coordinated - the rest of the forces that constituted the uprising were rallying the townspeople in various taverns, to rise up and support the raid on the castle. The numbers turning out onto the streets gradually swelled, whilst the small number of Zeleyanian guards on duty – Rosson had deliberately lowered the numbers that night – simply waited for instructions from their superiors, as they were unsure of what action to take.

Lieutenant Walker was still baffled by the fact that he had been gagged and bound by Rosson's personal guard, and had then been handed over to a group of mountain dwelling rebels. Rosson had previously told his officers that the invasion of Ur-Tokar had been called off, and that they had all been left stranded on the planet with no means of return to Zeleyan. He was in no real position to make sense of any of these events and simply followed the instructions of the armed rebels. His main concern was simply to stay alive; he figured he could work out what had actually happened in the fullness of time. As such, through the rest of the evening and into the early hours of the night, the troops simply followed his orders to surrender; the insurgents and the leading townspeople overseeing the entire disarmament of the diminished Zeleyanian forces, to be followed by the systematic destruction of all the advanced technology they had brought with them to the planet.

As Rogan's orange-yellow disc rose above the endless pine forests the next morning, and the early morning mists of Meridin lifted slowly over the fields, the town and its surroundings began to feel that it had finally returned to some semblance of normality for the first time in months. The farmers headed for their fields whilst the town dwellers went to work or the market, just as they always had done. However, the Mountain People were determined to press home their significant advantage whilst they were still in a position to do so – they had no desire to see the resurrection of the hated monarchist regime with all the attendant problems that could cause them - and immediately commenced their efforts to turn the new found situation to their advantage.

Firstly, the Zeleyanian officers were still being held in the castle dungeon, but they were unsure of how to deal with the failed invasion force. They needed to first ascertain whether Rosson's claim that the invasion fleet had turned around and was heading back to Zeleyan was indeed true. They were not able to do this themselves, but knew that the crew of the Opa-Loka would be able to help. If it was true, they needed to find some way of absorbing the Zeleyanian forces into their society. If it wasn't true, they would need to find a way of either isolating or eliminating the soldiers so the eventual invasion became far more difficult to execute. As such, they considered that they might keep the officers as hostages and attempt to strike a deal with the Zeleyanian Supreme Commander, though they suspected this was unlikely to be a successful plan. Dealing with Vartin, they had been told, was like dealing with the devil himself.

Secondly, that morning they convened a meeting with some of the leading figures in the town. They needed to put years of mistrust and conflict behind them, and find a means of uniting the two communities. They also needed to reach an agreement concerning the Zeleyanian problem. The meeting lasted the entirety of the day, but unfortunately they reached few concrete conclusions. This was frustrating for the Mountain People, but they figured there had been such great differences between their two peoples that they might need the dust of time to settle for a while before they could once again fully trust each other. They did, however, agree to a further series of meetings, but probably none of them, at this point, realised it would be several weeks before they could actually conclude the initial process of bringing their two communities together.

Arrival in Utopia

Zeta Kotlin – a message arrives from the Opa-Loka

Five and a half months after its emission, the message from the Opa-Loka that Zeleyan military forces were already on Ur-Tokar and with more on their way, finally arrived at the spaceport of Earth City on Zeta Kotlin. Unsurprisingly, this caused significant consternation amongst the world's inhabitants, as news filtered out across the various continents. The fascist regime on Zeleyan was held in very low regard and most of the population immediately assumed the worst. If Zeleyan was ready and willing to invade Ur-Tokar, it was highly likely they would soon have their sights set on Zeta Kotlin. There was little dispute over this – even those with only a rudimentary knowledge of political ideology, knew that all fascists despised and hated every aspect of the left and its beliefs. They were in no doubt whatsoever, that the Zeleyanian regime hated the socialist society of Zeta Kotlin, and would be extremely keen on implementing its destruction.

The main point of planetary discussion was how they would respond to this news, since virtually no one thought that this was a problem they could ignore, in the hope that it would simply go away. Doing nothing was clearly not a viable option. It was also widely assumed that convening talks and negotiations with a fascist regime would be utterly pointless – they were unlikely to find any common ground in such discussions, and could not trust them to keep their word anyway.

The main problem for the planet in preventing any invasion was the fact that they lacked any form of military or security apparatus. War and conflict – as originally planned by the 'utopian ships' that first colonised the planet – were entirely unknown, save for one brief dispute in the very early years of settlement. As far as the Zetans were concerned, they had successfully overseen the death of war. Their politico-economic system was a pan-continental one with no nations or class system. It was characterised by economic collectivism, direct democracy and the end of material scarcity. As such, they had effectively arrived at the end of History, with all that entailed. There were few disputes of any significant note, since ideological conflict was now over. The few minor disagreements that did arise were resolved peacefully and democratically. Their philosophy was generally one of live and let live. Therefore, they had no military forces.

Arrival in Utopia

The Zetans were always aware, though, of potential exogenous threats to their utopian way of life. During the early years of the departure from Earth - and the settling of many habitable worlds by the exodus ships - they had largely banked on like-minded stasis ships joining the colonisation of their new planetary home. Those of a different, possibly hostile, persuasion could simply head for planets that had already constructed a similar system to the one they were seeking to establish, or start their own entirely new ones somewhere else. Either by design or by luck, this approach had proven to be a successful one. In later years, as the planetary diaspora had settled down, they believed the long spatial and temporal distances between the star systems, and the relatively slow nature of space travel, effectively protected them from any potentially hostile worlds in the Nexus Cluster, or, indeed, from elsewhere in the near galaxy. Until now, this calculation also appeared to have been a successful one.

The people of Zeta Kotlin greatly valued their peaceful cooperative existence, and were always very careful to prevent any dispute escalating to the point where it might be threatened. Therefore, they were highly reluctant to establish any military institution, even for the purpose of defense against the Zeleyanians. A dissenting minority, nevertheless, concluded that – given the dire situation they faced - they really did need to establish a temporary military force, but one that could then be immediately disbanded, once the extra-planetary threat had been dealt with or had dissipated. The majority, though, feared such an institution might take on a life of its own and become a permanent feature of their planet. It had the potential to destroy their newly peaceful and progressive way of life, and they had no intention of letting in the past. And anyway, it was not part of the Zetan mindset to establish hierarchal institutions, let alone military ones.

Whilst this disagreement was being argued out, a planetary-wide investigatory committee had also been tasked with looking into the viability of developing a defensive shield system for the planet, based on a ballistic missile programme that could shoot down any arriving Zeleyanian stasis ships. However, a trawl through their historic data bases eventually showed that no such technology had been brought with the early settlers from Earth, and enquiries made amongst the newly arrived scientists from Alpha Fraczan indicated none had specialist knowledge in this area. The diversion of existing resources to such a huge and ambitious programme, the enquiry concluded, would be extensive and probably highly damaging to the wider economy. There were even concerns that they might actually destroy their way of life in the course of trying to defend it.

There were also concerns with how other worlds in the Nexus Cluster might regard the construction of a long-range ballistic missile system. Aware that some of the other planets in the system hated and despised their very existence, Zeta Kotlin had always been careful to do nothing that might be interpreted as a hostile inter-planetary action. They had never, for instance, sent spy satellites to the other worlds, despite knowing that the regime on Zeleyan had done so several years earlier – they had destroyed the one that was sent to spy on their own world – since this might be used as a pretence for initiating a military campaign against their civilisation. They had also ensured that their space programme was kept very low key and limited only to certain basic trading activities, for similar reasons.

Ultimately, the committee reported that a missile programme was a possible long-term contingency, but fraught with problems, and that other solutions would be preferable.

The regular community meetings at Kapal at this time were better attended than usual, since concerns over the situation on Ur-Tokar were running high – most of the community knew there were potentially dire consequences for their planet and were determined to be involved in efforts to thwart the danger.

The administrative committee met early one evening, shortly before Aequitas dropped behind the distant hills to the west. Its dappled late autumn light shone soft and pink across the alto-cumulus clouds high to the west in an otherwise cloudless sky. The dark purple crescent of Chixtos shone weakly to the north, whilst the smallest of the three moons, Xanthia, tracked more rapidly across the lower reaches to the south-east. The air over the plain of Xestron was still and peaceful as usual. The committee spent a short amount of time admiring the evening vista, and then set down to business.

'I always expected something along these lines,' Pedro stated, once the meeting had begun. 'The Zeleyanians are fascists and it's an inherent part of their ideology to invade and conquer other peoples. They think it makes them look superior, that they are some sort of master race that should conquer all before them. They forget about all the suffering, the misery and the hardship they cause. How can supposedly sensible people believe in such appalling ideas?'

'Well, they're not sensible people, they're fascists, and I think we're all agreed here that the Zeleyanians took the wrong path years ago; it's a real shame they've ruined such a lovely planet. But, I think our main focus needs to be on dealing with the potential danger they pose,' interposed Zhang Li, who always liked to keep discussions on track, and knew Pedro had a habit of going off at tangents that related to his various hobby horses. 'With any other civilisation I would have favoured talks and negotiations, but I fear that in this case, they would be completely pointless. We couldn't trust a single word they said – unless it was the doom and gloom they promised for us.'

'I understand there is some discussion of us developing our own military capabilities. I don't like the sound of that, at all. We've traditionally been a peaceful people and we need to consider how the other planets would regard such a development – they might see it as hostile action rather than a defensive one,' offered Catriona. 'I really don't like the idea of creating a military force – would we be forced to join up? That goes against all our beliefs. What if it became too powerful and imposed a dictatorship over us? I really think we should oppose any such idea when it comes to a vote on this issue.'

'Agreed, but I'm not convinced by the idea of a ballistic missile shield either. Surely that also holds potential dangers, never mind the resources and time needed to develop it,' offered Rishaan.

'And I don't believe we have the technology anyway. I cannot imagine the first settlers brought any such ideas with them, and we certainly won't have developed them since. I suspect that whole idea is a complete non-starter,' agreed Pedro.

'There's a move to push for some form of citizen's militia, where the whole planet is armed to resist the invasion, I believe,' offered Rishaan, who was coming round to this idea himself. 'I believe we do possess the technology and resources to establish that, if and when needed. And it would be much safer for our democracy if we were all armed, rather than just some privileged, hierarchal, military minority.'

'Won't we all need military training though?' enquired Catriona, who was not keen on engaging in any form of violence, though was now wondering whether this might be expected of her, in order to protect her planet. 'I've never fired any form of firearm in my entire life.'

'You won't need to. The weapons are all automated. They just lock-on to the target and you press a button - it's not particularly difficult. We just need enough people armed with them,' answered Rishaan. 'I doubt even the Zeleyanians can take on a whole planet that's fully armed!'

'What about the AI units, can't they do the fighting for us?' asked Catriona.

'They can, and I am sure they will – the Zeleyanian soldiers should constitute a very distinct target I should think, so there should be no concern about them shooting the wrong targets. We just don't have enough of them, so we need the people to be armed as well,' answered Rishaan.

'I'm still not massively keen on this idea either, but if it's that, or spending the rest of my life under a fascist dictatorship, then I guess there's not much choice,' said Catriona, expressing a viewpoint that was being commonly voiced across the planet.

'Is there anything our space ship - what's it called . . . oh yes, the Opa-Loka - can do to help?' enquired Pedro. 'I heard that Jiaying is back on board, though I thought she'd retired from all that space-faring stuff years ago,'

'I saw her some time ago in Earth City and she said she was doing one last mission and then retiring, though she wasn't sure where to. I'd be slightly surprised if she came back here, though. She always thought it was a bit boring,' answered Zhang Li. 'I believe the ship is doing its best to try and deter the invasion force, but it's just a trading ship, so I doubt it can actually do very much. The information we receive from them is, of course, many months out of date, so who knows what has actually occurred there in the meantime,' she added.

Similar such debates and discussions occurred across the many and varied communities of Zeta Kotlin, and the planet ultimately arrived at, and voted in favour of, the more radical and participatory solution that had been suggested. In the short-term, they would wait for news from Ur-Tokar. In the event of that planet being permanently occupied by Zeleyanian forces they would begin a planetary-wide mobilisation strategy. The mini-fabs would be programmed to mass produce armaments so that the entire citizenry of the planet could be armed in defense of the planet. In addition, much-needed resources would be diverted for the manufacture of extra AI units, and these would be programmed, along with the existing ones, with combat features, so they could form the bulwark of the defence against any invading forces. This was considered to be an acceptable sacrifice, and compromise with their established beliefs - since the continued survival of their very civilisation might depend upon such measures being taken.

In the meantime, the spaceport at Earth City devoted extra AI units to monitoring incoming messages and media output from the other planets in the Cluster. Unsurprisingly, there was an appetite for news of what was happening on worlds elsewhere, the movements of starships around the Cluster and a need to act quickly upon any further messages from The Opa-Loka. They also made the decision – after consultation with the General Council – to send an open message to the Opa-Loka with details of the preparations being taken in the event of Zeleyan sending an invasion fleet to Zeta Kotlin; fully aware that the Zeleyanians would also receive the message, and in the hope that it might actually deter them from doing so.

Zeta Kotlin – early history

From the very earliest of days, the people of Zeta Kotlin established their own historical account of the settlement and development of their planet, determined to forestall or preempt any inaccurate or hostile narrative from developing that might attempt to distort the actual story of what had occurred. In this, they were greatly aided by the existence of the planetary web, a system whereby all the communes across the various continents logged the details of their regular decisions and actions. They did this largely in the interests of transparency - to ensure that no community, through poor decision-making, was storing up difficulties in the future for the others. However, it also served to act as a world-wide store of useful collective knowledge and data from which communes, faced with new or complicated dilemmas, could refer to, in order to resolve their own particular problems and issues.

For Zetan historians – basically groups for whom this subject matter proved to be their area of greatest social interest - it had the accidental benefit of supplying a ready stream of data and knowledge by which they could collate and formulate an agreed history of their civilisation. And the version of history they established, was one that was widely accepted and agreed upon. In the absence of a class system or any other major social division or fault-line within their society, there was little of major note to disagree over - the collectivist nature of their society also lending itself towards such a process of generalised agreement and consensus.

Additionally, in their unified and egalitarian society, there had been an almost complete lack of conflict, no invasions of foreign lands, little in the way of major power struggles or political divides, and no rebellions by exploited and oppressed peoples, nor unacceptable and oppressive behaviour by over-mighty political leaders. Believing they had effectively already arrived at the end of History – there being no realistic prospect of any further stage of socio-economic development on the horizon – save for the gradual economic and cultural development of their civilisation, there was actually little for historians to record and comment upon. The following account is thus drawn from the largely consensual, Official History of the

Arrival in Utopia

Zetan People, agreed upon unanimously by the relevant Historical Committees, and approved of accordingly by a vote of the Zetan people.

The first of the stasis ships to arrive at Zeta Kotlin was one of the earlier 'utopian ships', the Wind of Change, and it was not long before the awakened skeleton crew realised they had been lucky enough to arrive at a world with considerable settlement potential. It was the second planet of a G class star – thus similar to the Sun – which they later named Aequitas. The star system itself, entailed an extensive range of asteroid belts and rocky dwarf planets, but in terms of larger celestial bodies, only possessed two large gas giants towards the outer limits of the planetary system, but little else of great note.

Zeta Kotlin itself possessed three medium-sized moons; the largest, slow-moving Chixtos, was a deep purple colour and took the greatest amount of time to orbit the planet. Xanthia was a small yellow moon that, by contrast, hurtled around the planet at a considerably faster pace, whilst the middle moon, the pale silvery-white Nacre, orbited at a rate somewhere between the two. This configuration gave rise to some interesting astronomical events and conjunctions, but also to a particularly complex tidal system across the planet's extensive oceans.

The newly-discovered world was, indeed, a largely oceanic one, but with nine fairly large continents spaced fairly evenly across the otherwise dark blue globe. The oceans were deep and extensive, whilst most of the continents possessed a significant range of offshore island chains on their respective continental shelves. Eight of the nine continents lacked any major mountain ranges, high plateaus or cordillera. They did, however, possess numerous areas of semi-desert, large open plains, low-lying plateaus, and extensive areas of softly undulating hills, occasionally cut through by deep gorges and river canyons. Only the large southern continent of Levalline possessed a significant mountain range, that of the extensive and towering Cascade Mountains, their gnarled rocky peaks mostly consisting of hard igneous and metamorphic rock structures.

Scans indicated that the core of the planet was still hot and active, though there seemed to be only limited volcanic activity across the surface of the planet, most occurring deep within the oceanic depths. Whether this was due to a prolonged lull in seismic activity, or indicated an ageing planet, had been a topic of debate ever since first landing, though one that currently remained unresolved.

The process of terra-forming the planet by the arriving 'genesis pod' had been a particularly fruitful one – presumably a result of the fact that many of the planetary conditions shared similarities with those on Earth. By the time the first settlers arrived, a fairly well developed set of ecosystems had already evolved across the various oceans and continents. Parts of the continents were already thinly wooded, and extensive grasslands had established in the drier areas of the continents. The shallower regions of the oceans were teeming with life whilst a range of insects, small reptiles and amphibians and other life forms were already flourishing on the land. Some of the later arriving stasis ships also added a small range of additional birds and mammals to the fauna of the planet. All in all, given the vagaries of planetary exploration, they could hardly have hoped for a better site to launch their utopian venture.

Initially, rudimentary communal settlements had been established on all the continents, predominantly at suitable coastal locations. However, almost immediately, it occurred to the new settlers that they faced a major logistical problem. Should they scatter their population thinly across the continents, or concentrate on populating one or two of them, with the intention of expanding across to the others later. Both approaches had possible problems. They debated as to what would happen if later arriving stasis ships - ones which might be hostile to their egalitarian and cooperative venture - occupied the uninhabited continents, or were able to dominate the existing thinly populated ones. Would they ultimately find themselves facing oppression, conflict, division and exploitation yet again, just as they had done back on Earth? They may well have travelled many light years across the depths of inter-stellar space for several decades, but almost all of that was in stasis. For the arriving settlers, the damaging, disastrous and catastrophic events on Earth were a very recent memory. They had no pressing desire to experience them a second time.

Ultimately, they realised that both approaches were potentially hazardous. They therefore decided to change the message in the transponder satellite left by the 'genesis pod', to one informing those stasis ships voyaging along behind them, of the type of society they were building, and for those with similar dreams and aspirations to come and join them in their utopian venture. In the event, in their desire to attract like-minded settlers they got lucky; for by that time, a significant proportion of the stasis ships leaving Earth in the later waves of the exodus were, in fact, 'utopian ships'. That, or at the very least, full of people who were thoroughly disillusioned with the materialistic and individualistic capitalist system that had eventually destroyed twenty-first century civilisation on planet Earth. In reality, the odds of attracting similarly-minded settlers had been reasonably good.

Throughout the following years, and for about a decade further, several more stasis ships – many of them 'utopian ships' - joined the colonisation event and, aided greatly by the productive nature of the planet, a thriving society and economy eventually developed across all nine continents. The early settlements eventually grew into small towns and the occasional small-scale garden city, and a range of economic sectors evolved to meet the needs of the inhabitants. The different continents, over the ensuing decades, developed a varied range of vibrant cultural outlooks; partly based on the particular origins of the colonists, but also as they adapted to the newfound environments, terrains and ecosystems that the settlers found themselves living within.

What was always insisted on, though, was that they all retain the basic ideological model of the original settlers. This involved retaining an economic structure where all activity, and particularly the use of AI units, remained under strict communitarian, and mostly local, control. No social class system was allowed to develop, and society was based on an entirely egalitarian and cooperative culture. Politically, government was highly decentralised and based on popular democratic control, usually through methods of direct democracy. A particular emphasis on working with nature, rather than against it, was also locked into the structures that constituted the new society. All the settlers agreed that they were determined not to be responsible for the destruction of a second planetary biosphere.

Throughout the early decades of its development, the process of creating a peaceful, prosperous and egalitarian civilisation, that would avoid the disastrous mistakes made on Earth, proved to be a highly successful one. For many of the arriving stasis ships, this was exactly the type of society they were looking for; their New Jerusalem, and they avidly and enthusiastically joined the project. Even those who arrived and were at first doubtful about the likelihood of success, were willing to give the new approach a try – especially as its social structures looked capable of avoiding a repeat of Earth's recent disastrous history. Slowly but surely, the new society embedded itself across the globe, firmly taking root across its ancient continents and islands.

It was not always plain sailing though. Mostly, those ships looking for a very different type of society to the one on Zeta Kotlin tended to move on fairly quickly. On a couple of occasions, however, a stasis ship arrived and decided to stay, though its occupants were not particularly willing to comply with the existing structures. On both occasions, the settlers occupied sparsely populated areas of one of the emptier continents and attempted to pursue the old, failed ways of Earth. This gave rise to intermittent political difficulties and periods of tension, and even one short - though only moderately damaging - period of actual conflict. However, the socialist majority had numbers, time, post-scarcity economics, institutional inertia and first occupation on their side. Additionally, in using a decentralised system, there was room to accommodate a certain amount of cultural variation; it was only the essential basic political and economic structures that they insisted on being respected. Eventually, majorities developed amongst the new arrivals wanting to integrate themselves into the existing society – one that to them seemed to be working extremely well – and as the century progressed, the planet achieved its original dream of creating a fully functioning socialist utopia.

Zeta Kotlin ultimately became one of the most successful of the newly colonised planets. For more than a century, the population across the hills, plains and islands of its nine different continents expanded steadily, though also sustainably and without suffering any form of population overload. Its civilisation grew to be quite unlike the one left behind on Earth. Material prosperity, shared equally amongst a set of inhabitants who also shared a genuinely equal political voice, gave rise to a quite different type of human being. Across the planet there developed well-adjusted, secure and self-assured individuals who felt confident enough to experiment with a whole variety of new lifestyle arrangements, safe in the knowledge that if it all went badly wrong, they had a secure and understanding community to fall back upon. Over time, different groups developed weird and wonderful new lifestyles in exotic new settlements, until a world was eventually created that was largely unrecognisable to a dweller of twenty-first century Earth.

Ur-Tokar – Lato after the uprising at Meridin

Whilst waiting the three weeks the AI units needed to fully repair the damaged engine on board the Opa-Loka, the crew engaged in a variety of activities to help pass the time and keep themselves occupied. Some of these involved performing routine preparations on the ship in readiness for their return to Zeta Kotlin. But it was easy to tire of these, whilst the appeal of further exploration on the world below them, and time spent with their new found acquaintances, proved considerably more appealing. Not surprisingly, the time they spent on the planet far outweighed that spent on the starship. This tended to involve both excursions to Lato and exploring areas much further to the east, particularly along the continent's highly indented and rugged coastline.

It was whilst exploring the latter, that Kahlil and Neema made a serendipitous discovery on one of the larger offshore islands - a series of unusual sea caves at the south-western end of the remote, entirely uninhabited and particularly mountainous island of Solnijar. At most times of day, the site was unremarkable save for the usual intensely deep blue-green colours of the ocean waters, and the steady procession of unusually-shaped icebergs drifting slowly southwards after calving from the giant ice sheet that flowed into the ocean further to the north of their position. In fact, in most respects, it was highly typical of so much of Ur-Tokar's many and varied coastlines.

On this particular occasion, the two were sat on the mainland close to the island one day, observing two seahawks soaring effortlessly around the lower peaks of the island, their brown and white plumage glinting superbly in the early morning sunlight, when they suddenly heard a series of strange but changing musical sounds emanating from the southern end of the island. Intrigued, they walked southwards along the sward, between the precipitous sea cliff and the edge of the forest, until, scanning the island sea cliffs intently, they discovered the source of the strange musical sounds.

It was high tide, and as the inflowing seawater rose up against the sea cliffs, it was being forced - at considerable pressures - high and deep into the caves and caverns of the sea cliff, and as it did so, the air it trapped was forced rapidly upwards and out through a serious of narrow fissures and small cave entrances that happened to pockmark the cliffs on the island. This had the fortuitous effect of creating a range of different musical notes, the sound of which travelled considerable distances. As they remained longer at the site, they also discovered that they varied according to the strength and height of the tide.

The two of them sat for some considerable time listening to the strange and unusual sea symphony. The range of caves and fissures on the sea-cliff was quite varied, and each one gave rise to quite distinctive notes, sounds and harmonic effects. One section consisted of high and narrow, almost pipe-like, pillar constructions which they called The Pan Pipes, since they emitted rising and falling notes of a fluting wind-like nature. Another section contained a particularly deep chamber with a series of vaulted rooves, which they nicknamed the Harmonic Hall, since it produced a range of clear bright notes reminiscent of tubular bells, whilst that of a deeper, more rounded one - which they called the Pulsing Cavern - gave a repeated and wavering series of vibrating notes that echoed and quivered around the deep cavern, and sounded both ominous and peculiarly uplifting at the same time. The overall result was an amazing array of musical notes and tones that left the two of them with the distinct impression that the sea was actually playing a symphony for them.

Once the tide had dropped and the symphony had ended, they returned to further exploration of the coastline, but so impressed had they been with the musical phenomena, that Neema and Kahlil made a point of informing the others of their remarkable find, and the crew visited on a number of occasions, discovering that the range of notes also varied according to the phases of the moon and the local weather conditions. On one occasion, when a thick fog - accompanying the rising tide - rolled in off the ocean, the sea symphony sounded particularly eerie and haunting; its notes lasting longer and deeper, seemingly far more mysterious, as they appeared to emanate from some considerable distance out across the dense sea fog.

As they listened to the strange and often variable sound show, the crew reflected that the more time they spent on the planet, the more they could understand why the spiritually-minded members of the Mountain People community believed that the planet of Ur-Tokar was actually a living, breathing entity. The spiritualists amongst the community believed that their world was entirely interconnected; a world in which the different life-forms looked out and cared for each other, where even the mountains, rivers and oceans spoke in subtle tones to those who knew how to listen. With so much of the planet in pristine condition and so vibrantly alive, the Zetans began to understand how a people who spent so much of their time engaged intimately with their environment, might arrive at such a conclusion. They all knew the singing sea caverns had a rational physical explanation, but their weird water music did genuinely seem to possess an almost otherworldly quality.

When not exploring the remoter parts of the landmass, the crew typically spent much of their time at Lato, where they were fairly well-known by now, and recognised as useful and trustworthy allies in the fight against their common enemy. As they became better known, and as they struck up a range of relationships with several of the locals, the communal nature of the small settlement began to remind them of the warmth and homeliness of their own communities back on Zeta Kotlin. Lato lacked the high levels of technology and material abundance they were traditionally used to, but the community spirit could sometimes be remarkably similar. Its culture, however, contained a complex mixture of the egalitarian and the hierarchal, the private and the public, and it often left them puzzled and bemused. It was quite easy to make social errors - and the crew frequently did so - though fortunately they found the locals were typically forgiving when they misunderstood their culture.

In addition, the settlement was a welcome source of proper home-made nourishing food and drink, and quite unlike the manufactured rations that constituted meals on the starship. The latter might be highly nutritious, but they were also invariably dull and uninteresting. Time spent eating, drinking, playing games and socialising in The Hall of the Mountain Grill was always time well spent, and a useful place to discover the latest comings and goings of the people they had come to know and include as their friends. The crew insisted on helping with local chores and other basic tasks, so as to contribute positively to their society, but they gained the distinct impression that as guests of the community, this was not actually expected of them.

Arrival in Utopia

One evening, as on so many other occasions, they found themselves in the Hall of the Mountain Grill eating, drinking and socialising. As was often the case, the wind was coming briskly down off the mountains, the trees were rustling loudly in the breeze, and the temperature of the night air was dropping quickly under the darkening cloudless skies. They gathered round the warmth of the blazing fire in the great hearth at the end of the tavern, and started discussing some of their recent experiences. Jiaying happened to mention their recent visit to the singing sea caves.

'Some of our people believe they are singing sea nymphs, relating the latest news from beneath the sea to any of our people who know how to listen,' Autumn told them, though they could also tell from her tone of voice that she was quite sceptical about this idea. 'The monarchists call them the Neptune Caves, since they believe the sea king uses them to converse with their people. Whatever you happen to believe, they're clearly a very special place and massively impressive. I've only visited them once, but I stayed for a second tide, to hear the musical performance all again. They are really amazing and unlike anything I've ever heard before.'

'Which reminds me, I've been meaning to ask you this for ages,' Kahlil said, 'why did the monarchists travel half way across the galaxy in a stasis ship for several decades, only to try and recreate an ancient period of Earth's history – and not a particularly good one, at that. What was the point of that?' he asked.

'Well, I'm not fully certain – as I've never had much to do with them – but I think they believed an economic system called capitalism destroyed the ecology of Earth. They thought the people who ran the planet were uninterested in caring about the land; they were not landowners and had no care or regard for the ecological systems they were destroying,' answered Autumn, a little hesitatingly, trying to remember what she had once been told. 'They simply came along and plundered the land and then departed. They believed that in a time before that one, the owners and stewards of the land were in control, and cared intensely for the environment and so preserved it in its traditional form. They wanted to recreate that time before, I believe, and thought our planet was perfectly suited for their ambitions.'

'Well, I can agree with most of the first part, but not the second - it's more normal to go forwards, rather than backwards, in time. On Zeta Kotlin, we went forwards with history, as is more usually the case. Protecting the environment is important, but so is progress and creating social equality. Also a lot of useful stuff was discovered and created during the capitalist epoch, why dispense with that, when it can be put to better uses - including ecological ones,' offered Kahlil, reflecting a commonly held belief on his home planet. 'An egalitarian society without material scarcity, like ours, is highly stable and offers a wide range of freedoms, but feudalism is a stage of history steeped in ignorance and suffering.'

Autumn was well aware of the Zetan disdain for the monarchists - one she shared, though for differing reasons - but was unfamiliar with the idea that history moved in a particular direction. 'I'm not sure we have any strong beliefs on the direction of history,' she said, unsure of her own view on the subject. 'I think we just see the world as sort of timeless and unchanging, except for the seasons and the various natural cycles, of course. I guess planets eventually grow old and perhaps die, that's a form of history, but it's also part of a cycle, as well.'

Kahlil decided not to mention dialectics, especially as he wanted to know more about the monarchists. 'But surely the monarchists knew feudal society was wracked by persistent plagues, famines and conflicts. How is that an appealing scenario? Why would they want to return to a time like that?'

'I heard King Alfonso mentioning this, when I was unfortunate enough to be in his esteemed presence,' Jiaying interjected, slightly sarcastically. 'He was very religious, and believed that these were all just part of God's natural order, some part of his grand plan, and so were unavoidable. Human's just had to endure them, he believed. They came out stronger in the end, or something like that, I seem to remember him saying. It sounded quite masochistic at the time, and I wondered if it actually had more to do with him using these unfortunate events to stay in power.'

'Yes, God created the universe, waited thirteen and a half billion years to create the extra-special humans - the chosen species - and then inflicted misery on them, so they could become a better species. All very logical,' added Kahlil, highly sarcastically.

Autumn enjoyed these types of conversations with the Zetans; they had an outlook on life that could be quite unlike that of her own people, and their views sometimes fascinated her. Warming to the conversation, she added, 'I guess that's why some of my people follow a more pantheist-type religion - it sees all parts of the planet as equally important. Humans don't have any special place within the world, we're just one creature amongst many others, and we need to share that ecological space, and make sure it remains in a condition from which we can all benefit.'

'Well, it is more logical, offered Kahlil, 'but I'd still like to see some evidence for these spirits that live amongst the rocks, rivers and the trees, and I suspect that's unlikely to be forthcoming. There are far more rational explanations for phenomena like the singing sea caves, you know.'

'Oh, and that reminds me,' interrupted Jiaying, 'I was talking to Mila earlier today and she's completed another of her research surveys today and is changing location yet again – she certainly seems to get about a bit! She is now planning to set up her next scientific station close to the singing sea caves tomorrow. Maybe the flying doctor could give you a lift there if you wanted to hear them again. I'm sure she could pop by on the way over there,' she suggested.

Kahlil had struck up a bit of a relationship with Autumn recently and looked at her, 'how about a visit, we could go for a day or two?'

'We don't do advanced technology, remember, so I will have to decline, though it was nice of you to ask. I'll just have to walk there again one day, arrive there through my own efforts – there's some great scenery along the way, so it's well worth making the journey. However, it is getting late now, so we could do a different shorter journey. How about an early night?' she asked Kahlil, smiling at him.

Kahlil and Autumn departed together a minute later. The others stayed some time longer, but eventually they too decided to call it a night, and after pairing up, left the tavern to return to the different cabins and houses they were staying in at various points across the settlement. They all stepped out into the cool mountain air of the night and Jiaying looked upwards, over the darkened mountains, and into the cloudless night sky. The purple moon of Arioch appeared small and distant this particular night, but the heavens were ablaze with starlight, as was always the case at this altitude. It was not long before a shooting star streaked across the star-studded sky, to be followed by another and then yet another.

They all stood quietly and remained still for a while, transfixed by the night sky and the meteor shower display high above their heads. Jiaying, in particular, stood absorbed and transfixed by the light show and soaked up the whole peaceful atmosphere – the mountains, the cool night air, the stars, the meteors, the moon and the occasional lights that littered the hillsides of the darkened settlement. She had already made the decision that her present mission would be her last one; that she wanted to concentrate on something more creative like painting or literature for her future life. She was toying with the idea of retreating to somewhere remote and idyllic on Zeta Kotlin, or perhaps to an island on Margalla. But now, looking at the calm nocturnal scene around her, she wondered if this was the ideal location for her new, more relaxed way of life. She clasped Rowan's warm hand tightly, and headed back to his place in the cool night air.

Early one evening, a few days after this, news filtered through to the tavern of the uprising at Meridin, of the defeat of the Zeleyanian forces, and the curious defection of their commander Vice-Admiral Rosson. The mood in the tavern and the settlement that evening was one of jubilation and talk of a bright new future for their people and its way of life. Their conflict with the lowlanders had been a long-running one, spanning across several years, and they were only too aware of the attritionally negative impact it had inflicted upon their society – raising levels of suspicion and mistrust, creating an inward-looking - almost bunker-like - mentality at times, and a stoic pessimism that had previously been uncharacteristic of their people. They now dared to hope that the end of the conflict was near, and a new understanding with the lowlanders - finally freed of their oppressive monarchist yoke – could create a fresh beginning, and form the platform for a freer and more productive future between their two peoples For the people of Lato and its surrounds, it was very much like the day a wall came down.

The accompanying news that the Zeleyanian invasion fleet had turned back, however, raised immediate suspicions amongst the crew. This was not the information being relayed from their ship and they checked with Janicka, who happened to be the crew member left minding the ship that day, whether this was in fact true or not. Janicka double and triple checked the ship's scans from the relevant zone, and replied later that day that the invasion fleet was, in fact, still on course for the planet and had not changed its trajectory in any way whatsoever. The crew felt like killjoys when they relayed this information to their friends in the tavern, but by that time, enough had been drunk for the locals to optimistically claim that they were a united people now, and they would defeat the invading forces anyway. The Zetans couldn't help smiling, but knew that this was massively overoptimistic, and that a great deal of defensive preparation was still required for them to stand even the remotest chance of repelling the fascist invasion successfully.

A couple of days later, Topaz, Indigo and several others returned to Lato following their part in the uprising at Meridin. They were joyously and warmly welcomed by everyone present and congratulated on their great success. Over the usual refreshments in the tavern, they discussed their recent nerve-racking experiences.

'So, you're semi-suicidal plan actually worked,' stated Savverio. 'I had major misgivings about the whole operation. It could all have gone so badly wrong at so many junctures.'
'Well, it turns out we got really lucky,' replied Topaz. 'Their commander, Rosson, had somehow discovered our plans, but fortunately he had his own strange plan, and used ours to make sure his worked even better. Otherwise, I think none of us would be alive to tell the tale. It's quite scary just thinking about it.'
'Yes,' chipped in Indigo, enthusiastically. 'I was so scared during the whole operation. I was just hoping against hope that it all went to plan. And now . . . it's almost embarrassing. Rosson must have found about it quite easily. It seems almost foolish now that we thought it would work.'
'Well, it was still very brave of you to get involved,' suggested Neema.
'Though there's a very fine line between bravery and foolishness,' stated Savverio, quite seriously.
The others looked puzzled. 'What do you mean?' asked Kahlil.
'Well, if it works, it was brave, and if it fails, it was foolish,' he replied.
The others were not sure if he was being serious or just facetious.
'So, why has this Rosson guy decided to go and live in the mountains?' asked Jiaying, genuinely perplexed.
'I'm not sure – someone said something about there being a power struggle amongst the Zeleyanians, but I've no idea what it was about or who was involved. It didn't look like he'd lost a power struggle to me,' replied Topaz. 'It does seem a bit strange, but I'm really glad he made that decision,

otherwise I'm sure I'd have been captured and executed, along with all the others.'

'And have some stayed in Meridin to formulate further plans?' asked Neema. 'I guess you've heard that the invasion fleet is still on its way.'

'Yes, we heard, it looks like Rosson lied about that. I wonder why?' mused Indigo.

'Those who stayed are trying to convince the lowlanders to adopt a way of life that is closer to ours, so we can prevent the reemergence of a new monarchy. It seemed to be slow going at first, but I think they're making some progress,' added Topaz. 'Of course, they'll now also need to work out a means of opposing the Zeleyanian invasion force. That's going to be a massive task. I think they're looking at some form of attritional guerilla warfare, as there's no hope of winning a straightforward battle. I guess we'll have to wait and see what comes out of the discussions.'

'That, I suspect, is the only strategy that has a real chance of working,' offered Savverio. 'Their forces will be very heavily armed. However, I think their military relies quite heavily on AI units to do the fighting, and they struggle to work out exactly who the enemy is, so that's a definite area of weakness which can be exploited.'

'Why is that?' asked Indigo.

'The reason is they are pre-programmed machines working according to algorithms. They cannot always calculate who is an enemy and who is a friend. For instance, they must be programmed not to shoot Zeleyanian soldiers, so if you wore their uniform, they would not shoot you. There might be other protocols you could discover and use to your advantage.'

'Ok, we'll pass that information onto the others,' said Topaz. 'But, let's not worry about that just yet. Let's gets some drinks in, as I've still not fully recovered from the scare we got the other night.'

'I'll second that,' added Indigo, 'I really could do with another drink.'

A few minutes later they were all downing large flagons of ale, and exchanging news of their recent adventures. There was much to relate about their recent experiences, as well as the need to make plans for the future. The reunion lasted well into the night.

Two days later, and the tavern that evening was filled with rumours that Vice-Admiral Rosson had passed surreptitiously through the village in the very early hours of the morning. Lato, due to its high and remote location, effectively acted as the gateway to the Zarozinian Mountains, as well as the difficult route to the sparsely populated forests of the far eastern provinces many days beyond. The rumors maintained that this was his eventual destination, though speculation as to why it should be so, came in many forms. Knowledge of his passage through the settlement came as something of a shock to the Zetans, though, as they had made a point of always avoiding the Zeleyanian forces, and of doing their best to keep their own presence on the planet a continued secret, and it thus sparked a concerned discussion amongst the group.

'Do we even need to still keep a low profile now that the base at Meridin has been defeated?' asked Neema. 'We're planning to leave soon, long before the invasion fleet arrives, so even if they know about our presence it doesn't really make any difference to anything anymore, does it.'
'I would say we almost certainly do still need to be very careful,' replied Jiaying. 'There might be renegade groups that have not fully accepted their defeat, and which could pose a danger to us . . .'
'But, if they believe that the invasion fleet is no longer arriving anymore, any rebellion is fairly pointless, I would have thought,' chipped in Neema, before Jiaying could fully complete her point.
'It's possible some of them know otherwise - we don't know if they still have access to advanced communications equipment or not. Equally, I would have thought that some of them will still want to return to Zeleyan, rather than staying on an unfamiliar planet which they may well dislike; so capturing us, or, more precisely, our ship, offers them a direct route home. I think we need to remain very vigilant, just to be on the safe side,' disagreed Jiaying.
'If that is the case - and I know we all like it here at Lato - maybe we should spend more time elsewhere,' offered Savverio. 'Mila and her companion's latest location looks good – they've moved on again! I had a good look around after landing them there. The climate's very pleasant – maybe a little on the cool side - but there's some interesting-looking hills that enjoy great views over a very scenic and large coastal lagoon. We could spend some time there exploring in order to keep out of trouble.'
'Mmm, sounds like a possibility,' commented Jiaying, though she wasn't overly keen, and was torn between a desire to remain in Lato, whilst also

wanting to remain safe. 'How are the repairs coming along?' she asked Savverio.

'A little slower than we expected, but we're getting there,' answered Savverio. 'There was an unexpected difficulty with one of the compression units which delayed the whole procedure, but that's been dealt with now, and the AI units have now moved on to the final section of the repairs. Another three or four days and I think they should be completed.'

'If that's the case, is it really worth leaving Lato, we'll be gone soon anyway. It'll be good to spend a few last days with Topaz, Indigo and the others – maybe have a bit of a party or something before we leave. What does everyone think?' asked Jiaying looking around, now finding a reason not to leave their adopted base on the planet. 'We can remain vigilant at the same time, and disappear early if it looks like there's going to be any trouble.'

'Well, this place is quite remote anyway, so I'm inclined to think we'll be safe here anyway, so that's fine by me,' agreed Neema.

'I'm also fine staying here,' added Kahlil, who had, like Jiaying, taken a liking to the village and its inhabitants, and wanted to spend more time with Autumn.

Savverio looked a bit more sceptical, but was clearly outnumbered, and was soon to replace Janicka on the starship anyway, so deferred to the wishes of the others.

In Meridin, a few days before this, some of the former Zeleyanian troops had also been assessing their possible next steps. The sudden capitulation of the Zeleyanian army leadership to a combined force of Meridinian townspeople and a guerilla army constituted by members of the Mountain People, had taken the Zeleyanian troops totally by surprise. Combined with the sudden defection of Vice-Admiral Rosson to the rebels, and news that the invasion fleet was now returning to Zeleyan without them, the troops were initially at a complete loss as to what they should do next. As the conference at Lato had correctly predicted, a group of men habituated to always dutifully following orders - rather than thinking for themselves - were not experienced decision-makers, and it took several days for the implications of their new and unique situation to become fully apparent to them, and to the fact that they needed to actually make some pressing decisions.

Fortunately for the troops, though, the inhabitants of Ur-Tokar, during the course of their prolonged series of meetings and negotiations, had discussed the situation of the demobbed troops. Their main concern was one of law and order, fearing the troops – with no immediate means of self-sustenance - might become roving bands of brigands terrorising the town and countryside. As such, they had decided to reach out to the troops and offer them either employment, land or help in building a new life on the planet. Meridin itself had suffered significant human losses during the first battle, and there was now a significant shortage of men. This meant there were potential opportunities for the troops, both in terms of employment and relationships – a few of the latter having already become established once the troops had occupied the town previously.

The cultures of both Zeleyan and the monarchist lowlanders were strictly patriarchal ones – their armed forces were entirely male affairs, for instance. The soldiers choosing to stay with the lowlanders would thus find social relationships to be little different to those on their home planet. For those joining the Mountain People, though, significant – and possibly lengthy - adjustments would probably be needed. Their culture in this matter, as in so many others, was, however, not a consistent one. Some followed a spiritualist and eco-feminist tradition verging on the matriarchal; one which worshipped a moon goddess and perceived femininity in all aspects of nature. Others – such as some of the cabin dwellers - had retained a somewhat more patriarchal approach, more typical of their ancestors on Earth. Most, however, like those at Lato, had embraced a generally more egalitarian approach to gender relationships, though it was not embedded in their society to quite the same degree as on Margalla or Zeta Kotlin, for instance.

The Zeleyanian troops were well aware that they faced dwindling food supplies – since their ferming units had been destroyed along with all the other forms of advanced technology they possessed - and could not prolong their decision for too long. Many of the troops were only in the army because they had been forcibly conscripted, or had performed poorly in the Zeleyanian education system and thus enjoyed limited career options. For these men, a return to Zeleyan offered them few, if any, decent prospects and the decision to start a new life on Ur-Tokar - either in the forested mountains or in the lowland valleys - was not a particularly difficult one to make. They did, though, all wonder what a life without advanced technology would prove to be like.

Others, though, were distinctly less happy at the thought of being unable to return to their home planet, to the communities, friends and families they had been missing for several months now. Rumours were also circulating amongst this group that Rosson's assertion that the invasion fleet had turned around, was actually a lie. The fact that the abduction of The Crusader several months earlier had not been immediately relayed to them by Rosson, but had only emerged through a process of hearsay and gossip, made such rumours all the more credible. Chief amongst the doubters was the Communications Officer Sub-Lieutenant Schultz, whose last scan of the relevant space quadrant before the uprising, had indicated that the invasion fleet was still on course for arrival at the planet in less than two months time.

Sub-Lieutenant Walter Schultz was not normally a rebellious person, but given his current circumstances he felt he had little choice. Deriving from a lower middle class background, he had experienced a very strict upbringing from disciplinarian and highly religious parents. An early and painful memory of being severely beaten for participating in a shoplifting incident as a small child had been burned indelibly into his mind, and he had remained a highly law-abiding, obedient and conformist individual ever since, though more out of a fear of punishment, than a belief that he was doing the right thing.

Through following the expected rules and norms of behaviour, Schultz had progressed steadily in life but had never particularly flourished – held back by a fear that any experimentation or unorthodox behaviour might result in further harsh punishments. On a number of occasions he found himself torn between doing the right thing, which might entail acting upon his own - possibly unacceptable – instincts, and behaving correctly, which entailed behaving in a manner he knew would be accepted and approved of. Invariably, he opted for the latter. A life in the known entity that was the military had thus appealed to him, and being of good background and from a well-respected family, he had experienced few problems in reaching the lower ranks of the officer class.

Here, however, he had reached his limits. Held back by a combination of personal caution and an inability to compete with the connections and sense of entitlement of those from a more privileged background, he had ultimately settled fairly comfortably into the role of Communications Officer. This, he discovered, largely suited his aspirations – a certain level of status, but without the difficulties involved in performing actual leadership roles. A few years later he was attached to the newly formed Space Fleet and had thus worked with Vice-Admiral Rosson ever since. Although he had been an early recruit to the space fleet when it had been first established, he was nevertheless looking forward to returning to his family, once his present tour of duty had been completed.

After the uprising, he had initially lacked access to any communication devices to confirm his suspicions, though he had previously cached one away in one of the anterooms inside the castle, and was hoping it had not been discovered and destroyed. Several days after the uprising he managed to create an opportunity by which he was able to access the anteroom and discover that it was - to his relief - still there. A hurriedly brief activation of the device – since he now lacked the means of recharging it once it ran out of power – showed that Rosson had indeed lied to them, and that the invasion fleet was still heading directly for Ur-Tokar. Schultz relayed the news to his associates and ordered them to keep quiet about his discovery, to bide their time, and wait for the fleet to eventually arrive. At this point they could retake control of the situation once the newly arrived troops had landed.

This left them with time on their hands, but after several unproductive days milling around the town and its environs, Schultz and three others decided to do a little further exploration of the planet. In the various taverns they habituated, they had overheard the name of a town called Lato being mentioned on several occasions, and had gained the distinct impression that it had played a significant role in the uprising against their base. A quick check of his maps showed the town to be several days journey from Meridin, but as they had little else to keep them occupied, Schultz decided to make the trip anyway. Any useful information they might glean from their visit would stand him in good stead with Supreme Commander Vartin, he figured, especially if it led to the capture of Vice-Admiral Rosson, who was now widely regarded as a traitor and a turncoat.

Arrival in Utopia

The journey to Lato proved to be somewhat longer and far more problematic than they had initially anticipated – non-automated travel was not something they were accustomed to on Zeleyan - and they made several wrong turns and overshot various pathways along the length of their journey. However, through a combination of walking, hitching lifts on travelling wagons and a lengthy boat ride down the River Kauai, they eventually arrived at the town several days later, tired, exhausted and hungry. Their plan, though, was a simple one - to pose as ex-troops interested in possibly starting a new life amongst the Mountain People if they liked what they encountered. As such, they found suitable lodgings in the main square of the settlement and, once recovered from their journey, set about discovering more about their destination.

In this respect they were in luck, as the recent festivities of the astrological new year meant there were more strangers around than usual, and the buzz from the recent celebrations had not fully ebbed away as yet. The village was still hosting the remnants of the festival goers and the Zeleyanians – no longer in the military uniforms that had been confiscated back in Meridin – did not particularly stand out from the assortment of other visitors. They were also in no particular hurry, so could afford to spend time socialising, mingling with the locals and visitors, and generally discovering more about all aspects of the settlement and its culture. Showing a general interest in an area that might prove to be the base for their possible future life was almost bound to lead to at least some information of relevance to their mission, Schultz figured.

The initial progress made by Schultz and his fellow soldiers, however, proved more limited than they had first expected. They soon discovered that the local people were also aware that the Zeleyanian invasion fleet was still heading for their planet and this, combined with the fact that they had learned to be circumspect with strangers during their long attritional conflict with the lowlanders, meant that many folk were reluctant to discuss anything that might have political or military implications. Nevertheless, the very fact that they knew that Vartin was still on course for Ur-Tokar, further fuelled Schultz's suspicions that collaboration with some form of off-world forces was taking place, and probably here in Lato, and so he decided they should persist with their efforts.

Arrival in Utopia

As the days and nights passed, they were able to pick up occasional snippets of useful information that did indeed confirm their suspicions that Lato had played some form of pivotal role in the uprising at Meridin. In addition, a rumour circulating that Rosson had passed through the settlement several days before their arrival, seemed to only further confirm this belief. However, this proved to be about the limit to what they could discover, particularly as they were concerned not to attract any untoward attention and thus kept their questioning to a very generalised level. After several days of surreptitious mingling, sight-seeing and socialising, Schultz wondered if this was as much as they were going to achieve, but a return to Meridin held no particular attraction, and he ultimately decided to persevere for a little longer.

His patience proved to be fortuitous, for one evening, whilst drinking in The Hall of the Mountain Grill in one of the side-rooms of the tavern, they spotted a fairly large group of young adults, amongst whom were individuals who looked distinctly unlike anyone else they had seen on Ur-Tokar up to this point in time. The people of the planet were almost entirely descended from white European settlers, yet this group was ethnically mixed, and additionally that they were wearing clothes and sporting hair styles that looked distinctly non-local. Schultz's suspicions were immediately aroused, and they decided to sit as close to the group as possible without attracting any undue attention. In the event, it proved to be sufficiently close to hear enough of the conversation for them to realise that they were indeed off-worlders and from Zeta Kotlin, though they were unable to discern the exact reason for their presence on the planet.

Later, back in their lodgings, Schultz explained his thoughts to his fellow soldiers. 'Whilst working for Rosson as Communications Officer we encountered several phenomena that simply made no sense. Firstly, no matter how many attempts we made, we could not access the satellite system left around the planet by the original genesis pod. Given that the Ur-Tokarans have such low level technological abilities, it was difficult to believe it was they who had implemented such a sophisticated locking system. Secondly, we intercepted a small number of messages from various spacecraft that seemed to have no obvious destination – we couldn't work out who they were being sent to or why. Thirdly, on at least two occasions I thought I discerned the movement of a transporter craft leaving the planet, but it disappeared before I could be fully certain. Mostly though, we just registered nothing – there was no stasis ship and nothing else to be suspicious about. Everything else just looked normal, so it was easy to believe that perhaps I was just mistaken.'

He paused for a while and then continued. 'All of this makes sense now. Zeta Kotlin used to have a trading ship, but we thought they had retired it about a decade ago, so we stopped monitoring its movements years ago. They must have restarted their operation, and their starship has been here all along, deliberately hiding from our – admittedly limited - scanning abilities, whilst working closely with these Mountain People. It explains all the anomalies we noted, and also who carried out the sonic attack on our base – those flares that signaled our presence to the monarchists. Those conniving socialists have been at the root of all the problems we've been suffering here, sneakily undermining our invasion plan right from the very start.'

'Right, so we need to take these bastards out, then, after all the problems they've been causing us. What's your plan?' asked one of the soldiers.

'I think we have three possible options. We could just return to Meridin, let the Supreme Commander know what we have discovered when he arrives, so that he can then capture the village and deal with the renegades. However, the Zetans might have departed by that point, and there will be no opportunity to bring them to justice. They might also still be trying to actively undermine the invasion plan. To prevent that, we could seize them, force them to take us to their ship and take control of their craft. I doubt there are many personnel on a trading ship and they're probably unarmed, so the four of us should easily be enough to overpower them. However, they clearly have many associates in this settlement and if our abduction goes wrong, we will certainly be overpowered. That option could be far too risky. The third option is that we follow their movements, find their landing craft and then take control of the situation from there, and that is the option I have decided we are going to follow. We need to be highly furtive so we are not discovered, but we can make a start tomorrow morning – there must be a suitable site for their landing craft somewhere near this settlement. We'll start by looking for that.'

Interstellar Space – the Zeleyanian invasion fleet receives news from Zeleyan

For Supreme Commander Vartin, aboard the Patriot IV, the three weeks since the arrival of the messages from Vice-Admiral Rosson and the Spirit of the Age had been particularly grim, and had passed excruciatingly slowly. After the messages, he could no longer face his two generals, and in a fit of temper had ordered them back into stasis. For the following days he had wallowed in self-pity and spent much of his time sleeping. Vartin had never followed the recommended fitness regime onboard: he was ageing, overweight and unfit and his body had failed to adjust to the low gravity environment of outer space. As a result, he suffered frequent bouts of space sickness, pounding headaches and severe stomach cramps. For much of the time out of stasis, he felt as though he had been the victim of a severe pummeling; his body ached and his head felt sore, whilst his increased use of painkillers made little or no difference to his condition.

As the level of self-pity diminished, though, he sought to rework his plans for the future. In a little over one month's time they would finally reach Ur-Tokar. He figured his forces – imbued with the spirit of patriotism - would still take control of the planet, though with a little more difficulty than he had initially assumed. The thought of fighting a long-term guerilla insurgency against highly dispersed forces filled him with foreboding. The terrain on Ur-Tokar was unlike anything his forces were familiar with on Zeleyan, and he feared that the defence of his newly established regime on an unfamiliar and semi-frozen world might prove to be a long and drawn out affair. The military forces with him – like so many of the Zeleyanian regiments – were dependant for firepower on AI units, and he worried that they might not cope in conditions they had never been tested for. He also wondered whether there was actually much in the way of habitation left to take effective control over; Rosson's failures seemed to have left a trail of destruction. He had made several attempts to contact his Vice-Admiral, but had received nothing in return – only a continued silence – despite the ship's computer assuring him they were now close enough to the planet for his messages to be received and answered within the space of a few short days.

Arrival in Utopia

Beyond Ur-Tokar, however, his future plans became increasingly uncertain. Throughout the whole endeavour, his main objective had been the destruction of Zeta Kotlin. Its very existence was an affront to everything he believed in and all his party stood for. But, the vastly greater distance that needed to be covered to invade Zeta Kotlin, meant only a surprise attack held any series possibility of success. His inability to acquire advanced space flight technology from Rorque 4 meant there could be no swift descent on the planet. His known presence on Ur-Tokar also meant the socialists would place themselves in a permanent state of readiness for his invasion. A successful attack on Zeta Kotlin now looked a very unlikely and distant prospect. This irked him considerably, but he could find no way of resolving his dilemma.

He was convinced that much of the recent political unrest on Zeleyan had been stirred up by left-wing agitators. They would undoubtedly point out the existence of the socialist alternative of Zeta Kotlin as a means by which to subvert his regime. They might even be in league with spies from Zeta Kotlin – his media outlets often claimed this to be the case. His view of the people he ruled over was a particularly low one – he believed the masses who existed below him were mostly stupid, inert, fickle and easily led. Without his firm leadership, who knows what idiocy they might succumb to? And, the masses, he further considered, were certainly stupid enough to believe this utopian socialist nonsense that was being disseminated. If he could either capture Zeta Kotlin - or at the very least destroy its decadent and depraved society - then this particular problem would be ended once and for all. There would be no empirical example of a supposedly better alternative any longer. But now, with a complex array of difficulties facing him, there was no realistic prospect of his dream being realised any time soon.

There were other planets, though. During this time, he had followed the constant flow of media transmissions emerging from Rorque 4 with increasing interest. It was abundantly clear the planet was in the midst of a major crisis. The economy was teetering on the brink and there was an impending climate catastrophe. The most recent emissions had shown the temporary closure of government – and he wondered how any society could even continue to exist under such circumstances. There were also tantalising hints in the media emissions of a possible mass departure from the planet.

For all he knew, the corporations might have already evacuated the planet – after all, he was receiving emissions that were breaking news a full two months ago. If this was the case, then Rorque 4 might be an easier target for invasion than Zeta Kotlin. But would it be worth invading and would it be controllable? This would need to be assessed as more information became available.

And then there was this small planet called Margalla orbiting the star of Sazhina. He had not been aware of any inhabited planet in that star system, until recent media reports from Rorque 4 had said as much. It sounded like a small, largely insignificant and lawless place. Was it even worth bothering with – he would also need to look into that matter at a later date – it might possibly hold some strategic importance, he considered. And finally, there was Alpha Fraczan – now uninhabited but restabilising; future colonisation was always a possibility, but would probably have to wait for greater planetary stability. In summary, there were still possibilities out there for his imperial expansion, but somehow they all seemed just out of reach. The situation he found himself in was an increasingly frustrating one; he had departed from Zeleyan full of optimism and certainty, but now he was wracked by uncertainty and doubt.

As further days passed though, his future plans of imperial conquest started to become the least of his concerns. He started to become aware of frequent transmissions by officials within his own government; ones relating to a renewed upturn in political unrest on Zeleyan itself. This was particularly annoying for Vartin, since he had previously believed that he had finally quelled the insubordination resulting from the implementation of the new working arrangements needed to pay for the space fleet bought from the Rorque Corporation. He had expected a certain amount of opposition to the new pay arrangements and working conditions, but had also expected the unrest to gradually die away over time.

He realised - now too late - that it had been a profound mistake to implement the new working arrangements across the entire supercontinent. He had become complacent and overconfident and had united the people against him, rather than behind him; a divide and rule strategy would have been far more successful, he realised with hindsight. And, if he ever needed a successful imperial invasion of Ur-Tokar, now was certainly the time - to serve as a major patriotic distraction, to draw people's attention away from their economic difficulties, and towards the glorious nature of his regime. This, he was sure, would have the desired effect of quelling the unrest.

With this in mind, he had ordered the separate media outlets in each region to step up their traditional divide-and-rule strategy of blaming one of the other regions – be it Outer Padnia, Nova Salazar or the Northern Alliance – for the particular difficulties that existed within their own region. He had observed over the years, that the people had always been stupid enough to fall for this before, and he saw no reason as to why they should not continue to do so. It always amazed him how easy it was to shift the blame for the shortcomings of his own government to some unfortunate group of outsiders or other marginal grouping. He guessed it was easier and safer for the public to blame outsiders than the government, but this was yet further evidence of the weakness of the masses, in his opinion, and of why they should be kept firmly away from political power.

The political unrest was, of course, nothing new, but Vartin found it particularly worrying that the centre of the unrest appeared to now be Novo Salzar – usually a beacon of stability, and, until now, largely immune from the political unrest. He had issued orders on how to deal with the rebellion, but was also aware that they would not arrive at Zeleyan for over two months – in addition to the fact that the news he was receiving was also two months old. He was presently entirely reliant on his appointment of General Plenge as acting chief commander of military forces to perform his patriotic duty, and maintain control and retain a sense of law and order. From this far out in space he suddenly realised he had little or no control over events in his own - now faraway - regime – a highly uncomfortable feeling for someone as obsessed with control as Vartin was. Such a feeling of powerlessness only encouraged him to keep an even closer eye on events on Zeleyan – his only means of feeling he was still in some form of control – but what he saw over the ensuing days was increasingly unsettling, and only added to his anxiety.

It was after a particularly difficult period of space sickness and intermittent periods of feverish sleep that he woke one day, and eventually worked out he had not received any emissions from Zeleyan for nearly three full days -

whilst emissions had still been arriving intermittently from elsewhere. Still slightly feverish, he wondered whether there might be some form of technical fault, and decided to leave his quarters and worked his way slowly through the corridors to the control room of the ship. Given his uncertain physical and mental condition, this took considerably longer than should have been the case and a couple of rest breaks while he took his bearings.

Once finally in the control room, he strapped himself into the commander's chair and looked around the wide array of technology surrounding him. The various screens and information panels all appeared as normal and seemed to be functioning correctly. He looked across to the viewing window and out at the thousands of multi-coloured stars that littered the cold darkness of space. The ship appeared to still be making steady progress, and the monitors indicated the continued presence of the two accompanying stasis ships close by. Nothing looked particularly untoward.

He checked with the ship's computer as to whether there was some form of internal or external communications problem, but received a reply in the negative. A data analysis showed all systems to be functioning correctly. Almost out of desperation he sent several messages back to his officials on Zeleyan - more from a desire to control the situation than for any useful purpose – but unsurprisingly there was no reply. He returned his gaze to the multitude of stars and galaxies studding the infinite blackness outside the ship. He looked long and hard, almost as if looking for help or inspiration, but the cosmic scene remained unflinchingly the same. He felt tired, alone and small in an unforgiving universe.

He dozed off for several hours during which the communications silence from Zeleyan continued, until he suddenly awakened to realise he was finally receiving something from his home world, though initially he struggled to place the newsreader or to understand what was being said. None of the information made any sense or related to events and people he knew, until the following summary was spoken by the broadcaster:

The Free Revolutionary Forces have now gained full control of Novo Salzar and the capital Zeleyan City. Significant sections of the military and security services have come over to our side, whilst those resisting have either been defeated or forcibly disbanded. The Revolutionary Council has reached out to the people of Outer Padnia and the Northern Alliance to join us in bringing down the hated fascist regime of Commander Vartin once and for all. They are ready to send revolutionary forces to assist in any such endeavour.

For Vartin, the penny finally dropped – it was not his own regime sending some strange emission, but that of left-wing revolutionaries who had seized political control. The emission continued on at some length as it explained recent political and military events, and the means and manner by which anti-regime forces had seized control of Novo Salazar. It was accompanied by extensive footage of revolutionary forces on the move, cheering crowds and defeated soldiers being marched to detention camps. There were scenes from inside a newly established revolutionary assembly, showing clips of revolutionary speeches being made by assorted left-wing insurrectionists and their idealistic plans for the future of Zeleyan.

Vartin stared at the emission in total disbelief, and continued to do so for over an hour in an almost masochistic exercise in self-torture. Eventually, though, he terminated the programme and slumped heavily into his chair. For several minutes he stared out into the infinity of space in complete silence. He gazed at the millions of stars that filled his vista. For all he knew, similar dramas to his own were being played out across the galaxy at this very moment in time. Millions of people facing their own personal crises, their untold dilemmas and moments of anguish – just like his own. Surely, he couldn't be the only person in the universe at this precise moment who was suffering such torment and torture.

For a long period of time he felt quite numb. He stared out at the infinite, cold, dark neutrality of space. He looked at the millions of stars and at the numerous galaxies – billions of stars clustered together, as if for protection against the cold harsh unfeeling reality of space. Its vastness was remorseless, impersonal and infinite. It neither knew nor cared of his misfortune, it did not hate or fear him, but its cold, unthreatening, implacable existence had ultimately defeated him. He had been vanquished by a far greater adversary, but he could take little comfort in that fact. He suddenly felt very small and very insignificant.

He did not know whether to cry, to be angry, to be disappointed, to be bewildered or even to be relieved. He emitted a long low groan of despair.

Arrival in Utopia

How had such a straightforward mission gone so calamitously wrong? Almost everything that could have gone wrong, had gone wrong! He had planned the invasion in meticulous detail - and yet it had turned out to be an utter disaster. There had been reversal, followed by reversal, followed by yet further reversal. How had his plans for imperial glory become such an abject failure, he wondered grimly to himself.

As a military commander he was all too familiar with the concept of imperial overstretch – that eventually even the most powerful empire invaded one territory too many; that their attempts to retain control over that final conquest ultimately spread their forces too thinly, leading to eventual internal collapse and external invasion. But that usually occurred after long and extended periods of glorious conquest, when a foolhardy leader finally took the reins of control, and overreached his own limited abilities. Vartin's own attempt at imperial conquest had fallen at the first hurdle, not at the final one. His pursuit of imperial glory had been one of the worst attempts in all of recorded history. How could that have happened? How could his carefully laid plans have ended in such utter disaster?

Vartin started to look for scapegoats for his own failings. Rosson was clearly one of the main culprits; he had been utterly useless as a spacefleet commander, and worse, a traitor to his nation. His incompetence had led to failings at every turn of the mission. His useless generals on Zeleyan had also failed in their patriotic duty, had failed him when he most needed them - and despite the high levels of trust he had placed in them. The double-dealers of the Rorque Corporation had also played their part – he would never trust such a dubious bunch of corporate swindlers for the rest of his life. And finally, there was that unholy social alliance of space bandits and computer cowards - scientists, Zetan socialists and other unknown subversives who had conspired against him in their usual underhand and deceitful manner.

Vartin felt the anger rise precipitously within him, and the decision as to what he should do next was suddenly and swiftly made. He issued direct orders to the ship's computer to turn back for Zeleyan, with the other two ships to immediately follow. He could use his old and trusted techniques to save the Northern Alliance and Outer Padnia. And, if they had fallen by the time of his return, there were still methods by which he could regain control of his world. He would leave Rosson to rot and die on Ur-Tokar, as he fully deserved. He would deal with all the other traitors later. And after three and a half months of space sickness he would finally get some proper sleep by re-immersing himself into stasis.

A few minutes later, the three stasis ships began a long and slow curve through the darkness of space, effecting one extremely prolonged and sweeping arc that ultimately resulted in a 180 degree turn, and placing them on a trajectory that would see the starships return to their original point of departure. In seven months time they would be back where they started from, arriving in orbit around Zeleyan, their home planet. The invasion of Ur-Tokar had been officially terminated. Vartin now needed to effect one of his own planet.

Rorque 4 – evacuation by the Rorque Corporation

As far as the Rorque Corporation was concerned, the procedures for effecting the departure of the corporation for its new planetary home located around the star Zarak 2 had run as smoothly as could possibly have been expected. There had been the expected anger from those who had not been offered a place aboard their stasis ships, and there was also some initial resistance from several of those who had. However, it was made abundantly clear to those concerned, that the corporation had already made its final decision on the matter, and would not be changing its approach any time soon. The thought of being abandoned, on what was clearly a planet facing an impending and seemingly intractable crisis, concentrated the minds of those harbouring lingering doubts about the decision, and eventually only a very tiny minority had decided to take their chances, and remain behind in the developing chaos of Rorque 4.

The designated employees and their possessions were transported out - mainly at night and in large convoys - to the spaceport at Mirivan, transported up to the starships, and immediately placed in stasis. As the whole procedure progressed, security had needed to be steadily and increasingly strengthened as more and more protestors and armed gangs attempted to attack the convoys and the spaceport. Sections of the population – considered completely undesirable by the Rorque Corporation - had demanded to be allowed departure on the spaceships, alongside those already chosen for the lengthy inter-planetary journey. The Rorque Corporation, of course, had no intention whatsoever of conceding these demands, but fortunately for their security forces, the confrontations tended to involve mainly poorly organised sections of the discontented populace.

In this they were aided by the fact that most of the underclass was actually far too busy securing clean freshwater and basic food supplies - whilst also attempting to survive the numerous fires, heatwaves and droughts that were afflicting their residential areas - to become engaged in protests and a potential insurrection. Of those that had taken notice of the recent news bulletins, many tended to regard the departure of the corporations as good riddance, and were looking in the future, to a time without their malign influence. As such, the security operation – largely consisting of the usual AI units - had been able to fend off the mostly minor disruptions.

Unbeknown to the Rorque Corporation, however, and shortly before the Margallans had left for the spaceport at Mirivan seven months previously, the departing crew had met with several of their newfound friends in one of the bars they had regularly frequented in downtown Shade Gate. Amongst the group was the ageing revolutionary Dave Shevecke, who they had first met at the psychedelic rock concert in The Aubergine that Ate Rangoon. He knew the Margallans were soon departing for their spacecraft, and they had, in fact, invited him to join them; to start a new and better life on either Margalla or Zeta Kotlin, whichever he happened to prefer.

He was sorely tempted to accept the offer – he had spent his whole adult life championing the egalitarian and communitarian cause - and understood why so many of his friends had chosen to do so, but he had informed them that he felt it was his responsibility to remain on Rorque 4, in order to further the revolutionary cause on his own planet. His analysis was that the corporations had been so severely weakened by the ongoing climate crisis, the long economic downturn and their failure to create an economic upturn through their newly created space endeavours, that they would probably decide to leave the planet in the proximate future. He was a fighter and an eternal optimist, he told them, and he believed that the people would find it much easier to rise up and take control in the political and economic vacuum that would follow their departure.

The Margallans were less sure of his analysis as they had seen little sign of any rebellion on the planet - other than amongst their close associates in Shade Gate – though they later conceded he was correct about predicting the corporate departure from the planet. The crew indicated they would miss him, and if ever wanted to drop in on their planet, he would be more than welcome. Before they departed though, he had asked them if they could supply him with some detailed scans of certain selected sites on the continent once they returned to their starship. The crew suspected - from various suggestive comments made by some of their other acquaintances - that Dave was involved with some form of armed underground resistance movement, and thus had a rough idea of why he might want such information. They promised they would send them as soon as possible, and duly followed through with their promise, once back aboard the Spirit of the Age.

During the course of the planned corporate departure, Dave had, indeed, been with his comrades in the underground movement, and they were making good use of the information sent to him by the Margallans. One of the scans had shown the existence of a well-guarded country retreat, hidden in a remote, secluded and steep-sided valley, a considerable distance from any major habitation and with no known roads in the vicinity. Yet, the officially published maps indicated there was absolutely nothing there. It was, additionally, a reasonably short distance from the spaceport at Mirivan, and there was quite clearly a cleared trackway passing through the highly secluded valley between the building complex and the outskirts of the spaceport. They had been discretely monitoring the area for some weeks now, and their suspicions as to its purpose had been confirmed by an increased level of activity at the location, particularly with the recent arrival of some of the leading figures in the world of business, law and politics.

On the final day of the evacuation procedure night had now fallen, and Colin Jamieson had been informed by the corporation's Head of Operations that embarkation onto the stasis ships had been fully completed. All but the security AI units were safely stowed away aboard the spaceships, all designated employees had been placed safely in stasis, and the ships were now ready to accept the corporate elite to fill the final compliment of places. The elite had gathered at the corporation's secret retreat, Woody Gate, a site established many decades before, in anticipation of the present eventuality. From this location, they were able to direct and monitor operations and finalise their journey details, whilst also making preliminary plans in anticipation of their arrival at their new planetary home, currently many light years away. The retreat also housed equipment and data they would need for the journey and beyond, but this had already been placed on the stasis ships earlier, partially hampered by what had been an unusually windy day.

The complex consisted of a number of luxury cabins positioned within a small, lightly wooded and relatively flat area at the base of the steep cliffs that formed the towering ravine sides. It was all surrounded by high fencing and a thin but dense line of fir trees making it difficult for intruders to gain access to the compound. Down in the valley itself, the ravine was sheltered from the high winds above, and the air remained calm and relatively still. Shortly before midnight, the various members of the elite began to emerge from their cabins – their luggage carried by their personal AI attendants - and made their way to a central point within the complex. The occasional greeting or nod of the head was made as they gathered, but mostly those present remained silent – perhaps, aware of the enormity of what they were actually doing, and of what lay ahead of them.

The gathered assembly looked around at each other in an almost knowing way and then, given the signal by the corporation's Head of Operations, one by one they climbed into the convoy of stationary vehicles waiting in front of them. Once they were all aboard the autocars and comfortably seated, their engines were started and the convoy commenced its relatively short journey along the low-lying makeshift track, hidden from the outside world by the steep-sloping sides of the valley ravine and the trees growing at the base of both sides. The convoy had been programmed to proceed at a relatively slow pace along the track – the various vehicles keeping a regularly maintained distance between each other - and so maintaining a coherently tight formation.

The members of the convoy sat mainly in silence, some looking at their consoles, others simply looking at each other. The headlights of the lead vehicle partially lit the trees to their sides and their shadows stretched high up onto the cliff walls. The journey continued quietly without incident for several minutes. Then suddenly, emerging from the night's dark silence and from the front of the convoy there came a deafeningly loud explosion – and the lead vehicle was totally ripped apart by an immense blast that scattered bodies and debris in all directions. Almost immediately, two further explosions had a similar impact at the rear section of the convoy. As the noise from the explosions subdued and the smoke partially cleared, armed men and women in dark clothing appeared from higher ground on both sides of the slope and raked the convoy with incessant gunfire. A small number of the security AI units had survived the explosions and returned fire, but they were hopelessly outgunned, and it was not long before the firing came to an abrupt halt, once it became clear that the ambush had been a very one-sided affair.

The bodies of those making up the convoy were left bloodied and bullet-ridden - the entire elite of the Rorque Corporation lay strewn across the trackway or slumped fatally in their vehicles. There was not a single survivor. The armed men and women descended down to the trackway and searched amongst the dead bodies that lay before them. After a short while they had ascertained, with considerable satisfaction, as to who exactly was present amongst the dead - Colin Jamieson, as intended, was one of their many victims. Dave Shevecke raised his assault weapon in the air above his head and declared, 'they got what they deserved. They've spent their entire lives enslaving us, oppressing us, exploiting us, denying our humanity and forcing us to live in poverty. They have destroyed this planet after their ancestors did exactly the same to Earth. But we have stopped them from repeating their wanton destruction on a further future planet. The galaxy is a far better place without them,' and all the insurrectionists around him cheered with loud shouts of 'Viva la Revolution'.

They then made their way rapidly on foot towards the spaceport. They knew the explosions would have attracted the attention of the security forces at the base, so they needed to act quickly. Fortunately, their location gave them direct access into the spaceport along the secret trackway and they - unlike the protestors and gangs on the outside of the perimeter fences - were able to attack the security positions from within the base itself. This gave them a significant strategic advantage, and eventually the edge, in the prolonged battle that ensued. Once they had subdued the AI units defending the base, they quickly set about torching all the transporter craft still present on the airfield, and then set fire to the main building itself. Dense smoke soon billowed out strongly from the spaceport, out across the surrounding lands of the plateau. As far as the insurrectionists were concerned, absolutely no one would be taking any stasis ships to wreck another planet now.

Rorque 4 – evacuation by Cosmic Solutions

Christine Sanchez gazed out of the self-tinting windows of her penthouse office for the very last time. In the distance she could see the smoke plumes from several brush fires rising into the lower atmosphere far beyond the city of New Galtsville. Here they met a high pressure temperature inversion and the smoke spread horizontally across the skyscape. Above the inversion, the sky was brightly lit with shades of electric blue; but below, a noxious haze was slowly developing and spreading downwards towards the settlement underneath - an acrid, reddish-brown smog that seemed to be sucking all the oxygen out of the atmosphere. It was a suitably apocalyptic scene for her last day on the planet.

She lowered her sights to the streets of the city down below, streets that were now almost completely devoid of any meaningful activity. The latest heatwave to spread across the city had been a particularly oppressive one, she could see the heat haze rising strongly from the pavements; the whole city seemed to shimmer below the thickening red-brown haze. The city almost looked as though it was melting in the baking heat of the summer sun – hotter, it seemed, than the forge of Vulcan. She wondered what would happen when the rising heat met the lowering haze, though she had no intentions of staying around long enough to see the actual result.

The idea of leaving Rorque 4, she now thought, actually seemed quite exciting. The corporation had achieved everything it had set out to do and more. The planet had served its purpose, but it was now time to move on - to depart for pastures new. Cosmic Solutions – first conceived of way back on Earth as a means of transferring business operations halfway across the Orion-Cygnus arm of the galaxy – had initially been highly successful. It had delivered more than respectable profit margins for the best part of a century – subject to the usual cyclical fluctuations, of course. But the recent long-term malaise – almost certainly resulting from a failure to open up any new and substantial markets – meant it was now time to start the whole process all over again once more. The climate difficulties the planet was experiencing, she had decided, were a warning sign that it was time to move on – a portent of worse to come, if they remained here for any longer.

Arrival in Utopia

The evacuation process was all but completed now. The whole process had been relatively pain-free, she had been told. The chosen employees had been informed of their status, provided with the appropriate information and security passes, assigned a stasis pod, and should now be in the deep state of wakelessness that stasis entailed. Most of the employees had accepted the new reality, though a tiny handful had chosen to remain. She could not imagine why they would want to make such a decision. The employment of those not chosen to depart with her on the stasis ship had been terminated. They would have to make their own way now, on the burning planet. But, in her opinion, that was their own fault. If they had been better employees they would have enjoyed a better future – the exciting opportunity of creating a whole new neoliberal economy on a planet just waiting to be colonised and developed. What could be more exciting, she thought to herself.

She left her office for the last time, and descended to the ground floor in her own personal, super-fast shiny metal elevator. The rest of her entourage was already in the huge, highly polished red-granite lobby hall that constituted the centre of the ground floor. She glanced across the group and recognised the numerous figures that constituted the elite of both her own corporation, and of United Rorque Technologies, who had recently joined them in their new endeavour – part of the political deal put together, following their recent electoral victory. The leading financiers, politicians, economists, judges, administrators and business leaders were all present, and accompanied by their closest relatives. She checked with her Security Chief that all was in order, and after he gave the all-clear, the entourage made their way to the convoy of heavily protected autocars waiting at the rear of the building.

The convoy initially snaked its way through the city centre streets – streets that were largely abandoned and with little in the way of traffic on them, now that the corporation had effectively ended its commercial activities on the planet. As the convoy moved towards the suburbs, it picked up speed on the straighter more direct roads of the westway, slicing their way through the urban sprawl that constituted the outskirts of the city - a largely soulless spread of suburban housing, high rise accommodation and isolated retail centres. Fifteen minutes later, and the convoy emerged into the dry, dusty, fire-darkened semi-desert that formed the hinterland of the city. The convoy gathered speed and blazed a trail across the flat dusty plain, a long plume of choking dust spreading out from behind the speeding vehicles.

The convoy made good time and fifty minutes later its members could begin to discern the raised, reddish-brown plateau upon which the shiny silver spaceport of Stratostan was situated. As they closed in on their destination, the steep, rugged granite sides of the plateau started to loom high above them. Slowly its huge bulk gradually blocked out the majority of the darkening sky, as the long convoy of black armoured vehicles approached its towering walls. The road led straight to a major geological fissure in the vertical cliffs and they began their ascent up and along a precipitously steep, narrow, dry and scrubby canyon that snaked its way up the side of the plateau, tightly twisting and turning as they gained height in order to reach the elevated level of the spaceport.

Initially, and for some minutes, the climb passed without incident, but as they approached the higher elevations of their ascent the lead vehicle suddenly alerted its passengers to smoke billowing towards them. The convoy was halted and a drone sent up to assess the situation ahead of them. Live footage was soon beamed back showing a wall of flames that was sweeping rapidly across the plateau towards them and with the spaceport already engulfed in smoke. AI units were running around the base frantically trying to deal with the fire. Earlier that morning, a strong wind from the low range of mountains to the north-west had swept down, curved in direction and then fanned out across the vast spread of the plateau. In the short space of time the convoy had spent climbing the narrow canyon, the wind – trapped under the inversion - had suddenly accelerated during its descent, and driven the numerous scrubby fires burning on the plateau in a strongly south-easterly direction, uniting them as it did so into one blazing inferno that now threatened the whole spaceport.

The convoy had no choice but to reverse and return down the narrow canyon, but the lengthy limousine-type vehicles struggled to perform U-turns in the narrow confines of the canyon - the vehicles struggling to reverse in such a tight situation, and blocked each other's progress as they attempted to do so on the steep and narrow incline. As they struggled to realign and head downhill, the accelerating wind sucked in fast moving air currents that swept the spreading flames down rapidly into the tinder dry canyon - the narrow gorge funneling the intense fire through the scrubby bushes and trees that grew along its twisting course. Within a few short minutes, the convoy was totally engulfed by the scorching intensity of the firestorm that swept down the canyon, and every last autocar became a burning death trap. Not a single person survived the raging inferno.

Fifteen minutes earlier, Anna Dubois had been sat in the spaceport waiting for the arrival of Alex Kim. She had arrived in an autocar late that morning, having stayed in a hotel in Motorway City the night before. Given the scale of the evacuation from the planet, she was surprised to find the spaceport largely deserted. Stratostan, because of its elevated position on a high plateau, had found it far easier to keep away angry mobs than had been the case with the spaceport at Mirivan, and the only people present were a few security personnel, a tiny number of passengers arriving late, and the usual complement of AI units that served the base. Almost immediately, she had felt uncomfortable and out of place, and it was not long before she was approached by security wanting to confirm her identity and purpose at the spaceport. Fortunately, the night before, Alex had informed the security system of her intended presence, and she was duly left to sit alone in the foyer of the main building.

She had chosen to sit near the front windows of the building in the hope of spotting Alex as he approached the spaceport. Shortly after her arrival, she had received a message from him informing her he had been running late, but was now on his way to the spaceport, but would still be later than he had originally indicated to her. She had also become aware, through the actions of the security forces, that a major convoy of vehicles was on its way and was expected to arrive any time soon. She assumed Alex was in the convoy, and walked out of the building to look out across the plateau to see if she could spot its imminent arrival. Brush fires had become so commonplace in recent weeks, that the one she noted further across the plateau had not really mentally registered with her initially, until it suddenly became apparent to her that it's flames were sweeping very rapidly towards her, looming higher and higher as they approached the shiny new spaceport. For a brief moment, she simply stood and stared at the oncoming inferno, until it suddenly registered that her life was probably in grave danger.

Arrival in Utopia

When Anna had first arrived at the planet on The Spirit of the Age at Mirivan spaceport, her landing craft had developed stabilisation issues during the descent and the craft had been instructed to land away from the main runway - in the event that any safety issues might arise - and head directly towards the storage and maintenance bays. As such, she became significantly more familiar with the layout of a spaceport than she had any real desire to do so at the time, but she had, despite the inconvenience, learnt that the landing craft were serviced in large underground storage bays, and it was to one of these that she made a determined and concerted dash. At one point she was convinced the flames were going to beat her to the entrance door; she could feel the heat of the flames, the crackling of the burning vegetation and the whooshing sound of the air being sucked into the flames around her, but she made it safely to the large iron doors, just in time. She grappled for a brief moment with the heavy side door but made it inside with seconds to spare, and slammed it airtight behind her.

Once inside, she spent a few moments gathering her composure, and then descended in the elevator to the storage bay below, where a number of AI units were standing around idly in the large empty hangar - all the transporter craft having been thoroughly prepared earlier, and were ready and waiting above ground for the elite motorcade that was due to arrive any moment soon. Some of the AI units were watching the monitoring screens that hung from the walls, viewing the alarming scenes unfolding above. She moved cautiously over to where they were standing, but they hardly gave her a second glance. The screens were transmitting pictures from above ground and now showed the fire blazing across the entire airfield and its several buildings. Small numbers of AI units were scurrying around trying to extinguish the flames, but to no avail as they themselves became victims of the blazing inferno.

For several minutes she stood transfixed and watched in horror at the scenes occurring above. One by one, though, the screens went blank – no doubt as the buildings they were located on were destroyed in the rapidly moving blaze – until only a single aerial drone camera continued to relay pictures to the ground. From its lofty perspective, she could continue watching the appalling scene until, finally, she could see that effectively nothing had escaped the fire – the buildings, the transporter craft and all else near them had been subject to such intense heat that only blackened, smouldering remains were left as the fire moved rapidly ever onwards. The fire then continued on its path and she could see it sweeping its way to the edge of the plateau. She looked at the AI units, but they did and said nothing – she presumed they were simply service and maintenance robots – and so she headed back towards the elevator.

Once above ground, she found the expected scene of devastation; the heat was still oppressive and she struggled to breathe in the hot dry air. The smell of smoke was everywhere, and the ground beneath her was blackened and smoking. She wrapped some material round her face to protect her from the smoke and the dry heat. Across the airfield, she could see the blackened hulks of the waiting transporter craft, and to her right, the blackened smouldering remains of the spaceport, its windows entirely destroyed and small fires still blazing away in the upper storeys of the building. Other than the drifting smoke and the flickering flames, there was no movement anywhere on the plateau, there were no people, no AI units and no transport craft; she walked dazed and alone across the airfield towards the service road – a lone figure in a desolate smoky landscape.

She wasn't sure why she was walking towards the road, but as she did so, she noticed a sudden uprush of flames from where the road entered the canyon on the edge of the plateau. Suddenly she remembered she was meant to be meeting Alex, and realised he would be heading towards the inferno and into serious danger. She took out her console and phoned him, for a few moments there was no reply and she wondered whether she was too late and he was already a victim of the fire. And then she experienced a sudden sense of relief as his voice sounded. 'Wow, are you still alive? That fire looks dreadful, I assumed it had destroyed the whole spaceport. How did you survive?' he asked, genuinely surprised that Anna – or anyone else for that matter - had been able to survive such an intense fire event.

'I hid in an underground cargo bay. Where are you? Has the convoy not reached the plateau yet?'

'I missed the convoy departure. I was held up last night on the motorway. I needed to collect various possessions and download large amounts of data in the laboratory this morning, before I could get to the corporation headquarters on time. The convoy is somewhere ahead of me, I'm not sure where. I'm currently on the road to . . . err, to a different approach route . . . err, I'm not too sure where, the autocar is trying to work out an alternative route to avoid the fire,' he replied, relieved she had survived the fire, but also confused as to what was actually happening.

'I think the convoy might just have gone up in flames, judging by the strength of the fire descending down the edge of the plateau,' she replied, though uncertain as to whether that was exactly what she had seen. 'There's certainly no sign of it arriving here, anyway.' She paused a moment to think, 'the southern service road is still passable by the looks of things, but everything else here is completely destroyed. The space station, the shuttle craft, everything. Would you be able to divert and pick me up? I have no other way of leaving here. It's total devastation; I think I'm the only survivor.'

Alex thought for a moment, 'sure, I'll instruct the autocar to come in from that direction. I think it's about an extra forty minutes. I'll see you soon,' and abruptly he was gone.

Forty minutes later and she was still stood by the side of the road waiting, her small case standing next to her. She wondered if Alex had decided not to come for her – after all, she didn't know him that well, and she had been something of an encumbrance for him in the last day or two. She wondered whether to phone him again, but thought that might make her look needy or, worse, untrusting. She continued to wait. She started to wonder what she should do next, and how she could leave the planet now, or whether it was even possible. And then, suddenly, she remembered something she had entirely forgotten about. It might be her way off the planet, but she would still need Alex to aid her. Ten minutes later, and she thought she saw movement at the southern end of the plateau, and sure enough, a moving object, dust spreading far behind it, gradually transformed from being a small dot on the horizon to an autocar that eventually came to a gradual halt right in front of her.

Alex stepped out and embraced her, 'wow, I thought you must have died,' he said, once more, 'until I received your call, of course.'

'I thought the same about you. I think missing that convoy has just saved your life,' she replied.

'Definitely, there's just been a traffic report – the entire south-eastern canyon approach is blocked by a multiple vehicle fire – it sounds like there were no survivors.' He looked around the spaceport and slowly took in the scene of utter devastation before him. 'There's no chance of us leaving from here, and the news bulletins early this morning said the Mirivan spaceport was completely destroyed by an angry mob. I really have no idea of what we should do next.'

'I've just remembered that the landing craft I descended in when I first arrived here, is still in storage at an industrial unit at my university. It malfunctioned as we were preparing for landing. The repair fee the spaceport quoted me was astronomical, so I had it flown to my university to have it fixed ready for when the Margallans left – I thought I owed them that much. The university didn't seem too happy at the time, though, to put it mildly. The Margallans departure occurred so quickly, though, that by the time I found out about it, they had already left orbit. It's still there, and no one ever changed the access codes; so I should still be able to access and use it,' explained Anna. 'Do you still have access to the ship you came on?'

'The Avante, yes, I think so. We sold it to Cosmic Solutions, but I was given restricted security clearance to access the vessel, as I needed a starship I could check some of my experimental data on. I went up there a couple of times, some while ago, so I should still have access – assuming my permission privileges have not been recently cancelled,' he answered.

'So, if we can get to Altair University, we have a chance of getting out of this hellhole,' she said, sounding somewhat relieved. She thought for a further moment, 'even better, we can head for somewhere without a neoliberal economy – every cloud has a silver lining,' she stated, sounding almost pleased with the latest turn of events.

Alex glanced at her questioningly, and then remembered her recent experiences. His time on the planet had been much better than hers, though admittedly it had also been very frustrating at times. He figured her reaction was probably understandable. And additionally, given the rapidly declining state of the planet and the recent shocking events, he too now shared her enthusiastic desire to leave, and preferably as soon as possible. They boarded the autocar, programmed in their destination – the ferry port at New Nozike – and moments later they were picking up speed, and heading rapidly away from the blackened and ruined spaceport.

Interstellar Space – The Spirit of the Age is awakened again

An AI unit made its way quietly and steadily from its station on the maintenance deck and through the long corridors that led to the vast stasis chamber that composed the huge central section of the starship. It did so in its usual unhurried, calm and methodical manner. The chamber was dimly lit by the low level strip lighting that flickered quietly and softly high above the corridors between the stasis pods, but this made no difference to the progress of the android. It passed the endless array of grey metallic piping snaking its way confusingly across the walls and ceilings, and then, periodically, it stopped at pre-selected stasis pods, keyed in the appropriate code and waited for the cover to slide back. It repeated this on six occasions, and then revisited each to ensure that the occupant was emerging without difficulty or mishap. In the background, the constant low level hum of the ventilation systems sounded continuously.

One by one, the crew of The Spirit of the Age woke from stasis, spent several minutes regaining consciousness, and then after building sufficient strength – both mental and physical – emerged somewhat dazed and unsteady from their individual stasis pod. The AI unit assisted with their waking and then their passage to the forward deck, where they gathered for renourishment and updates of the current situation and recent events from the AI unit. As they slowly acclimatised to a waking state, they all spent considerable amounts of the time seated quietly, slowly recovering and observing the star lit darkness through the viewing screen, though the vista before them remained largely unchanging as they did so.

The crew of The Spirit of the Age had previously decided to return to stasis for a period of two and a half months, once they had completed their dealings with the Opa-Loka and other matters. They had ordered the ship's computer to wake them as they approached Rogan's star system, with the intention of reviewing the situation and discerning whether their assistance might be needed for one reason or another. They had offered to help the Opa-Loka if it was in need of any such aid, and were curious to know if any relevant messaging had been logged. If it turned out they were unneeded, they had agreed they would return to stasis and simply remain on their pre-established trajectory for Zeta Kotlin.

They were also curious to know whether the Zeleyanian invasion fleet was still heading towards Ur-Tokar, though they were fairly sure it offered no actual threat to themselves, since their expected time of arrival at the star system was some considerable time before that of the invasion fleet. As the crew neared the end of the recovery from stasis, the ship informed them that the scanning system had - quite literally the day before - registered the Zeleyanian invasion fleet turning around and heading back in the direction of Zeleyan. Further scans had confirmed the observation. The crew all gave a big cheer and congratulated themselves on playing a part in thwarting the invasion plan.

'Yeh, bring it on home,' cheered Arlo, pumping his fist in the air, 'we've defeated the fascists. Now they're heading for the exit.'
'Wow, I can't believe it actually worked. Was it our message that made the difference, then?' asked Kiyona,
The ship informed them of news of the revolution that had broken out on Zeleyan, and that the invasion fleet appeared to have turned about shortly after they had presumably received news of that event.
The crew looked a little deflated, but still gave a smaller, more ironic, cheer.
'Well, I'm sure we played some role in helping to defeat the invasion, even if it was a small one,' expressed Akiko with a big smile, certain that the others were all thinking along the same lines. 'It's also great news that there's a revolution breaking out on Zeleyan. With any luck that will be the end of fascism on Zeleyan – the Nexus Cluster will be a much safer place, for all concerned. That's certainly one less problem we have to be worried about. Now that everyone knows of our existence, we need to start concerning ourselves with these matters.'
'Agreed,' added Xander, 'what's the news from Rorque 4?'
The ship then brought them up to date with the latest emissions from Rorque 4 and the imminent departure of the stasis ships for either Zarak 2 or some other distant but, as yet unknown, star system.
'Wow, the corporations are leaving the planet, and it sound like they're still competing with each other. They seem to be very slow learners in that respect,' exclaimed Zhavia. 'It doesn't surprise me they're leaving though – they've made such a mess of that place . . . and now they're just planning to do it all over again somewhere else. What a load of dickheads!'

'It's appalling that people can even think like that,' interjected Kiyona, exasperated at the thought of such behaviour. 'Why can't they just look after the place, what's so hard about that?' she asked, though not actually expecting an answer.

'Mmm, I think we've been through all that before', replied Zhavia, but offered his well-rehearsed answer anyway. 'The capitalist economic system is mainly driven by the desire to make profits. It moves into an area, extracts as much profit as it possibly can, and then, when the area's profitability has been exhausted, it simply leaves to repeat the process elsewhere. More often than not, it leaves environmental damage and resource exhaustion in its wake, but its desire to make profits elsewhere, and the expense of cleaning up the mess after it's left, means it does little or nothing about the destruction. It just leaves, and others have to pick up the pieces.'

The crew had all heard this before and had no real disagreement with his opinion, but, having spent almost their entire lives in a society that took great care of its environment, still could not get their heads round the fact that people would actually behave in this way. There was a period of silence as they contemplated their thoughts on the matter.

'Anyway, never mind that,' offered Xander, breaking the short silence. 'I wonder what Dave Shevecke thinks of the new situation – he did predict the corporations would leave the planet, and pretty soon. His rebel army might be able to take over once the capitalists have all departed.'

'Dave had an army, I didn't know that,' Arlo added, genuinely surprised.

'Well, not as such, but I heard from the others that he was involved in some form of underground rebel movement, and that it was probably well armed. Once the corporations depart, there will be a power vacuum, and potentially anyone could take over, I would have thought. Given that the rest of the population seemed so demoralised and apathetic, I would hazard a guess that Dave's group has as good a chance as anyone, especially if they're well organised and determined,' Xander explained.

'When you say take over, I assume you mean create a society more like ours, rather than seizing political power. Dave seemed to be very much an anarchist to me . . . although not exactly like people on Margalla, somehow a bit different, though I'm not exactly sure how . . . not quite so innocent, a bit more experienced, or something like that,' offered Akiko.

Arrival in Utopia

'Oh yeh, he definitely didn't like politicians, I would imagine that is what his group was fighting for,' Zhavia clarified. 'If they have any sort of success, then Rorque 4 might be another planet we no longer need to worry about. I wonder if there's any way of contacting them and finding out what's happening,' and so he duly requested that the ship's computer look into the matter.

'Computer, what's been happening on Ur-Tokar,' asked Akiko, changing the conversation and wanting to know more about their present situation, which was the main reason they had emerged from stasis.

The ship's computer promptly informed them of the departure of The Star Chaser for Zeta Kotlin two months previously, and related the fact that recent scans showed that the Opa-Loka had not yet departed from Ur-Tokar's orbit for Zeta Kotlin.

'I wonder why that is?' asked Kiyona. 'I thought they said their mining operation would be a relatively quick affair – it should be completed by now, and they should be well on their way back to Zeta Kotlin by now.'

'I wonder if they're still involved with the conflict on the planet in some way. There's still a Zeleyanian military unit down there, even if it is depleted. Maybe they're helping the locals finish them off. We should message them, to see if they need any help. We might be able to assist them in some way. Out here we are possibly of some help to them now,' Akiko offered optimistically, looking around the others and hoping they might agree with her.

She was beginning to get a taste for space adventure and the situation on Ur-Tokar might provide what she was looking for, she figured, though also nothing that was too dangerous, she thought at the same time.

'After all, we are very close to the star system now and communication delays are minimal. We should be able to work out the situation pretty quickly and come to a decision.'

The crew generally agreed; a short amount of time spent out of stasis might prove to be interesting and productive, they thought. So, now that they had finished receiving news of recent events and transmissions from around the different planets, the crew duly sent a message to the Opa-Loka, and settled back to wait for a reply, which they assumed would arrive fairly quickly, given their close proximity to the planet. Initially, though, there was only silence.

At first, they assumed the absence of any return message was simply due to the usual temporal delays they had become so used to in space, but after a while they began to grow a little concerned. As they were now closing in on the outer limits of Rogan's system, they instructed the ship to slow slightly and pass more closely to the star system. A further period of waiting still produced nothing, whilst further scans of the stellar system indicated that the Opa-Loka was definitely still orbiting Ur-Tokar, and also that there had been no significant stellar or planetary activity in the system that might cause communication difficulties. And just as they were wondering what more they could do, a message suddenly came over the ship's system:

Sorry for the delay in replying, but we have an ongoing emergency situation. Some of the crew have been captured by rogue Zeleyanian forces down on Ur-Tokar. I am trying to effect a rescue operation but there is a danger they will board and take control of our ship. Any help you can offer will be greatly appreciated. I will update you soon. Savverio.

'Oh no, that's dreadful. We must go and help them,' Akiko exclaimed with alarm, and certain that the others would all agree. She quickly instructed the ship to change direction and divert for Ur-Tokar.

At this point in time, they were literally skirting past the far reaches of Rogan's outer gravitational attraction zone, and so an immediate deviation in direction, followed by a rapid ship-shaking reversal of the engines – which was clearly going to do the starship no favours in the long-term - soon saw them rapidly decelerating through the planetary system of the diminutive star, whilst the crew continued to remain in urgent communication with Savverio. Approximately three hours later, they dropped into orbit around Ur-Tokar, approached the position of the Opa-Loka, and were still in close touch with Savverio.

Arrival in Utopia

Ur-Tokar – the crew of the Opa-Loka endangered

Two days before, the crew of the Opa-Loka had received the welcome news from Savverio that the engine of their ship was now fully repaired, and the completed diagnostic tests had shown it to be in full working order. Following the crew's return to the starship, they could finally commence their long delayed departure for Zeta Kotlin. Once they had decided when and where they wanted to be collected, he would inform Mila and her colleagues of their plans for departure, liaise between the two groups, and organise arrangements for a single transporter craft to collect them all from their respective locations and then return them to the starship. With everyone and everything on board, they could then commence departure.

A short time before this, he had taken great pleasure in excitedly informing them that the ship's computer had recently registered the fact that the Zeleyanian invasion fleet had performed a complete and hurried U-turn, so that the three ships were now following a trajectory through interstellar space that would see their eventual return to Zeleyan. He had run a series of repeat scans just to make sure the initial one was not a computer error, or in some way misleading, but they had all shown the three ships were quite clearly on a flight trajectory that would see them arrive back at Zeleyan in several months time.

The rest of the crew, who were all in Lato at this point in time, wasted no time in informing as many of the settlement's inhabitants as they could find of the great news, though also details of their imminent departure. As the news spread around Lato and beyond, it was decided that a celebration and farewell party should be organised, centring on their favourite tavern, The Hall of the Mountain Grill. Over the course of the following day, preparations were hurriedly made, so as the afternoon waned and the evening commenced, numbers slowly began gathering in both the tavern and around the settlement. The Mountain People had been engaged in a long, tiring, and, at times, demoralising conflict with both the lowland monarchists, and then lately with the invading Zeleyanian forces, but it now appeared to have all been resolved very much in their favour. They had a great deal to be thankful for.

Arrival in Utopia

The tavern was often busy in the evenings, but on this particular night it was packed to the rafters – the celebrations proving too great an attraction to miss for almost all those living in the immediate area and beyond. Throughout the evening and long into the night there was a long and great outpouring of joy and relief. The previous years had been like dealing with a deadly and persistent pandemic, a long and drawn out affair with intense periods of suffering, times when recovery seemed imminent, only for the harmful effects to return and the suffering to become even worse. But now, finally, the virus had been defeated, the worst was definitely over, and a long and peaceful period of recuperation could now be expected.

For some, though, the celebrations were also tinged with sadness, for the crew of the Opa-Loka were due to depart the next day, and some strong friendships were now about to be broken forever. There was little prospect of either group encountering each other ever again, or of being able to remain in touch, and the starkness of knowing this fact was difficult to countenance for some of them. They would only ever be able to wonder how time had treated their newfound friends and comrades, what lives they had lived, the relationships they had built and the adventures they had experienced.

Aware of this imminent parting of the ways, Topaz suggested a means by which they could all remember each other by, and brought out a very primitive looking needle gun. She had a small collection of very distinctive pieces of jewelry, studded with tiny dark purple amethysts, and one by one she pierced the ears of all those present, so that they could all easily remember each other at any future point in time. After this, they somehow felt better about the whole situation, and spent several hours discussing their relative plans for the future. And, in general, the joyous mood of the wider settlement and its celebrations prevailed, as the crew and their friends resolved to make the most of their final night together in the tavern. They all tucked in heartily to the food provided, large quantities of the local ales were downed, and later, favourite bands struck up, eliciting much singing and dancing. The celebrations lasted long into the night and eventually proved to be a joyous and raucous affair.

Finally, though, in the small hours of the morning, the numbers in the tavern dwindled as small groups and couples spilled out into the cold night air, the stars twinkling in the dark sky above, and the dark Zarozinian Mountains showing in the background, dimly lit by the pale purple moonlight of Arioch. They all made their different ways back to their houses, lodgings and cabins singing drunkenly and merrily, until, in the early hours of the morning, silence finally descended across the entire settlement.

Late next morning – aware of the likely condition of his fellow crew members – Savverio informed the transporter craft already located at Mila Lustrom's latest location that it should prepare for departure. Mila had been informed in advance of the departure time, and was ready and waiting with her colleagues and their equipment inside the craft. Before she entered the craft, though, she had taken one last look at the stunning scenery – an intoxicating mix of snow-capped purple mountains, lush green forests and turquoise blue-green alpine lakes – and then made her way quietly, almost reverentially, onto the craft. Once seated and secured, the craft lifted off and departed for Lato. It was being piloted by the AI unit that was aiding Mila with her research – this was considerably more straightforward than Savverio trying to control the operation from afar - and after its flight over the mountains and down into Lato for one final time, it would then be returning to the orbiting spacecraft.

Approximately forty minutes after leaving the alpine location, Mila could make out what looked like the Kauai river canyon down below, and close by, the settlement of Lato. The shuttle craft commenced its descent and circled slowly down to its usual landing spot in the meadow-like clearing, close to the settlement. Waiting below, standing on the edge of the clearing, were Jiaying, Kahlil, Neema and Janicka, all somewhat the worse for a night of prolonged drinking and then obtaining only a short amount of sleep. They had earlier said their goodbyes to anyone they could still find awake in the settlement, and were now feeling very mixed opinions about their imminent departure. On the one hand they were pleased to be returning to their home planet, but on the other, they were leaving behind some close friends and interesting adventures.

They watched as the craft landed safely in the late morning sunshine. The sky was clear and the air was cool and refreshing. There was the usual hum of insects sounding from the trees, which glistened and sparkled with dew in the bright morning air. A woodpecker drummed loudly from the trees along the edge of the clearing, and a cloud of butterflies lifted from the carpet of meadow flowers at the far end of the clearing as the shuttle craft came in to land. Once it was safe to do so, they started to make their way across to the centre of the clearing towards the transporter craft.

They were approximately halfway across the clearing when Jiaying heard the woodpecker emit a strident alarm call. She turned around and watched its undulating flight across the clearing, but as it flew across the clearing, she noticed two men walking rather hurriedly towards her. They were fairly stocky, with short hair and had a military-type look about them, and both looked vaguely familiar, though she couldn't quite place where she had seen them. Jiaying immediately sensed a potential problem, but hoped against hope that she might be mistaken. Almost immediately, though, her intuitive anxiety proved to be correct, as the slightly taller man took out a small pistol and leveled it at her head. She instinctively turned to see if she could make a run for it, but there were two more men carrying large knives advancing from the opposite direction.

'Stop right there. We're coming with you and don't try anything funny. We know how to work these craft, and at the first sign of any trickery I'll put a bullet through your brain,' stated the taller man in an authoritative voice, though also with a hint of nervousness, as he hurriedly advanced towards the crew.

It was at this point that it suddenly came to Jiaying's sleep-deprived brain where she had seen them before – someone had pointed them out in the tavern the night before as ex-Zeleyanian troops planning to start a new life amongst the Mountain People. She had made a point of keeping out of their sight, but she now figured that she must have been unsuccessful.

'But your forces have been defeated and the invasion fleet has turned round for Zeleyan. The war is over. You've lost,' stated Neema somewhat naively, having obviously never been in such a situation before, nor thinking through the situation fully.

Arrival in Utopia

'We know, we are fully aware of that fact. We were at the party you threw last night to celebrate our defeat,' Schultz, the taller man, replied with a hint of menace. 'You are our only means of leaving this backward frozen dump. We also have every intention of returning to Zeleyan, as well. Now open the doors to the craft, and we'll all enter slowly and calmly. Any false move and it will be your last one.'

Despite her hung-over state, Jiaying's brain started racing, and she made a quick calculation with regards to their possible options. Making a run for it was probably suicidal, and even in a completely fit state they were probably no match for four military men in a fight, she calculated. Their only option for the moment was compliance – they would have to think of something on the craft - or more likely back on the ship - if they were to get out of this alive and not end up dead, or even worse, end up on Zeleyan.

As Schultz had demanded, they opened up the craft and he led the way onboard, still brandishing his pistol, whilst his fellow soldiers guarded the rear of the group. They made their way into the passenger compartment where he was visibly surprised to see Mila Lustrom and her colleagues, who looked equally disconcerted at the sight of an unknown man armed with a pistol.

'Who are they?' he asked, pointing in Mila's direction.
'They are scientists from Alpha Fraczan; they've been studying the biology of Ur-Tokar,' replied Jiaying, wondering at the same time if a pack of lies might have been better; though after a moment, on second thoughts, she considered that lying might actually have made matters worse.
Schultz paused and thought a moment. 'Ah, your comrades in crime, the people who stole my ship The Crusader. Maybe we can find a way of arranging for them to bring it back. Well, it looks like they'll be joining you on our flight back to Zeleyan'.
At this, Mila suddenly clocked exactly what was happening. She opened her mouth and was about to tell them she was an astrobiologist, not a computer scientist or engineering technician, but then thought better of it and decided to remain silent.

Schultz looked around the shuttle craft and noted the AI unit piloting the craft. The presence of the scientists on board had slightly thrown him; he had expected only a single human or AI pilot on the craft, and was initially uncertain as to how he should deal with them all. He was also slightly concerned by the fact that he had noticed that whilst they were observing the Zetan crew in Lato, he in turn was being watched by the local inhabitants, and he glanced out the windows occasionally to see if any of the locals had followed them. Unable to see anyone in the immediate vicinity, though, he momentarily reflected on the fact that his plan, so far, was actually going much better than he had anticipated – he had always considered it a bit of a long shot – and he eventually decided it would be sufficient to just order one of the soldiers to keep a very close eye on the scientists. After all, it was highly unlikely any of them were armed.

Once they were all seated and secured, the AI unit was instructed to initiate take off and the craft accelerated, commencing its ascendancy for the short journey that would take them to their starship waiting in a low space orbit, some three hundred kilometers above the planet. Jiaying and the others all looked around them searching for possible means to enable their escape from captivity, but nothing in particular sprung to mind. The atmosphere in the cabin was tense and nervous, and not a few of them kept hoping - in their hung-over state, - that they might wake up soon to find it was actually all just a bad dream.

After what seemed like a lifetime to Jiaying – and an ascendency that seemed to last much longer than usual – the shuttle eventually arrived at their spacecraft, and the cargo bay doors duly slid open allowing the shuttle to land next to the other transporter craft. Schultz ascended from his seat, but indicated everyone else should remain seated.

'So, how many crew members are on board the ship?' he asked, almost threateningly.
Jiaying, before anyone else could answer, and as quickly and as confidently as she possibly could, lied, 'none, it's all fully automated. We were all down below for the party,' whilst hoping at the same time that Savverio was keeping to a plan they had formulated some months ago now, in the event of a Zeleyanian incursion on the ship.

Schultz, an experienced spacefleet junior officer, knew this could well be the case but, of course, had no knowledge of Zetan spaceflight procedures. He suspected they would be much less rigorous than their own, but was still sceptical about Jiaying's answer. He ordered Jiaying - who he had decided was their de facto leader - to give him control of the ship's computer. Again, she felt she had no choice but to comply and just hoped that Savverio had devised a plan to deal with the situation, particularly since the crew, so far, had come up with absolutely nothing themselves. Schultz ordered the ship to identify the number of personnel and passengers on board and it duly identified that number to be twelve – the same number as on the shuttle.

Schultz seemed to be fairly reassured by this information, but still ordered one of the soldiers to take a look around the cargo and stasis holds on the ship, just to ensure that the information was actually correct. He knew his position was not a particularly great one – lightly armed and with only three men at his command –and he was only a junior officer in the Zeleyanian spacefleet. He had suddenly found himself in charge of a situation he had never been trained for, was unused to taking decisions of such importance, and was now discovering it was somewhat more difficult than he had initially assumed. Nevertheless, so far he was quite pleased with the developing situation, as everything still seemed to be going to plan.

Once the soldier had departed, he ordered everyone to disembark slowly from the shuttle craft. Since there were eleven of them, they used the flight elevator to reach the highest floor, where the forward and control decks were located. As they made their way through the ship, Schultz noted that the design of the craft, as he had expected, was the standard mass-produced one of all stasis ships that had been constructed on Earth back in the late twenty-first century. To all intents and purposes it was very similar to The Crusader and, no doubt, to the ships the Zeleyanian spacefleet had bought from the Rorque Corporation. As they ascended up through the ship, he thought to himself he should have no problems in placing it under his effective control, and then piloting a successful return to Zeleyan.

Once they had arrived at the forward deck, he took the opportunity to change the security codes on the doors, and ordered the two remaining soldiers to keep guard over the captives, whilst he effected his own control over the ship and assessed the onboard situation. He was particularly interested in whether he could actually obtain full control of the ship's computer. He spent a considerable amount of time engaging in this task, until he believed he had finally dealt with it to his ultimate satisfaction. He seemed to be fully in control. He then checked the fuel levels and the general condition of the ship – both of which appeared to be perfectly adequate.

Whilst performing this task, though, he was also aware that he needed to urgently consider other pressing matters. In particular, he was unsure if he should simply take control of the ship and head immediately back to Zeleyan, or whether he should return to Meridin and order the remaining soldiers to join him on the return journey to Zeleyan. He wondered if he had the firepower and personnel to carry out the latter procedure in any suitably effective manner, since he was also aware that a percentage of the troops appeared happy enough to remain on Ur-Tokar, and might refuse to comply with his orders. If he chose this course of action it would also mean delays and possible conflicts and disputes, whilst the local inhabitants might try to destroy his landing craft, which would be highly difficult to defend. He considered this to be by far the riskier course of action; he simply did not have the numbers necessary to pull it off successfully. It would be much easier to simply head straight for home, although this seemed to him to be unpatriotic and the incorrect course of action. He worried that the senior command on Zeleyan might not accept his excuses for such inaction - with all the implications that entailed.

He was also unsure of how exactly to deal with his eight captives. As far as he was concerned, they had all knowingly engaged in the sabotage of the Zeleyanian mission to Ur-Tokar, and he believed they should all be placed on trial to answer for their actions. The Zetans had removed many of the stasis pods from the ship to make more room for the cargo they transported, but there were still easily enough for all his captives – and also any soldiers who could be persuaded to return – so it would be easy enough to put them all in stasis for the journey home. They could then all be placed on trial to answer for the crimes they had committed. However, he was concerned that they might have programmed in early waking mechanisms - by which they could retake command of the ship - or effected some other means of regaining control he had not considered. Simply eliminating his captives here and now might be the easiest course of action. Alternatively, they could be placed in an escape pod or transporter craft and simply returned to Ur-Tokar, and he would be rid of the entire problem. But, again, would senior command see this as the correct course of action? He was far from certain, and was finding it difficult to make a definitive decision on both these matters.

A short time before all this occurred, and as the unfortunate developments unfolded in the forest clearing near to Lato, high above them on the Opa-Loka, Savverio had been monitoring the progress of the shuttle craft, as it first collected Mila Lustrom's group and then, a short while later, his crew-mates at Lato. He was therefore immediately aware of the unfolding and alarming situation on the planet below, and as the ship's computer was able to monitor exactly what was happening within the shuttle, he also knew exactly what was happening, to whom and when. Soon after becoming aware of the developing problem, he had returned an encrypted message to The Spirit of the Age informing them of the crew's predicament; he wasn't exactly sure how they could help, but figured they might be of some possible use, especially as he now knew they were in close proximity to the star system, since they had messaged him shortly before the crew had been captured. He also wanted them to know they were close to a potentially dangerous situation.

From the Opa-Loka he had the ability to control the shuttle craft, and immediately slowed its ascendency so he had more time to work through his options. He considered diverting the craft to various locations on Ur-Tokar or manipulating its life support systems, but, with his crew members held hostage at gun-point on board, he decided this was far too risky. As it ascended, though, he quickly set about altering the security protocols on the ship's computer, instructing it to give him preferential access and over-ride all other control instructions, whilst also keeping this instruction fully hidden and encrypted. Once he had completed the alterations to the system to his satisfaction and issued a range of new instructions, he relayed their details in a further encrypted message to The Spirit of the Age, by which time he had become aware they were half-way across the stellar system now, and on a direct bearing for Ur-Tokar. The starship would soon be dropping into orbit around the planet.

Once he had finalised these alterations and communications, he quickly departed from the upper floor of the ship and made his way to an area close to the cargo holds. He was hoping the rest of the crew would remember an emergency plan they had hatched in the event of their ship being boarded by hostile forces. Before long he had taken up place in his new location; one where he was still able to monitor events closely as they happened, whilst also retaining his control over certain features of the ship's systems, though without any third party being aware of his presence within the system. Shortly after taking up position, the doors to the hangar opened, the shuttle craft arrived safely in the landing bay, and he was pleased to hear that Jiaying had remembered their plan, but also noted the orders given to one of the soldiers to check the ship in case she was lying to them.

Savverio tracked the soldier's progress as he made his way cautiously through the cargo holds and the huge hangar containing the remaining stasis pods. After finding nothing in either area, the soldier made his way towards the various operations rooms on the cargo deck which he began to check one by one, though not particularly thoroughly, Savverio thought. Presumably, the soldier was not actually expecting to find very much. Savverio had been hoping he would follow such a course of action, and it was thus a supremely easy task to remotely lock down one of the doors behind him, close down the internal intercom and effectively isolate him from the rest of the ship. Now they only had three Zeleyanians to worry about.

Savverio then returned his attention to the forward deck and control room up above him on the highest deck. Monitors allowed him to closely follow what was happening in both rooms and he was relieved to see that everyone was now together in this location and still very much alive. He carefully noted the positions of everyone in the two rooms and the weapons held by the Zeleyanian soldiers. He then considered the various options he had previously figured might work out in this situation.

The first plan he considered – inspired by their earlier success on The Crusader - had been to don a protective space suit so he could temporarily alter the life support systems on the ship to induce unconsciousness in all the others, giving him enough time to disarm and bind the three soldiers, before returning the ventilation systems back to normal. He had seen Petra achieve this with ease on The Crusader, but he was less sure of his own ability to manipulate the life support systems, in particular whether he could get the oxygen levels exactly right and implemented quickly enough to effect his rescue plan. As he surveyed the scene in the two rooms, he wondered how the guards and Schultz would react as they realised what was occurring and whether this plan was, in fact, far too dangerous.

He therefore decided to check on the possibility of following Plan B before making any final decision, and was extremely relieved to see that The Spirit of The Age had already launched a shuttle craft which would soon be approaching the doors of the landing bay. He had released the security protocols to them for opening the cargo bay doors, and their arrival – both earlier in orbit around the planet and now within the ship - was not being actively registered by the ship's control systems, since he had previously isolated these functions from the main section of the computer system. He took another quick look on his console to make sure the situation on the top deck was still as it had been before, and then headed as quickly as he could towards the landing bay.

Once the cargo bay doors had closed behind the incoming shuttle craft he made his way across the landing bay, and gave the thumbs up to the pilot he could see sitting in the control section of the craft. The doors at the side opened and more than a dozen people emerged one after the other. Savverio had been expecting four or five members of a skeleton crew at most, so was somewhat taken aback by the small crowd that quickly gathered in front of him.

'Hi, I'm Savverio, good to see you, though I wasn't expecting this many people,' he announced to the group.
'We brought some friends out of stasis whilst we were decelerating through the star system. We thought that greater numbers might give us the edge, especially as there's only four of them to deal with,' explained Akiko, who was situated at the front of the group.
Savverio looked around them and thought he could work out who had recently come out of stasis – several of them still looked a bit spaced out, bleary-eyed and groggy – but he still said, 'good idea, extra numbers are bound to help. They're down to three now. I've locked one away in one of the operations rooms - we'll sort him out later. The rest are on the top floor

and have one pistol and a few knives between them. Now that you're here, I've got a plan for how we can deal with them.'

Whilst he said this, he noted that some of them had emerged from the craft armed with flare guns, presumably the ones typically stored in transporter craft for emergencies. 'I'm not sure those are a good idea. They won't actually kill anyone, you know, and in a confined space they could cause mayhem. Can we leave those as a last resort please, if you don't' mind?' he requested, aware that they might do more harm than good to the plan he had devised.

He then signaled for them to follow him, and returned to the improvised control room he had recently set up. There, he showed them live pictures of the control room, where Schultz was still working, the forward deck, where all the others were located and then various other relevant locations, so that they all had a complete picture of the present predicament, and then guided them carefully through the details of his plan.

Back on the forward deck, Mila, Jiaying, Neema and Kahlil had all been waiting for some form of opportunity to wrest back control of the situation, but had, as yet, thought of very little that might resolve their predicament. Before Schultz had left the forward deck for the control room, he had ordered the soldiers to bind the hands and legs of all the captives. They had then been placed on the fixed chairs that backed against the walls to either side of the doors that entered the room. The soldiers – armed with the pistol and knives - remained on guard, mostly on the far side of the room, and were thus able to closely observe the entire scene and note any move they might make.

As such, no opportunities for action had presented themselves so far. Jiaying had thought of every diversionary tactic she possibly could – requesting to go to the toilet or feigning illness, for instance - but was far from convinced any of them would actually work. Ultimately, she was hoping that Savverio was managing better than they were, and as time passed, and the fourth soldier showed no sign of returning, she started to believe that maybe Savverio had indeed worked out a rescue plan.

Down in the depths of the ship, quietly and cautiously, Savverio led the motley crew of Margallan and Rorque 4 departees from his temporary operations room up through the various floors to their designated destination on the top deck. Despite the extra effort required, they took the much narrower and darker auxiliary flight-tubes rather than the more obvious flight elevators, as there was less chance of their movements being discovered, or of Schultz being able to halt or slow their progress if he had somehow discovered Savverio's manipulation of the ship's systems and implemented a means of overriding his control protocols. The dusty auxiliary flight-tubes had clearly seen little use over the years, and it was a relief to finally emerge out onto the side corridors of the top deck a little while later. Savverio held the group up whilst he checked the situation on his console, keyed in a few alterations, checked the console again and then motioned for the group to follow him to the main corridor and down towards the doors at the front end of the ship.

For those on the forward deck, so little had happened since they were first bound and seated, that the initial fears and alarm of the captives had now turned very much to boredom. When a knock on the door and the entrance buzzer sounded, it suddenly startled them out of their semi-torpor. The guard with the gun waved it menacingly in the air and told them not to make a move or sound. He moved over to the door and studied the monitoring screen. The image showed the fourth soldier waiting outside whilst saying something none of them could actually hear very clearly. Jiaying's heart sank - how had Savverio failed to deal with him, she wondered. And then her thoughts became even darker; she suddenly wondered whether Savverio had been discovered and killed.

The guard manually unlocked the door at exactly the same moment as Schultz entered through the doorway from the control room. 'I was wondering where he had got to, what took you so long to . . .' Schultz never managed to finish his sentence, as more than a dozen figures suddenly poured through the doorway shouting and screaming, diverging immediately into two distinct groups as they did so. The guard with the gun – taken completely by surprise - was quickly overpowered by one group before he could make use of his weapon, whilst the other group made directly for the second guard across the room and achieved the same result moments later. Within seconds, both guards were disarmed and firmly pinned against the walls of the room by several determined bodies.

However, the presence of Schultz in the room had been unexpected – the plan had been to deal with him once the two guards had been overpowered and the pistol captured. The sub-lieutenant, taken completely by surprise himself, simply grabbed the nearest person heading past him – who happened to be Akiko – and had attempted to return with her to the control room, whilst the others pursued the two guards. It took a few seconds to register exactly who Schultz was, but Savverio and Zhavia, who were now in possession of the pistol, had quickly diverted from the plan and managed to block his route to the connecting door as he wrestled only half-successfully in his attempt to pull Akiko across the room. Ultimately Schultz was left cornered in the room whilst holding a knife to Akiko's throat.

Savverio moved forward towards them, 'you need to let her go, there's nowhere you can escape to now. You've lost. I have actual control of the ship, and if you harm her, we'll do the same to you and your guards,' he stated, trying to sound as authoritative as he possibly could.
'I'm going back to Zeleyan,' Schultz declared with all the confidence he could muster, 'you need to release my men, otherwise she's dead and it will be your responsibility.'
'There's no point in you returning to Zeleyan; there's been a revolution. Your regime has fallen and the new one won't want you back,' replied Savverio, who, at the same moment used his console to bring up a recent Zeleyan news report on the bluescreen that dominated the far wall of the room, knowing Schultz was unlikely to actually believe him.
Schultz watched the report, initially with scepticism, but with growing dismay as it became increasingly apparent that the news footage was clearly authentic and not some form of Zetan trickery.
'It's probably why your Supreme Commander called off the invasion of Ur-Tokar. Presumably, he thinks he can save the situation, but your two wealthiest provinces are controlled by the revolutionaries, and the third looks like it's going the same way. By the time he returns it will be all over. You might as well surrender to us. We won't harm you – we'll put you back on Ur-Tokar and then we're leaving. Let Akiko go without harming her and this can all end peacefully.'
'I'm not staying on Ur-Tokar' Schultz fumed contemptuously, 'if Supreme Commander Vartin thinks he can save Zeleyan then I'm joining him. The

revolutionaries will be a disorganised rabble. We will defeat them. Now you've got five seconds to release my men, or the girl dies,' he stated coldly, pressing the knife firmly against her throat, whilst hoping that the Zetan belief in solidarity with their comrades and opposition to loss of life, was as strong as they always claimed it to be.

'1 . . 2 . . 3 . . 4 . .', it might have been only a split second in reality, but for Akiko, it seemed like the fifth second of forever. She closed her eyes and wondered what it was like to die. Time froze. She wished she had done more with her life, that she had made more of a difference. She thought of her home planet, the friends she would never see again, her time spent on Rorque 4, her travels on The Spirit of the Age, the stars and the planets she had stared and wondered at, and the deep dark cold depths of space they had silently zoomed through at unbelievably high speeds.

And then, suddenly, there was a large, bright and unbelievably loud explosion above her head. She instinctively crouched and put her arms above her head. Fortunately for Akiko, Schultz did exactly the same, and a number of figures surged across the room, seized the knife from Schultz's hand, and pinned him firmly against the wall. Kiyona had fired one of the flare guns and the magnesium flare had smashed into the wall directly over Schultz's head.

The crew of the Opa-Loka and Mila Lustrom were all quickly untied, whilst Schultz was bound along with the two guards and then taken to a lower deck housing the escape pods. After a short while, they were joined by the fourth soldier – also bound – and the four of them, still bound, were strapped into one of the escape pods. Savverio programmed in the destination coordinates of Meridin and promptly dispatched the capsule to return the four Zeleyanians back down to the planet below. The pod detached silently from the ship and Savverio watched it for a while as it dropped slowly and gradually away from the ship - a small perfectly round silver object diminishing slowly against the backdrop of the blues, greens and whites of the planet - the starkness of the capsule standing out against the organic naturality of the forests, clouds and oceans it was descending towards. Eventually the capsule shrank in size until was only a small dot, indistinct against the white clouds, and Savverio turned away from the scene and headed towards the flight elevator to join the others at the front of the ship.

Arrival in Utopia

He suddenly realised it had been a very long morning, and he really needed a long cool drink.

Rorque 4 - Anna and Alex travel to Altair University

The journey to Altair University for Anna Dubois and Alex Kim had proven to be a largely uneventful one. They had left the smouldering ruins of the spaceport at Stratostan far behind them, and travelled south-westwards across the long flat plain that stretched for hundreds of kilometers all the way to the ferry port on the coast at New Nozike. Much of the plain was now blackened by the extensive fires and it was noticeable that very little scrub remained – the semi-desert was clearly turning rapidly into a true desert environment.

The roads were now largely empty, and they made good progress with their journey along the length of the motorway. Flat wide open spaces stretched to the horizon in whichever direction they cared to look. They had both spent almost their entire lives on the mountainous planet of Alpha Fraczan and such vistas rarely existed there, save for the occasional plateau landscape. Alex occasionally commented on the fact that he had never really become accustomed to the vast and never-ending landscapes on Rorque 4, and to the open and empty skies that stretched above their heads – the absence of any significant mountains or hills meant there were no significant visual landmarks to use as a means of identifying exactly where you were, or how far you were from anywhere.

They both gazed out of the autocar and across the huge flat vistas, typically still and lifeless except for the occasional isolated tree that had somehow escaped both fire and commercial usage. From time to time, they passed huge wind farms consisting of thousands of tall erect turbines that stretched evenly spaced from horizon to horizon, or huge arrays of dark rectangular solar panels blanketing the plain gathering the harsh sunlight; both sets of constructions creating electricity for the numerous homes and offices across the continent. As with all the colonised planets, there were, of course, no fossil fuels available for energy production, and most also lacked uranium for nuclear fission power plants. Almost all relied largely on vast quantities of renewable energy and Rorque 4 was no exception in this respect. They noticed, however, that many of the energy fields looked to have been damaged by fire and many of the wind turbines were no longer turning. There were already signs of neglect and disarray setting in.

Arrival in Utopia

Anna wondered how much longer electricity supplies would continue for. The large corporations were all leaving the planet and terminating their business operations. They had dominated the energy markets, having either driven the smaller competitors out of business or bought them all up a long time ago. She wondered if the few remaining human technicians would be able to keep the operations going - the corporation AI units having all been transferred to the departing stasis ships since they were considered far too valuable to be left behind. She had been worried that the ferry between the two continents might have terminated for similar reasons, but travel reports indicated it was still working to schedule, though again she wondered for how much longer.

By mid-morning they had made good progress after by-passing Motorway City, and by midday they had reached the normally bustling ferry-port, which was now considerably quieter than usual, commercial traffic having ground almost to a halt. The journey on the fully automated ferry across the Straits of Nozike was short and uneventful, though Anna continued to worry about potential travel difficulties. Her contract with the Rorque Corporation had effectively been terminated, and she was now running low on credit, though she had wondered whether she might obtain an instant loan from some credit agency somewhere – one that she would probably never need to pay back, she hoped. Even this might prove impossible though, she considered, since the Rorque Corporation should officially have left the planet two days previously, and since they dominated business activities on her continent, she presumed they had probably closed down all their numerous operations.

On the short ferry journey across the straits, Anna and Alex took themselves to the rear outside deck of the fully automated boat, and stood together watching its churning wake and the small number of seabirds that seemed to habitually follow the vessel in search of feeding opportunities. Whilst doing so, it suddenly occurred to Anna that they had not discussed their eventual destination, assuming they could actually get into space successfully.

'So where should we head for?' asked Anna, looking at Alex, the breeze blowing strongly through her hair.
'What do you mean, I thought we were going to Altair University', he asked, a little perplexed.
'No, once we've boarded The Avante. Which planet should we head for?'

'Ahh . . . I've not really given that much thought. I have no idea where Zarak 2 is, and it looks like the expedition to Planet X is now terminated - wherever in the cosmos that might actually be. I guess we stay in the Nexus Cluster,' he answered, not entirely helpfully.

'Yes, I sort of assumed that, but where exactly. Unfortunately, I suspect I will not be overly welcome on Margalla, after what I did to their crew members and their ship, though it does sound like a nice place,' offered Anna, who had clearly given the subject more consideration than Alex. 'Zeleyan is definitely a non-starter, for just about every reason you could possibly imagine, and I'm not sure I want to dispense with modern technology, so Ur-Tokar is also out of the running, and so I think that just leaves Zeta Kotlin, which is ironic given we both chose to avoid going there with the diaspora in the first place.'

'I've heard the Margallans are quite an easy-going people – they might also be forgiving. It sounded to me from the media emissions that it's very much like a holiday resort, so it might be good to spend some time there at some point in the future. It could be a possibility, though probably not in terms of careers, research and work purposes.'

'Even so, I don't think I'll push my luck on that one, and, yes, I understand they have no universities, as such, so probably a non-starter for people like us anyway,' Anna added.

'So, it looks like we're heading for Zeta Kotlin then. Yes, that is ironic, though somehow it seems a lot more welcoming now. After experiencing Rorque 4 and its dysfunctional society, life on Zeta Kotlin almost sounds normal. You never know, we might adapt and fit in, and maybe all our dreams will come true there instead,' Alex offered optimistically.

'Well, at least we won't be treated like human robots anymore - that at the very least will be a bonus. We might actually be respected as human beings once again; no longer treated like a customer with a numbered ticket, to be processed as quickly as possible in order to boost their profit margins – I so hated that aspect of their society. And I can wear what I want to wear again, not what the latest fashion gurus are telling me is oh-so crucially important if I don't want to be seen as socially redundant,' added Anna, beginning to feel liberated. 'What about you, what won't you miss?'

'I'm not sure,' Alex replied. 'I'm still mostly concerned with advancing my work, so I'd like more time and less supervision and fewer pressures to hit deadlines – more like back on Alpha, though I did appreciate the better resources here. It's ironic that I had too much time and too few resources on Alpha, and too little time but adequate resources on Rorque 4. So I guess, what I really need is both time and plentiful resources once we arrive on Zeta Kotlin.'

'They claim they've achieved a post-scarcity economy, so that actually might be a real possibility,' replied Anna. She paused for a moment. 'Another bonus is that I won't have the credit agencies chasing after me any more either. I managed to rack up a fair amount of debt here – my salary never seemed adequate, so I borrowed to make up for it. I didn't realise the interest rates rose automatically as the weeks passed, so I owe far more than I thought I would initially.'

'You were heavily in debt here?' Alex stated questioningly. 'I'm not surprised you can't wait to get out of this place,' he concluded.

Once across the straits, they found that, fortunately, there were still autocars available and running. A fellow passenger they had met on the ferry maintained that the corporation was officially ceasing all operations at midnight at the end of the week – this was being done for accounting reasons - so they had a few days left before the economy ground almost entirely to a halt. Alex had sufficient funds to pay for the journey, anyway, and they were soon back on their way. Again, the motorways were largely empty, and they assumed this was because nearly all the AI units and the majority of the key workers were now firmly ensconced – and also stranded - on the stasis ships orbiting high above the planet. The rest of the population had always struggled to afford lengthy journeys, and so had never use this form of transportation much anyway.

In anticipation of her imminent arrival at the university, she messaged several friends and colleagues who she knew had also failed to secure a place on a stasis ship – or declined the offer - and informed them of their plan, inviting them to join her if they wanted a place aboard The Avante. Towards the end of the afternoon they arrived at Altair University - where security now seemed to be entirely absent - and so, without further ado, they immediately made their way to the industrial unit on the outskirts of the campus, where the transporter craft remained unattended and forgotten about in a large and otherwise empty storage bay.

Arrival in Utopia

For Anna, the ease with which they had arrived at Altair University had been something of a surprise; much had gone wrong for her in recent weeks, and she was still half-expecting some disaster or other to halt her progress at any given point in their journey. So far, surprisingly, all was going to plan. Her next potential obstacle was access to the industrial unit and she was fully expecting her security clearance to have been terminated, and so was already wondering what implements might be at hand to force entry to the hangar. Surprisingly, the door simply slid open as she approached – maybe her security privileges also expired at midnight at the end of the week, she thought to herself. One inside the unit, Anna knew access to the shuttle craft was not an issue, as she had never been asked to rescind control of the codes by the university – presumably they had just forgotten all about its existence, or simply had more pressing issues to be concerned with in these troubled times.

They both entered the craft without any difficulties and carried out a quick check of the cockpit, passenger area and cargo hold. It had clearly been cleaned and tidied by the AI units, but other than that, it was just as she had left it several months previously. She entered the security codes that were still in her possession and the ship's computer immediately came to life. They waited several minutes whilst all the various functions booted up; the computer then ran the standard series of diagnostic checks, and eventually declared that the craft was fully functioning, fully fuelled and ready for departure. Given it had been recently repaired and serviced, this came as no surprise to either of them. Anna then checked her console and noted that several of her colleagues had agreed to join her, and were now hurriedly making their way from the university's various accommodation blocks to join them on the shuttle craft.

Anna waited anxiously in the cockpit for several minutes, she was still sure there would be some unpleasant twist to their unauthorised escape, and was wondering whether it might not have been better for the two of them to have simply made a rapid exit, rather than complicating matters by inviting extra passengers. However, as her colleagues began to appear in ones and twos, she greeted them warmly and felt pleased that she had followed her original line of thinking, whilst they engaged in short conversations concerning the departure plan and recent events on the planet. A short while later, she did a quick headcount in the passenger section and figured that just about everyone she had contacted had arrived – a couple turned up as she was doing so - when she suddenly noticed a tall dark haired figure in the doorway leading onto the shuttle.

'So where are you off to this time, Dubois – hijacking another ship for your own selfish purposes,' a loud mocking voice proclaimed. 'Don't worry, I won't tell anyone, your secrets safe with me.'

It was Ralph Parker – just about the last person on the planet she wanted to see at this precise moment, or indeed any moment. Her numerous encounters with him had almost invariably been negative ones. His arrogant boasting and numerous put-downs had initially been irritating, but his attempted rape had left her despising everything about him, and she had attempted to avoid his presence whenever and wherever possible. He had, she was absolutely certain, undoubtedly played a key part in her demise at the university.

A brief moment of panic swept over Anna, as she assumed that Parker had followed her colleagues, and was acting in some form of official capacity to prevent their departure. Then suddenly she realised that someone of his status should have already been safely in stasis on one of the starships, or at the very least with Jamieson's ill-fated departure convoy. It suddenly dawned on her that Parker must have been denied a place on the stasis ships – maybe Jamieson had finally tired of his boorish and irritating personality, she thought. She could almost picture the cold glee of Jamieson deciding to dispense with Parker's services. Several thoughts whirred through her head as to what her next move should be, but ultimately she decided to just play safe.

'We're heading to Zeta Kotlin, not that that has anything to do with you,' she eventually replied, as firmly and confidently as she could manage, but without hiding her disdain for him. 'I doubt you'll want to come. They're really not your kind of people.'
'Well that's where you're wrong Dubois,' retorted Parker, a man who could not bear to be excluded from anything. 'I'm coming along for the ride. I'm through with this place and that jumped-up jerk posh-boy Jamieson. He

wouldn't recognise talent if it ran him over in the middle of the road. I need a fresh start somewhere new, and Zeta Kotlin's as good as any place to start.'

Anna had not expected this response, and she looked around the room for some help from the others. She could see from her colleague's faces that they too were not impressed with Parker's performance – no doubt they had probably suffered at his hands at some point, and they knew of the attempted rape and her defeat at the ensuing tribunal. But it looked as though no one wanted any trouble, and despite some mutterings, no one threw her a lifeline, so she felt she had no choice but to offer him a seat on the flight. This was definitely not the outcome she had wanted, though she figured Zeta Kotlin was a large planet – hopefully she would never see him again, anyway.

She kept well out of Parker's way and returned to the control room where Alex was scanning in the final details of their flight programme to the Avante. 'Everything ready?' she asked.
'Yes, all ready to go. What about back there?' he replied.
'Fine, except we have some dickhead called Parker on board, but apart from that we're all ready to go.'
He looked at her questioningly.
'I'll tell you all about it as we ascend. Let's get out of here before there are any other problems.'

Anna instructed the computer to commence departure and the shuttle craft moved slowly towards the large doors at the front of the building, which slid slowly open as the craft taxied towards the front of the building. She then instructed the craft to travel towards the open plain that lay to the north of the university complex. After some tricky manoeuvring between various industrial units, they eventually arrived on the outskirts of the complex, and moments later they were ascending rapidly through the atmosphere and heading for inner space high above the planet's surface.

Anna looked out the cockpit window as they did so, once again noting the vast flat plains and absence of hills or mountains of any significant magnitude. The plains looked largely lifeless, dry and parched, blackened in numerous places. She noted the pale blue of the shallow seas to the south and the long curve of the coastline as it ultimately headed in a north-westerly direction. As they gained height the blue curvature of the coast was eventually replaced by the thin blue curve of the planet's atmosphere, and beyond it she could see the dark blackness of space and the twinkling of the stars. On this occasion, it looked almost welcoming.

She looked below again at the reddish-brown planet and its occasional shallow seas and scattered white clouds. She was glad to be leaving; Rorque 4 had not been kind to her. Her time on the planet had been a largely difficult and problematic one, replete with setbacks, and yet after such a promising start. She had become a different person, though she wasn't sure it was necessarily a better one. She had lost an element of her confidence, though she now realised it had been a naïve and sometimes arrogant confidence, and although she also felt she had become a wiser – and perhaps a more understanding – person, she somehow still resented Rorque 4's treatment of her. She wasn't sure she could forgive the planet just yet; painful memories were too fresh in her mind for that.

The journey to the Avante was a relatively short one, during which Anna recounted to Alex some of her unpleasant dealings with Ralph Parker. Alex looked concerned, and was clearly not happy that such a character was aboard the shuttle craft, though there seemed to him to be little they could actually do about his presence for the moment. He made a mental note that Parker should be one of the first to go into stasis, where he would be unable to cause any further problems, either for them or for the rest of the group.

Upon their arrival at the Avante, Alex gave the ship's computer the appropriate access codes, and to his great relief they proved to still be the correct ones, since the hanger doors opened promptly and smoothly in front of them. The shuttle craft manouevred its way into the cargo hold, and after touching down was secured to the deck and thus they had all made it safely aboard the vast ship, despite their earlier concerns. The small party of scientists, plus Parker, made its way carefully out of the transporter craft and waited in a group for further instructions.

'We need the ship's computer to locate the empty stasis pods which are still available for you. While that's being carried out, I will prepare a flight plan with the ship's computer for Zeta Kotlin. Once everyone is safely placed in stasis, we should be able to depart within an hour or so, I would have thought. The flight to Zeta Kotlin will take approximately two years, but I guess you know that already. Is that ok with everyone, are there any questions?' asked Alex.

'Fine, except for one thing. I will be taking over from here on,' Ralph Parker stated, as he moved away from the rest of the group, pulled out a high powered pistol from his jacket and aimed it directly at Alex. 'We will not be heading for Zeta Kotlin and all those pathetic socialists moaning on and on about injustice and poverty and whatever else they have a problem with. We will be going to Zeleyan instead - a planet with proper people and proper ways of doing things. There's none of that namby-pamby whining about inequality nonsense there,' he stated. 'I will take control from here on.'

Anna opened her mouth and was about to say something derogatory, and then thought better of it. However, Parker had noticed her reaction.

'Yes, you all underestimated me, yet again,' he started, never missing an opportunity to blow his own trumpet. 'Just like Jamieson – and look what happened to him,' he continued, despite the fact that he had played absolutely no part in the demise of Colin Jamieson. Looking at Anna, 'I knew you'd come back for that transporter craft at some point; I just needed to sit tight and wait and see exactly when it happened. Thanks for doing all the security stuff, but from here on in, I'm making the decisions. Now, let's make a move towards the forward deck and I don't want any heroics as I know how to use this thing. If you end up dead, that's your fault, not mine,' he finished menacingly.

The group looked visibly disappointed, but not wholly unsurprised, and felt they had no choice but to follow his instructions. Accordingly, they took one of the larger flight elevators to the upper decks and proceeded to the main control area of the ship adjacent to the forward deck. Upon arrival, Parker, who had remained very close to Alex throughout, started to instruct him in how he wanted to proceed, whilst, at the same time, Alex tried to work through in his mind how he could slow down or sabotage the actions Parker was demanding of him, and then ultimately find a means of sabotaging his entire plan.

Colin Jamieson had employed Ralph Parker because he recognised in him an ambitious bully, but one who would unquestioningly follow his own personal orders, not because he respected Jamieson, but because he wanted to demonstrate to others how important he was. Jamieson was a shrewd judge of character, since he also knew Parker was no astute tactician or strategist and thus of no threat to him personally. Parker generally assumed that everyone else essentially thought in the same boorish and arrogant way he did, but that most others were simply too stupid, feeble or cowardly to act upon these beliefs, whereas he was not.

As such, he persistently overestimated his own abilities, whilst underestimating those of others. As with so many of his endeavours, his current plan had not been thought through properly, if at all. It was one thing to share an entire planet with only one Ralph Parker, but Anna and her colleagues had no desire to live on a world which was dominated by thousands of people who thought and acted in the same manner in which he did. On this occasion, he had definitely underestimated the group's opposition to him – regarding them as weak and ineffective - whilst dramatically overestimating his own ability to control more than a dozen people in close proximity to him.

As they entered the forward decks, Anna and her colleagues exchanged furtive glances and they all knew what each other was thinking. As Parker issued instructions to Alex and then finally ordered him to hand control of the ship to him, the group bided their time and waited patiently for their opportunity. On the first occasion Parker stopped watching Alex intently and became distracted by the computer projections of their flight plan, the nearest members of the group all rushed him at the same time. If it had been a lone individual, Parker would no doubt have dealt with them without problem, but six people all at once took him completely by surprise and he was quickly overwhelmed in the melee, smashed violently against the wall by the group, and the pistol unceremoniously removed from his grip.

As the group untangled and ascertained exactly what the outcome of the brief fracas was, they discovered that Parker had been knocked unconscious as he hit the wall with such considerable force. Anna was not only massively relieved about the outcome, but could not help think that this made their decision-making considerably easier. 'I can think of several things I would like to do to him, but what do we think is actually our best strategy?' asked Anna.

Arrival in Utopia

'We could flush him out of an airlock. Then it won't be just his ego that is inflated,' suggested Anouk, one of the biochemists Anna had worked with on occasions, and with whom she had formed a reasonably good working relationship with, before her various travails.

'Much as I dislike the scumbag and would love to be rid of him forever – and the universe will definitely be a better place without him - I'm not a murderer, so I'd prefer a different approach,' replied Anna, though she had to admit she was tempted by the idea.

'We could just put him in stasis; Zeta Kotlin might be good for him, he might actually learn to behave like a proper human being once he's there,' suggested Kwame, another member of the group and someone who looked vaguely familiar to Alex; he was fairly sure he was some form of engineer, though he couldn't quite place where they had met.

'I'm not sure the poor people of Zeta Kotlin deserve such a punishment. I would also be concerned that he might somehow find some way of emerging from stasis early, and then who knows what damage he might do on the ship if he gains control over it,' offered Anouk, and judging from the reaction of some of the others, they clearly shared her worries. Most of them had experienced the unpleasant side of Ralph Parker at one time or another, and could easily imagine the unpleasant actions he might be prepared to pursue.

'I think that's highly unlikely, but I do sort of share your concerns. I think it would be better if he was not on the ship, conscious or unconscious. All these ships have escape pods, you know,' Alex informed them, 'we can simply put him into one of the capsules and send him back to Rorque 4. That's the obvious solution, in my opinion. We can leave him there to work out a way to survive on an unpleasant world that was partially of his own making. That would be fitting justice, I would say.'

'Yes, as the great Twenty-Second Century thinker Voraka once said, 'the demented man, deserves the demented planet he is on,'' quoted Anna.

Alex looked at Anna, slightly questioningly, but again assumed that her recent experiences probably explained this particular turn of thought.

Alex's suggestion was clearly supported by everyone present, and so they transported the unconscious body of the unwanted man to one of the lower decks and placed him into the nearest available escape pod. Alex programmed in some coordinates that equated to a semi-desert area on the continent of Northern Thule and moments later Ralph Parker was descending smoothly and rapidly back to Rorque 4, back to where he came from. Alex watched the small silver capsule descend towards the area of desert he had selected, diminishing in size as it did so. Gradually, the capsule grew smaller and smaller, until eventually it was just a tiny silver dot disappearing against the dark red of the continent, and then finally, as Alex watched on, it completely disappeared.

Once Alex returned to the forward deck, his first priority was to find the location of the remaining empty stasis pods for the Alphan colleagues who had ascended to the ship with him and Anna. He soon discovered there were easily sufficient pods to go around, and with several more to spare - presumably because of a handful of non-arrivals and the fiery destruction of the Cosmic Solutions elite convoy. Once everyone in the group had said their farewells and readied themselves for the long deep sleep of stasis, the AI units led them to their appointed pod and then proceeded to take them through the standard procedures for entering stasis. A short while later, everything in the huge hangar had been completed, and the ship and its passengers were effectively ready for departure.

Alex and Anna would be the last to enter stasis. Firstly, though, they spent some time together in the control room finalising their preparations for the journey. Alex ensured the ship's computer was following the exact route and trajectory he wanted for their journey to Zeta Kotlin. He also checked that all the AI units were correctly programmed. Both he and Anna knew, from personal experience, what could occur if such checks were not actually undertaken. Once this was completed, they felt they could take stock of the situation and relax a little. Their day had been a long and eventful one, and during that time they had come to know and appreciate each far better than during their much more casual acquaintanceship back on Alpha Fraczan.

'There's thousands of people on this ship who will eventually wake up on a planet they were not expecting to be on,' Alex thought out aloud, suddenly aware of the implications of what he was doing.
'I know; we seem to be making a habit of doing this. How do we keep ending up in situations like this?' Anna replied. 'I wonder how they're all going to cope on Zeta Kotlin. I assume that all the passengers on this ship are mostly

go-getting, ambitious, obedient corporate types, and they're soon going to be on a planet committed fully to a system of egalitarianism and collective decision-making. I suspect it's going to be a huge culture shock for them.'

'I expect they will just have to adapt. After all, we became more like the people on Rorque 4 – I'm somewhat ashamed to say – you just have to fit in with your environment and the structures you're working within, I guess. Human behaviour is quite flexible and we're capable of rationalising all sorts of situations – assuming they're not too bizarre or harmful. If you don't adapt, well . . .' he tailed off, they both knew the problems they had recently encountered.

'It seems highly ironic that we both headed for Rorque 4 to pursue our own personal ambitions on a planet devoted to individualism, and now we're heading to one based on collectivism. Is that because we're individual failures or because we realise the failure of individualism?' Anna pontificated, as she watched Alex monitor one change after another on the data inputs - the ship's computer methodically working its way through yet another series of data. She was fairly sure now that the answer to her question was definitely the latter.

'Well the whole planet is falling apart, and I'm sure that excessive individualism is part of the reason for that. I don't think we were failures, though; it's just that we failed on their terms - terms we did not fully understand, until it was too late. On Alpha Fraczan, we would still be methodically working away on our research. If it produced insightful knowledge, we would be regarded as successful. It all depends on who's doing the judging, I guess,' replied Alex. 'I think I was quite naïve before I arrived here. I'd never given social structures much thought. I just thought that only science and engineering were important. I was obsessed with how machines work, with engineering techniques, aeronautical equations, rocket ships and other machines – a bit of a motorhead really. For me, it was a case of all hail the machine, as far as I was concerned. Completely lost in science! But now I've realised how crucial the elements of wider society are – economics, politics, social agencies and suchlike. They all affect how you work, and I never really realised that before. I've had problems here, but I think I'm a wiser person now, and I certainly now appreciate the more collegiate approach we had back on Alpha.'

Anna had the distinct impression this was something he had been thinking about for some time. 'How well do you think we will fit in on Zeta Kotlin, then?' she asked.

'Well, at least on Zeta Kotlin we will be treated like human beings, rather than corporate robots. I suspect the problem there might be needing to work at the pace of the wider team; it might be a bit slow and chaotic, I suspect. I guess we can forget about trying to be outstanding figures in our field, as well. Their measure of success is based largely on whether your work improves society as a whole or not,' he answered. 'That's not such a bad thing, though, I can live with that. Knowing I made a contribution . . . I don't think that's such a big problem.'

'And after what we've witnessed on Rorque 4, that really isn't such a bad thing,' added Anna. 'They really could do with a healthy dose of cooperation and more consideration for the wider population.'

'What about you, how will you cope on a socialist planet? What about your plans and ambitions?' he asked, whilst making the final alteration to the flight details, and then commencing the countdown for departure.

'My ambitions have changed entirely. I used to think it was all about rising towards the top, to gaining promotions and becoming more and more important – to be elevated above the rest, to gaining accolades and universal recognition. But now, I can't even remember why I wanted to do that - I guess it was just what my family expected, as I was growing up. On Alpha it was all fine, it just entailed holding higher positions of office, but on Rorque 4, it was damaging me as a person. I was expected to treat others as pawns in a game, rather than as real human beings. I had to treat people in ways I considered wholly unacceptable, and I found I just couldn't do it. I guess I'm just not cut out for that kind of elitism, so a socialist planet might actually suit me now.'

Alex nodded and smiled, and looked as though he fully understood her feelings, though he said nothing.

With that admission, she felt they had both done enough philosophising, but it also felt good to finally admit the truth to herself, and also to someone who could understand how she felt. And, she felt far more relaxed now after the travails of the long day, and the realisation that her ordeal had finally ended.

Arrival in Utopia

She moved over towards Alex. 'I was wondering something, though, have you ever made love in space?' she asked, smiling warmly at him.

'No, but it's something I've always wanted to try,' he replied, and as the ship began to lift out of orbit, so they made their way as casually as they could to the crew's quarters.

Outside in space, the starship accelerated rapidly away from the reddish-brown planet, past the sleeping Morpheus and away across Eleutheria's gravitational ambit; its asteroid belts, dwarf planets and Oort cloud, and then finally out beyond its outer influence and into the endless darkness and isolation of inter-stellar space. Inside The Avante, though, Anna and Alex were feeling far from isolated and spent the next few days -as so many space pioneers felt the need to do so - exploring the different possibilities that sex in a low gravitational environment offered, and against the backdrop of the entire star-studded cosmos. Their time together proved to be not just an exploration of each other and unusual sexual positions, but also a cathartic one, for as the two became one, they left behind the disappointments, the frustrations and the failings they had endured on the neo-liberal planet.

After several days of travel and togetherness, the starship – now fully locked into interstellar overdrive - was fully secure and safely on its long journey, first towards the centre of the Nexus Cluster, a trajectory that would ultimately take them past Rogan's star system and then onwards to Zeta Kotlin. Anna and Alex were in a much more comfortable place now – both physically and emotionally - and, despite the temptation to do otherwise, agreed it was now the right time to enter stasis and remain there until they reawakened on the far side of the Nexus Cluster. They made their way to adjacent stasis pods with the accompanying AI unit, kissed passionately, climbed into the capsules and followed the standard stasis immersion procedures. Before long, they were both in deep stasis, unconscious and hopelessly lost in the wastelands of sleep. Once certain that all was as it should be, the AI unit made its way calmly and unhurriedly back to the control room on the upper deck to help oversee the safe journey of the vast spaceship onwards to its ultimate destination.

Arrival in Utopia

Ur-Tokar – the departure of the starships

The mood on The Opa-Loka once the Zeleyanian soldiers had been returned to the surface of Ur-Tokar had quickly turned from one of high tension to huge relief and joy. Akiko, in particular, was full of admiration for the others and spent a considerable amount of time thanking them for saving her life. Her society was a highly communitarian one, but no one had ever actually risked their life to save her, and she felt eternally grateful for their rescue from what she had assumed was going to be certain death. The others all hugged and kissed her, also relieved the worst had not come to pass.

Once the mood had calmed a little though - and after Savverio had explained to the former captives how exactly their rescue had been effected - various introductions and welcomes were made between the two sets of crew members. Once these were completed, it slowly dawned upon the crew of the Opa-Loka that they could now finally contemplate the return journey home to their respective communities. There had been several false dawns with regards to their departure from the planet, but this time it felt like their time at Ur-Tokar was now genuinely and finally over. The Zeleyanians had been completely vanquished, the ship was now in good working order and their mining operation fully completed. There was nothing now that could prevent them from returning to their home planet of Zeta Kotlin.

Before they actually commenced their departure, though, Jiaying and Savverio wanted to spend some time with Akiko, Kiyona and the other Margallans and catch up on old times, exchange information and hear about their recent adventures. They had both visited Margalla on previous trading missions and had thoroughly enjoyed their time there, and wanted to know whether it was still as charming and friendly as they remembered. Together they all relocated to one of the larger crew quarters and, over food and drink, reminisced over their shared past, and the various boat trips, parties and gatherings they had shared together, in what now seemed like a lifetime ago.

As they did so, Jiaying, in particular, began to feel pangs of nostalgia for the time she had spent on Margalla. For her, the island archipelago had always been the perfect destination on which to spend time relaxing, sunbathing, swimming and partying – away from the difficulties of space travel. She remembered the warm kiss of the sun's rays, the soft evening breezes blowing across the sandy beaches, crystal clear waters, the friendly people, the warm relationships and the excellent, locally produced, food and drink. She could only ever remember enjoying herself there – it truly was a utopia, she thought to herself.

An idea then occurred to her. Both their spaceships were planning on heading to Zeta Kotlin, but there was no need for the Margallans to do so anymore. They could transfer all the minerals and ore from the Opa-Loka onto The Spirit of The Age, which could then continue onwards - with its complement of scientists still in stasis – to its original destination. Those wanting to journey to Margalla - which now included herself - would all remain on the Opa-Loka and travel there directly. They could eventually retrieve their respective starships at some convenient time in the future. She put this to the assembled gathering, who all decided this was a great idea, especially the Margallans, who were particularly keen to return to their communities after their long unwanted ordeal on Rorque 4.

The transfer of the minerals and ores took the AI units a while longer than was initially expected. The cargo bays and various holds on the lower decks of the space vessel had to be emptied of old and unwanted junk, and a number of walls opened up to obtain easier access and create much larger repositories for the ore. During this short delay, the Margallans, and their comrades from Rorque 4, took the opportunity to enjoy some sightseeing on Ur-Tokar, though they were ultra-careful to avoid any encounters with disaffected Zeleyanian troops or disgruntled ex-monarchists, and steered well clear of any of the planet's few habitations. They had already been stranded against their will on one planet and were in no hurry to repeat the exercise again. As with the Zetan crew members, they too could not help but be impressed by the stark, pristine beauty of the partially frozen planet, which was so unlike that of the sub-tropical island home on their own world.

Finally, once the transfer of mineral ores was complete, the respective parties headed for the particular starship that was heading to their chosen destination. Mila Lustrom and her colleagues, whilst tempted by what they had heard about Margalla, were keen to spend time with their fellow Alphans at whichever university they opted for on Zeta Kotlin, and to thoroughly analysing the data they had acquired on Ur-Tokar, in order to develop their new theories in astrobiology. Before changing ships, though, Mila indicated she was particularly interested in obtaining data from Margalla and requested that Akiko send her as much of her own research as possible. The two of them could liaise in future and compare evolutionary processes on their different planets.

The Margallans and their associates from Rorque 4 all chose to head for Margalla, with the sole exception of Arlo who fancied spending some time travelling and sightseeing on Zeta Kotlin before returning eventually to Margalla. Neema, Janicka and Kahlil were all looking forward to seeing their friends and returning to their communities on Zeta, but both Savverio and Jiaying wanted to spend some time relaxing on Margalla, before making any future decisions about their lives. Jiaying was already considering the idea that she might never leave – she had spent more than enough time in space, she possessed few strong ties on Zeta Kotlin, and she could think of no better place to retire from space travel to than Margalla's sub-tropical islands and beaches.

As they departed, they all exchanged goodbyes and promised to keep in touch and meet up again in the future. Those not needed for the departure crews were immersed straight into stasis, whilst the respective skeleton crews went through the standard departure procedures. A short time later, and the two ships were boosting their engines, accelerating, lifting out of orbit, and rapidly gaining speed as they headed in their respective directions. Both skeleton crews looked back at Ur-Tokar and wondered what the future held for the small, strange and beautiful planet.

The Opa-Loka passed the glitterball planet of Corusa as it made its departure, and the crew - just as Vice-Admiral Rosson had done only a few short months before - marveled at its unique and strange sparkling nature. Travelling on a completely different trajectory, the crew of The Spirit of the Age took in the strange beauty of Lapiz as they exited Rogan's diminutive stellar system. They too were intrigued by the way its outer blue-grey gaseous layer was being stripped slowly away, floating out into the wastes of space, and exposing the intensely violent electrical activity of the golden void shimmering below. Neither crew, though, attributed any strange or mystical explanation to the appearance of either planet.

Arrival in Utopia

Once well beyond Rogan's gravitational field, those aboard the Opa-Loka gathered on the observation deck for one last time before entering stasis. They took the opportunity to spend some time gazing out at the space scene that lay before them.

'I can't believe how beautiful space really is,' expressed Zhavia. 'At night, the stars and the Milky Way look impressive from the planetary surface, but up here they're quite spectacular. There are so many of them, and so many colours – reds and whites, yellow ones and even a few blue ones. And you can actually see some of the spiral galaxies and the amazing gas clouds. I don't think I could ever get tired of looking at them. It's just the most spectacular sight you could ever imagine.'

'And the sheer number of stars and galaxies, the distances between them and the age of the universe; it's impossible to get your head round the mind-boggling numbers,' added Zek. 'It's just utterly amazing.'

'I wonder how many now have human civilisations on the planets around them, and whether we'll just keep spreading across the galaxy, now that we've got properly started,' pondered Zhavia.

'I suspect that as civilisations rise and fall, we'll have no choice but to keep moving on occasionally. Judging by the experiences in our own star cluster, that's probably going to happen every now and again, I suspect,' offered Savverio.

'Which reminds me, what do you think will happen now on Ur-Tokar?' asked Akiko. 'Will the situation stabilise there?'

'It's difficult to say exactly. The Zeleyanians are completely defeated and there are very few of them left anyway,' answered Savverio. 'I suspect those left will be absorbed into the existing societies. There's also a lot of empty space for those wanting to live elsewhere. Whether the lowlanders adopt a more progressive form of society, now that the aristocratic class has been eliminated, is more difficult to say, but I guess it's possible, since the Mountain People have shown it can definitely be done.'

'Surely the peasants and townspeople won't want to be under the oppressive monarchist yoke again,' interjected Jiaying. 'Why would anyone in their right mind want to do that? Surely they can see the Mountain People's way of life is infinitely better. I'd take that any day.'

'I heard a rumour that you were thinking of staying with them permanently,' said Kiyona. 'Is that true?'

'Yes, I did seriously consider staying on Ur-Tokar. The planet is so beautiful and the Mountain People just intrigue me. I did really give it some serious consideration.'

'So, what changed your mind?'

'I think it was partly the frightening experience with the Zeleyanian soldiers, but, more importantly, I'm not sure I could give up all the benefits of modern technology forever. Their lifestyle is a beautiful one, but it's also quite hard work and has many difficulties and hazards. And then when the opportunity to head straight to Margalla arose, well, that decided it for me. How could you turn down retirement to a sub-tropical island utopia?'

They all laughed at this, and the Margallans were once again reminded of their good fortune.

The crew members spent a little while longer admiring the spacescape, but eventually, after further conversations, they ultimately decided it was time to become reacquainted with their stasis pods. A short while later, they all entered stasis and the ship was safely locked down for their long voyage home.

The two starships headed out, away from Rogan, into the long black corridor of interstellar space, their respective flightpaths taking them on diverging trajectories into the Near Sector of the Nexus Cluster. Outside their spacecraft lay nothing but the dark unending infinity of space, its stark bleakness and cold neutrality lay all around them, neither threatening nor comforting, just an unending nothingness. Inside, the human life forms remained warm and alive, the passengers safely cocooned in the torpor and deep sleep of stasis, oblivious to the billions of stars and galaxies visibly sprinkled across the frozen bleakness. Both stasis ships would journey through the immense unending darkness of space for a period of sixteen months, and then finally, departing from the nothingness, they would arrive at their respective destinations, back with their communities, back on the warm welcoming planetary islands that were little more than dots of light in that vast dark unwelcoming cosmos.

PART 4

All Change in the Nexus Cluster

Arrival in Utopia

Ur-Tokar – Rosson in the mountains

Former Vice-Admiral Rosson looked out across the broad and lightly forested valley that stretched far below his cabin, taking in the fantastic view that lay before him on yet another stunning Ur-Tokar morning. Somewhere behind him a woodpecker drummed loudly on a dead pine tree, and there was the constant buzz of bees and various other insects that had made his forest garden their home. High overhead, a thin line of stratocumulus clouds moved briskly eastwards, pushed along by the high altitudinal winds that were a prominent feature of the weather at this level of elevation.

The previous evening he had watched the pale purple moon of Arioch rise above the towering purple Zarozinian Mountains in the western skies. Clear nights of crisp cold night air – common at this altitude – allowed him a clear and spectacular view of the starry firmament high above in the darkness. Shooting stars were a frequent sight as they arrowed their way diagonally downwards only to end in a sudden darkness, their fiery trail extinguished by the planet's atmosphere. On occasions, particularly on the coldest winter nights, he was sometimes lucky enough to glimpse a bank of shimmering purple or green light in the northern reaches of the sky, hovering restlessly above the dim and distant northern icecap. On this particular morning he was watching Arioch disappear over the low-lying hills that bordered the distant eastern ocean.

The seasons where he had chosen to make his new abode changed slowly and subtly, almost indiscernibly. Located towards the higher reaches of the northern tropic zone – but on a planet distantly orbiting a smallish red dwarf star – the climate at this altitude was various shades of mild and cool, occasional snowy spells in the winter, and prolonged periods of warming sun under anticyclonic skies in the summer. Rainfall was infrequent but melting snow from higher altitudes provided all and more of the water he could possibly need. A very fine overnight sprinkling of soft powdery snow this morning indicated that autumn was finally giving way to the crisper cooler days of winter.

As was the case with nearly every day that passed at his new abode, he reflected once again on his decision to defect from the Zeleyanian spacefleet, and he came to the same conclusion as he always did – it was the wisest course of action he had ever taken. Despite this thought, the first few months had been a slightly nervous affair. The contacts he had developed amongst the Mountain People had recommended this area, far to the east of the precipitous Zarozinian Mountains – a sparsely populated region characterised by a further range of rugged snow-capped mountains, though on a significantly less grand scale. Further from the western oceans, it was accordingly drier, but still characterised by a mixture of upland coniferous and deciduous forest, fast-flowing mountain streams and areas of open mountain plateau. It had been considered sufficiently remote and hidden for him to evade Vartin and his security forces – on the then assumption that the Zeleyanians were continuing with their invasion plan - even from the planetary scans carried out by stasis ships high above in orbit.

Whilst he and his fellow deserters all possessed some rudimentary survival skills and outdoors knowledge, they had been very much reliant on help and advice from the other cabin dwellers in the valley for the construction of their new dwellings - close to mountain streams and suitable for developing small plots of land capable of supplying a reasonable percentage of their dietary needs. The local Mountain People had shown them the best areas for foraging, and also the forest foods that were suitable, safe and abundant enough for consumption. Rosson had frequently been impressed with both their local knowledge, and by exactly how much could be achieved with such limited levels of technology.

At all times they had impressed upon Rosson and his fellow Zeleyanians the importance of working with the environment - rather than against it - and the imperative of maintaining sustainability within the natural world. In particular, they stressed the importance of respecting the animal life as sentient life forms in their own right, as beings that had evolved over millions of years to suit particular environmental niches and perform vital roles within healthy working ecosystems. They were, under no condition, to be treated as beasts of burden, pets, a form of entertainment or purely as a source of food or clothing or any other type of selfish anthropic desire that debased their existence within the wider biosphere. This, they stressed, was where the human race had gone so badly wrong back on Earth.

Arrival in Utopia

On occasions, when there was little in the way of provisioning, foraging or building work needing to be dealt with, he joined either his fellow Zeleyanians or the local Mountain People on expeditions to scale the mountains to the north of them, usually for no other reason than to admire the spectacular views or to simply test his mountaineering skills. On other occasions he would hike through the forests, familiarising himself with the terrain, the plants, the animals and the subtle changes in the seasons. At the foot of the valley lay the River Naess, a medium-sized mountain waterway, its icy cold waters meandering slowly through the lower reaches of the upland region. Here he could spend long hours canoeing on the river far below the peaks that towered distantly on both its sides, fishing or simply absorbing the peace and tranquility of the river valley.

His life now was a much simpler one, and all the more enjoyable for it. He had passed through his winter of discontent and emerged successfully on the other side. He could luxuriate in the late afternoon sunshine as it warmed the mountainside, enjoy the exhilarating fresh mountain breezes and admire the amazing alpine vistas that lay stretching in all directions around him. Treks through the mountain forests invariably led to new discoveries and amazing surprises. The satisfaction he gained from the successful tracking of a deer or a wild boar, the delights of the forest fruits, nuts and berries he foraged and the cultivation of vegetable and grains on his land was - like the locally brewed beer – unlike anything he had ever experienced before. He had even learnt to work with nature and not against it; what once were seen as garden pests were now valuable aids in the small semi-artificial ecosystem that surrounded his cabin and produced so much of what he needed. Occasionally there were failures, setbacks and minor disasters, but these were all part of the learning curve he was determined to master.

The long and frequent days in the wilderness were also chosen, though, to refrain from occasional visits to the hamlets and mountain settlements farther to the west. He knew that even here the hills have ears, and was keen to keep his whereabouts a complete and total secret. At a later date, news that Vartin had called off the invasion and returned to Zeleyan had eventually filtered through to his community, though he was initially wary of believing that his fortunes had taken another major turn for the better. As time passed though, and the news of the invasion fleet's non-arrival remained consistent, he found he could relax far more and start to fully enjoy his new life in the mountains. Even after this news though, he tended to keep to himself and the company of his fellow Zeleyanians. Given his previous background, he was still unsure of how the lowlanders and some sections of the Mountain People might treat him, and he had decided to remain in the splendid isolation of his mountain retreat and its immediate wilderness, at least for the immediate future, anyway.

The relaxed pace of his new lifestyle did mean, however, that he was able to reflect on his past life at considerable leisure and over extended periods at a time. By no stretch of the imagination did he miss the oppressive nature of the Zeleyanian military. The rigid hierarchy, the stiff conformity, the endless giving and taking of orders, the starched uniforms and the pointless pomp and ceremony of the parades were all, for Rosson, a thing of the dim and distant past. He frequently reminded himself of how lucky he was in his newfound situation. He had always felt deep down as though he was a square peg in a round hole - the military system had slowly but inexorably damaged him as a person.

There had been the impelling drive to preserve the fascist regime at any price, at no matter what the cost, no matter how many lives were ruined or destroyed and no matter what the damage it caused to the individuals involved. The casualty list had been a long and painful one. And then there had been the unnatural responsibilities of leadership, the pressure from above to deliver, and the possibility of a sudden and dramatic fall from his lofty position; all this had led to a sense of semi-permanent insecurity and occasional damaging bouts of anxiety.

At the outset of his career he had been a relatively open, honest and trusting individual, but the political intrigues, deceptive conversations, shaded pretences and false appearances, the quests for promotion, and the shifting alliances of friends and enemies as he manouevred his way through the upper echelons of the hierarchy had all turned him into a more deceitful, mistrusting and suspicious person. He had constantly needed to watch his back, and develop the ability to second guess his rivals and enemies. None of this had come naturally and he had made some serious errors of judgement along the way; one of which, though - he reflected upon ironically - had fortuitously resulted in his current Arcadian lifestyle.

In his former life, he had been something of a Steppenwolf-like figure. On the outside he had been - to all intents and purposes - a civilised, perfectly respectable, typically urban figure with the correct manners, appropriate dress, polite conversation and respect for the rules and regulations in all their different forms. But on the inside there had been the inner rural wolf struggling to emerge, to be at one with nature, to do what came naturally, to live life under the moons and the stars, experience the shifting of the seasons and the changes of the weather - just as they were meant to be known. The two competing versions fighting within him had resulted in some strange decisions, distorted actions and displaced behaviours. He was now more than pleased that the inner wolf had finally succeeded and he could be the human he really wanted to be.

This reflection reminded him of the only part of his previous life he actually missed; viewing the extraordinary planets orbiting around the various stellar systems he had been lucky enough to visit. In particular, he remembered the impressive glitterball planet of Kristilla, circling the forgotten star of Necron, the shimmering firestorms of Corusa and the mysterious Lapiz, slowly but inexorably being stripped of its outer layers. He now wondered if this planetary interest had been a pure form of escapism – a means of mentally evading the rest of his oppressive life, or was he correct as he had thought at the time, that the planets held some form of a message for him – or even wider humanity – and that in some strange and intriguing way they had led him to his present blissful utopia. It was the nature of these things that he would probably never know, he guessed.

Nevertheless, he was planning to stay close to the planets in one particular way - he was constructing a telescope so he could watch the heavens, study the stars, follow the planets and just generally remain in awe of the wonders of space and the night sky. He was slightly worried it might be considered by others in his community as advanced technology, but he was only making a single instrument, and the metals and optics he needed were well within the capabilities of the local artisans, so he figured he could defend his decision to do so if he really needed to. He was keenly looking forward to developing his new found interest in astronomy. He had managed to locate his old home star of Hedilla in the night sky and was hoping for better views through his telescope, though he was not entirely sure why - probably for no other reason than curiosity.

On occasions, he also thought of his family, friends and colleagues back on Zeleyan, sometimes with a certain degree of nostalgia, but more usually he could only remember the superficiality of his former life and the relationships within it, especially when he compared them with the ones he was now cultivating and developing. His increasingly intimate knowledge of the land, his love of the flora and fauna, his close connection with nature and the passing seasons, and the companionship and solidarity of his fellow cabin dwellers and a shared passion for the wild were orders of magnitude better than those of his previous existence.

On occasions, whilst looking at the myriad stars in the night sky, he had wondered why the Zeleyanian fleet had called off its invasion and returned to their home planet. Had he himself played a significant role in the decision to cancel the imperial venture? Had it resulted from the various calamities, failures and upsets that he had been partly responsible for? Or was it the deterioration of their relationship with the Rorque Corporation, and an awareness that invasions of further planets, especially Zeta Kotlin, were likely to be a non-starter? He had later been made aware of the Zetan trading ship's role in the whole affair – how significant had their impact been on the unraveling of his imperial adventure, he wondered.

He speculated whether the multiple failures had eventually got to Vartin, to such a degree that he had finally cracked and made the decision to return home. He suspected not. Vartin was a single-minded, driven and ambitious man wanting to make his mark in history, to follow in the footsteps of the great one. It would take more than a few minor set-backs and failures to force his return to Zeleyan. He remembered the last news reports he had seen emanating from Zeleyan; they sounded suspiciously as though the regime was in increasingly deep trouble. He suspected Vartin had retreated to save his own regime – that seemed like a more plausible explanation for his sudden about turn. If he was correct and that was the real cause, he wondered whether Vartin had succeeded or failed. He suspected he might never know.

Arrival in Utopia

Zeleyan – the return of the invasion fleet

The speed with which the fascist regime on Zeleyan collapsed had been quite staggering. Historically, it had appeared strong and stable - at least from the outside - destined to last for decades or even centuries, even if what longevity it had managed to achieve was largely the product of fear and repression. The latter, though, meant that the regime held no authentic legitimacy, no genuine popular support, and once the people lost their fear - and the massed ranks of armed troops switched sides - the regime simply collapsed like a house of cards.

On the inside, the regime had been held together by an intimate and extensive network of bribery, nepotism, and cronyism; none of those at the top had arrived at their positions through merit, hard-work or by means of popular demand. When the regime collapsed, they all collapsed vertiginously with it. And a political vacuum quickly developed, one which was filled just as rapidly by the revolutionary groupings that mushroomed across the entire supercontinent during the course of the insurrection.

As is oft repeated, there is nothing quite as strong as an idea whose time has come, and the people of Zeleyan had grown thoroughly tired of authoritarianism, conservatism, repression and arbitrary brutality. The planetary civilisation had originally emerged in order to implement the dreams and desires of disparate right-wing nationalist refugees from Earth, but as the generations that followed waxed and waned, they in turn had developed an entirely different set of dreams and desires – ones shaped by their new environment and the circumstances of the planet they actually lived upon. They sought a society based on trust and cooperation, and on freedom and equality for all of its citizens, not just for a tiny privileged few. They were all Zeleyanians now, and that had been the case for several generations.

They wanted to share in the delights and the wealth of their new planet – benefits that should be enjoyed by the entire population, - and Zeleyan was a fertile, climatically pleasant and potentially wealthy planet. Over the intervening decades the economy had developed steadily; agricultural lands had been developed within the low-lying and fertile river valleys, whilst industrial centres had been successfully created along the coastlines – the iron dream having been finally realised. Development may have been a little slow – the security of the regime had always enjoyed preeminence in the hierarchy of considerations – but their civilisation was one now capable of supporting the entire population at a level of material non-scarcity, and the people somehow instinctively knew this.

Zeleyan City had fallen quickly and almost without bloodshed to a popular internal uprising. The city was easily defended from hostile external forces, but when the opposition came from within the city itself, its defense was an entirely different matter - especially once the troops had mutinied and summarily executed General Plenge. With the capital in the hands of the rebels, insurrection then swept through Outer Padnia and finally to the less developed lands of the Northern Alliance. The whole population knew that the Supreme Commander, large numbers of military AI units, and the hated Patriotic Guard – Vartin's elite regiment associated with the most brutal massacres by the regime – were absent and engaged otherwise with the imperial conquest of Ur-Tokar. It was the perfect time to dispense with the regime.

By the time the three tired space ships returned wearily to their home planet after the aborted mission to invade and colonise Ur-Tokar, the rebels were firmly and fully in control of the entire supercontinent. The political, military, economic and social apparatus were all now subject to genuinely popular control, and, whilst there were lengthy debates and discussions as to the exact nature of the society that should follow, they were all united in the belief that Vartin and his fellow travellers had absolutely no role to play in that future society. There was, though, a general feeling that they would seek and find ways to reimpose their authoritarian brutality, and could thus never be genuinely trusted. Other measures would be needed to deal with them.

Knowledge of the failure of Vartin's invasion fleet to reach Ur-Tokar and its sudden retreat back towards Zeleyan had already been widely disseminated across the planet. Initially, the revolutionaries had assumed that this was driven entirely by his desire to save his own regime, but over the ensuing weeks information had emerged strongly indicating that the forward military mission on Ur-Tokar had faced several operational difficulties, and that the regime's dealings with the dying economic system of Rorque 4 had ultimately proven to be a failure. It gradually became apparent that the whole imperial venture had been an utter failure – and a very expensive one at that. The spaceport at Gombos – now firmly in the hands of the revolutionaries - carefully tracked the position of the returning stasis ships and the planet readied itself for the return of the three military spacecraft.

Aboard The Patriot IV, Vartin had ordered the ship's computer to awaken only himself and three carefully selected junior officers from stasis, seven days prior to their expected time of arrival. He had not informed the officers of exactly why the mission to Ur-Tokar had been aborted, other than to explain that Zeleyan was facing a full-scale left-wing rebellion, and it was their patriotic duty to make a full and proper appraisal of the political and military situation on the planet and report back to him immediately. This they duly performed and he was shocked to discover the news that the entire planet had fallen firmly into the hands of the rebels. Even worse, the rebel forces seemed to be largely united and appeared to enjoy a high degree of popular support amongst the wider population.

Vartin – far too late – realised that the elite sections of his regime had become wholly disconnected from the mass of the people, and so his potential options were highly limited. He also calculated – almost certainly correctly – that he would be executed if he voluntarily handed himself over to the new regime. Nevertheless, he did still possess significant firepower aboard the invasion fleet, and he assumed there would be former regime forces that were now lying low on the planet; patriotic ones who would welcome his return and rally to his cause if he was able to engineer a successful landing. He thus devised the outline of a plan that entailed the disembarkation of troops as rapidly as was physically possible - and under the cover of night - at a strategic location close to the southern uplands of the Northern Alliance lands – a location that was reasonably remote, relatively easy to defend, but from which he could rapidly counter-attack from. However, his plan relied on the stasis ships being able to safely orbit the planet, and here he knew he was potentially very vulnerable.

The three starships decelerated rapidly as they passed through Hedilla's outer planetary system, through the vast icy outer Oort cloud and its scattered dwarf planets and then past the various distant asteroid belts that ringed the remoter regions of the stellar system. The gravitational inertia of the gas giant Keitzel was used to further slow the ships on their approach into the system – a standard manouevre – and as they passed the great blue gas giant, Vartin regarded the behemoth of a planet for a brief period from the viewing deck. Its enormity reminded him of the sheer unknown immensity of space that had defeated him so recently, and once again he wondered at his place in the cosmos. He suddenly felt very small and insignificant again, and so he quickly turned his attention to other matters.

A short time later, Vartin returned to the viewing deck and watched as the stasis ships made their final approach towards Zeleyan – the planet he once completely controlled and was determined to do so again. As they did so, he prepared a carefully crafted message to the planet that lay ahead of him. In this matter, though, he was at a significant disadvantage - he did not recognise a single name amongst the people who were now making the political running down below on the planetary surface, but he nevertheless attempted to imagine the mindset of those he would now be dealing with. His main aim initially was to buy himself time, create a deception, and hope that his message caused divisions to open up within the new regime. The message was duly sent:

We return to Zeleyan in peace and seek to negotiate - in good faith - some form of reconciliation with the leaders of the new regime. We offer no political or military threat to the new regime. The many troops of the mission to Ur-Tokar are looking forward to seeing their loved ones after so many months away from home. We seek to negotiate a gradual and peaceful disembarkation of those on board in order to achieve this. We await a reply that can form the basis of initial negotiations.

The revolutionary councils - which now dominated the political and economic systems of the supercontinent – decided to broadcast the message openly and immediately, in the spirit of the new society that had been created by the people. It was, unsurprisingly, the subject of huge debate and discussion within the councils and amongst the wider population. Most saw straight through what Vartin was trying to achieve by mentioning the large numbers of troops still ensconced in stasis on the spaceships, but, to a limited extent, it achieved one of his initial purposes – that of creating a division within the revolutionary society, and opening up a potential delay in their response to the fleet's return to Zeleyan's planetary surface.

A minority – those of a more forgiving nature or who had not particularly suffered under his fascist regime - were inclined to give Vartin the benefit of the doubt, believing that his main objective was to avoid execution or a long prison sentence. Perhaps he was seeking to achieve some form of quiet retirement far away from the political spotlight, they speculated. Others, however, were far more suspicious of a man who enjoyed a reputation for being a shrewd and manipulative operator. They suspected he might be playing for time in order to effect a later return to politics, a much unwanted development if it were to prove correct and actually occur.

Yet others – probably the majority - believed it was just a classic Vartin ruse designed to buy time, create divisions and ultimately return him to his old despotic role. Some of this group worried that naïve sections of the population might be successfully deceived and seek some form of reconciliation between the old and new regimes. A particular group within this section of the population - particularly concerned that the delay was designed to give Vartin time to organise counter-revolutionary manoeuvres - decided they needed to take matters into their own hands to ensure such a development effectively became impossible.

During the course of building up the invasion fleet bought from the Rorque Corporation, Vartin had also created - again at great expense - a small number of missile bases capable of firing ballistic missiles into space. He had taken this course of action as he was concerned about possible future extra-planetary reprisals, in the event of a successful invasion of Ur-Tokar and elsewhere. The technological know-how was already available in the data banks inherited from Earth, but a combination of expense and a lack of need, meant that they had never actually been constructed beforehand. With the new missile bases fully constructed, Vartin had felt far more secure about his imperialist venture.

One such base at Kondstad in a remote western area of Novo Salzar was under the control of a particularly militant revolutionary council of workers and soldiers. The council at its latest meeting – held specifically to discuss Vartin's message – had raised concerns that the message was a complete deception and, in reality, simply presaged a planned invasion of the planet by his fascist military forces. They too were worried that others across the planet might be duped by Vartin's message and seek some form of compromise with him. This raised the extreme danger of further fighting and the possible return of his fascist regime.

Whilst the meeting recognised the potential political problems of taking this highly important matter into their own hands - and thus preempting any wider super-continental decision - it also believed that quick and decisive action was needed if the new revolutionary society was to be successfully defended and fully implemented. At the end of the meeting, the popular council voted almost unanimously to put an immediate end to Vartin's deception once and for all, and to preempt any counter-revolutionary fightback planned by the imperial military forces. In so doing, they believed that their decision to do so would be retrospectively approved by the revolutionary councils across the supercontinent.

That evening, the weather systems over the western shores of Novo Salazar delivered a warm dry night with clear and cloudless skies. Any local inhabitant taking a walk along one of the largely deserted beaches on that coastline after the sun had set beyond the western horizon, would have marveled at the clearness of the star-studded firmament; thousands of tiny shimmering points of lights in a deep purple-blue sky. The small chromium red moon of Jasper was just visible above the hills in the north-eastern section of the sky, and in the far eastern sky the bright white star of Vega twinkled, as it always seemed to do.

Overhead, high above the observer, three small points of white lights made their way steadily westwards through the night sky, moving quickly through the multi-coloured stars that were scattered haphazardly across the firmament. And then suddenly, without any form of warning, the observer would have seen the first of those small white lights suddenly burst apart like an exploding firework, quickly followed by falling plumes of white smoke and trails of burning matter descending into the darkened atmosphere – an aerospace age inferno, a military starship blown into a million tiny pieces. The bright white trails of debris and swirling plumes of smoke circled slowly planet-wards down and down as they dropped quickly and silently through the warm night sky, finally to be swallowed by the cool dark waters of the inky blue ocean far below.

The missile base at Kondstad issued its own communique explaining the reasoning behind its course of action. The Patriot IV contained former Supreme Commander Vartin, members of the High Council, his elite military commanders, the hated Patriotic Guard and large numbers of AI units adapted for purely military purposes. There were very few – if any – ordinary soldiers onboard. It could only ever be a threat to the revolution and the people of Zeleyan, and nothing else. It was an absolute certainty that Vartin had planned to regain control of the planet at the earliest opportunity available. The end of the communique demanded that the other two stasis ships should immediately surrender or face the same fate as the Patriot IV.

Aboard The Destroyer, the commanding officer was still General Davila. He had only been woken from stasis three days previously, and then informed – with absolutely no prior warning - that not only were the ships not about to arrive at Ur-Tokar for the invasion, but that they had returned to a Zeleyan which was now entirely in the hands of revolutionary left-wing forces. Not surprisingly, this came as a huge shock to the General and it had taken more than a day for the implications to fully sink in. Davila had wandered about the great hulking ship in a state of disbelief trying to reconcile what had actually happened with how he had originally envisioned his future. Eventually, after much confusion, he came to the conclusion that Vartin – who had been highly selective with the information he supplied to the two ships accompanying the Patriot IV - would have a viable plan for dealing with this new and unwanted scenario. He sat back and waited for events to unfurl in a far more promising direction.

At least, he did so, until the destruction of The Patriot IV suddenly showed up on the large bluescreen that dominated the forward deck of his stasis ship. Davila stared at the scene with a mixture of shock and disbelief, and then slowly rising anger as it fully registered with him that he had just witnessed the demise of his Supreme Commander and the entirety of their elite forces. And then his hair stood on end and a wave of fear swept through his entire body as it suddenly dawned on him that his ship might be next. He froze in terror waiting for the deadly explosion of sound and light that would signify his doom. He waited and waited, an eternity seemed to pass, but nothing happened. And then a sudden beep from the ship's computer made him almost jump out of his skin. It was the arrival of the communique from the revolutionary council at Kondstad and Davila listened to it with growing dismay.

A range of thoughts passed quickly through his mind. Surrender would be the ultimate humiliation, he thought, the admission that for all these years he had been wrong all along, and that it was the people he had despised as a child - and ever since those early days - who had been the ones who were actually on the right side of history, and not he himself. He could imagine the gloating and the self-righteousness, and such a scenario filled his self-centred arrogance and sense of pride with dread. And then, alarmingly, he recalled the orders he had given to the forces he had commanded when putting down the strikes and rebellions of recent years - the shooting of unarmed civilians, the summary execution of suspected rebels. He was bound to face a humiliating trial and certain execution. Or, had they abolished the death penalty since the insurrection, meaning a long and protracted period of degrading incarceration instead. He then wondered if he could make a rapid departure from the planet, outpacing the missiles and flying the ship to safety, to some as yet unknown destination, though he could not think exactly where. He was unsure if it was possible, and anyway, it somehow seemed a cowardly course of action which risked the deaths of thousands of loyal troops on board the two ships.

He suddenly remembered where exactly he was and looked around him, the rest of his skeleton crew – mostly composed of various junior officers – were looking at him expectantly. He remained impassive, but he could guess what they were thinking. There was no viable means of fighting back, whilst surrender would mean they all retained their lives. As junior officers, they would face lesser punishments and fewer humiliations. He continued to say nothing.

Finally, he came to a decision. He was first and foremost a patriot, but the country he loved no longer existed. He only had one viable option left. As the remaining most senior commanding officer, he made the decision to officially surrender to the Kondstad base below. He then ordered his junior officers to proceed to the departure deck below where they boarded a landing craft and returned to Zeleyan to facilitate the surrender of the ships to the planet. A short while later, he sat all alone in the captain's chair in the centre of the viewing deck, gazed out into the infinity of space, pulled out his pistol and put a single bullet through his brain.

Rorque 4 – The End or The Beginning

Dave Shevecke, one time performer, political activist, rock musician, and of late, urban guerilla, sat on a low ridge overlooking the narrow coastal plain known as the Galtian Edge, reflecting on how life had brought him to this particular place, at this particular point in time. Dave hailed from a working-class background, and from a young age he had always shown spirit, inventiveness and determination. Despite a camaraderie and identification with those around him, he had, in so many different ways, never really fitted in particularly well with the somewhat pessimistic fatalism of the community he derived from; he had always been far too much of an optimist, and far too much of a free-thinker. It had only ever been a matter of time before he sought to spread his wings and head out into the promise of the wider world.

But even as he sought the greater opportunities and openings existing within the social classes above him, he instinctively knew the odds were stacked against him, he somehow always knew he would only really get a single chance, a single shot at fame. For, the rules were very plain for someone from his background - even if they were not openly stated - you very much needed to play the game, their game and on their terms. It was just that at the time, he hadn't quite realised exactly how crucial these rules really were, just how important it was to know the exact details of the game and its well concealed and hidden truths.

Initially, matters had started out promising for him. He made his career choice, and for a while he very much thought he had got it right. But, a brief and acclaimed period of success on the stage was soon cut short, following his involvement in the organisation of a performers strike against redundancies and reductions in pay at the beginning of the long downswing that was, even now, still impacting on the planet's economy. Those with power in the higher echelons of the hierarchy, effectively cut short his promising career. He had failed to play by the rules – their rules - and those on high were about to let him know that you only enjoyed success on their terms.

He always knew there was potential for trouble when you left your own backyard, when you entered into a new and more prosperous neighbourhood, but he had not expected to be blacklisted for the rest of his life. Ever since that time, he had been something of a lost Johnny, wandering through the entertainment districts of various rundown towns and cities, looking for relief, searching for some form of metaphorical valium, whilst baying at the moon during his frequent periods of frustration. But the long difficult years had slowly hardened him, and of late - above all else - he had devoted his life to searching for a chance to gain the upper hand over those who had cancelled his dream all those many years ago. It was a search for justice that had been the overwhelming motivation of these past few years, the chance for an opportunity to turn the tables and to finally play the winning hand.

As he sat deep in thought, mulling over recent events, he hardly even noticed the descending orange-red orb of Eleutheria as it dropped rapidly over the western horizon and sank inexorably into the shallow green waters of the Ricardian Sea. The day had been a particularly humid and energy-sapping one, and even once the sun had dropped below the horizon, the air remained sticky, hot and difficult to breathe. He and his accompanying group had travelled through hot and dusty terrain for several hours that day, before finally arriving at their present destination. It had been a long, arduous and, at times, difficult and dangerous journey.

It was several weeks now since their attack on the Rorque Corporation convoy and the destruction of the spaceport at Mirivan. His group had made their way somewhat erratically, at times hesitatingly, and often slowly, across the vast continent of Northern Thule into the area known as Nuevo Pelerin. They were in no particular hurry, but they were determined to arrive at their destination without experiencing significant losses or casualties. The present chaotic state of the planet meant, that on any one particular day, their journey and any associated activity they engaged in could, at one extreme, be fraught with numerous problems and dangers, or, at the other extreme, pass entirely without incident. There were, though, a number of continuous difficulties they faced whichever area they passed through.

The provisioning of resources was a continuous problem; acquiring food and water was particularly difficult. They had both been scarce on the planet for some time now; production levels were low as a result of the departure of the main corporations, and easily outstripped by demand - despite the rising number of casualties in the chaos that had ensued since the shutdown of the major corporations. On occasions, it had still been possible to find abandoned homes, retail units or eateries where small amounts of food had been stockpiled and even very occasionally with supplies of freshwater. As the days and weeks passed, though, these had proved to be in continuing decline and ever more difficult to procure.

Transport was equally problematic. Almost all the main sources of energy on the planet were renewable, so the various well-established systems were able to continue their generation of energy, at least those that remained undamaged. However, the energy networks had been staffed largely by AI units – almost all of which were now on the stasis ships orbiting the planet – and whether the various different sources of energy continued to operate now depended largely on local factors. In some areas, local groups of people had taken control of the energy production stations to ensure a continued supply of energy. In others, they had ceased to function entirely, whilst a tiny number even remained staffed by AI units – presumably overlooked in the rush to leave the planet.

This meant access to transport – on a planet where it was entirely automated and electrically powered – was a highly haphazard affair. Across certain areas of the continent they could travel for long distances with relative ease, using the still functioning and well established transport networks. In some parts, they needed to negotiate access with the local people, who might demand any manner of payment in return for access to vehicles. In other parts of the continent, they had no choice but to walk, though usually chose to do so in the cool of the night rather than the energy-sapping heat of the day.

The actual landscape and terrain of the continent had also broken down into distinct zonal areas, characterised according to the form of habitation and social structure that was emerging within them, now that the corporations had departed. Much of the deep interior of the continent had always been uninhabited, or at best sparsely populated, and this area - as with those regions that had been recently abandoned - was relatively easy to traverse, notwithstanding the fact that they were frequently areas of dry semi-desert with their concomitant problems. Here they could pass through with relative ease, assuming they had sufficient provisions with them as they initially entered the region.

There were other areas where the locals were predominantly peaceful and simply left them alone. The inhabitants of the region were far too engaged in trying to maintain the manner in which they had always lived, even if the absence of the corporations meant this had become increasingly problematic for them, and necessitated considerable alterations to their lifestyle. In other zones though - typically some of the wealthiest ones - armed vigilante gangs roamed, as the local inhabitants sought to deter outsiders from entering their territory and prevent any form of looting or land theft. A small number of these areas even resembled something of a war zone, as the armed groups fell out amongst or between themselves and sought to violently wrest control from each other in various violent and bloody turf wars.

This complicated patchwork of problems and different habitation zones had forced the group to follow a far from ideal route across the continent in an attempt to minimise casualties and confrontations whilst maximizing access to necessary resources. They had attempted to avoid the areas with armed gangs, lack of transport and minimal resources, whilst remaining within those that offered better conditions of passage. Their route had thus turned out to be much longer than initially envisaged, entailing several deviations, a degree of backtracking and numerous halts and interruptions. Not surprisingly, their journey had taken considerably longer than they had originally planned for.

On one occasion – against their better judgement - they had been forced out towards the ultra-dry, sparsely vegetated and sun-baked fringes of the Inner Pelerin Desert and happened to pass close to the once famous Golden Ingots of Pelerin – an amalgamation of highly rectangular-shaped structures, coloured bright golden yellow and spaced fairly closely together on one of the slightly more elevated and drier parts of the desert. They had been discovered by chance, many decades before, by an off-roading expedition travelling through the desert, and had soon attracted much public attention, including the long-term attentions of a quasi-religious sect.

Their artificial-looking appearance, combined with the fact that they were spaced out in a geometrical pattern, meant that, as on so many previous occasions – from the ancient lines of the Nazca to the sunken pyramids of

Itzakhan on the lost planet of Denizos – some investigators had inevitably leaped to the conclusion that they must be the product of an ancient civilisation of infinitely wise alien beings. Those of a more religious or spiritual persuasion saw the golden ingot-shaped structures as a guiding sign - that it was no accident that Rorque 4 had become the home of an unfettered and unbridled capitalism – and that in some unknown and mysterious manner, the first settlers had been guided fortuitously to the planet. These believers developed a theory of floating anarcho-capitalism that claimed aliens had somehow guided them to the perfect planet for pursuing their business operations and long-term ultra-capitalist ambitions.

Gatherings of the faithful soon became a regular feature at the site and a quasi-religious capitalist sect developed that combined the worship of money with the worship of the ancient aliens who had supposedly created the semi-magical site. The sect lost some of its lustre though when, not too long after, geologists studying the area declared that the ingot-shapes were made of a hardened form of the golden-yellow heliodor crystal and were probably laid down on some ancient shallow sea bed, the surrounding softer material having long been eroded. They were not fully certain of the exact process and why they should be quite so regular and uniform in shape, but sand-blasting from desert winds had undoubtedly smoothed their appearance over vast eons of time and added to their rectangular and lustrous nature.

Despite this minor setback, a small number of true believers had continued to worship at their newfound golden alter for several decades; a dwindling band of the old faithful who trekked out into the desert each year on the anniversary of the first landing on the capitalist planet to give thanks for their arrival. Towards the very end of this period, on every seventh year, the disparate members of the - by now severely declining - cult had gathered on the hill in the silvery moonlight, convinced they were soon to witness the end of the human race, and transferred to distant realms by a magical lord of light, in some form of latter day capitalist rapture. Unsurprisingly, it never actually happened and the cult eventually withered away into some form of mythical oblivion.

Neither Dave nor any of his grouping had ever made the journey out to the Pelerin Ingots – not surprisingly given they were the sworn enemies of capitalism – but as the rectangular structures glowed a lustrous golden yellow under the heat of the afternoon sun, they admitted to each other, as they passed the strange monuments, that they could see why they might have attracted some form of mystical worship and semi-divine attention.

Despite their best efforts, their attempts to by-pass conflict zones and avoid trouble had not always been successful, however. There had been occasional clashes between the group and the armed gangs protecting their highly treasured patches, and they had suffered a small number of casualties along their journey. The most aggressive and hostile people they encountered were usually those that had previously counted amongst the more wealthy and privileged sections of the populace. Faced with a decline in their fortunes they had become increasingly reactionary – their decline was, they believed, always the fault of those less fortunate than themselves, and more than anything they wanted a return to the traditional way of conducting affairs – of reestablishing the old unequal and prejudicial hierarchies.

Rather than accept or adapt to their new situation, they tended to complain aggressively about their misfortunes, in particular how they were no longer able to lord it over those they had always perceived as less important than themselves. They missed their ability to push around, insult, demean, criticise and denigrate those they had traditionally oppressed and exploited. Given that the planet was almost literally falling apart around them, this struck the group as not only supremely self-centred, but as highly ignorant and showing an alarming inability in respect to the matter of establishing priorities. The worst of these encounters had occurred after they entered a string of protected territorial zones, as they skirted along the eastern fringes of the relatively prosperous and low-lying Rothbard Hills, down through the Röpke River valley on a southwards turn in the direction of their journey.

As they passed through the apocalyptic-looking valley, the sight of dead bodies, abandoned autocars and burnt out houses was a frequent one, with the occasional dead body hanging prominently from the branches of a tree along the roadside – presumably as some form of gruesome warning to some relevant party. They had nicknamed the valley area Damnation Alley, due to the high number of casualties they encountered, and the numerous signs of sadistic violence they encountered along its long length. The going along the valley was always far from easy, and they frequently felt they were running a whole gamut of problems as they tried to make their way as furtively and quickly as possible along its entire length. Eventually, with the occasional big dose of luck, they got through the whole mess, though not without suffering some significant casualties, and were glad to leave the whole area well behind.

Much of what they saw during the course of their travels was profoundly depressing; they encountered numerous groups of refugees – usually small bands and family groupings - leaving areas of persistent drought and looking - often without success - for sources of freshwater. They had frequently seen abandoned towns and burnt out city suburbs, but had attempted to avoid such sites unless the need for resources was extremely pressing. Brush fires were still an intermittent hazard and heatwaves continued to strike whole regions in a highly erratic and unpredictable manner. There was clearly no sign of any let-up in the intense warming of the planet.

Nevertheless, there were also some positive signs of improvement. In a number of locations they passed through, the locals had banded together in a more positive manner than that pursued by the armed vigilante gangs, and were beginning to organise themselves in a more collective and democratic manner, with the aim of surviving and then flourishing in the post-corporate social vacuum. For Dave and the band of revolutionaries, this was a sign that their hope for a better society – one that they had been advocating for as long as any of them could remember – was now a real and credible possibility, for the first time in their lifetimes. They frequently put such groups in touch with each other in an attempt to strengthen this welcome social development.

Dave watched the last glimmers of light disappear from the darkening sky, and as he did so he remembered a conversation with an old socialist friend who was highly familiar with the intellectual teachings of the ancient Earth philosophers. One of them had apparently said that when capitalism met its final crisis and faced imminent collapse, the options were either to move forward towards socialism or regress back to barbarism. Unfortunately, he thought, after considering their recent encounters, the world seemed to be experiencing more of the latter than that of the former at the present moment.

This, though, came as no great surprise to him; the dominant regime on Rorque 4 had been devoted religiously to enforcing individualism throughout the entirety of its existence. It was hardly surprising that its inhabitants were still struggling to work together in a more cooperative manner. He suspected it would probably take many years to build the better society he had envisaged and agitated for; after all, it was still early days and he assumed matters would eventually take a turn for the better. His positive view of human nature meant he never stopped believing that people would revert back to a more natural cooperative and sociable way of organising their lives - one based on the idea of the survival of the friendliest, rather than its more dubious tautological counter-part - especially now the pernicious influence of the corporations was at an end.

The corporations had always claimed that the lack of popular rebellion was a sign of support for their ideological approach – the so-called silent majority - but he believed they had mistaken a subdued and begrudging compliance for passive support of the system. In reality, people had conformed because they were too scared to rebel; their compliance was actually borne out of hopelessness and a sense of despair, not out of any enthusiasm for the regime. They had not seen the possibility of effecting successful systemic change – no matter how much it might have been desirable - so had never bothered to even try and make it happen.

Throughout history, civilisations had risen, flourished and then eventually fallen. For a concerted period of time they had aggregated and centralised, they had built great cities, established the farming and transport systems needed to furnish them, and flourished for many generations. And then, suddenly, they declined and fell, for any number of different reasons. Collapse was not inevitable, but, as on Rorque 4, they typically made a series of incorrect decisions that eventually resulted in their demise. In this case it had been their insistence on persisting with an economic system that was singularly dominated by the drive for profit, whilst maintaining a state that was so weak that - when the markets spectacularly failed - it too proved incapable of moving in and dealing with any serious or persistent crisis.

But when civilisations fell they did not disappear; they dispersed outwards, disaggregated and decentralised, they adapted and evolved, and the peoples of the civilisation survived, only to organise in a distinctly different manner. Dave and his fellow insurrectionists – fuelled by their revolutionary vision - were determined to help shape and nurture that adaptation. They stood on the cusp of two very different worlds; a place in time that finally offered them the opportunity to implement what they had always been disparagingly told was their dangerous vision. One where people actually worked together on a cooperative and equal basis – a social alliance made from all sections of society and one that worked equally for all involved.

For these one-time urban guerillas, the days of the underground were now well and truly over - part of a past life they were putting firmly behind them. They were now in the open daylight and actively working to implement their cherished vision. The mood music had changed and they were now operating to an entirely different tune – they were singing a different song, a song for a new age. Their immediate target was to take collective control of the numerous desalination plants strung out along the coast of the western fringes of the Ricardian Sea, the coastline that they were now overlooking. If they could collectively run and control these and thus distribute freshwater for free to the general population, then they believed they were well on the way towards taking the first steps to creating their brave new society. Once this goal was established, the energy production systems would be the next on their long list of targets.

Dave's attention was drawn to the firmament high above him and the myriad of scintillating stars that carpeted its purple blackness. Low over the eastern horizon, the ochre-yellow moon of Saffron was beginning its long low arcing journey across the southern reaches of the night sky. He looked behind him to the west and eventually located the smaller jade green moon of Viridis which was already high in the northern sky slowly tracking eastwards into the lower reaches of the constellation of Leptos. For several minutes he was transfixed by the small green moon as he wondered at its strange uniqueness, its long and unknown history, and its dark pristine beauty.

He switched his attention to the myriad stars and purple-white mass of the Milky Way. It looked the same as it always appeared to him, like some enormous cloud that had been stretched and partially ripped open; the milky white sheen of its edges seeming to shine out from behind the dark and purple shading of its darkened centre. He wondered at the countless thousands of yellow-white lights, the occasional reds and blues, and the larger spiral galaxies. He found the phenomenon of luminosity, combined with the sheer enormity of the galaxy and its endless stellar variations, so difficult to comprehend, and yet its vast dark coolness and its infinite and endless celestial bodies held a calming and soothing impact that he found almost impossible to explain. He sat for several minutes totally absorbed by the entrancing space symphony, the stellar light show shimmering high above his head.

And then he caught sight of two small specks of white light moving steadily in concert across the southern night sky. They were just two of the several stasis ships still constantly circulating high above the planet. On board the huge starships lay tens of thousands of people still ensconced in their stasis pods, deep in torpor, lost in the wastelands of sleep, endlessly circling the planet, slowly going nowhere. The highly personalised security codes to the ships had disappeared with the demise of the corporate leaders and, so far, all attempts to access the ship's computer systems had completely failed. For the moment, he figured, both the ships and the unfortunate passengers aboard them would be remaining indefinitely in suspended animation.

And on the stasis ships, stored amongst the long rows of sleeping passengers, were endless numbers of AI units. Something was running through the back brain of his mind, and then he remembered what it was. It was a comment Zhavia had made to him at the Psychedelic Warlords concert, though he had taken little notice of the remark at the time. According to Zhavia, the fundamental difference between their two worlds was that on Margalla they all collectively controlled and owned the AI units, and on his world they did not. If the Rorqueans wanted to effect their own arrival in utopia, they would need to follow the Margallan example and replicate the beneficial economic organisation of their diminutive world. He looked again at the two specks of light and wondered how his band of revolutionaries might take possession of the precious cargo stowed away on board the ships circulating so high above him.

Zeta Kotlin – the spaceships all arrive – The Star Chaser, The Spirit of the Age and the Avante

At the other end of the Nexus Cluster, the eventual arrival of the three spaceships - fully laden with the scientists and their families following their travails on Rorque 4 and around Ur-Tokar - had provoked a great deal of comment across the varied communities of Zeta Kotlin. When The Star Chaser and The Spirit of the Age finally made orbit around the socialist planet, it had been a little over five years since the Alphan diaspora had initially dispersed from their troubled home planet. Six months later, and the Avante, with Alex and Anna aboard, eventually repeated the same procedure. Their arrival had been anticipated long in advance, and this time the Zetans had been informed of the exact numbers arriving aboard each ship. They were also broadly aware of the intentions of those on board, and the fact that they had no immediate plans to make further voyages once they had arrived. As such, there was much less concern than previously, and the whole episode was a rather more sedate and reflective affair than the original arrival more than three years previously.

At Kapal, as elsewhere, there was a great deal of satisfaction with the developments that had recently unfolded across the Nexus Cluster. The mood of the community – and across the wider planet - was a generally positive one, with a distinct sense of self-congratulation in the air. A new administrative committee had by now been selected to run the affairs of the community at Kapal, but the four previous members had resolved to meet up regularly, largely on the basis that they had very much come to enjoy each other's company and political discussions.

The weather forecast for the day of their chosen gathering was one of sunshine with light summer showers, the perfect conditions for a visit to the Dancing Pools of Xestron. As such, they had all taken an autocar together across the plains to arrive at the famous site for around mid-morning. The journey was not a particularly long one, and was spent discussing their recent activities and the various sites that were visible as they travelled across the lightly-wooded savannah lands. As they pulled in at their destination their arrival was lucky enough to coincide with a warm summer rain shower drifting slowly across the pools and they quickly left the autocar and joined those already present for their first experience of the morning.

The Dancing Pools of Xestron were a large expanse of sparkling crystal pools – the remnants of river deposition on the sea bed of a once small and ancient shallow inland sea. On the numerous sunny days that characterised the warm climate predominating over the plains, the myriad varieties of crystal shimmered crimson red, blood orange, indigo blue, lilac pink, golden yellow, violet purple, neon blue, turquoise green and, in fact, any other colour you cared to mention, in the bright rays of the daytime sunshine. Given its location on the wide sweeping flatness of the vast plains, the multi-coloured glow emanating from the shallow waters of the pools could be seen shimmering and shifting in the air above them over vast and impressive distances.

This was impressive enough for any onlooker, but when localised rain showers passed over the plain in the warm bright sunshine, the crystal pools took on a whole new dramatic dimension of their own. The light sprinkling of warm summer raindrops gave rise to magical arrays of twisting and turning psychedelic rainbows, shifting patterns of kaleidoscopic light, and endless variations of sparkling scintillations which seemed to emanate coruscating and glistening from the multi-coloured crystal formations, dancing in the patterned light of the sparkling sunbeam and raindrop showers shining from the skies above.

Unsurprisingly, Zetans had been irresistibly attracted to this fascinating phantasmagorical phenomenon - providing an ever popular attraction - and visitors travelled from far and wide to visit the pools and enjoy the unique natural experience. Whilst a small minority simply went to watch the natural light show, it had become far more common for visitors to dance to their favourite psychedelic music in the soft summer rain, choose a sexual partner and pop whatever sweet obsession they might be inclined towards in their mouth. As they danced together in the soft sparkling watery lights - the sweet smell of petrichor lifting off the dry parched plain - they could experience the full sensory experience of light, sound, smell, touch and taste in an overload of the senses that was effectively impossible to beat anywhere in the known galaxy.

The group's luck was in this particular day, and a number of light showers passed over the crystal pools during the duration of their visit, allowing several visits to the crystal dance floor until they had finally enjoyed their fill of the highly sensual experience. Afterwards, they sat by the pools eating a light lunch with the usual array of locally-brewed drinks and conversed a while, whilst they watched the other visitors still enjoying the experience. As the day became hotter and the rains drifted away ever eastwards across the plains, they ordered another autocar, and once it had arrived, they headed back to Kapal, agreeing to meet later in the day on one of the terraces overlooking the western plains, so they could converse further and watch the mid-evening sunset.

As such, later that day, they found themselves together once again, seated together on a wide grass-covered terrace and provisioned with a range of quality foodstuffs and drinks. The late afternoon air was still warm and dry, with a slight breeze drifting down from the north offering a degree of cool freshness in the late summer sun. Before long their discussion turned to recent events on the planet and the relative fortunes of the Alphan scientists.

'I bet they wished they'd never left our planet in the first place now. They've spent endless years in space, had a terrible experience on Rorque 4 – and we could have told them that was going to be the case – and now they've ended up back where they started,' Pedro exclaimed, somewhat triumphantly, but also with a touch of sympathy for the spacefarer's plight.

'To be fair, it's easy to be wise in hindsight, though I agree they really should have thought the whole idea through a bit more carefully,' added Zhang Li, who tended to be more reflective than Pedro on most matters. 'However, we do always say that experience is the best teacher; sometimes you have to experience the failures before you discover the more successful route through life. In the long run, it might serve them well to have lived and learnt. Once they are properly settled here, they are more likely to be committed to their new home and way of life and to engage more fully in the life of our planet.'

'I agree,' added Rishaan, 'since - unlike on Rorque 4 - our society allows for those failures. We've all experimented with life, especially in our younger years, and only eventually discovered what we really want to do through trial and error. We're allowed to make mistakes, since our society is far more forgiving. On Rorque 4 it sounds as though your life was always decided by the corporations – for many, there were simply no second chances. If the market didn't like what you were doing, then that was the end of that. I guess the leadership there saw mistakes as expensive and costly, so such a severe punishment acted as a deterrent to unwarranted personal experimentation. Everyone just played it safe instead. Fortunately, we have a more forgiving way of dealing with these matters.'

'And we've learnt a great deal from this whole episode as well,' added Catriona. 'It's helped confirm what we always believed – but had perhaps become a bit blasé about. You need to give people space and allow them time to progress, to make their own mistakes and understand what they did wrong, rather than to just be demeaned and punished when matters go wrong. From what we've heard from the Alphan scientists, it sounds as if everything was determined by deadlines, targets, promotions and profit margins on Rorque 4, and negative consequences followed if you failed to achieve any of these. How can anyone be a real human being under those conditions, how can anyone genuinely grow and flourish? Surely, it's just not possible.'

'And the amount of deceit, lies and broken promises must have been enormous under such a system. People must have gone to great lengths to cover up their errors and mistakes in order to save their status and their careers, especially if the consequences of failure were so great,' agreed Pedro, and then took a long sip from his drink.

'And yet everyone must have known about all this deceit if it was so widespread. So, I guess you were just expected to play along with the whole game, and as long as everyone knew where they stood, they just turned a blind eye to the whole sorry process,' added Zhang Li. 'It must be very bizarre living in a society where you are effectively expected to be an actor, just a player in a game. It must be impossible to be yourself under such circumstances!'

'So, it's not surprising such an intellectually bankrupt system failed to last; it wasn't even built on firm foundations,' concluded Pedro.

'I'm sure it wasn't,' agreed Catriona, 'but it sounds as though their downfall was ultimately down to a failure to respect the environment of the planet. By all accounts, it was always quite a fragile biosystem – possibly more so than most that have been created - and really did need special care and nurture.

According to the scientists, their willful damage and neglect of their biosphere played a large part in their own self-destruction. It's a salutary lesson showing that we too need to be very careful and make sure we don't repeat their mistakes.'

'Looks like some people never learn their lessons though. What was it one of the ancient Earth philosophers once said; 'history repeats itself first as tragedy, and secondly as farce.' They really should have known better after what the human race did to Earth's ecosystems before we all left that old place,' offered Rishaan. 'This does definitely sound more like a farce than a tragedy, given what we all know,' he added.

'On the upside, though, it does mean the Nexus Cluster is now a much safer place, what with the demise of Rorquean capitalism and the successful revolution against fascism on Zeleyan. And, we've been a bit too insular in the past, in my opinion - possibly with good reason - but from now on we should start to be more outward looking and engage with the other planets on a more frequent basis,' suggested Zhang Li, reflecting a viewpoint that was beginning to become more widespread across Zeta Kotlin. The local inter-stellar configuration had recently altered in a manner unseen since the earliest days of its colonisation, and the newly emerging situation was giving rise to a whole proliferation of new and emerging viewpoints.

'Yes, visiting other planets, exploring different worlds, discovering exotic cultures and meeting new people should all be very interesting,' remarked Rishaan, suddenly wondering if there were opportunities there to satisfy his wanderlust. 'It would also have a reciprocal effect upon us as well, I assume; I wonder what the benefits for our society and those we engage with might be?'

'Not for me, space travel sounds unpleasant; long journeys, space sickness and endlessly stuck in stasis – doesn't sound like fun to me. I'm quite happy down here on Zeta Kotlin, there's plenty to be getting on with here, enough to keep me happy anyway,' chipped in Pedro, who was definitely the least likely amongst the group to engage in any such adventures.

'Each to their own, but Zhang Li is right that our corner of space is now a much safer and happier place. We've actually done very well out of this Alphan diaspora – we've gained new ideas and technologies and its helped end two unpleasant civilisations. I suspect they would have probably gone that way anyway sooner or later – they were, after all, following their own self-contradictory logic - but the diaspora seems to have perhaps speeded developments along and nudged them in the right direction,' offered Rishaan.

'We also have considerably more stasis ships now; we might want to think about putting them to good use. If Zeleyan needs any help or extra resources we should show our solidarity with their revolution and newly created society. I would say we should make some gesture of goodwill, just to show our support and forge better relations with them,' suggested Pedro, who had, like many other Zetans, also become a little less insular than had been the case before the whole affair.

'Definitely, if we can help to firmly establish and prolong their new society, that has to be a positive for all of us. I've often felt that since our arrival all those years ago, we, as a society, have become too cautious and timid – we were far too worried about what sort of threat other planets might pose to us, rather than offering our approach as a model for others. We were too hung up on worrying about being seen as imperialists or thinking that we knew what was best for others. Our little corner of space is much more promising now, we should start to reach out more and work with the other planets. There are nuanced and consensual ways to influence others, without sounding superior or arrogant. It's always possible to offer advice to others – it's their choice as to whether to accept it,' offered Rishaan.

'Sounds good to me, as long as we are careful about how we proceed with all of this,' responded Zhang Li. 'And we might want to start with the situation on Rorque 4. Whilst I admit that the information we're receiving is very patchy and sometimes contradictory, it does sound as though their world has descended into chaos and confusion. There might be some scope for us to help their inhabitants create a better society, especially if they ask us for such help. We're clearly in a position now to offer all sorts of different help. Sending a stasis ship with resources or some form of other help should be well within our capabilities,' offered Zhang Li.

'I agree,' said Catriona, 'and we might even be able to offer some ideas about dealing with their environmental crisis; we've developed considerable expertise in this area over the decades. I suspect it's going to be a huge task, but, at the very least, if we offer some relevant advice they should be able to ameliorate some of the worst features of the environmental crisis there, if nothing else.'

Arrival in Utopia

'We should raise all this at the next community meeting. I suspect other communities are thinking along the same lines as us. We need to formulate some concrete ideas and send them to the General Council for consideration; it would be good for the planet to make some decisions on these matters,' Rishaan suggested optimistically.

At this point, Aequitas was dropping quickly towards the horizon, and the shadows of the thinly scattered trees that haphazardly littered the extensive plains were visibly lengthening, and so the group stopped talking so they could better admire the large orange-red orb as it descended slowly and inexorably over the low hills of Outer Kextos far to their west. As it did so, the lightly clouded sky became a fascinating mixture of pinkish-purple clouds intermixed with long striations of liquid yellow light, shining softly, but slowly fading as the star finally disappeared behind the distant dark hills.

As the last of the light finally extinguished and the vast multiplicity of stars that constituted the Milky Way lit up the darkness of the cool night sky, the group waited for the next great spectacle of the day, and they were not to be disappointed, for this was a 'three moons night.' The silver-white shine of the slowly moving Nacre was the first to become evident, as it rose gradually from out of the north-eastern reaches, casting its pale pearly light eerily across the quietness of the plains. A short time later, less noticeable, but more intriguing against the darkness of the night sky, emerged the deep dark purple of the giant moon Chixtos, rising almost indiscernibly across the lower reaches of the atmosphere. And then, finally, and in stark comparison to the other two moons, the light mustard yellow Xanthia almost zoomed across the higher reaches of the firmament, quickly reaching its zenith, only to then follow a long shallow eastwards decline until it was lost in the far distance of the nocturnal darkness. The group marveled at the spectacle and talked long into the night.

Arrival in Utopia

Zeta Kotlin – Janicka, Mila, Anna, Arlo and Alex visit Kapal

After her return to Zeta Kotlin aboard The Spirit of The Age, Janicka had decided to spend some time with some friends in a commune on the outskirts of Earth City, whilst she contemplated what she would do with her immediate future. She had decided that she had experienced enough space travel for the moment, and was looking for her next big experience in life. Her cumulative experiences, both before and during her mission to Ur-Tokar, meant she now felt she had developed sufficiently as her own person, she was now very much more of an autonomous human being, and so she was looking for something somewhat more permanent to do with her life. The only problem was deciding what this should be.

Neema and Kahlil - inspired by their time on Ur-Tokar - had decided to head for the southern continent of Levalline to explore the Cascade Mountains for an indeterminate amount of time, and though Janicka had been tempted to join them, she felt it was not quite what she wanted at this moment in time. She had, however, made a point of trying to keep in touch with some of those she had met and worked with during her time in space. Before leaving the stasis ship, she had encouraged Mila Lustrom and her close colleagues and also Arlo to visit her at some convenient time in the near future.

Mila had initially decided to join the Natural Sciences department at Earth City University, for no other reason than that it was conveniently close to the spaceport she had arrived on the planet at. There were already a number of astrobiologists at the university, including some who had been in touch with Akiko on Margalla for several years now, and so she was able to integrate into both her work and social life with relative ease. Mila - and her colleagues from The Star Chaser - were keen to work through the data they had collected on Ur-Tokar, and to study comparative data from Alpha Fraczan, Zeta Kotlin and Margalla in an attempt to discern which forces were imparting the greatest impact on the evolution of Earth-originating life forms, and whether the comparisons could help create a generalised theory in their chosen field. Their work, Mila believed, was progressing at a promising rate, though she did at times find it difficult to adapt to the more socialistic practices of her new colleagues – especially the more relaxed work rate.

691

Arrival in Utopia

A few months into this process, and following the arrival of the Avante, Mila made a point of meeting up with Alex and Anna, intrigued by tales of their recent experiences on Rorque 4 and wanting to confirm that the situation really was as bad as her fellow passengers on The Spirit of The Age had earlier maintained. Both Alex and Anna also made the decision to research and teach at Earth City University, and partly for similar reasons to Mila. Anna had quickly teamed up with some former colleagues from Seven Mountains University now working in the biochemistry department, whilst Alex felt he needed to be close to an active spaceport as was physically possible.

The near space of Zeta Kotlin now hosted a whole fleet of stasis ships – effectively the new arrivals had all become the collective property of the entire planet – and Alex was still keen to improve their flight capabilities. As the group of friends at Kapal had earlier anticipated, across the whole planet there had been considerable debate as to whether the Zetans should now use their stasis ships in some more immediate and purposeful manner – thus largely breaking with their decades old tradition of semi-isolation - or whether they should continue to effectively remain parked in orbit to be used for some as yet unidentified future emergency. Alex was keen on the former idea, and was hoping to play a significant part in establishing a more active space programme based out of Earth City. The planet had already collectively agreed to establish better relations with Zeleyan, and was waiting to see what aid or resources they might supply them with, if such a request arrived.

Of the three scientists, Anna had probably found her intellectual situation the most problematic. Medical approaches on Zeta Kotlin were heavily focused on preventative medicine, whilst treatment for those who did become ill and injured tended to only use biochemical approaches as a last resort. As such, Anna was still trying to make a decision about her future research; she had toyed with the idea of becoming better acquainted with more therapeutic approaches within the field, but was also thinking of putting her biochemical knowledge to good use by linking up with Mila's research on evolution in non-human life-forms. Alternatively, she was wondering whether to study the chemistry of the oceans – a subject she had become interested in on Rorque 4. On Zeta Kotlin, she had the luxury of knowing there was no great hurry to make a decision, and so she was taking plenty of time before making any definitive decision.

One morning, Janicka woke to discover a message from Zhang Li on her messaging system. After discovering that Janicka was staying temporarily at Earth City, Zhang Li suggested that any time she wanted to visit Kapal she would be more than welcome. She was intrigued as to how Jiaying had fared on her recent mission to Ur-Tokar and whether she was planning to remain on Margalla, and was hoping Janicka could fill in some of the details. Janicka had happened to mention the Dancing Pools of Xestron to her new group of friends on an earlier get-together, so when she mentioned her invite to Kapal to Alex, Anna, Arlo and Mila they were all keen to make a combined visit to the pools and the ridge settlement of Kapal. Janicka made a point of closely observing the weather forecasts and eventually selected the morning that looked most apposite for their intended psychedelic experience.

And so, a few months after their previous get together, the group of friends at Kapal once again gathered for their regular social gathering, though this time joined by the group of former space travellers. Following a successful and rewarding morning at the Dancing Pools of Xestron, the invited group found themselves settling down for lunch at Kapal. The visitors arrived shortly after midday, and the whole assembly decided to sit outside on one of the western terraces in the warm afternoon sunshine, once a further brief shower had passed overhead. The intoxicating smell of petrichor still hung heavily in the warm air as they organised the seating and distributed a variety of drinks and a wide array of foodstuffs.

From their elevated position, the visitors stood on the terrace and marveled at the vast and spectacular views across the Xestron plains, from the distant dark foothills of Outer Kextos far to the west, to the equally distant reddish-brown darklands of the Zeratxusian cordillera just about visible beyond the vast flat reaches of the eastern plains. In both directions, acacia trees were widely and thinly scattered across the sun-drenched plains, interspersed with areas of scrub and the occasional shallow depression, freshly watered by the recent showers. Only a small number of animals had been brought to Zeta Kotlin by the original settlers, but the visitors noticed that those that did exist seemed to be increasingly plentiful on the largely protected plains.

Arrival in Utopia

As well as wanting to hear news of Jiaying's latest adventures, the former spacefarers had also been invited by the group because the situation above Rorque 4 had now become a hot topic of conversation amongst the widespread communities of Zeta Kotlin. Knowledge of the stranded stasis ships had now become common knowledge and there had recently been calls from sections of the population for the planet to effect a rescue operation of the hapless passengers, still deeply ensconced in the torpors of stasis.

'So, is it genuinely true that there are thousands and thousands of people in stasis on all those ships, simply orbiting the planet, going round and round in circles and potentially forever?' asked Catriona, not quite able to believe that anyone could allow such a bizarre situation to have actually occurred in the first place.

'Well, I'm not sure about forever, but certainly the ships are all locked into orbit, and there is no likelihood of them going anywhere anytime soon,' answered Anna. 'Their AI units will keep them in the correct orbit and functioning efficiently, and they can maintain that for several decades at least, I assume, but I'm not sure at what point that no longer becomes feasible.'

'The problem is that the security codes for the ships were highly personalised, and died with the leaders of the corporations,' added Alex. 'Cracking encrypted codes like those is effectively impossible. The only way onto the stranded stasis ships is through forced entry. AI units could be programmed to do this, but I doubt anyone on Rorque 4 has the capability to achieve that, and there are no shuttles there anyway - they were all destroyed in the fires at the spaceports. Unless a rescue is effected from Zeta Kotlin - or possibly Zeleyan could also do this now - then the ships will remain in orbit indefinitely, until they begin to disintegrate. The AI units can constantly re-energise the engines, so they won't fall out of the sky, any time soon, but that won't last forever.'

'And I really think we should be doing something about this. We can't allow those poor people to be left in stasis for perpetuity. We need to mount a rescue operation to save them. We have the starships and the AI units now, so we are in a position to be able to do something about this, we just need to get the operation organised. Even if there are no volunteers, I'm sure this is something that could be done entirely by AI units,' suggested Catriona.

'But what about the people down below?' raised Pedro, expressing support for the position that had caused so much disagreement across the communities of the planet. 'The people down on the planet are in a much worse situation – they're facing drought, fires, starvation and warfare. They're in a much worse situation than those on the stasis ships. At least the ship passengers are safe. It's the unfortunate people still on the planet below we should really be helping.'

'I'm still not totally sure about that idea. Our general approach with regards to other planetary systems is that we respect their right to self-development, unless it impacts negatively on our own civilisation. We don't interfere with their societies, and hopefully they won't interfere with ours. Invariably we don't fully understand the situation elsewhere, so it can be dangerous to intervene in the affairs of another civilisation. We might even achieve the opposite of what we want if the locals resent our intrusion and rebel against us. We need to be very careful about any intervention, no matter how bad the situation might be on their planet,' offered Zhang Li.

'Even if they ask for our help?' asked Catriona.

'Well that might be different, but we would still need to be very careful and make sure we were helping the right people in the right way. Even that could be tricky, there are different factions there and if the other groups decide to oppose what we are doing, we could be dragged into a damaging civil war. We would need a complete understanding of what is occurring on the planet, in order to help in a very targeted manner, and that could be highly difficult to achieve given the apocalyptic conditions on the planet. Ultimately, we cannot liberate other peoples, they can only do that for themselves,' she replied, slightly defensively. 'At best, we could offer some help, but we would need to be very careful about how we did it.'

'But if they want to be liberated, I'm sure we can help them,' added Catriona. 'We should be able to help both groups of people – those suffering on the planet, and those isolated on the stasis ships as well. We certainly have the resources for the latter, and we might be able to help with the former, if we're careful like you say.'

'I believe we should concentrate on helping those down on the planet, since they're the ones who have suffered the most. They're the forgotten underclass, the dispossessed and the downtrodden. They've spent a lifetime being oppressed and exploited. They're the ones we should be helping the most,' interjected Pedro. 'But I'm not sure about those on the stasis ships; they were the privileged corporate types - ambitious and selfish go-getters, promotion-seeking yes-men and yes-women. I can't see them adapting particularly well to the ways of our planet – it will be a huge culture shock for them to come and live here. They could cause us all sorts of problems.'

'I seem to remember you said something similar about the Alphans before they arrived here,' Rishaan said, smiling.

'Well, they turned out to have useful skills and technical abilities, and they also arrived from a semi-collectivist society, so adaptation to our ways hasn't been too much of a problem for them. I'm not sure that will be the case for out-and-out, ultra-competitive, neo-liberal individualists,' and he glanced at their visitors, hoping for some moral support.

'It's possible they might choose to go elsewhere. If we rescue them, they don't have to follow our ships back to Zeta,' offered Zhang Li.

'And I'm sure our civilisation is strong enough to cope with a few go-getters and wannabes,' replied Rishaan. 'I know there were some issues with those on the Avante, but I think that's largely blown over now. Is that right?' he asked, turning to Anna and Alex.

'It was quite a mixed picture,' answered Anna. 'We had to explain their entirely unexpected situation to them at considerable length. We also had to explain how we thought Zetan society worked and how they could fit in if they chose to do so. There were a number of areas we were very unsure about. There were a few who, I think, were quite relieved to discover that the whole stressful corporate lifestyle was finally over for them and that a more relaxed alternative was readily available. I believe these people have integrated quite well into your society. There were others – possibly a majority - who were unconvinced and highly sceptical, but effectively everyone dispersed from the starship over the next few days, so I'm not sure exactly what happened to all of them. I've heard a few rumours. They're probably all quite talented and resourceful individuals, but whether they can throw off their neo-liberal social conditioning and adapt to your egalitarian collectivism . . . well, we'll probably just have to wait and see. I'm not sure what their other options would be. We managed to work out the original intended destination of the Avante – from the flight plans - but we didn't pass on the information. Even if we told them, I'm not sure they could start a new civilisation with just half a starship full of people, and the stasis ship now effectively belongs to the people of Zeta Kotlin, so they would need to resolve that problem, as well.'

'Mmm, okay, so maybe the jury's still out on that one,' conceded Rishaan. 'But, anyway, the scientists from Alpha Fraczan seem to have adapted well to our society, so I'm sure others can as well.' He turned again to Alex, Anna and Mila, 'what have been the main challenges for you, how have you managed the process?'

Mila paused for a moment and thought carefully. 'My initial expectations of your society were largely wrong. I thought your world would be one that discouraged ambition and independent thinking. I thought I would be stifled by a collective group-think that barred new ideas and alternative thinking. I've slowly discovered that's not the case, in fact, I'm increasingly inclined to think it's the opposite here. I've heard some very bizarre ideas since I've been here; if anything, there's possibly too much discussion. Sometimes I wish people would just come to a quicker conclusion and get on with the task at hand.'

At that point Anna chipped in and added, 'yes, and there clearly are ambitious people here, it's just that they're ambitious for the whole of your society, not just for themselves or other individuals. I also thought I would be prevented from developing new theories and advancing my knowledge here, and I think in some areas that can and does happen, but that's because the ideas are deemed to have no useful wider application, or it's feared they will unfairly benefit selected groups. But if the ideas look promising and might help wider society, then they tend to be genuinely welcomed and are acted upon.'

'We were used to living on a world that rewarded talent with greater status and material advantages, but that's only important on a world where there is material scarcity and a relative shortage of resources,' interjected Alex. 'Here, there seems to be material prosperity and plenty for everyone, so individual material advancement seems fairly pointless and, in fact, almost ridiculous – like a child that wants too many toys. Living on Rorque 4 was a real eye-opener for me; I'd never really given these issues much thought before, but it's shown me just how damaging individualist materialism can be, especially when it's taken to the excessive levels their elite was engaging in,' he added.

'And even worse than that, for a socio-economic system that described itself as libertarian, there seemed to a highly authoritarian streak running right through the middle of it,' interjected Anna. 'If you openly opposed those in charge – the shareholders, the corporate leaders and their managers, or the security forces that protected them – you soon very quickly discovered a distinct lack of liberty and freedom. For a supposedly libertarian society, it possessed a huge prison population. I'm not sure how locking people up and depriving them of their freedom for extremely long periods of time in appalling conditions is considered to be libertarian.'

'So how did they justify that?' asked Zhang Li, genuinely perplexed.

'Usually something about them being a threat to other people's liberties, so they deserved to be there. In other words, it was liberty for some, but incarceration for others. You would have thought that a society with a completely genuine commitment to liberty would have found a more freedom-based way of organising its affairs,' Anna replied.

'What was really bizarre, and I still can't quite get my head round this idea, is that on Rorque 4 they exalted individualism and individual freedom above almost all else, but, in reality, their society was based heavily on people conforming in all different areas of life. You couldn't really be yourself. People dressed the same, behaved in the same way, thought similar ideas and did as their superiors told them to do. They were selfish, that was true, but not truly individual. I've notice that here, with your emphasis on the collective and the importance of society, people are more like true individuals and just think and say as they please. Your communities are quite distinct, so is your architecture and also the cultures on the different continents; there's far more diversity and difference here,' Anna said, somewhat perplexed.

'I think that's because a collective and egalitarian society is a safe and secure one, so individuals know they are valued for who they are and that they are understood by their communities, so feel safe to experiment and be different within them. On Rorque 4, mistakes could be very costly in terms of finance, status, careers and promotions, so most people just played safe and conformed. Being different was potentially disastrous, especially if you got it wrong,' added Alex, reflecting on his own different experiences on both Rorque 4 and Zeta Kotlin, and believing he had arrived at a satisfactory explanation for an observation that had puzzled him for some time.

'Even worse, it also seemed to me that there were people who tried to conform as individuals, especially to the requirements of the corporations, but, for whatever reason, couldn't seem to get it quite right. Instead, aware that it was clearly not working out for them, they developed a desire to be something or somebody else. But rather than try to become their true self and develop their real identity - because, for them, they thought that was at the root of their problem – they tried to take on a completely new and different persona.' Anna paused briefly to think of some of the individuals she had met at the university. 'Ironically, though, they typically opted for some form of stereotype constructed by Rorquean society, an identikit character frequently depicted in the media - essentially a packaged identity being sold to their consumers, for whatever reason. These individuals thought they were being different and developing a true and individualised identity, but they were just buying an off-the-shelf identity, a supplied identity – they were simply purchasing yet another product, a prepackaged media conception. If anything, they were becoming even less like themselves, just at the time they thought they were creating their own new and real identity. In reality, they were just buying further and further into the system – the one that was damaging them so badly in the first place - but if you tried to tell them, they just didn't want to know, so convinced were they that only they knew the real truth.' Anna shook her head, remembering some of the fraught conversations she had been involved in, believing she was helping people, only to have it all thrown back in her face.

'It sounds like a grim place to live, so much unnecessary alienation. I suspect you're glad to be well away from all of that. It sounds like you've all settled in quite well at Earth City, what about the rest of your community?' asked Catriona, wanting to know more about the new settlers on their planet.

'Well, there's always a few complaints and grumbles, and the usual cultural misunderstandings, but most of them, like us, have been pleasantly surprised. The people here are generally quite understanding and welcoming and also forgiving when you make genuine mistakes. That's made the whole process go far more smoothly. On the whole it's been a success, I would say. I think the priority for most of us has been being able to continue with our research and teaching – it was, after all, our planet's entire way of life - and whilst adaptations have been necessary to reflect our new circumstances, and the different way in which decisions are taken, most have coped quite well, as far as I can see,' replied Mila.

'Didn't some of your starships head off to a completely different star system? How are they getting along, have you heard anything from them?' asked Rishaan, changing the conversation, as he was intrigued by the boldness of this particular venture and wanted to know more.

'That was Itzel and the three ships that voted to support her idea of leaving the Nexus Cluster. They wanted to start another purely university-based civilisation. They're heading for a star called Alchemy which is about ten light years away, I believe. Our cosmologists are keeping an eye on their progress. So far, they are still on course according to their observations. I think they still have another twenty-five years or so before they arrive,' answered Mila.

'I wonder what they will think when six fascist soldiers turn up shortly after them, completely lost in space and with no idea as to why they are there,' said Janicka, and the former space travellers all burst out laughing. They had to explain the joke to the inhabitants of Kapal who looked very puzzled.

'Have you ever wondered about ever returning to Alpha Fraczan? I've heard the planet has stabilised now,' asked Catriona.

'We've been monitoring its progress; yes it does seem to have stabilised, but the rivers are still re-establishing their new routes, coastlines are in a state of flux and there are still signs of continuing volcanic activity. We assume the vegetation zones will all take a while to adapt to the new circumstances and so will the limited wildlife that is still hopefully there. It could become habitable in the near future, but we assume all our universities have been destroyed or are completely in ruins,' answered Mila. 'It's not a very practical proposition to go back.'

'Theoretically, it is possible to return, but I think if we did it would be mainly for reasons of nostalgia,' added Alex. 'It is, after all, our home planet and we all grew up there - and I do sometimes miss it - but much of it is probably unrecognisable now. From the point of view of our research and studies, well, most of that can be done here now, so I'm not sure how many would want to go back and start all over again. It would be a huge task to rebuild an entire civilisation and very time-consuming.'

'One possibility is a sight-seeing expedition once we think it has fully stabilised,' suggested Anna. 'I know it's a long way to travel, but I for one would like to go back at least once, just to see exactly what has happened to our old home. Once we've done that, we could possibly establish some form of base there for visitors who want to explore or study the planet. But, I agree with the others, I think there's little prospect of any immediate recreation of our civilisation. Future generations, might have other ideas, possibly,' she suggested.

'I'm still working on advanced rocket engine technology and we are finally making some small advances in terms of improving acceleration and thus eventual inter-stellar speeds. My time on Rorque 4 did actually produce some useful science after all, and I'm still hopeful of making further progress – just at a slower pace than I originally envisaged,' Alex laughed, remembering how impatient he had been only a few years ago. 'If we have further successes, regular travel between here and Alpha might actually become a more realistic prospect.'

'If you're successful and we could travel between planets far more quickly, it could mean better inter-planetary relations; we could get to know our neighbours better, help each other resolve our problems and exchange ideas and cultures. We've been too isolated and inward-looking for far too long, in my opinion, it would benefit us enormously to become a more outward-looking planet,' suggested Zhang Li, returning to a subject that was being discussed more and more frequently. After the recent favourable planetary developments, the public mood was swinging behind the idea that a cosmopolitan inter-stellar approach was now looking like a much more attractive prospect.

'I agree, and it will be much easier and safer now that the appalling regimes on Rorque 4 and Zeleyan have fallen,' added Rishaan, 'thanks, in part, to some of those present with us today,' he added, as he looked around at their guests.

'I'm not sure we played that significant a role in their demise. I suspect they were heading for collapse at some point in the near future anyway. At best we might have nudged them along their doomed trajectory more quickly – acted as a catalyst, if you like – but not much more than that, I suspect,' Janicka offered, in the standard non-egoistic way that was so characteristic of Zetans.

'Ah, I think you're being too modest. The event you engineered at Meridin definitely helped save Ur-Tokar from invasion; it brought down the monarchy there and eventually contributed to Vartin calling off his fascist invasion of the planet. That might have also helped weaken the fascist regime and strengthen the opposition forces on Zeleyan as well,' offered Mila, who had rather enjoyed her role in the whole proceedings, even if it had been a very minor one.

'I think you're probably right about Rorque 4 though,' added Anna looking at Janicka. 'The planet and the economy were already in a critical state when we arrived, and that was the product of over a century of neo-liberalism. I don't think there was any real prospect of there ever being any fundamental regime change there – the opposition forces seemed so weak, highly disorganised and lacking in confidence. At best, our inability to help their economic projects speeded up their demise, but I don't think we actually played any major role in the collapse of their civilisation.'

'It's extremely difficult for individuals or small groups to effect major change, especially if you have little wealth, power or influence,' interjected Arlo, 'we discovered how powerless we really were whilst on Rorque 4. We couldn't even find a means of acquiring rocket fuel to leave the planet, never mind contributing to the collapse of a whole civilisation. Even powerful figures like Sanchez, Vartin and Jamieson ultimately failed to shape the future in the way they wanted it to pan out.'

'Agreed, it's the actions of the masses that really matter – on Zeleyan they acted and changed their future for the better, whilst on Rorque 4 they seemed to have done very little and largely accepted their fate. That's why their futures have become so different,' offered Rishaan. 'In many ways that's how it should be; it's more democratic that change occurs in this manner. Imagine if small groups and individuals could actually effect massive and significant changes on a regular basis – without the consent of the people - it would be so unfair and so undemocratic. Change should be done on a widespread and collective basis by the masses, not by tiny groups of individuals.'

'And that is effectively what we practice here; democratically agreed decisions directed by the votes of the whole people. We're free to make the small changes to our own lives, but the big stuff is decided by the whole population, as it should be,' confirmed Zhang Li, wanting to bring this subject to a close and move on to other matters. She turned towards Arlo, 'I believe our Jiaying is now living on your home planet. Do you know how she's getting on; as per usual she's not very good at keeping in touch with us. I've heard much about what happened at Ur-Tokar, but I'm not sure about Jiaying's exact role in the events there, nor about her new life.'

'I've not heard anything directly from her, but I know she's living with Akiko, who contacts me occasionally. The last I heard, everything was going very well, but then not much goes wrong on our planet, anyway. She always enjoyed her visits to Margalla and invariably stayed as long as she could get away with, so I would imagine she's planning to stay for good. She already has some good friends there and our laid back lifestyle really suits her temperament. I suspect that if you want to see her again, you might need to get the next starship to Margalla. I believe there is a departure being planned within the next two or three months. I might be on that flight myself,' he answered.

'What about yourself – how are you finding Zeta Kotlin?' asked Catriona.

'It's great, there's so much to see and so many different places – not like our little archipelago on Margalla. There's so many different continents, hills, plains, plateaus, rivers, seas and whatever else. It changes dramatically wherever you go. I've tried to see as much as possible, and it's all been great. And some of the towns and their buildings are quite spectacular – out of this world, even. I'm really enjoying myself and everyone is so helpful and friendly. They just spend hours talking to you, wherever you go. The Dancing Pools of Xestron were excellent, I've been three times now, it gets better every time. I'm planning to visit the subterranean rivers of Ankajor next; I've been told they're fantastic.'

'They are, and the lighting effects installed recently used to illuminate them are great,' said Rishaan. 'You can travel quite long distances, visiting vast caverns, huge underground halls and submerged waterfalls - some tumbling over crystal-embedded rock-faces. Parts of it are quite spectacular. Take some good music with you and the experience is unforgettable.'

'Yeh, that's what I've heard. I'll visit there, travel around a bit more for the next couple of months and see where it all takes me.'

'And then you're heading back to Margalla, by the sounds of things,' asked Zhang Li.

'I'm not sure; probably, but it depends on exactly when the stasis ship is scheduled for departure. I'm not in any great hurry to leave, and want to see as much of your planet as I can first. I've not got any definite plans as yet. I could always take a later ship, if it proves necessary.'

'What about the rest of you?' asked Catriona, 'it sounds like you've ultimately made your peace with this place.'

'Yes, I certainly have, and it's highly embarrassing when I think about some of my past decisions,' admitted Alex. 'I was far too ambitious for myself and far too impatient. I can't believe I hijacked a whole starship just to pursue my own personal career, with no regard for the lives of anyone else on board. What was I thinking? It was completely outrageous and selfish! I messed up so many people's lives and I still feel really bad about it when I think of what I did. I wish I could do more to make amends for my actions, but I'm not sure how I would even begin to do that,' he said. 'I still sort of avoid certain people – I'm not sure they've fully forgiven me,' and Alex grimaced as he said these last words.

Anna also looked somewhat ashamed. 'And I did exactly the same, though for different reasons; I was more concerned about losing the status and privileges I'd acquired on Alpha Fraczan. I've also lost respect from my colleagues as a result of my selfishness and made far too many enemies. Ironically, on Rorque 4, I was then on the receiving end of similar treatment, but carried out by operators far more ruthless than myself, and much more experienced in behaving in that manner. They were desperate to out-compete me, in fact, anyone else they regarded as a potential threat. They were unbelievably single-minded in their ruthless ambitions and drive for power. Though I guess they were simply a product of their environment, but when the whole planet was visibly falling apart around us, it did make you wonder how just how myopic anyone could be. It made me realise just what the real priorities in life actually are. I sacrificed friends and community to pursue personal status and ambition, and it was a huge mistake.'

'And now that we're living here, what we did just seems so completely pointless,' said Alex. 'I was embarrassingly naïve about the social sciences before these events. I just assumed that all people took sensible and rational decisions, and to advance in life I just needed to pursue my own individual goals, and not concern myself with anything else. On both Alpha and Rorque 4 the opportunities and positions for advancing were quite limited and scarce, so I needed to get ahead of the competition and be competitive. Here, it's different; everything is organised collectively, so there's sort of unlimited opportunities. I can just work with those who have similar ambitions, I don't need to impress a senior authority, compete with others over limited positions, jealously guard power once I've obtained it, or keep having to meet targets and objectives set by others and over which I have little or no control. I genuinely didn't realise a system such as yours could function or even exist, but now that I've seen it in action, I'm quite impressed. It's not perfect, but . . . well, I it's better than anything else I've experienced.'

'Yes, anyone wanting complete perfection – whatever that is – will die an unhappy person waiting for that to happen. I think we've managed to create something of a utopia here - it's not perfect in the literal sense - but it's probably about as good as it gets,' offered Pedro.

'I had similar reservations to Anna and Alex, but again for different reasons,' explained Mila, feeling it was her turn to make a contribution to the conversation. 'I had a fairly pessimistic view of human nature. I just didn't think people could be enlightened and cooperative enough to create what you've established here. I thought there would be no genuine freedom of thought and action, just lip service paid to it. I assumed there would be a fairly ignorant and poorly educated majority that would use their collective voice to stifle and limit free thinking and new ideas. I've discovered, if anything, that it's almost the opposite. There are probably too many ideas knocking around – it can sometimes be slow going trying to make organisational and theoretical advances. Everyone wants to have their particular opinion heard, and sometimes there are so many ideas it can be difficult to know which to actually start with. I understand it makes for good social inclusion and occasionally I hear a brilliant idea I'd never thought of myself, but it can be time-consuming and on occasions bewildering.'

'Well, we're rarely in a hurry here, often there's all the time in the world, so just take your time. People are generally sensible and they usually reach the right decision in the end after a genuinely free and frank discussion of the issues. It's probably just a case of acquiring a more patient persona,' replied Zhang Li.

'Which seems to be a common and noticeable approach here, and, after my experience on Rorque 4 where everything had to be completed in double-quick time, it's something of a relief, though it can also be frustrating when you think you've worked out the best approach and just want to get on and actually get something completed,' added Alex, thinking about some of the engineering tests he was planning for the near future. 'I suppose I still need to work on developing a more collectivist mindset.'

'And when you do, it all seems to work. I'm impressed by how everyone seems to eventually find the niche that suits them, and just gets on with what they want in life without creating difficulties for others. I'd always believed that most people just couldn't achieve that by themselves, that they needed leadership to guide them, or even force them to behave in acceptable ways when necessary, but here it doesn't seem to be a requirement. On Rorque 4, I discovered how damaging hierarchies can be when you're at the wrong end of them, and how arbitrary and unfair they can be. They never looked so bad when I was at the favourable end of the arrangement. And I also discovered on Rorque 4 how much damage they can do to the people at the top. Yet here, you effectively have no hierarchies and it still works really well – in fact, much better in so many ways, so why not just dispense with such a damaging arrangement,' Anna explained, still quite surprised that she was now thinking along this lines, after a lifetime of effectively doing the opposite.

'And, it also helps enormously that you collectively control all the AI units; that they do all the basic stuff that is either too hard or too boring for humans, and that the wealth that is generated is collectively and equally distributed. It means people can take it easy, take their time and decide what they really want to do with their lives. Under those conditions, people are far more likely to be reasonable human beings. We had an element of that on Alpha, though the university authorities typically had the final say on how they were used. It's totally unlike the economic arrangement on Rorque 4, and the society it produces is so radically different, it's amazing how much difference it makes,' added Alex.

'And I still don't fully understand why the people of Rorque 4 don't switch to our system when there are so many clear benefits,' Rishaan mused out aloud. 'Is it simply down to repression?'

'It's partly due to strict laws which control the way in which they can be used, and harsh punishments if those rules are breached, but there's also the matter of obtaining enough money in the first place to acquire your own AI units. It's beyond the means of most ordinary people,' Anna replied. 'But you also need to consider all the psychology, social conventions, culture and traditions. If people did acquire AI units, they would probably just replicate the way in which the corporations use them – for no other reason than it would be the easiest course of action. The idea that the corporations own a share of the work that anyone performs is so ingrained in their culture that it is rarely even discussed. It's taken for granted that they skim off a certain percentage to maintain their own highly privileged and luxurious lifestyles. I think most people don't even believe there is any viable theoretical alternative, never mind an actually functioning one here on Zeta Kotlin. And so, they just conform. It's ultimately easier not to rebel, even if it's self-defeating for most people in the long run.'

'Wow, that's just given me an idea,' and Janicka suddenly jumped up from her seat. 'I think I know what I'm going to do next with my life. I just need to check some stuff on the space web,' and with that she headed off to the communal area of the nearest commune.

The others looked around at each other slightly puzzled, but were at a loss as to exactly what had suddenly inspired her brainstorm, though there was an assumption that some form of plan for intervening in the situation on Rorque 4 had just occurred to her.

The discussion then returned once again to the issue of what, if any, action should be taken with regards to the people left on or above Rorque 4, and it soon became clear it was going to be a lengthy discussion. Mila, Alex and Anna made their way over to a balcony overlooking the escarpment and looked westwards out across the plain. Evening was beginning to fall and the first stars in the clear night sky were appearing. They scanned the sky searching for Gannexon. Although it was a red dwarf, its relative proximity to the brighter Celestrina meant it was usually easy to locate, and they soon found it without too much difficulty, low in the sky above the distant Kextos foothills; a small red star twinkling amongst its brighter white cousins. They gazed at the star of their home world for a while.

'What do you think, is it worth going back?' asked Alex.
'Well it would be nice to see Cerula and Amaranthus in the night sky once more, so I do sort of miss the place,' replied Anna.
'Mmm, possibly,' mused Mila, 'bit I'm not in a huge hurry. I quite like it here.'
'Maybe some time in the future then.'

Earth Calling – was it worth returning?

In the year 2207, the esteemed sage Cabremar Kemi, seated in the great university of Altan Major on the planet of Kronos, made his own philosophical contribution to why the human race had spread across the near galaxy from the late twenty-first century onwards. 'Why do we travel into space? Despite its relentless darkness, its cold neutrality, its vast unfeeling endlessness, why do we traverse this never ending infinite blackness? Deep in our minds we are all looking for something, a hidden clue, an end to a certain sorrow, an answer for tomorrow. We enter that dark endless void, we take the path through that long dark night, for on the other side we will come across an ancient realm of light. That is why we travel into space.'

The children of the Sun had dispersed across the known galaxy in a series of migratory waves that had brought them to new homes on distant worlds around strange stars they could only have ever previously dreamt about. A whole generation of space travellers had encountered the vastness of interstellar space, its cold, dark and soulless nature, the unbelievably vast distances between the stars and the absolute silence of its stillness. Some had been woken en route and wondered at its sheer scale, its stark beauty and its cold terror. Some had met a premature and icy fate in that vast still darkness. Most had traversed the vast distances ensconced in a deep cold sleep, unheeding and oblivious to the endless darkness around them.

The inter-stellar diaspora had led to human encounters with stars ranging across the entire astral spectrum. Vast blue and white giants brilliantly dominating their particular corner of space, the numerous red dwarves and their small brown dwarf cousins, and interspersed amongst them, the more familiar and sought after standard class of white and yellow stars. The space travellers could only marvel up close at what for generations of humans had been nothing more than distant twinkling points of light in the vast darkness of the infinite night sky.

The sheer variety of planetary systems they had encountered and the novelty of the planets discovered within them was simply never ending. From the breathtakingly spectacular and stunningly complex to the ordinary and the mundane, no two were ever the same. Enormous ice and gas giants, sparkling ice dwarves, bare rocky worlds with pockmarked surfaces full of craters, some with moons and some without, stunning ringed formations, hot gaseous atmospheres, frozen icy surfaces, cold rocky plateaus, towering mountain chains, flat lifeless deserts, vast blue oceans, shallow dried out seas – the combinations were infinite and endless.

And across this vast plethora of celestial objects, civilisations of all kinds and sizes had been founded. Some had flourished and delivered the utopia their founders had sought so long to establish - peaceful and prosperous societies characterised by affluence, freedom and equality. Others had been marked by repression, death and despair – a space age nightmare for those suffering under the weight of newly oppressive regimes. Many replicated the societies left behind on Earth, doomed to make the same mistakes and doomed to meet the same fate. Others had never stood a chance from the very start, collapsing as quickly as they had been constructed; their decaying remains abandoned to become the dust of future ages. Some had risen and some had fallen and some had prevailed.

What they all possessed in common though, was the discovery that across the galaxy the preservation of life was at best precarious, but more typically a battle against overwhelming odds. Of the myriad and varied planets that constituted this newly expanding astral civilisation, none had yet been found that was as uniquely suited to human life as that of Earth, for how could that even be the case. Earth was the planetary home on which humans had slowly but successfully evolved over countless millennia, the one unique place in the universe that enjoyed the specific conditions for which humans were specially adapted to survive and flourish within. No other planet possessed such a specialised set of conditions as that enjoyed by the third rock from the Sun – its temperature, gravitational pressure, stabilising moon and protective sister planets.

The human exodus had dispersed far and wide across the near galaxy. But in every civilisation they created, they had all, at some point, stopped and stared into the dark star-filled night sky of their new home and wondered exactly where the yellow-white star known as the Sun lay within that stellar array, and then speculated on what had become of their distant planet of origin. The early settlers had been too preoccupied with founding and developing their new civilisations to give the matter any prolonged consideration or thought, and none had seriously entertained the idea of returning to their former home. Most were simply glad to have been released from its troubled grip.

But for future generations – those that had known nothing other than their new planetary home – many amongst their number had wondered what life had been truly like on the ancient planetary home of their species. For those in the newly established utopias, this was often little other than idle speculation. But in some civilisations, particularly those where the new reality had not lived up to expectations or had produced yet another dysfunctional dystopia, a nostalgia for old and better times had seeped into their decaying societies, a desire for a return to ancient haunts and homes. They had travelled a different path, they had paved their alternate way, but now their endless dreams of lazy wasted summer days had slowly faded away. In their place, an anger and a fear of being lost and alone in space had reawakened within their desperate peoples.

Thoughts of a proposed return to Earth awakened old memories and ancient images - the smell of the dust and the summer heat, the orange autumnal breeze and the weak wintry sun. The seers and the prophets amongst their disillusioned number spoke of changes in the stars, of strange scenes they could not explain, of the shifting, altering hands of fate. They foretold of a time, of a date with destiny, of a return to their ancestral home. They would pass back through the celestial door to see if they could cheat in life's final game, to see if a forgiving Earth would finally take back its long lost prodigal children.

But could Earth take back its wayward offspring? Was it still the picture of a nightmarish hell told and retold by their forebearers – a world engulfed by endless greed and selfishness, of willful ignorance, civilisational decline and climatic breakdown – the fable of a failed race? Or had it recovered and returned to the once vibrant green oasis occasionally glimpsed in rare flashes of nostalgia expressed by the first settlers as they struggled in the face of adversity, bravely enduring trying times of stress and difficulty, building their precarious new homes and towns amongst the stars? Such later generations asked how their ancestors could have been so reckless and so careless to have destroyed their one and only true home – a dazzlingly live blue jewel set in the dark icy blackness.

Such generations could only stare at the night sky and speculate as to what had become of life and the human race back on distant lonely Earth. The eerie silence that emanated from its small corner of the galaxy was widely interpreted as a signifier of doom. Numerous theories abounded. A runaway greenhouse effect had resulted in a planet that now bore a close resemblance to its Venusian sister – unbearably humid, vastly overheated and entirely hostile to life. Others were only slightly less catastrophic. Outpourings of toxic sulphurous gases released from the depths of anoxic oceans had delivered a sixth great extinction; life battled on, but amongst its diminished forms and numbers, humans were definitely no longer present. The last woman and the last man on Earth had long since drawn their last Earth breath.

Others were more hopeful and optimistic. At the time of the great exodus, for those looking in the future it was well known that for the Earth's inhabitants who did manage to survive, they would very soon be facing a completely different planet to the one upon which humanity had evolved over its many millions of years. The equatorial zone would no longer be one of luxuriant rainforests and coral reefs teeming with endless marine life. Instead it would be an unbelievably tempestuous region characterised by constant and endless monsoon-like downpours and fierce torrential storms. Supersize and super-powerful hurricanes – the like of which humanity had never experienced before – continuously circled the planet destroying everything in their path. Constant mudslides, continent-wide flooding and collapsing continental shelves meant that no complex life-forms could survive for long in this zone of endless pluvial destruction.

Moving both northwards and southwards from this zone, stretching far into the higher latitudes of the former temperate zones, two widening bands of intensely dry desert would have developed. Fiercely high temperatures, intense heatwaves, enormous sandstorms and permanent drought meant that these too were effectively uninhabitable for humans and most other life-forms. Across these inhospitable latitudes of sun-drenched inferno lay the abandoned settlements of human civilisation, cities of rust and broken concrete constantly swept bare by searing desert storms, their parched fields and ancient transport systems buried under the drifting desert sands. Coastal settlements, their ports and industrial facilities, their beaches and their marshy lowlands, had long since submerged under the rising seas of a completely ice-free planet.

Only in the former polar regions and the higher latitudes of the temperate zones would human habitation and food production remain a possibility - the cold temperate and subarctic conditions now replaced by sub-tropical temperatures, lush verdant forests and warm water seas. But had human life been able to cling on here successfully, eking out a living in a much changed and diminished landscape, its numbers drastically reduced and its options dramatically reduced. Amongst the more optimistic spacefarers, there numbered those that hoped that the highly centralised civilisations of the twenty first century had collapsed, giving way to more dispersed and decentralised forms of society, hanging on precariously in the now verdant former arctic and subarctic zones. Humans still lived on the planet, but were now living in a very different manner, at one with nature and no longer destructive of the environment. This explained the enduring radio silence.

Or had this region too become devastated and devoid of life by an unthinking and wayward human race, uncaring of its precious green home, desperately exploiting its ever dwindling living space as it fought a losing battle against its own stupidity – a planet too easily damned by the curse of man and doomed by the misfortune of women. For some, the silence emanating from the planet spoke volumes. Humans had died out and that was the end of the matter. There was nothing more to discuss. Others, though, speculated of degenerated civilisations, of brutal, highly secretive and repressive regimes - ones that had turned well and truly inwards, seeking only isolation and retrenchment, completely abandoned to any thoughts of further engagement with an inter-stellar space they had now firmly turned their backs upon.

Still others conjectured that the planet was currently uninhabitable, and of those left behind, all had been placed into stasis. They had entered the sleep of a thousand tears, an opportunity to reflect on the devastation and disaster they had brought upon themselves and their only true home, a period of prolonged and solemn reflection. Eventually, though, after long years, a message would emanate across space from the ancestral planet, 'we are not dead . . . only sleeping', and then, having passed through the tunnels of darkness and transcended the worst of the crisis, the ascent of man and woman would once again come to pass. The survivors could awaken in their newly renewed and reinvigorated home and once more prosper on a recovered and now verdant planet.

Whatever the particular theory they favoured, to be or not to be existing, was the crucial question they asked themselves about the fate of the human race on their ancient planetary home. Occasionally, the spacefarers would turn from their enquiring, their unknowing and endless speculation, to the possibility of actually planning a return expedition. Those fancying themselves as erstwhile space explorers mooted the possibility of a return voyage to Earth – to finally lay to rest the endless conjecture, idle rumours and myriad possible theories that had long been proposed and debated. Others suggested AI units would be far more suitable for such a long and arduous journey – a voyage that might take generations for anything or anyone to return with answers to the endless speculation.

Others questioned the wisdom of making such a journey. What if their worst fears proved to be founded? Did they really want to discover an Earth laid to waste by a destructive humanity; all life at an end, the last human soaked in the last blood of the Earth? What would be the doom-laden implications for their own fragile and still developing civilisations? If they found a degenerated and barbarous remnant of the once flourishing human race, what would they do – simply turn around and return home. Had they considered the vast distances involved and the eons of time spent in stasis – time spent away from their communities, from friends and relatives they would almost certainly never see again. Did they really want to know what had become of human life on Earth? On some planets, the fate of Earth had become a taboo subject. So far, none had chosen to return, none had gone in search of that ancient realm of light.

Arrival in Utopia

Margalla – the spacefarers return

Some weeks after The Spirit of the Age had finally dropped into orbit around Zeta Kotlin, the Opa-Loka skirted past the yellow-white star of Sazhina, using its significant gravitation pull to slow its approach on the way to its final destination of Margalla. The skeleton crew had been wakened a couple of days beforehand and was excitedly making frequent visits to the viewing deck in anticipation of the ship's imminent arrival at their home planet. As they made their approach, and the small blue dot that constituted their home grew gradually in size, the glistening white of the northern icecap slowly became discernible, to be followed by the numerous cloud formations that swirled around the upper reaches of the planet's atmosphere, white against the azure blue of the vast ocean.

In comparison with some of the fantastically strange and exotic planets they had observed on their travels, Margalla appeared somewhat ordinary, even a bit boring - a small blue watery world, with few distinguishing features and thus unlike any other they had recently visited or viewed. In the grand scheme of things, it almost seemed insignificant. Even within the Nexus Cluster it was a little known location, until very recently assumed by most to be uninhabited. Nevertheless, the crew knew that their communities, their loves, their lives, their histories and their futures all lay on that small azure blue dot, and, after their unexpected travails and adventures, they were very much looking forward to some sun-drenched relaxation on the archipelago's wonderful beaches.

They were also pleased to have played a small - even if relatively unimportant - part in probably the most significant historical development to have ever occurred in the Nexus Cluster. The differing planetary changes had led to a significant rebalancing of political forces in their small corner of space, to the point where there were already those within the Cluster who were looking for ways and means to extend and consolidate these progressive changes. Most of the crew were keen to relate their recent inter-stellar experiences to their friends and communities, and were looking forward to some interesting social gatherings and extended conversations. Nothing like this had occurred on Margalla before.

Arrival in Utopia

Once the Opa-Loka was safely in orbit around Margalla, the five Margallans plus Savverio and Jiaying woke the few dozen friends, associates and comrades who had accompanied them on the voyage from Rorque 4. As usual, it took the latter some time to fully recover from the torpor of stasis, but once completed, the members of the group made regular visits to the viewing deck to take a good first look at what was likely to be their new home for some time to come, given Margalla had only very infrequent contact with the other planets in the cluster. Initially, they were somewhat underwhelmed by the vast expanse of blue water – Rorque 4, for all its faults, at least had significant amounts of continental landmass to gaze down upon – but all that was to change after they had made their uneventful descent to the small chain of sub-tropical islands.

The first priority for the returnees and their Rorquean friends was to find vacant accommodation in a commune as near as possible to where they now wanted to be located – invariably this amounted to a desire to being close to their old friends and associates. Effecting this was not particularly difficult, since all the islands maintained a policy of providing and keeping more accommodation than was actually needed, to ensure free movement between the communes as and when was needed. Once this was achieved, they went about integrating the Rorqueans into their communities, again not a particularly difficult process, given the generally open and friendly nature of the islanders. The Rorqueans, through a process of trial and error, found they needed to make some significant social adjustments to their behaviours – and some adapted more quickly than others – but given their favourable views towards egalitarian collectivism, this was a task they were more than willing to undertake and seek to succeed in.

The new arrivals from Rorque 4 nearly all chose to settle into a couple of communities on Kaalvert, the largest and most interesting of the islands that made up the archipelago. Despite its relatively large size, it was still really only something of a sparsely populated island with just a small number of significant-sized communities, nestled amongst considerable stretches of open woodland intermixed with land used for agricultural purposes. The terrain was largely hilly and a range of artificial freshwater pools had been established in the lower lying areas to supply the freshwater needs of the islanders. It had a reputation for growing some of the better exotic fruits, but also for the best cannabis plants and for interesting social gatherings. As the largest of the populated islands, it was less of a culture shock for the previously urban dwelling Rorqueans than would have been the case on some of the smaller islands.

Despite their longtime political support and advocacy for a more egalitarian society back on their home planet, it still took them a while to adjust to an actually existing one. Some of the implications of living in a utopian society, especially after having only known the hierarchal individualism of a neo-liberal capitalist economy, they found quite surprising and unexpected, and only became truly apparent to them through their day-to-day experiences. Nevertheless, they were all more than keen to adapt to their new circumstances, and were certainly not missing their old and unloved planet.

Over time, they gradually become accustomed to living in an economy where they controlled the AI units – not the other way round – and where all relationships were constructed on the basis of mutual respect, rather than establishing your position in some oppressive pecking order, and where they all made a genuinely equal contribution to the functioning and development of the society they lived in, rather than feeling like cogs in a machine they effectively had no control over. Slowly, but surely, they established new lives and integrated fully into Margallan society, just as the five Margallans also reestablished their old relationships, and the two Zetan voyagers became reacquainted with old friends and lovers.

As the weeks and then the months passed easily by, the four years spent in space become an increasingly distant memory for the seven travellers, almost as though it had happened in a former life. But despite this lengthening temporal distance, all knew they had learnt something about themselves, about each other, their world, their beliefs and those of the wider Nexus Cluster. And as the days passed by and the magnitude of what they had actually experienced slowly sunk in, so their minds began to make increasing sense of their adventures, and thus they began to gradually form a better understanding of what had actually occurred to them.

And so, approximately eight months after their return, the former space travellers decided to organise a gathering for themselves and their friends to meet up once again, not just for old time's sake, but also to reestablish old ties and relive old memories, to see if the others had arrived at similar conclusions to themselves about their travels. The gathering was organised to take place on one of the remoter beaches on the island of Verdeluza and they assumed that the socialising would last the entirety of the day.

They had all spent the intervening period recovering from their travels, reflecting on their adventures, reacquainting themselves with their communities and reengaging with the projects they had formerly been involved with, and so they figured they had plenty to discover and discuss. Additionally, Savverio, Kiyona and Jiaying had all recently decided to move into Akiko's community at Ascaso and - although they were all previously acquainted with each other - had begun to establish firmer and more long-lasting relationships that - although they were not yet to know this - would endure for many years and decades to come.

On the day of the arranged gathering, the various groups of friends started to arrive on the beach from around early afternoon onwards. Much of the initial period was spent exploring the coastline, swimming in the sea and playing games on the beach. But as the shadows began to lengthen and the warm sea air began to discernibly cool, so they eventually got down to the business of eating and drinking the ample quantities of food and drink they had brought with them for the occasion. Then, as the late afternoon passed into evening, and the alcohol continued to flow, and the evening air filled with the scent of cannabis smoke, the emphasis shifted to socialising and reflecting on their recent experiences. Many of those at the gathering had not seen each other for several months and were keen to catch up on recent developments in their personal lives, the changing nature of their relationships, how they were settling into their new communities, their plans for the future and what they thought of Margallan society.

Akiko had spent most of the day mixing and mingling with their friends from Rorque 4, but as the evening progressed, she made a point of seeking out her fellow space travellers from the Opa-Loka and The Spirit of the Age. Several months had passed since their adventures, several months in which she had considered and reflected upon her experiences; the social environments she had visited, the occasions she had participated in and the varied people she had encountered. She wanted to know what the others thought about her ideas and the conclusions she had recently arrived at.

Initially, she was unable to find Jiaying, Xander, Zhavia and the various others and she spent some considerable time wandering along the shoreline and the sand dunes backing onto it as she searched for the group. By this point in the evening, the light was beginning to fade and she glanced up into the night sky, quickly spotting the red and green moons of Rosa and Jade, both traversing slowly across the lower reaches of the eastern sky. As she scanned towards the south she spotted the brilliant white star of Aequitas, always one of the first stars to appear in the night sky, and she wondered how Arlo was faring on Zeta Kotlin.

A short while later, and further down the beach, she eventually stumbled upon the gathering of former space travellers, already assembled around a small fire they had built on a gently sloping scrubby sand dune that overlooked the beach at the farthest end of the bay. They all waved to her as they spotted her slowly ambling towards them, and after various greetings and numerous hugs and kisses, she sat down amidst the centre of the group and was given a plate of food and a large drink once she was seated comfortably.

'Oh, I've been meaning to ask you for some time, what happened with regards to your shark problem?' asked Zhavia.
'Good news, they're back and in larger numbers,' Akiko replied. 'I was really worried. We have very few keystone species on Margalla and I was really beginning to become extremely concerned. If we lost one key species, well, what if the others went the same way? We might be facing some form of catastrophic ecosystem collapse. We're a very isolated and insulated group of islands - if one part of our ecosystem degrades, it could have all sorts of cascade effects, and invariably most of them are going to be detrimental ones. And it's not like we have anywhere to flee to if it all goes wrong – well, not unless we completely leave the planet.' She paused for a moment. 'And I'm not sure how we could return the islands to good ecological health, we don't really have the full knowledge of how to do that – I guess we would just have to hope the ecosystems could regenerate by themselves. It just highlights how important it is that we really nurture and take care of our

island ecosystems, otherwise we could be in really big trouble,' she explained, pleased with her recent fortunate discovery, but still not totally optimistic about the future.

'Yes, not like on Rorque 4. If ever there was a living demonstration of how not to go about matters, that is your prime example. The lack of respect and care for their planet was quite staggering, it was a real eye-opener. We sometimes think we could do better here, but compared with the Rorqueans we have nothing to be embarrassed about,' added Kiyona, who had also spent a considerable amount of time reflecting on her time away from her home planet. She now felt she had matured on her travels and somewhat awakened as an individual. She had seen a great deal, learnt much about wider society, and now felt far more confident about voicing her opinions on political and social matters. She had come to the conclusion that her upbringing on Margalla had equipped her with all the educational skills she needed, but there had never been much reason to actually put them to good use. The problems encountered on their voyage had left her with little choice but to hone and develop them. Her new found confidence meant she now felt she could hold her own intellectually with anyone now. 'Do you have a theory as to why the sharks came back?' she asked.

'I've been in contact with some of the marine biologists on Zeta Kotlin and they have recorded similar observations, but they managed to discover where their marine animals had migrated to. The location they headed to made little logical sense, but when they checked through the old data banks from Earth they worked out that the marine animals on Zeta were still following an old migration pattern established way back on Earth, probably one from hundreds of thousands of years ago. They suggested the sharks here might be doing the same. I've worked out some possible coordinates, and if they disappear again I'll scan the relevant area to discover whether we are experiencing the same phenomenon,' Akiko answered, with a confidence that would have surprised her before her pre-spacefaring days. The group rescue of her on The Opa-Loka had dramatically boosted her belief in herself, and these days she went about her life as if she was driven by a new found source of strength, as if she had laid an old ghost to rest.

'I wonder how much of old Earth *we* still have in us?' asked Savverio, who had occasionally discussed this question back on Zeta Kotlin and formulated his own ideas on the matter, but was wondering what the Margallans might think about the subject.

'Well, it's the planet we evolved on over millions of years, so we must, by definition, be best suited for that world. Life on the varied planets we have colonised can clearly be quite precarious – just look at Alpha Fraczan and Rorque 4 for how contingent existence can be on the different inhabited worlds. I know what happened on Alpha Fraczan was beyond their control, whilst the desolation of Rorque 4 was almost certainly avoidable, but it does show that we can never take our newly formed civilisations for granted,' answered Kiyona. 'It's made me think about our idyllic life on Margalla in a completely different manner- I think I took it all far too much for granted before.'

'We also have considerably more free will than sharks, I think it's fair to say,' Jiaying offered, 'so we are significantly more adaptable and can thrive in a wider range of environments. Having experienced three planets in my lifetime now, I can't help thinking that in some way the civilisation on each of them very much reflects the nature and geography of each planet. On Zeta Kotlin, with its many and varied continents, we have developed a range of very diverse cultures, on Margalla you have your sub-tropical idyllic beach culture on a small island archipelago, and on Ur-Tokar, most of which is frozen and uninhabitable, they had a quite restricted and limited culture,' she suggested, voicing an idea she had developed to make sense of the different worlds she had experienced in the Nexus Cluster.

'But Ur-Tokar had two distinct cultures on the same planet. I know they both rejected modern technology, but they developed into two very different types of society. There must be factors other than geography, geology and nature at work to explain that,' replied Savverio.

'Possibly, though that particular situation on Ur-Tokar might have only been a temporary development. When we departed, only the civilisational approach of the Mountain People was still surviving, so they just have the one civilisation now. I know it's kind of an odd one, but I came to quite like it once I understood it better. It sort of fits well with their planet, even if it is a bit esoteric; it's certainly better than the dreadful monarchist approach of the lowlanders,' Jiaying replied.

'Maybe, though I detect an element of bias, and I'm also not fully convinced that their deep ecologist approach is a completely stable one. I can't help feeling that the first major crisis they face, a charismatic leader could easily emerge who claims to have the all the answers to their problems, and if he or she attracts a widespread following, then what is there to stop him or her becoming a new monarch, especially if they are well armed and popular. It's also worth remembering that the monarchist society was destroyed by external forces – the Zeleyanian army - so nothing to do with the planet itself. I still think you need to consider factors other than geography to explain different civilisations,' replied Savverio.

'And none of this explains what happened on Rorque 4,' added Kiyona. 'They created a civilisation that was totally unsuitable for their planet and then pretty much destroyed it as a result. No forces ever emerged on that planet to rectify their destruction, so it cannot just be down to geography.'

'That's because the general population had no real power, they had no control over their lives and therefore their planet in general. Their political system was a farce – it, like everything else, was controlled by the corporations. The corporations called all the shots and they didn't care about the planet. They were controlled by greedy selfish individuals who cared only about making profits and maintaining their elite lifestyles. Whilst they were in power, the nature of the planet was never going to be the main factor in shaping their civilisation. It's ultimately about power and who is in control,' concluded Akiko.

'How does Zeleyan fit in with this? I'm not too familiar with the nature of their planet, but from what I can see there seemed to be a correlation. One large power dominating one large continent,' asked Jiaying, not yet willing to fully abandon her theory.

'I'm not saying there is no link between geography and the nature of any given planetary civilisation, but you also need to consider other factors, like power, for instance, as Akiko says. The Zeleyanian regime, remember, has also collapsed, and the people there appear to be adopting a form of socialism, as far as I can tell from the media emissions emanating from the planet,' interjected Savverio. 'They also had a capitalist economy, controlled by the selfish and the greedy, and dominated by a small elite that was desperate to cling on to power. Admittedly the state played a much larger role on Zeleyan, whereas on Rorque 4 it was very weak, by contrast, and the corporations effectively took over the usual functions of the state. Both have now collapsed and that's because elitist civilisations are, by their very nature, unstable and thus likely to be temporary. There's a massive imbalance of power and a lack of stabilising equilibrium, so there are always countervailing forces pushing back against the elites, trying to level things up and create more equality. It's pretty much a law of nature.'

'They both went very different ways, though. I mean, when they collapsed the results were very different on the two worlds,' Akiko interjected. 'To me, they both overstretched themselves and tried to achieve grandiose ambitions that were well beyond their abilities, but the impact was different when they collapsed. One has moved to socialism, whilst the other has descended into chaos. Why was that, then?'

'Whilst I was on The Opa-Loka I spent a great deal of time monitoring the media emissions of the two worlds and it looked to me like it was simply down to recent circumstances,' replied Savverio. 'Zeleyan's economy was developing fairly steadily and was mostly improving. The general population was employed, enjoying rising affluence and was quite confident and optimistic about the future, as a result. Vartin's big mistake was to impose his new economic conditions - those he needed to pay for his space fleet - on the whole population at the same time. Most rulers rule through divide and conquer strategies, but Vartin forgot that – maybe he became complacent or overconfident over time, I'm not sure. Whatever the reason, when suddenly economic conditions deteriorated for everyone, after long years of rising expectations, the people rebelled as one, they rose up united and confident against his regime and defeated him. Admittedly, it helped a great deal that many of the troops weren't there, but the people were optimistic, forward-looking and confident, so their chances of creating a better society were high.' Savverio paused, 'by contrast, on Rorque 4, the economy had been mired in depression for decades. The population was impoverished, divided, disorganised, fighting amongst themselves and thus demoralised and full of despair. When the regime collapsed, the people were unable to organise any form of coherent opposition and so their society has just descended into barbarism, and the reports coming out from the planet indicate this is still the case.'

'So, does that mean the nature of a civilisation depends on the people within it - that people do control their own destinies, that we do have free will, and that we make our own futures?' asked Xander, who wasn't entirely sure he was fully following the conversation.

'To some extent that's correct. All the peoples who left Earth had their own belief systems - their own idea of what a utopia was - and tried to implement them to the best of their efforts on the destinations they happened to arrive at. It certainly helps if you have a good quality planet – on Alpha Fraczan they were unlucky in not having a stabilising moon – so geography, and environmental factors in general, are important. But, if your planet is a suitable one, then to a large extent it's possible for the people to shape their own destiny. I'm sure the nature of our genetic legacy on Earth means that ultimately some forms of civilisation are possible and some are not, but we are quite an adaptable and flexible species and have a significant degree of free will. We can build all forms of different society, and across the galaxy we clearly have done so, developing many different kinds of civilisation,' formulated Savverio, finally arriving at the crux of his thesis.

'But there are clearly limits to free will, as your environmentalist explanations of the differing fates of Rorque 4 and Zeleyan undoubtedly demonstrates,' said Jiaying. 'Clearly the material circumstances any civilisation faces are a significant factor in anything it is able to achieve. Free will cannot transcend that; only shape it within certain already well-defined parameters.'

'And your mention of genetics is also telling,' added Akiko. 'Whilst we were on Ur-Tokar, Mila Lustrom told me about a school of thought known as Social Genetics which was being developed by some of her colleagues at her former university on Alpha Fraczan. They maintain that genetic studies have definitively shown that humans are highly sociable and an inherently collectivist species. This is why they talk about survival of the friendliest – that those best at making friends and engaging in frequent sexual relationships are the ones most likely to pass on their genes and to flourish successfully within society. So, according to their theories, humans have a natural inclination towards cooperation and to transmitting it to future generations. Mira seemed to think this was why Zeta Kotlin is so successful, contrary to what she had originally expected'

'History would seem to back them up on this,' stated Zek suddenly, making a rare contribution to the discussion. 'Throughout our entire existence, no matter where we have lived and what our culture is, we have always, without exception, lived in groups – tribes, villages and towns, sometimes extremely large cities. It's about the only constant in human history. Humans really don't like living isolated and lonely lives.'

'I don't disagree with those last two points, but aren't we forgetting our own civilisations in all this,' interjected Kiyona. 'Both Margalla and Zeta Kotlin have proved remarkably stable, whilst remaining prosperous and freedom-loving civilisations. That's because we are not just collectivist but also egalitarian; power and wealth are evenly distributed, so no one feels excluded and thus the desire to rebel against our system or against other humans. In addition, our social structures prevent any one person or small group from acquiring excessive power and profoundly damaging our societies and the environment. Whilst we were on Rorque 4 we constantly saw the exact opposite of all that, and that's why their civilisation collapsed. No doubt Earth also collapsed because of its huge power imbalances.'

'Exactly,' said Zhavia smiling at Kiyona, as he remembered their disagreement on this subject aboard The Spirit of The Age. 'But to achieve all of that it's essential that the economy, and in particular, the AI units are owned and controlled by the entire community. You need egalitarianism, but also collectivism. To me, whilst we were on Rorque 4, it became increasingly obvious that their main problem was one of rampant individualism and selfish consumerism. With a tiny elite controlling nearly all the AI units, this spelt disaster for the wider population. By contrast, our civilisations, which have implemented genuine collective economic control, have created widespread prosperity, become truly egalitarian, control their own destiny and remain politically and socially stable,' he summarised. 'As I said to Dave Shevecke; if they wanted to successfully change their world for the better they needed to take collective control of the AI units. Who controls the AI units, controls the nature of society. I wonder if he remembered.'